"I know of your love
for your people,
Princess Mika,
peasants and nobles alike,
and your love
for your nation.

When the time comes,
you will use your love
to free the people
from tyranny
and oppression."

Website: http://www.jasverenightsstudios.com
Twitter: http://www.twitter.com/JasvereNights
Facebook: http://www.facebook.com/JasvereNightsStudios

Edited by Shelley Holloway
http://www.hollowayhouse.me/

Cover Art by Joyce Ann Martin
http://www.inkgizmo.com/

PROLOGUE

THESE ARE PERILOUS DAYS. EVEN now, as I add to this chronicle each day, I am still just a child. I haven't lived very long in this world. And yet, my eyes have witnessed far more violence, chaos, war, and death than most children my age.

The nation of Melodice, one would expect, should be a proud nation. But a great majority of the population live in unbearable poverty. The population is divided into two groups. First, there was the lowborn, or the working class, more commonly known as the Peasantry, an outdated term that has persisted for centuries, since that time when we lived in an agrarian society. Second, there was the Nobility, also known as the highborn, or the upper class, a small minority of the nation's population. The Royal Family, the highest of the Nobility, ruled over the entire nation. However, the full support of the Royal Family was enjoyed by the Nobility, who stood on the backs of the peasants while hording much of the nation's riches, and taking advantage of all that luxury had to offer. The peasants were ruled through tyranny, and mercilessly oppressed by the Nobility.

I was born into the Royal Family. My home was the Scarletia Royal Castle, located near the centre of the capital city of Scarletia. In my clueless ignorance of the real world, I had lived a life overflowing with luxury. I had enjoyed what all highborn little girls delighted in, such as soft and shimmering dresses made of the finest silk and lace, loyal maidservants who waited on me, ready to gladly obey my every command, and a place to call home that was grand and beautiful. I was educated by the finest professors in the areas of science, economics, mathematics, sociology, politics, and many others. I was also born as one of the rare few who had an affinity with magic, trained by one of the most powerful Magic Knights in the nation.

However, I had also lived a life where the truth about the world was hidden from me. I had thought I would always enjoy the life of a Princess. I had always believed I would live a life of peace and harmony. But one day, all that changed for me. I remember that day that was the turning point of my life, one that changed my fate, and set me on the path not to a life of constant peace and harmony, but to the chaotic and terrifying path of war and death.

Melodice, Our Path to Salvation: 3566 – 3569
(pp. 24 – 25)
Mika Silveraine (b. 3554)

CHAPTER 1:

ASSASSINS

UNDER COMPLETE DARKNESS, THE SOUNDS of the rustling of clothing competed with those of animal hooves that struck the ground as they walked and the grinding of wooden wheels against a hard surface. Someone was searching in the dark but was having difficulty. Eventually, he found what he was looking for.

"Hey, Kiran, is that you fumbling around over there?" someone asked from beyond the darkness.

Kiran blew out a sigh. "Yeah, it's me, Athrel. Why?"

"Are you all right? What are you looking for?"

"I'm fine. I was only reaching for my sword. It's so dark and cramped in this fucking crate. I can't see a thing."

Another spoke from a different direction, and his voice hinted authority. "Kiran, Athrel, be quiet. By the sound of the cervid hooves on the pavement, I can tell we're nearing the gates of the castle. The knights will inspect the cargo very soon."

"Damn! This had better work," said Athrel.

A fourth voice came from elsewhere in the darkness. "No one has tried anything this insane for a very long time. Hey, Joris, do you think these crates will hold up against the inspection?"

"It'll work, Radeth. Trust me. These crates will hide us well. After all, I designed them myself," answered a fifth voice.

Radeth chuckled sarcastically. "Yeah, sure. As long as

those bastard knights don't remove the top shelf full of vegetables. You had *better* be right about this."

Joris snorted, dismissing Radeth's concern. "Ah, you worry too much."

The authoritative voice spoke out once more. "I suggest you all be quiet and stop worrying. We're here to fulfill the most important mission of our lives... for our nation of Melodice."

* * *

"You can't catch me!"

Mika Silveraine, the young Princess of the nation of Melodice, was a painfully timid and shy little girl of eleven years, but she felt most comfortable around a ten-year-old boy named Mirin Gothwald. There were many children who lived in the castle, but around him, she felt more relaxed and found it much easier to express herself.

"Oh yes, I can!" said Mirin who, though neatly dressed in his standard attire of trousers, dress shirt, and waistcoat, was able to outpace the young Princess.

The two children ran along a concrete walkway, one of many set in a grid pattern all around the Scarletia Royal Castle. On this late spring day, the bright glow of the sun gently warmed their cheeks.

The area around the castle, commonly referred to as the Grounds, was a very large expanse of open spaces, gardens, and walkways. The entire property was surrounded by walls of white stone three metres thick and at least ten metres high. Every twenty metres or so, the length of the wall was interrupted by watchtowers fifteen metres tall. Armoured knights watched over the surroundings as they patrolled the top of the walls.

Mika ran away from Mirin as fast as she could, but he gained on her. Their innocent laughter sang in the gentle breeze.

Mika was a petite girl for her age, with straight, smooth, mid-back-length, light-blonde hair and curious brown eyes that hinted of wisdom beyond her years. But along with her soft and delicate facial features, her eyes revealed her very meek personality. In her thin, knee-length, white dress of silk and lace, a pink ribbon in her hair that fluttered in the wind, white sheer stockings of woven silk, and a shiny new white pair of flat shoes that hampered her potential to run a little faster, she was quite a beautiful young girl.

Attached to the gold necklace around Mika's neck was a flat, circular, deep-blue diamond that sparkled in the late morning sunlight. Called the Princess Gem, it was the physical and legal representation of her identity as the Princess of Melodice, given to her by the Queen soon after she was born. It was handed down to every girl in the Royal Family by their mothers.

"No, no, you won't catch me!" exclaimed Mika, as she looked back at Mirin. As she followed the walkway around one of the corners of the castle, she suddenly ran into something... or, rather, someone. She gasped with surprise as she fell back onto her buttocks. When she looked up, she saw the thin but towering figure of Helen Renier.

"Mika!" Mirin caught up to her, seeing the young woman she'd just run into.

Helen was not particularly tall, but from Mika's perspective, she appeared quite intimidating, especially since she often looked down at her with a very serious expression. Awkward discomfort took hold of Mika as she noticed the deep frown Helen regarded her with for running into her just now.

Helen was sixteen years old, and therefore was of the age of majority. She had recently become a member of the Scarletia Royal Guard, and was the youngest among them. In her snug black trousers tucked into her dark knee-high boots, she stood with authority. The rounded collar of her white blouse peeked out from beneath her black knee-length cape, which she wore partially buttoned and tied with a thin ribbon. For sixteen, she appeared rather distinguished. The long knife strapped to the side of her right shin and the scabbard that hung from her leather belt added to her dignified appearance. As befitting the military style of her position, her smooth, mid-back-length, red hair was pulled back into a ponytail.

As Helen stared down at her with irritation, Mika felt the older girl's obsidian eyes pierce right through her body. She tried to speak, but the words couldn't come out, so she forced herself to swallow. Only then could she speak. Her voice quivered. "Miss Helen."

"Should the Princess of the great nation of Melodice be running around in her lovely little lace frock with not a hint of care?" asked Helen.

Detecting a sneer in Helen's voice, it was Mirin's turn to frown.

Mika was speechless.

Helen shook her head. "Is the Princess of the great nation of Melodice aware that the walkways can be quite dirty? Surely, your dress would be stained by now."

Mika was too busy feeling frightened of Helen to realize this until now. As she hastily tried to get back up, Mirin helped her. "I'm sorry, Miss Helen," she stammered as she avoided Helen's gaze. "I ran into you. I was being careless. I'm so sorry."

Helen frowned again, annoyed by Mika's tendency to apologize excessively.

However, Mirin was not at all intimidated, unlike his best friend. "Helen, you are so rude! You forget yourself! You do know you're talking to Princess Mika, don't you?!"

Helen rolled her eyes. "I know perfectly well who I'm talking to, Mirin. Didn't you hear me? You would do well to unclog your ears." A small smirk appeared in the corner of her mouth.

Mirin growled. "Why, you...."

Mika gently put her hand on his arm. "It's all right, Mirin." She turned back to Helen. "It won't happen again. I'm sorry for running into you."

"Perhaps this won't happen again, but surely, I will find irritation in *something else* you will do eventually," said Helen.

Mirin was shocked by her behaviour. "Helen, stop talking to the Princess like that! You could get punished! You should show more respect!"

"Mirin!" whispered Mika, hoping he would stop his outburst.

Helen suddenly straightened up, straight as a stick, her heels clicked together. She raised her chin, and looked straight ahead, right over Mika's head. "Your Highness, I apologize for my behaviour! It was rude of me to speak to you with such a careless tongue! I humbly and respectfully request that you pardon my insolence and forgive me because I would very much like to keep my head attached to my shoulders! I also apologize for standing in your way as you were running! If I once again find myself blocking your path, I will use my magic, and fly away with utmost haste!"

Mika was taken aback. She tried to think quickly for a response, but it was obvious from Helen's tone of voice that she was still mocking her.

"You don't know how to fly, Miss Helen. I don't think you've learn that skill yet," Mirin whispered with great irritation.

"Oh... um... it's all right, Miss Helen... I think..." said the Princess.

"Thank you, Princess! Now, if you will please excuse me, I must make haste as I head to the lavatory! I am sensing the call of nature, and it is quite urgent!"

Mirin covered his face upon hearing Helen's brazen attempt at sarcasm.

Mika felt awkward as she stammered again. "Um, all right! Of course, you're excused, Miss Helen! I'm keeping you too long! I'm so sorry!"

"Thank you, Princess!" Helen walked away as if her whole body was stiff in a highly exaggerated soldier's march.

Mika and Mirin watched her as she left them.

"If I didn't know her any better, I'd be laughing, but she has to be saying that on purpose," said Mirin.

Mika shook her head, put a hand on her forehead, and grimaced as if she felt a headache coming on.

Mirin noticed Mika's discomfort. "Are you all right, Mika?"

"I'm fine! I'm just, it's just... I feel so scared whenever

she's around me. Ugh, sometimes I can't bear it!" Mika sighed to calm herself. "I don't mean to sound blunt, but she can be so—what word should I use?—difficult. Whenever she's near me, my words are lost, and anxiety gets the better of me. I feel like I'm irritating her all the time, even when I don't mean to."

Mirin smiled, and took Mika by the hand. "Don't worry so much. She's no longer here." He directed her attention to her necklace. "Wait. Your Princess Gem... it must have slipped out from under your collar."

Mika reached up for her necklace. Since the neckline of her dress was loose, the necklace must have found its way out of her dress while she was running earlier. The Princess Gem, nearly the size of her palm, gleamed as she cradled it with her fingertips. She put it back under her collar. She smiled up at Mirin. "Let's go to the front of the castle."

* * *

"I can't believe it! We passed the gates! When those knights opened the crates for inspection, I thought we were done for!" exclaimed Athrel. "Your fancy design worked, Joris! They only found the vegetables!"

"As I expected, there was no need to worry. That means we're safe for now," said Joris.

Radeth laughed. "Amazing. I'm starting to think we might be able to do this."

Kiran chuckled in the darkness. "We should celebrate!"

Their leader's voice called out to the others from the darkness. "Gentlemen, it's too early to be celebrating. In fact, you all know it won't be us who will be celebrating. It'll be the people of Melodice."

Remembering their purpose, Kiran agreed. "That's right. We need to stay focused, and remember that what we're about to do today, we do for our people."

Radeth let out a deep sigh. "Yeah, well, I've done everything I wanted to do in this life. I have no regrets. I don't know about the rest of you."

Athrel laughed. "Come on, Radeth. Aren't you still a kid? You sound like an old man all of a sudden."

"What?! I'm twenty-four! And Joris is younger than me! Shut the hell up, Athrel!"

"Ah, both of you, shut up and focus on what we have to do next," said Joris. "It's almost time to kill some of those noble bastards. After that, our mission will be complete."

As Kiran pondered the words of their leader, he made a suggestion. "Dalemar, when the time comes for us to attack, could you possibly call out our names... one by one... you know, like a battle cry? Let those fucking tyrants know who's come to fight for the people of Melodice. After all, if everything goes well... it'll be the last time we hear them. What do you think?"

The leader of the group searched around for his scabbard. "As you wish. Is everyone ready?"

"As ready as we'll ever be," said Joris.

"Good. Now, ready your swords. We have rehearsed this plan many times, to the point that it's become second nature to you. Judging by the amount of time that has passed since we came through the gates, and by the sound of the cervid hooves, I can tell we're on the Valderia Pathway, which means we're getting closer to the front of the castle. Be sure to calm your nerves."

The other four responded in unison. "Yes, sir."

"Ellis will stop the carriage right before the front of the castle. As soon as we get out of here, things are going to move very quickly. Your lives might even be over in a flash. However, you're all here because you volunteered for this, because you are loyal to our nation. Your commitment and pride for the nation that you love is truly admirable. Our people, our families, and the citizens of our city and nation will honour our names for generations to come."

There was a moment's pause as they reflected on their fate. Everyone was silent as they neared their destination, their breathing heavy and their hearts beating rapidly in anticipation. The only sounds they heard were those of the hooves of the cervids that pulled the carriage along and the grinding of the wheels against the pavement.

Dalemar chuckled. "Today is a good day to die. Wouldn't you agree, gentlemen?"

"Yes. For our people," said Kiran.

Joris. "For all our children... for our future...."

Radeth. "For our nation...."

Athrel. "For Melodice...."

* * *

"You shouldn't feel so intimidated by Helen, Mika." Mirin often called her by first name instead of Princess or Princess Mika. Earlier in their childhood, Mika had insisted that he address her informally, and he was the only child in the castle who was allowed to do so. That was how close they were.

"I know..." said Mika. "But I can't help it. She's... she always speaks to me with a mocking tone. I don't feel comfortable whenever she's near me."

"I think she mocks you because you're very shy around her to begin with. Perhaps she sees that, and then uses it to her advantage."

"Perhaps you're right."

"But you've always been that way."

Mika nodded in agreement. "That's just how I am."

"But you're the Princess! You deserve every respect, and hers is no exception!" Mirin exclaimed with his childish energy. "She's only a knight and has been one for no longer than a season. Granted, she's a Magic Knight as well, but that doesn't matter. She's a Private Enlist in the Scarletia Royal Guard. You could order her to govern her tongue! And if she doesn't, a night in a dungeon cell might teach her proper behaviour."

Taken aback, Mika regarded Mirin with disapproval. "What? But that's terrible. It doesn't quite work that way."

Mirin blinked, confused. "Why? What do you mean?"

"If I threatened to throw her in the dungeon for her words, what sort of Princess would I be? I can't just punish people for being rude to me. If I did that, I would be like a tyrant who ruled her people using fear and intimidation.

Such a ruler wouldn't be at all inviting, and her people wouldn't feel comfortable with her. That would be wrong."

Mirin was silent. The Princess had a point.

"Who would want to be ruled by a tyrant Princess? If anyone actually wanted that, I'd be worried they'd caught a fever and had become delusional."

"You're probably right."

Mika put her arm through his as they continued their walk.

* * *

Two large, powerful beasts called cervids, their forward-pointing antlers moving up and down with every step they took, pulled the long wooden carriage, driven by a lone merchant, down the Valderia Pathway, the wide street that led from the castle gates to the front of the castle proper. Behind the carriage, the castle gates, made of steel and heavy algerwood, slid on steel tracks embedded across the width of the street back to their closed position. The knights who guarded the gates had already inspected the carriage.

Mika, watching the carriage coming down the street, reached into a pocket at the side of her skirt, and pulled out a golden timepiece. "The daily merchant carriage's arrival is late by one hour today."

Mirin was puzzled. "What do you mean?"

"I've noticed that the merchant carriage arrives every morning at about 9:00 without fail."

Mirin shrugged his shoulders. "So... what about it?"

Mika shrugged as well, as she put away her timepiece. "Nothing. Just a minor detail I noticed."

Mirin smiled and shook his head. "There you go again, always fussing over minor details. It's not like what it carries isn't going to arrive. In fact, it's here now."

Along the street and the walkways that branched off of it, nobles engaged in pleasant laughter and conversation, enjoying the warm spring day. The gentlemen and boys, in their dress coats over waistcoats and trousers, socialized alongside ladies and girls, in their elaborately designed dresses of various styles. Children were told by their fathers and mothers to be careful as they playfully ran underneath cloudless skies.

The carriage stopped short of the front of the castle as Mika and Mirin approached it from the side. They paid no further attention to the carriage as they were about to pass it.

Mirin tapped Mika's shoulder, and took several quick steps away from her to give himself a head start. "Tag! You're it! Now it's your turn to chase me!"

Mika gasped as she stood in the middle of the street a short distance behind the carriage. "No! That's not fair! I wasn't ready!"

Mirin laughed. "Tag is never a fair game!"

"I can never catch you! Please don't run too far ahead!" pleaded Mika, as a well-dressed gentleman was about to pass between her and the merchant carriage.

Mika caught movement in the periphery of her vision. A man leapt out from the back door of the merchant carriage, a short sword in one hand, its blade shining in the sunlight. As he lunged towards the gentleman, Mika turned her head to see more clearly what was happening. One slash with the sword was all that was needed. Drops of blood sprayed out, and the gentleman fell dead beside her.

"Ellis, Radeth, Joris, Athrel, Kiran, kill as many as you can!" shouted Dalemar.

A few short seconds seemed to happen in slow motion. Mika and Mirin's eyes were wide with shock and fear.

Four more merchants leapt out of the back of the carriage, all brandishing short swords. They saw Mika, standing before them in her bloodstained white dress, but ignored her. The driver joined the other merchants as they began to chase down innocent men and women around them. Women and children screamed with intense fear. Some of the men tried to protect themselves and their partners, but not a single one of them was armed, and each was instead cut down. Those who were farther away saw what was happening and ran, desperate to escape from the scene of carnage.

Farther down one side of the castle, Helen was kneeling down beside a patch of vibrant red and blue flowers, admiring their beauty. When she heard the terrified screams from the front of the castle, she stood up and turned towards the source.

"What's going on?"

She began running down the walkways as fast as her legs could take her.

Behind the merchant carriage, Dalemar stood with his bloodstained short sword at his side. Blood pooled on the street underneath the gentleman he had just killed. To either side of him, his companions slashed away at innocent noble civilians, men and women alike, without care. Dalemar looked down at the frightened little girl in front of him, spots of blood on her face and hair.

Mika stared back at the merchant, her body frozen with fear.

"It would be in your best interest to run away now, little girl. You don't need to see any of this!" He grinned at her, and then focused his attention on the civilians nearby, rushing to join his companions. "Kill as many as you can, gentlemen! Kill them in the name of our great nation of Melodice!"

A well-dressed couple tried to run away, but the long dress the woman wore hampered her ability to move quickly, tripping her.

"You're done for, bitch!" Kiran stabbed her in the back, cutting off her terrified scream.

"No!" Seeing his wife felled, the distraught man beside her tried to attack Kiran with his fists.

With one powerful swing of his sword, Joris let out a battle cry, and decapitated the man from behind. Children in the area stared in shock as their parents were brutally felled, but the merchants ignored them.

Mika tried to move her feet, but they wouldn't respond. Mirin shouted to her, but she could not understand him. His voice sounded like it was far away.

Mirin could not move his body either. He was far enough away from the merchants that he was not in immediate danger. He wanted to go to Mika and take her away, but that would mean putting himself at a much greater risk. He desperately called out to her. "Mika... run away! Run away, Princess!"

Mika blinked, and then heard his voice, but she was still frozen.

Dalemar heard the boy calling out to the little girl. "Princess?" He turned to look at the girl in the white dress, still standing where he'd seen her last. He stared at her from head to toe. She was dressed quite elaborately, like most of the little girls and women out here. He saw nothing on her that identified her as the Princess, but hearing the boy screaming for her and calling her Princess was good enough for him. He turned to his companions. "Everyone, today truly is a good day to die, for we have a Royal out here we can exact our revenge upon! It's the Princess of Melodice!"

Mirin gasped. *No... what have I done?!*

Mika heard each and every terrifying word.

In the distance, Helen ran hard towards the Princess. "Damn you, don't you dare touch her...." She quickly pulled out her long knife from the side of her shin.

Dalemar walked up to Mika, towering above her, and raised his sword above his head.

Mika felt her heart racing. Her eyes shifted to the blade, and saw blood dripping down from it. She shut her eyes tight. *I'm... I'm going to die?*

The merchant leader stared down at her with a hateful smile. "For our people... for our nation... for Melodice!"

Helen threw her knife towards Dalemar.

Dalemar moved his blade back to gather enough momentum to split Mika's tiny body in half. Suddenly, his head jerked to one side. The blade of Helen's knife was embedded in the side of his skull. His grip on his short sword weakened. It slid out of his grasp, and clattered loudly against the concrete.

Mika was startled as she gasped, opened her eyes, and jumped all at the same time. Almost immediately, the merchant closed his eyes, and fell on his side, never to move again. Mika drew in quick breaths, not realizing she had been holding them until now. She stared at the dead merchant, the man who was going to kill her.

As Helen approached, she unsheathed her long sword.

The other merchants looked around in confusion when they saw Dalemar dead. Athrel saw movement in the periphery of his vision, and when he looked, he was alarmed as he saw a young woman with a long sword. "Ellis!"

Too late. Helen moved so swiftly that, before the other merchants realized what was happening, Ellis was felled with a quick slash to the face. Almost at the same time, a pink magic circle appeared in the air as Helen held up her free hand in front of Athrel. Unrecognizable characters, symbols, and shapes lined the sides of the magic circle. It glowed brightly, and a blast of fire threw him a long distance. His hands and face were burned.

"Miss Helen!" Mika called out.

Mirin looked on in surprise and amazement.

It was more than enough of a distraction for Helen to take advantage of. She took Mika by the hand. "This way!"

Mika's feet finally obeyed her as Helen pulled her away from danger. As soon as Mika and Helen got to Mirin, all three of them ran.

As Helen watched the civilians running away from the danger, she looked back toward the scene of the attack. "The knights of the Royal Guard... where the hell are they?"

As if on cue, from both sides of the castle, twenty knights mounted on cervids appeared, and galloped towards the three remaining able-bodied merchants, who continued to kill or at least injure as many noble civilians as they could. As soon as the merchants saw the approaching knights, they stopped targeting the civilians, and charged for the mounted knights on foot.

"For Melodice!" shouted the merchants, raising their short swords.

Between the two forces, there was no contest. A mounted knight threw a spear that impaled Radeth, sending him flying backwards. Joris made a run for the knights, but his sword arm was cut off, while another knight behind him charged in, and decapitated him with a long sword. Kiran clashed blades with one knight on a cervid, and because he was distracted, another knight came up behind him and stabbed him in the back with a long sword. Athrel, lying on the ground injured, was pierced in the chest with a spear by another mounted knight.

* * *

On the grass, Mika, stricken with terror, sat with her legs folded back on either side of her, looking down at her white dress now stained with drops of blood.

"It's over now, Mika." Mirin put his arms around her, and tried to comfort her as she sobbed loudly. He tried to wipe away her tears, now mingling with the drops of blood on her otherwise unblemished cheeks.

Helen walked towards the scene of carnage. The six merchants lay motionless on the ground along with several noble men and women. There were a few children scattered nearby, sitting on the ground, crying over their dead parents. Other civilians stood around in shock, staring at the aftermath of the scene. The knights had dismounted from their cervids to assess what had happened. Helen counted the dead bodies. In addition to the merchants, there were fifteen civilians, nine men and six women. There were several injured as well. She regarded the children nearby.

Helen thought to herself. *Death could have come for the children as well. They were near when these people were killed. The merchants targeted only the adults. But for the Princess... it was different.*

She heard Mika's sobs behind her and turned. Although the merchants had not targeted the children, one of them did target the Princess. Had Helen not been there.... She thought about that for a moment. The only difference between Mika and the rest of the children was that she was of the Royal Family.

A large, distinguished, armoured gentleman passed

through the massive double doors of the Scarletia Royal Castle, accompanied by several knights. His hair receding, his moustache and beard faded to white, he held his head high with an air of authority as he walked down the stairs leading from the front of the castle to the Grounds below.

As soon as Helen saw him, she called out to the other knights. "The Supreme Captain arrives!"

Every knight stopped what he was doing, and stood tall at attention.

The Supreme Captain of the Scarletia Royal Guard and the Royal Army of Melodice, Terren Rinaldia, nodded to Helen to silently thank her. "As you were," he commanded, prompting the knights to return to what they were doing previously.

Terren was a heavily built man, his armour fitted larger to accommodate his muscular build. Without a helmet, he otherwise wore full armour, black and gold in colour, covered by a black cape with gold trimmings. He assessed the situation around him, his enormous broadsword sheathed at his side, with one hand resting on its hilt. His immediate concern was the presence of civilians—men, women, and children alike—still standing around, looking at the massacre.

He issued his orders to the knights. "Give our noble dead their final dignity. Cover them up. Cover the merchants as well. And ensure that the injured receive the proper medical attention."

"Yes, sir!" Some of the knights dispersed to gather blankets to cover the dead.

Terren approached Helen, and at the same time, he looked back at Princess Mika. He noted the stains of blood on her white dress. "The poor girl." He next turned to Helen.

Helen stood up straight at attention. "Sir."

"Are you all right?" he asked.

"I am unharmed, sir. But I fear the Princess may have been traumatized."

Terren sighed. "I agree. The Princess is eleven years old, a child, just a few years away from the age of majority, yet still a child. This is not for a child to experience."

"Yes, sir," said Helen.

"Tell me what happened from start to finish."

Helen complied with the Supreme Captain. She told him what happened, from when Princess Mika ran into her while playing, to when she heard the screams, to when she killed the man who tried to take the life of the Princess, to when she rescued her from the scene of carnage, to when the knights came and finished what she started.

"Thank you, Miss Helen. You have saved the Princess. All of us are grateful. Surely, our King and Queen will not let your heroic act go unnoticed."

Helen bowed her head slightly. "Such is my duty, Sir Terren."

Terren was impressed by Helen's attitude towards duty. Another knight passed by them, and Terren stopped him. "Young man, what is your name?"

The knight stood at attention, nervous from being addressed so suddenly by the Supreme Captain. "Sir, Valias Garan, Private Enlist."

"What have the civilians over there told you so far about what happened?"

"They told us the merchant carriage stopped where it is now. The driver and five merchants, who emerged from the back, attacked the civilians, killing nine men and six women. We rode out, and then killed the rest of them before they could harm anyone else. I killed the last one, the one lying on the ground with burns on his face."

Terren expressed his disappointment by shaking his head slightly. "So the last one was injured and could no longer fight? If you had let him live, we might have been able to take him prisoner and interrogate him."

Valias was taken aback, his voice filled with uneasiness. "My apologies, sir. But in the heat of battle…."

"What's done is done. Continue, Sir Valias."

"Yes, sir. There were children in the area as well… but, fortunately, their lives were spared."

"Yes, and we were fortunate they were spared," said Helen. "They attacked only the adults. The merchants ignored all the children except…."

Terren knew what Helen was going to say next. "The Princess...."

Helen nodded. "One of the merchants saw the Princess. He was well aware of her presence. While he and his companions ignored all the other children, he did not ignore Princess Mika. He raised his sword, ready to cut her down. To kill her was his intention."

"Why? Why did he decide to attack the Princess? Did he know who she was?"

Helen shook her head. "I'm uncertain, sir."

"Mika!" a woman cried out, clad in a long red dress that reached to her ankles. The heels of her high-heeled, knee-high boots made hollow sounds as she ran down the steps that led from the castle doors, holding on to the front of her skirt with both hands. Jewels were sewn into her low neckline, and her necklace and earrings sparkled under the sun. She had the same colour eyes as Mika and long light-blonde hair that fell to just above her knees. She held a greater air of authority than even the highly distinguished Terren, but her face was full of worry and fear for her daughter, the Princess of Melodice.

"Her Highness, the Queen, arrives!" announced Terren.

All the knights, including Helen, acknowledged with their stand of attention.

Mika saw her mother, Queen Maiya Silveraine. "Mother!"

"Mika!" The Queen ran past the soldiers without giving them a single look. It was her daughter, who had been subjected to the threat of death, she wanted to see.

"As you were," Terren announced again, and all the knights went back to what they were doing.

As Queen Maiya approached, Mika reached out for her, prompting Mirin to stand back. Her mother took hold of her, and hugged her tightly. Mika pressed her head against Maiya's chest, and held onto her arm with trembling hands while tears streamed down her cheeks.

"Mika! Are you hurt?"

"I'm fine. Mother, I'm not... I'm not hurt." True, Mika had not suffered any bodily harm. But she had stood in sheer terror as those events unfolded before her, and she was still quite frightened. She felt like she was going to die. However, her mother was here for her now.

Maiya pulled away, looked her over, and saw the bloodstains on her dress, as well as what were now smeared drops that remained in her hair and on her face and neck.

"Blood? Please tell me this isn't yours...."

Mika quickly shook her head. "No... no, Mother... I'm not hurt. It's not mine...."

Maiya breathed a sigh of relief as she took hold of Mika again, and held her tight, her own tears finally let go. "I'm so glad you're not hurt."

Mirin watched the Princess and the Queen as he slowly approached Helen and Terren. "I'm worried about her."

Terren heard his words of concern. "Your dear friend, the Princess, will be fine, Sir Mirin."

Maiya stroked Mika's head, shoulders, and back to comfort her. "It's all right. It's over now, Mika."

"They killed everyone, Mother." Mika's eyes were wide with fear as if it were all still happening in her mind. Everyone nearby heard her.

Helen listened intently to her words, which sent chills down her back.

"Mother... they killed everyone... they're all dead... they died in front of me.... I saw them kill them... they killed them...." Even after Mika's voice trailed off, her mind continued to scream the same words she uttered as the terror she experienced pierced deeply into her heart.

They killed them all... and they were going to kill me... he was going to kill me....

CHAPTER 2:

EYES OF THE PRINCESS

SEC 3566, Demetre 80

After two days, the deeply frightened and disturbed Princess Mika calmed down enough to be able to speak about the incident. She had spent much of that time in her bedchamber sleeping. As expected, Queen Maiya and her father, King Ralphen Silveraine, were quite concerned. Mika's maidservant, Angelica Ruviel, came in to her bedchamber often to see to her needs. Mirin often asked about her, hoping to see her, only to be told she was still recuperating from her experience. Mika had wished she could see him, but had been told that it was best for her to be surrounded by her immediate family for now.

However, two days did not seem very long to Sir Terren. While surprised by the short time span, he was relieved as well. In a room called the King's Conference, he mentioned this to the King and Queen.

"She is a highly resilient little girl."

The Supreme Captain leaned forward in his chair, resting his elbows on the side of a grand circular conference table made of rare and expensive algerwood. Instead of armour, he was in the typical uniform of the Scarletia Royal Guard, which consisted of black trousers, matching boots, and a black coat over a gold waistcoat. He also wore a black cape with gold trimmings.

"The Princess experienced a terrible tragedy no child should ever witness. Unfortunately, fate was not on her side that day. But after just two days, her fits of panic have not manifested without provocation. She may be easily frightened, but I must praise her for her resilience."

The King listened as he leaned back in his chair directly across from Terren, cross-legged, his smooth black hair combed straight back, his serious facial expression accentuated by hard features. His black waistcoat was in stark contrast to the white collars of his dress shirt underneath, both balanced out by the neutral gray of his long coat and trousers. His cape was similar to Terren's, and his black shoes had been recently polished.

The Queen stood beside Ralphen, and expressed her agreement with Terren. "Our little Princess does have a far stronger heart and mind than she cares to admit. She may be timid and easily frightened by even the most benign scares... but she's able to recover from situations that are challenging to her." Maiya paused for a moment. "However, this is the most difficult situation our sweet daughter has ever faced in her young life. I pray she recovers fully, both in mind and spirit."

"I don't doubt she will, My Lady," said Terren.

King Ralphen leaned his elbows on the edge of the table, shifting forward in his seat, which had a much higher back than the other twenty chairs that surrounded the table. "I am grateful, Sir Terren, that you think very highly of our daughter's strength of mind. I believe Mika has had plenty of time to recover from the incident. But we need to determine what caused this tragedy... and who is responsible."

"Agreed, My Lord."

"Have you found more on those... so-called merchants who attacked our Nobility and our Princess?"

"Yes, My Lord. And apparently, they were, in fact, merchants. The same merchants who delivered goods from the city proper and into the castle every day. They were of the Peasantry. The merchant carriage is one of several scheduled to arrive at 9:00 each morning, and this schedule was honoured without fail... until that fateful morning. This particular carriage arrived one hour late. Instead of delivering a cargo of vegetables, it delivered assassins."

The King narrowed his eyes. "Did the guards not inspect the carriage? How could a cargo of assassins simply pass through unchecked?"

"As a matter of fact, the guards did inspect the cargo. The merchant carriage, as expected, carried several large wooden crates. When they were opened, they appeared to be filled with vegetables. However, what the eyes see on the surface isn't always the truth. The crates had been specially modified. There was a top shelf inside the crates on which the vegetables lay. The assassins hid inside the crates underneath the shelf. Therefore, from the perspective of the knights who performed their routine inspection, nothing was amiss."

Ralphen's expression turned to that of anger. He clasped his tense hands together on the table. "These damn peasants... animals, they all are. And, yet, they were able to outwit our guards. How peasants can outwit a noble knight escapes me. It should not be possible."

"Nevertheless, My Lord, these merchants were able to pass through the gates, and perform their deadly act of mass murder."

Queen Maiya noticed her husband's anger, and put a hand on his shoulder. "It was fortunate that the knights were deployed when they were."

After a moment, Ralphen nodded. "Yes, that's true." He paused to try to calm down. "But what could have possessed these fools—these merchant assassins, I suppose we could call them that—to do this? Didn't they know the Royal Guard would be deployed to subdue them? Didn't they know they themselves would die?"

"I believe they did, My Lord," said Terren. "We've determined that these merchant assassins had only one purpose for infiltrating our castle. That one and only purpose... was to kill as many nobles as possible before they themselves were killed. They didn't expect to survive. When our mounted knights were deployed, the merchant assassins willingly charged on foot, equipped with only short swords. Our knights were in full armour and had superior weapons. There was no contest. They knew they would die."

Maiya, shocked by what she heard, put a hand on her chest. "Why would they kill our noble civilians? Didn't they know how meaningless it was?"

"We're not certain why, My Lady. Not yet," answered Terren.

"Isn't it obvious?" Ralphen let out an impatient sigh, his hands clasped together on the table even more tightly than a moment ago. He stood up, and then approached the large windows at one side of the room that overlooked the Grounds in front of the castle. Down on the Grounds below, he watched as noble civilians socialized as if the incident from two days ago never occurred. "They were nothing but peasants... but they infiltrated our castle to murder as many nobles as they could, and they knew perfectly well they were going to die at the hands of our knights."

He turned towards Maiya and Terren, and then made his way towards the bar at the other side of the room, where several liquor bottles were neatly arranged. As he continued to speak of the peasants with animosity, he poured himself a glass of sparkling spirits.

"The Peasantry have always hated the Nobility and the Royal Family. Many times throughout history, they have attacked our people and our way of life. They're an inferior sub-species of the race of Humans, their level of competence only a step above animals. But because of their nature, they look upon us with a collective inferiority complex, and use that as an excuse to attack us."

Terren drew back his hands, placed one of them under the table on his knee, and made a hard fist that shook slightly, but his face held no hint of a reaction. He watched Maiya nod with agreement.

Ralphen took a sip of his beverage, and then turned back to the Supreme Captain. "Sir Terren, in addition to questioning Princess Mika about the event from her perspective, I have some orders for you."

Terren relaxed his fist, and then stood up. "Yes, My Lord."

Ralphen set his glass down on the bar, and then approached Terren. "These damn merchant assassins killed fifteen of our people, injured several others, and threatened the life of our daughter. There had to be a plan behind this tragedy, and that plan was conceived by peasants who are out there, at this moment, walking the streets of Scarletia, thinking they're somehow victorious. They had to have leaders who put it into motion, and others supported them. I want these bastards who threatened our Princess found. Find their families, their women and children. When you find them, bring down justice upon them. All of them. Leave none alive."

There was a long pause as Terren, without any outward facial expression, stared into the King's furious eyes. Despite his calm exterior, he was full of turmoil inside, but he did his best to keep it in check. If he were to let the King know what he truly felt about his order, he himself would be executed. For a brief moment, he shifted his eyes to the large paintings on the walls that depicted armies, military leaders, warfare, and scenes of butchery.

Find them? Find their families, their women and children, as well? Once again, you mean to bring death upon innocents? You damn bastard of a King. Someday, you will get yours. Someday. I swear it as the Knight of the Dark.

However, the King noticed the Supreme Captain's pause, and he wondered what he was thinking about. "Are my orders clear, Sir Terren?"

"Yes, they are, My Lord. As you have ordered, it shall be done," said Terren, his voice loud and clear.

Ralphen patted Terren's shoulder. "Thank you, Supreme Captain. You bring honour to us, to the Nobility of Melodice, and to the Royal Family, as you always have."

Terren bowed his head slightly. "Such is my duty, My Lord. If there's nothing further, I'll proceed with finding these... people who committed this hateful crime. And when I find them, justice will be brought down upon them as ordered." He turned towards the Queen. "My Lady, later today, I will proceed as previously ordered to question Princess Mika. As you know, it might be difficult for her. When she is prepared...."

Queen Maiya nodded. "Of course, I will let you know, Sir Terren."

Terren bowed his head, and then exited the King's Conference.

* * *

Mika's bedchamber was elegantly feminine, though in a child-like manner, and elaborately decorated, as expected of a Princess. The room was large, and its ceilings were high. Artwork covered its walls, depicting a flower garden with small furry animals among grass, little birds flying or bathing in ponds of water, and a pink sky with white clouds. Windows occupied the entire length of one wall, overlooking the side of the castle, where there were real flower gardens five floors below. Long, flowing curtains covered half the windows. Her bed, on a frame of expensive algerwood with intricately carved designs of flowers and hearts, was enormous, covered in luxurious blankets and pillows.

Elsewhere in the bedchamber, a door led into a large wardrobe, and another beside it led to the lavatory and the bathroom. Bottles of body creams, lotions, and perfumes, as well as hairbrushes, hair ribbons, and boxes of jewelry, were arranged neatly on a wide dressing table, with chests of drawers at either side of it. The large mirror on top of the dressing table reflected the bright glare of a kerosene lamp and the gentler glow of candles.

Mika sat with the Queen on a white leather couch, while Terren sat on another couch directly across a rectangular algerwood table. On each couch were three soft pillows with flowery designs.

Mika's maidservant, the young and beautiful Angelica Ruviel, stood serenely nearby in an elegant dark blue and black maid's dress, the soft fabric of its long sleeves reaching just past her wrists, its hem falling just above her knees. Her large blue eyes hinted at a fierce devotion for her Princess, and her silky brown hair, which she refused to tie into a ponytail despite her occupation because she felt more attractive not doing so, fell to just above her waist

Tonight, Maiya had asked her daughter if she was ready

to be questioned by Terren, who needed to understand the events of the other day from her perspective. Mika had told her mother that she was. Maiya had repeatedly asked her if she was all right with this, but the Princess had assured her she would be fine.

"Thank you kindly, Princess Mika," said Terren. "I'm glad to know you're feeling well enough to be able to speak of the events from two days ago. It was tragic and frightening, and I would understand if you weren't feeling up to answering some questions. But you were standing right next to the merchant assassins. You had a unique perspective. It's important that we understand what you experienced with all your senses. If, at any time, you wish to stop, please do not hesitate to let us know."

Princess Mika said nothing for a moment, still somewhat uncertain of herself. Soon, she nodded. "I should thank you, Sir Terren, for being here with me."

Terren smiled, as did Maiya and Angelica. "Of course, My Lady. You are surrounded by two of the people in your life who are closest to your heart, your mother, the Queen, and your beloved maidservant, Miss Angelica, and that should put you at ease. Let me know when you're ready."

Mika nodded again as Maiya stroked her long hair to comfort her. "Please... proceed with your questions, Sir Terren."

"All right." Terren leaned forward on the couch. "I want you to close your eyes. Take your mind back to that day, that morning."

After a short moment of hesitation, Mika did as he asked.

"I want you to focus on your thoughts and feelings, what went through your mind and your heart, with each passing moment. Let us go to before this tragedy even occurred. What were you doing before that?"

"My friend Mirin and I were playing tag. I was running away. He was chasing me.... We were having fun."

"That's good, Princess."

"I ran into someone. Miss Helen. I was... somewhat frightened of her. Sometimes, she can be quite intimidating.

She's so beautiful... and she carries herself with great confidence. Sometimes... sometimes I wish I were more like she is."

Without her realizing it, Mika's facial expression turned to that of slight annoyance. A hint of envy was in her heart. From her perspective, Helen was more beautiful and overflowing with confidence, and she had all the characteristics Mika wished she had.

"She said she needed to go to the lavatory so I excused her. I felt... sorry for running into her. I must have annoyed her. Mirin and I headed for the front of the castle." Mika smiled, and a faint blush appeared on her cheeks. Her voice temporarily dropped to a soft whisper. "His hand was soft. I... I like holding his hand...."

Terren raised an eyebrow. He noticed Maiya doing the same, while Angelica smiled and blushed.

As Mika continued, she talked about what she went through internally. "The merchant carriage... it was one hour late. I checked my timepiece to be sure. I thought it was strange. It was different from when they usually arrived."

Terren was impressed. "You are very skilled at pointing out even small details like that, Princess. I'm truly amazed, and I must say I'm proud of you as well. You are truly a brilliant little girl."

Mika kept her eyes closed. Hearing those words from Terren gave her some confidence.

"Mirin and I were behind the merchant carriage. He tagged me, and he started running away. I thought... he was cheating, that... he was being unfair. I can't run very quickly. He's much stronger than I am, and he can run much faster for much longer than I can. Oh... there was a gentleman beside me. He was... he was walking between me and the carriage. I didn't know him. He didn't recognize me. My Princess Gem was underneath my collar. Because of that, he didn't know who I was."

Terren observed Mika's hands tense as they held onto the front of her skirt tightly. He could see that Maiya was trying to resist the natural motherly impulse to hold onto her daughter to comfort her.

"There was another man. He... jumped out of the back of the merchant carriage. He... had a... he was holding a sword. He jumped at the gentleman beside me... and he slashed him." Mika gasped with fright. She almost felt drops of some imaginary liquid sprayed at her as she pushed herself back on the couch, startling both Maiya and Angelica.

Maiya reached out to try to hold her, but stopped when Terren put up his hand to discourage it for now.

"How are you feeling, Princess?" asked Terren.

Mika's voice quivered with fear. "Blood... there was blood on my dress... on my face, in my hair. The merchant killed that gentleman. He killed him...."

Blood... red... on my white dress.... Her breathing became shallow, and she grimaced as she shook her head vigorously. She let out a soft whimper as she opened her eyes briefly, causing tears to stream down her cheeks.

As she came close to panicking, Maiya and Angelica became increasingly worried about her. Maiya put a hand on her shoulder. "Mika, perhaps we should stop for now."

Mika opened her eyes again, looking up at Maiya. "No! Mother!" she cried out, surprising her mother. "Please... please let me do this. Please...."

Maiya looked up at Sir Terren, who glanced back at her silently. She knew what he was wordlessly asking her. After some hesitation, Maiya nodded for him to continue. She put one hand over Mika's, and used her other hand to stroke her hair again. Maiya felt the tension in Mika's trembling hand.

"Please continue, Princess Mika," said Terren.

With some hesitation, Mika closed her eyes again. She breathed deeply several times before she continued, listening to the rapid beats of her own heart. *I need to calm down.... I can't think properly and I can't help Sir Terren if I can't calm down. He has been so good to me. Calm down, Mika....*

After another moment, Mika regained most of her composure, even after nearly giving in to panic, surprising Terren, Maiya, and Angelica.

"The first merchant I saw... the one who killed the gentleman beside me... perhaps he was their leader. I could tell, because... he called out the names of the other merchants with him and ordered them around. He told them to kill as many as they could. He saw me... he looked at me... he grinned. He said... I should run away... that I didn't need to see any of this. He told the others again to kill as many people as they could... in the name of Melodice."

Mika paused for a moment. *Killing in the name of our nation? What...?*

"The others... the other merchants... they started killing people nearby."

"You mentioned the first merchant, the leader, called out the names of the other merchants. Do you remember the names?" asked Terren.

The details were so vivid in Mika's mind that she did remember, except for the leader, whose name had not been mentioned within earshot. "He called out five names. They were... Ellis... Radeth... Joris... Athrel... and Kiran, in that order."

Terren repeated the names in his mind to memorize them.

"Then... I heard Mirin. He sounded like he was far away.... I didn't understand him. I was frozen.... I couldn't move. I was frightened. I wanted... to move my feet... to run away... but I couldn't move. He called out my name...."

"You mentioned the Princess Gem was hidden under your collar. When the merchant leader told you to run away, he didn't see you as the Princess. That means he didn't know you were the Princess. Is that correct?" said Terren.

Mika slowly nodded. "Yes... he didn't know. He couldn't have known."

"What did Mirin call you? Did he call you 'Mika' or did he call you 'Princess'?"

Mika hesitated. "First... he called me 'Mika'. And... then... he called me 'Princess'."

Maiya's eyes widened. "That means...."

"The man turned to me. He heard Mirin calling out

to me. He said 'Princess' as well, like he was surprised. He was very surprised. And then... he turned to the other merchants, and said...."

Terren noted Mika's fearful hesitation. "What did he say?"

"He said that today was a good day to die, because they had a Royal to exact their revenge upon. The Princess of Melodice...."

Wait... revenge? A Royal to exact revenge upon...?

Other thoughts crept into her mind, other feelings. What did he mean by revenge? But she needed to focus on what Terren asked her to do. She needed to continue to remember what happened, focusing on her thoughts and feelings each moment.

"The man held his short sword in front of me. He raised it above his head. He stared at me... his eyes... they looked angry. Angry eyes... but more than just anger. His eyes didn't just look angry... he looked sad as well...."

Queen Maiya was puzzled. "Sad? What do you mean?"

Terren continued listening.

Mika was too focused on what she was recalling to acknowledge her mother's question. "But... but he was going to kill me. He was ready to kill me. There was blood all over his sword... it was dripping down. When he was about to... suddenly, he just stopped. His head moved a little to the side. It was like something hit him. Then... then I saw a knife in his head. The same knife I had seen on Helen's shin before that... when I ran into her. I recognized it. The man... he dropped his sword... it made a loud noise. I was startled by the sound of his sword hitting the ground. He fell... he was dead... and then someone took my hand. It was Miss Helen... she took my hand... and we ran away." She opened her eyes. Although she was calmer than earlier, tears streamed down her cheeks.

Maiya put an arm around her. "Mika...."

Mika's voice dropped to a whisper. "Miss Helen saved me... she saved my life."

"It's all right, Mika. You're fine now," said Maiya.

Terren smiled at Mika. "We have a brave Princess. Thank you very much. You did very well, much better than I had hoped. I'm very impressed with you keeping yourself together while recalling these difficult and painful memories. Nicely done, My Lady."

Hearing Terren's words, Mika nodded as she felt warmth within her heart. "Sir Terren... you have taught me many things as the Supreme Captain, so I want to help you in return. I hope you can always depend on me."

Terren was pleased with Mika's kind words. "Thank you again."

Maiya looked down at Mika. "Sir Terren is right. You were very brave, Mika. You have been most helpful to him." With a proud smile for her daughter, she glanced up at Mika's maidservant. "Don't you think so, Miss Angelica?"

Angelica smiled. "That she is, My Lady. The Princess is very brave," she said with a soft, humble voice. She reached into her pocket, producing a shimmering white handkerchief, and knelt down beside Mika. "May I wipe your tears, My Lady?"

Mika straightened up. "Thank you, Miss Angelica...."

* * *

Terren and Queen Maiya spoke some more after having Mika recall the events she experienced. When they were done, they left Mika's bedchamber.

Angelica closed the door behind them. She leaned against it, and stared at the Princess for a moment, an awkward hesitation in her voice as she spoke. "Princess Mika...."

Mika, still seated on the couch, turned to her maidservant. "What is it, Miss Angelica?"

"I thought you wanted to keep it a secret."

Mika blinked, confused. "Huh?"

Angelica sat down beside Mika. "When you recalled the events you experienced, you also recalled holding Mirin's hand. You said his hand was soft. You said you liked holding his hand. You said this in front of the Queen and the Supreme Captain, while smiling and blushing like a little girl in love."

Mika's eyes widened as her cheeks became red. She fell on her side on the couch, grabbed a pillow, and put it over her head. "Oh no.... I do remember saying that! That's so embarrassing!"

"Oh my!" Angelica laughed as Mika overdramatized her embarrassment.

After a moment, Mika sat up as she held the pillow in front of her. "I can't believe I said that. I hope they don't tell Mirin."

"I don't think they would do that. Sir Terren wouldn't think much of it. As for the Queen, she might talk to you about it at some point later on, since she is your mother. She didn't say she was going to, but she might, if she remembers."

"I hope she forgets. It's still a secret, so please don't let anyone know."

Angelica laughed again. "However, Princess Mika, you did very well. You nearly panicked at one point, but you kept yourself together. You were able to recall everything you could and tell Sir Terren all about it. The information you provided will be helpful to him."

Mika thought about Angelica's praise, as well as the praise given to her by her mother and the Supreme Captain. She did not feel right about it somehow. "I don't deserve any of that."

Angelica was surprised. "What do you mean, Princess?"

"I don't deserve your praise, Miss Angelica. I don't deserve Mother's praise, and I don't deserve Sir Terren's praise either."

"Why? Why would you say that?"

Mika hugged the pillow, resting her chin on top of it. Her voice became very subdued and held deep regret. "I'm... I'm just a weakling... and a coward."

"Princess Mika...." Angelica was surprised that Mika thought of herself this way. She tried to think of what to say to convince her otherwise, but she was having difficulty finding the right words.

Mika put the pillow on the couch, leaning her head on it as she lay down on her side. "I remember Miss Helen... she protected me from them. She saved my life. She's not only a knight. She's also a Magic Knight. She's very proficient with a sword. Her magic is quite powerful as well. Miss Helen is the one who's brave... not me. Apparently, by definition of that term... I am also a Magic Knight."

Angelica nodded as she sat closer to Mika, putting a comforting hand on her arm. "Yes... that's right, Princess."

"But that term is just something people invented out of convenience. It's not an official term. You just have to be very proficient at magic to be called a Magic Knight. There's nothing that says you have to be a certain age to be one. But, still, I would think... at eleven years old, I'm too young to be one."

"But you do have very powerful magic as well, and you're highly knowledgeable when it comes to it. You are extremely proficient, as much as Miss Helen."

Mika thought about that for a moment. She knew that everything Angelica mentioned just now was true. However, she continued to doubt herself.

"But I couldn't protect myself... and I couldn't protect the people around me. I could have defended myself and everyone else there. I had the power to protect... but I was so scared. I was too scared to do anything."

Angelica was speechless.

"Those people who died... they died because I couldn't protect them. The Princess of Melodice was too scared to protect her own people." She closed her eyes, her regret etched deeply into her heart.

* * *

Later that evening, back in the King's Conference, Ralphen struck the top of the table with his fist, startling Maiya, who was seated closest to him. The King was burning with anger after hearing the testimony from Mika through Sir Terren, who did not react at all to his fury while seated directly across from him.

Supreme Commanders Collin Gagnier and Maleth Arlistia stood beside Terren. Sir Collin and Sir Maleth were both knights of the second-highest rank in the Scarletia Royal Guard. They reported directly to the Supreme Captain. Collin was in his early thirties, and Maleth was just a few years younger.

"Those bastard merchants... bastard peasants... peasant animals!" Ralphen stood from designated his chair so furiously that it fell backwards. "They spared the children around them as they killed our people... but they discovered that one of the children near them was the Princess of Melodice! Because she was of the Royal Family, they decided to target her! They decided to try to kill our daughter! I will not stand for this, Sir Terren!"

Both Collin and Maleth stole a quick glance at Terren, who still had no reaction, so they decided they would do their best to follow suit.

"They infiltrated the Grounds to kill as many nobles as they could. Like you said, Sir Terren, they did this knowing they would be killed. But they found luck on their side that morning... when the Princess was right next to them! And that's when they decided they would try to kill her!"

"We are fortunate that Miss Helen was nearby, as she was able to save the life of the Princess," said Terren.

"Yes, we certainly are fortunate, and I am grateful. We all are. We will commend her for her honourable actions that day. But as for these... filthy peasants who tried to kill our Princess. You know your orders, which I gave you earlier today. Seek out those who were involved in this crime! Find them and their families! Gather them up like the animals they are! Their possessions, their homes, raze them to the ground! Bring down justice upon them! Kill all of them! None may be allowed to live!"

The Supreme Captain resisted the temptation to give the King a death stare as he stood. "As you have ordered, My Lord, it shall be done."

"Good. Bring honour to our Princess and to our noble dead."

Terren turned to Collin and Maleth. "Gentlemen, you may proceed before me. You may begin making the necessary preparations in our search for these criminals."

"Yes, sir," said Collin. Both he and Maleth bowed their heads to the King and Queen, and then left the King's Conference.

Terren turned back towards the King. "I would like to speak with you freely and privately, My Lord."

Ralphen was puzzled. He glanced towards the Queen. "Maiya, if you would be so kind as to give us a few minutes."

"Of course." Maiya held onto the front of her long and heavy skirt, and then headed for the exit, closing the door behind her.

"Proceed, Sir Terren," said the King.

"I would like to ask you about this order you have given me, to seek out those who were involved, and bring down justice upon them. I understand it is necessary to do this, to bring justice to the people who were responsible for this crime, those who were involved. I vow that these people will be found, and I will deal them the rewards they have earned. But I'm not certain I understand doing the same to their families, their women and children, and to destroy their property."

Ralphen eyed the Supreme Captain with suspicion. "Are you questioning my order, Sir Terren?"

However, Terren remained dispassionate. "That's not the case, I assure you, My Lord. I merely wish to understand the necessity of dealing justice beyond those who were directly responsible for this crime. I wouldn't believe that someone's wife or child would be responsible for threatening the life of the Princess."

Ralphen stepped closer to Terren, staring into the Supreme Captain's eyes with a piercing glare, but Terren would not have it, and simply stared back. "I disagree with you, Sir Terren."

"How so, My Lord?"

"Their families were in every way just as responsible as those who planned this attack. They had to have known about this plan to infiltrate the Scarletia Royal Castle Grounds and attack our people and our Princess. But did they do anything to stop it? Of course, they didn't, because here we are. Those who were directly responsible, they had chosen to participate in this crime, and they'll have their reward. But those close to them did nothing to stop them, and for that, they had chosen to support the execution of their plans. They were indirectly responsible, but responsible nonetheless. They will have their reward as well, Sir Terren."

"What of their children, My Lord?"

"Older children have the ability to choose for themselves, and they had chosen to support this plan by doing nothing. Younger children may not have the ability to choose, but terminating their lives will send a strong message to those who are planning to attack the Nobility of Melodice. Everyone who was involved must be dealt with the harshest punishment possible! They tried to take the life of our daughter! If she is to be subjected to the threat of death, then so should their children!"

The King is a mad man. There's no reasoning with him. Terren nodded to Ralphen. "I understand now. As you have ordered, My Lord, it shall be done."

"Thank you, Sir Terren. If there's nothing further...."

"That is all, My Lord." Terren bowed his head to the King, and then headed for the door.

Ralphen watched him as he was leaving. "There is one more thing, Sir Terren."

Terren turned back towards Ralphen. "Yes, My Lord."

"I should remind you that your retirement is in ten days." Ralphen took a few steps towards Terren. "You have had a long and distinguished career with our Scarletia Royal Guard and the Royal Army of Melodice. You have earned a rich and luxurious retirement. But... please do remember one thing."

"What is it, My Lord?"

Ralphen regarded Terren with a warning stare. "I advise you to be more careful when you ask questions regarding my orders, questions that could be misinterpreted as insubordinate. Remember that, although you've earned a retirement of luxury and riches beyond your imagination, all that can be taken from you with one simple order."

Terren resisted the temptation to speak out with

hostility. That was not just a warning. That was also a threat. "Although it wasn't my intention, if you believe I've asked questions that could be misinterpreted as insubordinate, My Lord, I do apologize. I meant no offense. I merely wished to understand. By understanding, I'll be able to carry out your orders with more efficiency."

"Very well," said King Ralphen. "You are dismissed."

Terren bowed his head one more time, and then continued his exit. He made sure the doors were closed behind him as he proceeded down the hallways. To his right, windows lined the walls, through which he could see the front section of the Grounds. He thought back to his exchange with the King, an exchange that could be considered as a thinly-veiled confrontation.

"Honour has forsaken these lands."

CHAPTER 3

THE SCARLETIA ROYAL GUARD

SEC 3566, Demetre 83

HELEN SAT ALONE AT A square wooden table that was made for four people, located in a corner of a large mess hall, one of many within the Scarletia Royal Castle. Elsewhere in the mess hall, knights of the Scarletia Royal Guard ate and socialized together, many of them in their uniforms, while others not on duty chose to wear civilian clothing. Helen largely tuned out the chatter that came from all directions. A steaming bowl of soup sat on a steel tray on her table, but she had not yet started on it. She was too busy examining the contents of a flat, rectangular, black cardboard box. Within the box was a silver medal that reflected light from the bright kerosene lamps mounted above her on the walls.

The King was so busy with the search for the merchant assassins that he didn't have time to personally give this to me. The commendation medal for saving Princess Mika's life on the day of the incident.

The silver medal was slightly ovoid in shape. The figure etched onto its front was of a knight raising a sword and shield to protect a helpless civilian on the ground behind him. There was an inscription as well.

*The Commendation Medal of
The Royal Army of Melodice*

For Safeguarding the Defenseless

Issued SEC 3566
Helen Renier, Private Enlist

Helen could not help but smile as her thin fingers gently caressed its smooth surface. Along with the medal, she also received a handwritten letter from the King of Melodice, congratulating her on receiving the medal and telling her that she should accept it with honour and pride. In the letter, folded on the table beside her food tray, the King also thanked her for saving the life of the Princess of Melodice.

Four knights in uniform stopped at her table as they were passing by. When Helen sensed their presence, she glanced up at them with her usual calm and cool demeanour.

"Good morning, Miss Helen."

Helen recognized the knight who greeted her as Tanari Desalia, one of the female knights of the Scarletia Royal Guard. While a vast majority of enlisted soldiers in the Royal Guard were male, a small but significant percentage of the members consisted of women. She nodded to Tanari. "Good morning, Miss Tanari."

Tanari smiled with delight. "I see you received the commendation medal for saving Princess Mika's life. Congratulations!"

"Thank you."

Silence. Helen stared at Tanari, as if waiting for her to continue.

Tanari felt uncomfortable almost right away. She tried to think of something to say but nothing came to mind.

The other knights behind her very soon felt the same way.

"Um... why are we here... still?" asked the knight directly behind Tanari, the one who Helen recognized as Reland Salvien. He kept his voice low, but Helen could still hear him.

Tanari frowned at him. "What? I was just being polite." She turned back to Helen. "Miss Helen, I heard some of us will be joining the Supreme Captain later today. Those who were involved in planning and organizing the attack by the merchant assassins and endangering the life of Princess Mika were found. We've been ordered to raid multiple locations at once. Will you be joining us?"

Helen shook her head. "No. I haven't received orders to take part in the raid."

"Truly? Have you been outside in the city, Miss Helen?"

"No. Had I been ordered to take part in the raid, it would have been my first time seeing the city of Scarletia beyond the castle gates."

Tanari acknowledged with a nod. "By the way, we were just going to get some food, and I was wondering... if you're interested and if you're not terribly busy... why don't you sit with us?"

Helen was taken aback, because she rarely, if ever, received offers from her colleagues in the Royal Guard to sit and eat with them. She thought about it for a moment, but her train of thought was soon interrupted by the other two knights.

"Forget it, Tanari. She's not going to accept your invitation."

Helen recognized him as Palind Emarias, whose tone of voice she didn't like.

"Besides, she's just a child. She's the youngest in the entire army. She should go home and play with her dolls. I don't care if she's a Magic Knight and is proficient with a sword. A little girl has no place in the elite Scarletia Royal Guard."

That last knight made Helen frown. She recognized him as Belian Soraisa, who often taunted her for being the youngest in the Royal Guard, and she hated him for it. She wanted to get up and give him a taste of her fist, but that would not be in her best interest. She didn't have her sword with her. However, she always had her magic to back her up, and despite her smallish stature and slim frame, she could probably take both Belian and Palind on her own, but the consequences would not be welcomed. She might start a brawl in the mess hall. Eventually, she would be restrained by the other knights in the room. After that, there would be disciplinary actions from her superiors.

Tanari was visibly annoyed at both Belian and Palind. "What are you talking about, Belian? That's so rude! So what if she's the youngest member of the Royal Guard?"

"I'm... pretty young myself. I'm only nineteen," said Reland.

Belian shook his head. "You're not sixteen, Reland. You're fine. She may have just reached the age of majority, but sixteen years old is too young to be a member of the Royal Guard. Don't you think so, Palind?"

Palind nodded as he spoke with stinging crudity. "Agreed. And I'm not about to sit down and eat with a little girl, because I don't wish to hold back some of the occasional vulgarities that come out of my mouth."

Belian laughed. "You see, Tanari, Reland?"

Tanari attempted to counter their rude behaviour. "She reports directly to Supreme Commander Collin."

"What of it? There's something wrong with that picture. How does one who recently joined the Royal Guard with the rank of Private Enlist suddenly report directly to one of our Supreme Commanders?" asked Palind, his voice calm but condescending. "That doesn't make sense to me. Do you know the answer to that, Tanari?"

Tanari stopped, frustrated. "Well... I...." She shifted her eyes towards Helen, hoping she could provide an answer, but Helen said nothing.

Reland chimed in. "Um... maybe it's because of that old Magic Knight Sir Galner? I heard he convinced the King to have her report to Sir Collin."

Belian let out a mocking belly laugh. "Only because she's his special little student of magic. He may have power and influence, but he knows nothing of respect for authority. Do you sometimes hear how that old man addresses Sir Collin?"

Palind shook his head, and then continued. "Supreme Captain Terren will be leading a company later today into the city. I'm not surprised she hasn't received orders to take part in the raid. Perhaps Sir Collin deemed her too young to see the city of Scarletia for the first time, and the reason for that is obvious. Little girls like her shouldn't be subjected to gruesome scenes."

Belian shrugged. "Come on, let's just move along now. Let's go, Palind."

Helen glared at them with barely contained irritation.

As they began to leave, Palind pushed Reland forward. "Go, Reland. Stop getting in the way."

Reland gave an apologetic look towards Helen.

Tanari watched them as they left. She awkwardly turned away to follow them, stopped after taking one step, and turned back to Helen. "My apologies for that. Um... if you'll excuse me." At that point, she turned, and then followed the other knights.

As Helen watched them depart, she shook her head. Being shunned by her fellow knights was a daily occurrence. She hadn't truly had a chance to socialize with any of the other knights since she'd joined the Scarletia Royal Guard. Many of the knights did not wish to make any time for her, because they judged her for being so much younger than all of them. They regarded her as not much more than a little girl with a sword and knowledge of magic.

What the hell? I'm old enough to be a member of the Scarletia Royal Guard. I'm a legal adult. I can do whatever I want.

Helen put the King's letter inside the cardboard box with the silver medal, and then gazed around the room. Over a hundred knights filled the mess hall, all of them chatting and laughing while eating and generally having a good time with each other. Helen proudly smiled to herself, because she had achieved something that most of them had not.

"I don't see many of you with commendations from the Royal Family of Melodice. Damn fools," she whispered to herself, as she leaned forward, inhaling the tempting aroma of her soup, filled with slices of chicken, cabbage, and bean sprouts. Soon, she began digging in with a silver spoon.

* * *

A late spring rain gently fell on the cracked and weathered city streets, which had not been repaved for decades. In one of the many old and dilapidated residential areas of the city of Scarletia, houses made of common wood, brick, and mortar defied the elements and stood the test of time. Dogs sniffed through piles of trash at the sides of the muddy street, but when they heard people screaming, they ran away.

The people of the Peasantry, clad in dirty, old, worn-out clothing that were of extremely poor quality, ran towards a major intersection, their morbid curiosity conflicting with their sense of dreadful anticipation. Their typical attire, which consisted of short jackets, trousers, smock-frocks, cloaks, skirted jackets, and petticoats, did little to keep out the rain. Children and elderly, some of them dressed in rags, joined the group of people at the intersection to see what was happening. The onlookers watched as the fully-armoured knights of the Scarletia Royal Guard rounded up frightened peasants in the middle of the intersection.

Nearby, a group of knights forced a family out of a house. They pushed the father onto the street, and he fell on the mud. The mother was threatened with a sword if she refused to join her husband, so she complied. They were already deeply terrified, but they panicked when they saw their children dragged out of their house by their arms and legs screaming.

The mother screamed. "No, no, not our children! Please!"

The father forcefully tried to get to their children. "No, please, stop!"

"Get back!" A knight punched him in the face with a metal gauntlet.

The father fell to the ground, half-conscious, his nose and mouth bleeding, as he heard his wife and children scream.

A line of peasants was forced to walk down the street. Knights pushed and prodded some of them, ordering them to walk faster. They were led to another group of peasants that was corralled together at the intersection by more knights, who threatened them with spears and swords.

More men and women were tossed out onto the streets. Their hands were tied behind their backs so tightly that their wrists bled. Their children were not exempted from this harsh treatment. At the intersection, entire families were rounded up and forced to kneel down, scraping their knees against the rough pavement.

Sir Terren was accompanied by Sir Collin as they walked past the peasants who were guarded by the knights. They stopped some distance away from the peasants.

Terren watched the peasants, the screams of the men and women and the cries of the children ringing in his ears, but he could not shut them out. The only sign of his intense internal turmoil was a deep sigh. "So this is everyone?"

"As far as we have determined, sir," said Collin. "These are all the people who were deemed responsible, either directly or indirectly, for attacking the Nobility of Melodice and Princess Mika Silveraine on Demetre 78."

Terren looked behind him, and he saw another group of peasants, onlookers who observed what was happening. Some knights, mounted on cervids, brandished spears threateningly to hold them back. The observers were a good distance away from the intersection, but they could still see clearly what was happening. Terren saw young children in that group. There was a boy who was in the middle of his adolescent years, along with a few others who were younger than he. Terren's eyes looked farther up, and saw an ancient stone tower rising behind some buildings, taller than even the watchtowers at the Scarletia Royal Castle. It stood against the backdrop of gray skies, watching over the terrible scene.

The Supreme Captain turned back towards the peasants they had rounded up as he heard them plead with the knights.

"We are the ones responsible, not our children!"

"Please spare them!"

"Have mercy on them! Please!"

In desperation, a man tried to get back up onto his feet. "My wife had nothing to do with this! Please let her go!"

A knight grabbed him by the front of his shirt. "Shut your mouth, you filthy peasant! Or I will shut it for you!" He struck him hard on the side of his head with his gauntlet. The man was forced to kneel down again, one side of his face scraped and bloodied.

The sorrowful wails of a terror-stricken young woman nearby drew the attention of a knight, who grabbed her arm and twisted it so hard that she screamed. "Enough with the crying, you bitch!"

Terren turned to Collin, and spoke to him with a hushed voice. "I asked you earlier to count them up specifically. How many, Sir Collin?"

Collin hesitated, confused by Terren's request. "Sir...?"

Offended by Collin's reaction, Terren raised his voice. "How many, I said!"

Collin complied quickly. "There are a total of sixty-two peasants, fifty of the age of majority, twelve below that. Of the age of majority, there are thirty-five men and fifteen women. Of the children, three of them are still very young, and one of them is an infant."

Terren stayed silent for a moment as he watched the peasants. They were all gathered together in three rows of about twenty persons each, all knelt down on the muddy street with the rain soaking through their clothes. He saw fathers deeply worried for their families, mothers who wanted to take hold of their children, and children, little boys and little girls alike, who were petrified by the scene they were caught up in.

A woman was forced to let go of her crying infant covered in a tattered gray blanket. She reached for the knight who took her child. "No, please, don't take him away from me! Give him back to me!"

The knight grinned mockingly at her. The other knights forced her to kneel, and then tied her hands behind her back.

"No! Give him back!"

"Quiet! Shut your mouth!" shouted one knight from behind her. He twisted the rope that restrained her hands so hard that she yelped with terrible pain.

With a loathsome grin, the knight in front of her cradled her infant child in his arms. "Well, well, aren't you a cute little one?"

There were elderly in the group as well, frail old men and women, their physical states weakened, no longer with the strength to fight back, but equally mistreated by the knights as the more able-bodied adults. Terren watched them all with a heavy heart.

In all my years as the Knight of the Dark, I've never seen the nation of Melodice sink this far. Melodice was once a proud nation... but that was long before my time of existence. We've sunk farther into the depths of barbarism. What has become of our once-proud nation? What has become of our people, our culture, our way of life?

Terren waved a female knight over to him. The knight obeyed as she carried a metal bowl half-filled with water and a hand towel draped over her left arm. "What is your name, soldier?"

"Tanari Desalia, Private Enlist, sir."

Terren stared into her eyes for a moment, seeing a hint of uncertainty in them. As he observed all his knights around him, he could see there were those who were eager and willing to brutalize the peasants, but there were also those who were hesitant in doing so. Of course, the number of knights who did not hesitate to harm the peasants was a far greater number indeed.

He turned back to Tanari, and then lowered his voice as he spoke. "Do the things you see trouble you, Miss Tanari?"

Tanari hesitated as her eyes shifted quickly to the peasants, then to the other knights, and back to her commanding officer, debating whether she should lie and make herself appear as if she agreed with the way the peasants were treated... or be honest with herself and Sir Terren. She opted for honesty. "Yes, sir."

"Good. As they should." Terren thought to himself regarding Tanari's response. *If only we had more knights among our ranks like Miss Tanari, then we would regain our honour.*

Tanari was nervous, wondering whether she had answered him correctly.

The Supreme Captain noticed her anxiety. "Thank you, Miss Tanari. Do not be troubled. I appreciate your honesty. Watch carefully as you bear witness. This was ordered by our King. As such, I will wash my hands of it."

Tanari, along with Collin, watched Terren as he slowly removed his gauntlets, and then his gloves, giving them to Collin to hold on to.

Terren watched as the rain made ripples in the bowl. He placed his hands in the bowl as Tanari held on to it carefully. Terren rinsed his large hands, the water cold to the touch. After that, he used the hand towel to dry his hands. Terren noticed Tanari's confusion over what he had just done.

Collin, however, knew the reason behind the Supreme Captain's actions just now. This was Terren's way of ridding himself of the terrible guilt that was about to befall him.

Terren took one more look at the men, women, and children. Only some of the adults were responsible for the crime of attacking the Nobility and the Princess of Melodice. Most of them, including all the children and elderly, were completely innocent.

He watched Collin, observing his reaction. "Sir Collin."

Collin turned to Terren. "Yes, sir?"

"Does this trouble you as well?"

The Supreme Commander hesitated for quite a long moment.

"Your answer, Sir Collin?" Terren stared hard into his eyes, as if prodding for an answer.

After a moment, Collin swallowed. "Our King has ordered us to do this, sir, and my opinion on this matter is surely of no consequence."

An uneasy silence. Terren took his gloves and gauntlets from Collin, whom he regarded with a piercing stare as he put them back on.

Collin began to wonder if he had said the wrong thing.

"Sir Collin, you may proceed as ordered," said Terren.

"Yes, sir."

As Collin turned to the knights, Terren walked away, his back towards the peasants and the rest of the knights.

Collin drew out his long sword, and the other knights followed suit, their blades screeching against their scabbards, frightening the corralled peasants. "Knights, proceed with the execution!"

Terren headed towards his waiting cervid. He heard the screams behind him, screams from the men, women, and children, screams of fear and trepidation.

The knight carrying the crying infant gave a mocking grin to the mother, who shrieked as he threw her son high into the air, still wrapped in his tattered blanket. Another knight raised his crossbow, aimed for the infant, and fired. When the crossbow quarrel met with the infant in the air, the boy's cries were cut short... and his lifeless body fell to the muddy streets. Blood stained the blanket and smeared against the pavement, mixing with the rainwater that flowed along its surface.

The mother became hysterical, but her deafening cries of anguish were interrupted almost right away as the knight beside her stabbed her in the back with a long sword, its bloody blade protruding through the middle of her chest.

The civilians who watched from far away saw this, and they were repelled by the sheer brutality. Some of them broke away from the crowd, and ran as fast as they could. For all they knew, they could be next on the list of peasants who were going to be executed.

Terren did not look back, but he heard the cries of the men, women, and children that would soon be cut short. He listened to the cruel sounds of blades striking flesh and bone as he climbed onto his cervid. He urged the cervid to a slow trot, its head hung low and its sharp antlers pointed forward, as if intimidated by the deafening screams. No one was near him, and because of this, Terren was free to speak his mind. His heart filled with fury, he narrowed his eyes, clenched his teeth, and firmly held onto the reins.

"I must calm down. This is not the right time. Not yet."

CHAPTER 4

SIR TERREN'S GOODBYE

SEC 3566, Demetre 90

THE SCARLET CHAMBER WAS THE main audience room of the Scarletia Royal Castle, where the King and Queen presided whenever an audience was required of them, and one such event was the Retirement Ceremony for Supreme Captain Terren Rinaldia.

Near the back of the room, the red and gold thrones were decorated with intricate designs, and behind them was a wide doorway that led into another room, partially covered by red curtains. The entire floor was covered in a soft red carpet. Enormous stained-glass windows, many of which were opened to provide a view of the hallways beyond either side of the Scarlet Chamber, decorated the walls at either side of the room.

The audience consisted of members of the Nobility of Melodice who held high positions in government, along with several high-ranking knights, including Sir Collin and Sir Maleth, who were decked out in their formal uniforms. Helen, who wore a similar uniform as her commanding officers, stood beside Collin.

"Miss Helen, I'm glad you were able to attend this event," said Collin.

Helen responded with her usual serious tone. "I'm honoured, sir. Thank you for inviting me."

Collin lowered his voice, ensuring that no one else heard his attempt at flattery. "The dress uniform suits you, by the way. But I would think an elegant lady's dress would suit you even better."

Helen turned to him, confused. "I'm a knight of the Scarletia Royal Guard, sir. If I were to dress that way, it would be considered casual wear, and would be looked at and frowned upon as unbecoming."

Collin smiled. "I only jest."

King Ralphen and Queen Maiya stood at the top of a short set of steps, while Sir Terren, who was decked out in his most formal uniform, faced them, standing tall with his hands clasped together behind his back.

As the King and Queen spoke to the audience and to him, through the corner of his eye, Terren saw a man in a black and white robe. The man was not of this city, but his position as the Royal Representative of the Cerulean Magic Academy from the nearby city of Cerulean meant that he was stationed at the Scarletia Royal Castle. He was Galner Ciannar, one of the most powerful Magic Knights in the nation and a professor of magical studies. Tall in stature, his hair was gray and thin, and his strong, piercing, deep black eyes held the wisdom of a thousand mages. As a professor of magical studies, he personally taught Helen Renier and Princess Mika Silveraine.

Terren focused his attention back to the unbearably long speech the King and Queen had in store for him and the rest of the audience. He was, however, relieved to realize that they were almost finished when they began speaking to him directly.

"Sir Terren, as I have already mentioned and as everyone in this room is aware, you have had a long and outstanding career with us as the Supreme Captain of the Scarletia Royal Guard and the Royal Army of Melodice," said King Ralphen. "In your long and distinguished career, you had won many battles and fought against many trials and tribulations. You helped forge Melodice into one of the greatest nations of this world."

One of the greatest nations, you say? Terren thought with sarcasm.

It was Queen Maiya's turn to speak. "Sir Terren, you are definitely the most powerful knight in this entire nation. You're also the most powerful Magic Knight of all, the Knight of the Dark. You have extraordinary skills, and you're a skilled tactician."

Ralphen smiled. "That he is. The last time you flew overhead, you flew by so quickly and made such a thunderous sound that I honestly believed the world was about to end."

Some nobles in the audience laughed. Terren smiled, although deep inside, he did not find it funny at all, not one bit. *The King's attempt at humour is as pathetic as ever. I wonder if the nobles in this room who laughed just now probably felt they had to laugh. Perhaps it's not just the peasants who are being oppressed.*

"I still wonder how this name Knight of the Dark came to be," said Maiya. "Care to comment on that, Sir Terren?"

Terren shrugged slightly. "Apparently, it was a name my enemies used when they referred to me in the past, when I was much younger, because I had a tendency to lead companies into battle during the night. Those who were in the higher ranks in our military at the time heard of this name, and then started calling me the same."

"Very interesting." Maiya turned to Ralphen pleasantly. "Well, then, King Ralphen, what do you think? Perhaps it's time to impart the Royal Message to our honourable Sir Terren."

Ralphen nodded with agreement. "I believe you're right."

The King and Queen turned towards the doorway behind their thrones. Terren and everyone else in the room focused their attention there as well.

Just beyond the doorway, Angelica whispered to a small shadow in the corner. "Princess, it's time."

Princess Mika emerged through the doorway, holding a scroll, and immediately saw the large number of people. Her eyes widened, and she felt her rapidly beating heart sink to her stomach. Without realizing it, her feet took her to behind the Queen's throne instead of to where she was supposed to be.

Maiya was amused. "Princess Mika, you can come out now."

Mika heard the laughter of a few nobles in the

background. Though they may not have meant to ridicule her, she felt extremely disconcerted.

However, Ralphen did not find this amusing. He turned, his large red cape flowing around him, and headed quickly behind the thrones. He stared down at Mika, clad in a white silk dress with flower designs and rosettes. The Princess Gem sparkled in front of her dress.

Mika gasped softly as she held a frightened expression upon meeting her father's angry gaze.

"What the hell are you doing, Mika? Stop wasting time or I will give you a tender beating," Ralphen said with a hushed but firm voice. He grabbed her by the arm, and pulled her out from behind the Queen's throne.

Mika grimaced as she felt some pain in her elbow and shoulder. The wreath of silk rosettes on her head nearly fell, so she held on to it, making sure it was centred.

Terren, who watched the King's rough handling of the Princess, narrowed his eyes for a brief moment. *A tyrant King who brutalizes his own people... and a bastard father who does the same to his own child....*

Ralphen headed back to his place beside the Queen, who shook her head at the brief exchange between the King and the Princess, slightly annoyed.

Mika slowly headed to where she had been previously told to stand, which was in between her mother and father, and directly in front of Terren. She kept her eyes downcast, avoiding the gazes of the people in the Scarlet Chamber. It was already bad enough that she was out here in front of them. Now, she was about to impart the Royal Message to the Supreme Captain from the scroll, around which her trembling hands felt cold and tense. She hesitated for a moment, and then slowly opened the scroll.

Helen watched the frightened Princess, shaking her head. "They're having her recite the Royal Message? This'll be a fine mess."

Collin heard her. "The Princess is shy, but I'm sure she'll do fine. You should show more confidence in her, Miss Helen."

Public speaking was certainly not part of Mika's skill

set. With everyone in the audience silent, all she could hear was the rapid beating of her heart. She looked up at Terren, who smiled at her, and gave her a small but encouraging nod. That gave her a slight boost in confidence, and calmed her down a little as she looked back down at the scroll. She cleared her throat.

"To… our dearest Sir Terren Rinaldia, Supreme Captain of the Scarletia Royal Guard and the Royal Army of Melodice, also known as the Knight of the Dark, from the Royal Family of the great nation of Melodice," she recited. She tried to speak as loudly as she could, but her voice was naturally soft and did not carry very far. "We thank you from the bottom of our hearts for your many years of service to our nation. You had served the Royal Family, the Nobility, the Scarletia Royal Castle, the city of Scarletia, and the nation of Melodice with great honour.

"For many years, you led with courage and bravery, and your knights looked to you for guidance, wisdom, and leadership. They respected and honoured you, and they followed your orders with due diligence. You protected… served the Royal Family, the Nobility, the Scarletia Royal Castle…." *Oh no, I'm reading the wrong line!*

Everyone noticed Mika's very prominent pause. She stammered at where she was supposed to be in the message, but was lost for a moment in the block of text.

Ralphen closed his eyes, and bowed his head slightly as he felt terrible embarrassment.

Maiya's only reaction was a small smile, for she knew that her daughter was doing her best, despite her nervousness.

"You… I mean, yes, you protected us from the dangers of the world. You protected us… from the…." Mika could sense her father's disappointment nearby and the blank stares of the audience as she heard her own voice quivering. "You protected us from those who sought to take away our freedom and dignity, from those who attacked our way of life. Thankful words uttered or written are not enough to express the heartfelt gratitude of the Royal Family, the Nobility, and the nation of Melodice.

"We hope that... that your retirement will be most enjoyable, and that you will be able to fulfill all the plans you have laid out for yourself in order to take full advantage of what life has to offer. To live one's life to the fullest is always an admirable goal. We hope you will be able to attain this goal, and live a life of peace and harmony."

Mika glanced up from the scroll and met Terren's gaze. He smiled at her again to encourage her, so she smiled as well. She knew the last words on the scroll, and no longer needed to refer to it.

"Sir Terren, we thank you for your services, and hope that you will keep us in your heart as we keep you in ours." Mika gently closed the scroll.

"You are most welcome, My Lady," said Terren, and then he glanced up at the King and Queen. "My Lord, My Lady, you are most welcome. I'm honoured by your message."

Mika breathed a sigh, but still felt nervous standing here in front of everyone, even though her job was done.

Terren turned to face the audience. "Ladies and gentlemen, I promise not to bore you with a long and sentimental parting speech, so I will keep this brief. I thank you all for your support. My forty-one years of service with the Scarletia Royal Guard and the Royal Army of Melodice have been a most enriching experience. I had fought many battles, saved those who were in danger, and protected those who could not defend themselves. My time with you all and those before you had been most enjoyable. Some of you were not even born when I became a knight. I protected your parents and grandparents, and here you are now, alive and well, enjoying a life of peace and harmony."

He walked farther down as he spoke, and stood in the middle of the Scarlet Chamber. Surrounded by the leaders of his nation and the Royal Guard, he continued to speak with an air of gentlemanly grace, dignity, and authority. He paused for a moment, as he needed to choose his next words carefully.

"Everyone... you should all be proud of your nation. You should be proud of your people. You're all of different professions in life. Some of you advise the Royal Family on political matters, some of you are leaders in the Royal Army of Melodice, some of you manage maidservants, and some of you are just beginning your lives as you have recently reached the age of majority. It matters not what you do in life, because what you do contributes to the well-being of our nation. You might believe you don't contribute very much, but a multitude of small contributions can combine to maintain a great nation.

"As you realize this, I say again, be proud of your nation. Fight for the honour of our people, our culture, and way of life. Fight for respect and dignity, and protect those who can't protect themselves. Safeguard the innocent. Treat everyone around you—every man, woman, and child of all walks of life, regardless of their status—with respect, honour, and dignity. Always do what's right for others.

"Ladies and gentlemen, thank you. I wish you all well."

Everyone in the room gave applause, King Ralphen and Queen Maiya, Collin, Maleth, Helen, and many others.

Mika hesitated as she mulled over some of the words Terren used, words which she thought were beautiful.

Maiya noticed her daughter's blank stare. "Mika, you need to give applause."

Startled, Mika placed the scroll neatly on the floor in front of her glossy white shoes, straightened up, and gave applause. She smiled as Terren shook hands with some of the nobles in the room, including Collin and Maleth.

"Keep up the good work, gentlemen," Terren said.

Maleth chuckled and smiled. "We will continue your legacy, Sir Terren."

"Thank you, Sir Terren," replied Collin.

Terren shook hands with Helen as well. "And you, young lady, you're doing very well with yourself after just recently reaching the age of majority. Be proud of what you do, Miss Helen Renier."

Helen smiled. "Thank you, Sir Terren."

Next, as Terren shook hands with the civilian members of the Nobility around him, his thoughts mocked them.

The Nobility of Melodice... people who are filled with corruption and stand on the backs of the lowborn. They heard my message just now... but perhaps not a single one of these fools actually listened. It's a damn shame.

Terren turned back towards the Royal Family. The King and Queen continued to applaud. The Princess did as well. She appeared tiny as she stood between her parents. From the way she appeared on the outside, although she was always well-dressed and beautiful, she was still just another little girl. However, he knew more about her than she knew about herself... and what she was truly capable of doing.

Perhaps, Princess Mika, you're the only one here who understands... and even if you don't understand now, I pray that you do as soon as possible... or our nation is lost.

* * *

SEC 3566, Morrighan 1

Shortly after breakfast in her bedchamber on this first day of summer, Princess Mika, clad in her thin, sleeveless, silk nightgown, held a rose stem in one hand, and carefully reached for one if its thorns using a small pair of scissors with the other. She stood by a window, where a few potted flower plants rested on the windowsill. The windows of her bedchamber faced east, allowing the mid-morning sunlight to provide ample light, which helped her with her task. The thorns were many, some large, most of them tiny, and some were even difficult to see. The thorns fell on a white cloth on the windowsill as she snipped them away. She intended to give the rose to Sir Terren.

The former Supreme Captain, Sir Terren, is leaving today. He has taught me so many things, so many valuable lessons. I don't have very much to give back to him... but I hope this is good enough.

Mika turned the rose stem in her hand. Unfortunately, she failed to notice one tiny thorn as it pricked the middle of her left forefinger. She gasped, dropped the rose on the windowsill, and put the scissors down. A tiny drop of blood appeared. She covered it with her left thumb as she reached for a handkerchief, which she used to cover the wound, and kept pressure on it for a few minutes until it no longer bled.

The Princess knew exactly what to do. Mika pulled out one of the drawers of her dressing table, where she found pieces of cotton cloth, a small bottle of alcohol, and some small white bandages. She used the alcohol and the cloth to clean her wound, and she grimaced with discomfort as the alcohol stung her. She used a thin white bandage to cover the wound, and tied it around her finger, but had to tighten it using her teeth and her other hand.

There was a knock on the double doors of her room. Mika turned. "Miss Angelica?"

One of the doors opened slightly, and Queen Maiya's head poked through. "Actually, it's me. Your mother. Queen Maiya Silveraine."

Mika smiled. "I'm sorry, Mother. Good morning."

Maiya, clad in a long red dress with a low neckline that revealed prominent cleavage and jewels sewn into the ends of her sleeves, opened the door fully, and entered. "Good morning, Mika. How are you this morning? Has Miss Angelica served you your breakfast?"

Mika nodded. "I'm fine, thank you, Mother. Yes, Miss Angelica had already served me breakfast. I finished eating a while ago, in fact."

"Very good." Maiya sat down on one of the couches.

Mika wondered why her mother was visiting her this morning. "Um... how are you this morning, Mother?"

"I'm well." Maiya smiled. "Why don't you have a seat here beside me, Mika?"

Mika did as she asked. She gazed at her mother with a curious expression.

Silence. Maiya played with Mika's hair.

"Is there... something you wanted to talk to me about, Mother?" asked Mika.

"There is. In fact, I was meaning to talk to you about it on the day when Sir Terren questioned you about the incident with the merchant assassins, but I was so busy that I couldn't find the opportunity. I didn't think it was the right time either. For a while, I forgot about it. But, fortunately, I remembered it this morning."

Mika stiffened. *She didn't forget? It's about that mistake I made, isn't it? I was hoping she'd forget about it! This is... so embarrassing!*

"So I heard you mention that you liked holding Mirin's hand. Is that right? Did I hear that correctly?"

Mika gasped, leaning away from her mother.

"You were even blushing and smiling when you said that."

Mika stammered. "Oh... um... well...."

"So did I hear that correctly?"

The young Princess hesitated, her eyes wide, her mouth hung open. She watched her mother, who stared at her with little facial expression, but she could tell she wanted an answer. Mika cast her eyes down on the table in front of her, and clasped her hands together on her lap. "Um... I... I suppose so... yes, you... you did hear... correctly."

Maiya suddenly laughed, surprising Mika. "Truly? So you like holding his hand, then? Well, you and Mirin have been friends for about three years now, I believe... and it looks like you both have become very close. You're together all the time. Is that right?"

Mika hesitated again before she nodded. "Yes, Mother."

"How do you feel about Mirin?"

No, wait, this is not going the way I want it to. I have to think... think quickly. Mika sighed for a moment. "He's my best friend, Mother."

"Well, yes, I'm aware of that. But I would just like to understand, since I don't see you as much as I would like. I have many duties and responsibilities as the Queen of Melodice, and you have yours as you train and prepare yourself to become a future leader of our nation. I don't always know what happens in your life, so I'd like to know."

Mika leaned back, her eyes meeting her mother's. "All right, Mother."

Maiya hesitated for a moment, as she felt and appeared awkward, trying to find the right words to say to her daughter, or to find the right question to ask. "So... is there... how should I say this? Is there... perhaps a special relationship of some kind?"

Feign ignorance. If I do that and pretend I'm a clueless little girl who doesn't know anything, then maybe she'll stop asking me about Mirin. "What do you mean?" asked Mika.

"Well... it's because... you know, boys and girls... well, actually, usually girls... when they reach this time of their lives, the way they see boys becomes... somewhat different. Sometimes, girls begin to see boys as... their potential partners... as in...."

"Huh? Partners?"

"Romantic partners. Many girls around your age begin to view certain boys in a different light. You're of that age now, Mika. Do you... feel a sort of attraction between yourself and Mirin, some kind of affection that you've never felt before?"

Mother... you can be so blunt all of a sudden! Mika tried to stop herself from blushing, but perhaps she was only partially successful as she looked away for a moment, and then back at her mother. She did think of something that might help her stop her mother from asking any more questions. "Mother... I don't think it's like that... with Mirin and I."

"Oh?"

Mika looked up at Maiya with her sweetest and most innocent smile. "Well... I'm not too certain about any kind of attraction or affection between boys and girls. I'm probably far too young to understand anything like that. What I do know for certain is that Mirin is my best friend. In fact, he's my only friend in the castle, except for Miss Angelica, of course. He's the only one close to my age who's my friend, and I treat him the way I would treat any other friend."

Maiya was taken aback.

Mika wondered if she was not convinced.

"And, yet, you both hold hands and are always together? I don't see too many boys and girls your age holding hands... unless they claim to love each other as a couple."

Mika shrugged slightly. "Would it be strange if I had a female friend who was my age and I always held hands with her?"

"No, of course not. That wouldn't be considered strange at all."

"So... why is it strange if I hold hands with a friend who is a boy and is my age?"

Maiya was speechless for a moment. "Well... I suppose it just doesn't happen very often. I mean... a boy and a girl around your age... who are simply friends... holding hands."

"Maybe it *should* happen more often. Girls who are close friends with each other are always holding hands and embracing. I'm a very sensitive and very affectionate girl myself. Whether my best friend was a girl or a boy, I'd always want to embrace them and hold hands with them. Why can't a girl do the same with a boy who's as much a close friend as another girl who's also a close friend?"

"It's just different. You're a girl and he's a boy," answered the Queen.

The Princess was unconvinced. "But how is it different? How does that matter?"

"Uh... well...." Maiya rubbed her forehead for a moment, as if a headache was coming on. Mika's questions easily exhausted her, and at this point, she had already run out of things to say. "Hold on, Mika, where's my timepiece?"

It's working, isn't it?

Maiya found her timepiece in her pocket. "Wouldn't you know, it looks like I have an upcoming meeting with Shelia Talsien, the Premier of the Department of Agriculture. I need to get ready to meet her. We'll talk about this some other time." Of course, in reality, she had plenty of time before her meeting with Miss Shelia. She stood up from the couch to leave.

However, Mika was not fooled at all. *Yes... it did work.*

"Mika, don't forget. We're meeting Sir Terren at the front of the castle later today."

Mika smiled. "Of course, Mother. I'll be ready by then."

Maiya nodded. "Good. I'll see you in a little while."

"Yes, Mother."

Maiya smiled one more time, somewhat uncomfortably. She hastily headed for the door, and exited to escape from her daughter's prodding questions.

Mika sat back on her couch, leaned back, crossed one leg over the other, and smiled proudly with satisfaction. She reached up and played with her smooth hair.

"Well, then... I did better than I expected."

* * *

Mika had chosen a thin dress of white silk with a sash tied around her waist into a knot just above her left hip. The Princess Gem, attached to her golden necklace, sparkled under the summer sun. She held a red rose in her left hand, and held onto the side of her skirt with her right hand as she gingerly walked down the steps from the front of the castle.

Among those who were about to say their final goodbyes to Sir Terren were King Ralphen, Queen Maiya, Sir Collin, Miss Helen, and Sir Galner. Mika joined them quickly near the bottom of the steps, and stood beside her mother.

Terren, no longer the Supreme Captain, was in civilian clothing whose appearance was just as distinguished as his military attire. In a light blue waistcoat and white dress shirt that peeked out from underneath a long dark blue coat that matched his trousers, and black boots that had been meticulously polished, he stood with just as much gentlemanly confidence, grace, and dignity as before today, when he still held his title. Behind him, two cervids waited in front of an unmarked carriage, onto which his belongings had already been loaded.

Mika saw a glimpse of Mirin, walking with Angelica, who was his legal guardian. She discreetly waved him to come over.

Mirin pulled away from Angelica. "I'm going to Mika."

Angelica frowned and shook her head. "Oh my.... They're saying goodbye to Sir Terren. Don't do or say anything that could result in you embarrassing yourself in front of them."

"Of course, I wouldn't!"

Mika pulled away from her mother, and headed to the side of the group so Mirin could join her without passing the others. She blushed as Mirin took hold of her hand, but she could tell he had done that without thinking.

Maiya watched them as she remembered her discussion this morning with Mika, a discussion she had to interrupt because she didn't know how to proceed further with it.

The King shook hands firmly with Terren. "I'm slightly disappointed to see you go, Sir Terren. Retirement doesn't mean you have to leave us, after all. You could have stayed as one of over ten thousand noble civilians living in the castle who have chosen to make this place their home."

Terren smiled. "My Lord, it would be wonderful if I could stay at the castle. But, as you know, I do have plans to live my life to the fullest in my golden years. I no longer have to complete reports, manage whole armies, or do any sort of work."

"What are your plans, Sir Terren?" asked Maiya.

"One of my goals is to travel the entire nation and beyond, My Lady, to see the world before age finally catches up to me."

"That sounds like a wonderful idea." The Queen shook hands with him as well. "In that case, I wish you good health in your travels."

"Thank you, My Lord, My Lady."

Terren turned to Galner.

"Sir Galner, we may not have had very many opportunities to talk over the years, but I wish you well."

"Of course, Sir Terren." Galner shook hands with Terren. While several years younger than Terren, his voice sounded older than his actual age. He was as tall as the former Supreme Captain, but was physically weak. However, he was one of the most powerful Magic Knights in the entire nation. His white long-sleeved dress shirt and gray waistcoat was visible through the front opening of his long dark gray robe, and his matching trousers were tucked into his black boots. "I hope you'll have an enjoyable retirement. Hopefully, my Retirement Ceremony will be as grand as yours when it's my turn."

Terren smiled. "You are the personal professor of magical studies for the Princess of Melodice and for our very own Helen Renier. Surely, you have the Royal Family's favour. Yours will probably be grander than mine. I'm certain of it. Please continue to provide the best education and training as you always have for these lovely young ladies."

Mika and Helen stole a glance at each other when they were mentioned, and as soon as they met each other's gazes, Mika nervously cast her eyes down, causing Helen to frown.

"Your words honour me, Sir Terren," said Galner.

Terren next faced Collin, and they shook hands firmly. "Sir Collin, I believe you're next in line for my office."

Collin smiled and nodded. "I believe so, sir, but that office will still be yours. Should you come and visit us, please feel free to use it as your own."

Terren shook his head. "No, no, Sir Collin. That office will be yours soon enough. You deserve it. I have recommended you for promotion to Supreme Captain. You have done well, and I believe that position suits you. As a Supreme Commander, you have demonstrated most of the qualities of a great leader. The one and only thing I believe you still need to work on is to stop holding back on what you truly think and feel. You have your own opinions, just like everyone else."

Taken aback, Collin hesitated, and then cleared his throat. "Thank you, sir. You've taught me a great deal, and I will do my utmost to carry on your legacy."

Terren turned next to young Helen. "Miss Helen, I'm glad you could make it to this little gathering."

"I'm glad to be here, sir. Sir Collin was kind enough to invite me."

"That's good," said Terren, as he offered his hand, which Helen shook firmly.

Mika observed Helen. Her handshake was that of a

confident young woman, a handshake she believed she could never hope to mimic. Helen looked like she had soft and delicate hands, and yet, they were strong and firm.

"Continue to do your best. I have heard many good things about you from Sir Collin. You may have just begun your career as a knight, but you have proven yourself to be highly skilled, and news of the commendation you received for protecting our Princess has reached all of the Royal Guard."

"Your words are kind, Supreme Captain… I mean, Sir Terren." For a moment, Helen forgot that Terren no longer held that title.

Terren smiled with amusement. "You have great potential as a knight in our army, as well as a Magic Knight."

"Thank you, sir," said Helen.

Terren walked over to Princess Mika, and noticed Mirin beside her. "Well, now, young man, I'm glad to see you here. What a pleasant surprise."

Speechless, Mirin could only smile.

Terren patted him on the head. "Someday, you'll become a man, and you'll be a strong man who will protect the Princess. Will you promise to do this for me, Sir Mirin?"

"Yes, sir, I will do that. I promise," said Mirin, feeling very confident. No boy his age would normally be addressed as Sir by an adult. Children sometimes did refer to each other using Sir or Miss. However, few children, like Princess Mika, always used them to address other children.

Terren extended his hand, and Mirin shook it with a firm grip. Terren laughed with pride for the young boy. "Sir Mirin, you have a strong handshake."

Lastly, he turned to Mika, who stepped closer to him as she held a rose in front of her with both hands. She was so much smaller than he was. Because of this, he knelt down on one knee in front of her so his face was at the same level as hers. Palm down, she held one hand out to him, which he took in his.

"Princess Mika, My Lady, it's time for me to say goodbye to you." Terren bowed slightly, and kissed Mika's small and delicate hand, as it was customary. A gentleman kissing the hand of an unmarried Princess was honourable, but kissing the hand of a Queen was considered inappropriate, especially in the presence of a King. This was why he only shook hands with Queen Maiya.

Mika spoke softly as she smiled. "Know that you go with my blessings, Sir Terren."

"Thank you, My Lady."

She held up the rose. "I picked this rose from one of the flowering plants in my room. It was the most beautiful rose I had. I'd like you to have it as a parting gift from me."

Terren accepted the rose. The petals were a bright red, and the leaves were a vibrant green. He noticed the thorns had been trimmed meticulously, as well as the small white bandage tied around Mika's left forefinger when he looked down at her other hand.

"You are very kind, Princess. Thank you for this."

"You're welcome. I wish you the best of luck," said Mika. "I hope you'll be able to fulfill all your future plans."

Terren grimaced slightly at the mention of future plans, and he thought deeply about that for a very brief moment. He was almost amused by it. He smiled as he looked into her kind and gentle eyes. "My Lady, my future plans... I certainly do hope I'll fulfill them with great success. I'll do my best."

Mika wondered what he meant. He sounded like he was unsure of himself for a moment, which was out of character. "Um... Sir Terren...."

"Yes, My Lady?"

She cleared her throat, and cast her eyes down for a moment, searching for the words she needed to express. When she met his gaze again, she found some of her confidence. "I'd like to thank you for everything you've taught me. You've taught me many things in the areas of politics and... even areas that are related to the military, like tactics and all. I don't believe I'll be able to find a better professor when it comes to these."

"You're most welcome, Princess Mika. And you're probably right. Perhaps you may never find a better professor when it comes to these areas of study. However,

I do encourage you to continue by way of self-study and refine your knowledge. This is how I learned many of the things I know."

Mika nodded. "Self-study. I see. I value your advice, Sir Terren, so that's what I'll do."

"Very good. Tell me one of the sayings I taught you."

She thought for a moment. "To know your enemy, you must become your enemy."

"Give me another."

"Um...." She sensed all eyes on her, including Mirin's. "Appear weak when you are strong, and appear strong when you are weak."

"One more for good measure, My Lady."

"All warfare is based on deception."

Terren laughed with pride. "Good. I have taught you well."

Mika blushed and smiled.

"Now, then, Princess Mika, remember my words well. You're a far stronger individual and have far more courage than you give yourself credit for. You may think otherwise, but you shouldn't put yourself down the way you sometimes do. My Lady, your courage comes from your love of others. You're far from a weakling. You yourself are highly proficient with magic, like Miss Helen."

Mika was speechless. She was tempted to say that what he said was not true, that she really was a coward and a weakling, but it would be inappropriate to question the wise words of the former Supreme Captain, who she knew meant well.

Terren moved his face closer to hers, his mouth near her ear... and began to whisper.

Ralphen and Maiya watched from where they were, puzzled, but they could not hear what Terren was saying. Neither could anyone else, not even Mirin, who stood closest to them.

"I know of your love for your people, Princess Mika, peasants and nobles alike, and your love for your nation. When the time comes, you will use your love to free the people from tyranny and oppression."

Terren pulled away, and smiled at Mika, amused by her confused expression. He stood up, and then stepped back. He noticed the puzzled expression King Ralphen held, and knew it was time to leave... before he started asking questions about what he had just whispered to Mika.

"Everyone, I wish you well. Goodbye," he said with a confident air.

"Farewell, Sir Terren," said the King, biting his tongue.

Terren nodded, and then headed for his carriage.

Mika took a step forward, her hands clasped together in front of her. She wanted to ask him what he meant by his last words to her, but he didn't give her the chance.

Terren climbed onto the cervid carriage, and grabbed hold of the reins. His scabbard was at his side, in which his large and powerful broadsword was sheathed. He urged the cervids to begin their trot, and the carriage lurched forward down the Valderia Pathway towards the castle gates. Because there was no one else around him now, he felt free to whisper what was truly on his mind.

"It's not over yet. There's still much work to be done. The legendary Knight of the Dark will someday return."

* * *

King Ralphen and Queen Maiya were about to go back inside. They had just seen the castle gates in the distance open to let Terren's carriage through and then close.

"I hope this is not the last we'll see of Sir Terren," said Maiya.

"I'm certain we'll see him again, Maiya. Besides, just now, I didn't have the chance to ask him what he said to the Princess." Ralphen looked towards Mika, thinking about asking her instead.

Maiya took him by the arm. "You need not worry about it. I'm certain he was simply giving her words of advice like he always does. You know that the former Supreme Captain always meant Mika well."

"Yes, that's true." However, Ralphen suddenly recalled his exchange with Terren in the King's Conference, when he believed that the former leader of the Scarletia Royal Guard was questioning his order to hunt down and kill those who were responsible for the attack of the merchant assassins, including their families. He began to wonder if he should somehow keep an eye on Terren.

Collin waited for the King and Queen to move on ahead.

"Sir Collin, we will soon need to promote you to Supreme Captain," said the King.

Collin agreed. "Yes, My Lord."

Galner passed by Collin, and gave him a pat on the shoulder. "You look so tense, boy. I'm sure you'll be a fine Supreme Captain. Sir Terren said so himself."

Collin narrowed his eyes at Galner. "'Boy' is what you call someone who hasn't reached the age of majority, Sir Galner. I'm certain you wouldn't appreciate it if I called you that."

Galner chuckled. "I only jest, Collin."

As Ralphen and Maiya headed back into the castle, Collin and Galner walked together behind them.

Helen stole a quick glance at Mika and Mirin. Mika stared at the castle gates far ahead of her. Helen wondered what Mika was thinking about. She wanted to ask her out of curiosity. However, because Mika would probably jump with nervousness if she asked, she decided not to. She headed back into the castle.

Mirin stood beside Mika, and put a hand on her shoulder, startling her. "Are you all right, Mika?"

Mika put a hand on her heart for a moment. "I'm fine."

"Is something on your mind?"

You could say that, thought Mika. She repeated Terren's last words in her mind, and wondered what he meant by them. She smiled at Mirin as she put her arm through his. "No, not at all."

Mirin was skeptical. "Are you certain?"

"I'm fine. There's nothing on my mind... except perhaps a bowl of ice cream."

Mirin smiled, amused. "Oh? Is that so?"

"Yes. Would you like to share one with me?"

"Sure, that would be nice."

"Good, because I can never finish a bowl on my own."

Together, they both headed back for the castle.

CHAPTER 5:

PREOCCUPATION

SEC 3566, Morrighan 7

PRINCESS MIKA, SUBMERGED UP TO her neck in warm, soapy water in a cast iron bathtub, stared intently at the oil lamp that burned brightly on a wooden stand at the other side of the bathroom. She observed the oil within the glass tank just above the base of the lamp and the flame just above it. Her curious stare hinted at the intensity of her internal thought processes. She knew through the study of science that the flame was burning the oil, and that it must be causing some material, probably in gaseous form, to exit the lamp through spaces between the glass chimney and the metal covering above it. She assumed that the oil must turn into some kind of gas, and then leave a residue on the underside of the covering. But, soon, her meticulous scientific analysis was interrupted by the opening of the bathroom door, causing the little Princess to snap out of her thoughtful trance.

Angelica entered the room with a large kettle on a wooden cart, and wheeled it over the cold ceramic tiles. "More warm water for you, My Lady."

Mika leaned forward. "Thank you, Miss Angelica."

Angelica stopped beside the bathtub. For a young woman with a small frame, she was strong enough to lift the kettle and pour the water into the bathtub.

Mika watched her with amazement as she carefully stood up in the bathtub, water running down her smooth skin. She scratched her nose as water dripping gently down from her hair made it itch. "I could never hope to lift that."

Angelica laughed, handing her a soapy washcloth while holding another. "I suppose I've grown accustomed to lifting something as heavy as this, My Lady. It's certainly not a problem for me."

Mika compared her arms to Angelica's. "I'm too thin. I don't think I can ever have the strength to lift anything that heavy."

As Mika watched from the front, Angelica washed her from behind... and noticed her unusual silence.

"You seem somewhat preoccupied today." Angelica poured water over Mika's shoulders using a metal container, rinsing away soapsuds.

"What do you mean?" asked Mika.

"But then again, you usually are preoccupied."

Mika giggled as Angelica helped her out of the bathtub. Angelica splashed water at her lower legs to remove more soap. Water made its way across the floor tiles, and seeped into a drain nearby.

"You're probably right. I'm always thinking. My mind never stops thinking. Mirin tells me the same. He tells me I'm always thinking deeply." When Mika mentioned Mirin, her voice trailed off.

Angelica simply smiled. "It must be Mirin that's on your mind, Princess."

"You could say that. In the last several days, since Sir Terren left us, he has seemed somewhat... subdued. Is there something on his mind that he's not telling me?"

Angelica's expression became somber as she used a towel to dry Mika's body. "He told me he's still preoccupied by what happened that day... when those merchant assassins came."

"I see," said Mika. "I'm... I'm worried about him. I remember him calling out my name in front of the leader of the merchant assassins. The man didn't know who I was. He didn't know I was the Princess. But then... Mirin called out to me using my title. He called out 'Princess Mika'... and at that moment, the merchant assassins knew. They knew who I was. I wonder... if he's feeling regretful about that."

Angelica was taken aback. "I hadn't thought about that, My Lady. I'll talk to him about it later tonight."

"I don't think he needs to feel guilty about it. He didn't know what was going to happen if he did, and it's not like it would be bad in any other situation. He had no reason to think they were going to kill me if they realized I was the Princess. I hope... he'll understand that I don't blame him for anything." Mika sighed as Angelica wrapped a towel around her chest. "I'm very worried about him."

"You're always so affectionate whenever you speak of Mirin, My Lady."

Mika blushed and stammered. "No! That's not it! I mean... no, I mean, uh... that's not what I meant! I do love him, but... no, it's not like that!"

Amused by Mika's embarrassment, Angelica laughed. "You're so cute, Princess!"

"Oh never mind! Well... you know how I feel about him. It's hard to say it sometimes... but you're right. I love Mirin."

Hearing Mika's affectionate words regarding Mirin, Angelica felt a warm blush on her cheeks as she smiled sweetly. "I'm glad, Princess. I always love to hear you express your affections for Mirin."

Mika cast her eyes down for a moment. "I love him... but he doesn't love me. Well, maybe he does, but not the way I do."

Surprised, Angelica lost her smile. "What?"

"He doesn't know how much I like him. I mean... he knows I like him but... to him, I believe he regards me as a close female friend. A very close and very affectionate female friend. That's all. He holds my hand, and he hugs me. He lets me walk with him side-by-side with my arm through his. But I think... despite all that, he only sees me as a close female friend."

"Oh... I see...."

"I try to show him how I feel. I'm always affectionate with him. I love to hold hands with him. When I'm tired, I sit beside him, and put my head on his shoulder... and he lets me. I suppose you could say I can't keep my hands off him. I don't believe he notices at all. He's so dense! It's very difficult for me because I feel so awkward about my feelings towards him!"

Angelica nodded with agreement. "Yes... I understand your frustration, My Lady. But there's something I must remind you of."

Mika was puzzled. "What is it?"

"Mirin is ten, and you're eleven. He's more than a year younger than you are. Please remember one of the main differences between boys and girls. Girls mature much faster than boys do at around this time of their lives. So, Princess Mika...."

Mika reached up to touch her hair out of habit, water dripping from it down her chest and soaking into her towel. She looked at Angelica, who knelt down in front of her.

"Please be patient with our little Mirin. You're maturing much faster than he is, simply because you're a girl. I'm certain you haven't bled yet unless you're not telling me."

Feeling slightly awkward, Mika blushed. "I haven't. The moment I start bleeding, I will let you know."

"Well, you are quickly approaching your child-bearing years. He still needs to grow a little more, and then things will change. Eventually, maybe in a few more years, he'll see you as an attractive young woman, not just as a lady friend. Let's be patient with him."

Mika smiled and nodded. "Yes, you're right, Miss Angelica."

Angelica smiled as well. "Now, let's dry your hair and get you ready for bed." She offered to take her hand, so Mika let her.

As they were about to exit the bathroom, Mika stopped at the oil lamp, puzzling Angelica. Mika looked underneath the metal covering above the flame inside the glass chimney. Her hypothesis had been correct. She saw a residue on the bottom of the metal covering.

Mika smiled. "Exactly as I suspected."

* * *

Mika sat on the chair in front of her dressing table at

an angle so Angelica could kneel down beside her and brush her hair. Angelica poured a conditioning lotion into her hand, and ran her fingers through Mika's hair, while Mika applied body lotion all over. She gave the glass bottle of lotion to Angelica, who applied it on her back. Mika finished her evening beauty routine with a luxurious perfume.

"All done, Princess Mika. You are so beautiful! Your skin is so soft and is as smooth as silk," said Angelica, who arranged the bottles of various lotions on top of the dressing table.

Mika stood from her chair, and stared at her nude reflection. She was small for her age. She put her hands on her waist, examining her curves… or the lack of them. Her hands reached up to her breasts, which showed no signs of growing. As Angelica retrieved her clothes for the night, Mika thought to herself that she was far from becoming a woman, and felt a little disappointed.

Angelica pulled a sleeveless nightgown over Mika's head after she had her put on knickers, and then brushed her hair once more. As she did this, Angelica could not help but notice Mika's continued preoccupation.

"What are you still thinking about, My Lady? Are you still thinking about Mirin?"

Mika shook her head. "No, not this time."

"What else is on your mind?" Angelica led Mika to her bed. She made sure the sheets were nice and soft as she pulled back the blankets, and arranged the pillows in the manner which Mika was most comfortable with for sleeping.

Mika hesitated for a moment. She climbed onto her bed, and sat down, her knees together and feet dangling over the edge. "I'm still thinking about that day when the merchant assassins came."

Angelica joined Mika, sitting beside her. Saddened, she spoke softly. "I'm certain it'll disturb you for a long time. I wish I could erase it from your mind, My Lady."

Mika was confused for a moment. "You mean the fact that they tried to kill me? Yes, of course, it will. I'm definitely disturbed by that, too. It truly was very frightening…."

Angelica was taken aback by Mika's words, realizing that she was talking about something else. "Wait, Princess, you mean that's not the only thing on your mind? It sounds like there's more."

"You could say that. There is... something else that's bothering me."

"Please tell me. You're aware that you can always confide in me. You can tell me anything that's in your heart, anything that disturbs you in any way. I've been your trusted maidservant for the last three years, and I'm very glad to have had this privilege. To wait on such a sweet young lady such as you is an honour. I'd like to think I've come to know you personally. So I hope you can trust me with anything that causes your heart restlessness... and it's my hope that I can help you."

Mika felt warmth within her heart as she smiled at her beloved maidservant, reaching over for her hand. She thought about what was bothering her just as much as the attempt on her life. She thought back to that moment, when the leader of the merchant assassins discovered that she was the Princess of Melodice. She remembered his exact words, as if it had happened only yesterday.

"I remembered the words of the merchant assassin who was going to kill me. During the interview with Sir Terren, I told him the merchant's exact words. Do you remember what I recalled, what the merchant said to me?"

Angelica tried to think back. She shook her head slightly, so Mika recited the words, the exact words from start to finish. Hearing those words made Angelica's heart skip a beat.

"He hadn't intended to actually kill me. If I had been any other child, he would have left me alone, just like the other children that were there that time. He only wanted to kill me once he discovered that I was the Princess." Mika looked up at Angelica with a very serious expression, one that made Angelica slightly uncomfortable. Her deep thought processes were very visible in how she behaved and spoke. "They were going to have their revenge on a Royal. In other words, me. I just happened to be present.

I was... going to be the target of their revenge. What... what did he mean by revenge? I've been thinking about this for quite some time now. What is this revenge that he spoke of?"

For a long moment, Angelica was speechless as she hung on to every word spoken by the Princess, words that made her uneasy. Eventually, she shook her head, and put an arm around Mika to rub her back and shoulders.

"Princess, please don't think too much about what happened. Don't think too much about what those... people... said to you. Peasants... often say incomprehensible things, things that don't make sense to us. The merchant assassins were nothing more than a group of criminals. Their words were meaningless." Angelica stood up, quickly changing the subject to dispel the serious tone of their conversation. "I have fluffed your pillows for you, My Lady, and your blankets are nice and warm."

Mika said nothing as she watched Angelica pull her blankets back and fold them neatly at the foot of the bed. Something puzzled her just now. "Miss Angelica...."

"Yes, My Lady?"

"Did... you really mean what you said just now?"

"Huh?"

"About the peasants often saying incomprehensible things that don't make sense to us. By 'us', do you mean you and me, or do you mean the Nobility?"

Angelica was confused by Mika's question. "Why, the Nobility, of course. I'm not... quite certain I understand the question. I'm sorry, My Lady. What did you mean exactly?"

Mika was silent for a moment, thinking it odd that Angelica changed the subject so abruptly. She also thought about Angelica's confusion over her question, which she thought wasn't confusing at all. But what bothered her most of all were the words her maidservant used to describe the way peasants spoke. Incomprehensible, she says?

After a moment, Mika smiled and shook her head. "Um... nothing. It's nothing. Maybe I should stop thinking for tonight. It's rather late."

Angelica responded with a smile and a quick nod. "I think that's a good idea."

Mika drew her legs up, and crawled into the most comfortable part of her bed. Her maidservant tucked her in, putting pillows beside her under the blankets, and made sure she was as comfortable as she can possibly be. She felt her head sink into her cozy pillow and the softness of her blanket between her thin fingers.

"Thank you, Miss Angelica."

"You're most welcome, My Lady. I trust you're comfortable?"

"Very comfortable." It was so comfortable in her bed that she could already feel her entire body relaxing. It would not be difficult for her to fall asleep.

"As always, you know where I am." Angelica stroked Mika's hair.

"Don't forget my kiss," said Mika.

"I wasn't going to forget." She leaned over, kissing Mika on the cheek, and Mika returned it with a soft one on hers.

"Good night, Miss Angelica." Mika hugged her nearest pillow as she turned to her side.

"Good night, My Lady." Angelica turned off all the lamps in the room, and then blew out the candles. Soon, she left Mika's bedchamber.

With the curtains drawn back, there was still some light in the room. Two moons, their silvery phases nearing full, hung like bright jewels in the sky on this clear summer night.

Peasants often saying incomprehensible things? I'm sorry... I don't think I like what you said just now, Miss Angelica. It sounds... somewhat insensitive.

As Mika drifted to sleep, her thoughts were of the words spoken by the leader of the merchant assassins, words that referred to some kind of revenge. She continued to mull over them, even as sleep took hold.

* * *

SEC 3566, Morrighan 8

"What do you want to do after this?" asked Mirin.

Mika stared at the sky while lying down on the

grass next to one of the gardens of the Grounds. She thought she heard Mirin ask her something, but she was too preoccupied with her experience with the merchant assassins to understand him. Her hands played with the sides of her bell-shaped skirt, part of a long white dress that reached her ankles.

"Mika!" called out Mirin, lying down on the grass beside her.

Startled, Mika turned her head towards him. "What is it?"

"I'm trying to talk to you, but you're ignoring me. What's going on?"

Mika suddenly realized this. "I'm sorry! I didn't mean to ignore you."

Mirin shook his head. "I was asking you what we should do after this... or later on. It looks like it's going to rain any moment now."

Mika glanced at the thick clouds of varying shades of gray that progressively darkened as they moved across the sky. "I don't know."

"What about later in the afternoon?"

There was silence. Mirin turned towards Mika again.

After a moment, Mika did manage a response, but not the response he was looking for. "Whatever you want, Mirin. Just tell me what you'd like to do."

Mirin frowned. "What about just before dinner?" he asked a little more firmly.

"I'm not sure. Maybe... we can eat together...."

"What? Maybe we can eat together before dinner when we're already eating during dinner to begin with?" It was obvious to Mirin that she didn't understand him at all, which was completely out of character. Unless, of course, she was thinking deeply once again. "Um... Mika, is there something wrong? Something must be on your mind yet *again* because you're not making any sense."

Mika blinked, and turned towards Mirin again. "I'm sorry, pardon me?"

"What's going on? I've been asking you what you want to do later today and before dinner. You're not listening to me."

"I'm sorry!" Mika said quickly. "I'm sorry. I didn't mean to sound dismissive or uninterested."

"It's all right. What's on your mind this time?"

Mika stared at him silently for a long time as she thought about the best way to tell him what was on her mind. She thought about the merchant assassins, or rather, what their leader said in front of her. Since last night, that was all she thought about. "Mirin... do you know what revenge means?"

Mirin was taken aback. "Revenge...." He tried to remember what he'd learned in school so far. "I don't think I've learned that word yet. Language isn't exactly one of my favourite subjects. What does it mean?"

Before Mika answered, Mirin felt a drop on his forehead, and his hand instinctively reached up to feel what it was. It was wet.

"Ah... what was that?" asked Mirin.

Mika looked towards the sky, and saw two raindrops fall into the grass at either side of her head. Very soon, more raindrops fell.

"It's raining! Come on!" Mirin stood up from the grass quickly. The rain intensified.

"Mirin!" Mika tried to get up, but her oversized dress made it difficult for her. She held out both her hands for him.

Mirin took hold of them, and helped her get up. "Come, Mika!"

Mika used one hand to lift the front of her heavy skirt. Her other hand in Mirin's, they both ran to the side of the castle, where they found shelter.

Heavy rain fell onto the garden, giving life to the plants, flowers, trees, and grass. The bright flash of a distant lightning bolt startled Mika, and she jumped when she heard the rumbling thunder that came shortly after it. Near one of the side entrances, there was ample shelter, because the upper floors that protruded from the side of the castle provided cover. Water dripped down from Mika's hair and into the back of her dress. For Mirin, the water darkened the shade of his gray waistcoat.

As they watched the rain, Mika turned her eyes upon Mirin, admiring his strong and quiet demeanour. She smiled as she slowly reached for his hand. When her hand touched his, his hand moved... and went around hers, causing Mika to blush. Mika hoped they could stay like this for as long as possible. She wanted to stand beside him and lean on him, and she wanted him to put his arms around her... but that might be asking for too much at this point. For now, having him hold her hand like this was good enough. Mika turned towards the rain again.

"I wonder... does the city of Scarletia... outside the castle... do they have any gardens?" Mika asked, almost thinking to herself. "I've never seen the city."

Puzzled, Mirin turned to her. He remembered what they had been talking about before the rain started. "Mika, you were asking me if I knew what revenge was. What is it?"

Mika stood closer to him. "Revenge is the act of inflicting punishment out of resentment on someone who had done a perceived wrongdoing."

Mirin thought about the definition for a moment, trying to understand it. "So... I suppose if I did something bad to you, revenge would be like... you punishing me because you were angry at me for doing something bad to you."

"Yes, that's right. But I'm sure you'd never do anything bad to me, and I would certainly not get so angry at you that I'd want to punish you to that extent."

"Of course not."

"But the punishment is often not according to the law. It's about taking the law into your own hands, and dealing your own form of punishment, and oftentimes, the punishment is unfair or unjust."

Mirin cast his eyes down for a moment. "I think I understand."

"Given your relationship with me, if I had died that day when the merchant assassins came, if that man had killed me, assuming you survived, what would you feel? Would you feel terribly angry?" asked Mika.

Feeling uneasy, Mirin thought about that for a

moment. "That's a rather frightening thought. Um... I suppose I'd feel many things, and anger would be one of them. In fact, I'd be terribly angry. I'd be so angry that I'd want to do something."

"What would you have done to those people who killed me, if they had survived?"

"I suppose I'd want to go out, find them, and kill them myself. I suppose you could call that revenge."

Mika remembered again the words of the leader of the merchant assassins, words that disturbed her greatly. "That man who tried to kill me. He said there was a Royal who they can exact their revenge upon. He was going to kill me out of revenge... but wouldn't you seek revenge on those who wronged you? Have I... have I wronged anyone so badly that they'd want to kill me?"

Mirin turned to her, his voice raised. "No, you did nothing wrong! Absolutely nothing! And those merchant assassins, you didn't do anything wrong to them! You didn't even know who they were!"

"They didn't recognize me as the Princess until they heard from you that I was."

Mirin's eyes widened, his painful guilt from that day welling up from within. He let go of her hand, turned towards her, and put his arms around her.

Mika gasped with surprise as her cheeks became red.

"I'm sorry... I still feel terrible about what happened. I called you Princess in front of them. Because of that, they found out who you were, and then they tried to kill you." Mirin closed his eyes, his voice subdued. When he opened his eyes again, he looked angry. He was angry with himself.

"Mirin...." Mika put her arms on his shoulders, looking into his eyes, seeing his terrible guilt. Seeing him like that made her heart ache.

"At that time, the Princess Gem was under your collar. They didn't see it. They didn't know you were the Princess, until I gave your identity away. They didn't know what you looked like. They had never seen you until that day, until that moment."

"But I know you didn't mean to do it, Mirin. It was an accident." She leaned her face on his shoulder affectionately, her face next to his. Being this close to him made her heart beat faster. "Please... don't feel bad. Don't feel guilty. You did nothing wrong."

Mirin closed his eyes, resting the side of his head against Mika's, finding comfort in her soft and affectionate hold. They stayed that way for a few minutes. He was glad for a moment that he had no friends who were boys, and that his closest relationship was with the Princess of Melodice, not just any other girl. Otherwise, he'd be teased to no end.

Oh my... please don't stop holding me like this. Mika sighed, her breathing a little shallow. She listened to her heart racing, and she felt the warmth in her cheeks. She looked up at him again as Mirin raised his head. "Mirin...."

Mirin smiled and nodded. "Yes, you're right... and I do know I did nothing wrong. Everything you said is true. It truly was an accident, but... I suppose it's been a little difficult for me to think that way."

Unfortunately, to the great disappointment of the love-stricken young Princess, Mirin soon let go of her, and then turned back towards the rain. Mika lost her smile. She forcefully pushed her disappointment away by thinking more about the words of the leader of the merchant assassins. "But do you know what this means, Mirin?"

"Huh?"

"What if a different Royal had been there at that moment? What if it had been my mother, but, somehow, nobody knew she was the Queen? What if they initially ignored her as they started killing people? If they realized she was the Queen, would that merchant assassin have said the same thing? From the words he chose, it sounded like... it was not me specifically he wanted to kill. He just... simply wanted to kill a Royal. I just happened to be at the wrong place at the wrong time."

Mirin thought about that. "That's true. If he wanted to kill you specifically, he'd have said something else. He'd have said something like today is a good day to die, and they have you, Princess Mika Silveraine, to exact their revenge upon. Instead, he had said they had a Royal out there to exact their revenge upon, and he mentioned you after that, like you were an example. Am I right?"

Mika nodded as her eyes widened with surprise. "Yes, that's right! Mirin, you're very good at this! I had no idea!"

"I believe your frightening tendency to think deeply is rubbing off on me." He held up his thumb and forefinger with a small space between them. "Just a little though."

"So... it's not me they targeted. They realized they had a Royal near them, and wanted to kill that Royal so they could exact their revenge... and it just so happened that the Royal was me. But then... revenge for what? What did they mean by exacting their revenge upon a Royal? I didn't do anything wrong. But they couldn't have been referring to me. Were they referring to someone else? Were they referring to someone else in the Royal Family of Melodice? Or were they referring to the Royal Family in general? Did the Royal Family do something to them? If that's true... then what did the Royal Family do?"

Mirin stared blankly at Mika as she asked all these questions of herself. She looked straight at Mirin as she did this, so it appeared to him as if she was asking him instead. "Mika...."

"What is it?" she asked.

"You're giving me a headache. That's far more questions than I can handle."

"I'm sorry."

Mirin shook his head. "Mika, you think far too deeply for your own good. Don't do that. You'll exhaust yourself. In fact, sometimes you do. I've never met another child close to my age who thought as deeply as you."

"I know but... this is something I want to figure out for myself. I need to understand why this happened to me. I think that's the best way for me to cope with it." Mika clasped her hands together at her heart. "I still feel frightened when I recall those events. I sometimes have nights when I can't sleep, or I wake up and I start crying in my bed. I need to understand... why this happened. Or I'll never recover from it."

"But there's something you're forgetting, Mika.

Those merchant assassins... they were nothing more than peasants. They were just criminals. I'm sure they were just delusional when they talked about revenge. It's not worth mulling over too much."

His words were similar to what Angelica said last night. Nothing more than peasants? Criminals? Delusional? Mika felt somewhat disturbed by them as she stared at Mirin for a long time. Except for the rain that fell on the garden and the distant sounds of rumbling thunder, there was silence between them.

You're thinking like Miss Angelica as well? Why? Is this what everyone thinks?

Mirin was puzzled. "Um... what's wrong?"

After a moment, Mika shook her head and smiled. For now, she no longer wanted to talk about this with Mirin or Angelica. "Nothing... nothing at all. Perhaps you're right... and I'm thinking too deeply about this."

Mirin chuckled. "I would think so."

But I know I'm not. I'm not thinking too deeply. Something... doesn't feel right.

CHAPTER 6:

THE EXCURSION

P RINCESS MIKA DID NOT NORMALLY wear shoes with taller heels, but today, she decided she would try a pair with four-centimetre heels as she walked down the wide hallways of the castle. She quickly found out to her disappointment that it was not an easy task. She certainly felt more womanly wearing them, but also found them much more challenging to walk in than she'd anticipated. On this warm afternoon, she headed down one of the hallways that would lead her to the office of Galner Ciannar. She had been called to his office just moments ago.

Two little girls, who were close to Mika's age and clad in beautiful dresses, were about to pass as they walked the opposite direction. Mika recognized them immediately. For her general studies, they attended the same classes as she did.

It's Miss Taria and Miss Sheena, she thought, as the girls paused for a moment, and then curtsied.

Sheena was younger than the Princess by almost a year. Sweet, quiet, and humble, she smiled at Mika, her hands clasped together in front. "Hello, Princess Mika."

Taria was the same age as Mika. The total opposite of her friend Sheena, she stood with one hand on her waist and her nose high in the air, her personality bursting with pride. "How are you this morning, Princess?"

Mika gasped softly, and gave a shy smile. Because they

greeted her, she was forced to stop for a moment, nearly tripping again. She grimaced, feeling a very slight pull within one of her ankles, but fortunately, she supported herself against the wall just in time. Alarmed by near-injury, she stared down at her shoes with widened eyes.

Sheena and Taria both noticed her discomfort.

"Um… are you all right, Princess?" asked Sheena.

"I'm… I'm fine, thank you, Miss Sheena." Mika stiffened, feeling very timid. She tried to meet their gaze, but had difficulty doing so. She wasn't sure what else to say to them.

Taria noted the tall heels of Mika's shoes. "Are your shoes bothering you?"

Mika quickly shook her head. "No—um, well, no, not at all, I—uh… I'm sorry… I have to see Sir Galner. I was summoned to his office."

Confused, the two girls stole a glance at each other.

Taria glanced back at the Princess with a hint of annoyance in her eyes that she tried very hard to conceal. She found Mika's timid personality annoying. "If you say so, Princess."

Sheena simply smiled. "If you'll excuse us, we'll be going now."

Mika bowed her head to them slightly when they curtsied once more. She watched them walk away, more quickly this time, until they disappeared around a corner. Keeping her hand on the wall to steady herself just in case she fell, she thought about her encounter with Sheena and Taria just now.

They must always think I'm strange. None of the girls in my classes like me. I can always sense it. I don't know how to talk to them, and they think I'm pretentious because of it. I wish they could understand me.

Mika thought about Mirin. Unlike those two girls she ran into earlier, Mirin was a very close friend to her, but he was a boy. To him, she was a close friend, but to her, he was more than that, a boy for whom she has affection. The only female friend she had was Miss Angelica, who was nineteen years old, eight years older than she. Mika had no female friends her age, and in this castle that was home to over ten thousand nobles, there were many girls her age.

When Mika reached Sir Galner's office, the large double doors were closed. There were comfortable chairs along the wall outside the doors. Mika took one step towards one of the chairs, and felt her ankle give way. She gasped as she nearly fell sideways, but she managed to regain her balance. She looked behind to see if anyone had seen her just now. Sure enough, there was a noble couple that did see her. When she met their gazes, they immediately looked away, and then kept walking.

"Ugh... this is so embarrassing," she whispered as she looked up at the ceiling with frustration. She carefully sat down on one of the chairs nearby, next to the doors. As she waited, she sat farther back in the chair, crossed one leg over the other, and clasped her hands together on her lap.

After a few minutes, Mika noticed someone else coming down the hallway. She heard the echoing footsteps of someone's boots. As soon as she looked up at the approaching young woman, Mika stiffened, wishing she could become invisible. She cast her eyes down at the tips of her shoes to avoid the piercing gaze of Helen Renier as she stood outside the doors of their professor's office.

Helen was in the regular knight's uniform for women, but without the black coat or cape on top of her white blouse. Her black trousers were snug around her figure. She sat down on the chair across from the Princess on the opposite side of the hallway, crossing one leg over the other.

Mika kept her head down, but watched Helen, observing every detail of how Helen carried herself as a young woman and how she dressed. Everything about Helen, Mika wished she had. She was strong and toned, yet was very slim. Her hips were wide, her waist was narrow, and her breasts were the perfect size for her body type, not too large and not too small. Mika unconsciously put her hand on her chest, discreetly feeling up the size of her flat breasts. She sighed with disappointment. She had a long way to go.

Miss Helen is so beautiful, so womanly. I wish I was as

beautiful as she is. I feel like I'm so far behind in every way. When I turn sixteen, will I be as womanly as Miss Helen?

Helen suddenly shot a glance towards Mika, who looked away just as quickly. Mika pulled her hand away from her chest, and clasped her hands together on her lap again.

"Is there something on my face, Princess Mika? You've been staring at me since I arrived here," said Helen.

Startled, Mika froze for a moment. When she found her words, she spoke quickly. "I'm... I'm sorry, Miss Helen. Please forgive me."

"Did Sir Galner summon you as well?"

Mika tried to look up at Helen again, but as soon as their eyes met, she shifted her gaze away again. She nodded quickly. "Yes... yes, he summoned me. I suppose you're here for the same reason?"

"Of course, I am. Didn't you hear what I said?"

Remembering that Helen said "as well" in her previous sentence, Mika was startled again. "I'm sorry!"

Helen leaned forward. "Will you please stop apologizing?!"

Startled, Mika forced herself to be quiet. In front of Sir Collin or Sir Maleth, she knew that Helen would never yell at her like she did just now. Such behaviour would cause quite a commotion. But they were the only ones here right now, and Mika was not one to complain that someone yelled at her. Mika forced herself to stop apologizing. It was true that she apologized too much, and often for no reason. Mika was always worried she was offending someone, and with Helen, she was worried about that more with her than with anyone else.

Helen leaned back. "Forgive me. I should govern the tone of my voice."

Mika gazed up slightly, and this time, she did not feel too intimidated. She couldn't believe her ears. Helen actually apologized to her. "It's... it's all right. I probably deserved it just now."

"Princess...."

"Yes, Miss Helen?"

"Why do you always have to look away from me like a frightened rabbit whenever I look at you?"

Mika was startled by that question. When she slowly glanced up at Helen again, she saw that she still had a firm expression. Mika opened her mouth, but no words came out. She wasn't sure how to answer Helen's question.

"You don't have a legitimate reason for being frightened of me. I'm your knight, and you're my Princess. In fact, we're far closer in age than all the other knights. And I'm female. I had also saved your life. Also, we're colleagues in the study of magic under Sir Galner. There's no reason for you to be afraid of me."

She was right. As Mika thought about that, she realized she had no reason to be scared of Helen. She also realized it was her timid personality that caused her to act this way.

Mika allowed herself to smile just a little. "I suppose… you're right, Miss Helen."

Helen was surprised by Mika's smile. She closed her eyes, and then casually rubbed the bridge of her nose, her hand covering her face to hide any possible outward hint of envy.

Damn! I wish I could smile like that! Despite her youth, she's far more beautiful than I am. I wish I had been as beautiful as she is now when I was eleven years old….

At that moment, the double doors to Sir Galner's office opened. The professor of magical studies appeared at the doorway. Mika and Helen stood up.

"Ah, Princess Mika, Helen, thank you for coming." Without his robe, Galner appeared even thinner in only his dress shirt, waistcoat, and trousers. However, he did not appear unhealthy, and was perfectly capable of opening the large double doors into his own office, which were heavy. "Please come in."

Princess Mika was about to enter through the doorway when her ankle gave way slightly. Helen was about to go in after her, but she stopped. Mika cast her eyes down, her shoulders tensed. "Please go ahead, Miss Helen."

Helen looked down at Mika's high-heeled shoes. She kept her amusement hidden. "Practice makes perfect, Princess. You should go ahead of me."

Mika hesitated, but it sounded to her as if Helen insisted that she go on ahead. She regained herself on her awkward shoes, and then walked into the office. Helen followed her in.

Galner turned back briefly as he headed for his large wooden desk. "Please close the doors behind you, Helen."

Helen complied as Galner sat on the leather chair behind his desk. Other than some sheets of paper with notes, and a pen and bottle of ink, his desk was quite neat and tidy. In front of his desk were two leather chairs, but not as high-backed as the one in which Galner sat. Shelves heavy with books lined every wall, except the one behind Galner, which had windows and a door that led to a balcony. In the middle of the office, two long couches faced each other, separated by a table. The carpet underneath Helen's boots felt soft as it muffled her footfalls.

"Please have a seat here in front of my desk," said Galner.

Both Mika and Helen did as he asked.

"You have a fine office, Sir Galner," said Helen.

"Thank you. It's not bad at all, is it? How are you both?"

Helen and Mika glanced at each other for a moment, as each wondered if the other was going to respond.

Because Helen said nothing, Mika was forced to respond. "We're doing well, thank you, Sir Galner. I trust that you are well? We've been practicing our most recent lesson like you asked us to."

"I'm also doing well, and I'm glad you're practicing the lesson I gave. I assume there are no difficulties?"

Helen stiffened, glancing at Mika.

Mika stiffened even more so, meeting Helen's gaze.

This time, Helen took the initiative at answering. "Sir Galner, I've been practicing the lesson you gave. But I must admit that the lesson... escapes me. This lesson on magical flight... is quite challenging."

"Ah, I see." Galner turned to Mika. "Princess, do you find this most recent lesson challenging as well?"

Mika hesitated, but she had to admit it. "Uh... yes, Sir Galner. I'm also having some difficulties with it. I'm not sure I completely understand the lesson. I'm having a problem visualizing it."

"Ah, I see," the professor repeated.

"I'm sorry, Sir Galner!" Mika stammered.

Helen stared at her with widened eyes, wordlessly telling her to stop apologizing unnecessarily.

Mika continued. "I'm... having difficulty understanding the lesson. I think... perhaps... I may not be competent enough for the lesson on magical flight."

"I respectfully disagree, Princess. Both of you are highly proficient in the use of magic. You're both extremely talented, and have power that could be considered almost unlimited. Both of you, it's your own potentials that escape you, not the lesson on magical flight. You're perfectly capable of understanding this ability. All it takes is time and practice. Don't be so hard on yourselves, especially you, Princess Mika. With time and practice, you'll be able to better visualize this ability, and you'll be able to understand it, and then use it to your own advantage. It'll become part of you, like all the other abilities you have learned up to now."

"Your confidence in us is appreciated, Sir Galner," said Helen. "I hope we'll be able to understand this ability sooner rather than later."

"You will. I'm certain of it. Admittedly, this can be a difficult magic spell for some. It truly depends on each person."

"How long will it take for us to learn it, Sir Galner?" asked Mika.

"That's not something I can tell you. Only you can answer for yourselves. Every student is different. Some students learn certain spells faster than others. Some still struggle with simple spells, and yet are proficient with ones that are more advanced. You will learn magical flight in your own time, at your own pace. Some students do understand it very quickly while others take much longer, and it matters not how proficient they are with magic in general."

Mika's voice became subdued. "Oh... I see."

"I expect you'll understand it very soon. Take your time. And more importantly, be careful, and don't do anything that could cause injury. There have been a few students in history who have forced themselves to learn magical flight by subjecting themselves to a life-threatening situation, like jumping out of a building."

Mika gasped, her hands clasped together at her heart.

Shocked, Helen leaned forward. "Truly?"

"Yes. Some learned it somehow as they were falling, and saved themselves. Unfortunately, for some others, either injury or death resulted. Please do not jump out of a building. I highly disagree with this method."

Mika shook her head. "I could never do that...."

Helen leaned back in her chair. "Likewise."

Sir Galner leaned back as well. "Good. Now, let's talk about something else: the reason why I summoned you both here. You're familiar with the Cerulean Magic Academy, although neither of you has set foot within its walls, correct?"

"Yes, Sir Galner," said Mika.

Helen recalled what she learned about the Cerulean Magic Academy. "It is a revered institution of learning. Located in the great city of Cerulean, it was established well over a thousand years ago. In fact, it's not known exactly when the Academy was established, but legend has it that it was the realized dream of a woman who was a member of the race of Spires."

"You know your history well, Helen. That's correct, or at least, that's what we believe. Records are difficult to come by, but we believe, based on current evidence, that a woman named Muriel from the land of the Spires came to visit our race of Humans, and bestowed upon some of us the ability to learn magic. By doing this, she helped establish the Academy. However, back in those times, it wasn't called the Cerulean Magic Academy. The city of Cerulean was built around it over many years, perhaps centuries, after the fact. It's a legendary place of learning with a rich history."

"I've read many books about the Cerulean Magic

Academy. I'm always amazed by everything I read about it. To the entire nation, it's considered legendary," said Mika.

"I'm glad to hear that. Now, the reason why I'm telling you this is that I'll be heading to the city of Cerulean for a major conference with professors such as myself that will last for five days. I'd like to use this opportunity to take you with me to show you the Cerulean Magic Academy."

Absolutely surprised, Mika and Helen wondered if they were imagining this. They were being invited by Galner to the Cerulean Magic Academy.

"Sir Galner, it would be an honour!" exclaimed Helen.

Mika nearly jumped out of her seat. "Sir Galner, I would love to accompany you to the Cerulean Magic Academy! I've only read about it in books and seen illustrations! I would be so happy to see it in person!"

"As would I, Sir Galner. Like the Princess, I've never seen the Academy in person. This would be a wonderful opportunity, and I wouldn't miss it for the world."

"It's the one and only school of magic in the entire nation of Melodice, in fact, this whole continent of Alenshire. The Academy is the envy of other nations nearby. There are other schools of magic in the world, but they're few in number and located in distant lands. Nearly all of them are in the land of the Spires."

Galner was amused by the excitement expressed by his two young students. To him, Helen appeared to be trying her best to contain herself, but was having trouble doing so. She appeared almost like a child herself. Mika, of course, was not so reserved.

"Princess Mika, Helen, you're both among the best students I've ever had the pleasure of instructing. I'm very proud of you. This is the reason why I'd like to show you the Cerulean Magic Academy. I'm sure you will both appreciate it."

"As I said, we are very much honoured, Sir Galner."

"Good. Then I will make the necessary arrangements."

Princess Mika stood up. "Sir Galner, may I tell my parents now so that they're aware? I'd like to obtain their permission as soon as possible."

"Why, of course, Princess, please go ahead. I'm certain they'll be happy for you as well and allow you to go."

The delighted Princess smiled. "Thank you so much!" She started quickly for the doors, forgetting that she was wearing high-heeled shoes. One of her ankles gave way again, and she nearly fell sideways. She would have fallen if she had not been able to use the back of one of the couches for support.

Galner noticed the sudden difficulty the Princess experienced and wondered what happened.

Mika looked back, and then saw Helen and Sir Galner staring at her.

"Are you... all right, Princess?" asked Galner.

"I'm fine, Sir Galner." Terribly embarrassed, Mika straightened up, and started walking again, this time with a little more care. She opened one of the doors just enough to let her tiny body through, and then closed it behind her.

Galner stood up to look at the part of the floor where Mika nearly fell over. "Might I have dropped something on the floor? I don't see anything."

Helen got up, ready to leave. "It's... not that, Sir Galner."

"Do you know what just happened?"

"The Princess appears to be having some difficulty with her new high-heeled shoes."

Galner laughed. "Ah, I see, Helen. Well, she is a young lady, and I'm sure she'll become accustomed to them in the future. I do see young women sometimes in shoes with tall heels, and I wonder how they can walk." The professor paused for a moment as he changed the subject. "Now, as for this excursion to the Cerulean Magic Academy, I'm glad that both of you will accompany me. Of course, the Princess should definitely seek the permission of her parents, as she's doing now. I would suggest that you should at least let your mother know."

Helen paused for a moment, regarding Galner with a serious expression. "May I ask why?"

Galner was taken aback by her reaction to his suggestion. "Well... it might be a good idea. She might appreciate it if you let her know, and hearing that you'll be traveling to the Academy, she might be proud of you."

"I'm sixteen years old. I'm of the age of majority. I have a profession I'm proud of, and I'm able to live on my own. I have no need to be approaching my mother for anything."

Although Helen had a point, Galner thought it was somewhat harsh. He shrugged. "You don't have to let her know. It was only a suggestion."

"Thank you, Sir Galner. Well, then, if there is nothing further?"

"That is all, Helen. I will see you and Princess Mika at our next lesson."

Helen bowed slightly, and then headed for the exit. She fumed as she approached the doors. As she exited, she ensured the doors were closed behind her, and in the hallway, she frowned with annoyance.

"That woman... I don't have to tell her anything. She wouldn't be interested anyway."

* * *

Mika was able to obtain the permission of her parents, and when they gave their blessings, she was absolutely elated. She had to tell Mirin about this... but the first thing she needed to do was change her shoes.

Seated on her couch in her bedchamber, she removed her shoes, and then gently threw them on the couch directly opposite of her as she let out a huge sigh. They bounced off the cushions, falling onto the floor. Not only were they difficult to walk in, they also made her feet hurt. She didn't even want to count the number of times she could have sprained her ankle.

Mika left her bedchamber, intent on finding Mirin. Wearing the flat shoes she normally wore, she was much more comfortable as she headed to the door that led to Angelica's room. Using the door ring, she knocked, but there was no answer. She knocked a second time. They were not home.

Mika proceeded farther down the hallways, and eventually came upon one with windows that overlooked the front of the castle. Looking out the fifth floor windows, she could see quite far away. She watched nobles socializing and taking a walk on the Grounds. She tried to see if Mirin was among them, but he was nowhere to be found.

She continued down the hallways and then some stairs as she headed down to the lower levels. She wondered where he might be, so she tried to think of the places where he would normally go. He might go outside and play in the Grounds. He usually went outside with her, and if it was not with her, it would be with Miss Angelica.

Eventually, when Mika exited through the castle doors, she heard her name being called out almost right away.

"Mika!" Mirin ran along the bottom of the steps that led up to the castle doors. He stopped there, smiled, and waved at her.

Mika's cheeks felt warm as she saw how handsome he was in his gray trousers and white dress shirt with loose sleeves. His black boots were somewhat dirty from soil that he must have stepped through at some point. Mika smiled, waving back. With the shoes she changed into, it was much easier going down the steps. As soon as she reached the bottom, she ran over to Mirin, embracing him.

Mirin was taken aback by her sudden display of affection, but he put his arms around her to return it. "You look like you missed me after not having seen me for years."

Mika blushed. "I'm sorry...."

"Don't be sorry. You can always hug me."

At the mention of that, Mika blushed even more as she cast her eyes down.

"But what was that for?" he asked.

Because I love you. Mika shook her head, smiling. "No reason." She remembered why she wanted to see him, and became very excited. "But I was looking for you! I need to tell you something!"

Mirin lit up with curiosity. "What is it?"

"Do you know about the Cerulean Magic Academy?"

Mirin nodded. "Yes, of course. It's the one and only school of magic in all of Melodice, and it's the only one of its kind in this part of the world. It's the envy of our neighbouring nations."

"Sir Galner invited me and Miss Helen to accompany him to the Cerulean Magic Academy!"

Mirin was surprised. "Truly?"

"Yes! I've always wanted to see it! It's in the city of Cerulean. I've read about it in books and seen illustrations, but I've never seen it with my very own eyes. It's legendary! Almost all of the students of magic in the entire nation study there. This will be my first excursion, beyond the castle gates, beyond the city itself, and into another city, and it'll be to see the Cerulean Magic Academy! I'm so excited that I don't know how I'll be able to sleep tonight!"

"So I see...." Mirin crossed his arms against his chest.

It was obvious to Mika that he was not particularly excited. In fact, she noted right away that he appeared slightly annoyed. "You don't sound happy for me. Are you all right?"

"Why is Sir Galner inviting you and Miss Helen?"

"Um... well, he said he was going to attend a major conference, and wanted to take this opportunity to show us the Academy." Mika stared at him for a long time. She knew him well enough to be able to see what he was feeling. "You seem annoyed, Mirin. Is... something the matter?"

Mirin just shook his head. "No, no, I'm not annoyed. I'm happy for you, actually."

It was obvious to Mika that Mirin was denying it. She wondered if he was annoyed because she was going to an excursion without him. A part of her wanted to ask him if that was the reason why he felt the way he did. However, Mika knew that if she kept on asking, he might get angry with her. Such a situation had happened once before, and she remembered not being able to stand it. That time, she felt terrible, and she did not know what to do.

"Well... all right, Mirin." Mika smiled, putting a hand on his arm very gently. "Um, would you like to go inside and have some tea and biscuits with me?"

Mirin simply nodded. "Sure, let's do that."

Mika smiled sweetly, and took him by the hand. They walked up the steps to the castle doors, and entered.

* * *

SEC 3566, Morrighan 15

Soon, the day of Princess Mika's excursion came. Decked out in pure white, she was ready to go in her silk and lace dress that had a slight shimmer to it and felt luxuriously soft and smooth on her skin. The ribbon in her hair was mid-back in length. Her stockings were smooth and opaque above her low-heeled, knee-high boots. Her cape reached down just past her knees, buttoned and tied around her neck with a thin ribbon, covering the Princess Gem. Underneath her cape, she carried a leather handbag with its strap across her shoulder.

Mika checked herself in front of the dressing table mirror one last time while Angelica arranged her hair as perfectly as possible. On the floor beside her bed, a sturdy wooden travel chest contained all the belongings she planned on taking with her, such as clothes and shoes. The doors to her bedchamber were wide open.

Helen appeared at the doorway, along with two knights. "Well, Princess Mika, are you almost ready?"

Mika was startled as she turned around. She was about to avoid Helen's gaze, but she stopped herself. "Hello, Miss Helen. I believe I'm ready now."

"Good." Helen wondered why there were two knights here. When they met her gaze, she gave them a blank stare. She recognized them as Caylen Malavers and Aldrian Triska.

"Pardon us, My Lady," said Sir Caylen, who cleared his throat, feeling slightly uneasy because of Helen's stare. "We were advised you had some luggage you needed brought to the carriage that's waiting outside."

"Yes, sir, I do." Mika quickly walked over to the chest beside her bed. "It's this one. If you could please bring this to the carriage, I would greatly appreciate it. It's far too heavy for me. I hope it's not too much trouble."

"No trouble at all, My Lady," said Sir Aldrian, who smiled, thinking this was going to be very easy. Even though it was a travel chest, a young girl's things shouldn't be that heavy to carry, should they? He and Caylen headed for the chest.

Mika joined Helen at the doorway.

Helen regarded Mika with curiosity. "Princess, I believe we were told to travel light."

"I *am* traveling light. Why?" asked Mika.

It became obvious very quickly to Helen that Mika's definition of light traveling consisted of a minimum of one travel chest. She shook her head.

As the knights bent down to pick up the chest by the handles at both ends, they were surprised. They glanced at each other, puzzled. It was heavier than they imagined, but they still managed to easily lift it up.

"Aldrian," whispered Caylen.

"What is it, Caylen?" replied Aldrian.

"This chest… don't you think it's heavier than it should be, assuming it carries only clothes, shoes, and other things women normally carry with them on excursions?"

Aldrian agreed. "That's what I thought as well."

Mika stiffened slightly when she heard their conversation, but she regained her composure quickly, and pretended she didn't hear. She watched the two knights carry the chest through the doorway. "Thank you."

"You're most welcome, Princess," replied Caylen.

As the knights left, Helen could not help but comment further on Mika's luggage. "As I said, we were told to travel light. Seeing how those knights carried your travel chest, it didn't appear light to me. Are you taking your entire wardrobe with you?"

Mika shook her head. "No, of course, not. I'm not carrying all that much luggage, am I?"

"You need to rethink your definition of traveling light."

Mika, being more sensitive than most girls her age, felt like she had been stung by Helen's words. "I'm sorry. I've never traveled before."

"Well, that's a lesson to remember for next time. I

better head to the carriage outside. Sir Galner is waiting. I'll meet you there."

Mika simply nodded.

Helen passed through the doorway, and was about to head on her way when she saw the Queen approaching. She stopped, and bowed slightly. "My Lady, I hope you're well."

Mika raised her head upon hearing Helen's words. She heard her mother's voice down the hallway.

"I am, Miss Helen, and I hope you are as well," said Queen Maiya.

Helen continued on her way.

Maiya appeared at the doorway, and saw her daughter, beautifully dressed from top to bottom. "Ah, there you are, Mika. Come here."

Mika smiled as she approached her mother, who took hold of her by the shoulders, and then lovingly stroked her soft cheek and her smooth hair.

"Look at you. As always, you are so lovely. I am so proud of you. This will be your first excursion, one that will take you to the outside world to the Cerulean Magic Academy. I have visited there before, and I'm certain you'll enjoy it. You won't forget your first visit to the Academy for the rest of your life. It'll be wonderful."

"I'm excited, Mother. I've always wanted to see it in person." Mika was almost bouncing on her heels with anticipation.

Maiya gave Mika a kiss on the cheek, and then embraced her. "I pray that your journey will be safe, and that your excursion will be most enjoyable."

"Thank you, Mother." Mika returned her kiss and embrace. "I can't believe I'll be seeing the outside world. Going beyond the castle gates for the first time. I've never even seen the city of Scarletia. From the upper floors of the castle, I can only see a few taller buildings far away over the walls."

"Yes, that's true. You'll have to travel through the city of Scarletia. Sir Collin has chosen a fine group of five knights who will protect you, led by Sir Maleth. They're among the best and most highly skilled. They will ensure your safety, as well as the safety of Miss Helen and Sir Galner."

Mika was curious. "Mother, may I ask why do I need to be accompanied by such a large number of highly skilled knights, led by the great Sir Maleth, and a group of knights personally selected by the great Sir Collin himself?"

Maiya was confused by her question. "It's a natural necessity, Mika. When your father and I traveled, Sir Terren often accompanied us, along with several knights, and not just any random knights either. Our former Supreme Captain always selected from the best. They ensured our safety as we traveled."

"I understand," said Mika.

Maiya knelt down to embrace Mika again. "Be safe, Mika. I love you."

"I love you, too, Mother."

Mika and Maiya parted ways. As soon as Maiya was no longer with her, she wondered where her father was. He did not come to bid her farewell, to wish her well, or to embrace her and kiss her, like her mother did. Mika wondered if her father was angry with her again, if she had done something wrong, but she could not remember doing anything that might have disappointed him lately.

Or... perhaps... to my father, in general, I myself am a disappointment?

Angelica approached Mika, and knelt down beside her. "Everything's ready, Princess. The only thing outstanding is our dear Mirin. He's nowhere to be found. I had told him that he should be seeing you off."

Mika stiffened again, but she did her best to remain calm. "Wasn't he in your room this morning?"

Angelica shook her head. "He had left our room very early this morning. I was still half-asleep when I heard the door close. At first, I thought I had been dreaming, but apparently, I was mistaken."

Mika giggled. "Mirin is... probably somewhere in the castle doing the usual things he does. He loves to be up and about, after all."

Angelica shrugged. "Yes, you're probably right. However, I can't help but be disappointed. He should be seeing you off. I'll have a talk with him when I see him."

"That's fine. I'm not going to be angry with him or anything of the sort. I'll be seeing him as soon as I return."

Angelica smiled. "Of course, My Lady."

Mika smiled as well. She put her arms around Angelica, and kissed her on the cheek. "I love you, Miss Angelica. I'll see you soon."

Angelica felt warmth in her heart as she returned her embrace. "I love you, too, Princess Mika."

A moment later, Mika walked down the hallway, the sounds of her boots echoing on the marble floors. She walked like the lady she was, with her back straight, her head level, and her hands clasped together in front of her. Mika took a deep breath, barely able to contain her excitement. The Cerulean Magic Academy was waiting for her.

* * *

When Mika saw the carriage, she immediately thought it was large. Its rectangular cabin had doors at either side, windows at the front, back, and sides, and four large wheels. A platform with a roof was behind the cabin, where two knights could be comfortably seated and cargo could be stored, including her travel chest, which rested on the floor, tied to the beams and railings that surrounded the platform. At the front of the carriage was space for two drivers, and in front of them, four cervids waited patiently, two at the very front and another two immediately behind them. Intricate designs were carved into the wood of the carriage itself. At either side of the cabin, near the front and just behind the drivers' seat, ladders led up to the roof of the cabin. A large space was carved into the roof where two more knights could be seated so they could watch over their surroundings with ease.

Mika saw Helen and Sir Galner talking at the bottom of the steps in front of the castle. She proceeded down the steps, and joined them.

Helen regarded her with her infamous frown. "You finally came."

Mika opened her mouth, ready to apologize, but she stopped herself. She remembered Helen getting angry with her for apologizing too much. "I was saying goodbye to the Queen and Miss Angelica."

"That's fine," said Galner, then he regarded the travel chest at the back of the carriage. He ignored it for now, intending to talk to the Princess later about it. "Shall we go?"

Mika, Helen, and Galner headed for the carriage. One of the knights, who Helen recognized as Valias Garan, opened the left door for them. Galner, though he appeared thin and physically weak, climbed into the carriage effortlessly, surprising Mika with his stamina. Mika carefully stepped up onto the beam below the door, and went inside.

Helen met the gaze of the one female knight in the group, Tanari Desalia, who smiled at her, so Helen returned her silent greeting with a nod, and then entered the cabin right after Mika. The door was closed behind them.

Sir Maleth was now the sole Supreme Commander for the Royal Guard, since Sir Collin had been promoted to Supreme Captain after the retirement of Sir Terren. His black hair was trimmed almost bald, and he had a thin beard and moustache that were meticulously shaped. He wore a full set of black and gold armour, but without the helmet, and his long black cape was tied below his neck.

Maleth approached his five knights. "Gentlemen and lady, shall we go?"

"Yes, sir," said the five knights, all of them equally armoured as their commanding officer. Their helmets were on the carriage, but they had no need to wear them right now. Unlike their commanding officer, they did not wear capes.

Maleth climbed onto the carriage at the front, where he was joined by one of his knights. "Samal, you and I will be driving the carriage. Let's show the lovely Princess Mika Silveraine those fine driving skills."

"Yes, sir," said Samal Evastian. Hearing the encouraging words of Maleth, he smiled. Not counting Maleth, he was actually the oldest of the knights in the group.

Tanari and Aldrian ascended the ladders to the roof. Caylen and Valias climbed onto the platform at the back, and took their seats at either side of Mika's travel chest.

Inside the cabin, two large seats, upholstered with red wool, faced each other, each as wide as the width of the cabin and could accommodate four people, for a total of eight. Underneath each seat were spaces for luggage and other items. All hard surfaces were made of polished deep brown algerwood. A table was attached to the cabin floor between the seats. The curtains at each window were drawn back.

Galner sat on the seat at the front of the cabin so he could easily communicate with the drivers if he needed to. While Helen sat comfortably at one end of the seat which faced Galner, Mika positioned herself as far away from her as possible at the other end of the seat.

Galner had earlier intended to ask Mika about her luggage, and now was his chance. "Princess, please pardon me for saying this, but I believe I had asked both you and Helen to travel light. It appears you have brought an entire travel chest with you."

Helen closed her eyes for a moment. "I was telling her the same thing, Sir Galner."

"I've... never traveled before," Mika stammered.

Galner leaned back in his seat. "Well, in any case, I'm sure we can live with that. Storage space on this carriage is limited, however. We have to make do with what we have. We're fortunate that you're not carrying too much with you, Helen."

"I only brought a large travel bag. It's underneath this seat. I'm not one to bring too many things with me." Helen turned to Mika. "So, Princess Mika, I noticed your little beau isn't around. What happened to him?"

Mika spun around towards Helen with shock as her cheeks turned a deep red. "Huh? My what?! Uh... it's not like that! And I don't know what happened to him!" She realized she had raised her voice with great embarrassment as she cast her gaze down. "I'm sorry... I wasn't yelling. But it's not like that at all! It's... not... I mean, ugh...."

Galner was confused by this sudden exchange between Mika and Helen. "A 'beau'? What do you mean by 'beau'?"

Mika gasped. "Sir Galner, he's not… I mean, it's not like… it's actually… I mean, it's more like…." She lost her words, and tightened her fists, no longer in a good mood, as she looked up at Helen briefly. She saw Helen's mocking grin, which appeared very briefly, and then it disappeared.

However, Helen was not done with teasing Mika just yet. "Isn't he always with you? I'm surprised he wasn't with you today. I see the two of you together quite often, and I believe I detect a little hint of…."

Mika felt intimidated by Helen, whose teasing struck a more personal aspect, which she did not appreciate. Mika looked up at Helen with slightly teary eyes.

Galner sighed, somewhat impatiently. "That's enough, ladies. Miss Helen, please don't tease the Princess. It's unbecoming of someone of your position. And you do realize, of course, that this is the Princess, not just any other girl."

"I apologize, Sir Galner."

Galner heard a knock on the opened window behind him, so he turned towards it.

It was Sir Maleth. "Sir Galner, we're ready to proceed. Is everything in order?"

The professor nodded to the Supreme Commander. "We are ready here, Sir Maleth. Please proceed."

Maleth and Samal coordinated with each other in urging the cervids to begin their trot. The carriage move down the Valderia Pathway towards the castle gates.

Inside the carriage, Mika dabbed her eyes with her handkerchief. One hand clenched tightly around the soft fabric of her skirt, she let out a frustrated sigh.

I let her make fun of me. She's so… ugh, I don't know what to say! I truly am a coward and a weakling if I can't defend Mirin and my relationship with him from her teasing!

Mika slid the window beside her partially open, and she felt a gentle breeze tug at her hair and ribbon. She watched nobles taking a walk on the sides of the Valderia Pathway as the carriage moved by, socializing pleasantly under clear azure skies. Looking towards the front, she saw the enormous castle gates. Shortly, they will part to allow the carriage through and into the city of Scarletia proper. Then, they will travel through the city, into the countryside, and eventually to the city of Cerulean, where the Cerulean Magic Academy waited for her.

Mika would very soon see the world beyond the castle gates for the first time in her life. All she has known until now was the world within the gates. A sense of excitement filled her heart as she smiled with anticipation.

CHAPTER 7

THE CITY OF SCARLETIA

MIKA STARED INTENTLY THROUGH THE window beside her. The city of Scarletia, as it appeared beyond the castle gates, was not quite what she expected. Her excitement waned, replaced with a sickening feeling she could not quite describe yet.

The rays of the summer sun beat down on the dilapidated buildings, the tallest ones no more than three floors high, many of them made of rotting wood and cracked brick and mortar, worn down by weathering for years, decades, perhaps centuries. In some places, garbage littered the streets, and in others, a powerful fecal stench, whose source Mika could not determine, assaulted her sense of smell.

Mika watched the people. There were far more people out and about in the city proper than within the Scarletia Royal Castle. There were places so crowded that the carriage had to slow down to wait for people to pass or make way. The appearance of the people surprised Mika. At the most basic level, the men, women, and children dressed similar to those who lived in the castle, but the clothes they wore were dark, plain, dirty, old, and worn out, as if no one had any replacements.

As they proceeded down the Valderia Pathway, a large shadow loomed from above. Mika did not take long to find its source, a white stone tower that stood far taller than any other building in the entire city and even the watchtowers of the castle. The stone it was made from was different and far more weathered, but at the same time, far stronger and in better condition than all the buildings Mika has seen so far, suggesting that it was ancient, that it has been watching over the city for a very long time.

Galner leaned back with his eyes closed, resting. He had earlier reminded Mika and Helen that the trip to Cerulean would take about two days.

Helen stared out the window, speechless. She was just as shocked as the Princess was with the appearance of their surroundings. This was also her first view of the world outside the castle gates. However, Helen did not outwardly express her reaction.

Mika looked outside again. Unlike Helen, she would not stay quiet. "Sir Galner?"

Galner opened his eyes. "What is it, Princess Mika?"

"I'm curious." Mika looked at the buildings. "Why... why do the buildings look so worn out? They're very old, and it looks like they haven't been kept very well. I'm afraid that some of them will collapse and cause injury and death."

Helen, hearing Mika, glanced up at Galner.

The professor casually waved his hand in a dismissive fashion. "The buildings out here are of no particular importance to anyone. If they do collapse, that wouldn't be a problem."

"But I'd think that would be a problem for the people inside them."

Galner was confused. "Pardon me? What do you mean?"

"If they collapsed, the people inside could die."

Galner laughed. "Not to worry. The buildings can be rebuilt."

Mika and Helen stole a bewildered glance at each other. Galner didn't say anything about the people inside the buildings should they collapse. He only mentioned the buildings and what would be done if they did collapse.

Mika regarded the streets next. "The streets are dirty, and there are cracks and holes everywhere. Why are they like that?"

"Well, just think about what happens during the winter, when there's ice on the ground. I believe you have learned this in your science lessons."

Mika remembered immediately what she learned. "Yes, I believe so. In the winter, the temperature hovers above and below the freezing point of water. Ice will thaw into liquid... seep into the cracks in the street... and then freeze again, but it expands when it freezes. I suppose it pushes the street apart?"

"Correct," said Galner.

"But it looks like the streets haven't been repaired for a very long time. I'm afraid that, someday, they might open up and swallow everyone."

"There's nothing to worry about, Princess. If we need the street repaired, I'm sure we can spare some workers to repair it. But I suppose there's no immediate need to repair them. It's not as if we use this road frequently."

"But I see the people using this road, and they look like they use it all the time."

"What people?"

Mika stared at her professor, nearly speechless. She swallowed hard. "The people outside," she replied.

Galner raised an eyebrow. "Are you talking about the peasants?"

"Is that what they are?"

"Yes. But, Princess, I'm confused. You're referring to *them*?"

Mika nodded.

Somewhat perturbed, Helen stared at the professor intently, taken aback by his words, but she remained quiet.

Galner frowned slightly, and then leaned forward. "Why? I don't understand."

Mika was not sure what to say. His question of why did not make sense to her either. To Mika, the peasants outside looked like they used the street all the time so the street must be important. Therefore, it did not make sense that the street was not being repaired for them. She looked outside again.

Galner leaned back but kept his gaze on her, trying to determine for himself what she was going on about.

Mika soon continued with her observation of the city. "The streets are so dirty. There's garbage everywhere, and it's filthy. I even smelled a stench a couple of times that

113

I've never experienced in my entire life, and it was so bad that, for a moment, I thought I was going to suffocate."

"Those must be the open sewers. And yes, I do agree that the streets are dirty with garbage," said Galner.

"But, Sir Galner, why isn't anyone cleaning up the garbage? Why isn't anyone repairing the sewers?"

Galner was even more confused. "These are not important tasks. I'm rather puzzled to...." He came to a sudden realization and smiled. "I see. I do apologize, Princess. I forgot that this is the first time you're seeing the city of Scarletia outside the castle gates. It does appear vastly different from the castle. The buildings and the streets are not quite as lovely. Far from it, in fact. It's the same with you, Helen."

"You're correct, Sir Galner." Helen leaned her head against her hand with her elbow against the windowsill beside her.

"I understand that you both might be very surprised. But, I assure you, there's nothing to be concerned about."

Mika regarded the people outside, the men, women, and children. "Their clothes are old and worn out. They're very plain compared to mine. Can't they make or buy new clothing for themselves?" She saw a few examples. "That little girl, it looks like her dress is too small for her now. It has stains everywhere, and there are parts that are torn. That elderly woman there, she's wearing a frock that looks like it's made of the same material as the cloth that Miss Angelica uses to wash the floors with, only worse because hers is so badly worn out that it might just fall off any moment."

Galner chuckled. "These are peasants, Princess Mika. They dress differently from us. That's simply how they look."

Helen frowned, but let Mika do all the talking and questioning.

Mika saw something else that disturbed her. A small group of elderly men and women were seated on the side of the street, holding out empty metal cans. Mika saw the glint of a couple of pieces of Crystium in them.

Someone passed by and gave a flat piece of Crystium to one of the old women by putting it in the can she was holding. The woman attempted to nod with gratitude, but the steady shaking of her entire body made it difficult for her. Mika wondered if she was ill with something. Like her companions around her, she was thin and frail, but she was in the worst condition. With hollow cheekbones and protruding collarbones, her entire body was like a living skeleton.

"Are they... asking for money? Begging for money, rather?" asked Mika.

"Ah, you must be referring to the beggars at the side of the street. You are correct. They are begging for money."

Mika glanced at Galner. "Why?"

Galner raised his hands beside him. "I don't know. Does it matter?"

Yes! If they are begging for money, that must mean they have none!

However, Mika did not voice what she wanted to say. Not yet, anyway. Also, it was not just the elderly that Mika saw doing this.

"That's horrible. The children are begging for money as well?"

Mika observed the children, huddled together at a street corner, dressed in tattered clothing. The oldest appeared to be a girl who was perhaps a year or two older than her, holding an infant that cried from hunger pangs. Mika noticed a slight bulge in the girl's abdomen, and concluded that she was pregnant. No doubt the screaming infant was her child as well. There were three slightly younger boys with her who held out their hats that contained a few pieces of Crystium. Occasionally, strangers donated what little they could, but most walked past them without a second look. Two much smaller girls sat on the pavement, their faces somber. All of them were thin and frail from malnutrition. Mika glanced at the oldest girl, and knew right away that her unborn child would not survive given her current physical condition. Mika felt her heart ache as she watched their desperate situation.

Next, Mika observed a woman selling flowers from a basket with a baby strapped to her in front. The baby was quite small so she must have recently given birth. The problem with the flowers she was selling was that they were dull and almost lifeless. How she expected to make any sales with the flowers, Mika had no idea. If this was the flower seller's only source of income, Mika concluded that she would not be able to feed her infant child adequately. As Mika observed her, not a single person stopped to buy a flower from her.

As the carriage rode down the street, Mika and Helen, on both their sides of the street, saw workers pushing small wooden carts. The workers, shirtless and clad in boots and trousers, were blackened with dirt. Sweat trickled down their muscular backs, and glistened under the sun. Mika and Helen looked at their carts filled with a strange-looking, crumbling black rock that glimmered under the sunlight.

Galner saw this through the window beside him, and let out an uneasy breath.

Outside, Maleth and Samal, driving the carriage, regarded the workers.

"This is perhaps a little too close for comfort," said Maleth. "We need to move to a different street."

"Why, sir?" asked Samal.

Maleth ignored his question.

They heard a tapping sound from inside the cabin as Galner called for their attention. "Sir Maleth, we need to steer clear of these workers."

Maleth agreed. "That's precisely what we'll do next. For our own safety, we'll proceed with a detour."

Samal was confused. "Our safety, sir?" He looked up at Tanari and Aldrian above him, but they returned his glance with a puzzled shrug.

Tanari leaned forward slightly to pose a question for Maleth. "Sir, what was that rocky material the workers were handling?"

Maleth simply shook his head. "Nothing important."

Samal, Tanari, and Aldrian stayed quiet. If they needed to steer clear of the workers for their own safety, it was obvious that there was something dangerous back there, likely the black rocky material... but Maleth seemed unwilling to tell them anything.

A short distance later, Maleth and Samal urged the cervids to head around a corner, and then continue on another street, away from the workers and their carts.

Helen looked back through the window as they distanced themselves from the workers. "What was that, Sir Galner? What happened?"

"It would seem that some of the peasants in that area were miners," replied Galner.

Mika tilted her head with curiosity. "What were they mining?"

Galner leaned back, his tension from earlier subsided. "I'm assuming you both saw the black rocks in the carts those miners were pushing along? The Spires refer to the material as Starstone."

Mika was puzzled. "Starstone?"

"Yes. It's a highly combustible and explosive rocky material. Some say it's not a true rock at all, despite its name. It can explode and burn at extremely high temperatures, and the deep-blue flames generated are so hot that water cannot extinguish it. If you try to douse a flame caused by the combustion of Starstone, the water will almost instantaneously evaporate. There's no known method to extinguish such a flame. It's best to steer clear of the material for our own safety."

Helen was appalled. "Why is such a dangerous material being mined in the first place?"

Galner became silent for a moment, staring at his students with all seriousness as he thought about what he could and could not say.

Helen stared back at him with perturbed curiosity.

Mika was puzzled as well by his pause. "Sir Galner?"

"It's being mined as a potential energy source. It might be possible to burn the Starstone in a controlled environment. Doing so can generate energy that is far more efficient than coal, oil, or kerosene. It's also much more abundant than any material we're able to extract from the ground. If we are able to harness this energy source, our society's level of technology may advance significantly."

Mika thought that might be a good reason to mine such a material. If it could safely be harnessed as an energy source, then it had a legitimate use. However, she thought about the workers who handled it. "Sir Galner, is it easy for the Starstone to ignite, explode, and cause a fire?"

Galner nodded. "Very much so, Princess. It's extremely dangerous to handle with our current level of technology."

"But then... what about the safety of the miners?"

Galner was confused again. "The miners? What do you mean?"

"The Starstone could harm the workers who are mining it. If it explodes and burns, they could all die or, at the very least, could be seriously injured. It didn't look like they were handling or transporting the material safely. What about the safety of the workers then?"

Perplexed, Galner paused for a moment as he regarded the Princess. "If what I'm hearing is correct, and you're worried about the peasant workers, Princess, I must say that your concern is misplaced. There's no need to be concerned for their safety."

Mika's eyes widened.

Helen tried not to react at all, but she was just as surprised as Mika was to hear such a response from Galner.

"Why not?" asked Mika.

"They're merely peasants, Princess Mika. If anything were to happen to them, they're simply replaceable." Galner shook his head as he regarded their surprised stares. However, he did not fault them too much for how they reacted. He understood that this was the first time they were seeing the world outside the castle, after all.

Mika's mind was full of thoughts that questioned everything she had seen and heard so far.

The peasants... are replaceable? Why? People are not replaceable! Why would people be replaceable?

She remembered Angelica's and Mirin's words. Angelica had mentioned that peasants often said incomprehensible things, and Mirin referred to the merchant assassins as nothing more than peasants.

Miss Angelica and Mirin both uttered similar words about the peasants, just not nearly as harshly as Sir Galner. Is this how everyone thinks? Why is everyone thinking this way?

Mika glanced at Helen, who directed her gaze out the window again. Mika wondered what she was thinking about. After a while, she noticed that Helen was behaving differently. She was much more quiet and subdued than usual, and she spent much of her time looking out the window, her face turned away as if to hide her face from Mika and Galner. To hide facial expressions? This behaviour started when they passed through the castle gates. If Mika did not know any better, she would say that Helen was disturbed as well, probably as much as she was, but Helen was trying her very best to suppress it.

The carriage was about to pass by a trio of knights who were in a confrontation with a man outside his house. They were close enough to the side of the street that Mika heard them talking. Mika gasped as the knights suddenly grabbed the man, and then threw him to the ground. One of them kicked the man in the ribs, and he yelled out in pain.

"What's wrong with you? You know that evading taxes is a criminal offense!" shouted one of the knights.

"I'm sorry, sirs!" The man tried to sit up. "Please forgive me! We had to use the money to feed our kids! They were hungry! I'll pay the taxes as soon as I can! Please!"

"You impertinent and filthy peasant, that's not an excuse!" Another knight struck him in the face with his gauntlet, and the man fell sideways to the ground.

Mika saw the man's wife and children at the doorway, all of them frantic. "That's horrible!"

Startled, Helen turned towards Mika, wondering what happened.

Galner wondered as well as he sat up. "What's horrible? What happened?"

Mika turned to Galner. "Sir Galner, there was a man being beaten by our knights! They were beating him because he couldn't pay his taxes! But he had to feed his children first! He probably didn't have enough to pay the taxes because he had to feed his children!"

Relieved, Galner let out a slow breath, leaning back again. "Ah, I see. Yes, evading taxes is a crime. This peasant man deserved his punishment."

Helen narrowed her eyes for a brief moment.

Mika stared at Galner with shock. "Sir Galner! He had to feed his children! Isn't that more important?"

Galner rolled his eyes. "Princess!" he said firmly, startling Mika. "Yes, you're probably right. You should definitely feed your children first before you pay your taxes. After all, your children will go hungry if you don't. This applies to us. This does *not* apply to the Peasantry."

"Why not?!" asked Mika.

"Because that's the way it is!" exclaimed Galner. He saw right away that Mika had been somewhat frightened when he raised his voice, forgetting for a moment that the Princess was quite the timid girl. He realized this, and breathed deeply to calm down. "Please pardon me for raising my voice."

Helen made a fist, but she hid it beside her thigh. Galner's words made her burn inside with anger. *I've never been more disturbed in my life. Not even killing a man for the first time disturbed me this much. The Princess must be in turmoil.*

Mika turned away, and returned her attention to the outside. The people lived and worked in conditions that were unhealthy and unsafe. The entire city around her was in a state of ruin, and the people were suffering from it. If the people had nothing but old and dirty clothes to wear, if elderly and children were begging on the streets for money, if women were selling wilted flowers with infants strapped to them... then, for Mika, there was only one conclusion. She spoke very softly, almost to herself. "Extreme poverty... that's what this is...."

Galner heard her whisper. He stared at the Princess with barely contained irritation, the muscles in his jaw tensed. The way she behaved annoyed him greatly.

"My life is different from the peasants. I live with standards that are different from theirs... but why? Why is it that... their lives are different from mine? This doesn't look right. Something... something's not quite right."

"That is enough." Galner suddenly got up from his seat.

Helen looked up, alarmed.

Galner slid the window beside Mika to its closed position, frightening the Princess. He grabbed the curtain to cover the window so hard that the curtain rod broke. He stopped himself, realizing he had just lost his temper. He held the curtain and the broken curtain rod.

"Well, this is just fine." Galner dropped the curtain and the broken rod on the floor of the carriage, kicking them under his seat, as he sat back down. "Princess, please forgive me for losing control just now, but I must be honest with you. I grow weary of these questions and comments from you."

Mika, her hand on her heart, tried to recover from her fright, casting her eyes down and away. Through the periphery of her vision, she could still see through the window. As Galner lectured her with a condescending tone of voice, she refused to meet his gaze.

"Princess, as I mentioned before, I understand you're seeing the world for the first time. This is how the city looks like beyond the castle gates. Yes, it's very different from what you're accustomed to, but this is truly how the world looks. Please don't let it trouble you too much. Eventually, you will grow accustomed to this. The Peasantry of Melodice live a different kind of life compared to you, the Royal Family, and the Nobility. It might appear to you that their kind of life is not normal, but it is, I assure you. This is how they live, in poverty and in filth. That's their way of life. It is simply different from ours. It's truly not difficult to understand, and it's something you simply have to accept eventually."

Helen stared at Galner as he uttered those words, words that made her blood boil, but she had to do her very best to remain professional, because she was still a knight of the Scarletia Royal Guard.

Mika kept quiet for now, afraid that she might anger Sir Galner more than she already had. But his words disturbed her even more. *How is this normal? Their lives are different from mine, but why and how is it different? Why is Sir Galner talking about the Peasantry as if they aren't people? I don't understand any of this.*

As the carriage continued on in silence, Mika caught a glimpse of a small boy that slightly resembled Mirin and appeared to be about the same age. She watched the boy as he held out a hat to some people on the street, begging for spare Crystium, while standing at the side of the street. As the carriage drove by, Mika's and the boy's gazes locked for a brief moment.

* * *

Shortly after Mika saw the little beggar boy, the carriage passed by several alleyways between buildings. Mika continued to stare through the window without a word. Galner closed his eyes to resume his rest. Helen observed the awful scenery from her side of the carriage.

As Mika passed by one particular alleyway... her eyes widened. "Oh my...."

In the alleyway that was wide enough that it might have accommodated the size of a building sometime in the past, a young woman was in great distress, her dress ripped open at the front, exposing her brassieres, and the side of her long skirt torn open, revealing thigh-high stockings similar to Mika's. Three men in the alleyway tried to grab and restrain her, but she fought back, punching one of them in the face and spitting at another.

"Stop the carriage..." Mika said softly.

Helen looked in her direction. Galner opened his eyes.

Mika raised her voice. "Stop the carriage!"

"What is the matter, Princess?" demanded Galner.

Mika slid the window open beside her and, knowing that her soft voice did not carry well, called out as loudly as she could. "Please... stop the carriage!"

Maleth heard. "What?!"

"The Princess has requested to stop the carriage!" Tanari said loudly from above.

Maleth and Samal pulled on the reins as hard as they

could to force the cervids to come to a complete stop. The carriage shook as it came to a halt.

Mika opened the door on her side of the carriage.

"Princess!" exclaimed Galner.

"What's going on?!" shouted Maleth.

The Princess jumped out of the carriage.

Helen was startled. "Princess Mika?!"

Tanari saw the Princess right away from above. "My Lady?!"

"Princess, please get back inside the carriage immediately! For your own safety!" shouted Galner.

"Those men are violating that woman! Please save her!" Mika clamoured with a high-pitched, distressed voice. She forced herself to shout as loudly as she could, causing the pitch of her voice to go higher than it already was, and her own vocal cords to ache from the stress.

Caylen shouted from the back of the carriage. "Where?!"

People on the crowded street took notice. Women who peddled fruits and vegetables, men who pulled on carts filled with various wares, children who chased each other while playing, and elderly who begged for spare Crystium, all of them stopped what they were doing, and turned towards the source of the commotion, hearing the desperate scream of a highborn little girl.

Helen saw the commotion in the alleyway, and was angered that the knights did not see it. "Damn it!" She gritted her teeth, grabbed her scabbard from underneath her seat, and jumped out of the carriage.

Alarmed, Galner shouted. "Helen!"

Helen ran by Mika so fast that all she felt was wind.

The knights saw Helen run into the alleyway, where they saw the three men with the distressed half-naked young woman.

"Why did we not see that?!" Maleth and the other knights jumped off the carriage.

Galner was alarmed by the action of the knights. "Stop this!"

Helen drew out her long sword, and threw her scabbard backwards in one smooth motion, narrowly missing Mika who had to step sideways to avoid being hit by it. The loud noise of the scabbard hitting the side of the wooden carriage startled her.

Although the three men heard the screaming of a well-dressed, noble little girl and saw the carriage behind her, they had little time to react to the young woman who came at them with a long sword.

Helen slashed in front of her, nearly beheading the first man, who screamed and fell backwards.

The distraction gave the woman a chance to escape. She gasped with great surprise as she turned and ran down the alleyway, frantically holding onto the torn side of her skirt with one hand and covering her brassieres with the other.

A glowing magic circle appeared in front of Helen's free hand, causing the second man to be blasted by a sudden chill. The man fell on his side, shivering from terrible cold, his hands and face turning blue.

At that moment, the woman passed the knights, who ran by her in the alleyway, drawing out their long swords.

Helen yelled out a battle cry as she slashed at the third man, purposely missing his chest as he screamed and struggled backwards, and was eventually trapped by the wall behind him. He looked up, beads of sweat running down the sides of his dirt-smeared face. The sword's deadly tip was in between his terrified eyes.

The woman tripped outside the alleyway on some loose debris that was the remains of a wooden crate long discarded. She fell on her hands and knees a short distance in front of Mika. She struggled to keep together her tattered clothes.

Mika hurried to the woman. She quickly unbuttoned and untied her cape, exposing the gleaming Princess Gem around her neck, and covered the crying woman with her cape to preserve her modesty.

Samal and Aldrian grabbed the first man, pushed him down, and restrained him, but he continued to fight and struggle in a desperate but hopeless bid to escape.

"Stay down!" ordered Aldrian, holding the blade of

his sword near the man's face. Terrified, the man finally stopped moving.

Tanari, followed closely behind by Valias, held her sword above the second man, who was barely able to move from the ice that formed on his hands and face, the result of Helen's magic. She lowered her weapon, prompting Valias to do the same, and turned the other knights. "This one's down!"

Helen glared at the third man, her voice barely containing her rage as she spoke. "If I ever see you again, I swear, I will cut off your manhood."

Eventually, the three ruffians were ordered to stand by Maleth and his knights while their hands were bound behind their backs. Galner felt a headache coming on as he rubbed his forehead while he stood beside the carriage.

Mika watched as Helen walked out of the alleyway with her long sword at her side, perfectly calm. She could not help but be amazed by her while knelt down beside the woman they just rescued. Helen retrieved her scabbard, and then sheathed her sword.

The woman saw the bright sparkle of the Princess Gem, worn by the little girl who covered her.

Tanari turned to Mika, as the three hooligans were led away by the knights and made to stand at the side of the street. "Princess, what should we do with these cowards?"

At the mention of little girl's title, the woman's eyes widened as she drew in a quick breath.

Mika suddenly felt very unsure of herself. "Um...." Her words were lost, and quite severely this time.

Maleth saw the uncertainty of the Princess, so he stepped forward, and approached the other knights. "Summon the knights patrolling this area. There should be a patrol station nearby. I believe there's one down the street we just passed. Have them take away these bastards."

Aldrian volunteered. "Yes, sir. I'll take care of this."

Maleth nodded. "Thank you, Sir Aldrian."

Aldrian proceeded down the street as quickly as he could.

Galner stepped forward, infuriated. "This is ridiculous! A complete waste of time!"

Mika and Helen were startled. Maleth and his knights turned to Galner.

"You knights need to follow my direction! We should leave these damn criminals and be on our way!" He pointed at the woman who Mika held with her cape the same way he would point at an unruly dog. "Get that half-naked whore out of here!" He next pointed at all the knights. "All of you get back on the carriage!" Lastly, he pointed at Mika and Helen. "That goes for both of you as well!"

"Sir Galner!" Maleth called out with a raised voice full of authority.

Galner turned to Maleth.

"I strongly suggest you govern your tongue and calm the tone of your voice in the presence of Princess Mika Silveraine! I'll remind you that you're a civilian! The Princess gave the order to stop these criminals and rescue this poor young woman! The Princess's order is absolute! It's the Princess who has the highest authority here, not you!"

Galner, his fists clenched underneath his cloak, gave Maleth a furious glare. He knew that the Supreme Commander was correct. He was only a civilian. While he had power and influence because of his position, it did not mean he could give out orders. He said nothing more.

Helen turned towards Mika and the woman. She saw the look of great surprise on the woman's face. The eyes of the woman shifted between the Princess Gem and the Princess herself. Mika may not have noticed this, but Helen certainly did. Helen next saw the peasant civilians from all around them watching. This incident had caught the attention of everyone in the area.

Mika tried very hard to speak to the woman with a quivering voice. She immediately noticed that she was quite beautiful, her long black hair was as smooth as silk, and her red eyes hinted at a powerful resolve, the kind of person who refused to be a victim. Mika remembered that this woman tried to fight back when the men tried to violate her. She could not help but be filled with admiration. "Um... are you... are you all right, miss?"

The woman stared wide-eyed at Mika.

She looks terrified! She must have been so shocked. What should I do? Oh... maybe I should.... Mika wondered what she should say... and after a moment, she figured she could ask for her name. "Um, may I ask your name, miss?"

The woman closed her eyes for a moment, trying to calm down. She looked up at Mika. "Valeria... Tannlar."

Mika smiled. "My name is Mika. Are you all right now?"

The woman hesitated. She thought back to what just happened. She had been rescued by the young girl's companions. "Thank you for saving me," she whispered.

"You're welcome," said Mika.

Valeria began to stand, but she felt pain in different parts of her body, including her knees, which made it difficult for her. Mika and Helen helped her get up.

Helen drew Valeria's attention to her injuries. "You have a few scrapes and bruises that are forming. It would be wise to seek some medical attention. Can you walk?"

Valeria nodded. "Yes, I can still walk. Thanks." She glanced up at Helen. "Um... what's your name, miss?"

"Helen Renier."

Valeria regarded the two young ladies, not knowing how to react in front of them. She had regained her senses fully after the shock she just experienced. She thought back again to what happened. Helen took down the men who tried to violate her, and Mika cared for her and covered her with her cape to preserve her dignity.

"Thank you, ladies. I... I should be okay now," said Valeria with a soft voice. "Thanks for helping me."

Mika smiled and nodded. "You're most welcome. You can keep the cape. It might be best to use it right now since your dress is torn."

Valeria stared at the Princess for a long time, as if receiving the greatest surprise of her life. "Uh, thanks. I... guess... I guess I should be heading back now. Goodbye."

"Be safe," said Helen.

Valeria walked away with a slight limp, but it was nothing she could not handle. She held Mika's cape around her, which was rather small because it was sized for a little girl, but it was sufficient to cover the parts of her dress that had been torn open.

As she walked away, Helen and Mika noticed the growing number of peasants gathering around and watching.

Helen observed the eyes of some of the peasants. They were directed towards the Princess. The Princess Gem dangled in front of her dress. "Princess, perhaps it would be wise to hide the Princess Gem."

Mika noticed right away what she meant by that. Because she no longer had her cape, her diamond, which represented her identity, was visible, so she placed it under her collar.

Galner, Maleth, and the knights also noticed the growing crowd.

"I suppose they're curious about what happened," said Mika.

As Helen was about to walk back to the carriage, she discreetly whispered to the Princess. "That was initially their reason for gathering around, but it is no longer. Now, their attention is on you, My Lady."

Galner frowned as he stepped closer to Helen and Princess Mika. "I suggest you get back inside the carriage for your own safety," he said more calmly, trying to watch his words more carefully for now.

Mika started for the carriage along with Helen, who was ahead of her. As Helen was about to pass Galner, he put a hand on her arm, and she stopped, causing Mika to stop behind her as well. Mika looked up as Galner spoke.

"I hope you both realize that your actions here have been very rash. We're on a journey. We're not here to save distressed women from criminals. That's the job of the knights who are patrolling this part of the city. These are mere peasants and nothing more. What you both did was completely unnecessary."

Helen's blood boiled as she stared at Galner for a moment. *What the hell did you want me to do? Did you want me to stand idly by and watch as that woman was raped?* Galner released his hold on her arm, and she climbed into the carriage fuming. As soon as she sat down, she kicked her scabbard under her seat.

Mika could see she was angry now, hearing those words from Galner. Mika stepped onto the carriage, avoiding Galner's gaze. *Sir Galner is disappointed in me. What else could I do? Miss Valeria was in distress, and I reacted in the way I thought I should react. I was scared, but somehow, I reacted. I did the right thing... didn't I?*

As Mika took her seat, she clasped her hands together in front of her, leaned her forehead on them, closed her eyes, and sighed. She had been frightened. She had exposed herself to possible danger. However, she still felt that what she did was right. Unlike that day when the merchant assassins attacked, when she was too frightened to protect anyone... this time, she was able to protect someone for the first time. She contributed to the rescue of Valeria Tannlar. Had she not reacted, Valeria would likely have been murdered.

* * *

The cervid carriage was not going to move anytime soon, because they had to wait for one of their own to return with the knights from the local patrol station to hand over the three criminals. Valeria observed this as she walked away from them. She watched the girls who introduced themselves as Helen Renier and Mika as they entered the carriage. The three men who tried to violate her were made to sit down on the side of the street. The knights stood around, along with the cloaked man who appeared to be a mage.

Her walk became faster, and it soon changed into a jog, then a run, despite the pain she felt in her legs. She thought back to the little girl who wrapped her in the cape she was now wearing. When she introduced herself, she did not mention her full name. But Valeria knew who she was. She wore the Princess Gem, an item which she recognized from illustrations. That was the first time she'd seen it in person. She remembered reading that it was the legal representation of the identity of the Princess of Melodice. That was not just some well-dressed, highborn little girl named Mika.

That little girl was Princess Mika Silveraine.

"I can't believe it... that was the Princess of Melodice. Princess Mika Silveraine. A Royal," she whispered.

Valeria drew a few odd stares as she ran with a white silk cape that was too small for her while using her free hand to keep the tear in her skirt closed. People brushed past her on the crowded streets. She rounded a street corner, nearly running into a carriage pulled by a cervid, its sharp antlers dangerously close.

The driver shouted at her. "Get out of the way, lady!"

Valeria gave the man a dirty look as she went around the carriage, and then crossed the street. As she ran, she headed for an inn, whose wooden sign above the door read "Traveler's Paradise." The inn was located in an old brick and mortar building, discoloured by over a century of weathering.

Valeria entered the inn. A group of rowdy men passed her to exit, leaving behind the stench of liquor in their wake. She headed straight for the bar, where the owner of the inn polished a plate with a cloth.

The man's dress shirt, waistcoat, and trousers were of a little better quality than the clothes of most of the men in the inn, but nevertheless, his clothes were still old and somewhat worn. As he held the plate at an angle under a bright kerosene lamp, examining it for defects, the darkness of his eyes held the look of a man who would not hesitate to give a brutal beat-down to anyone who causes trouble in his inn. The prominent lines in his face had resulted not just from the healing of very old injuries, but also from an unceasing fury. This was a man who has been seething with vengeance in his heart for a very long time.

"Reid!" Valeria called out to him as she reached the bar.

Reid Alviana saw Valeria, and was surprised by her decrepit state. "Valeria... what the hell happened to you? You're a real mess!"

"Never mind that." Valeria went behind the bar, and grabbed him by the arm. She spoke to him with a hushed voice to keep from being heard by anyone else. "Listen. There's a Royal outside."

Reid was taken aback. "What?"

"It's Princess Mika Silveraine."

"Are you sure? What's going on, Valeria? What happened?"

Valeria held on to his arm tightly and desperately. "Come on. We need to do something. Among the Royals... she's the most vulnerable. I had no idea that the Princess was just a kid, and that's what makes her the most vulnerable. If we want to further our goals, we have to do something *now*."

CHAPTER 8

PRINCESS OF MAGIC

AFTER A LITTLE MORE THAN a half hour, several more knights came to the scene to join the knights led by Maleth. The criminals were handed over to them and taken away. No doubt, their punishment would be severe.

As Maleth approached the carriage, Tanari joined him. "Sir, I have a question."

"What is it, Miss Tanari?" asked Maleth.

"When we caught those men, I asked the Princess what we should do with them. As she's of the highest rank here, I thought it would be appropriate to do so. But the Princess didn't know. Was it appropriate that I asked her? Might she have been offended?"

Maleth laughed. "No, of course not. The Princess is not one to be offended by such a question."

"I see, sir."

"She simply didn't know how to answer your question. She may be a Princess, but she's still eleven years old. She's still growing into her role of leadership. It may take some time, but be assured that in a few years, she'll be able to carry herself with confidence, and master some of the basics of leadership. We don't expect her to command whole armies, but we do expect that she'll be comfortable with asserting herself, and giving basic orders. Right now, she does have authority, but she's not yet confident enough to assert herself."

Tanari nodded with acknowledgment. "I understand, sir. It's as I expected. But I wanted to be certain."

"Eventually, the Princess must become an adult. Give her time."

As one of the doors of the carriage swung open, Galner looked outside, searching for Maleth. As soon as he saw the Supreme Commander, he made sure to let his growing impatience be known.

"Sir Maleth, I believe we are long overdue in continuing our journey."

Maleth sighed for a moment, keeping his voice down as he spoke. "And, unfortunately, Miss Tanari, someday, the Princess will be forced to listen to complaints from this old man. I'm certain he will have some for the King and Queen to happily listen to as soon as we return to the castle."

When Galner closed the door, the knights gathered together and boarded the carriage. As soon as everyone was ready, Maleth and Samal urged the cervids to a slow trot, and the carriage gently lurched forward.

Galner rolled his eyes as he sat back in his seat inside the cabin. "Finally. We have wasted enough time here."

The carriage moved past peasants on the street as the four strong cervids pulled.

However, because of the crowds, the knights didn't notice the suspicious movements of a few men who stood in the alleyways on the other side of the street. Clad in large cloaks and hoods that concealed their faces, they pulled on their own cervids by the reins. As the carriage moved, one of the men urgently made a hand signal to a small group of people who watched the carriage as well from across the street. They climbed onto their cervids, and rode down the alleyways.

* * *

Another quarter hour passed. The carriage continued down the Valderia Pathway. There were so many people on the street that Maleth and Samal were forced to slow down even more than they already had. This meant that the knights needed to watch their immediate surroundings with more scrutiny. It was possible that a peasant may attack the carriage, since such events did occur occasionally. However, they were not likely to attack a carriage that was heavily guarded by six well-armed knights... or at least, that was what they hoped.

As Galner fumed over the events from earlier, Helen and Mika stayed quiet.

"I'm extremely disappointed with what happened earlier," said their professor. "I cannot believe what you both did! It was completely unnecessary."

Mika sat up straight, and thought to herself, her gaze cast down on the cabin floor. *I don't mean to seem rude but... how I wish he would stop talking. I'm growing weary of this.*

"These people are nothing but peasants. Their lives are different from ours. We are like two different types of Human. The difference between them and us is that they are lower on the evolutionary scale than we are. We are the highborn, the Nobility! They are the lowborn, the Peasantry! We have nothing in common with them, and we shouldn't be associating ourselves with them. Princess, what you saw earlier is common among the Peasantry. It happens all the time. Events like those are the business of the peasants and not of ours.

"It's regrettable that we had to be involved in that ruckus. I very much hope it doesn't happen again. We're the Nobility of Melodice, Princess Mika. You're a member of the Royal Family. We don't associate ourselves with these lower forms of life. Do you understand what I'm trying to tell you?"

Mika was lost in her thoughts. *He's talking about them like they're animals... like they're not even Humans. I... I never realized that the professor was like this.*

Galner noted Mika's silence. "Princess, are you listening to me?"

Mika nodded as she met his gaze. "Yes, Sir Galner. I'm listening."

Galner turned to Helen. "Don't think you're exempt from my lecturing, Helen. You're just as guilty as the

Princess for wasting our time, delaying our journey, and involving us in matters that don't concern us. The matters that are of concern to the unwashed masses of inferior scum are not our own. We have nothing to do with them."

Helen leaned against the windowsill as she thought to herself. *Your words disgust me. I didn't know you were like this.*

"Do you understand what I'm saying, Helen?"

Helen hesitated as she stared blankly at the professor. "Yes, Sir Galner. I understand you perfectly well."

"Sir Galner?" said Mika.

The professor turned back to Mika. "Yes, Princess?"

Mika tried to think of her words carefully, so she would not anger him again like she had earlier. "I'm... I'm sorry, I'm just trying to understand all of this, since... as you said... this is the first time I'm seeing the world."

"That's quite all right."

"But there's something I would like to ask of you. It's... purely out of curiosity."

The professor let out a small chuckle. "Curiosity is one of your strong points. What is it, Princess Mika?"

"Are your opinions of the Peasantry also the opinions of the Nobility?"

Galner stared at Mika, the muscles around his jaw tightening as he attempted to keep a calm exterior.

Mika stared back as she waited for an answer.

Helen stiffened with surprise over the Princess's words as she watched them both. *That's a very bold question, Princess. I'm very surprised!*

Finally, Sir Galner spoke. "These are not my opinions, Princess, as they might sound to you."

"What are they then?" asked Mika.

"These are *well-known facts*!"

Mika gasped softly as she looked away.

Helen continued watching both the Princess and their professor as she stayed quiet, intrigued by their exchange and Mika's unexpected show of assertive questioning.

Galner leaned back and closed his eyes, trying his best to calm down. After a moment, he spoke with a more appropriate tone of voice. "I apologize again for raising my voice. However, as I said, these are not my opinions, nor are they opinions of the Nobility. This is simply the way these people are. Don't ask me why they are the way they are. As far as our leading scholars have determined, the Peasantry are an offshoot of the race of Humans, one that's inferior in all aspects. They haven't kept up with evolution as we have. It has been theorized that in about ten thousand years or so, they'll have fallen so far behind in evolution that they'll become a race completely separate from us, the Nobility. We will still be Humans. What they will become, we don't know. And it's not for us to concern ourselves with."

Mika thought about the troubling words Galner used. She leaned back against her seat, placing her elbow on the windowsill and resting her chin on her arm as she looked outside. She did not want to say anything more, because she knew that Galner would just become angry with her and hurl more hateful words about the Peasantry.

If Sir Galner considers his opinions of the Peasantry as so-called facts, and the entire Nobility think the same way, then... there is truly nothing more I can say to him. What he tells me... disturbs me. I feel like I'm going to be sick from hearing this. So this is the way it is? I'm sorry... I'm not certain I am able to accept that. To me... it simply doesn't seem right.

Mika continued to watch the images of extreme poverty from her side of the carriage, as if there was no end to them. Everywhere, peasants begged for money, were harassed by knights, or lived and worked in terrible conditions.

* * *

Maleth and Samal pulled on the reins, urging the cervids to slow down even further, to avoid trampling on peasants in front of them.

Annoyed, Maleth shook his head. "Perhaps the Royal Family should think about the population problem of the city of Scarletia."

"I agree, sir," said Samal, his voice carrying a little too much.

"Don't agree so loudly, Samal. You and I could be accused of insubordination if anyone heard us say that."

"I'll keep my voice down, sir."

As the cervids walked, they drew dangerously close to some peasants.

"Dammit, stop them, Samal. Come to a complete halt." Maleth pulled on the reins. He and Samal forced the cervids to come to a stop as the people moved back and forth in front of them.

Sir Galner, inside the cabin, noticed, and opened the window at the front. "Sir Maleth, what's going on? Why are we stopping again? We need to get through this most unpleasant part of our journey as quickly as possible."

"My sincerest and most humble apologies, Sir Galner," said Maleth, purposely dropping hints of sarcasm through the tone of his voice. "There's an enormous crowd of peasants in front of us. We need to wait for it to clear just enough so that the cervids can get through without trampling anyone to death."

Galner let out a sigh of frustration. "This is unbelievable!"

From both sides of the carriage, Mika and Helen watched outside. The ocean of Humans was vast indeed. People walked past them, back and forth, and across each other, each of them headed for their own destinations. Mika and Helen wondered how they managed to navigate through the seemingly endless crowd.

Eventually, the crowd thinned out ever so slightly. Maleth and Samal once again urged the cervids to slowly and carefully move forward. Aldrian and Tanari looked ahead from their unique perspective on the roof of the cabin.

Tanari saw something out of the ordinary. "Supreme Commander, there is... a blockade up ahead."

Maleth needed a better view, so he stood up to look over the cervids and the crowd ahead of them. The crowd definitely thinned out, but he saw some commotion. It was as if the people in the crowd were being told to move out of the way.

Maleth grabbed onto the reins that Samal held. "Stop the cervids."

The carriage once again stopped.

Galner's irritation knew no bounds. Through the window, he saw Maleth standing. "What the hell is the matter, Sir Maleth?"

"There's a large group of peasants in front of us, Sir Galner. They seemed to have formed a blockade," said Maleth.

Mika and Helen were surprised.

"A blockade?" said Helen.

"Why?" asked Mika.

Galner slammed his hand on the windowsill, and poked his head through the window as if doing so would emphasize his demand. "Tell them to move out of the way, Sir Maleth! How difficult can that be? They are only peasants!"

Maleth sighed heavily. As he looked ahead of him, he could see that there was still a significant crowd between him and the blockade.

"To the people blocking the Valderia Pathway in front of us. I humbly request that you let us pass so we can continue our journey in peace! Please move aside!" Maleth announced, the sound of his voice carrying far.

There was no reaction among the people that formed the blockade. The crowd in front, to the left and right, and behind the carriage thinned out further. At the same time, Maleth and the knights heard loud and angry shouts among the crowd as people were told to move along.

Caylen and Valias, positioned at the back of the carriage, stood up and held on to the beams for support as they watched behind them.

"Supreme Commander, there's a blockade behind us as well!" shouted Caylen.

"And to our left and right!" Aldrian pointed to the peasants who had gathered at the sides of the street.

Maleth looked around them, as did the other knights.

The blockade encircled them. Eventually, the crowd thinned out further, fully revealing the extent of the blockade. The groups in the front and the back stood no closer than thirty meters or so, while groups that lined the sides of the wide street were at least fifteen meters to the left and right of the carriage.

The situation gave Maleth a feeling of dread. "Surrounded...."

"What's going on, Sir Maleth?" asked Galner.

The peasants who formed the blockade began to shout angrily.

Maleth kept his voice calm. "It appears we have been targeted."

Mika's heart was beating much faster long before Maleth made that declaration. Eyes widened with fear, she covered her mouth with both hands as she moved away from the window beside her. Her voice quivered as she spoke. "What... what's going on?"

Helen saw the lines of peasants at the front and the back.

The angry clamours of the peasants grew louder. It did not take long for Mika, Helen, Galner, Maleth, and the knights to start picking out specific words from the crowds.

"We know there's a Royal in that carriage!"

"Bring out the Royal!"

"We demand you bring out the Royal!"

"Bring her out! Bring her out!"

Mika heard them, and knew they were referring to her. Her hands shook as she placed them at her heart. She asked herself why they demanded that she be brought out.

"Answer for your crimes, noble criminals!"

"The crimes of the Royal Family will be met with justice!"

"Get out of the carriage and face your crimes, you Royal bitch!"

"Face the crimes of the Nobility against the nation of Melodice!"

Galner chuckled. "What incomprehensible things are these peasant dogs trying to say? They're the criminals here, blocking our path!" He once again spoke through the window at the front of the cabin. "Maleth, order them to get out of the way! They're spewing rubbish!"

Helen reached for her scabbard underneath her seat, and as she straightened up, she felt Mika's side against hers as Mika moved further away from the window on her side of the carriage. Helen looked down at her. Because Mika's body was against hers, she felt slight vibrations as the young Princess trembled with terrible fear.

"Princess..." she whispered, but Mika did not hear.

Maleth watched the blockade. He assessed their level of agitation, which increased by the minute. "Everyone, we don't wish to cause any trouble! Please move aside so we can be on our way!"

But his words did nothing to alleviate the situation. The anger of the peasants only intensified.

"This is not going to work." When Maleth looked down at Samal, he saw his trembling hand slowly reaching for his scabbard under their seat. He grabbed the knight's arm. "Don't... Samal. Not yet."

Samal looked up at Maleth with widened eyes as the people continued to hurl their angry demands. The young knight felt scared himself. "Sorry, sir...."

"Bring out the Royal!"

"Let her face the crimes of the Nobility and the Royal Family!"

"Noble bitch, face your crimes!"

"Come out of that carriage and face justice!"

Those words of anger and hatred from the peasants stabbed at Mika's heart like a thousand knives. Her breathing was shallow, and her skin felt cold to the touch.

Helen could see that she was on the verge of a panic attack. *The Princess is frightened. This is just like the day when the merchant assassins attacked. What should I do? Is there anything I can do for her? I can protect her as a knight. But what else can I do?*

"Princess Mika." As Helen held her scabbard with her left hand, she wrapped her right arm around Mika's frail body, and held her close.

Mika gasped, and blinked a couple of times, then looked up at Helen. "Miss Helen...."

"Stay close," whispered Helen.

Mika hesitated, and eventually nodded. Helen's act of wrapping one arm around her calmed her slightly.

Helen asked herself why she was holding the Princess like this. *Well... I'm her knight. I'm sworn to protect her, after all. Such is my duty. Whatever I can do, I will try.*

"Why... why are they saying such angry words?" Mika whispered. Soon, her whispers became louder, and Galner and Helen heard them. "What crimes are they talking about? What do they mean? What crimes? What did I do? I don't understand."

"You did nothing, Princess," said Helen.

Galner waved a dismissive hand. "Nothing more than rubbish."

Maleth rested his foot on a metal beam in front of him as he continued to assess the crowd. He watched the cervids in front of him, noting their calm. The cervids paid no attention to the crowd in front of them, to the sides, and behind them. They were so heavily trained that they were focused on controlling the carriage and obeying the commands of the drivers. The cervids were not intimidated by the angry crowd, and considered their clamours to be nothing but noise. Unfortunately, for Maleth and the knights, it would not be so easy to ignore them.

"Knights." Maleth looked at Samal beside him, then at Tanari and Aldrian above on the roof of the cabin. "You don't need to be reminded. Your first duty, above all else, is to protect Princess Mika."

Aldrian nodded. "Agreed, sir."

"We will protect the Princess at all costs, sir," said Tanari.

Maleth looked down the side of the carriage, and toward the rear at Valias, who heard Maleth just now and acknowledged with a nod.

"Samal, my helmet and scabbard," said Maleth.

Samal reached down to retrieve the Supreme Commander's helmet and scabbard as ordered. He reached for his as well. Above, Tanari and Aldrian put on their helmets, and reached down for their scabbards and bows and arrows. At the rear, Valias and Caylen did the same.

Inside the carriage, Galner looked through the left and right windows, shaking his head. "Damn peasants. They don't understand Maleth's orders. It's a testament to their limited mental and intellectual capacity."

Helen struck the floor of the cabin with the tip of her scabbard, making a loud thud that startled Mika. "When the time comes, Sir Galner, I will protect the Princess, for such is my duty."

"Of course, I would expect nothing less from you. It appears we may have to use more than just words to pacify this threat."

"I would hope it doesn't come to that," said Helen.

"But I believe it will. We are dealing with animals, after all."

Helen glared at him, but she caught herself before she could say anything she would have regretted. "As I mentioned, I will protect the Princess at all costs. I will add that I'll do whatever is necessary to protect her. This means, if we're attacked, that's when I can counterattack and not before."

Mika gasped softly. Hearing those words from both Helen and Galner meant that things were about to become violent.

Helen released her hold on Mika, and put her hand on her shoulder. "Princess, I suggest you stay low."

Terrified, Mika did not want to see any bloodshed. She had already seen it. She remembered that day when the merchant assassins attacked. She still remembered the drops of blood that flew at her as someone was killed in front of her.

"Everyone... please... be careful." Mika slid off the seat, and knelt down on the floor.

Helen and Galner positioned themselves behind the doors on both sides of the cabin, and opened them at the same time. They stepped out of the carriage, and quickly closed the doors. At that same moment, Maleth got off the carriage, as did the other knights, helmets donned, bows and arrows held at their sides, and their scabbards mounted at their waists. They all watched the crowd of furious peasants. Galner stood with Samal, Tanari, and Caylen at the left side of the carriage, while Helen stood with Maleth, Aldrian, and Valias at the right side.

Mika tried to take a peek outside through one of the side windows, and saw Helen and Maleth. She listened to the accusing words of the peasants. They continued to demand the Royal, specifically her, to step out of the carriage. Mika could barely stand it as she moved away from the window, and knelt down at the table. She put her head down, and covered her ears, trying in vain to block out the angry shouts.

"Allow me, Sir Maleth, to continue where you have failed," said Galner.

Maleth gripped his bow hard, wishing he could get away with swinging it at Galner's face. "Be my guest, Sir Galner, if you believe you can do better."

Galner stepped forward, staring down the peasants like he would unruly dogs. "That is enough! I order you lowborn dogs to step aside, and make way! Make way, or you will suffer the consequences!"

His order, while he spoke with as loud a voice as possible, did nothing to intimidate the peasants, who shouted right over him.

"Shut your mouth, old man!"

"Bring out the Royal!"

"It'll be you who will suffer the consequences!"

"You bastards of the Nobility are the true criminals!"

Galner was furious. "What the hell is this? They're ignoring me! They dare to ignore the orders of the Nobility?! I don't understand!" He shouted to the peasants again. "I order you all to move aside! I am a member of the Nobility, and you peasant dogs will do as I say! If you don't obey the orders of a noble, you will be punished!"

The peasants ignored Galner's pretentious words.

"Get out of our way, and bring out the Royal bitch!"

"The Nobility will pay for their crimes!"

"Let justice be served against the Royal Family!"

"Justice will be served today!"

Maleth shook his head. "I'm disappointed in your skills of persuasion, Sir Galner. I had such high hopes that you could do better where I had failed."

"Still that tongue of yours, Sir Maleth," said Galner, feeling his inflated noble ego being stepped on by the peasants, a feeling that he could barely stomach at this point.

"To hell with the Nobility and the Royal Family!" shouted the peasants.

"Take this, you filthy noble maggots!" One young man took a step forward from within the crowd located behind the carriage, holding a tall but narrow glass bottle with kerosene inside. A cloth was partially stuffed down the bottle's narrow opening, its exposed part burning with a bright yellow flame. He hurled the flaming bottle at the carriage with as much strength as he could muster.

Valias was alarmed. "Incendiary!"

Maleth reacted immediately. He aimed his bow and arrow at the flying bottle, and fired. The metal tip of the arrow struck the bottle mid-flight, breaking it, and causing its contents to ignite. Flames and pieces of glass fell onto the street.

Suddenly, several large men emerged from the crowds to the left and right. They ran for the carriage, brandishing long knives and short swords.

"Permission to counterattack if attacked, sir?" Tanari quickly aimed her bow at one of the approaching men.

Maleth reloaded his bow immediately with another arrow. "Permission granted!" He fired, felling a man with a short sword as the arrow struck him in the forehead.

Tanari released her arrow, which embedded itself into the heart of another man. The other knights fired their arrows. More violent peasants brandishing blades fell on the street, some dead and others severely injured.

Inside the carriage, Mika screamed, and shut her eyes as she heard the sounds of arrows being fired. She heard shouts, screams of pain, and final clamours of death. She covered her ears, trying again to block out those awful sounds, but it was useless. Mika put her hands on the table, and pushed herself up to look through the windows to her left and right. She saw the peasants charge for the knights with crude weapons, but the knights continued firing arrows at them. Mika's eyes were wide with shock as she watched even more death than when the merchant assassins attacked.

The attacking peasants were now too close for bows and arrows.

"Swords!" ordered Maleth.

The knights threw their bows underneath the carriage, so the attackers would not be able to pick them up, and, along with Helen, drew out their long swords, their blades screeching against the metal inside their scabbards. Long swords clashed against short swords. The fine steel blades of the knights reflected the afternoon sunlight. Peasants who came too close were cut down by the superior swordsmanship of the knights.

Helen not only used her sword to fight back, she used her magic as well. Every so often, a magic circle appeared in front of her free hand, and a blast of flame appeared, burning beyond recognition any attacker that was unfortunate enough to be in front of it.

Galner looked on around him, standing back from the fighting, and although he looked calm, he was seething with fury inside.

"Fire the incendiaries!" someone shouted from the front.

Someone else in the crowd relayed the order. "Fire the incendiaries!"

The order was repeated until it reached the crowd in the back. After a moment, about twenty peasants came out of the crowd from all directions, all of them holding flaming bottles.

"Fire!"

The flaming bottles flew.

Mika gasped as she saw flames in the sky through both windows on either side of her. Many of the flaming bottles were aimed for the roof of the carriage. If they were to strike the carriage, it would be consumed in flames while she was still inside it. Mika closed her eyes, anticipating a fiery death.

The knights watched helplessly. Even if they were still equipped with their bows and arrows, they would not be able to stop all of the incendiaries.

"Fools." Galner held a mocking grin.

An enormous blue magic circle appeared on the street below the cervid carriage. It was huge, covering an area quite a distance around the carriage. A semi-transparent dome of light, as wide as the magic circle, appeared and hovered above the carriage and the knights and peasants who fought. The dome acted as a barrier as the flaming bottles struck it, exploding and causing flames to spread outwards. Pieces of glass and flames bounced off the dome, and rained down on the street all around, farther away from the carriage. Some of the glass injured peasants that were too close, slicing through clothes and cutting through faces. Other peasants were burned by the falling flames. They collapsed on the ground screaming, their clothes set aflame.

The knights realized very quickly that they had all been protected from the flying projectiles by Galner's magic. They continued their fighting, defending the carriage and their Princess. The bodies of the peasants piled up in some places as they were felled. Some of the peasants who had been injured tried to crawl away, only to be stepped on by more peasants who charged in to attack.

A peasant had his arm cut off as he charged for Tanari, and he fell to the ground. Another one charged for Aldrian, who stabbed him with his long sword. Aldrian had to kick him off his sword to get rid of him. Another man lost his balance as he was nearly slashed by Caylen, and stumbled towards one the cervids, falling against its side. The annoyed cervid struck the man with its large antlers, throwing him back into the crowd. Though the cervids were trained to ignore such external disturbances, on occasion, they took notice and reacted.

Mika could not count the number of dead piling up on either side of the street. She saw blood, severed limbs, and bodies with bloody gashes. She shook her head, and covered her mouth. "No more... please stop this." Tears came down her cheeks as she opened her eyes. "Please stop the killing!"

Galner slowly moved from where he was while a strange wind blew around him. He took a few steps towards the charging peasants, his glare full of hatred.

Inside the carriage, Mika felt a strange sensation, the presence of very powerful magic. Words were not enough to adequately describe the sensation of something that existed but in a different space, something that surrounded her but could not be felt unless one was proficient with magic. At best, she could only describe it as a tingling sensation, but not on her skin. She quickly went to the other window to see what was happening. She realized that Galner was getting ready for a very powerful magic attack.

Galner stepped past the knights. "You peasant dogs have attacked us, and threatened all our lives, the lives of the Nobility, including the life of the Princess, a member of the Royal Family. You'll be rewarded for this loathsome criminal act."

A peasant man was about to strike him down with a short sword, but Galner glared at him without concern.

A gigantic magic circle appeared on the ground, circled around the group of peasants on the side of the street. The man who was about to attack Galner did not have enough time to react as he saw the edge of the magic circle under him. It was so large that it was not just under the attacking peasants and the blockade but also the crowd on the side of the street, innocent bystanders who watched from behind the blockade. Part of the magic circle was also underneath a couple of buildings in that area.

Mika watched with horror. The blue magic circle, along with its many strange shapes and symbols, glowed brightly, and a giant wall of raging flame suddenly appeared. The wall of flame reached into the sky from the edges of the magic circle, while inside that wall, a massive fiery explosion occurred.

Peasants watched with great shock, as did Helen, Maleth, Aldrian, and Valias, who saw the hellish flames behind them and the terrible rumbling sounds that came with them. Horrified, Tanari, Samal, and Caylen stood back from Galner.

The people inside the circular wall of flame were burned alive. Their dreadful screams struck terror in the hearts of all those who watched. The flames consumed one whole building with three floors and parts of two others of the same height. The wood in the building that was completely consumed burned while the brick and mortar cracked, and very soon, it collapsed on top of some of the peasants in a cloud of fiery debris.

Mika watched as people were crushed by the falling rubble. She saw peasants writhing as their bodies burned, the colour of their skin turning into a sickening mix of black and red. But that was not all she saw. She also saw a woman with a baby strapped to her as she carried a basket of flowers. Mika had seen her before. The woman and her baby were consumed by flame.

"Damn you, Galner..." whispered Maleth, as he watched the awful scene.

Helen watched with her eyes wide, her voice subdued. "Not... all of those people were attacking. Some of them were innocent bystanders, not part of the blockade."

The peasants were in mass chaos. Some who had charged towards the knights ran away. Others continued their attack while the knights defended accordingly. Many tried to force their way through the crowd to escape, but others stood their ground.

"Don't stop fighting!"

"Stand your ground!"

"Are you insane?! You people are mad!"

"That old man's got the power of magic on his side!"

At the other side of the carriage, opposite of the flames, the crowd thinned out slightly, revealing a woman in a plain smock-frock and a long crossbow strapped to her back.

Valeria Tannlar quickly forced herself back through

the crowd, and gained entrance into a building. The inside of the building was mostly empty, as the people inside had evacuated, hoping to avoid the dangerous situation nearby. There were still some in the building, watching through the windows with a strange curiosity.

"Get out of the way!" Valeria ascended the stairs, passing several people who rushed to leave.

Valeria made it to the third and highest floor. Just below an opened window, she knelt down and looked at the scene below, loosening the strap that kept her crossbow in place. She watched the chaos as some peasants tried to get away while others continued to fight. The dead continued to pile up around the carriage. The young woman who saved her from being violated and introduced herself as Helen Renier fought the peasants who attacked with swordsmanship and basic magic. She saw the flames on the other side of the street, and was aghast by the amount of death she witnessed. She glared at the man who had unleashed the magic attack that caused it. She remembered him referring to her as a half-naked whore.

"That pretentious bastard of an old man. I'll make sure you don't survive this, you damn murderer."

As the knights continued to fight nearby, Galner walked towards the front of the carriage, passing the cervids that watched the massacre around them with little concern. He stopped just a few steps ahead of the cervids, and glared at the blockade in front of him.

The peasants were struggling to keep the blockade as solid as possible, but it did not help that people were trying to go through them to escape, and even some of the people who were part of the blockade were themselves trying to get out, only to be told to stand their ground. There were people running within the blockade as well, and one of them happened to be a little boy who tripped over his own feet and landed on the street.

The fallen boy grimaced in pain as a lower portion of one of his flimsy trouser legs had been torn, revealing a large scrape on his knee.

Galner raised his hand, pointing towards the boy as another large magic circle appeared on the ground.

Seeing the magic circle, the boy realized that the old man was pointing directly at him, and drew in a quick breath.

Mika gasped as she sensed the presence of powerful magic again. She rushed to the front window of the carriage and saw Galner, readying another magic attack. She saw that Galner was aiming straight for someone, a small boy, the same boy she had seen earlier begging for money on the side of the street. Mika noticed that Galner was using him to target his magic, but his real intention was to keep his upcoming magic attack as straight as possible. He was really aiming at the blockade in front of him, but by unleashing this magic attack, he would not only kill almost everyone in the blockade, but everyone that gets caught between him and his intended target, including the small boy.

"No, that's enough... stop already, please!" shouted Mika.

Of course, Galner would not be able to hear her from outside amidst the chaos, and even if he did, she knew that he would probably just ignore her. Mika shut her eyes.

I... I have to do something... I have to try... I'm the Princess of Melodice... I can't let this killing continue... it has to stop... I have to stop it!

Mika did not know what to do, but she knew in her heart that she must do something, anything to stop this senseless killing. She remembered the merchant assassins and how she was so frightened that she couldn't move as the merchants attacked the civilians around her and killed them. She remembered telling Angelica that she thought of herself as nothing more than a coward and a weakling, because she couldn't do anything to protect the people around her, even though she had the power to do so. Despite her intense fear, she knew she had the power to protect others. She had the power to stop this killing now, not only because she was the Princess, but also because she wielded the power of magic.

A bright sphere of light appeared in front of Galner's hand. The light became brighter and the sphere larger as more power was gathered. Very soon, bolts of lightning appeared, furiously lashing out from the sphere of light in all directions.

Mika looked up as a small pink magic circle appeared on the cabin floor. "All this senseless killing... I have to stop this!"

"Peasants... I, Galner Ciannar, an honourable representative of the Nobility of Melodice, order you, all of you! Die!"

Mika disappeared from the cabin in the blink of an eye, along with her magic circle. One of the doors suddenly opened at the exact same moment.

Enormous bolts of lightning exploded out of the sphere in front of Galner like fingers that could tear Human flesh. They lashed out towards the blockade of peasants, but first towards the small boy, who quickly closed his eyes and threw up his hands as if to defend himself one last time, before his life was taken. The lightning bolts were so bright that almost everyone nearby—peasants, Helen, Maleth, the knights—had to shield their eyes, and the sound it made was loud and terrifying, a rumble that shook the ground.

Valeria, in the building just above them, covered her ears, and looked away as the brightness intensified.

But something happened that Galner did not expect. The bolts of lightning struck an invisible surface, and were redirected upwards at an angle. It was so bright that Galner could not see what was happening in front of the lightning bolts, but he could tell that something was not quite right. The magic attack streaked through the sky for quite a distance before it dissipated.

A pink magic circle glowed on the ground near the small boy, who opened his eyes, and realized that he was still alive. He saw the large magic circle... and very soon, he noticed someone standing in front of him, a beautiful girl clad in a white dress.

"What is this...?" Galner felt his heart sink. He was absolutely shocked by what he saw, as were Helen, Maleth, the other knights, and all the peasants around them.

Princess Mika stood in front of the small boy in the centre of the magic circle, holding up one hand towards Galner. In front of her, a pink, rectangular, semi-transparent barrier of magic was angled in such a way that it would redirect skyward any beam-like magic attack that struck it.

"Princess Mika." Helen watched with great surprise, her voice subdued. She wondered what the Princess was thinking... and what she had done.

Valeria watched from the building above. "What... just happened? Did the Princess just...?"

Reid Alviana appeared beside her, joining her at the window. "What the hell just happened out there? What's going on?"

Valeria was not sure how to answer his question, for she herself had just witnessed something that, in her mind, was completely out of the ordinary.

Galner glared at Mika. "Princess... what the hell is the meaning of this? What are you doing?!"

Mika looked up at Galner. Although she was frightened, her determination to stop this attack was too great this time for fear to take over her entire being. With a voice that stammered and quivered, she asserted who she truly was.

"I am... I am... Princess Mika Silveraine... and... I command that you stop your attack on my people!"

CHAPTER 9

BY ORDER OF
THE PRINCESS

EVERYONE—THE PEASANTS WHO HAD FORMED the blockade, those who attacked the carriage, innocent bystanders, Sir Maleth, the knights, Helen, and Sir Galner—watched as the greatest unexpected event they had witnessed in a very long time unfolded before their very eyes. Princess Mika stood in front of the peasants, in front of the small boy... and protected them against the magic attack that had been unleashed by Galner. Mika was visibly shaken and physically drained by what she had just done. Her magic barrier held up like a solid wall, impenetrable to even Galner's powerful magic attack.

Mika cried out to them. "Please... stand down, everyone! Stop killing!"

However, Galner was furious. He began to walk towards the side of the magic barrier, intent on getting around it. "Ridiculous! Princess, it is you who needs to stand down! Get out of the way! I must stop these peasant dogs!"

"Galner!" Maleth pointed to the knights who were nearest him, Samal and Aldrian. They quickly got in front of Galner, and then held their swords in front of them, forcing Galner to stop.

"What the hell is this?!" shouted Galner, glaring at the knights.

"It is the Princess who ordered you to stand down!" said Maleth. "Stand down, or I will convince you to obey her order in a way you won't soon forget! Obey the Princess!"

Galner did not move, but he glared at Maleth.

The fighting had stopped around them. The confused peasants all looked on. Those who still held their weapons did not know what to do as they stood staring at the Princess, the one who they had demanded to come out of the carriage. She most certainly came out of the carriage, as they had previously demanded, but not in the way they imagined. The only sounds they heard were the raging flames on the other side of the street.

From above, Valeria watched the scene, agape. "She saved them. The Princess stopped the attack from that old man, and saved the peasants."

Perplexed, Reid narrowed his eyes as he observed the actions of the Princess. "You can't be serious. Why would a Royal defend peasants?"

The pink magic circle disappeared, along with the magic barrier, when Mika was sufficiently satisfied that no one was going to fight any longer. Relieved, she put a hand on her heart, and closed her eyes for a moment. She turned around, and she saw the small boy on the ground behind her.

The boy stared up at the beautiful girl in front of him with widened eyes, unable to fathom what had just happened. But if he could believe his eyes, it looked to him like the Princess, a member of the Nobility and the Royal Family, the most hated people in the entire nation, had just saved his life.

Mika felt the cool, hard surface of the weathered street through her stockings as she slowly knelt down on the street in front of him, and regarded him with concern. "Does it hurt? Your knee... it looks like you injured it," she said with a very gentle, soothing voice.

A long hesitation and silence, and eventually the boy nodded. "Um... yeah...."

"May I see?" Mika reached out with her hand. "Please?"

More hesitation. The boy nodded again. After a moment, he lifted the remains of his trouser leg, and grimaced with pain.

Mika moved closer to him, and covered her mouth for

moment, as if she herself was experiencing the pain of his injury. The boy's knee was very red as it bled slightly, and some of the top layer of skin had been scraped off. Mika pulled out a large silk handkerchief from her handbag. "I'm going to wrap this around. Is that all right?"

The boy nodded.

Looking at him, Mika thought he really was about the same age as Mirin, although somewhat smaller, which made him closer to her height. Mika gently wrapped his knee with the handkerchief. The boy grimaced again. Mika gasped, seeing his pain, so she stopped for a moment. "I'm sorry...."

The boy kept his gaze on the handkerchief. He took a couple of breaths as the pain subsided. He met her worried gaze, and then nodded to her, prompting her to continue.

After wrapping the handkerchief three times around his knee, Mika tied a knot. "There you go. I hope it heals very soon."

The boy reached down to touch the makeshift bandage. Its silk fabric was soft and smooth to the touch. When he looked up, he saw the surprised and confused faces around him. The peasants watched, not knowing how to react to the Princess tending to his wound. "Um... thanks," he said softly, as he looked up at Mika.

Mika smiled. "You're very welcome."

A voice called out from among the peasants. "Tyrel!"

Mika heard the voice, and turned towards the direction from where it came, as did the young boy whose name, she noted, was apparently Tyrel. There was another boy who ran towards them, a few years older and quite a bit taller as well. Mika stood up, and Tyrel followed suit, grimacing as he rose.

"Jaren," said Tyrel.

The older boy grabbed him as soon as he arrived, and worriedly looked him over to see if he had any other injuries. "Damn. Thank goodness you're all right." He saw the bandage around Tyrel's knee, and regarded the Princess with a frown.

Mika shrank back, feeling somewhat intimidated, and

cast her eyes downward as she clasped her hands together in front of her.

Tyrel pulled on Jaren's sleeve. "Don't look at her like that."

Jaren calmed down, and realized the way he had been staring at the Princess just now. Though he was tempted to be hostile with her, he remembered what the young girl had just done a few minutes ago. "You... you saved my little brother... and everyone else here."

Mika barely met his gaze as she looked up, answering with a very soft voice. "Yes... I did."

"But... you're a noble... and a Royal. Why? Why would you save us?"

"Huh?" Mika was confused as she tilted her head slightly with curiosity. "I'm sorry... I'm not certain I understand...."

Tyrel was taken aback by her response. "You stopped the magic attack just now that would've killed my little brother and everyone else behind him. You saved his life and everyone else's. I'm asking you why you did that. Why did you do that?"

Mika saw the peasants staring at her. The ones nearby heard Jaren's question, and she was sure they wanted to know the reason as well. She understood what Jaren asked her, but what confused her was that he even asked.

They didn't expect me to save them. I think... they might have expected the exact opposite. But what else can I say? It's obvious why I saved them.

"Because... I'm your Princess." Mika took a deep breath, and smiled brightly. She spoke more loudly, feeling a little more confident. "Because you're my people. I'm your Princess and I love all of you."

There were loud gasps among the peasants as well as whispers. Surprise washed over them like a wave. The brothers Jaren and Tyrel were taken aback as well. It was definitely unexpected. This young girl, who, in their minds, represented everything they hated more than anything else in the entire world, the Nobility and the Royal Family, told them that she was their Princess, and that she loved them as her people.

"Is this real?" whispered Valeria.

Reid, who stood with her at the window, was so shocked by what had happened and what the Princess said that he could not close his mouth for a moment. "That can't be right. Tell me I'm dreaming this."

Galner's eyes widened with great shock, but kept his voice down as he spoke. "No... this can't be. Why, Princess? Why would you say that?"

Maleth and the knights simply watched the exchange between Princess Mika and the two young brothers. Helen watched as well, and began to smile just a little, and if Mika had seen that, she would have been ecstatic.

"Princess... My Lady," said Jaren. "I guess I can introduce myself and not get killed. Um, my name is Jaren. Jaren Balias. And this is my little brother Tyrel."

Mika extended a hand out towards them, feeling shy and timid, but at the same time, she was naturally friendly as well. "I'm very pleased to meet you, Sir Jaren, Sir Tyrel."

Jaren hesitated as he looked down at Mika's hand. He felt Tyrel tugging on his sleeve, urging him to shake the hand of the beautiful young Princess. Eventually, Jaren held out his hand, and he and Mika gently shook hands. Her hand felt soft, small, and warm in his, and because of that, he felt a very slight blush coming on, one that he hoped the Princess did not notice.

Mika felt warmth in her heart as she became acquainted with the first two peasants she had ever met.

Jaren, in attempt to keep his composure, cleared his throat. "I never thought I'd be shaking hands with a member of the Nobility, let alone the Royal Family. I know your name and that you're the Princess... but today's the first time I've ever seen you. I had no idea you were just a kid."

Mika simply giggled. "I'm eleven years old, in fact."

"I'm fourteen. You're older than you look. I thought you were my little brother's age, maybe younger... and he's ten."

"Truly? I've been told I'm small for my age, so, yes, I am certainly older than I look. My best friend is ten as well."

"She must think you're a great friend, then."

"He, actually," said Mika.

Tyrel was startled by that. "Your best friend's a boy?"

Mika was confused. "Huh? Um, yes… why?"

Jaren rubbed his younger brother's head roughly. "Who cares, Tyrel?"

Slightly annoyed like nearly every young boy would be when handled by an older sibling in such a manner, Tyrel pushed Jaren's hand away. "Leave me alone."

Mika heard a low rumbling sound. It was definitely not the flames that raged in the background, because it came from Tyrel's direction.

Tyrel blushed with embarrassment.

Placing her hands together at her heart, Mika simply smiled, immediately realizing the source of the noise and the reason behind Tyrel's reaction. "Are you hungry?"

Tyrel hesitated, wondering what he should say. The rumbling of his stomach spoke for him, and he wasn't sure whether he should deny it or agree with it. Eventually, he gave in to what he was truly feeling, and nodded.

"Hold on. I think I have some bread with me." Mika opened her handbag. As she rummaged through it, she found a package wrapped in a cloth and tied with a ribbon. She opened the package, revealing a large bun. "It was going to be a snack, but… I'd rather you have it. It's much too big for me to finish. Here!"

Tyrel stood speechless and motionless as Mika offered him the bun, along with its cloth wrapping. After some hesitation, Tyrel eventually took it.

Jaren was once again surprised, as were all the peasants around them as they watched. Now the Princess was giving food away to one of their own.

Tyrel smiled excitedly. "Thanks, Princess!"

"You're very welcome," said Mika.

Seeing that the knights were still holding their swords, Maleth issued them an order. "Knights, stand down."

Helen was the first to comply. "Yes, sir."

The knights, while somewhat uncertain at first, sheathed their swords. When the peasants holding short swords saw this, they hesitated for quite some time as they looked at each other with confusion.

Noticing their ambivalence, Maleth turned to them. "The Princess ordered us to stand down. You should as well. Remember that she just saved your lives a moment ago. Remember the words she uttered and the kindness she has shown one of your own."

Mika's words were spoken with the love of a Princess for her people, and her actions had shown that. One peasant put away his short sword, then a second one, and soon another, and another. Very soon, all their weapons had been sheathed. At this point, there was no longer any reason to fight.

Galner watched with shock. "What is this?" He glared at Maleth and the knights. "Don't sheathe your swords! You're still surrounded by these peasant dogs! They are a danger to the Princess!"

Valeria gritted her teeth as she held the crossbow at the windowsill, glaring at Galner. "I want to kill that son of a bitch so badly right now."

Reid raised his hand to stop her. "Hold on. Don't just act on your own."

Maleth returned the glare from Galner as he shook his head. "There is reason no longer for anyone on either side to be fighting, Sir Galner! The Princess is not going to allow any further killing to take place! I suggest you calm yourself!"

Mika heard the exchange between Galner and Maleth, but did not turn to watch what was going on. She simply sighed when she heard Galner's hateful words. It was good to know that Maleth appeared to be on her side.

Jaren exchanged uneasy glances with Tyrel. He looked back at the Princess. "We better go now."

"All right," said Mika. "I'm glad I met both of you. I hope we can see each other again some time."

Jaren nodded. "I hope so, too." He put his arm around his little brother's tiny shoulders. "Come on, Tyrel."

Tyrel stole a quick glance at Mika, smiled, and waved his hand. "See you soon, Princess Mika."

Mika smiled back, and then watched them leave. Eventually, they disappeared among the crowd. "I'm glad I met them."

Helen watched her surroundings, at the confused peasant civilians all around them, at the baffled peasants equipped with short swords, now safely sheathed in the scabbards that hung from their belts. She exchanged relieved glances with Tanari and Caylen. Even from where she was, she could feel the heat of the flames on the other side of the street. Reassured by the relative calm that replaced the violent chaos just moments ago, she soon joined Mika.

"Princess Mika, I believe it's time to return to the carriage. I'm certain there will be no further violence."

Mika nodded. "Yes, you're right."

* * *

Valeria held her crossbow on top of the windowsill. Using the sights on her weapon, she eyed Galner, aiming the dangerously pointed tip of a steel quarrel straight at him. "I have that bastard in my sights. I'm sick of the things I'm hearing from this old fool. He killed a lot of our people. I'm ready to put him out of his misery."

"Don't miss now, Valeria," said Reid.

"I never miss. This will not be the first noble I've sniped."

As Galner spoke nonsense under his breath, Maleth told him off again. The knights stood around, awaiting orders.

Reid observed the red-haired young woman who had no armour but was fighting like a knight. The young woman spoke to Princess Mika as both of them headed back for the carriage. He heard their soft voices but he couldn't make out what they were saying, nor did he care. He observed the young Princess for a moment, and then he shifted his eyes to Valeria. He watched as her finger gently began to pull back on her crossbow's trigger.

"Hold on. Wait."

Valeria pulled her finger away from the trigger. "What now?"

Reid rubbed the bridge of his nose, his eyes suddenly narrowed, the muscles around his jaw tensed. He watched the Princess again as the images of her using magic to save the lives of the Peasantry just moments ago flashed briefly in his mind. He hardened his heart, and pushed them away, remembering his burning hatred of the Nobility of Melodice.

"Kill the Royal."

Valeria stopped, confused, her concentration now lost. "What?"

Reid repeated his order. "I said kill the Royal."

"Wait. Hold on a moment, Reid." She stared at Reid with a hint of disgust. "You're telling me to kill the Princess?"

"That's what I said, Valeria."

"You're telling me to kill Princess Mika. A child. A child who just happened to save the lives of hundreds of people just now. She protected them. And she's a kid! She's a little girl!"

Reid frowned with irritation. "A little girl who is a Royal."

Valeria shook her head. "When I said she was the most vulnerable of the Royal Family, I wasn't thinking about killing her. I was thinking... maybe we can take her prisoner somehow. I didn't even know the Princess was a kid until I saw her!"

"Listen!" Reid put a hand on her shoulder firmly, his obsidian eyes aflame with hatred and anger. "I didn't know the Princess was a kid either, but that doesn't matter. I don't give a damn if that pretty little bitch is a child. She is *still* a Royal, a representative of the Royal Family. This is our chance to avenge the nation of Melodice! For the thousands who died before us, hundreds of thousands throughout the decades, it's time for this nation to have its revenge! We don't know when we'll have another chance!"

Valeria stared at Reid for a long time, hesitating, not knowing what to do.

"So I'm telling you, Valeria... kill her. Kill Princess Mika Silveraine."

Part of her agreed with him, that the nation of Melodice needed to be avenged, but she was not quite sure about this method of obtaining that vengeance. She looked again, this time, not towards Galner... but towards Princess Mika. She moved the sight of the crossbow from the mage to the Princess.

Valeria sighed. "I can't believe I'm doing this...."

"As soon as you fire that quarrel into her stuck up little head, the others will fire as well." By that, Reid meant other crossbow snipers just like Valeria, waiting in the other buildings nearby, out of sight.

Valeria shook her head slowly. "Funny, she didn't seem stuck up at all when she held me and wrapped me up in her cape."

"What's the matter with you, Valeria? You're turning soft on me. You can bet it was all just an act to fool you. Nobles can't be trusted."

The blockades in front of and behind the cervid carriage had dispersed. Mika headed back to the carriage with Helen. At the same time, she looked at the piles of dead bodies, at least fifty of them, lying in pools of blood. Some of their decapitated heads still had their eyes open, staring at her as if they were accusing her of something. Dismembered arms and legs littered the streets. Then, there were the flames on the other side of the street, where over a hundred people were burned alive by the magic attack unleashed by Galner. As Mika approached the carriage, despite the early summer, she felt cold, so she crossed her arms against her chest, rubbing her shoulders.

Helen noticed the paleness of Mika's face, and was immediately concerned. "Are you all right, Princess?"

"I'm... I'm fine, Miss Helen," Mika said very softly.

As Mika and Helen reached the side of the carriage, Galner approached them quickly, his mood the worst it had been in a very long time. "Princess Mika!"

Mika was startled, but did not look up at Galner.

"This is unbelievable, Princess! If you were my child, I'd give you the worst beating of your life!"

At the mention of those disrespectful words, Helen

glared at him. Maleth and the other knights, hearing what he just said, turned towards him.

"How many times did I tell you? These peasants are nothing more than animals! They are the Peasantry and we are the Nobility! We have nothing to do with their pathetic lives! They can live in the filth they always have for all we care! It is not our concern!"

While Galner was in the middle of his outburst, Maleth quickly approached him.

"Your actions have been contrary to the status quo! I will make certain that the King hears about this, and he will be furious when he does! This will not be tolerated! You are the Princess of the great nation of Melodice! I expect you to behave better than this!"

"Galner!" Maleth grabbed his shoulder, and forced him to turn around.

Galner was surprised. "How dare you, Maleth!"

Maleth, with his face in Galner's, pressed a clip on his scabbard, which caused his sword to push out slightly, exposing part of the blade.

Galner noticed the sword, and glared at Maleth with shock.

"Govern your tongue, Sir Galner, or I will cut it out of your mouth," said Maleth.

Galner's gaze burned with fury. "You're threatening me?"

"Yes, I am. You are in the presence of Her Highness, the Princess of Melodice, and you *will* govern your tongue."

Mika was having trouble paying attention to the hostile exchange between Maleth and Galner. In fact, she was having trouble paying attention to the lecture Galner was giving her a moment ago as well. It was like his voice was far away. Mika could see the dead bodies in the periphery of her vision. She felt as if something was welling up from inside her, some kind of sick feeling.

Helen reached out to put her hand on Mika's shoulder. "Princess?"

Up above, Valeria stared through her crossbow's sights with the side of Mika's face as her target. "Princess Mika, please forgive me in the afterlife."

Mika felt it. Something really was welling up from inside her. Her stomach felt queasy. She grimaced as she put one hand on her mid-section.

Reid grinned ominously as he watched in anticipation, the lines of his face twisted by his pure hatred. "This will be the greatest sacrifice of all. For our future, for our people, for Melodice...."

Valeria pulled the crossbow's trigger.

Mika fell to her knees, her other hand on her mouth... out of which came her half-digested breakfast, which made a puddle on the ground in front of her. At the same time, Mika heard and felt an ominous wind blowing past her, behind her head as she fell to her knees. She heard a loud sound, as if something sharp struck something rigid. Mika immediately turned her head... and saw a crossbow quarrel, its tip embedded in the side of the carriage.

Valeria gasped. "Damn!"

"Sniper!" shouted Helen.

Galner, Maleth, and the knights were alarmed, but Helen's warning came too late. More crossbow quarrels flew, three of them striking Samal, Valias, and Aldrian in the neck, one of the areas where their armour was weakest. The three young knights fell on the street, never to rise up again.

Horrified, Maleth pushed Galner away towards the carriage door while waving Helen and Mika away. "Get inside!" He turned to Caylen and Tanari as he rushed for the driver's seat. "Knights, on the carriage!"

"Go, Princess!" Helen opened the side door and grabbed Mika, pushing her into the carriage, almost throwing her in.

Mika made a couple of yelping sounds as she fell on her knees, but she struggled to get farther into the cabin at the same time as quickly as possible, hitting the side of her head against the table and putting runs in her stockings.

Helen jumped into the carriage, followed by Galner, who closed the door.

Quarrels flew again, striking the wooden exterior of the carriage. Caylen and Tanari jumped onto the platform at the back of the carriage, holding on tightly.

Maleth, narrowly evading a quarrel, jumped into the driver's seat. He grabbed the reins, just as one of the cervids was struck in the side by a quarrel. The cervid felt pain, panicked, and started running, panicking the other three cervids and forcing them to start running as well. The carriage lurched forward hard, throwing Mika and Helen onto the floor, while Galner held on. Caylen and Tanari nearly fell off, but they held onto the beams behind the carriage.

One of the ropes that secured Mika's travel chest was struck by a quarrel that was deflected by Tanari's gauntlet. The travel chest became undone, and the momentum of the carriage caused it to slide off the platform. Caylen tried to grab it by one of the handles, but he missed as it fell onto the street.

Another set of quarrels flew. Some of them embedded themselves into the sides or the roof of the carriage, while others struck the large and powerful bodies of the cervids. Although they ran as if the quarrels were nothing to them, they actually felt quite a bit of pain. The few peasants still in the area, taking notice of the flying quarrels, ran into buildings for cover.

A quarrel struck one of the windows, breaking the glass. Mika screamed as Helen grabbed her, and put her in a corner. Several shards of glass were scattered all over the table, into which the quarrel embedded itself.

"Stay away from the windows!" exclaimed Helen.

"You don't have to remind me!" said Galner, as another quarrel struck the window closest to him, cracking it, but not breaking it. However, one more strike would certainly break it to pieces.

Caylen watched Mika's travel chest as they distanced themselves from it, but he stared at it intently as it opened up by itself... and inside was a boy who started screaming for help. He came to an immediate realization. He, along with Aldrian, had lifted up the chest, and both of them had commented that it seemed heavier than it should be. Now he knew the reason why.

"That's why the carriage was heavier than it should be!"

Tanari saw as well, and her eyes widened.

"Help!" shouted Mirin. "Help me! Someone help!"

A few peasants heard him or saw him, but none were in the position to do anything.

In the carriage, Mika and Helen heard the familiar scream. They both jumped onto the back seat, and looked through the back window.

Mika gasped. "Mirin!"

Galner looked up with confusion, hearing the boy's name. "What?"

Helen grabbed her scabbard, opened the door, and leapt out of the carriage, rolling onto the side of the street to minimize injury, and then got up and ran for Mirin. A crossbow quarrel struck the street and bounced off as she ran, almost hitting her. She ran as quickly as she could, at the same time mounting her scabbard to her belt.

In the building above, Reid slammed his fist against the wall beside the window with anger and frustration. "Dammit! We failed to kill the Royal! We're done here! Come on, Valeria!"

Taking her crossbow, Valeria got up from under the window and left with Reid.

Mirin screamed when a quarrel struck the side of the travel chest. He pushed himself against the inside of the chest, causing it to tip over and spill its contents, which included some of Mika's dresses, nightgowns, stockings, knickers, socks, shoes, bottles of lotion and perfume, hairbrushes, ribbons, small jewelry boxes, and a myriad of other small feminine items.

When Helen arrived at the travel chest, she saw fear written all over his face. "Come, Mirin! Onto my back!" She grabbed him, and threw him over her shoulder.

Another quarrel narrowly missed them as it embedded itself into the travel chest. As far as Helen was concerned, the peasants could have Princess Mika's belongings. She ran back as fast as she could towards the carriage, which continued forward. She had to catch up to it.

Tanari went around the side of the carriage, and then called out to her commanding officer. "Sir Maleth, Miss

Helen has rescued one of our occupants! She needs to get back on the carriage! We need to slow down!"

"What happened back there?" Maleth shouted. Of course, not having any time for explanation, he pulled on the reins to urge the cervids to slow down. Fortunately, they complied. However, slowing down made them more vulnerable to crossbow fire.

"Don't tell me, Princess Mika, that you stowed Mirin away in your travel chest?!" exclaimed Galner.

Mika barely heard him as she watched Helen running back towards the carriage with Mirin over her shoulder. She was not catching up fast enough, even though the cervid carriage was slowing down. Soon, another set of quarrels flew, bouncing off the ground.

Helen felt one pass her shoulder, narrowly missing her head and Mirin.

"I have to…" Mika said softly, and then shut her eyes hard. "Miss Helen and Mirin… I must… protect them!" She opened her eyes, watching Helen and Mirin, as a pink magic circle appeared on the floor of the cabin.

"What are you doing, Princess?!" Galner demanded.

A semi-transparent magic barrier, spherical in shape, appeared around Helen and Mirin, moving along with them. Another much larger one appeared around the entire carriage, including the cervids.

"Princess, thank you…" said Helen, as she continued to run.

A quarrel was headed their way but it bounced harmlessly off the magic barrier. Another set of quarrels flew at the carriage, but they bounced off was well. Mika's magic barriers offered complete protection.

Galner was astounded by Mika, who maintained two magic barriers around two moving targets at the same time while she herself was moving and was having difficulty concentrating. Such an act would quickly drain any novice magic user physically and mentally, but Mika fared quite well. However, Galner knew she would not be able to keep this up for long. He also noticed that the magic barriers Mika created where of a higher level of magic. Normally, magic barriers protected against magic attacks only. Mika's magic barriers also protected against physical attacks such as crossbow quarrels.

"I can't believe it," whispered Galner. "This is... Forbidden Magic. I didn't expect this. These magic barriers are... her magical skills are... truly impressive."

Caylen held out his hand while holding onto a beam. "Miss Helen, throw him to me!"

Helen used her momentum to throw the screaming Mirin towards Caylen.

Caylen leaned precariously away from the platform, and caught him by wrapping his arm around his waist. He pulled himself and Mirin to safety.

Tanari held out her hand to Helen as she used her other hand to hold onto the beam closest to her. "Come, Miss Helen, take my hand!"

Helen took her hand, and used perfect timing and momentum with Tanari as she jumped onto the carriage, placing her foot exactly where it should be. A quarrel bounced off the magic barrier as Tanari pulled Helen to safety.

"Everyone is on board, Sir Maleth!" Caylen shouted.

At that moment, Maleth urged the cervids to go faster, as fast as they could go.

Mika dropped the magic barriers. She fell on her side on the seat, her eyes half-closed, exhausted.

Maleth briefly turned towards the front window of the cabin. "We can't continue this excursion! Sir Galner, we're heading back to the castle!"

Galner was forced to agree. In their current situation, with the carriage riddled with crossbow quarrels, the cervids injured, three of their knights dead, a stowaway from Mika's travel chest, and the current emotional state of the Princess, it would not be possible to continue. They must return to the Scarletia Royal Castle.

As the carriage sped down the Valderia Pathway, a total of twenty knights mounted on cervids joined them from nearby patrol stations. Hearing about the chaos that ensued, they had tracked down Mika's cervid carriage, and intercepted it to give escort. Unfortunately, they were far too late to provide assistance with the earlier attack.

As Mika lay on her side on the seat in the cabin, she covered her face with one hand, and sobbed quietly over what had occurred. She thought about the peasants and the attack on her carriage, the words Galner used to describe the peasants, words that were full of condescending hatred, and wondered how any of this could be normal.

"I don't understand... why?"

CHAPTER 10

TURMOIL

SEC 3566, Morrighan 16

"DAMN THESE BASTARD PEASANT ANIMALS from hell!"

The rage King Ralphen felt could not be contained as he slammed his fists on top of the heavy algerwood table in the King's Conference. But it no longer surprised any of the people who attended the meeting regarding the series of incidents that had occurred around Princess Mika on her failed journey to the city of Cerulean. Queen Maiya sat beside the King, while Sir Collin and Sir Maleth were directly across from them. Sir Galner was also present, seated closer to the Queen.

Ralphen leaned forward, his eyes aflame. "They've attacked us again! Our daughter was attacked and nearly killed! I want the animals who tried to assassinate Princess Mika found, and I want them all executed!"

Collin exchanged uneasy glances with Maleth for a moment, and then leaned forward in his seat. "My Lord, we will certainly do our best to find these criminals. When we do, we will bring down justice upon them. After obtaining the report of this incident from Sir Maleth, it appears that there were two groups involved. The first was the blockade, or rather, the peasant mob. The second was the group of snipers. So that I am clear, are you referring to the snipers who attempted to assassinate the Princess?"

"What do you think, Sir Collin?!" shouted Ralphen. "Of course, I'm referring to them! You have a large role to fill after the departure of Sir Terren, and it would be in your best interest to fill that role well!"

Maleth cleared his throat, and leaned forward from his seat as well. "My Lord, the problem we have with finding these people who tried to kill the Princess is that we did not see them. They were in the buildings, firing crossbow quarrels from the windows, out of sight."

"Well, then, you can start with the peasant mob. I'm certain they're related. Haven't you thought that perhaps the blockade was set up so that those snipers would have the opportunity to kill the Princess? I believe they're one and the same group."

Collin agreed. "Yes, My Lord. It's likely that they're the same group, or perhaps, even two groups working together. The peasant mob set up the blockade, and attacked the Princess and her companions, while the snipers were in the buildings, waiting for the opportunity to assassinate her."

The King stood from his chair, and slowly walked around the table towards the knights. "Sir Collin, this will be your first major duty as the Supreme Captain of the Scarletia Royal Guard and the Royal Army of Melodice. Sir Terren spoke highly of you and recommended you to be his replacement, and here you are. Your orders are to find these people who were involved with the peasant mob, which will ultimately lead you to the snipers. I want you to find these people... and execute them! Kill all of them and all their families and relatives! None may be allowed to live!"

Collin did his best not to appear as if he was overwhelmed with the task assigned to him as the new leader of the Royal Guard. "Judging by Sir Maleth's report, you do realize, My Lord, that there were at least a thousand peasants who could possibly be involved. Perhaps more."

Queen Maiya turned towards the King. "He's correct, Ralphen. That's... a very large number of people to search for."

"That shouldn't be a problem," said Ralphen. "I don't care if there are thousands of them or tens of thousands. I want them all dead! Torch their properties as well!"

It was obvious to Collin and Maleth that the King was so furious that he was not thinking about the consequences of ordering thousands of people to their deaths. There was nothing that either could say about it, but there was one person in the room who could.

Maiya regarded the King with all seriousness, raising her voice, which prompted him to turn towards her. "Now, Ralphen, think about this for a moment! You cannot be executing thousands of people all at once. You cannot seek out that many people, and have them all killed along with their families and burn down their homes and expect few or no consequences. It's possible that a significant labour shortage would take place, and I believe you're aware of what would happen if that occurs. It's also possible that you might incite rebellion among the Peasantry, and to stifle a rebellion would be much more difficult."

Ralphen leaned against the table with both hands, and cast his eyes down. "Yes, yes, I know, dammit," said the King, his voice lowered. "It's difficult to accept that our daughter was targeted for death... not once, but twice."

Maiya, saddened by the situations Mika has faced recently, looked down. She got up from her seat, and walked over to Ralphen to comfort him, her hands on his shoulders. "I know, Ralphen. And we should definitely search for those who are responsible, and bring justice upon them. That would be the right thing to do. But we should seek out those who are responsible, no one else. I suspect that these peasants had leaders who organized this incident. We should seek them out."

Ralphen nodded, and approached Collin, this time more calmly. "Sir Collin, you heard the Queen's words. These peasant criminals have leaders. At this point, they will be the ones we'll seek out. Find them, and capture them!"

However, there was something else that Collin had thought about, and he decided to share it with the King. "Yes, My Lord. However, this assumes that everyone in the peasant mob were members of a very large rebel group. If it turns out that a majority of the peasant mob were civilians rather than members of a rebel group, what then?"

Ralphen was taken aback by this possibility that he had not thought of. "I find that highly unlikely, Sir Collin. I do believe that the crossbow snipers and everyone in the peasant mob are either one very large group or two groups working together. If that's the case, you will seek out their leaders and deal with them, as your Queen has suggested. However... it's possible that you may be right. If finding the leaders of these peasant criminals leads you to a rebel group, and if it turns out that only some of the bastards in that peasant mob are part of that rebel group, then you may not only execute the leaders, but everyone in the group as well. That will send a strong message to the civilians who participated in the mob that we have no tolerance for the existence of rebel groups. They have been causing problems for the Nobility for the longest time. Bring them the rewards they have earned!"

Collin nodded with acknowledgment. "I understand, My Lord. As you have ordered, it shall be done."

"Very good. Now, Sir Maleth." Ralphen circled around the table to stand close to the Supreme Commander.

"Yes, My Lord," said Maleth.

"I've not had the opportunity until now to show our gratitude for what you did. The Queen and I thank you for protecting the Princess. Because of you, she is alive and well."

Galner glared at Maleth.

Maleth bowed his head slightly. "Such is my duty, My Lord. However, I am deeply regretful."

"Regretful?"

"Yes, My Lord. While I did my best to protect the Princess, three of our most talented knights did not survive. Samal Evastian, Valias Garan, and Aldrian Triska. All of them were quite young, their lives cut short so tragically."

"I understand." Ralphen put a hand firmly on Maleth's shoulder. "My heart feels heavy for these fine young men and their families. But we'll remember their sacrifice, and honour them. I will issue commendations for each of them to be given to their families. They fought well, and they defended the life of the Princess with their own." He next turned to Galner. "And you as well, Sir Galner. I'd like to thank you. You subdued many of the criminals who attacked our Princess."

Galner bowed his head slightly. "It was only natural for me to do what I did, My Lord. However, I'd like to remind you of my complaint."

It was Maleth's turn to glare at Galner.

Ralphen remembered Galner's complaint. He looked at the ceiling for a brief moment with impatience. "Yes, of course. You complained that Sir Maleth antagonized you, and then threatened you."

"That's correct, My Lord." He shifted his accusing eyes to Maleth. "His words were not becoming of the Supreme Commander of the Scarletia Royal Guard."

Maleth turned to the professor, his eyes narrowed but his voice a dead calm. "Perhaps you should have stilled your tongue, Sir Galner. You raised your voice, and insulted young Princess Mika several times. Your words were not becoming of a member of the Nobility."

Galner slammed his palms on the edge of the table as he stood up, feeling his pride as a member of the Nobility of Melodice being attacked. "How dare you!"

Ralphen raised his hands. "Gentlemen! That's enough."

Galner turned to the King. "My Lord, you read through my complaint, so you're aware of the reasons why... I uttered the words I did."

Ralphen nodded. "Yes, I'm aware, Sir Galner." He turned to both men, and urged them to calm down. "Gentlemen, I'm aware of both your concerns. Sir Galner, you may not know this, but Sir Maleth also filed a complaint against you."

Surprised, Galner nearly took a step back. "Against me?! I have said and done nothing that warranted a complaint!"

"I'm afraid I will have to disagree with you, Sir Galner," said the King. "Your behaviour towards our young daughter was unnecessarily harsh. If you had been anyone else, I would have had you locked up in the dungeon after a lashing."

Galner clenched his fists as he straightened up with a defiant frown. "I see."

"But... I'm aware of your reasons for reprimanding Princess Mika. According to your complaint, her words and her actions were... quite disturbing."

"So you agree that my concerns were legitimate. The words that Princess Mika uttered made me uncomfortable. They turned my stomach, My Lord. I apologize for my harshness, but I do believe that her words and actions were irrational. She questioned the normality of the world around her. It's understandable because it was her first time seeing the world outside the castle gates. Nobles, especially noble children, are often shocked to see it for the first time, but they quickly learn to accept it. But the Princess... she was something else, My Lord. She poked and prodded with every question, surpassing what the imagination was capable of conjuring.

"And then, there were the irrational actions she took. She ordered the rescue of some dirty young whore in the alleyway. She took it upon herself to comfort this peasant woman, and wrapped her up in her cape. The questioning did not stop after that. The Princess was greatly disturbed by her surroundings, despite the accepted fact that everything around her is just the way it is. She refused to accept that fact. And then, during the attack of the peasant mob, the Princess physically stopped my magic attack! I was going to subdue the criminals in front of us when the Princess used her magic to give herself a temporary boost in speed, appeared in front of me, stopped my magic attack, and redirected it, protecting the lives of these peasant dogs! I don't understand why she did such a thing. She even acquainted herself with two unwashed little peasant boys! She shook hands with them, and gave food to them. It was quite... disgusting, My Lord. And let's not forget that she stowed a civilian away in her travel chest. Mirin Gothwald. He could have been killed! Had he been killed, I'm certain you will agree with me, My Lord, that delivering the news of his death to his guardian, Miss Angelica Ruviel, would have been most unpleasant."

The muscles around Ralphen's face hardened with anger as he listened to Galner's words. "I'm not too concerned with the boy. What I am more concerned about is everything else Mika said and did. I haven't forgotten about her words and actions, and I'll make certain that I... speak to her about them."

Maiya stiffened upon hearing the pause in the King's words. "Ralphen."

The King turned to her.

"Remember that Mika is still recuperating from her ordeal. If you should discipline her, you should do so at a later time. She was deeply traumatized by her experience, as you should be aware."

Ralphen nodded. "Yes, of course, Maiya. I'm well aware."

"I'm simply reminding you. Don't forget," said Maiya.

The King turned to Galner and Maleth. He paused for a moment. "However, gentlemen, regarding your complaints against each other, you both had legitimate reasons for saying what you did. You were both subjected to a highly stressful situation. In situations like these, sometimes we say things we don't normally say. This is what I believe happened. I will remind you, Sir Galner, Sir Maleth, that professionalism is important when dealing with stressful situations, so you must both attempt to keep a level head. You are members of the Nobility, so you must take pride as nobles, and display professionalism at all times. Other than mentioning this, I can't find reason to fault either of you. I have no reason to pursue either of your complaints any further, and consider the matter dropped. We shall speak of this no more."

"Thank you, My Lord," said Maleth.

Galner hesitated for a moment. "Thank you... My Lord."

* * *

SEC 3566, Morrighan 28

Thirteen days after the traumatic ordeal, Princess Mika remained in her bedchamber. During the first few days of her recuperation, her appetite left much to be desired, but Angelica noted that there had been some improvement lately. She never left her room, not even for a moment.

This morning, Mika sat across the width of a club chair that was next to one of the windows, her legs dangling over one side, her back leaning against the armrest on the other side. Her arms crossed against her chest, she stared intently through the window at the sky outside, her face expressionless.

The sky slowly changed to varying shades of red, orange, yellow, and blue as the shimmering globe of the summer sun rose from the horizon, partially covered by distant dark clouds. Watching the sunrise instilled a calm feeling within Mika. She turned her attention briefly to two of the moons in the sky, now waning crescents.

Still in her short, sleeveless, white nightgown, Mika had awakened about an hour ago but could not go back to sleep. In her mind, she repeated the events of that day, starting from when she, Helen, Galner, Maleth, and the knights first left the Scarletia Royal Castle, then through the gates that took them into the city proper, and ending with the attack of the snipers, and having to make a desperate escape from the area. From beginning to end, she constantly replayed the events, literally hundreds of times, seeing all the violence and death in her mind, to the point that she felt somewhat numb.

"Why were the peasants so angry? Why were they so angry that they wanted to kill me?" Mika asked herself with a very soft voice, as she closed her eyes for a moment.

They wanted me to face some crimes, but what crimes were they referring to? I know I did nothing wrong. So what did they mean by that? Those accusations... couldn't be directed personally at me, could they? I don't understand.

She remembered the demands of the peasants. They knew there was a Royal inside the carriage, but they couldn't have known it was she, specifically. That was the first time she had ever been seen in public. Up until that day, she had never set foot beyond the castle gates. The peasants were seeing her for the first time, which meant....

"They didn't know I was in the carriage. All they knew was that there was a member of the Royal Family inside. It just happened to me."

So, again, just like with the merchant assassins, I think their true target wasn't me specifically... but rather, the Royal Family and the Nobility, groups that I represent.

Mika remembered the woman they rescued named Valeria Tannlar, and wondered what became of her after she was rescued from those men who attempted to violate her. From what Mika remembered, Valeria seemed quite thankful that she and her companions, Helen, Maleth, and the knights, were able to rescue her.

The fighting was still fresh in her memory. The peasants attacked, the knights counterattacked, and much blood was spilled. Mika knew that the first duty of the knights was to protect her, and that was what they did, which meant they had no choice but to kill the peasants who attacked. However, she remembered the actions that Galner took. He used his magic not only to kill several attacking peasants, but also to kill many innocent bystanders. It was true that his intention was to protect her, but Mika was greatly disturbed by his methods and by the fact that he also killed more than just those who attacked. He would kill innocent peasants as though they were nothing more than animals.

"That's what he thinks of them. Sir Galner thinks of the peasants as nothing more than animals."

Mika remembered the mother who had been trying to sell dull and lifeless flowers and her baby which had been strapped to her, both of whom were burned within the range of Galner's magic attack.

"He even killed a defenseless mother and her baby."

Mika closed her eyes again and put a hand over her forehead. *He even used the boy I met, Sir Tyrel, as a target for his next magic attack. I was so relieved that I was able to use my haste spell just in time to put myself in front of his attack and deflect it into the sky.*

She remembered the two young brothers, Tyrel and Jaren. To her, they seemed like very nice young boys. Tyrel had been injured, so she wondered how he was faring. She also hoped he was not going hungry at this moment. Because of the general state of extreme poverty she found the peasants to be in, she was certain that Tyrel and Jaren were also living the same way, with little money and food.

After the fighting between the peasant mob and the knights was stopped by Mika's own order, she remembered seeing the piles of dead bodies. She remembered becoming sick to her stomach. During the first few days after those events, whenever she remembered the death that surrounded her, she felt ill, and sometimes vomited. However, in the last few days, she had been able to manage some of the grisly images in her mind. She could remember them, and dwell on them without feeling sick.

I almost died that day, that moment when I became sick. If I hadn't fallen to my knees, the crossbow quarrel would have struck me in the head, and I would be dead right now. Those snipers attacked with crossbows. Sir Samal and Sir Aldrian and Sir Valias were killed. I was almost one of them.

Remembering Mirin in her travel chest, Mika clenched her fists against her thighs, holding the hem of her nightgown. She turned to her side, and stared at the window.

"I wish I hadn't let Mirin convince me to let him go with me."

She had been calm, despite thinking about the disturbing events of that day, but soon, tears came down, soaking into the armrest of her club chair as she rested the side of her face in one hand. Her thoughts turned to Mirin.

He almost died because of me. I had him hide inside my travel chest so he could come with me. But I put his life in danger.

However, a thought occurred in the back of her mind as she blamed herself. It was true that Mirin's life was endangered, but there was no way the Princess could have predicted the future, and expected a peasant mob and a group of crossbow snipers to attack them. Whether he was inside the travel chest or in the cabin, he would still have experienced the same danger. But, at the moment, she did not want to entertain that thought, and blamed herself instead.

When Mika's carriage had returned to the castle that day, it was riddled with at least thirty quarrels, some on the roof and others on the sides. The cervids had been shot by the quarrels as well, and all four of them had to be put down, because they did not receive medical attention in time. Even if they had received the proper treatment, they would have spent the rest of their lives as animals that performed light work instead of riding and traveling. Cervids loved to run, and not being able to run every once in a while would cause them to become depressed and die anyway.

After a few minutes, Mika wiped her tears away, swung her legs around, and sat up. She went to the window and stared outside, not looking at anything in particular. Her hands and forehead on the cold glass, she thought again about Galner's spiteful words, about the attitude that even Angelica and Mirin had expressed regarding the peasants, and the anger of the peasants and their hatred towards the Nobility and the Royal Family.

"I don't understand. Why is everything like this? Why does everyone think it's normal? It can't be. People are suffering. How can this be normal? Something... is not right. This is not right at all."

CHAPTER 11

FURY OF THE KING

SEC 3566, Morrighan 32

FOUR DAYS LATER, PEASANTS, MOST of them men while some were women, were dragged out of the inn called Traveler's Paradise screaming, and thrown onto the dusty streets by several fully armoured knights. Threatened by long swords, spears, and crossbows, they were led to another group that was forced to walk down the street to an intersection, where Sir Collin and Sir Maleth waited. As soon as the peasants joined the group, their hands were bound behind their backs so tightly that the ropes caused bloody scrapes on their wrists. They were forced to kneel down on the street, grimacing in pain as they felt the rough cracks in the pavement, and if they did not obey, they were beaten mercilessly by the knights.

Collin stiffened as he observed the brutality inflicted by some of his knights, but he forced himself to retain his calm composure, reminding himself that he was the Supreme Captain of the Scarletia Royal Guard, and must remain resolute in front of his soldiers. "So... this is everyone directly involved?"

Maleth nodded. "Correct, Sir Collin. The crossbow snipers and those who organized the peasant mob were one and the same group, a rebel group that consisted of at least two hundred members. Except for a few who may have escaped, we've captured all of them."

"We can't do much about the ones who escaped. So it's true that most of the people in the peasant mob were actually civilians who agreed to follow the direction of this rebel group, not part of the rebel group itself. Their role was to form a blockade to encircle Princess Mika's carriage, and shout their demands angrily, but no more than that. Although they were an accessory, the civilians did not directly attack the Princess."

"Precisely. The people you see before you are the members of the rebel group only. They were the ones who actively attacked the Princess."

Collin was relieved, knowing that he did not have to hunt down any innocent men, women, and children, people who did not attack Princess Mika. Forming a blockade was one thing, but attacking the nation's young Princess and her company was another. But this opinion, he kept to himself. "Very good. It would be much more difficult to seek out and capture those who were part of the peasant mob. You said there were...."

"I estimated about one thousand civilians were in the peasant mob," said Maleth.

As Collin watched the peasants, his eyes shifted to several groups of people farther away, held back by groups of knights on cervids who pointed spears at them threateningly. They were onlookers, people who had gathered with morbid curiosity. No doubt, some of them may have been part of the peasant mob.

As Maleth looked over the peasants, he saw someone familiar, and felt a chill down his back. The knights approached with a woman in a smock-frock. She screamed in pain as they tied her hands behind her back. Maleth approached her.

"Sir Maleth?" Collin wondered what he was doing.

Valeria Tannlar was forced to kneel down, and grimaced in pain as her knees scraped against the rough pavement. She felt the ropes cutting into her wrists as she saw a surprised Maleth arrive. She stared at him as he stood in front of her for a long moment.

"Miss Valeria. I don't understand."

Valeria simply sighed. "Of course, you wouldn't understand."

One of the knights pulled her hair, causing her to cry out. "Watch your tongue, you little bitch!"

Another was made to kneel down beside Valeria, an older man who held a defiant expression, despite two hard punches in the face given to him by the knights.

"Reid!" said Valeria, silently asking him if he was all right.

Blood trickling down from his nose and lips, Reid responded with a smug grin. "Don't worry about me."

Collin joined Maleth as one of the knights approached them to relay some information.

"Sir Collin, Sir Maleth, this man here is the leader of this rebel group. It was under his direction that the peasant mob was organized and the crossbow snipers attacked Princess Mika Silveraine. Reid Alviana is the bastard's name."

"Thank you, Sir Serian," said Collin.

The young knight bowed slightly to the Supreme Captain. "Such is my duty, sir."

Collin stood in front of the kneeling Reid. "So you're the criminal who planned the attack on our Princess. You must be a talented leader, Sir Reid, for being able to put together such an organized attack on our Princess in such a short amount of time. I'm guessing you had planned this beforehand, but hadn't had the opportunity to actually implement it until that day, when the Princess was riding through the streets of Scarletia for the first time in her life."

Reid smirked, cocking his head. "And you, sir, are very perceptive. I planned this long time ago, but hadn't had a chance until now to actually go through with it. My group and I were at the right place at the right time. Your little Princess was also at the right place at the right time. It was a perfect opportunity." He chuckled. "Unfortunately, for you, you were too late to figure out my plan. You couldn't stop us at all. Your knights were almost helpless under our crossbow snipers."

"Still, the Princess came out of it unscathed. Unfortunately, for you, you will not be as lucky as she was."

Reid laughed coldly, and then spit blood that had

collected in his mouth onto the ground in front of him. "It doesn't matter what you do to me now! I will gladly accept my execution. I've done a great service to the people of Melodice! When you kill me, I'll be sure to die with pride and honour and dignity! I will hold my head up high in defiance of your tyranny! One day, the Nobility and the Royal Family will be punished for their crimes against the nation! The people of the Peasantry are tired of being oppressed by the likes of you!"

Collin struck Reid hard on the side of his head with his gauntlet, causing him to nearly fall sideways, but two knights forced him to stay up. More blood came out of his mouth.

"You, Sir Reid, speak in nothings." Collin turned to Maleth, and watched him gaze at the woman in front of him. "Someone you know, Sir Maleth?"

Maleth nodded. "Yes. Miss Valeria Tannlar."

Serian had more information. "Sir, we also determined that it was this woman who fired the crossbow at the Princess."

The Supreme Commander stared hard at Valeria. "Is that true?"

Valeria nodded after a long hesitation. "Yes. I took the shot."

Maleth paused for a moment to ensure he did not react on impulse. "But... why, Miss Valeria? As you may recall, it was Princess Mika who saw you being violated by three men, drew attention to your predicament, and ordered us to save you. Had she not done that, we wouldn't have noticed you. We rescued you from them. Who knows what those men could have done to you if the Princess hadn't noticed your distress? They might have killed you. You could say we saved your life."

Valeria was silent as she cast her gaze down, knowing full well that Maleth's words were true.

"The young Princess Mika Silveraine, who you met for the first time, showed you gentleness, kindness, and compassion. And how did you return it? You returned it with a crossbow quarrel."

Valeria looked up again at Maleth as her eyes began to tear. "I was just... it's not like that at all!"

Collin turned towards Valeria. "Someone ordered you to do this."

"Yes!" She nodded vigorously as tears came down her cheeks. "I didn't want to kill her! Even if she's the Princess, she's still a child!"

Maleth let out an angry breath. "Who gave you the order to kill the Princess?" He pointed at Reid. "Was it him?"

Reid did not bother to let Valeria answer, as he responded with a mocking laugh and a raised voice. "That's right! It was me! I ordered her to take the shot! I ordered her to kill the little Royal!"

Clenching his teeth, Maleth glared at him. "Damn you."

Reid smiled with ominous obsidian eyes. "I was the one who did it! And I would do it again if given the chance!"

Tempted to separate the rebel leader's head from his body, Collin put his hand on the hilt of his sword, sheathed in his scabbard at his side, as he gave Reid a deadly stare.

Valeria watched Reid's eyes and the lines of his face that were twisted by his vengeful rage. She had to admit deep within her that he looked frightening.

"If given another chance... I'd shoot the Princess myself. Maybe an arrow in the leg or in the arm, you know, not to kill her, but just enough that she'd feel excruciating pain. And then, I would capture her, and take her away. I'd take her someplace where no one could find us. I'd strip off all her fine clothes, all that silk and lace, I'd tear it all from her body, put myself on top of her naked body, right between her thighs, and then I'd rape her hard until she screamed and bled! I would impregnate her, wait until she gave birth, and take her child! I would force her to watch as I piss all over it and then skewer it to death! And then lastly, I would take the Princess, rape her some more, stab her with a sword up her tight little cunt, cut her body into pieces, and feed each piece of her to the wolves!"

As nobles, Collin and Maleth were both trained to deal with some of the harsh and vulgar things one might say. However, nothing in their training prepared them for the hate-ridden words Reid had spouted.

Even Valeria was shocked. She felt sick to her stomach.

"You vulgar bastard." Maleth made a fist, and stepped forward, about to give Reid a deadly beating, but Collin stopped him with a hand on his arm.

However, Reid was not quite done. "But, you know what? The kind of pain I want to give to that little bitch of a Princess of yours is nothing compared to the pain that the Nobility and the Royal Family have given the people of Melodice! So even if I'm not the one who fucks your little Princess, it'll be someone else!"

Collin gritted his teeth, his eyes filled with rage. With one smooth and quick motion, he grabbed the hilt of a long knife on his belt, pulled it out, and swiped the blade across Reid's neck.

Valeria, along with a few nearby peasants, screamed as his blood became an ominous red rain that sprayed out of his neck. She watched as the knights pulled Reid away, letting him bleed to death on the street, his face twisted by excruciating pain.

Collin put away his knife as he glared at the dying Reid one more time.

Reid's face held an expression of horror during the last several seconds of his life, surprised by what had just been done to him. He had expected the standard execution, where he would be beheaded or stabbed with a sword or spear while knelt down. He had been hoping to die with his head held up high with defiance and pride. Instead, he was killed without warning with a knife across his neck, a disgraceful death. Very soon, life left his body, and he became motionless, his eyes still open.

Collin turned to the rest of the peasants. "You all heard what this man said! Your leader is not a Human! He's a monster!"

Maleth noted the terrified expressions of the peasants, and wondered if they truly wanted to follow such a man like Reid Alviana, a man who was full of hatred and bitterness.

Collin turned to Maleth and the other knights. "We're

finished here. Give them the rewards they have earned."

With that final order, Collin began to walk away as Maleth and the other knights drew out their long swords. Cries of fear from the peasants became louder.

As Valeria watched, she saw her companions being executed. Some of them were speared, others were stabbed, and still others were decapitated. Their final clamours of death rang cruelly in her ears, impossible to shut out with her hands restrained. Tears streamed profusely down her cheeks as she sobbed loudly.

"Miss Valeria." Maleth held his sword at his side as he stood in front of her, his voice saddened.

Valeria gazed up at him, her previous expression of defiance replaced by that of terrible fear and resignation.

Maleth regarded her with pity. This woman saw Princess Mika as a child, and never truly wanted to kill her. She had been ordered to by a man whose only concern was vengeance. He wondered what could have possessed her to join Reid and his rebel group. Nevertheless, her crime for attempting to take the life of the Princess of Melodice was punishable by death.

"Please forgive me, my dear, in the afterlife, but I cannot allow any attack on our young Princess to go unpunished."

Valeria closed her eyes as Maleth raised his sword. With one swift sideways motion of his blade, her head was separated from the rest of her body, and fell on the street. Her body fell backwards, as others around her were executed in front of hundreds of onlookers.

* * *

SEC 3566, Morrighan 33

Night began to fall outside. Princess Mika, in a short, pink nightgown with thin straps, was seated at her dressing table in front of her mirror, brushing her hair.

"Will you be all right, My Lady?" asked Angelica, as she was folding clothes while seated on one of Mika's couches. "You haven't stepped out of your bedchamber for quite a while now, not even once."

Mika glanced up at Angelica's reflection on her dressing table mirror. "I'm sorry. I've... been doing a lot of thinking. Maybe tomorrow, I can go out. How's Mirin?"

"He's fine, but he's worried about you."

"Oh... I see." Mika sighed. "I can't apologize to you enough, Miss Angelica, for taking Mirin with me on that day. I put his life in danger. I wouldn't fault you at all if you hated me for doing such a thing."

Angelica shook her head. "Princess, how many times do we have to talk about that? It's over and done. Yes, of course, I was very disappointed and terrified. I was scared for both of you! But I was glad you and Mirin returned to the castle. I was so relieved. I could never hate you, My Lady. You know I will always love you."

Mika smiled, feeling warmth surround her heart. "Thank you, Miss Angelica."

"There was only one thing I wished you had done, My Lady, and that was to use your authority as Princess to invite Mirin with you instead, even if Sir Galner had not invited him to that excursion to Cerulean. I don't mind Mirin going with you to places far away, as long as it's not stowed away in a travel chest."

Mika nodded. "The next time I go anywhere, I will invite him, and he will sit with me in the cabin."

"Thank you."

The doors to her bedchamber suddenly swung open to their fullest extent, causing a loud thud as they struck the walls at either side. King Ralphen strode into the room, glaring at his daughter.

Mika gasped, sat up from her seat, and turned around. The fiery anger she saw in her father's eyes frightened her deeply.

Angelica, startled, stood up from the couch, dropping some of the clothes she was folding from her lap. "My Lord!" She bowed slightly.

"Get out, Angelica," Ralphen ordered firmly.

Angelica nearly jumped out of her skin as she looked

down. She took one quick fearful look at Mika, who glanced back in the same fashion, then scurried past the King like a frightened fox, closing the doors behind her. The King had barged into the bedchamber of the Princess. Unfortunately, both Angelica and Mika knew what this meant.

Mika clasped her trembling hands together at her heart as she cast her widened eyes downward.

"Eighteen days have passed since that attack. I think you've recuperated sufficiently," said the King, who stared at her for a long time, as if waiting for a reaction.

Mika did not know how to react, but eventually, she gazed up just a little at her father. "Um... is... is everything all right... Father?"

Ralphen sat down on one of the couches, pushing Mika's clothes to the side, and gestured for her to come and sit on the couch that was directly across the table from him.

Mika hesitated for a moment, but if she delayed obeying, he would probably come over, grab her, slap her, and force her to go there. She slowly walked over to the couch, and sat down in the middle, directly across from Ralphen. She did not meet his gaze as she kept her eyes on the top of the table. She clasped her hands together tightly, trying to stop them from shaking, and placed them on her lap as she sat up straight with her knees together.

"Now, then," said the King. "After spending this many days recuperating, you should now be able to answer some questions for me. I need to understand what happened that day. I'm somewhat confused, so perhaps you can enlighten me."

"Um... do you mean, why the peasants attacked?"

"No, Mika. Your professor, Sir Galner, had reported to me some disturbing words and actions from you. There's a long list of things you said and did that don't make sense to me. I will have an explanation for each."

Oh no... I have to explain what I said? For some reason, I'm not surprised... and I'm certain I know what he's going to say. If what my professor thinks of the peasants is any indication, my father will probably think the same way.

"Do I make myself clear, Mika?"

Mika hesitated for a second too long.

"Answer me!"

The terrible yell reverberated throughout the entire bedchamber, startling Mika, making her heart skip a beat. "Yes, Father."

Angelica, who was listening from out in the hallway, put one hand at her heart, fearing for her poor, sweet Mika.

"Tell me what went through your mind when you saw the city of Scarletia for the first time. What did you think about it?"

Mika dared not hesitate this time as she forced herself to think quickly. "Uh... when I first saw the city, I was very shocked."

"Why?"

"Because... everyone lives in a state of extreme poverty and the city is in various states of disrepair." After saying those first few words that described what initially went through her mind, she found it a little easier to continue, though it did nothing to prevent her from feeling extremely anxious. "The streets of Scarletia are dirty, and there are cracks everywhere, as if they haven't been repaired for decades. Garbage litters the streets, and there are open sewers in some places. The buildings are old and crumbling, as if they haven't been maintained for a very long time, and I'm afraid that some of them will collapse on top of the people inside them."

The King leaned back in the couch, and crossed his arms against his chest. "From your tone, it sounds to me like this greatly worries you."

Mika nodded. "The people of Scarletia are all very poor. I saw elderly and young children begging on the streets for money. Some of them were even dressed in clothes that look like they were made of rags. Some of them were going hungry, and they were begging for money so they can at least buy something to eat, but no one's giving them money, likely because the people around them don't have much to begin with. They have to look after themselves first, and I can't fault them for that."

"Sir Galner told you that all this was normal. Didn't he?"

"Yes, he told me it was perfectly normal."

"But you don't quite agree with that, do you?"

Mika shook her head. "I don't understand how that can be normal. People are suffering out there in the city. They are living and working in terrible circumstances. I feel so sad for them. I saw a man who was being beaten by our knights, because he couldn't pay his taxes. But he couldn't because he needed what little money he had to feed his children first. Sir Galner told me that he was being punished, but I don't approve of such a punishment. Shouldn't they ensure that their children are fed first before they have to pay their taxes? And even if he can't pay his taxes, why are our knights beating him?"

Mika continued to speak while her father stayed quiet. She found it easier after a while to speak about what was on her mind and in her heart the more she spoke.

"I saw peasants handling a material called Starstone. Sir Galner told us what it was, and from what I've heard, it appears to be an extremely dangerous material. When I saw the peasants handling it, I was scared for them, for their lives. If anything were to happen, it could explode and burn them, and no one would be able to save them. Sir Galner told me, if that were to happen, that the miners were replaceable. But... I just can't think of people as being replaceable. If someone dies, they can't be replaced. Some of those men are fathers to children while others are children of fathers and mothers. Surely, they can't be replaced in the eyes of those who love them."

Ralphen raised a hand, signaling her to stop talking.

Mika obeyed immediately.

"You mentioned you don't understand why things are the way they are, Mika. You don't understand why the Peasantry are living in these conditions, why they are being punished in the way you saw them, why they are working in an unsafe manner. There are many more things you mentioned you don't understand, according to Sir Galner. I could list them all, but we'd be here discussing them all night. So allow me to clear up some confusion for you."

Mika listened intently. What was her father going to say? Was it going to be different from what Sir Galner had mentioned to her already?

"Sure, I could tell you that these things are normal, but that would probably not satisfy your inquisitive mind. You want a simple and straightforward answer. And I will give you one."

"What is it, Father?" asked Mika.

Ralphen leaned forward, leaning one arm on his knee.

Mika held her breath with anticipation.

"Simply put, they are the Peasantry. Nothing more." Ralphen leaned back again.

Mika stared with confusion. *That's the simple and straightforward answer I'm looking for? I'm more confused than before. What does he mean by that?*

"You look like you're wondering what I'm talking about. In that case, allow me to elaborate my simple and straightforward answer for you, Mika. Simply, it is their nature. It's the nature of the peasants to be inferior to us, the Nobility. They are inferior to us in every way. They are inferior physically, emotionally, mentally, socially, intellectually, and in all other aspects. Do you understand?"

Mika said nothing, partially because her father did not give her a chance to respond as he continued, and partially because she did not know what to say to that even if he did let her say anything. She clasped her small hands tighter on her lap as the cruelly condescending words her father used to describe the Peasantry stung her.

"You see, there are two kinds of Human in this world. The first is the Nobility, far more advanced and evolved. The second is the Peasantry, whose development in the aspects I mentioned are sorely lacking, and have fallen far behind ours. In the distant past, there were multiple branches of Human evolution, and we're at a point where the last branch of the Human species is slowly splitting into two. Eventually, there will be two species of Human. Given more time, of course, because of the inferiority of these... people that we call the Peasantry, they will become extinct, no longer able to keep pace with the passage of time and the course of evolution. And that, Princess Mika, is the more scientific explanation of why the peasants are the way they are and live the way they do.

"Everything about the Peasantry is testament to their evolutionary inferiority, from the decrepit way they appear, the barbaric manner in which they speak, their obscene behaviour, their inability to reason, their inability to look at the sky and ponder and dream of what is beyond, to their hostility and their aggressive tendencies which you have experienced firsthand. It's as if they are animals that we're meant to stand on, useful criminals that can at least provide cheap labour, replaceable when required."

Mika heard the pounding of her heart as her tension kept her completely motionless. Her father spoke with a calm voice, as if teaching a child about the ways of the world. Mika wondered if that was what her father believed he was doing. However, to her, it was something else entirely. Had she been half her age now, she probably would have believed him. But at this point in her life, she was old enough to form her own opinions and think critically. His explanation made absolutely no sense to her.

The peasants are an inferior form of Human? I don't remember this ever being taught in any history or science lesson or written down in any of the books I've read. Perhaps it's not written anywhere, and if it's not written anywhere... then where did this information come from? Father, what you're saying disturbs me... just like what Sir Galner said to me.

"Those miners you saw handling Starstone, as Sir Galner already mentioned to you, are replaceable. We're aware of the dangers of handling Starstone. We're aware that the workers handling it can be killed or at least severely injured if the Starstone exploded or burned, but this is not a problem. Peasants are replaceable."

Ralphen leaned forward again, his elbows on his knees as he stared into Mika's eyes. His expression hardened.

"Now, let's discuss what happened when the peasant mob attacked you and your company."

Mika's hands felt cold and clammy as she rubbed them against her thighs. She held the hem of her nightgown a little too hard, causing her fingers to ache. Mika noticed her father's voice getting louder as he spoke.

"When the peasants attacked you, Sir Maleth and his knights did their best to protect you. They defended you against those who sought to kill you. Sir Galner did the same. He used his magic to protect you, to defend you against those who sought to terminate your life! He was about to finish off these peasants when you interfered! You used your haste magic to get in front of his magic attack, and deflected it! You protected the peasants! Why did you protect the peasants? Explain your actions, Princess Mika!"

Mika clasped her hands together again hard. The words that had flowed easily out of her mouth were now lost. Seeing her father's furious eyes, she could feel the heat of his anger from across the table. She cast her eyes down. She opened her mouth, her lips quivering with fear, and tried to speak... but nothing came out.

"Look at me when I'm talking to you! I demand an explanation!"

Mika was startled again by her father's raging yell. She forced herself to meet the gaze of the King. "I protected them because...."

"Why, Mika?"

"Because... because they're my people."

Ralphen narrowed his eyes. "What are you talking about? I don't understand you referring to them as your people. These are peasants. They are to be treated as such. That is what they are and nothing more."

After all that has happened, after all she has witnessed, after all she heard from Galner, Angelica, Mirin, and now from her own father, the King of Melodice, Mika felt all kinds of emotions. She had been in turmoil, ever since the attack of the merchant assassins, but as she spent enormous amounts of time thinking about these things, her emotions become clearer to her. Sadness for the peasants and their circumstances, fear of what could happen to them should their circumstances continue, disappointment because of what she has heard from other members of the Nobility, regret over not being able to do anything for the peasants, and to her own surprise, anger for how they were being treated and being referred to as nothing more than animals and criminals that were replaceable.

No... I can't let things continue like this. Now that I know these things... I can't just let it be this way. I am the Princess of Melodice. Surely, there must be something I can do... something, anything....

Mika slowly looked up into Ralphen's eyes, despite being frightened over what might happen to her at the hands of the King. "Father...."

"What is it? Are you experiencing regret over your actions?"

Mika hesitated at first, trying her best to choose her next words carefully.

To his great dismay, Ralphen watched her slowly shake her head.

"I'm sorry, Father... but I must disagree. They are my people. They are the people of Melodice, and I'm the Princess of Melodice, and therefore, they are my people."

Ralphen put his head down for a moment, and rubbed his temples as he felt a headache coming on. His daughter easily exhausted him mentally despite her age. He gazed up, trying to calm himself, but he was having great difficulty doing so. "Sir Galner told me you protected a little peasant boy. You tended to his injuries. You became acquainted with him. You gave him food to eat."

Mika nodded slightly. "Yes, Father. He was injured. He was also hungry. That's why I tended to his injury, and gave him bread to eat. He was very sweet, and I liked him, which is why I became acquainted with him."

Ralphen stared hard at the Princess. "Mika... I don't understand any of this. Why would you do all these things for the sake of peasants?"

Mika silently drew in a slow breath as she closed her eyes. She slowly let it out as she opened her eyes, and tried to appear as calm as possible. However, the slight trembling of her hands betrayed her composure.

"Because... Father, the peasants are just as much my people as the nobles are. I love them because they are my people and I'm their Princess."

Angelica still listened from the outside, her ear against one of the doors, wondering what was going on as the room fell silent.

Mika had explained herself to the best of her ability, and expressed the basis of all her actions. Simply put, it was love. That was all it was, and yet, it was powerful enough to give her the courage to do what she has already done. Mika cast her eyes down at the top of the table in front of her, not knowing what else to say or do.

Eventually, Ralphen spoke as he leaned forward some more, seated at the very edge of the couch. "Lean forward, Mika."

Mika looked up, puzzled over the calm of her father's voice. She leaned forward to the edge of the couch, placing one hand on the table to keep from falling forward. She could not have been any less prepared for what was coming to her.

Mika felt a stinging sensation as her father slapped her. She yelped as she was thrown sideways, and fell from the couch and onto the floor, her hair covering her face. Her eyes widened with fear.

The slap was hard enough for Angelica to hear it from outside, causing her to jump and take a few steps back.

Ralphen stood up from the couch, and shouted down at her. "You speak to me with such insolence! You always were a stubborn little girl with strange ideas in your head!"

He grabbed Mika by the back of her flimsy nightgown, tearing its delicate and soft fabric as he lifted her up... and slammed her tiny body, front side down, against the table. Mika's face missed the table, but her chest, abdomen, shoulders, arms, waist, and legs were not so fortunate. Ralphen next kicked the corner of the table so hard that all four legs gave way.

Outside, the terrified Angelica heard the loud crash, and wondered what it was. She leaned against the wall, and covered her face with her hands.

Mika could hardly move her body as tears streamed down her cheeks, the side of her face against the carpet. Pain racked her entire body from head to toe.

Ralphen stood above her, staring her down as if he was glad that she was in pain. "The rebel group responsible for organizing the peasant mob and the attack on you and your company was found. Every member we could find of that rebel group was executed yesterday by Sir Collin, Sir Maleth, and their company of knights. They have earned their reward. Let's see if you can take a guess as to who we found with that rebel group. It's someone you met while traveling through the city of Scarletia. Who do you think it was, Mika?"

No, it couldn't be Sir Tyrel! No, he's too young. Oh no, please don't let it be Sir Jaren!

"You don't know? Or perhaps you don't remember? Does the name Valeria Tannlar sound familiar to you?"

Miss Valeria? No, it can't be! We saved her from being violated! Why would she...?

"This criminal was part of the rebel group. You had ordered her rescue from a group of immoral men. If you hadn't ordered her rescue, she would have been raped and possibly killed, and she wouldn't have been able to run back to her leader. Her leader wouldn't have organized the attack on your company. You would've been safely on your way to the Cerulean Magic Academy!"

So it's my fault this happened? I ordered her to be rescued and then... but hold on, why would she do that at all? We saved her! She was thankful, wasn't she? But then... why?!

Ralphen knelt down on one knee beside Mika, his boot in front of her eyes, but she looked past it as more thoughts raced through her mind, and a flurry of intense emotions assaulted her heart.

"There's more. It also turns out that Miss Valeria was a skilled crossbow sniper. She was trained as one in secret. As for the crossbow she used, it looked like standard army issue, so it must have been stolen at some point. She was the one who aimed a crossbow at you and tried to fire a quarrel into your skull, Mika! She was the one who tried to assassinate you!"

No! Why would she want to kill me? Someone had to have told her to! No... no more... I don't want to hear anymore! Please stop!

Ralphen raised his voice again as he grabbed her hair and pulled, lifting her face slightly, and causing her to grimace in pain.

"These are the peasants that you claimed are your people, people that you claimed to love! They didn't give a damn if you rescued them! Their only purpose was to do one thing and one thing only! To kill you!"

He let go of her hair, and her face fell against the carpet. The King stood up furiously, and screamed at her from above.

"Rid your mind of these... disgusting and deviant ideologies, Princess Mika! The Peasantry are nothing to us, and you are to treat them as such! They are *not* your people!"

Ralphen walked away from her, took a few steps towards the dressing table, and screamed with great rage as he pushed all her beauty items from the table. Many of the glass bottles of creams, lotions, perfumes, and scented oils flew off the table, but fortunately, none of them broke when they struck the soft, carpeted floor. He grabbed a flowerpot of roses, from which Mika had cut a rose as a goodbye present for Sir Terren Rinaldia, and threw it with all his might against the dressing table. With a terrifying sound, the mirror broke into a thousand pieces, shards flying everywhere.

Mika screamed as she heard these sounds of violence.

The King straightened his coat, and turned around, causing his cape to fly around him. He headed for the double doors, and swung them open. As Ralphen stormed out of the bedchamber, he saw Mika's maidservant.

Angelica leaned against the wall with tension and fear, her hands clasped together at her heart, tears in her eyes. She nearly met his gaze, so she cast her eyes down and away.

Ralphen walked down the hallway with loud and furious steps that echoed on the marble floor.

As soon as he was gone, Angelica rushed into Mika's

room, and saw Mika on top of the collapsed table lying face down.

"Princess Mika!"

Angelica rushed over to Mika's side, and helped her turn so she could be face-up.

Mika winced in pain as she did so. She was only able to turn on her side. "Miss Angelica...."

"Princess Mika!" Angelica examined her quickly. The left side of her face where she had been slapped was red. She had bitten her lip when she had been slapped, causing it to bleed. Her hair was disheveled. The front and back of her nightgown had been torn down the sides and below the straps, forcing her into a state of half-undress.

Her vision blurry from tears, Mika saw the opened doors of her bedchamber, so she struggled to move one arm to cover her exposed breasts. In her pitiful state, she did not want to be seen by anyone.

"Everything hurts..." Mika whispered, but physical pain was the least of what was hurting her at the moment.

Angelica cried, tears coming down her cheeks, as she held Mika, stroking her hair. "I can't believe the King would do this to you, My Lady! Why is he always beating you? This is the worst he's done to you so far! I can't stand it!"

Mika's tears soaked into the carpet, as well as on the remains of the table. Her sobs became louder as she struggled to speak.

"What is it, My Lady? What is it?" Angelica strained to hear what the Princess was trying to say as she knelt down closer to her.

"They are my people... they are... my people."

The image of Sir Terren flashed in Mika's mind. She remembered giving the Royal Message for him, his farewell speech for everyone, and his final goodbye outside the castle. Mika remembered him kissing her hand, giving him a rose as a goodbye present, and then... words he uttered that were peculiar to her at the time.

They made sense to her now.

Mika concluded that Sir Terren knew these things would happen. He knew the way she thought, the way her mind worked, and the way she felt in her heart. By the words that she has said and the actions that she has taken so far, she has already planted the seeds of a growing rebellion in her heart.

"They're *my people*... I can't abandon them."

I won't. I won't ever stop loving them. I am their Princess, and I will be the one who will protect them!

"Because... because I am... *I am....*"

I am the Princess of Melodice, Mika Silveraine!

CHAPTER 12

SECRECY

SEC 3566, Morrighan 37

A FEW DAYS AFTER THE BEATING she received from her father, Princess Mika limped through the halls of the castle. Her physician had told her to stay within the vicinity of her bedchamber, but Mika, always the stubborn little girl, ventured out farther than she was supposed to. Her entire body still ached, mostly on the front side from her chest and shoulders and all the way down to her knees, and even some parts of her ankles and feet. The prominent red and black bruise beside her left eye ached. She was fortunate that her bones were intact. The neckline of her silk, pink and white dress was high, completely covering the bruises on her chest, and her long sleeves fell below her wrists. Because the hem of her dress stopped only just below mid-thigh, she hid the bruises on her legs and thighs with opaque black stockings. As always, when she was not in her room, she wore the Princess Gem around her neck.

Mika had not seen her father or mother in the last few days. She wondered if this was also her punishment, being shunned by her parents and not being seen by them. As she continued down the hallway, she used the wall for support, while pain accompanied each step she took.

Mirin was about to walk down an intersecting hallway, but stopped when he saw the Princess, limping away down another hallway. "Mika!"

Mika stopped to turn towards where the voice came

from. As soon as she saw Mirin, her facial expression became bright. She waved at him.

Mirin rushed over to where she was, and noticed right away her slight limp and the bruise around her eye. He heard from Angelica what the King had done, and it made him angry and afraid inside. "Are you all right? Is there a lot of pain?"

Mika shrugged, which made her wince. "I'm… fine, Mirin. My body will heal, as it always does."

"I can't believe the King would do this to you. I know he does this quite often, but this is the worst so far. After all these beatings, I'm surprised he hasn't broken any bones yet. You may be scrawny but… I'm surprised at how your body can just take all that."

Mika smiled. "I am built pretty tough."

"Oh? All jesting aside… still… I'm worried about you."

"I know… but, Mirin, if you don't mind, I would rather not talk about that."

"I'm sorry."

Mika tried to walk towards him, releasing her hand from the wall as she limped. Mirin went closer to her, and she rested her hands on his outstretched arms. She stood in front of him, close to him.

"Don't be. Besides, I'm very happy that, at least, you still talk to me. The King and Queen haven't seen me for days now. Perhaps the beating from my father was only half the punishment, and the rest of it is…." Mika shook her head, realizing what she was doing. "Never mind, I told you I didn't want to talk about it, and here I am talking about it."

Mirin chuckled. "That's fine. Well… I suppose the plan we put together didn't quite work out. I wanted to see the Cerulean Magic Academy as well, even though I'm not Sir Galner's student, even though I have no magical ability."

A blush formed on Mika's cheeks. "I can't believe I put you in my travel chest with all my clothes. I hope you didn't touch anything… like my undergarments, for example."

The thought of being that close to the Princess's undergarments while inside her travel chest made Mirin's cheeks turn red with embarrassment. "How was I supposed to avoid touching anything when I was cramped in a small space like that? Especially when I was covered by some of your dresses just in case anyone opened it. It was cramped and hot in there. The only reason I could breathe was because there were small gaps between the wood panels."

"But we never did make it to our destination, let alone leave the city."

Mirin nodded. "Yes, you're right. Terrible things happened that day. It's a miracle that we came out of it alive."

Silence fell between them. Mirin wondered what was on her mind while Mika stared at him for a long time. He stared back questioningly, asking her silently what was wrong.

Mika leaned her head on his shoulder. Her voice dropped to a whisper. "I'm so sorry…. I'm sorry, Mirin…."

"What? What's wrong?" asked Mirin, surprised.

"I put you in so much danger. I wish I hadn't put you in my travel chest. When it fell from the carriage, you were still in it, and I was so scared that something might happen to you. I honestly thought you were going to die. If I had just convinced Sir Galner to take you with us, as Miss Angelica had suggested to me because I had the authority to invite you, even if he didn't agree, then you could have sat with us in the cabin, instead of you having to endure the cramped interior of my travel chest. If you had died that day… I don't know how I would deal with it. I wouldn't be sure how to tell Miss Angelica that you had been killed. I would be far too disturbed by it. I might not… want to live anymore if you were taken away from me, if you had died."

Mirin put his hands on her shoulders, and made her look up at him. "Mika, come on now, don't say that. First of all, if I had died, I would want you to keep living. Second, you couldn't have seen the future. I would have been fine in your travel chest for the entire trip, as long as you gave me food and water in secret. We didn't know we were going to be attacked by a peasant mob and crossbow snipers. If I had been riding in the cabin with you, I would still have been in the same danger."

Mika was taken aback by what Mirin said, because that was exactly what had been nagging her in the back of her mind, a part of her that tried to convince her that she was not at fault. It was a thought she had tried to push away. Hearing it from Mirin validated it. "I suppose you're right."

"Of course, I'm right. In fact, I'm alive because of you. Helen is alive because of you as well. She carried me as she ran back to the carriage, and you used your magic to protect us from the quarrels. We could have been killed, but you protected us both. I haven't had the opportunity to tell you how thankful I am, since you've been in your bedchamber all this time, but thank you, Mika."

"I'm glad you're fine. Miss Angelica must have been angry with you, but I hope she didn't yell at you or anything of the sort."

Mirin simply laughed. "No, she didn't yell at me. She was angry, yes, and she was disappointed and scared, but she was fine. She cried a few times, and kept hugging me over and over again though."

"That's because she loves you. You may not be related, but she loves you like a mother loves her son."

"Yes, and I do love her, too."

Mika nodded as she smiled sweetly. "I'm glad."

"By the way, Helen is thankful as well," said Mirin.

Mika was suddenly confused. "Huh?"

"When you surrounded us with the magic barrier, she whispered something, and I could hear it because she was carrying me. She said 'Princess, thank you.' I was surprised when I heard it."

"She said that?" asked Mika.

Mirin chuckled, amused by Mika's state of disbelief. "She did! She truly did!"

Mika's smile returned. She was surprised to hear this from Mirin. Even though it was gratitude from Helen, it felt nice. It was not something she expected. "I wonder... that's not something she would say in front of my face, I'm certain."

Mirin shrugged with a grin. "Probably not. I wouldn't bring it up with her either, if I were you. We know how she is."

"I wouldn't dream of it. I'm happy she felt that way though."

A few civilians passed by in the hallway. Normally, they would have greeted Mika. However, they noticed that the Princess was in conversation with her friend, so they passed her by without greeting, because doing so would be considered interrupting a conversation between a Royal and someone else. It would be considered rude.

Mika noticed their long glances, and knew that they saw the bruise around her left eye. She pulled away from Mirin for a moment, and leaned against the wall.

"Are you all right, Mika?"

"Please... don't worry about me." Mika looked up, and saw someone in the periphery of her vision down the hallway.

It was Helen. In her usual knight's uniform, she walked down an intersecting hallway slowly enough that when she turned her head, she saw the Princess. Helen gazed at Mika, who gazed right back. In just a few seconds, she disappeared.

Mika took Mirin's hand. "I need to talk to you about something."

"What is it?" Mirin asked.

"Not out here. Come."

Mika limped down the hallway, putting her arm through his. They headed down another wide hallway, and found a narrow corridor that led to one of the storage rooms.

Mirin was puzzled. "Why are we here?"

"The halls are busy with people going back and forth. Here, not so much. I don't want anyone hearing our conversation."

"Oh... but why? You said you needed to talk to me about something? What is it?"

"I don't know if you saw it, but when I stopped the magic attack from Sir Galner, I protected a boy named Tyrel

Balias. I tended to his injury, and I gave him some bread to eat because he was quite hungry. I became acquainted with him and his older brother whose name was Jaren Balias."

"I didn't see it, but I heard about it. Miss Angelica told me everything that happened. She was told by one of the lady knights that she's acquainted with—I think she said her name was Miss Tanari. What of them, Mika?"

There was something Mika wanted to tell Mirin, something she wanted to do, in fact, but she was worried about how he was going to react to it. But he was the one person whom she trusted more than anyone else in the entire castle. Because of that, she thought he may be able to understand.

"I want to find them and their family."

Greatly surprised, Mirin looked around, making sure there was no one around them. "Why?!" he asked, trying to keep his voice down. "You want to see peasants?"

Mika nodded. "They're not just peasants, Mirin. They're people as well."

Mirin looked perplexed. "What do you mean?"

He really doesn't understand. I guess he was taught to think of them as being inferior like the rest of the Nobility. But he needs to at least understand what I want to do and why I want to do it. Please, Mirin....

Mika collected her thoughts as she put her hands over her face for a moment. She leaned her back against the wall for support. She gestured for him to stand against the wall beside her, as close to her as possible, so they could speak softly, but still hear each other.

"I want to know the truth about the state of the people of our nation."

"The truth?" said Mirin. "I'm confused. What truth?"

"When I saw the city of Scarletia for the first time, I realized that everyone out there, all the peasants, live in extreme poverty. It's horrible. Their homes look like they could collapse any moment because they're in such a decrepit state. Elderly and children are begging for money on the side of the street. Some of them can't even afford to pay for new clothes, so they wear clothes made of rags. The knights would punish them by beating them, just because they fed their children before they paid their taxes. Everyone is living in harsh circumstances. Somehow, they're surviving, but barely.

"When I asked Sir Galner and my father about the things I saw, I was told that it's normal, that this is the nature of the Peasantry, and that this is their way of life. But it doesn't make sense to me. How is it normal for so many people to be suffering and living in poverty? Is that normal, Mirin?"

Mirin was not sure how to answer. "Um… well, I suppose it is… but when you say it that way… I suppose I think it's normal because the adults have always told me that it's normal."

"We usually believe what the adults tell us. But what if the adults are wrong? People can be wrong sometimes, so why can't adults?"

"Um… I suppose you're right… they can be wrong as well. I've been told that no one is perfect."

"It's apparently an accepted fact that the Peasantry live the way they do, and are naturally inferior to us. We are told that things are just the way they are, and that it's all normal. Hasn't anyone questioned the normality of what I saw? Like I said before, how can it be normal for people to live with such suffering? In such poverty? We don't live with suffering. We have food readily available to us and plenty of money. We have the finest clothes that we can wear and beautiful rooms to sleep in. We live differently from the peasants. But why is it different? Because they're naturally inferior? Because that's just the way things are? That doesn't make sense to me. Again, how is that normal?"

Mirin remembered a brief discussion with one of his professors regarding the Peasantry, where the professor shared with him and his classmates what was considered to be an accepted fact. "Well… I learned a short while ago that they're apparently a different type of Humans. Miss Aryn said so."

"Truly? Miss Aryn told you? Did she show you from a book?"

Thinking back, Mirin shook his head. There was no book.

"I thought so. Miss Aryn is a member of the Nobility. She'll tell you the same thing that everyone else has been telling me about the Peasantry. But how is that true? They don't look any different from me. Their faces look like ours. They have two arms and two legs and a head. They speak the same language as we do. They smile when they're happy, and they cry when they're sad. They built homes, and they worked hard to support their families and feed their children. They must love their children the way nobles do. They're able to...." Mika hesitated for a moment before continuing, swallowing the lump that formed in her throat. "They're able to plan an assassination attempt, so they must have the same level of intelligence as we do. They can slip past armed guards on a merchant carriage unnoticed. Surely, they must be just as intelligent as we are. So how are they different? How is it that they're considered to be different—even inferior—from the rest of the race of Humans? By the way, I've never read any of that in books on science and history, and you know that I read many, many books. I'm not certain I can believe what Miss Aryn told you."

Mirin was thinking as well, listening and trying to hang on to Mika's words that were full of wisdom. He tried to keep up with her train of thought as much as possible, though he had to admit that it was very challenging. She was only a year older than he was, and yet, she could think like this.

"So, again, how is that normal?" asked Mika.

"When you think about it that way, no, it doesn't sound normal at all. It sounds very strange. It doesn't make sense," replied Mirin.

"And whenever I ask, I'm told that there's nothing for me to be concerned about. But I've recently thought about whom I was asking... and I've been asking members of the Nobility. I've been asking people who are biased and see themselves as being more important than the peasants somehow. That's why... I need to find out the truth. But to find out the truth, I can't ask a noble. I want to hear the truth from the peasants. That's why I want to find Sir Jaren and Sir Tyrel and their family. I want to talk to them. I want to hear their side of this terrible story. I want to hear it from the mouths of peasants."

"But, Mika, surely you can find a noble that... might share the same opinions as you. It's a huge castle with ten thousand people living in it. There must be at least a few."

"That's not the same as hearing it from someone who has actually experienced it. And there's something else I'm thinking about."

"What is it?"

"I've been thinking about what the peasants said to me, the angry ones. I remember what the people in the peasant mob were shouting. They were talking about punishing me for the crimes of the Royal Family and the Nobility against the nation of Melodice. They called us criminals, and said we need to face justice. They say we have tarnished our nation."

Clenching his fist, Mirin remembered the words of the angry peasants, which he had heard while stowed away in Mika's travel chest, words that made his blood boil. "But those peasants were criminals! That's why the Nobility are saying they're inferior! They don't know what they're talking about!"

"Truly?" Mika spoke quickly, her words completely free of her tendency to stammer. "Why would so many people share the same anger and shout the same accusations? If they feel that the Nobility and the Royal Family have committed crimes against the nation and that we are all criminals, what do they mean by that? When I think about it, I think about their poverty. I think about the way they're living, about how everyone seems to be referring to them as peasant dogs and animals, about how they're being classed as inferior to the Nobility, how the knights are treating them, and how Sir Galner and my father talk about them. Do you know what I think, Mirin?"

Mirin stayed quiet. He still wanted to convince Mika that the people who attacked her were criminals, but he was unable to find fault in her words.

Mika stared at the wall across the corridor they stood in, her expression dead serious as she paused to choose her next words carefully. However, no matter what words she thought of, she could not find a less controversial way to say what she needed to next.

"I think... the Peasantry are living in suffering... because the Nobility and the Royal Family have made it that way."

Mirin stared at her, shocked by what she had just said. If he did not know any better, he could have sworn she had just accused the Nobility and the Royal Family of wrongdoing. It was something completely frowned upon.

"That's... a very bold accusation, Princess Mika."

Mika was silent for a while as well. If word of this were to reach her father, he would be furious. A beating would be the least of her worries. "Yes... it is a bold accusation. That's exactly what it is. I want to know the truth from the peasants, specifically Sir Jaren and Sir Tyrel and their parents."

"How do you propose to do that, Mika?"

"I have to leave the castle."

Greatly surprised, Mirin grabbed her by the arm. "No! You can't leave the castle. It's dangerous out there. And ever since the attack of the merchant assassins, there have been more armed guards at the gates. They're not just simply going to let you through, even if you're the Princess. Only the King or the Queen can allow you to go through."

"I know it's probably almost impossible to leave the castle of my own accord. But I have to find a way," said Mika. "Come, let's go back, Mirin."

Mika and Mirin stepped out of the side corridor, Mika's arm through Mirin's. However, as soon as they stepped out of the corridor and into the hallway, Mika gasped, startled.

"Miss Helen!" said Mika, her eyes wide.

Mirin was startled as well. "Helen!"

Helen stood against the wall of the main hallway, at the edge of the wall that gave way to the narrow side corridor where Mika and Mirin had been. Her arms were crossed against her chest, and her expression was an ominously dead calm.

"Princess Mika, you should take more care in choosing your words, and find a more appropriate place to discuss your intentions."

Mika and Mirin stiffened with anxiety. Mika stared up at Helen, somewhat frightened. "Um... you... you heard what we were talking about?"

"Every word," said Helen, keeping her voice down. "If I didn't know any better, I would think your words are prelude to treachery. Are you, by any chance, thinking of inciting a rebellion?"

Mika was taken aback. "No! Why would I do that?" She looked down and away from her, casting her eyes on the carpeted hardwood floor of the hallway, her hand clamping around Mirin's arm a little more tightly. "That's not what I was thinking about."

"All right, let's see about that. You just went on a long speech questioning the normality of the living conditions of the Peasantry and how it's different from the Nobility and a multitude of other things that I don't care to recite for you. Frankly, My Lady, for someone who is quiet, reserved, shy, and timid, you talk too much. Also, you, the Princess of Melodice, have just accused the Nobility and her own Royal Family of being the very cause of the suffering the Peasantry is experiencing. If that doesn't sound like the beginnings of a rebellious streak, I don't know what does."

Mika's heart skipped a beat as she gazed up at Helen with a frightened expression. "Are you... going to tell Sir Collin?" If Helen told Sir Collin, the King would hear about it next. If her King were to hear about her words just now, he would probably have her executed.

"You better not," said Mirin.

Helen smirked. "No, of course not. I wouldn't tell Sir Collin," she said softly, and then turned towards Mika and Mirin. "I'll be honest with you, Princess Mika, and what I'm about to tell you remains between the three of us."

"Huh? What is it?" asked Mika. She exchanged curious glances with Mirin.

Helen looked around to make sure there were no nobles nearby. "I'll admit I was also greatly disturbed when

I saw the city of Scarletia for the first time in my life and the state of the people living there. The peasants are living in such horrid conditions. I saw everything you saw, the children begging on the streets, the elderly emaciated as if they had not eaten for days, and many other things that turned my stomach."

Mika gasped. "So you agree with me."

"Earlier, you were wondering if there are other people in this castle who share your opinions about how the peasants are being treated by the Nobility and the Royal Family." Helen noticed a few nobles coming down the hallway.

When she stopped speaking, Mika and Mirin heard their footsteps from behind, but did not look back. All three of them waited for the nobles to pass them. After that, Helen went into the corridor where Mika and Mirin had been, motioning them to come with her. They followed her into the corridor, farther down than they originally were.

"As I was saying, you wondered if anyone else thought the same way as you did. I will tell you that there are some who have seen the Peasantry and how they are living, and they do believe they're being oppressed by the Nobility. I don't know who they are for certain, but I've heard about them from other knights. The other knights who have told me about them may or may not be among those who share this opinion. If they are, they need to protect themselves, so they may feign speaking of the peasants as criminals. You're not the only one. In fact, I will tell you right now, I share your thoughts and opinions."

Mika began to smile, and for a moment, she no longer felt intimidated by Helen's presence. "Miss Helen...."

"As I said before, this stays between the three of us."

"We wouldn't tell a soul," said Mirin.

"Of course," said Mika.

"While we were in the carriage with Sir Galner, there were many times I wanted to question him as well, but I wouldn't have been able to do so in the same manner as you. I would've been much more hostile, and I would've started telling him exactly how I felt. There would have been consequences for me as soon as I returned to the castle. I would have probably lost my position, and then locked up in the dungeon right away for uttering words of treachery. I had to stay calm, and I couldn't say anything. There were many things he said that irritated me, but I had to control myself."

"I understand, Miss Helen. It must have been very difficult for you. I'm sorry that you had to experience that."

"You should not be the one to apologize, My Lady."

Mika let go of Mirin's arm as she clasped her hands together in front of her at her heart. "You truly meant everything you said just now? You agree with me, and you do see that there's something not quite right about any of this?"

Helen nodded. "Yes, I do. And I also agree that you can't truly ask a noble if you want to know the truth about the world. They've been brought up to believe certain things. They're convinced that everything is as it should be, and they're taught to accept it all as fact. It's similar to your mother telling you that your name is Mika, and then you just take it as fact. But what if you're not? Not saying that you're not, because you are. But what if you were any other child? What if you had been adopted by a noble family, and they gave you a name? It wasn't your original name because your real mother gave you a different name first, perhaps a peasant family, but you didn't know about it, and you didn't have the awareness back then. You accepted the name that was given to you by your noble family as your true name, and didn't question it. You saw no reason to question it. That's the name you gave to others when they asked you for your name. That's similar to the rest of the Nobility and perhaps all Humans as well, including peasants. You're told something, and you're told that it's a fact, and you accept it without question. Then you tell others the same thing, and the cycle repeats."

Mika hung on to every word. She understood everything Helen said.

To Mirin, it went over his head. He did not expect Helen to have such deep words.

However, Mika was not surprised at all. "But then, Miss Helen, every so often in history, someone always comes along who questions the accepted facts, and tries to find out the truth behind them. That's how some people have made their discoveries, for example. They made discoveries that changed the world around them, usually for the better."

Helen smiled. "That's right. Without such discoveries, our civilization would not have progressed the way it has."

Mika was surprised by Helen's smile, which was certainly more prominent than usual, and not the kind of smile Mika was used to seeing. *I've never seen Miss Helen smile so fully. More often, she smirked at me or held a mocking grin. A real smile this time. Miss Helen is so beautiful when she smiles like this. She should do it more often.*

"It would appear that you and I think similarly, Princess Mika."

"I agree." Mika giggled in front of Helen. When she realized she did that, she was surprised at herself.

Completely bewildered, Mirin blinked a few times. "I didn't understand any of that just now. Miss Helen, you think odd thoughts, just like the Princess."

"The Princess has more odd thoughts than I do," said Helen.

"Rude as always, aren't you, Helen?" countered Mirin.

"I would think someone who's on a first-name-only basis with the Princess is rude as well."

Mika watched as Helen and Mirin exchanged witty comments, with Helen's being even more so than Mirin's. She thought about Helen and what she learned about her just now.

Miss Helen agrees with me. She also believes it's not right for the peasants to be treated as they are. Does that mean... she's on my side? If she's on my side, does that mean she would be able to help me? There's no one else in the castle I can ask for help, is there? She's the only one I know who shares my thoughts. She's a knight, as well as a Magic Knight, with great talent in swordsmanship and magic. Miss Helen... she doesn't think very highly of me. She intimidates me, sometimes with purpose, and she teases me. She sees me as a coward and a weakling, which is how I see myself as well. But… there truly is no one else I can ask for help. She's the only one who can help me.

"Miss Helen," said Mika.

Helen and Mirin stopped.

Mika opened her mouth, but the words would not come out. She wanted to ask Helen. She tried to force herself from within, but her timid nature was trying to stop her. She began doubting herself. Is it something that Helen would agree to? Agreeing with her opinions and thoughts was one thing, but agreeing to help her with what she needed to do was something else entirely.

Helen frowned at Mika after that long moment of silence. "You look like you want to ask me something. Speak up, Princess."

One hand on his waist, Mirin pointed an accusing finger at Helen. "See what I mean? Rude."

"Still your tongue, Mirin," countered Helen, without giving him a look.

Mika was taken aback by how obvious it was on her face that she wanted to ask Helen something. She sighed heavily, trying to calm down. She clasped her hands together in front of her… and as she gathered her thoughts, her words began to flow more easily.

"Miss Helen?"

"What is it?" asked Helen.

"As the Princess of Melodice, I would ask you if you could be of assistance to me."

"Assistance?"

"I would like to understand my people better. As you're aware, I became acquainted with two peasant boys, Jaren and Tyrel Balias. They must live somewhere in the city of Scarletia, perhaps near the area where I met them, and they must be living with their mother and father. I'd like to meet with them, talk with them, and find out from them the truth about the world from their perspective."

Helen stared at Mika for a long time, surprised by her request.

All this time, I always thought she was a coward and a weakling. Lately, she's been showing signs of courage. Perhaps the ordeals she has lived through are forcing her to mature. I'm impressed.

She turned to face the Princess. A small smile appeared. "You're my Princess. You're also my colleague in the area of magical studies. We share the same opinions about the suffering that the peasants are being forced to endure in the name of the Nobility and the Royal Family. I will help you."

The surprised Princess gasped. "You will?"

"That's what I said."

"Thank you!" Mika resisted the urge to hug Helen, because she was fairly certain that she would not appreciate it, not with her personality.

Mirin was surprised as well. "You truly will help her, Miss Helen?"

"Must I say it a third time?" Helen rolled her eyes with impatience. "However, in order to find the Balias family, we'll have to act covertly. We can't arouse anyone's suspicion, or neither of us will live to tell about it, Princess Mika. But if we were to find them, you would be able to meet with them, and gain the understanding you are searching for. Perhaps I will as well."

Mika nodded, and smiled brightly with excitement. "Agreed. But how will we be able to leave the castle and find the Balias family? I don't know where they live. I only assumed they live near the area where we were attacked. I don't know how to navigate the city."

"You can leave the technical details to me. There are many ways to exit the castle covertly at different times of the day and night. The library contains census records, so we'll be able to determine who they are and where they live. There will also be maps of the city streets that we can use."

Mirin crossed his arms against his chest, and smirked at Helen. "Well, then, Miss Helen, it appears to me that you've finally decided to show the Princess some respect."

Helen shot him her cold, infamous frown.

Mirin was surprised. Being subjected to the frown of Helen Renier was not something you wanted. He stiffened, but he stared back at her, trying to look defiant. Slowly, he observed her frown give way into a sneer as she bent down to rest her hands on her knees, putting her face at the same level as his.

Mika watched them, and wondered what was about to happen.

"So, Mirin, you were in Princess Mika's travel chest with all her feminine finery. Not just her finery, but also items of the more private category," said Helen, the tone of her voice mocking.

Stunned, Mirin took a couple of steps back until he hit his head against the wall behind him. He grimaced as he felt an ache that lasted a moment.

Mika was shocked as well, as she covered her mouth with both hands.

A blush appeared on Mirin's cheeks. "What... what are... what are you talking about?"

"Don't tell me you don't know, Sir Mirin. You were lying either on top of or next to some of the things the beautiful Princess Mika Silveraine would wear underneath her pretty little dresses. These are the kinds of items that girls and women wear, by the way. Have you come up with a favourite so far? Was your interest piqued by the smooth nylon and elegant designs of her thigh-high stockings, or were you more interested in the simplicity of her plain but luxuriously soft cotton knickers? You do know she's wearing them right now, don't you? In fact, all girls and women do. I wear them all the time as well, even now. But when it comes to the Princess, which kind of young man are you, Sir Mirin? Soft and smooth knickers or elegant thigh-high stockings?"

Mirin growled as his cheeks became even redder. "Why, you?!" he exclaimed furiously. Helen was mocking him in the most embarrassing way. He wanted to say something, but no words could counter Helen's.

But no one was more embarrassed than Mika herself. She backed away several steps, staring at Mirin with shock, her face red from deep embarrassment. "Are you... are you that kind of boy, Mirin?" she asked, her voice quivering. "It was embarrassing enough to have you hide in my travel chest... but... but were you touching my undergarments after all?"

"What are you insinuating? No!" Mirin ran his fingers through his hair with frustration. "Mika, please, don't think of me that way! I'm not like that! I promise you! I didn't touch anything!"

Helen put her head down, and covered her mouth, then turned away from them, as if trying to hide her face. She leaned into the opposite wall, her back to both Mika and Mirin. She made a strange sound, as if she was almost sobbing, but it was not quite that.

"Miss Helen?" asked Mika, puzzled by the sounds she made.

Mirin stepped closer to Helen, and went around her to see what was happening to her. When he realized what she was doing, he turned to Mika with an annoyed expression. "She's laughing at us."

Mika was taken aback. After a moment of recovering from some of her embarrassment, she sighed. Helen may have been making fun of both of them, especially Mirin, but at least she agreed with Mika about the peasants. Mika could not help but smile a little while Helen was hiding her laugh.

But now, Helen had become Mika's ally. Mika was now much more confident that she would be able to find out the truth about the world around her.

CHAPTER 13

UNDER DARKNESS

SEC 3566, Morrighan 38

THE NEXT NIGHT, ANGELICA TUCKED Mika into bed, wrapping her up in her warm blankets, fluffing up the pillows on which she laid her head, as well as the pillows at either side of her to prevent her from rolling off the bed. Mika sometimes still did this, despite her age, and if reminded of this, she would deny it to no end. The only lights in her bedchamber were a few candles and one bright kerosene lamp.

Mika briefly glanced at the windows to look outside. There was no hint of moonlight in the late night sky. *It's very dark. The night is perfect.*

"Are you comfortable, My Lady?" asked Angelica.

Mika nodded, pulling the blanket up to her chin, and feeling its softness between her fingers. "Very much so, Miss Angelica, thank you."

"I'm glad." Angelica stroked Mika's hair. "I'm going to blow out the candles and take the lamp, Princess. Good night and sweet dreams."

Mika pushed down the sheets just a little, her skinny arms reaching out to Angelica for her usual hug and kiss. Angelica bent down to allow the Princess to embrace her. Mika kissed Angelica on the cheek, and Angelica did the same.

"Good night, Miss Angelica," Mika said with a slightly melancholy tone.

Angelica laughed as she pulled away. "You sound like you won't be seeing me for a long time, Princess."

Hearing that, Mika stiffened as Angelica turned away. Mika watched her blow out the candles and take the kerosene lamp with her. As she opened one of the double doors on her way out, she turned to face Mika, and gave a slight curtsy. "See you in the morning, My Lady."

Mika waved at Angelica, who closed the door. The absence of the lamp and candlelight made Mika's bedchamber significantly darker. She let her eyes adjust, observed her surroundings, and listened. There was complete silence. One of the windows was opened, allowing the summer night's air to enter, cooling the room. She saw the rustling of the curtains as a light breeze played with them.

"I hope this works."

From underneath her pillows, Mika pulled out her timepiece. In the almost impenetrable blackness of her room, even with eyes adjusted, she struggled to determine the exact time as she held the timepiece at different angles to see the position of its hands. Eventually, she found the right angle, and watched the hands as they ticked away. She had to wait another quarter hour, so she used that time to contemplate.

Am I doing the right thing? I'm betraying the Nobility and the Royal Family. I'm going against their wishes. If I head out into the city with Miss Helen, we could both be in great danger. It's possible that we'll be attacked, just like what happened to me, even though we'll be under the cover of darkness. I could just stay in this bed, where it's safe. After all… I'm just a little girl.

But what would happen? Nothing would happen. I still wouldn't know the truth. I still wouldn't know the story of the world from the perspective of the peasants. Everything would be the same. The peasants would still be suffering, and the nobles would continue to look down upon them. I may be just a little girl who is frightened easily by many things, and I'm certain many people think I'm a coward and a weakling… but I also know who I am.

No, I have to do this. I must do this! For my people! For such is my duty… as the Princess of Melodice!

The minutes ticked by slowly. Mika thought about the plan she and Helen had put together last night.

We have to blend into the darkness of the night. Miss Helen mentioned I should dress in black. But the problem is I don't have very much black clothing. Oh wait, I have a cloak. It's somewhat old and I don't like it. It's not completely black either because it shimmers somewhat. That might be a problem. Miss Helen also told me I should dress as casually as possible. Basically, she's saying to try to dress like a peasant. How am I supposed to do that? I don't have any old clothes that are black and worn out. That's probably the most black I can get! But it's still much too elegant for a girl pretending to be a peasant.

At exactly 11:00, Mika pushed away the blankets and pillows, swinging her legs over the side of her bed. In her pink nightgown, she ran for the doors, instantly regretting it as she felt pain shoot through her legs, so she slowed to a careful walk. Even in the darkness, she navigated easily without hitting her knees or feet on anything, because she knew the exact layout of her bedchamber. She knew what each dark shape was as she passed them by. The back of one of the couches to her left. The chair at her dressing table to her right. At the doors, she placed her ear against the smooth algerwood surface, and listened for any hint of stirring outside. There was none.

She returned to her bed, and arranged the pillows, pulling the blankets over them to make it look like there was someone—her—still sleeping in the bed. It was just in case Angelica came by to check on her during the night.

Mika went to her dressing table, where a new mirror had been installed to replace the one her father had broken. She lifted up her nightgown to pull it over her head, grimacing as she felt pain in her arms and shoulders. She stared at her dark reflection, nude except for knickers. Though she could not see her bruises in the dark, she knew they were still there, all over her chest, shoulders, upper arms, waist, and thighs. She also knew that they had faded slightly. Even so, they were taking a long time to heal. She touched the area around her left eye, still feeling some pain, even though the colour was back to normal.

The Princess headed into her wardrobe, but it was darker in there than the rest of her bedchamber. She rummaged around for the black cloak she knew she had, and after a moment, she found it on a hanger at the very back of a row of hanging clothes. She found more clothes she needed, and took them to the club chair near one of her windows so she could see more clearly. She looked at her timepiece again. She was late.

Mika quickly pulled on white stockings to just above mid-thigh, but in her haste, they were not quite as smooth on her legs as she would like. She chose a simple white dress with a high neckline in order to hide the bruises on her chest and a hem that stopped just above her knees. Mika had some black shoes, but could not find them, so she instead opted for a pair of flat white shoes. She found her Princess Gem at the dressing table, attached it to her golden necklace, and put it on. Over her dress, she put on her black cloak, buttoned it, and tied the ribbon at her chest to cover her diamond. She asked herself why she stood in front of the mirror as she weaved a black ribbon through her hair, since she could hardly see anything anyway. To do this, she relied only on finger dexterity. She kept the hood off her head for now.

At the double doors, she looked back at her bedchamber. She was about to venture out into the dark hallways of her castle and to the outside, where Helen was probably waiting for her by now.

"I will do this... I must," she whispered to herself as she inhaled deeply and exhaled slowly in an attempt to alleviate her tension. With one gentle pull, she opened one of the doors, making sure it made no sound when she closed it. At last, she left her bedchamber, and limped down the hallway, right past the room which Angelica and Mirin shared.

Mika had already planned her route. She knew which hallways to use, many of which were still lit up by a few lamps mounted on the walls. Occasionally, she encountered a noble civilian still awake and strolling through the hallways, so she hid. She listened and looked carefully through the darkness to avoid being discovered, moving from one shadow to another only when it was safe to do so. Her small stature was also to her advantage. She could hide very easily, and her soft footsteps could not be heard.

She descended a stairway that led to the first level of the castle. Fortunately, by this time of the night, most people had retired to their rooms. The hallways were almost completely empty. Once she reached the first level, she limped off the stairway, and leaned against the wall, feeling aches all over her body. She stopped to catch her breath and calm the pounding of her heart, while making sure she was still under the cover of darkness.

After a moment, Mika continued down the gloomy hallways. She eventually reached one of the side exits. She looked behind her to make sure there was no one, and as soon as she was certain of that, she opened the door. Mika stepped outside into the night, feeling the gentle coolness of the air brush past her cheeks.

"You're late."

Mika gasped, letting go of the door as she turned around. She saw Helen sitting on a wooden bench along the path that led from the side exit. She realized right away that she'd let go of the door, so she grabbed it by the handle before it could close and make a loud sound. She eased it gently to its closed position.

"Do you know how long I've been waiting, Princess Mika?" asked Helen.

Mika approached her, seeing there was no one else nearby. "I'm sorry."

Helen's appearance was surprising. Mika had never seen Helen in a dress. Clad in all black, she could blend into the darkness of the night much more easily than Mika could. Her silk and lace dress with a somewhat low neckline and a hem that reached just above her knees was simple in appearance, but Mika thought it was pretty nonetheless. Her cloak was similar to Mika's, but it was plainer. She also wore shin-high boots over stockings. Helen sat on the bench, her arms crossed against her chest.

"Miss Helen...."

"What?"

"I like how you look right now. You're very beautiful," said Mika.

Helen stared at Mika, and then looked away, feeling her cheeks turning warm. If it were daytime right now, Mika would be able to see her blushing. However, Helen was not about to let that happen, nor was she going to let it affect her right now. She stood up from the bench as the Princess joined her, and eyed Mika's attire for a moment. Mika's cloak was of sufficient size and length to cover much of the dress she wore underneath, but through the opening at the front, Helen could see her white dress. She also noted Mika's white shoes and white stockings.

"I thought I told you to wear all black," said Helen.

"The cloak is probably the only thing I have that's black. I don't have very many black clothes. Almost everything is white. I have some that are light blue or pink or some other colour, but most of my clothes are white. Almost all my shoes are white as well. I couldn't find any of my black shoes."

Helen shook her head. "Fine, then. This will have to do." She got right down to business as she produced two sheets of paper from one of the large pockets inside her cloak, and showed them to Mika. "Are you able to see this, even though it's dark out here?"

Though Mika's eyes had adjusted to the darkness, it was still difficult to see what was written on the paper. One of them was a hand-drawn map with streets arranged in a grid-like fashion, complete with street names and an arrow pointing towards the north. The other sheet of paper had writing. She read the information, and realized it was a list of the members of the Balias family, with names as well as an address.

"Dellen Balias, his wife Zima, and his two sons, Tyrel and Jaren. Avencial 560. You found out where they lived?" said Mika.

"Didn't I tell you? The library contains census records. I found the family name, and then the names of the boys, and eventually the names of their parents and where they live. Census records are updated every year, and it looks like the family's been living in the same house for several years. I'm certain they're still there, since peasants don't typically have enough money to afford to move. I drew a map as well. It's quite detailed, if I do say so myself. I did have to stay up late last night to make sure no one would find me in the library looking for this information, writing it down, as well as drawing the map."

Mika smiled as she gave the papers back to Helen. "That's wonderful, Miss Helen. You're very good at finding information."

"Thank you." Helen put the papers back inside her cloak. "Keep your hood off for now, because it'll hamper your peripheral vision. It's enough that we're covered in darkness, not just in our apparel, but by the environment as well."

"So how will we exit the castle?"

"Let's proceed to the back. As I said before, there are several ways to exit the castle, depending on the time of day or night. You might think that the obvious route is directly through the gates, right through the group of knights guarding them. But there are less obvious and more subtle ways of getting through the gates. I'm certain you remember how the merchant assassins gained entrance into the Grounds."

Mika nodded as they walked side-by-side along a path closest to the side of the castle's stone exterior. "I was told they hid inside crates, and how they managed to go undetected even when they were inspected, I still find it strangely ingenious."

"It certainly was, and we will use a similar method, perhaps not quite as sophisticated, but it should work nonetheless."

Mika and Helen took quite some time to get to the back of the enormous castle. Mika looked up to see any hint of moonlight, but there was none, not even a faint glow among the clouds. Even the clouds themselves were not visible, and their presence could only be inferred from the lack of moonlight. The only lights they could see were the distant bonfires on top of the walls that surrounded the castle, lighting the paths of the soldiers that patrolled them. Very soon, they rounded a corner and stopped.

"We're here. Stay down." Helen knelt down on the ground, and looked around the corner.

Mika followed suit beside her. She felt the cool earth on her knees, while the soft blades of grass tickled her fingers.

There were at least twenty large carriages. Some of them were arranged in rows and columns, while others were scattered randomly. They all appeared the same, all made of wood, with four large wheels. Each carriage had a door at the back. At the front of each carriage were two cervids, resting as they stood side-by-side. None of the carriages had drivers at the moment.

From where Mika and Helen were, they heard voices from far away. Men were talking, but the girls could not make out what they were saying. Their talking was interrupted by occasional fits of laughter. Unfortunately, the men could not be seen, so Helen was not completely certain if it was safe for them to come out of hiding.

Mika kept her voice down to a whisper as she observed and listened. "I've never seen carriages like these. What are they for, Miss Helen?"

"These are supply carriages. They're carrying empty wooden crates. Every night, shortly after midnight, these carriages are loaded with empty crates. The carriages take the crates back into the city to have them refilled at one of the storehouses. The crates are refilled during the early morning hours before sunrise, and then the carriages bring them back to the castle."

"I see." Mika committed this new knowledge into memory. "What's the plan, Miss Helen? Based on what you mentioned, I'm assuming we're going to ride one of these carriages, and hide inside the crates?"

Helen chuckled. "For an eleven-year-old girl, you are extremely perceptive, Princess Mika."

Mika wondered if Helen was being sarcastic, which happened often enough for her to assume that was the case.

"And, yes, you're correct. We'll do what the merchant

assassins did. We will board one of the carriages through the back, and hide inside the empty crates."

Hearing that plan, Mika closed her eyes for a moment, feeling apprehensive. She felt the rapid thumping of her heart again. "Are the crates large enough for us to fit in one?"

"If a large man can fit in one, both of us should fit in one. You're quite thin and small for your age, and I'm quite thin myself. That shouldn't be a problem," replied Helen.

"What about the storehouse? Do you know which storehouse they'll be heading to?"

"No, but I'm not planning to go into a storehouse. We should exit the carriage while on route. Otherwise, we will fail."

Mika placed one hand on her heart, her fear escalating and threatening to take control of her, but she pushed it away in her mind, pushed it away several times, as many times as she could. "I'm worried...."

Helen glanced at Mika.

"I'm worried we might be caught. What if someone inspects the crates? Surely, they would catch us inside. If that happens, we'll both be arrested by the knights."

"The supply carriages and the crates they hold are inspected only on the way back into the Grounds."

Mika thought about that for a moment, and came to a quick realization. "I see. There's no reason to inspect them when they leave the Grounds. But the knights would have reason to inspect them when they enter the Grounds, in case there may be people hiding in them."

Helen nodded. "Again, very perceptive."

Mika was silent for a moment, thinking that Helen was probably mocking her again.

"That was a compliment, by the way."

The Princess blinked, confused. "It was?"

"Yes. Be thankful, because I don't give compliments often."

Mika smiled and giggled. "That's very kind of you, Miss Helen."

"Would you like me to take it back?" Helen's voice was soft but held barely concealed irritation.

"I'm sorry. Thank you." Mika was still surprised. She thought to herself it was probably the first time Helen had ever complimented her. If she has, Mika neither remembered nor noticed, since Helen concealed her possible previous compliments with sarcasm.

"Peasants may use the carriages as a way to attack the Nobility, gaining entrance into the castle the way the merchant assassins did," said Helen.

Mika nodded, fully understanding everything Helen explained. She held her breath for a moment as she and Helen remained still. Other than the distant conversation and laughter of the men somewhere beyond their range of vision, they heard nothing. Mika felt the fear within her trying to take control again as she clasped her hands together at her heart, closed her eyes, and breathed out. "I'm scared...."

Helen looked down at Mika. "Princess?"

Mika's cold and clammy hands trembled. "I can't believe I'm doing this. In fact... I'm not even certain I *can* do this."

Helen looked around the corner, and then behind them to make sure there was no one nearby. It was just the two of them in the darkness. She hesitated for a moment before placing her arm around Mika's shoulders and her other hand on the little girl's trembling hands.

Surprised, Mika met Helen's gaze with widened eyes.

"Princess... at this point, it's up to you what you want to do. If you find yourself too frightened to continue, we can always go back. If you choose to continue, there's a possibility of being discovered or even attacked. Whether you choose to continue or not, there will be consequences. I would hope you have thought about those."

The trembling of Mika's hands lessened with Helen's hand over them. Mika looked back at the carriages.

"I know the consequences, whether I go or not," whispered the Princess. "I've already thought about this. If I go, I can meet the Balias family. I can find out from them what I need to know. But it's possible we might be caught by these people driving the carriages or by the knights patrolling the city streets. We might even be attacked by the peasants if they discover that we're of the Nobility. But I've also thought about what will happen if I don't go. I won't meet the Balias family, and I won't find out the truth about this world. I can go back into the safety of my bedchamber, and nothing will change. The Peasantry will continue to suffer through a life of extreme hardship and poverty. But having experienced some dangerous and traumatic events that enlightened me to their world, I can't just ignore them."

Mika calmed down somewhat. Her hands no longer trembled as Helen pulled away. The young Princess was successful in pushing back some of the fear that was stopping her. Of course, not all of it could be pushed back.

"I'm still terribly frightened. But I'm... I'm the Princess of Melodice, Mika Silveraine. I have to... no, I must do this. Because they're my people."

Helen smiled a little. "All right, Princess Mika, in that case, we will continue."

Mika smiled as well. "Yes, let's do that."

Both Helen and Mika continued to observe their objective for another minute. The men were still talking and laughing, immersed in their social banter.

Helen pointed at one carriage that was perhaps the third closest to them, its back end slightly to the side and facing away from the castle. "We run for that carriage, and enter through the back." She stood up from the grass.

Mika stood up as well, but felt aches all over her body as she did so. "Running... might be difficult for me, I'm afraid."

Helen turned to Mika. "What?"

"Remember that my father punished me. I'm still recovering."

More like beat you, thought Helen. *What the hell kind of a father does this to his child? That's not a punishment. That's abuse.* She was tempted to voice her thoughts, but did not want to make Mika feel more uncomfortable than she already was.

"I'll have to carry you," said Helen, "just like when I carried Mirin."

Mika was taken aback, and almost responded by telling her that it was not necessary. However, given their current situation and what they wanted to do, it was probably for the best. It would not be possible for her to make a run for the carriage without pain or further injury. The possibility of getting caught would also increase. "Um... all right."

"The longer we wait here, the higher the chances of being discovered. We have to go now. Come." Helen knelt down on the grass on one knee.

Mika stood in front of her, facing her. "Miss Helen?"

Helen sighed with impatience. "What now?"

"Um... in case we are attacked by anyone, do you have... anything?"

"You mean a weapon? I have a long knife strapped to my thigh under my dress. Normally, I'd carry a sword... but it would appear suspicious since I'm not in my uniform. I would prefer not to take any unnecessary risks."

Mika nodded in agreement. "I see."

"Now, are we ready? No more questions?"

"No more questions."

"Good. Now, if you would be so kind as to come closer so I can put you over my shoulder, and make a run for our target carriage."

"All right." Mika complied. Helen put her arms around Mika's waist, and lifted her up over her shoulder, causing Mika to gasp. "Please be careful...."

Helen was surprised by how light Mika was. It was true that Mika was quite thin, but she was somewhat lighter than Helen expected. She looked around the corner again, and listened carefully for the next few seconds. She also watched for any shadows that might be moving, suggesting the presence of people.

"Out of curiosity, Princess, from one young woman to another, what's your weight and height?" asked Helen.

"Huh? Um... twenty-four kilograms and one hundred twenty-seven centimetres," answered Mika. "Why?"

"You truly are small for your age, aren't you?"

Mika blushed. She was not given the chance to respond as Helen dashed for the target carriage as fast as she could, her footsteps barely audible on the soft, trimmed grass. Helen and Mika looked in the direction of the voices. Eventually, they saw a small group of men talking while standing around a bright kerosene lamp. They all stood close to a set of double doors that were wide open. The doors led into a storage area inside the castle. Several empty wooden crates were scattered around the men. Helen carried Mika to the side of their target carriage, and set her down on her feet.

Mika's heart was beating so fast that she felt as if it would jump into her throat. She leaned against the side of the carriage, and took a few deep breaths. "I'm truly not... accustomed to... this kind of risk-taking."

"Quiet." Helen peeked around the carriage to make sure no one had noticed them. She went to the back of the carriage, and then opened the door. "Come on, let's go."

Mika joined Helen, and was about to climb gingerly into the carriage when Helen pushed her into it. Mika felt a few aches in her knees, and let out a gasp of pain as she was all but catapulted into the carriage. Helen followed, and then closed the door behind her. Mika could not see anything in the darkness of the cabin, which was even darker than outside. Small glass windows on the side walls did little to illuminate the cabin.

"I can't see anything," said Mika.

Helen reached out to feel for the Princess, and took her by the arm. "Hold on to me. I'm going farther in."

Eventually, Helen's knee struck the side of something that was unmistakably a wooden crate, based on its shape, size, and texture. After a moment of feeling around, they ended up at one side of the cabin.

"Can't I use my magic to make some light?" asked Mika.

"What do you think will happen if you do that?"

Mika thought about it, and discarded the idea. "Never mind. I suppose someone would see it from outside, and it would look suspicious."

Eventually, Helen found a crate in one corner of the cabin farthest from the door. "Here, Princess. Be careful with the sides. I'll help you go in, but feel around to make sure you don't fall into it."

With Helen's help and Mika feeling around for the sides of the crate, she eased herself in. She made sure to sit on one side. The hard wooden surfaces of the crate's interior felt rough on her hands. For a moment, she was worried that she might scrape them.

"I'm going in next. Watch out." Helen went in right after, though much more easily. She was careful not to step on the Princess, but not as careful with what Mika was wearing.

Mika felt Helen stepping on her cloak and a part of her dress so she pulled to try to tug herself free. "Miss Helen...."

Helen felt the pulling motion underneath her boots. "What are you doing?"

"I'm sorry... but... you're stepping on my dress and cloak."

"Who the hell cares? Make room." Helen knelt down, and felt around for the padlock that would keep the cover of the crate closed. She found the padlock, and found something else along with it. "Fortune must be on our side tonight."

"Huh?"

Helen felt the padlock and the key that was attached to it. Of course, it had little to do with fortune. Every crate in the cabin had a padlock with a key inside. There was no need to remove the keys from the padlocks since the crates did not contain anything. Helen closed the crate's lid, and used the padlock and key to keep it closed from the inside by curling the shackle around two wooden beams, one on the crate itself and the other on the lid. She locked the padlock, and kept the key in the same pocket inside her cloak along with the list of the Balias family.

Mika carefully felt up the inside walls of the crate, and found that there were several narrow spaces that could allow her to see what was outside, but they were useless in the near complete darkness at the moment.

Helen leaned back on the side of the crate with her legs curled up, her knees almost against her chest. "Princess, you're fortunate for having a small stature."

Mika, feeling Helen's shoulder snug against hers, curled her legs up to her chest as well. She thought about when Helen asked for her weight and height and stated that she was small for her age. In this tiny wooden crate, she was not too uncomfortable, but Helen might be having a less easy time, being significantly taller.

"Um… may I ask you, one young woman to another, your weight and height then?" Mika said, somewhat imitating how Helen had asked her the question earlier.

"Forty-six kilograms and one hundred fifty-nine centimetres."

"You're much taller than I am so I hope you're not too uncomfortable."

"It's rather uncomfortable, but I must endure it."

Mika rested her chin on her knees. "I suppose we'll be here for a while. I hope no one finds us."

"Yes. We'll have to wait. I can hear those men still talking and laughing from this far away. Very soon, they'll start driving the carriages out of the castle, through the gates, and into the city proper."

Mika had brought her timepiece, but it was useless in the darkness. She assumed the time was probably very close to midnight. As she waited, she asked herself again if she was doing the right thing, but she once again reminded herself that she must do this, for the sake of her people, despite her fear. There was no question about it. It was simply the right thing to do.

* * *

SEC 3566, Morrighan 39

About a half hour passed.

Startled, Mika drew in a quick breath, and felt Helen's hand over her mouth almost immediately to stifle any fearful sounds she made. The door at the back of the carriage had been swung open. They both heard a couple of men talking and the sounds of wood scraping against wood, as if something was being lifted up, gently set down, and then pushed along the cabin floor, likely another crate.

One of the men mounted a kerosene lamp on a hook hanging from the ceiling close to the door, pushing away much of the darkness.

Narrow shafts of light entered the crate in which Mika and Helen hid. Mika's eyes were wide as she leaned away from the side of the crate's interior against Helen. They made no noise as the two men loaded up the carriage with a few more empty crates.

"I believe that's all of them."

"Good. That means we can finally be on our way to the storehouse."

The men took the lamp, and stepped out of the carriage, closing the door behind them. Their voices receded as they walked away.

Helen removed her hand from Mika's mouth. "It's likely to be past midnight by now. It sounds like they're ready to go."

Mika leaned her head back against the crate's interior, closed her eyes for a moment, and inhaled and exhaled several times to calm the pounding of her heart. She pushed herself back against the inside wall of the crate so she could sit up straighter. Even though she was able to fit inside the crate with Helen, not being able to move very much was causing her body discomfort, especially since she was still recovering from her bruises.

"My whole body is aching more than it was before," whispered Mika.

Helen shrugged. "Well, Princess, you need to be more patient. We have to endure this in order to fulfill your plan."

Mika nodded. "Yes, I know...."

Helen chuckled a little.

Mika turned to her, somewhat puzzled. "What is it?"

"I was just thinking about something interesting."

"About what?"

Helen turned to Mika, her face beside hers. "Well, all this time, I've been... I should admit that I've been teasing you a little because you're so shy and timid. I always thought of you as a weakling and a coward."

Mika did not know what to say to that. It was obvious, but Helen just confirmed what she had been doing.

"But you're starting to change, Princess Mika."

That, Mika did not expect. "What do you mean?"

"I never thought you'd put yourself in the situation you're in right now. You snuck out of the castle, and you stowed away in a cramped little wooden crate. We're only vaguely aware of which part of the city this carriage will head to. You've been taking some risks lately. You've decided on your own to do this. No one is convincing you to do anything you don't want to do. You've been showing signs of maturity and bravery."

Mika paused for a long moment. She was doing something that could be considered insane. She thought that no person, let alone a child her age, would do something like this. She was putting herself at risk... and she knew it. Her reason for putting herself at risk, however, greatly outweighed the risk itself.

"You're definitely capable of much more than you think," said Helen.

Mika smiled. "I always thought myself a coward and a weakling."

"Perhaps you shouldn't be so hard on yourself, and I shouldn't be either."

"Why do you think that?"

"Do you mean why do I think you're braver and more mature than you believe yourself to be?" Helen felt the nod of Mika's head beside hers. "I'll remind you of your words to the Balias brothers, Jaren and Tyrel. You told them you loved them as your people, as their Princess."

Mika remembered her words. She remembered getting acquainted with the peasant boy Jaren Balias and his younger brother Tyrel. Jaren had asked her why she protected them and the people around them, the rest of the peasants. She remembered her response.

"Love is what's making you do what you're doing now. That's what's giving you the strength and the courage to do what you feel must be done."

Mika could feel warmth in her cheeks.

"Because of all this, I believe I'm starting to understand you, Princess Mika."

"Thank you," whispered Mika. "You seem to care about others around you, including the peasants. You don't see them as being any different from the nobles, do you?"

"No, and how could I? I don't understand how they can be treated differently from us based on the belief that they're somehow inferior to us. To me, it's wrong. And right now, I'm doing something that I myself could be arrested for. I'm risking myself just as much as you are. But I certainly don't agree with Sir Galner and his words, and I'm very much against his having murdered so many innocent civilians that day. Many of those people were not attacking us at all, and in fact, were innocent bystanders. Sir Galner used that opportunity to kill not just those who attacked, but also those who were innocent. Killing innocent civilians is very much contrary to justice. That is absolutely *not* one of the ways to resolve any conflict. He only needed to target those who were hostile, but that is not what he did."

"I see. I believe I'm starting to understand you as well, Miss Helen."

Helen smiled. "Thank you, Princess Mika."

Both Mika and Helen hushed themselves when they heard the voices of men approaching. Someone climbed onto the carriage, probably at the front where the driver was supposed to be.

"I think we're finally about to move," said Helen.

Soon, the carriage lurched forward as the cervids pulled on it, urged by the driver who took hold of the reins at the front. They moved slowly, and turned to face a different direction. The carriage, along with all the others, moved down a path that would take it towards the Valderia Pathway at the front of the castle. The line of carriages was on its way towards the main castle gates, their destination being the city of Scarletia proper outside.

Mika thought about what was happening. There was only one direction she could go now.

There's no turning back. I will do what I must.

CHAPTER 14

INTO THE CITY

HELEN REMOVED THE LID OF the crate in which she and Mika hid, and carefully climbed out, holding on to anything she could get her hands on to prevent from falling over. It was not a smooth ride on the streets of Scarletia, as the carriage shook while driving over cracks and potholes. The streets in this part of the city were even more worn than the paths that Mika and Helen had taken during their failed excursion to the city of Cerulean. Helen moved over to one side of the carriage, and looked through the glass windows, but kept herself low so that no one outside might see her, even if that chance was remote because of the darkness.

Mika knelt inside the crate, holding on to the sides, as she watched Helen's dark shadow against the windows. "Do you see where we're headed, Miss Helen?"

"Somewhat." Helen found that the window could be opened from the bottom because its hinges were at the top. She unlatched the window, and pushed it open ever so slightly, just enough so she could poke a bit of her head through, and see what was in front and behind them.

Helen could see a little better from the window because of the lamps that lined the sides of the street outside. The street lamps, each about four metres tall, contained large supplies of kerosene within them. The bright flames within their glass chimneys illuminated the areas around them, occasionally interrupted by a lamp that had exhausted its fuel supply. Towards the back, Helen saw the sides of many carriages, and the same when she looked ahead. A dark shape loomed in the distance, the unmistakable bulk of a large storehouse.

Helen closed the window, and turned to Mika. "We're approaching the storehouse. It's time for us to exit this carriage."

"Why are we leaving now? If we go into the storehouse...."

"We will have a much harder time getting out of the storehouse if we go in. There will be many people in it, such as the drivers of these carriages, and anyone else who will be helping them, and all the exits will surely be guarded."

"But are you...?" Mika stopped. She wanted to ask Helen if she was sure about this, but did not want to sound like she doubted her.

"I don't know for sure if the storehouse will be crowded and guarded. If we assumed it wasn't, and it actually was, then we'd be caught. I would rather err on the side of caution. We can't take that chance. We have to leave now."

With Helen's help, Mika eased herself out of the crate, though she was very awkward because of the aches and pains throughout her body, not to mention her small stature and the loose fabric of her dress and cloak. Mika nearly fell when she climbed out of the crate, but Helen held her.

"The carriage is still moving. How are we going to get out?" asked Mika, as she headed for the side window, and watched the dark scenery that passed.

Helen went to the back door, and peered through the window there. "We'll have to jump out."

Mika turned to Helen with shock. "But we'll get hurt!"

"We don't have a choice, so I suggest you don't get hurt."

Mika tried to find her courage again, and certainly thinking about what she needed to do helped somewhat.

Helen watched through the back window, seeing the carriage behind them and the two cervids that pulled on it. She could barely see the driver through the antlers of the cervids. The cervids were just tall enough that they obstructed the forward view of the driver, giving them a chance to open the back door of the carriage and exit. However, even though it was dark outside, it was still possible that the driver might see dark silhouettes coming out of the carriage in front of him. The chances of being seen were actually higher than not. "Not very good odds."

"Huh? I'm sorry, I couldn't hear you," said Mika.

"Princess." Helen waved Mika over.

Mika complied, and stood close to Helen, holding on to the wall of the carriage to keep from losing her balance.

"You'll need to go first."

Mika was taken aback. "Why?!"

"The person who exits first is less likely to be discovered, and you're smaller than I am, so you will be even less noticeable. If you go first and you're discovered, I'll be coming after you anyway, and I can still protect you. It would be far worse if I went first and I was discovered. You'd be left behind. I would no longer be able to protect you."

What am I thinking? I must be insane, thought Mika, as she took a deep breath, putting a hand on her heart. "All right... please tell me exactly what I should do."

"I will open this door just enough so you can go through it. Jump down onto the street below, and make sure you roll to the side to minimize injury. As soon as you're on the ground, run to the side of the street. Be aware of your surroundings."

Mika was terrified by this risky method of escape. She was also terrified of being alone on the street. She felt the trembling of her hands almost right away. "What about you? You're... you're coming right after me, aren't you?"

"I am. I'll be right behind you. As soon as you're clear of the carriage, I'll follow you."

Mika was very uncertain of this plan. "Miss Helen...."

Helen put a hand on her shoulder. "Princess, please trust me. I will not allow anything to happen to you, but you need to do exactly as I say."

Mika knew Helen was trustworthy with these kinds of situations. She knew exactly what she was doing. She had been trained in the ways of the warrior, a young knight with excellent skills that would be very useful for what they were trying to do. The Princess nodded to Helen as she stood by the door. "I suppose I'm ready."

Helen acknowledged with a nod. She turned the handle without opening the door, and waited a moment, watching the driver on the carriage behind them. Soon, she noticed him reach out for something beside him. At that moment, she opened the door.

Mika, her eyes widened and her mouth agape, stared at the street below, passing by far more quickly than she would like.

"Go, Princess."

But Mika froze.

Helen was alarmed. She watched the driver again, who was still looking for something beside him. He was probably having trouble in the dark, but he would look up very soon. She turned back to Mika. "Go!"

Mika forgot her fear for a split second due to the urgency of their situation. She held onto the front of her cloak and dress, and jumped down, landing on the street. She rolled to the side, heeding Helen's advice, but as soon as she did that, she felt pain throughout her body and stinging sensations in her hands as she scraped them against the rough surface of the pavement. In the middle of the street, Mika felt the compulsion to cry like a small child who had just hurt herself, but she resisted it as hard as she could.

Helen's eyes widened as she saw the cervids of the carriage behind them approaching Mika, who was still on the ground.

Mika heard the thundering hooves of the approaching cervids, looked up, and gasped. Despite the pain in her body, she rolled out of the way, and the powerful hooves of the cervids missed her. The cervids were heavy enough to crush her to death if she had not moved out of the way. On the street, she tilted her head up, and saw Helen at the back of the carriage, the door opening up a little more. Their gazes met.

"Miss Helen, jump," she whispered.

Helen jumped out, at the same time as the driver in the carriage behind her looked forward.

It was too late.

The man saw Helen's dark figure as she exited the carriage. He was alarmed as he stood up, still holding onto the reins. "Who's there? You! What are you doing?!"

"Damn!" Helen jumped up, and ran down the side of the street, seeing Mika a short distance away, trying to get up as well. Helen ran right past the carriage that had been behind them.

The man shouted with his fist waving in the air. "Stop right there!"

As Mika got up, the pain in her body made her almost fall back down again as she grimaced, but she was able to keep her balance somehow. She saw Helen running towards her, and she gasped as she felt Helen's strong arms wrap around her waist. Helen threw Mika over her shoulder, and continued to run.

As Helen ran past closed storefronts, looking for an alleyway they could hide in, she could hear the receding voice of the screaming driver.

"Guards! We have a stowaway!"

Because Mika was over Helen's shoulder, she could see what was happening behind them. She saw the cervid carriage they were in stop, forcing the carriages behind to stop as well, including the one with the man who had discovered Helen.

Very soon, Helen found an alleyway, and hid around the corner of one of the buildings. Helen put Mika down. They poked their heads around the corner to see what was happening.

The driver had gotten off the carriage, and a few guards in leather armour ran to his vicinity. They were underneath a street lamp, so Mika and Helen could see them. The man was pointing down the street in the direction that Helen ran.

"We have to go," said Helen. "Come on. I can't always be carrying you. Please tell me you can run."

With a desperate tone in her voice, Mika agreed. "Despite the pain, I suppose I have to."

Helen took Mika's hand. They ran down the alleyway, which led them to another street that was perpendicular to the one on which the carriages travelled. They tried to avoid the street lamps as much as possible. Mika could not run as fast as she normally could as she grimaced with pain. They crossed the street to the other side.

"That alleyway there." Helen pointed to an alleyway that she hoped would take them to another street.

Up above, the clouds in the sky had thinned, revealing two of the moons that appeared like lamps covered by thick black veils. The darkness of the night was now slightly illuminated. Mika and Helen went into the alleyway a short distance, and then stopped, leaning against the wall of an old building. Helen looked around the corner, still holding on to Mika's hand. No one was on the street. It was empty and quiet.

Mika tried to catch her breath, feeling the rapid beating of her heart. "This is terrifying. I'm not certain how my heart is able to take all this. I've never experienced so much danger in my whole life."

Helen held Mika's hand a little tighter. "Princess, please remember that I'm with you. I'll protect you with everything I have."

Mika nodded, though she still appeared terrified. "Thank you." She looked down at her aching hands. "I think I hurt my hands... when I jumped out of the carriage."

Helen examined Mika's hands. "You only scraped them, and there's no blood. Nothing but scratches. You're fine."

Mika's breathing was still somewhat rapid as she turned away from Helen, and stared down the dark alleyway, leaning her head against the wall. The cool hardness of the aged bricks felt rough on the side of her head.

Helen waited for Mika's intense fear to abate. She looked around the corner again, and stared into the night, her eyes well adjusted. She saw a shadow moving on the other side of the street so she watched it carefully, soon realizing it was just someone who was probably taking a walk.

* * *

After Mika had calmed down a bit, she and Helen continued down the alleyway, hoping it would lead them to another street. It was much darker in the alleyways than the streets. Their only sources of light were the two moons above that were still partially hidden behind thin clouds.

As they walked down the alleyway together, Helen continued to hold Mika's hand. The only sounds they heard were their own footsteps, which echoed on the cracked and weathered pavement. Various types of debris composed of wood, metal, paper, and other random materials littered the sides of the alleyways. In some places, Mika and Helen coughed and held their breaths for a moment as they encountered the offensive stench of rotting garbage. They stared with revulsion at the emaciated form of a dead cat that lay next to a pile of detritus. No doubt it had recently died from malnutrition, unable to muster the strength to crawl to a place where it could die without being seen. It was not only peasants who suffered from the conditions of poverty. Mika covered her mouth as she held the expression of shock.

Helen shook her head to rid herself of the sad image for now. "We need to get to a street so I can look at the map I drew. Using that, we can find the street where the Balias family lives."

Mika turned her eyes away from the dead cat, and pulled her hand away from her mouth. "Do we know where we are right now?"

"No, I'm afraid not. I was more concerned with making an escape from the carriage. Now that we have escaped, we're tasked with finding our way through the city. First, we need to orient ourselves."

Mika nodded. "That could take us a while, if we don't initially know where we are."

"We'll be fine," said Helen, as they rounded a corner, and went down another dark alleyway.

After a few moments, Helen saw shadows in the distance, so she stopped.

Mika stopped beside her as well. She peered into the darkness, and saw the shadows moving.

"What the hell?" Helen whispered.

Mika saw right away what Helen was concerned about. The shadows became close enough for her to see. They were people, and it did not take them long to realize that the shadows were approaching them.

"Let's go back," said Helen.

Mika nodded, her heart rate increasing again as she listened to the footfalls of the approaching figures. She and Helen began to head back the way they'd come, but they stopped again and saw more shadows, shadows of people who were approaching. They were trapped.

"Well, well, well. Look at what we got here."

They were young men dressed in shirts and trousers made of rags, and a couple of them did not wear shirts at all, exposing their slim but muscled upper bodies. Mika gasped. She and Helen looked in front and behind them. There were ten of them, five in front and five behind. These men were not going to let them get away.

"A group of street thugs," whispered Helen.

Mika held onto Helen's arm tightly, her hands trembling and her knees feeling weak. She wondered what these people were going to do to them. They glared at both of them with expressions that suggested they wanted to do something against the law.

Helen kept calm as she watched every move they made no matter how small it was.

"Have you, by any chance, completed the lesson on magical flight, Miss Helen?" asked the terrified Princess.

"I haven't learned how to do that, and neither have you," Helen replied.

One of the thugs stepped forward, his hands in his pockets. His face was twisted by a deep knife scar that had long since healed. "You look like a couple of rich young girls. We could use some money. Care to help us out?"

From behind them, another one said, "They're awfully well-dressed. These aren't our own."

"Yeah," said yet another. "Wearing clothes like that... I think these two are a couple of nobles."

"Nobles, huh?" said another member of the gang. "You're probably right."

The first thug chuckled. "Damn nobles, huh? Taking a walk on our streets?"

"We should teach you a lesson. We were going to anyway."

Several of the men laughed.

"Yeah, I bet they're a couple of sweet, young virgins. And if they're carrying some cash, we'll get paid for our pleasures!"

Helen clenched her teeth.

Mika gasped. She remembered Valeria Tannlar and the three men who tried to violate her. The same thing was about to be done to them. The hooligans took a few steps closer. Mika was so terrified that she was frozen in place, her cold, trembling hands clasped together in front of her heart, her body leaning against Helen.

"You pretty little bitch, come here!" one of the shirtless ruffians growled as he tried to grab Helen.

Helen dodged, and struck him on the side of the face. Her attacker was stunned. Helen's blow struck him so hard that he fell to the ground on his side. Another tried to attack Helen, but she fought back with a knee into his abdomen and an elbow into the middle of his back. The thug screamed in pain as he fell, and tried to crawl away as quickly as possible.

With Helen no longer beside her, Mika fell to her knees as they weakened.

"What the hell is wrong with you? They're just a couple of girls!" said one of the gang members, annoyed that one of their potential victims was able to fight back so easily.

"I'll take the little one!" shouted another member of the group.

As Helen fought off a third attacker with kicks and punches, Mika saw one of them coming towards her, intent on grabbing her and having his way with her, whatever that might be.

Helen was alarmed. "Get away from her!"

Just as the thug was about to seize Mika by the

shoulders, she closed her eyes tight, and put her head down. He was so close to her that she could smell the hot stench of his breath. Although her body was frozen with fear, another part of her reacted.

"No!" screamed Mika.

A pink magic circle appeared on the ground on which her assailant stood. He was alarmed by the bright circles that contained strange symbols, shapes, and characters, all rotating about a common centre. More magic circles appeared underneath each member of the gang. Suddenly, they all found themselves unable to move.

"What the hell is this?!" shouted one of them.

"It's... magic!"

Helen was shocked herself as she watched the thugs around her, their bodies completely motionless.

Mika looked up at the man in front of her. He was in a pose to grab her, but he was frozen in place. Mika screamed as she pushed herself backwards, ending up on her buttocks.

"You did this, didn't you?!" the thug screamed at Mika.

"You bitch!" yelled another.

"Magic-wielding whore, we'll fuck you, and then kill you!"

Mika could not hear the curses they hurled at her as she watched what she had just done without thinking. She had cast her magic upon all of them at once. She used a magic spell that could stop people from moving.

"Stop acting surprised at what you did and run!" Helen grabbed Mika's hand, and helped her to get up. They ran past the angry thugs who continued to yell curses at them. They went straight down the alleyway, the end of which led to yet another street.

When they were far enough away, Mika released the magic spell, and the magic circles disappeared. The thugs could move again.

"Come on, after them!" said one of members of the gang.

Mika stopped, and then looked back, hearing what they said.

"Princess!" Helen stopped as well, looking down the alleyway and at the thugs who were making a run for them.

"I can't... let them... get near us again!" shouted Mika, raising her voice incrementally at the end of every word. An enormous magic circle appeared on the ground where she stood. She held out one hand towards the thugs.

"Hold up! Wait!" said one of the thugs.

They all stopped.

"Let's get out of here! We don't know what she can do!"

"She might kill us! Run! Let's go! Go!"

They all ran, quickly rounding a corner and disappearing into another alleyway.

Mika released her magic spell, and the magic circle disappeared. She breathed deeply several times, trying to recover from her fright, her hands on her knees. She nearly gasped when she felt Helen's arm around her. They stayed that way for a few moments.

"Princess Mika, I'm impressed. You scared them away."

"I was the one who was scared. I was so scared!" Tears streamed down Mika's cheeks as she knelt down on the ground, her knees feeling the cool hardness of the pavement, on which she felt dust underneath her hands. She continued to watch the alleyway, hoping that those young men would not come back.

Helen knelt down beside her. Behind them, she saw another street just a short distance away. Across the street, she saw a couple of people walking, minding their own business. She turned back to the Princess, and spoke to her with a calm, soft voice. "It's all right, Princess. I'm certain they won't come after us again after seeing your magic, or at least, a small sample of it."

"I just... I just reacted. I could have hurt them just now. That would have been terrible." Mika used her sleeves to wipe her tears away.

Helen shook her head. *Princess Mika, I'm so sorry you have faced such terrible experiences lately, this being one of them. However, I can see you're getting stronger because of them. I just wish you could become stronger in less stressful and less dangerous circumstances.*

After a few moments, Mika had calmed down sufficiently. She got up from the pavement with Helen's help, and wiped the dust off her hands on the sides of her cloak.

"Are you all right, Princess?" asked Helen.

Mika gazed up at Helen slowly, and a small smile appeared. "I was so scared, but... I have to get through this. It's dangerous, but I know we can do it. I'm so glad you're with me, Miss Helen."

"We will get through this together, My Lady. Come. We have a street that looks like it's close to a residential area. We should consult our map."

Mika and Helen walked out of the alleyway and onto the sidewalk. Someone passed them by, a middle-aged man in baggy trousers and an old long-sleeved shirt under a waistcoat that looked like it had not been washed in over a month. He gave Mika and Helen a funny look for a moment, noting their appearance, but continued on his way when he passed them. A handful of people walked down the sides of the streets, but they all minded their own business.

"We should check our map now. Wait. I almost forgot." Helen pulled the hood of her cloak over her head, concealing some of her face. "You should put on your hood. We need to draw as little attention as possible, even if that might not be easy with our somewhat beautiful cloaks. We should at least conceal our faces."

"Yes, of course." Mika followed suit.

"Excellent. Let's go, Princess."

Helen and Mika started on their way. The two young ladies walked down the side of the streets, appearing like two dark shadows.

CHAPTER 15

CONFIDENCE

MIKA STOPPED AT AN INTERSECTION, and noted the wooden sign mounted on a steel pole at the street corner, on which the names of the streets were painted. The lamps at the intersection were brighter than those that lined the streets, illuminating the street signs well. Standing beside the sign, she turned around to face Helen.

"Look, Miss Helen. This street is Arelia, and that one is Medeas."

"Let's see where we are." Helen stopped underneath the lamp to examine her map.

Mika tried to look, too, but Helen was quite a bit taller than she was. Standing on the tips of her shoes, she could see only a few streets on the map. "Did you find where we are?"

"Hmmm... yes, there it is. I made it quite detailed, after all."

"It looks like you copied a quarter of the entire city. How long did it take you to draw the map?"

"I did have to stay in the library for a good half the night. However, this is not a quarter of the city. I only drew the part of the city map between the castle and the Balias family home, as well as anything to either side just in case we were taken off course. And from what I can tell, we're not too far off course." Helen pointed down the street called Arelia. "Let's go that way, Princess. This should lead us to yet another street called Dalieth, and from there, we'll take a few more side streets, and finally get to our destination."

They were in a quiet residential area. Houses made of brick, wood, or both lined the sides of the streets, all of them one or two floors high, all of them very old and in desperate need of repairs. The state of poverty extended throughout the entire city, and the residential area was not exempt from that. Mika could see that some of the houses did not appear particularly safe and could collapse and crush the occupants inside at any time.

As she walked beside Helen, Mika smiled a little. "Miss Helen, you certainly are a very resourceful individual."

Helen raised an eyebrow. "Oh?"

"I'm impressed by how much you prepared before this. You found the Balias family's whereabouts, and you even copied a map of a large section of the city that would help us navigate our way there. You're even able to make plans depending on the situation, such as when we had to escape from the carriage, for example."

"You just have to plan accordingly, My Lady, either ahead of time or as the situation calls for it. But I'm also impressed with you."

Mika blinked, confused. "You are?"

"I was very impressed when you stopped those thugs who attacked us. You literally stopped them in their tracks with your magic. We were able to get away from them, and when they tried to chase us down, you scared them away with your magic. They didn't know what you were capable of, so they ran away."

"I was desperately hoping that I wouldn't have to cast any offensive magic. I suppose... I reacted without thinking. I wanted to... I didn't want them to hurt us, so I reacted out of self-preservation. That's the first time I have done that."

Helen smiled. "You did well, My Lady."

A small giggle came from Mika. "Thank you."

"Do you know what time it is?"

Mika reached inside her cloak to check her timepiece. "It's 1:30 in the morning. I've never been awake this late before. Midnight was the latest I've stayed awake until now."

As Mika and Helen walked the dark streets of the residential area, they said nothing. Their surroundings were so quiet that the rustling of leaves in the gentle breeze could be heard even from far away. The sounds startled them both. Mika was relieved when she realized it was only the leaves among the trees that made the sounds and nothing else.

"Princess Mika," said Helen.

"Yes, Miss Helen?" asked Mika.

"I have a question for you. I've been wondering for quite some time, but I've never truly thought about asking you until now."

Mika was curious. "What is it?"

"What is your relationship with young Mirin?"

Mika blushed, wide-eyed, as she stared up at Helen. "What? My relationship with Mirin? Um... what do you mean, Miss Helen?"

Helen shook her head. "You know what I mean, Princess. I'm just curious."

"Curious? Why?" *Please don't tell me you're curious, too, like my mother was.*

"Well... the two of you are almost always found together. Whenever I see you and Mirin, I see you both holding hands... and quite affectionately, I might add. When you look at him, your facial expression changes, and sometimes the way you speak also changes. There's just... something different about the way you behave whenever he's near. Because of that, I've always wondered about your relationship with him."

Mika was speechless, and her cheeks felt warm. She was thankful for the darkness of the night, because it concealed the blush on her cheeks.

"So what is your relationship with him?" asked Helen.

Mika cast her eyes down on the sidewalk. "Miss Helen?"

"What?"

"I just want to make sure of something... before I tell you anything."

It was Helen's turn to be curious. "Huh?"

"I want to be sure you're not... teasing me or anything of the sort."

"I'm not teasing you. That's not my intention. I see you together often, and I'm simply curious. It appears to me that you both have been close friends for a long time. At least, that's what I'm seeing from my perspective."

Mika hesitated for a moment. "Uh... well...."

"You don't trust me?"

Mika looked up to meet her gaze. "That's not it!"

"Have I not helped you tonight with what you need to do? We've come this far, and I've been with you every step of the way. I even let you know how I truly feel about the kind of life the Peasantry of Melodice are suffering through at the hands of the Nobility. If my superiors knew how I truly felt, I would be branded a traitor. But I believe I can trust you with that information, since we both appear to have similar opinions. I even told you my height and weight when you asked me."

"I know! I'm just...." Mika looked down. "I'm just embarrassed... I suppose. I'm sorry. Well, the truth is...."

Helen stayed quiet, waiting for Mika's next words.

"I love him," whispered Mika, the blush on her cheeks becoming more prominent as she cast her eyes ahead.

"Truly? I'm... glad to hear that, Princess Mika," said Helen, her voice soft.

Mika was taken aback. "You are?"

Helen nodded. "That's actually very nice. I'm glad for you."

"There's only one problem," said Mika.

"What is it?"

Mika answered with a wistful voice. "Even though I'm very much in love with Mirin, I don't believe he feels the same way. Miss Angelica knows about my feelings towards him. He seems to love me as a friend, but no more than that. My love for him is greater than that. But he doesn't realize it. I'm always holding his hand. Sometimes I lean on his shoulder. I'm always touching him affectionately. Still, he doesn't realize how I truly feel about him. Miss Angelica told me that it's because he's a boy and that he's younger than I am."

"I believe Miss Angelica is correct. This is due to

adolescence, when changes occur in the mind and body as a child slowly transforms into an adult. In general, boys his age are not nearly as mature as girls of the same age... and you just happen to be older than he is. Let's also add that you're extremely mature and far more so than typical girls your age. In terms of emotional maturity, Princess, you are literally several years ahead of him."

Mika nodded. "I know... and I understand that. But I'll continue treating him the way I always have. Perhaps... someday... he'll realize it."

Helen smiled. "I have no doubt he will."

"By the way, Miss Helen, this is supposed to be a secret. As far as I know, the only other person who knows how I truly feel is Miss Angelica. My mother suspected that I have feelings for him, but I denied it. And I believe I may have unintentionally let Sir Terren know. Other than them, no one else knows or suspects. At least, I hope so."

"You can trust me to keep this information in confidence, Princess Mika."

"Thank you," said the Princess.

"How long have you known Mirin? I'm afraid I don't know very much about him."

Mika thought back to when she first met Mirin, and remembered how long it has been. "Um... I suppose it's been about three years. I met him shortly after Miss Angelica became my maidservant, just after she turned the age of majority. She's nineteen years old now, and would have been sixteen back then. Mirin was seven, and I was eight."

"Does he not live with Miss Angelica?"

Mika nodded. "Yes, he does. They live in the same room."

"But they're not related, are they?"

"No. Miss Angelica is Mirin's legal guardian. She takes care of him."

Helen became even more curious about Mirin's life. "Hmmm... interesting. How did this living arrangement come to be? I don't believe I've ever heard anything about his parents."

"Mirin started living with Miss Angelica about three years ago as well."

"Everything seems to have occurred around that time. You became friends with him during that time, and Miss Angelica became your maidservant around that time...."

Mika's voice and facial expression became very calm as she thought more about Mirin and his life, and how it was related to her maidservant. "A long time ago, shortly after Mirin was born, something happened to Mirin and his parents. They died before his memories started to form."

Helen was taken aback. "I'm sorry to hear that. If his memories had not formed, he must have been very young, perhaps an infant."

"Yes. I don't know what happened. That's what Miss Angelica told me. Because of the relationship between Miss Angelica and Mirin, I believe Miss Angelica knows what happened to them, but I didn't feel right asking her. I didn't believe it was my place. I felt so terrible when she told me they had died when he was so young. Mirin doesn't remember ever seeing his parents. Basically, he never knew them."

"I can't imagine not knowing your own parents," Helen said softly.

"When Miss Angelica turned the age of majority, she became a maidservant, and was assigned to me. I hadn't had a specific maidservant prior to that, but several did wait on me. When we first met, I liked her very much. She was very sweet and kind to me, and we instantly became very close. She moved into the room next to mine, which was reserved for the Princess's maidservant and her family, if she had any, and brought Mirin with her. It's the same size as my bedchamber but arranged differently and can comfortably hold up to four people. Mirin had already been living with Miss Angelica at the time. He had moved in with her when she became his legal guardian, shortly after she'd turned sixteen. So that's when I met him, and we became friends. He didn't really have any friends back then, and I didn't either."

Mika thought about the life that Mirin led despite his

young age. She stared ahead into the dark night. While she was quiet for a short moment, she heard nothing but her footsteps and Helen's and the occasional rustling of leaves. Helen kept quiet as well. Soon, Mika continued.

"I've known him for three years, but in all that time... I've never asked him about his life before Miss Angelica became his legal guardian. Between the time when his parents died and the time when he and Miss Angelica became close, I don't know how he lived. Who did he live with? He must have lived with someone during those years. Who took care of him? And where was he living? I don't remember ever seeing him before we became friends. Was he living in the castle or was he somewhere else?"

"If you're curious about that, Princess Mika, I could take a look at the census archives in the library as well. If you'd like...."

Mika shook her head. "No, that's fine. But thank you for your offer, Miss Helen. I think it might be more appropriate if I found out from either Mirin or Miss Angelica, on their own terms, rather than me asking them or looking into census archives in the library."

"As you wish," said Helen. "I had no knowledge of the life he's had. It's very unfortunate." *Perhaps I've been insensitive towards him as well, almost as much as I've been with the Princess. I'm such a fool. I should know better.*

"Please don't tell anyone about this, Miss Helen. This is as much a secret as my true feelings for Mirin. And please don't let Miss Angelica and Mirin know what you know either. It would appear very inappropriate if they found out that you know."

Helen nodded. "Of course, Princess Mika, I would keep this information in confidence as well. You can trust me with it."

Mika smiled when she met Helen's gaze. "Thank you. I'm sure they will tell me on their own time. I can't imagine living without knowing who my mother and father were. I suppose if I had lived a life where my parents had died before my memories formed, I would have no emotional attachment to them. And to me, it wouldn't be sad at all, but it would be on a different level, just not on a level that I can comprehend."

"Others would feel sad for you even if you didn't."

Mika and Helen continued navigating the residential streets. Very soon, the clouds parted. Two of the moons, hanging brightly in the sky like shining jewels, provided better illumination in the night. They occasionally saw someone taking a walk or heading someplace perhaps once every quarter hour or so. Otherwise, it was quiet.

* * *

After another half hour, Mika and Helen reached the part of the residential area they were looking for. It did not look any different from other parts of the residential area they had been. If there were no street signs, it would be easy for them to become lost. Fortunately, Helen was very good at navigation, and used her map to their advantage on top of that.

"I believe this is the area," said Helen as she examined her map underneath another street lamp. "What's the name of the street?"

Mika saw the street sign. "Avencial."

"There it is." Helen smiled at the Princess. "This is the street where the Balias family home is located. We just need to find the house."

"What's the house number?"

"It's 560. And it's that way." Helen pointed behind her.

There were sidewalks on either side of the street in this part of the residential area, and Mika and Helen took advantage of them. As they walked past houses, they watched the house numbers, but many of them were difficult to see in the dark. The houses were farther away from the street lamps because of the sidewalks. The house numbers were painted on the doors with the same type of paint as on the street signs.

Mika watched the numbers increase... 108, 110, 112, and so on. "This must be a very long street. It might take us a while to arrive at 560, judging by how slowly the numbers are increasing as we're walking."

"Nevertheless, we'll get there. Keep pace with me. We should walk faster."

Mika complied. "But please don't walk too fast. My whole body still hurts."

Helen slowed down somewhat, despite her impatience. She wanted to tell the Princess to move faster, but even if she told her that, Mika would not be able to.

"I sincerely hope Miss Angelica doesn't check on me during the night," said Mika.

"What do you mean?" asked Helen.

"I put some pillows underneath my blankets on my bed to make it look like I'm still sleeping. If Miss Angelica opens the door to my bedchamber and checks on me without actually going to my bed and lifting the covers, she will think I'm still sleeping. But if she goes in and checks the bed, it's likely that she'll discover I'm not there."

"We can only hope at this point that she doesn't check on you. That would be extremely unfortunate right now. I'm hoping we can return to the castle unseen somehow before she checks on you in the morning."

Mika nodded. "I hope so as well."

"That's also something we'll need to plan very soon."

As Mika observed the house numbers increasing, she noticed they were getting closer to their destination. Mika could also not help but sense her nervousness increasing as they neared the house they were looking for.

After several more minutes, Helen started calling out the house numbers. "Let's see... 556... 558.... There, 560."

Mika and Helen stopped on the sidewalk in front of the house. Mika stared at it for a long time. There was nothing special about it. It looked like all the others in the area, old and run-down. From the sidewalk to the front of the house was a paved area, completely bare and with cracks in the concrete. The house was made of mostly wood, but the foundation appeared to be of brick and mortar.

Helen noted the size of the entire house. "I can't imagine how four people can live in that house. It is very small."

"If all peasants are poor, they probably can't afford to

live in larger homes." Mika put a hand on her heart, and closed her eyes for a moment.

Helen glanced down at Mika. "How are you feeling?"

"I'm nervous."

"Again?" said Helen, her tone impatient. "Princess, we've come this far, and you know there's no turning back."

"Yes, I know. It's now or never." Mika stared at the front door of the house, unassuming and ordinary, but somehow it felt unwelcoming. "I sincerely hope everything goes well, and that they'll understand what I'm trying to do. These are my people. I can't turn back on what I'm doing, and I certainly can't turn my back on them. Like I said before, nothing will change if I do nothing." She stepped onto the pavement in front of the house, and walked slowly towards the door.

Following closely behind Mika, Helen stole a glance behind them to make sure there was no one nearby. The streets were as quiet as they had been.

As Mika approached the door, she thought about the time. What time was it anyway? She had not looked at her timepiece for a while, but it was obvious that she was about to visit someone at a very uncharacteristic hour. Mika paused, her eyes on the door ring.

"I'm coming at a terrible time. They are surely sleeping right now! I'll be waking them up and bothering them!"

"Princess, this is the only way you can meet them. Would you rather leave the castle during the daytime? You'd be caught. We can't even have you order the knights to open the castle gates for you. They would open them for you, but the Supreme Captain would be notified soon afterwards, and the King and Queen would know about it soon after that. That would just cause us more trouble than is necessary. And besides, we're here. We can't just stop now."

Mika hesitated, and then she nodded, her eyes going back to the door ring. "You're right. I'm so sorry, Miss Helen. I keep hesitating and second-guessing myself, telling myself that I can't do this. But I have to remind myself of what I'm trying to do, what I want to know and to understand. To understand, I have to meet with them. They're my only acquaintances among the Peasantry at the moment so it has to be them."

"That's right. And all you have to do is knock on their door."

Mika stepped closer to the door. She reached out for the door ring, held it for a moment... and knocked very softly.

Helen frowned. "How do you expect the people inside the house to hear you when you're knocking like that, Princess Mika?!" She stepped towards the door, prompting the greatly surprised Mika to draw her hand back from the door ring, which Helen used to knock much louder and harder. The sound echoed throughout the entire house.

Mika's eyes widened. "Miss Helen, please don't do that! They might get angry with us!"

Helen calmly stood back as she finished knocking. "There. That should do it."

Mika turned back to the door. She anticipated a very large and angry man opening it, his muscles bulging and his face half-asleep but with a very grumpy expression, staring down at her with terrible annoyance. Her hands trembled. She turned to Helen.

"Oh... um, Miss Helen, what do you think I should say when they answer the door?"

Helen gave another one of her infamous frowns. "Can you please stop being foolish? Just do what you need to do so we can go home! Speaking of going back home, we haven't planned that yet, and we need to do so. I suggest you finish what you need to do as soon as possible so we can start planning our way back."

Mika and Helen heard some unusual sounds, as if something was being moved against the inside of the door. The door unlocked and swung inwards. Mika gasped, completely startled, while Helen stood up straight with her hands clasped together in front of her.

Mika looked up at the man who did not appear the way she had anticipated. He looked like a gentle man, his sleepy face clean-shaven. His long-sleeved shirt and trousers made for sleeping were old and wrinkled. Mika stared up at him for a moment, not knowing what to do or say, frozen.

Soon, the man's sleepy expression turned to one of confusion, as he regarded the two young girls, one of them clearly a girl in her teenage years and the other a little girl, both wearing beautiful black cloaks, their faces partially concealed by their hoods, knocking on his door at such an unusual hour.

"Um... can I help you?" said the man, his voice gentle.

Mika continued to stare, her eyes wide open.

Helen sighed.

The man saw the frightened expression of the little girl in front of him, and he sighed as well, seeing that her older companion did the same out of annoyance. The older girl's cloak was plain while the little girl's cloak shimmered and had elaborate designs. Why was the older girl standing back while the little one was at the door? The younger girl was obviously meant to be the one to greet him, though she appeared terribly shy. He wondered what these two wanted. Since the little girl who was meant to greet him appeared like she had frozen herself into a frightened statue, he decided to take the initiative.

"What can I do for you at this strange hour?" the man asked again, his voice a little less groggy this time.

Mika's eyes blinked as she started breathing again. She tried to gather her courage. She looked the man over, and had listened to his voice. He was not the freakish man that had appeared in her imagination a moment ago.

"Uh... um... I'm... sorry for bothering you this... this evening, sir." Mika tried to clear her throat. "But... uh, is this the residence of... of Tyrel and Jaren Balias?"

The man was puzzled. "You're asking about my boys? Is there a problem?"

Helen remembered the information on her sheet of paper. *This must be the father. Dellen Balias.*

Mika gasped, and quickly shook her head. "Oh, no, no, sir... there's no problem. No problem at all!"

"Okay, so what's this about?" he asked.

Mika hesitated. She stole a glance at Helen, silently asking for guidance, but Helen had no facial expression. If this man wanted to know why she was knocking on his door asking about his sons at a strange hour, she had better convince him that her presence meant serious business. She tried to think quickly... and remembered that she wore the Princess Gem.

"I'm... truly very sorry to bother you, sir." Mika pushed back her hood, and loosened the front of her cloak by pulling on one ribbon, revealing the shining Princess Gem.

Dellen Balias was alarmed at the sight of the diamond, something he had only heard about and seen in illustrations. Only the Princess of Melodice could wear the Princess Gem. He was so alarmed that he took a few steps back.

Helen watched him, hoping he would not trip himself and fall backwards.

Mika now knew she was seen as the Princess, and that gave her a little confidence, as she clasped her hands in front of her, standing like the proper young lady she was. Her voice still slightly timid, she introduced herself to him.

"I'm... Mika Silveraine. I suppose you know me as the Princess of Melodice." Mika glanced at Helen, and then back at Dellen. "This is my guard, Miss Helen Renier." Now that she was feeling a little more confident, she remembered the paper Helen had shown her, the one with the names of the Balias family members. "You must be... you must be Sir Dellen Balias, the father of the two boys I recently met, Jaren and Tyrel Balias."

Dellen swallowed, somewhat frozen, and still with an expression of great shock. He also could not help but feel a sense of dread. "Uh... yeah...."

"I apologize for coming to your home at such an unusual hour."

Dellen did not know how to react. A member of the Royal Family, the highest of the Nobility, was at his doorstep. It did not matter that this member of the Royal Family was a very young girl. This situation still gave him a sense of trepidation.

"Would it be all right if I could have a chance to speak with you tonight?" asked Mika.

Dellen was taken aback. "Speak with us?"

A woman appeared from farther inside the house, clad in a long nightgown that was old and worn. She joined Dellen. "Dellen, what's going on?" However, as soon as she saw Mika standing at their doorstep, wearing the Princess Gem, she gasped with shock, her hands flying to her mouth.

Mika remembered her name from the paper Helen showed her. *She must be Miss Zima Balias, the wife of Sir Dellen Balias.*

"The Princess of Melodice?!" Zima stammered.

"Zima, stand back." Dellen held up his hand, as if to protect her.

Mika still felt nervous, so she closed her eyes, and took a deep breath that she let out slowly, and when she opened her eyes, she felt even calmer and a little more confident in herself. She looked up at Dellen and Zima with a gentle smile.

But despite her present demeanour, both Dellen and Zima were wary and cautious.

"What do you want from us, Princess Mika Silveraine?" asked Dellen.

Mika hesitated for a moment, so she glanced back at Helen, who nodded to her to encourage her. She turned back to Dellen and Zima, and found herself not looking directly at them. Instead, she found herself gazing more towards the floor in front of them, so she forced herself to look up.

"I was hoping I could chat with you about something. I sincerely hope I'm not being too much of a bother, since I'm coming to your home at this time of the night, but if I am, I do sincerely apologize."

Helen let out a sigh. *Can you stop apologizing so much? How many times is that now?*

Dellen hesitated, wondering what she meant by that. He sized her up. She was just a little girl. He thought to himself that she could very easily be overpowered and restrained. When Dellen's and Helen's gazes met, Dellen knew right away that she was observing him, that she knew what he was thinking. The look that Helen gave was almost as if she was telling him not to try anything that could be considered hostile. Helen, from his perspective and judging from her stature, did not appear threatening. However, the look she gave him definitely was. He figured that she could be hiding something underneath her cloak, perhaps a knife or a sword, if what the Princess said earlier was true, that she was indeed her guard.

"What... do you want to chat with us about?" asked Dellen.

"There were some things I experienced recently that I found highly disturbing, Sir Dellen. By visiting you and your family, and learning about your life, I hope to gain the understanding which I am seeking."

CHAPTER 16

UNDERSTANDING

PRINCESS MIKA HAD BEEN GIVEN the chair at the head of the rectangular kitchen table, both of which were made of a cheap wood that creaked whenever they were nudged. She shifted uncomfortably in the hard chair. Both Mika and Helen had hung their cloaks on a coat rack near the front door. A few candles lit the kitchen, but what gave the most light was the large kerosene lamp at the centre of the table. Black curtains covered the windows, but they were not true curtains. Rather, they were large pieces of cheap cotton that had been cut out from something much larger, and then hooked on to nails partially embedded in the wall above the windows.

In one corner of the room, the wood inside a firebox glowed orange as it generated heat, which warmed the steel plate on top of it, on which there was a kettle filled with water. Eventually, steam escaped from the kettle. Zima lifted it up, and poured hot water into a decorated white ceramic cup with a chip on the side just above the handle.

"I hope you'll like this, Princess Mika." Zima sprinkled herbs and tiny dried leaves into the cup. She carefully set the cup on a decorated platter, and placed it on the table in front of Mika.

"Thank you, Miss Zima." The Princess smiled sweetly. Observing the cup and the platter, this was probably their most expensive among their collection of tableware. Mika saw other cups and mugs in the kitchen, and most of them appeared to be made of clay.

Zima stood back a few steps to stand near her husband

Dellen, who was leaning against the wall next to a window with his arms crossed against his chest, observing the Princess and her companion. He was still unsure what was going on and why the Princess of Melodice had knocked on their door.

Helen stood leaning against the doorway that led into the kitchen, carefully observing Dellen and Zima.

Mika lifted the cup to her lips and sipped carefully. It was hot, but after she blew on it a bit, she was surprised by its aroma and its smooth flavour. "This is very good green tea, Miss Zima."

Zima was taken aback by Mika's response. "I'm... glad you like it, Princess." She exchanged puzzled glances with her husband.

Mika sipped on her tea, smiling to herself, for it made her feel good inside. This was tea given to her by peasants... and it was good. It did not taste that much different from green tea that was served at the castle. She concluded, as she expected, that the peasants and the nobles drank the same green tea.

Zima leaned against Dellen gently, whispering to him. "She's drinking our tea."

"I know. A noble in our kitchen drinking our tea. I'm surprised as hell," said Dellen.

Mika tried to stifle a giggle, for she could still hear them, despite their whispering.

Dellen continued. "But I'm surprised by more than just that...."

"What do you mean?" asked Zima.

"Isn't it obvious? She's a member of the Nobility and the Royal Family. I've always thought of them as nothing but oppressive tyrants who look down on us and abuse us. But this girl... the Princess... she's...."

Zima thought about the demeanour of the Princess. She was definitely unlike most of the nobles she has come across. The nobles that have crossed her path included mostly knights, but sometimes also civilians, most of them pretentious and hostile towards peasants, seeing them as nothing more than cheap labourers. But the little girl who was the Princess of Melodice completely defied the expectations she and Dellen had.

"She's very sweet, speaks with a kind voice, and is polite," said Zima. "But she seems very shy, quiet, and reserved, and she stammers when she speaks sometimes. It's as if she lacks the confidence to express herself. I noticed she kind of has a difficult time looking into our eyes."

"Yeah, I know, but you'll pardon me if I'm still somewhat... skeptical. You know how it is," said Dellen.

"I know, I know." Zima approached Mika again. "I'm glad you're enjoying the tea, Princess."

"Thank you again, Miss Zima. I do appreciate your hospitality," said Mika.

Zima smiled and nodded but with hesitation and confusion. Despite the kindness and gentleness that the little girl Princess of their nation showed, Zima was still wary and cautious. Mika was, after all, a member of the Royal Family. *Why is she here?!*

At that point, Helen saw the oldest of the Balias brothers, Jaren, appear at the doorway.

"Princess!" exclaimed Jaren.

Mika, Zima, and Dellen turned to the doorway. The younger brother, Tyrel, joined Jaren almost immediately. Both boys were clad in long nightshirts.

Tyrel exclaimed as well. "Princess!"

"What are you boys doing awake?" asked Dellen.

"Father, we heard you and Mother talking, so we got up." Jaren regarded the Princess. "But I didn't expect to see the Princess here!"

Tyrel seemed excited as he left Jaren's side, and quickly approached Mika, remembering that she was only a year older than he was. "Princess Mika! What are you doing here?"

"Tyrel!" Zima gave him a warning look, and then shifted her gaze back to Mika. "I'm so sorry, Princess, if he's bothering you."

Mika shook her head. "No, it's quite all right." She turned to Tyrel. "I'm just here... to talk, I suppose, with your parents about some things."

Jaren walked farther into the kitchen. "Don't you remember, Mother, Father? Princess Mika saved us all that one day. She protected us with her magic against that old man who was going to kill a lot of people."

Tyrel chimed in. "Yeah. You saved me, Princess. You saved everyone."

"And I thank you again as well, Princess Mika," said Jaren, trying to sound like a noble by changing his speech.

"You're welcome," said Mika, smiling sweetly, remembering the day when the peasant mob surrounded her cervid carriage, and when the peasants attacked her and her companions, including Helen. She also remembered the chaos and death, more than anything else. She remembered Sir Galner and his magic attack that killed so many. She remembered deflecting another attack from him and protecting the peasants behind her.

Dellen nodded. "I remember that."

Zima smiled towards the Princess. "I remember that, too. We weren't there to see it, but we heard what happened. You saved our boys, Princess. You have our everlasting gratitude. Thank you for protecting them and everyone in the area."

"I did what I had to do." Mika's expression turned to one of sadness. "I had to protect everyone. That was my duty as the Princess. But, still, so many people died. I will... I will mourn that day for the rest of my life. Whenever I remember that day, I become very sad, and I feel a sense of dread. It was... extremely disturbing to me."

"I'm sure it was," said Zima. "I'm sure you've never seen anything like that before."

Mika nodded with agreement. "All my life, I've lived in the castle. I had not ventured beyond the castle gates. I'd never seen the city of Scarletia... until that day when I left the castle for an excursion to the city of Cerulean, to the Cerulean Magic Academy. That was going to be our destination. Miss Helen was with me. That was the day I saw the city for the first time. It was totally unlike what I had expected. I expected it to look more or less the same as within the castle gates, but it was completely different."

While Zima sat down on a chair near Mika, Dellen stayed where he was, observing the Princess. His look was one of skepticism.

Both Mika and Helen could see his suspicion. Mika did not say anything about it or look back at him, for she felt somewhat intimidated. Zima was far easier to talk to, along with their two sons.

"When we were on our way to Cerulean, we were surrounded by an angry mob, and it seemed like they were very angry at me. They knew that a member of the Royal Family was in the carriage. They wanted me to come out, and face my crimes, or rather, not my crimes, but maybe someone else's. They attacked, and the knights that were with me fought back."

Mika's sadness intensified. Zima and the others in the room listened intently as she continued.

"I saw the peasants being killed. And then, my professor of magical studies, Sir Galner, he... he killed so many people with his magic attack. I remember every detail of what happened as if it happened just a moment ago, and I still feel sick whenever I see those images in my mind. Dead people everywhere, some of them burning, some of them with missing legs and arms... and missing heads, and terrible injuries that they died from. There were many injured, crying out in pain. I was so frightened. For a while, I couldn't do anything. I was too frightened to act, until Sir Galner targeted Sir Tyrel with his magic, and I could see he planned to kill more people. I had to stop him. I cast a magic barrier to deflect his attack. And, after that, just when I thought everything was fine, a group of crossbow snipers starting firing quarrels at us. I was almost killed. They killed three of the knights who were escorting us. We had to escape."

Zima regarded her with sympathy.

"So much death. I was so frightened," said the Princess.

Everyone in the room was quiet. Helen wondered how the Princess was feeling, and was hoping she would not break down and dissolve into tears as she often did. But considering what happened to her, she would not blame her if she did. It truly was a frightening experience for her. When she looked up at Dellen, he appeared completely calm and unmoved by Mika's story.

Tyrel and Jaren looked on, not knowing what to say, and feeling uncomfortable because of the seriousness in the room. The Princess, despite her age, could speak like an adult, and the serious tone of voice she used made them feel very uneasy.

"I'm so sorry you had to experience these frightening things, Princess Mika. But I hope you understand that this is the kind of thing we experience regularly," Zima said softly, expressing her sadness as well. She remembered that the Princess mentioned earlier that she wanted to understand something, which was the reason for her visit. "Princess, what was it you said you wanted to understand?"

Mika tried to calm herself as she looked up at Zima. "I want to understand the truth about the state of our nation."

"Huh? Pardon?" said Zima.

Dellen was puzzled as well.

"I have to admit... I don't know anything about the world around me, despite what I've learned from professors and books and constant studying. They've taught me many things. But I feel that they're not telling me everything. When I ventured out into the city for the first time, it was completely different from what they taught me, or perhaps I should say there were many things that were left out. I knew the city was bustling with the activity of many businesses and industries, and people living and working to support the nation. This is what I was taught. However, I wasn't taught that those people were living and working in such terrible conditions. I only found out on my own, by seeing the city with my own eyes."

Mika leaned back in the chair, her hands clasped together on her lap. She continued to speak, her gaze locked with Zima's, her confidence increased by the opportunity to speak her mind. She spoke with a calm but melancholy tone of voice.

"There have been two attempts to take my life. The first was by assassins disguised as merchants. One day, before the beginning of summer, a merchant carriage entered the Grounds, and stopped in front of the castle. A man leapt out of the back of the carriage, and killed another man that was standing right beside me. His blood sprayed all over me, all over my dress, my face, my hair. That man was the leader of the merchant assassins. He and his companions tried to kill as many noble civilians as they could, knowing that they themselves would be killed by the knights once they came. When the leader found out I was the Princess, he turned to me, and he readied his sword, intent on killing me. Fortunately, Miss Helen saved me.

"The second time was the attempt by the peasant mob and the crossbow snipers. They demanded that I be brought out of the carriage, because they wanted me to face some crimes. They were so angry that they attacked us and threw flaming bottles, and even had armed peasants attack our knights. Once again, I was surrounded by images of chaos and death. A sniper was ordered to take my life. I later learned that the sniper was a woman whom we had saved from being assaulted earlier that same day. She nearly killed me, and the only reason why I'm alive right now is because I became sick and fell to my knees. The quarrel that was aimed for my head missed me.

"So one of the things I want to understand is... why are the peasants so angry at me? So angry that they want me dead. And is it me specifically, or is it because I'm of the Nobility and the Royal Family? I have witnessed many things in this past half-month. When the merchant assassins attacked, that was the first time I'd ever seen a person killed. Then, when we drove through the city, I saw poverty unlike anything I'd ever imagined. I was told by many people, the King of Melodice, my professor of magical studies, and several others that everything I saw in the city was perfectly normal, and it was just the way it was. I was told that I shouldn't have to question it. They said this was how the world was, that this was how it worked, that the nobles ruled over the peasants, and that was the way it was. But... recently, I've become very skeptical about that. I believe my skepticism began when I saw the city proper with my own eyes.

"I want to know the truth about the world around me. It's useless for me to ask those closest to me: my father and mother, my maidservant, my own best friend, my professor, or anyone else in the castle. They all think what I'm seeing is normal. But I can't just accept things the way they are just because they say that's the way it is. I decided, if I wanted to understand the truth about the world, I couldn't ask the nobles who appear to have biased opinions. I needed to talk to the peasants who are living in the world that was hidden from me until now. Sir Tyrel and Sir Jaren were the first peasant boys that I became acquainted with. Because of that, I'm able to talk to you, Miss Zima and Sir Dellen. I was hoping that... I could find answers to my questions from you."

"That's enough, Princess," Dellen said abruptly, but Mika had already finished with what she wanted to say. Helen, Zima, Tyrel, and Jaren all turned towards him, and Mika looked up to meet his gaze, a gaze that stared her down with distrust.

Zima wondered about his tone. "Dellen?"

Dellen approached the kitchen table, and sat down on a chair directly across from Mika. He rested his arms on the table, and held his hands together, his expression serious. "Don't take this the wrong way. I do understand you saw the world for the first time, and I'm sure it was disturbing. Your reaction wasn't all that surprising. I don't have a problem with you coming to our home to see us and to find out what you want to know and understand. But I also need you to understand where I'm coming from."

Mika was confused, trying to figure out what he was trying to say.

"I don't know you very well, My Lady, since this is the first time I've ever seen you. I've only heard of you. I don't know if you really are the sweet little girl that Zima thinks you are. For all I know, this could all be an act, and there could be knights coming here right now intent on capturing us and killing us."

Jaren frowned deeply. "Father, what are you saying to her?"

"Wait just a minute," said Dellen, gesturing with a hand motion to calm Jaren down. "Everyone, just hear me out, including you, Princess Mika. I'm not trying to be disrespectful or anything, and if I sound that way, please forgive me. But I have no idea what's going on here. You just showed up on our doorstep, and started telling us these things. Why? You say you want to understand, but to what end? My wife seems to like and trust you, but I have to protect my family first. I hope you understand what I'm saying, Princess. Is there something you can tell us or show us that would convince us we're not being led into a trap?"

Helen glanced towards Mika. "Sir Dellen has a point, Princess."

Mika looked down at the table in front of her as she leaned forward. She watched the tiny remnants of tea leaves sinking to the bottom of her teacup. *Yes, you're right, Miss Helen, he does have a point. What reason does Sir Dellen have to believe what I'm saying? From what I've seen, it looks like the Nobility and the Royal Family have been oppressing the Peasantry for a long time. He's of the Peasantry, and I'm of the Nobility and the Royal Family. He has no reason to trust me. The peasants don't trust the Nobility. Why should they after being treated the way they have?*

"So what'll it be, Princess Mika Silveraine?" asked Dellen, waiting for a response.

Mika looked somber as she gazed up at Dellen. *It pains me to do this, but perhaps I should show him… all of them. That's the only thing I can think of that might convince him.*

Mika slowly pushed herself out of the chair, feeling a few aches and pains all over her body as she stood up, and supported herself against the table.

Tyrel was closest to her. He saw her struggle, so he took her arm. "Princess, are you okay?"

Mika nodded. "I'm fine."

Zima and Dellen were confused. They wondered what she was planning to do. Why was she getting up? And why did she look like she was in pain just now?

Helen was just as confused as the others. "Princess?"

Everyone looked on while Mika headed to the centre of the kitchen, facing all of them with sad eyes. She wrapped her arms around herself, feeling not just physical pain, but also a deep shame and embarrassment that she forced herself to get over. Otherwise, she would never be able to convince them. Her voice quivered slightly as she spoke.

"Sometimes... sometimes my father gets angry at me when I do or say something that he doesn't like. I don't necessarily do anything wrong, but it just seems like everything I do and say is wrong somehow. I suppose... parents have to discipline their children."

As she spoke, Helen was alarmed, because she knew what the Princess was talking about, while everyone else was confused, trying to figure out what she was doing. The white dress Mika wore had a high neckline, but did not go all the way to her neck. It was a kind of dress that she could slip into easily by putting it over her head. However, there were three strings at the back that were tied into bows. If she pulled on them, the top of her dress would loosen, and would open up in the back. This is precisely what she did. She pulled on the strings.

"Princess, what are you doing?" asked Helen, her eyes wide.

Mika continued speaking. "Several days after I returned home from the attack of the peasant mob and the crossbow snipers, my father came up to my bedchamber to see me, and he wasn't happy with me. He was angry at me for questioning the world around me, for protecting the peasants, for becoming acquainted with Sir Tyrel and Sir Jaren...."

With the ties of her dress undone, Mika let it slip off her shoulders, allowing it to fall just to her elbows. She used both hands to hold up the front of the dress to keep it from exposing her breasts. Her shoulders, upper arms, and much of her chest were exposed. Dellen, Zima, Tyrel, and Jaren, all shocked, saw the light and dark bruises of varying shapes and sizes all over her skin.

Mika's eyes began to tear as her voice dropped to nearly

a whisper. "He was very angry at me so he punished me. These bruises... will take some time to heal. They're all over the front of my body. I still feel a lot of pain whenever I move."

"Princess," whispered Zima, her own eyes beginning to tear as well.

Dellen looked on as he stood up from his seat.

Tears came down Mika's cheeks as she cast her eyes down. "I'm not lying to you, Sir Dellen. I'm not lying to any of you. When Sir Jaren asked me why I protected them... I told him it was because I was their Princess and that I loved them as my people. When I said that, I meant it. I meant it then as I do now. You are all my people, and I'm your Princess."

"The King... did this?" whispered Jaren.

Helen stood beside Mika, her heart filled with several emotions at once. She was worried about Mika, and she was angry at King Ralphen for physically abusing his own daughter. She wanted to put an arm around Mika to comfort her, but at the same time, her hand formed a fist that wanted to go to the King and punch him out... but that would probably be her last day on this world, because she would be executed if she tried anything like that.

"Tell me, Sir Dellen, as a father, do you consider this punishment?" Helen asked.

Dellen responded right away. "No, Miss Helen, this is not punishment. This is abuse. This is what the King does to the Princess? This is how he disciplines his daughter, whether she actually did anything wrong?"

"Correct, and this occurs every once in a while. These are the worst injuries the Princess has endured so far. I fear it may become worse as she gets older."

"The nobles see themselves as superior to us peasants, but they treat their children with barbarism? I don't know of any parent among the Peasantry who does this to their child. Not a single one."

Despite her tears, Mika almost laughed as she spoke a little louder. "Sometimes I think of myself as a coward and a weakling. I'm probably useless as well, because I'm too scared to say or do anything. I may be a Princess, but I'm still just a child because I don't know much about the world around me." Mika tried to pull her dress back up.

"Allow me, Princess Mika," whispered Helen.

"Thank you, Miss Helen...."

Helen pulled Mika's dress up over her shoulders, closed it at the back, and retied the strings that kept the top of her dress together.

"I may not know very much... but there's one thing I do know more than anything else," said Mika, trying her best to be more determined. "I do know that I love my people... and because I do love you, then perhaps I can do something. But... but I don't know what to do, because, as I mentioned, I'm still a child. I know very little about how the world works and how to interact with it."

Dellen cast his eyes downward on the wooden floorboards, feeling a heavy heart.

"I don't want to stand by anymore and see my people suffering the way they are." Mika wiped her tears with her sleeve, because she had nothing else on her she could use to wipe them away.

Dellen was surprised. "Huh?"

"I can't allow my people to suffer any more than they already have. I want to help them. As the Princess of Melodice, that's what I have to do, because that's my duty. That's what I want to do."

Dellen paused for a long moment, taking in the words of Princess Mika. He questioned for a moment if he was hearing this right, but she spoke clearly and was not stammering. From how she expressed herself just now, he could tell she was not just spewing words of idealism that maybe a naive child would.

Mika knew what she was talking about, and knew what she wanted to do. She knew it deep in her heart.

"Princess... I hope you realize what you're saying. If you keep on saying and doing the things you have, even if you're a member of the Royal Family, even if you're the Princess of Melodice, you're going against what's considered by the government, by the Nobility, and by the Royal

Family, to be status quo. If you're caught, you'll be charged with treason, and the sentence for that is execution. You do realize that, I hope."

Mika nodded. "I do! I know I could die by my own father's hand. I'm frightened. I'm so scared I feel like my heart might stop, even at this very moment. But… but I still want to help. If you knew that a loved one was being oppressed by someone else, wouldn't you want to help your loved one, Sir Dellen? Wouldn't you want to save them, even if it meant putting your own life in danger?"

Dellen thought that Mika's words were wise, despite her age. He began to acknowledge her words. "Yes. You're right, Princess."

Zima got up from her seat, and went to kneel down in front of Mika. "Princess Mika, you're so kind and wonderful to us. You're very different from most of the nobles we've met. A few were kind to us, but you're the kindest one I've met in my entire life."

Mika smiled. "I'm simply doing what I feel is the right thing to do."

"Thank you, Princess." Zima stood up, and looked at everyone around her in the kitchen. "Well, then, as you asked, I think it's about time for us to tell you the true state of the nation of Melodice. What we will tell you might surprise you… or it might not, since you've already seen some of the suffering we have to endure. These are the kinds of things that the people of your castle will not tell you, because they're ignorant and honestly aren't aware, or they think it's just the way it is and it's not worth mentioning, or they think you simply don't have to know because they think it's not important."

So this is it, thought Mika. *The cold, harsh reality, I will know about it, not from the nobles who see themselves as superior to the peasants, but from the experiences of the peasants themselves.*

* * *

Dellen and Zima told their two boys to go back to sleep.

They had wanted to stay in the living room, where everyone else was, to listen to what their parents revealed to Princess Mika and Helen. The living room was close to the front door of the house. It had old couches arranged around a low makeshift table that was really an old wooden crate, now repurposed. The upholstery was almost threadbare from years of use, torn in some places. Dellen brought the kerosene lamp into the living room for light, and set it in a corner.

Although the front door was locked, Helen noticed that there were steel braces mounted with screws on the walls at either side of the door. A heavy wooden beam rested against the wall beside the door. She remembered hearing the sound of something moving past the door before Dellen had opened it for them earlier. She concluded that the door had been barricaded.

Mika and Helen sat beside each other on one of the couches, which were so low on the ground that Mika was able to sit like an adult, with her thighs level to the ground and her shoes touching the floorboards, but due to Helen's height, her knees were almost up to her chest. In order to preserve her modesty, she sat diagonally, keeping her knees together, because her black dress didn't go below her knees. It wasn't too bad with Mika, who dressed similarly. Across the table from them, Dellen and Zima were seated on another couch facing them.

What Mika and Helen were about to be told about the state of the nation was going to surprise them greatly. They were young ladies who were brought up in a protected environment with the true nature of the world hidden from them; their reaction would only be natural to Dellen and Zima.

"Have you studied anything about economics, Princess Mika?" asked Zima.

Mika nodded. "Yes. It's one of the subjects that my professors teach me at the castle."

"Good. And I'm assuming it's not a common subject they teach to children your age. It's likely because you're of the Royal Family. They'd be teaching you economics, and probably the more advanced aspects of it."

"Um… I suppose so. I do study basic economics with other children who are close to my age in one class. I also study the more advanced aspects with a different professor."

"Very good," said Zima. "You seem to be pretty intelligent, Princess, so I'm sure you'll understand what I'm about to tell you. In the study of economics, specifically financial economics, you'll know that the nation has a certain amount of financial resources. You know this, right?"

Mika nodded again. "Yes, I do."

"I don't know exactly how much money the entire nation has, but we know it's not infinite. Nobody can have an infinite amount of money, and nations are not exempt from that rule. It's impossible. Now, let me tell you that, out of all the money the nation has, about ninety-nine percent of that money, those financial resources, is owned by the Nobility. The one percent that's not owned by them is owned by the Peasantry. You do know about percentages, don't you, Princess?"

"Yes. Mathematics is a subject I learn from my professors as well, and I believe I'm quite proficient at it."

"Okay, that's good. I'm impressed, by the way. Do you know how many people live in the nation of Melodice?"

"About twenty million," replied Mika.

"That's right. When you compare the percentage of the population that's of the Nobility and the percentage of the population that's of the Peasantry, there's a huge difference. About ninety-nine percent of the population is of the Peasantry. The remaining one percent is of the Nobility. From those percentages, would you happen to know how many people are nobles and how many people are peasants?"

"Um… let me see." Mika thought for a very short moment as she calculated the numbers in her highly developed mind. "One percent of twenty million is two hundred thousand, so that's how many people are of the Nobility… and about nineteen million eight hundred thousand are of the Peasantry." Her expression became very much subdued as she understood what did not make sense among those numbers.

Dellen noticed her reaction. "You see now what's wrong with this picture?"

Mika looked up at Dellen and Zima. "That doesn't make sense. Why is it that such a huge proportion of the nation's financial resources is owned by such a small proportion of the nation's population?"

"Because the small proportion of the population, that is, the Nobility, is in control of those financial resources, Princess Mika," said Zima. "They control the flow of money. If they control the flow of money, they control the flow of goods and the provision of services. If they control all those things, then they control how much of the financial resources, goods, and services can be allocated to the Peasantry."

"I see... so the Peasantry are left with almost nothing, even though they are the majority of the population," whispered Mika.

"This is why the peasants are living in a state of poverty. Also, taxes are very high. Again, taxation is controlled by the Nobility. The cost of living in our nation is also very high. Everyone, regardless of whether they're nobles or peasants, pays the same percentage of taxes. Everyone pays the same percentage given whatever goods or services they purchase. The cost of living is the same for both. However, if peasants and nobles are paying the same amount of taxes and they're paying the same amount of money towards the cost of living, what does that tell you, based on what you've heard so far?"

Mika thought quickly about that as well. "It means that the Nobility can afford the taxes and cost of living, since they have much more money, while the Peasantry have a much more difficult time. They can't afford it as easily, or they may not be able to afford it at all, since they have much less money."

Mika remembered the man she'd seen while she was traveling through the city of Scarletia. He was being beaten by knights because he failed to pay his taxes, but the reason he could not pay his taxes was because he had to feed his children first.

Zima smiled. "You have a brilliant mind, Princess, for someone your age."

Mika blushed for a moment. "Oh... thank you. But... how long has it been like this? Surely, it couldn't have been like this throughout the entire history of Melodice. Our nation has existed for a very long time. There are many people who are proud of our nation. But then again... all the people I know who are proud of our nation are of the Nobility."

"I can tell you that the Peasantry are just as proud of their nation as the Nobility are, if not more so. And yes, you're right. It wasn't always like this. There was a time when the gap between the upper class and the working class was much smaller."

Mika remembered some of things the peasant mob had said to her when they surrounded her carriage. From the words they chose to use, it sounded like the crimes they referred to where against the nation and the people. She remembered what the leader of the merchant assassins had said to her just before he was about to strike her down with his sword. He was going to kill her for the nation of Melodice.

"How long has it been like this?" Mika asked.

"Just over a century now. Something happened back then that somehow gradually increased the gap between the upper class and the working class over many years. I can't... remember exactly, but I'm sure you yourself can research it and find out very easily."

Zima paused for a very brief moment, staring into Mika's eyes, as if she wanted to say something, but she did not know how to say it. She cleared her throat, and continued.

"Eventually, the Nobility began to see the Peasantry as a separate people. They began to use the peasants as something like slave labour. The only reason why we're not called slaves is because we're paid a little for our labour. Also, while the Nobility began to regard the Peasantry as a separate people, they also started to see us as inferior to them in every way. They began to control us, and treat us like we were criminals in some sort of prison. Knights would patrol the cities, and hand out harsh punishment to the peasants, sometimes not because they did anything wrong, but because they felt like it. They asserted their so-called superiority by making the peasants suffer. Peasants who made simple mistakes were also punished very harshly, sometimes with death."

Mika remembered being told about the execution of the people who were involved with the attack of the merchant assassins. It was not just the people who were involved that were killed. Their families, including women and children, were also executed by order of the King.

"Princess Mika, we're living under tyranny and oppression. Because of this, throughout the past century, countless revolutions have occurred all over the nation."

At this point, Mika was confused. She tried to search her memory on what she has learned of history. "I can't... seem to remember learning anything about revolutions."

"What about civil wars?"

Mika shook her head. "I don't remember anything about civil wars either."

Zima looked up at Helen. "What about you, Miss Helen? Since you're the Princess's guard, you might know."

Helen was as confused as Mika was. She shook her head. "I'm sorry, Miss Zima, but I don't remember hearing about revolutions or wars either. As far as I have learned, the nation has lived in peacetime for a very long time, several decades, if I remember correctly."

"Well, then." Dellen laughed sarcastically. He leaned back, crossing his arms against his chest. "I guess I'm not surprised. You're both young, so I'm sure you've been kept from learning the truth. Revolutions have occurred within our city in your lifetimes. You just haven't been told about them."

"That's right," said Zima. "Revolutions have occurred all over the nation, not just in our capital city, within your own lifetimes. All these revolutions have occurred between peasants and nobles. Why do you think you have such an enormous standing army within the castle during peacetime?"

Helen was surprised at herself for not thinking about that. "Come to think of it, that does seem rather odd. I've never truly paid attention to it until now. We're living in times of peace, but knights are always keeping watch from the walls. There are about two thousand knights permanently stationed at the castle, with another one thousand in the city proper."

Mika felt disturbed. "That's true. I've always thought the knights were just there to keep the peace."

"That's an awful lot of knights permanently deployed in your castle just to keep the peace," said Dellen.

Mika noticed Zima turn her gaze to Dellen, as if asking him a silent question, which he responded to with a nod of his head. She wondered what that meant, if anything.

Zima turned back to Mika and Helen. "Within our city, there are rebel groups who are always fighting on behalf of the peasants. They fight against the Nobility and the oppression and tyranny that they represent. In fact, they're not just within Scarletia. They exist in every city and town in every part of the nation. They're everywhere, but they're in hiding, and keep their operations secret."

"Rebel groups?" asked Mika.

"Yes. There are two main rebel groups in the city of Scarletia. There are also several other much smaller rebel groups scattered throughout the city. One of those minor groups was actually the group that organized the attack on you and your companions while you were traveling through the city."

Mika gasped at hearing that.

"Almost all the members of that group were found, captured, and executed. Usually, when any attack like that occurs, an attack on the Nobility, knights are deployed to find those responsible. They find and execute not only the ones who are responsible, but their families as well... and that includes innocent children."

Mika's hands covered her mouth as she leaned forward, her elbows on her knees.

Helen closed her eyes.

"Sometimes," said Dellen, "we wonder if we're next in line to be found and killed. It could happen anytime."

"Princess Mika," said Zima, "apparently, our family is somewhat more fortunate than most of the peasant families out there. However, we still barely make enough money to make ends meet. We're barely making enough money to send Tyrel and Jaren to school."

"It's been calculated that the average working-class civilian takes home about five hundred Crystium every year. Compare that to the average income of a noble, which is about fifty thousand Crystium, about a hundred times more than the average peasant."

"Our combined income, for my husband and I, is just enough to feed our children for the entire year and to provide for their education, but there are a lot more things to consider. We have to pay our taxes. We have to make sure that our children have clothes to wear after they've outgrown them, and we have to make sure they're healthy. We simply don't have enough money to handle all the things that life typically throws at us."

Dellen leaned forward towards Princess Mika, his elbows on his knees. "Princess, you earlier talked about these merchants who infiltrated the castle and tried to kill you."

Mika nodded. "Yes?"

"They were part of a rebel group, another minor group, far smaller than the one involved with the mob of peasants. They were found, but it wasn't just the people involved that were found. All of them, including their wives and children, including at least one infant, were slaughtered by the knights. Our son Jaren was there to see it."

Mika, one hand over her mouth, closed her eyes, turning her head to the side. She could not begin to describe what she was feeling deep in her heart.

"He told us," continued Zima, "that the knights took the baby away from his mother, screaming, crying hysterically. The mother was in agony when she begged the knights to spare her son. When the order to execute them was given, the knight who held the baby threw him into the air, and another knight shot him with a crossbow. The screaming of the baby stopped mid-air. He fell to the ground, still wrapped in a blanket. The blanket was stained with blood. It was the most dreadful thing he had ever seen, and he still has nightmares because of it. After that baby was killed, the other knights slaughtered everyone... men, women, and children."

Mika opened her eyes for a moment, and tears came down her cheeks and onto her hand.

Helen tried to be as calm as possible, but she could imagine the events taking place in her mind as Zima described them. Seeing Mika cry made her want to cry herself, but she tried as hard as she could to look calm.

"This was ordered by the King of Melodice, King Ralphen Silveraine," said Dellen.

Mika could not take any more of this as loud sobs came from her throat. She turned away, and closed her eyes tightly, covering them with her hands, trying to stem the tears that streamed down profusely.

Dellen hung his head low, staring down at the floorboards, feeling a heavy heart.

Zima stood up from the couch, and walked around the table, kneeling down in front of Mika. Zima held out her hands. "Princess Mika...."

When Mika saw them, she put her small hands in Zima's, and when she looked up at Zima, she could see that she had started crying as well.

"This... this is our reality, my dear Princess Mika," said Zima, her voice soft and breaking as she spoke through her tears. "I am... I am so sorry that you had to see it."

Mika shook her head. "No, please, please don't be sorry. I'm the one who's sorry. I'm sorry that this world is so ugly. I'm sorry that it's treating you and everyone else like this. I'm so sorry...." Loud sobs came as Mika put her head down on her knees, her hands holding onto Zima's tightly.

Despite Helen's exceptional self-control, she could not take any more of this. She quickly stood up, and spoke in a whisper. "Please excuse me. I'll be outside."

Dellen looked up at Helen, and nodded with acknowledgment. However, he noticed that she immediately avoided his gaze as she headed for the front door to exit, and wondered if something was wrong.

As soon as she was outside, Helen leaned against the door. Under the dark skies, she did not care if there was anyone else walking on the street right now. She put her head down, and covered her face with one hand as tears streamed down her cheeks.

"Dammit... why am I crying...?"

However, she knew deep in her heart the reason why, after hearing Dellen and Zima's words and seeing Princess Mika cry over them. After a moment, she looked for a handkerchief in one of her skirt pockets, and wiped her tears away. She tried to calm herself.

"Stay in control, Helen... this is not the time."

Inside, Mika was also trying to calm herself down, but it was taking her quite some time. She saw Jaren and Tyrel hiding around a corner. They had been watching what was going on, and listening to everything that was being said. As soon as Mika saw them, Jaren pulled Tyrel back, and they both disappeared.

After a moment, Helen went back inside the house, and sat down beside Mika. "I'm sorry," she said, apologizing for leaving so suddenly and coming back the same.

When Mika saw Helen's eyes, she suspected that she must have cried as well, but Helen was doing an extremely good job of making it look like it never happened, except for what she could not control, which was her reddened eyes. Mika wiped her tears away with her sleeves as she began to sit up straight again. "Please forgive me for crying so much."

Dellen's voice was hushed. "You don't have to apologize for that."

Mika clasped her hands together on her knees as she glanced at everyone around her, Miss Helen, Sir Dellen, and Miss Zima. "This nation is so ugly, the way it has treated all of you. The Nobility have been oppressing the Peasantry for a long time, and this has been happening without my knowledge. The truth was hidden away from me. And now, Miss Zima, Sir Dellen, I do understand.

This is what I was seeking, the reason why I set out into the city this late into the night. I've heard the truth from you, from the peasants, from the people who personally experience that truth. Thank you."

Zima smiled sadly at Mika. "I'm glad you understand now, Princess Mika. You don't know how much it means to me, how much it means to my husband, to our family, to be understood by you."

"Same here, Princess," said Dellen. "I think... for a member of the Royal Family to understand our situation, it means so much to us, more than you'll ever know. This may be a small thing that's happened, your understanding... but it's probably the single greatest thing we've seen happen for a very long time."

Mika wiped her eyes again with her sleeves to remove any residue of tears. She was no longer crying, but her eyes were red. "I'm... I'm going to change our nation...."

Helen looked up suddenly, wondering if she heard right.

Zima and Dellen were surprised as well.

"Now that I understand, there must be something that the Princess of Melodice can do. I'm going to put a stop to this ugliness." A quiet determination began to surface through Mika's voice as she spoke a little louder. Her hands tightened on the hem of her dress. "That's what I'm going to do. I'll change this nation. The problem is I don't know how to go about it. I may not know what to do in order to achieve that goal, but I know what I want to see, and what I want to see is the end of the suffering of the Peasantry. I know I need help, because I don't know very much. I'm just a child, after all. I need the help of people who I can trust."

Mika and Helen watched as Zima looked back at Dellen again, as if asking another silent question, but they said nothing about it, nor did they react at all outwardly. Dellen responded with a nod.

Zima turned back to Mika. "Princess Mika, if you want to help the peasants, I think that's extremely honourable of you. If that's what you want to do, as the Princess of Melodice, there are people in this city who will be able to help you."

Helen felt a sense of dread somehow, but she was not sure why just yet.

"People... who can help me?" said Mika.

"Yes. All you need to do, if you want to, is tell them what you want to do, that you want to change this nation, for all your people who you love so much. That's all you need to do. That's the very first step. If you want to, you just have to take that first step."

Sir Dellen, Miss Zima... they're part of a rebel group, aren't they? Both Mika and Helen thought this at the same time.

Mika held her hands together on her lap as she thought.

Take that first step. That first step would be to talk to the people who are willing to help me with what I want to do. That means... I might be talking to a rebel group. Who else would have the resources and cunning to be able to help me bring about the changes I want to see? It wouldn't be ordinary peasants. If they're able to help me reach my goal, if they're able to help me free the peasants from tyranny and oppression... yes, they're the only ones who can help me....

Helen was also thinking about this.

Wait a minute. Princess, now that you understand, it's very honourable of you to want to help the peasants and bring to them a brighter future. It's very honourable of you to want to change the nation of Melodice for the better so the Peasantry can live a better life. But... wait a minute. We're talking about people who are willing to help you if you just tell them what you want to do? No nobles can do that for you, and certainly no ordinary peasants... only rebels can. Princess Mika... you don't mean...?

Mika gazed up at Dellen and Zima, her eyes filled with a new determination welling up from within. "I'll change our nation for the better. I promise."

CHAPTER 17

DECISION OF THE PRINCESS

A S HELEN LEANED AGAINST THE wall near the front door, she watched Mika, who was taking a short nap on one of the couches, covered up to her chest with a thin blanket that Zima had placed on top of her earlier. The Princess had been asleep for the past half hour. She was exhausted from all she'd learned tonight, and it was very late, a few hours past midnight. A quick nap should do her some good.

"Princess," whispered Helen. She was deeply disturbed by what Mika had said earlier.

So you want to change our nation. That's fine, but… but what are you planning, exactly? From what I've heard, it seems that either Sir Dellen or Miss Zima is a member of a rebel group, or both, or perhaps just Sir Dellen, most likely. So there are people willing to help you realize what you want to see happen? Princess, from what I'm seeing, there can only be one direction this can lead. This was not part of tonight's plan!

In a few more hours, the sun would rise. Helen approached Mika, and knelt down close to her. She shook the Princess gently by the shoulder. "Princess, please wake up." She shook her a little more.

Mika opened her eyes. She slowly pushed herself off the couch, and then sat up, rubbing away sleep from her eyes. She pushed away the old blanket, whose threads were coming loose down every side. Despite that, it still felt soft and comfortable, as if it was an old stuffed animal. She was surprised at how alert she was. She had expected herself to be extremely sleepy.

"How are you feeling, Princess?" asked Helen.

"Very well, Miss Helen," answered Mika. "I'm surprisingly wide awake now."

"This is why they call them power naps. I believe that is the term used by the peasants. It works quite well, in fact."

"I see."

"Anyway, I'm concerned with how much time we're spending here." Helen looked up just in time to see Dellen and Zima coming back into the living room. "Sir Dellen, Miss Zima, I believe we are overstaying our welcome. It's imperative that we return to the castle as soon as possible."

Dellen looked at his timepiece. He was the only member of his family who owned one. They could not afford more than one. "It's very late. And sunrise will come in a little more than two hours."

"Exactly." Helen turned back to Mika, who was still sitting up on the couch with her legs folded back on either side of her, her shoes on the floor. "Princess, we still need to plan on returning to the castle from here."

"Oh my," said Zima. "You told us earlier, Miss Helen, how you both managed to sneak out of the castle to begin with. It was very bold and daring, not to mention dangerous."

Mika kept quiet, staring down at the floorboards underneath the old wooden crate in front of her that served as a table. She stared at her white shoes, now stained from her recent adventures through the city of Scarletia. She thought about what she said earlier, about wanting to change the nation of Melodice, about needing help to change it, about not knowing what to do or how to do it. She remembered what Zima told her, that there are people who would be willing to help her if she just asked.

"And it'll be even more dangerous when we go back." Helen sighed at the insurmountable task that was given to them. Getting back into the castle was going to take a miracle. "I've been trying to think of a method that would help us return unnoticed, but I must admit that it's extremely difficult."

Dellen shook his head. "You should have planned your return to the castle just as thoroughly as you planned getting out. But I understand you might not have had enough experience in planning something like this, given that you're still quite young, Miss Helen. When taking on a mission as a soldier would, you should always have an escape plan. You should take into account any and all possibilities."

Helen frowned slightly as she felt her pride taking a hit. She knew he was right "I admit we didn't plan as well as we should have."

Zima had an idea. "I guess you can try to do what those merchants did, the ones who attacked the Princess. Sneak into the castle inside wooden crates, just like how you snuck out of the castle to begin with."

"But if we do that, it would be much later in the morning before we can actually return to the castle, because they run on a schedule. And I'm certain it would look very odd to the people who will unpack the crates, because the delivery will be not of fruits and vegetables, but rather a knight in casual apparel and the Princess of Melodice."

"That's true." Dellen crossed his arms against his chest as he tried to think as well, but even he could not think of any ideas.

The quiet Princess was deep in thought. *There's something... there's something I must do....*

Helen continued. "In the approaching daylight, the Princess and I would no longer be able to maintain our cover. Our cloaks are of expensive and high-quality fabric, and are in sharp contrast to the clothes the peasants are wearing. They will notice us."

Dellen agreed. "That's right. And it won't just be the peasants who'll notice. The knights who patrol the streets might notice you, too."

Helen stood up. "This will be the most challenging thing I've ever done. I sincerely hope for success. Otherwise... I don't even want to think about the consequences."

"Miss Helen," whispered Mika, still staring at her shoes.

Helen glanced down at Mika. "What is it, Princess Mika?"

Mika slowly met Helen's gaze. She gathered the courage to say what she needed to say. "Please return to the castle without me."

Taken aback, Helen was not sure if she heard that correctly. "What?"

"You can return without me," Mika said again.

Dellen and Zima looked on with surprise.

Helen's eyes widened with shock. "Princess Mika! What exactly are you trying to say? Are you saying you're staying here?"

"Yes, Miss Helen, I am."

"What? Wait...." Helen tried to speak but something happened to her that rarely happened. She was speechless for a moment. She was so shocked by what the Princess told her that she did not know what to say or think. A flood of emotions overwhelmed her from within.

"It would be far easier for you to return to the castle on your own, Miss Helen."

Helen gritted her teeth as she knelt back down in front of the Princess. "No! I don't care if you're the Princess! I'm telling you what I think, and I think that's a terrible idea! What the hell are you thinking?!"

Mika shrank back, her eyes cast down and away, as Helen yelled at her.

"We both have to go back, Princess! We must return to the castle! We left together! We have to return together!"

"I'm sorry, Miss Helen...." Mika looked up at Helen again. "But please think about it for a moment. If you were to go back to the castle on your own, you could simply walk up to the castle gates, and ask the guards to let you in. They'll most likely let you in, almost right away, since you're one of them. They might ask you what you were doing outside the castle, and you can probably conjure up a story. They'll most likely believe you. If we return together, it would look suspicious. You might be disciplined, and your career as a knight would be threatened. I might receive an even worse beating from my father. We may have been able to escape from the castle without letting anyone know... but returning together unnoticed would be impossible without consequences."

Helen's surprised expression was now mixed with a look of anxiety, worry over the Princess and her well-being. "What about you, Princess? What are you doing, exactly? Why are you...?"

Dellen and Zima stole a glance at each other, for they could see where this was going. Zima appeared regretful that the Princess had made this decision so quickly, while Dellen kept a calm exterior.

Helen agreed inwardly that it would be much easier for her to return by herself, but it was not for her own well-being that she was worried.

"Miss Helen, I appreciate your concern over me." Mika leaned forward, her face closer to Helen's. She tried to look calm, in contrast to Helen's uncharacteristically emotional expression. Usually, it was Mika who was more emotional while Helen was calm. It was as if they had switched places.

"But... Princess...."

"I'm going to stay here with my people. I'm their Princess."

Helen sighed heavily as her anger and frustration exploded. Glaring at Mika, she slammed her fist against the top of the table beside her. "No! This is wrong!" She stood up, and loomed over Mika, who gasped. "Not everyone among the Peasantry will be as understanding of you as Sir Dellen, Miss Zima, and their family! Not everyone will be as sympathetic towards you as they have been! If they see you and realize who you are while you're out here on your own, some of them will not hesitate to kill you! You know that, don't you?! Please tell me you know that!"

"I do know that!" Mika answered, her voice raised. However, the Princess was not angry. She raised her voice to try to convince Helen that she knew what she was doing. She got up from the couch, and stood in front of Helen, placing her hands gently on her arm. "I do know that the peasants are angry at the Nobility and the Royal Family, and if they see me, some of them might capture me and take my life. And you know, I'm very scared, Miss Helen! I'm scared that might just happen to me!"

Without her realizing, Helen gently placed her own hand on Mika's arm as well. "Then come back with me."

Mika spoke with a quivering voice. "I can't. I have to be with my people, Miss Helen. I'm their Princess. Yes, I'm scared of what might happen to me. But if... if I'm going to die, I think I would rather die by the hands of the peasants than by the hands of the nobles. The nobles would probably kill me because I've done something that is against their status quo. If the peasants are to kill me... it won't be before I tell them that I love them as my people, because I'm their Princess. I would hope that my last words, when I die, would be of love for my nation, for peasants and nobles alike, for my people." Mika held onto Helen's arm very gently, trying to comfort the older girl from her emotional turmoil. "Please, I do beg of you, please return to the castle."

Helen stared into Mika's eyes, her worry for her so great that she wanted to grab her and force her to come with her. "Princess Mika... I...."

"Please don't make me order you to go back without me."

Helen was still angry, but that last thing Mika told her made her anger worse. She pulled away from the Princess, and took a few steps back. "Why are you doing this anyway? Was I right in asking you before if you had the beginnings of a rebellious streak in you?! I understand that you want to help your people, but what you're doing is not the right way to do it! There are other ways to help the Peasantry, far safer ways, ways that will not include you risking your life!"

"Why even ask me why I'm doing this when you know why, Miss Helen? You know why I want to help the Peasantry as the Princess of Melodice."

"How the hell do you propose to help them?!"

Mika shook her head. "I... I don't know, Miss Helen. I told you already, I don't know what to do just yet. I have to find out how to do it and who will help me. Miss Zima told me that there are people in this city who would be able to help me if I simply asked them."

"Don't be so naive!" Helen wanted to take her and get out of here as she screamed in her mind. *Damn, you stupid little girl, what are you thinking?! If I take her, I could get arrested, even if the Princess defended me, and she would, knowing her. What the hell do I do?!*

"Please, Miss Helen," said Mika.

Helen took a deep breath, regaining most of her composure after a moment. She looked down at the Princess with her usual seriousness. "No, Mika."

"Huh?" Mika was surprised, especially since Helen addressed her so casually just now.

"I'm not going anywhere without you. I'm your knight. You're my Princess. We're colleagues in the study of magic. In a way... you could say we're partners in that regard. We're not too far from each other in age. We've... even started to understand each other... and maybe, someday...." Helen shook her head. "No, I can't just leave you here on your own."

Mika felt warmth in her cheeks. *She called me by my first name... and she said we're partners... and we've started to understand each other? Does that mean... maybe someday...? Miss Helen, please don't be angry with me for too long. I didn't want to have to do this... but... right now....* "I'm so sorry, Miss Helen... but... that means I have to give you an order... as the Princess of Melodice."

Helen was shocked, but she had a feeling this was going to happen. She was trapped. There was nothing else she could do now. The tone of her soft voice pleaded as she shook her head. "Please, Princess Mika...."

"Please... return to the castle without me. That's an order."

Helen clenched her fists at her side with utterly helpless frustration. As the Princess stared at her, she sighed heavily, her heart full of turmoil. After a long, silent moment, she took a few steps back.

"As you wish, Princess Mika." Helen sighed with regret. She hesitated one more time as she and Mika exchanged a long gaze. Mika was not going to change her mind, and she was not going to see it her way. Helen turned to Dellen and Zima, and gave them a small bow of her head. "Thank you for your hospitality."

Dellen nodded. Both he and Zima were speechless.

Helen approached the front door. She put on her cloak, and took one more glance at Mika. "All I can ask of you right now is for you to please try very hard to stay safe, Princess Mika. As much as possible. I beg of you. Will you at least promise this?"

Mika nodded. "Of course, Miss Helen. I will do my best."

With that, Helen left the house, closing the door behind her.

Dellen stepped closer to Mika. "Princess... you're sure you want to do this?"

As Zima joined Dellen, Mika hesitated at first, thinking about his question. There could no longer be any other answer, as she thought about it. She nodded with determination. "Yes. Absolutely. Because I'm your Princess, I will do anything to change our nation for the better. I will do my very best. And I will start here in the city of Scarletia."

"I know that... but... it's just...."

Mika was puzzled. "What is it, Sir Dellen?"

With one look at Dellen, Zima could tell exactly what was on his mind. "I think Dellen is just worried about you, Princess Mika. In fact, I am, too. We're worried about you... as parents would be."

Dellen nodded with agreement. "Yes, exactly. I can't overlook the fact that you... that you're a child, Princess. How old are you, exactly?"

"Eleven," answered Mika.

"You're still a kid, still years away from the age of majority. But... you're deciding on your own what you think you should do, and it could be dangerous for you. You're putting your life at great risk for the sake of the people. You do know that's what you're doing, don't you? I can't really agree with a child knowingly putting her own life in danger like this, because, as a father, my first thought would be that a child your age doesn't always understand...."

"I know what I'm doing, and I do understand. Didn't I come here to seek understanding? I've gained that understanding," said Mika. "I know I'm putting my life in danger. But if it's for the sake of my people, then I must. I'm terribly frightened. But I don't have any other choice. Now that I'm out here, I have the opportunity to change things around me. I've told myself countless times that nothing will change for the better if I stay in the castle and do nothing. If I did nothing, I would be safe, but everyone would still be suffering. For the suffering to end, I have to do something. I have to... because that's my duty."

Dellen and Zima thought of her words, which were full of wisdom. This little girl who was the Princess of their nation was well-educated and had many times proven that her wisdom far exceeded that of other children her age.

"Okay, Princess Mika," said Dellen. "We're glad you're on our side."

Mika smiled. "I'll always be on your side."

* * *

Even though it was still dark outside this early in the morning, Helen put on her hood to conceal her face. She looked back at the house of Dellen and Zima Balias. Leaving Mika behind in that house, she was furious with the Princess, but she was also furious with herself. She ran down the quiet street, intent on returning to the castle, seeing that she had no other choice.

"This is ridiculous! I can't believe this! Stupid Princess Mika! You truly are a stubborn little girl!"

As she travelled, Helen looked back on that day when she was sitting outside of Sir Galner's office, waiting with Mika. Mika had smiled at her after Helen told her that she should not be so frightened around her. When Mika smiled, she looked so beautiful. Helen had thought to herself that the Princess was beautiful, even more beautiful than she was.

Then Helen recalled the day of the excursion to the Cerulean Magic Academy, when they were attacked by the peasant mob and the group of crossbow snipers. Helen had protected Mika that day. She had also shared in Mika's great disappointment when seeing the city of Scarletia for the first time, the city whose peasants lived in extreme poverty. She shared Mika's opinion that the peasants were being oppressed by the Nobility and the Royal Family.

And then, there was tonight. They were able to speak to each other several times without interruption. They had gotten to know each other more. They had shared with each other some intimate details, such as Helen's true feelings towards how the Peasantry were being treated by the Nobility and Mika's secret affection towards Mirin.

Helen generally thought of the Princess as a coward and a weakling because of the way she usually acted. Mika was easily frightened and moved to tears. But since that first day in the city, Mika had shown a bravery Helen had not witnessed before. She had strength and determination. However, she was also a sweet and kind little girl. There were many traits about the Princess she found to be annoying, but at the same time, there were many traits she found to be endearing. She thought about the intimate details they had shared together. As she thought about her exchanges with Mika, she thought those were the kinds of things that only friends would tell each other.

"You're doing something that's absolutely ridiculous and stupid! What do you hope to accomplish? You're putting yourself in so much danger, and it shows how young and immature you really are. Do you truly understand what you're doing?"

Helen looked around as she ran to make sure no one was nearby to hear her talking to herself with great frustration and irritation. She reached an intersection, remembering which way she was supposed to go in order to return to the castle. She proceeded down another street.

"And ordering me to leave you here? Have you lost your mind?"

As Helen ran, she felt fatigue coming on, so she stopped for a moment, her hands on her knees. More houses surrounded her, lining the sides of the street in front of her and behind her. She saw someone taking a walk but no one else. Otherwise, nothing stirred, and she heard no sound.

"I have a bad feeling about this," whispered Helen. She continued running.

Because Helen took the shortest possible path, and was alternating between running and walking, she was able to make it to the Valderia Pathway, which led straight to the castle gates, in about an hour. The castle gates loomed large in front of her as she approached them.

"Who goes there? Please identify yourself, miss." A knight mounted on a cervid approached her from the shadows beside the gates.

Helen stopped, and pushed her hood back. She gazed up at the knight with utter seriousness. She clasped her hands together in front of her. As the knight moved closer on his cervid, his face became more visible under the silver moonlight. It was Belian Soraisa, the annoying knight who sometimes taunted her for being the youngest knight in the entire Scarletia Royal Guard and the Royal Army of Melodice.

"It's me, Sir Belian. Helen Renier."

Belian was surprised. "Miss Helen!" He cleared his throat. "What are you doing out here at this hour? It's not safe beyond the gates. In fact, how did you—?"

Helen interrupted him, because she knew he was going to ask how she managed to leave the castle. "I was taking a walk. I couldn't sleep, and I needed to clear my mind so I took a stroll throughout the city for a few hours."

"I see." Belian shook his head. "I'm tempted to say that a young lady shouldn't be out here by herself, for it could be dangerous. But... as you are Miss Helen Renier, you would be able to protect yourself against any peasants who might attack you, I suppose."

"Perhaps I'm not the little girl you think I am, Sir Belian, as you are quite fond of pointing out at times."

Belian smirked. "Perhaps not. Regardless of what I think, what possessed you to do something so dangerously foolish? I'd hate to see a pretty young face ruined by peasant thugs, even if you do manage to fight them of. They crawl the city alleyways and attack anyone, noble or peasant."

Helen frowned. "As I said, I couldn't sleep, and needed to clear my mind."

"Humph. Well, then... care to come back inside?"

"Yes, please."

Belian led Helen to the castle gates, where a few other knights were stationed. "Open the side door."

Someone from the other side complied.

"Thank you," said Helen.

Stepping through the side door that led her back onto the Grounds, Helen thought again about Mika's actions. As she stepped back onto the Valderia Pathway, she gazed up at the Scarletia Royal Castle ahead of her.

"Damn. What am I supposed to do now?"

* * *

The sun had risen about one hour ago, its warm rays filtering in between the black makeshift curtains in the kitchen. Mika pushed back one of the curtains, and felt the gentle rays warm her cheeks. She could hear Zima humming to herself while cooking. The smell of fried eggs and bacon filled the air. Two pans with a bit of cooking oil in each one rested on an extremely heat-conductive metal plate above the firebox, which was full of burning wood, their furious flames heating the metal plate above them, cooking the food. The smoke from the firebox did not enter the house. Instead, it was directed into a chimney, allowing it to escape to the outside.

"Okay, boys, breakfast is almost ready, so have a seat. It's the most important meal of the day," Dellen called out. His sons dashed into the kitchen ahead of him. Tyrel was first, as he was the fastest and the most eager to have his breakfast.

Mika turned around to face them, holding her hands together in front of her, her feet together, and her back straight, in her usual ladylike demeanour.

Tyrel's eyes lit up when he saw Mika. "Princess, you're still here?"

Jaren shook his head. "Don't be so rude, Tyrel."

Mika giggled. "Please don't worry."

"Where's your guard? Her name was Miss Helen, wasn't it?" Jaren asked.

"That's right. She left for home already. She should be back at the castle by now," answered the Princess.

"Why did she leave?" Tyrel took his seat.

"She's a knight. She has to report for duty."

Jaren raised an eyebrow, puzzled. "Isn't it her duty to stay with you as your guard?"

These are hard questions, I must admit. What am I supposed to say? "To be honest, I sent her home."

"Why?" asked Tyrel.

"There are... some things I want to do out here in the city, but I want to do them on my own. That's why I sent her home."

"But she's supposed to protect you, isn't she?" asked Jaren.

Mika smiled. "I can protect myself just fine, actually."

Tyrel looked on with confusion. "I guess it's because you can use magic, right?"

"You could say that," said Mika.

Dellen smiled with amusement as he sliced some bread and put it on a large plate.

Zima, finishing up her cooking, giggled at hearing their conversation. She placed the eggs and bacon on another large plate, and set it on the kitchen table. She looked up at Mika. "Princess, why don't you have some breakfast as well?"

Mika nodded. "Thank you, Miss Zima. I appreciate your hospitality. Your home is cozy and warm, and I take great pleasure in being your guest."

Zima blushed. "So glad you're enjoying our company, Princess Mika."

"Sit here, Princess!" Tyrel pointed at the seat beside him.

"Tyrel, say please!" commanded Jaren.

Tyrel frowned at his older brother. "What?"

Mika was amused by the brothers as she took her seat. Dellen placed slices of bread on three smaller plates, which he passed to Zima, who placed two eggs and four slices of bacon on each. They served the plates to Mika, Jaren, and Tyrel.

"Thanks," said Jaren

"Thank you!" shouted Tyrel.

Mika was much more serene with her gratitude. "Thank you."

"Not a problem." Dellen removed one of the curtains from the nails that held them in place above the windows to allow sunlight to enter and brighten the room. After that, he and Zima both took their seats. They poured themselves cups of coffee as Tyrel and Jaren began to eat.

As Mika began to eat her breakfast, she noticed the boys eating quite voraciously, drinking from their cups of water every couple of mouthfuls. In fact, they were already almost halfway done, and she was quite surprised. She figured that they must be very hungry right now. She smiled as she watched them eat. In a way, they kind of reminded her of Mirin.

Mirin.... I wonder how he's doing right now. He's the only other person who knows that Helen and I left the castle last night.

Mika had never eaten with peasants before. It was just like eating breakfast with Mirin and Angelica. There was nothing different about it at all. She asked herself again why nobles thought of them so differently. The bacon, eggs, and bread tasted exactly the same as what she would have had back at the castle. They ate the same food. They ate their food just like nobles did.

As Mika took another mouthful, she noticed that Dellen and Zima were not eating anything. They were just having coffee. "Sir Dellen, Miss Zima, you're not going to have breakfast?"

"Pardon?" Zima glanced up from her steaming cup of coffee.

Mika noticed Jaren and Tyrel stop and look down as if feeling ashamed for some reason. If she did not know any better, she could have sworn they wore expressions of guilt.

Dellen grinned. "Don't worry about us, Princess. We'll eat later."

Mika looked at the food on the kitchen table. Before they started eating, there were a total of six eggs, twelve slices of bacon, and three slices of bread. There was no more of the bread either. It was only she, Tyrel, and Jaren who were eating. She came to a quick conclusion.

Miss Zima only prepared enough breakfast for her children and for me. There's not enough food for her and Sir Dellen.

The young Princess glanced down at her plate, with its one and a half eggs, three slices of bacon, and one slice of bread that had a tiny little bite in it. There were two other plates, large ones, one of which had been for the bread and the other was used to hold the bacon and eggs. Both plates were now empty.

Mika got up from her seat, puzzling the entire family. They watched, speechless, as the Princess took the two large empty plates. She cut up her slice of bread into three evenly sized pieces, placing two of those pieces on the two empty plates. She put one slice of bacon on each plate. Finally, she cut her one whole egg in half and put each half on each plate. With a plate in each hand, she walked around the table to where Dellen and Zima were, and standing between them, she placed one of the plates on the table in front of Dellen and the other in front of Zima.

"Um, Princess, what... are you doing?" asked Zima.

Mika smiled at both of them. "I believe Sir Dellen mentioned that breakfast was the most important meal of the day."

Jaren and Tyrel both smiled as they watched.

Mika turned to the brothers. "Wouldn't you agree, Sir Jaren, Sir Tyrel?"

"Agreed," said Jaren.

Tyrel nodded and smiled. "Agreed."

Both Dellen and Zima felt warmth in their hearts. Zima wanted to give Mika a hug, but she did not know how the Princess would react to that just yet. Of course, unknown to her, Mika would not have minded that one bit.

"You are something else, Princess." Dellen smiled with pride.

"Thank you, Princess Mika," said Zima.

* * *

At the end of their breakfast, Mika observed Dellen walking into the living room and pushing back a curtain to look outside, as if he was waiting for something... or maybe someone. She followed closely behind, with Zima beside her.

Mika's voice was wistful and timid as she hesitated. "Um... Sir Dellen?"

Dellen closed the curtain, and turned to Mika. "Yes, Princess?"

Mika wanted to say something but she was not sure how to say it. She cast her eyes down on the floor.

Zima saw her hesitation. "What is it, Princess Mika? Something wrong?"

Mika calmed down, and then forced herself to meet Dellen's puzzled gaze. "Um... I was hoping... I mean, I'm... I'm hoping you won't be angry with me...."

"Angry? What do you mean?" asked Dellen, confused.

Mika looked around to make sure that Jaren and Tyrel were nowhere nearby. They had returned to their room to change their clothes.

"There were... there were a few things I noticed about you. I noticed it while you and Miss Zima were explaining the truth about the state of the nation to me and Miss Helen earlier. I... was wondering... it sounds like you're part of one of those rebel groups you mentioned, perhaps one of the two major ones. Am I right?"

Mika stiffened, and cast her eyes downward, afraid that he was about to get angry with her. She saw Zima surprised, but Dellen looked like he had no reaction.

After a moment of silence in the room, Dellen simply chuckled. "You're a very perceptive little girl, Princess Mika. And, no, I'm not angry. I'm just amazed you were able to figure that out just by observing our mannerisms and listening to the words I used."

Zima was relieved. "Well, then… yes, my husband is part of one of the major rebel groups. Not me though. But I do support him in whatever he does." She looked behind her for a moment to ensure her sons were not around. "Our sons don't know about this. It's best that they don't know, so please don't say anything about this in front of them."

"I wouldn't. I made sure they weren't nearby when I asked," said Mika.

"Thank you."

Mika smiled. "Then… you will be able to help me explain my goal to the people who can help me accomplish what I want to see happen. I can make it happen through you, Sir Dellen. That is, of course, if they accept me. I hope they can accept me and believe me."

"I wouldn't worry too much about that, Princess." With a smug look, Dellen smiled.

CHAPTER 18

MISSING PRINCESS

A s Mirin stepped out of the room he shared with Angelica, the doors to Princess Mika's bedchamber suddenly opened. Angelica stormed out of the room, and ran down the hallway, panic on her face.

Mirin called out to her. "Angelica?"

Angelica turned around to face him. "Mirin, stay here!"

Mirin watched as Angelica turned, and ran away with great distress... and he became distressed himself, but his reason for feeling this way was much different from hers.

"She knows now. This is... not good," he whispered.

Angelica ran down the hallway, nearly running into a few noble civilians along the way, the heels of her shoes echoing against the stone floor whenever she did not step on carpeting. After running down another hallway, she saw her destination, which was the office of the Queen of Melodice. As soon as she reached the large double doors that led into the office, she frantically knocked using the door ring.

Queen Maiya, as always, was elaborately dressed, no matter what part of the day it was. Ready to start with day-to-day business, she was in a long red dress as she sat on a large chair behind an enormous algerwood desk, flipping through the pages of various reports. She was startled by the loud knocking. She looked up, somewhat annoyed.

"It's too early in the morning for this." Maiya raised her voice. "Come in!"

One of the doors swung open, and Angelica came running into her office. "My Lady!" She ran to the Queen's desk.

"Miss Angelica! What's wrong?"

When Angelica reached the Queen's desk, she rested her hands on its edge, and bowed her head, but respect was not the only reason why she did this. She struggled to catch her breath after running down the hallways.

Concerned, Maiya went around the desk, and put one arm around Angelica. "What's wrong, Miss Angelica? Tell me what happened. What has made you panic so much?"

"My Lady!" Angelica had not sufficiently recovered from her running, but she was doing a little better after a moment. "Princess Mika... she's...!"

Maiya paused at the mention of her daughter. She suddenly felt a sense of trepidation. "What about Mika?"

"She's not in her bedchamber, My Lady!"

Maiya's eyes widened.

"When I went into her room with her breakfast, I thought she was still sleeping. I saw what I thought was her form underneath the blankets. I called out to her, but there was no answer. I tried to wake her up, but... but when I lifted the blankets... it was her pillows. They were all arranged neatly, as if placed there to make it look like she was still sleeping. The Princess... she's gone!"

Maiya tried very hard to contain her shock. She placed her hands on Angelica to comfort her, but she wished someone else would do the same for her. "Miss Angelica, please summon Sir Collin! Summon him immediately!"

* * *

It did not take long for the entire castle to enter into a state of alarm. As soon as Sir Collin was informed of the disappearance of Princess Mika, he ordered his knights to search high and low for her.

Mirin observed his surroundings as he walked down the hallways of the castle. He watched as servants moved from one room to another, escorted by knights. They asked people whether they had seen the Princess or any sign of her. They checked rooms that were empty as thoroughly as possible. Mirin stiffened.

He nearly jumped when someone tapped him on the shoulder. He turned around, and faced a tall knight and a maidservant.

"Mirin," said the maidservant, who was older than Angelica by a few decades. "The Princess is missing! Do you know anything about this? Do you know where she could have gone? Have you come across any sign of her at all?"

Mirin vigorously shook his head, his eyes wide.

Frustrated, the maidservant turned to the knight. "Come on."

As the maidservant and the knight left, Mirin stood against the wall, distressed. "This wasn't part of the plan." *Mika and Miss Helen were supposed to head out into the city late last night, and then come back before sunrise. What happened to Mika... and to Miss Helen? What's going on? Something's wrong!*

Mirin headed down the hallway again, and ascended to the fifth floor, where their rooms were located. He passed by a couple of knights, who paid no attention to him, as he headed for Mika's room. A short distance away from his destination, he stopped, and put his hand against the wall. At the entrance into Mika's bedchamber, a few knights stood around talking with maidservants, including Angelica. Mirin watched as Angelica and two other knights disappeared into the room. They were probably looking for clues as to what might have happened to Mika. Mirin turned around, and walked away.

What am I supposed to do? Mika didn't come back! What about Helen? Where is she? She didn't come back either?

Mirin spotted Helen walking down an intersecting hallway well ahead of him, and he gasped as soon as he saw her. He ran down the hallway to try to catch up with her, and stopped when he reached the intersection.

"Miss Helen!"

Helen turned around, clad in her usual knight's uniform with a cape. When she saw Mirin, she waited until he finally caught up to her.

"Helen, what's going on? Where's Mika?!" asked Mirin, a little too loudly.

Helen was alarmed as she looked around to make sure no one was nearby. There were a couple of civilians farther away, but they did not hear what he said. She glared at him, clenching her teeth. She grabbed him very firmly by the arm, and held him against the wall. "Shut up! Don't speak so loudly!"

Mirin realized that he had mentioned Mika's name too loudly, and in this situation, if he had been heard, trouble would have followed him soon afterwards. "Sorry. But what's going on, Helen? You're back, but what happened to Mika?"

"She stayed with them!"

Mirin was shocked, drawing in a quick breath. "What?"

"Listen to me!"

Helen put her face closer to his, grabbing the fabric of his waistcoat near his neck. She glared at him in an intimidating fashion, much more so than usual, and much more serious. Her glare was so full of frustration and anger that even Mirin, who was usually defiant in her presence, actually felt intimidated, almost as much as Mika would be. Helen spoke softly, but that did nothing to make her anger any less frightening.

"You're the only other person in the entire castle who knows that the Princess went out into the city and met with a peasant family. She was supposed to return to the castle with me, but she ordered me, as the Princess, to return on my own. Do not speak to anyone about this. If anyone asks you, pretend you know nothing about it! And if I ever find out you've talked to someone about this... trust me, you do not want to see me truly furious, because you don't know what might happen to you!"

Helen let go of him, turned around, and continued on her way with a quickened pace.

Mirin stared at her, his eyes wide, as he watched her walk away. "Mika... you stayed with the peasants? Why? What's going on?"

* * *

Over twenty knights, in full armour, mounted on cervids, rode down the Valderia Pathway on the Grounds towards the gates to join the guards already patrolling. The knights dismounted when they reached the gates. Several ascended the steps at either side of the gates, steps that led to the top of the wall, where more knights were already deployed.

Within the hallways of the castle, servants continued to check every single room while accompanied by knights. Noble civilians were questioned briefly, but none of them knew anything about the whereabouts of Princess Mika. Security was made tighter within the castle as well as on the Grounds and at the gates. No one was going to be allowed to exit the castle, let alone enter it, without being scrutinized by the patrolling knights.

In the King's Conference, King Ralphen pounded his fist on the table, and shouted his orders, startling Queen Maiya who was seated close to him. "Search every corner of this castle! Continue searching until you find the Princess!"

Sir Collin, who was accompanied by Sir Maleth and a few knights, stood tall and acknowledged the order of the King. "We will find her, My Lord! Such is our duty! Our knights will leave no stone unturned!"

Maiya leaned forward in her seat, resting her forehead in her hands for a moment.

Angelica, along with a few other servants, noticed the Queen's discomfort. Angelica was ready to head over to her to ask her if she needed anything, but one of the older maidservants put an arm around hers, and discouraged her.

But Maleth also noticed the Queen's expression of worry. "My Lady, are you feeling all right?"

Maiya looked up sharply. "I'm assuming you ask your question in the physical sense, Sir Maleth, and to answer your question, I'm fine. But I'm deeply worried over my daughter's disappearance."

"My apologies. We will find her, My Lady. Security has been increased throughout the castle and around it. No one would be able to enter or exit without being searched or questioned, no matter who it is."

"Sir Maleth is correct, My Lady," said Sir Collin. "I

understand you're worried about the Princess. I give you my word that we will find her safe and sound."

The King pointed his finger at Collin with barely contained fury. "You had better understand, Sir Collin."

"Is it possible that she could have been abducted?" asked Maiya.

Collin thought about that for a moment, and admitted to himself that he had considered that possibility. "If the Princess was abducted, I can't see how that could have happened."

Not appreciating the possibility she mentioned being dismissed so quickly by the Supreme Captain, Maiya became somewhat more agitated. "Well, it is possible, isn't it? There were two attempts on her life. Each time, she came very close to having her young life taken away from her!"

"If someone abducted her," said Maleth, "they would have to go through the castle which is populated by ten thousand people. If they had somehow slipped through unnoticed, they would still have to contend with the dozens of knights that patrol the castle gates. Leaving the castle with the Princess held captive would be an extremely daunting task for any potential abductor, My Lady."

Clearly, the possibility was remote, and Maiya could see that. "Of course, Sir Maleth, Sir Collin. I hope I don't seem like I think less of your abilities to protect this castle and all the people in it, including Princess Mika. I know you're both more than capable."

"Thank you, My Lady."

Ralphen shook his head. "This is likely not an abduction. Leave nothing undisturbed, Sir Collin. From top to bottom, in every corner, search this castle and the Grounds as well! You must find the Princess!"

"We will, My Lord! I swear it! I will find the Princess!"

* * *

SEC 3566, Morrighan 40

Somewhere in the city of Scarletia was an unassuming inn

called Ethereal Daydreams that occupied an entire brick and mortar building with two floors and a basement, popular among the peasant civilians in the area. The building was old but somewhat better kept than most of the surrounding buildings. The first and second floors were open to the public, but the basement never was. It was always locked up, and the entrance was not through the front or within the first floor via descending stairs, but through the back within an alleyway, where several young men who looked like thugs kept watch. But these were not truly thugs. They only appeared and behaved as such.

A total of seven riders on cervids, five men and two women, all of them clad in dark gray robes, slowly walked down the alleyway, ignoring the thugs, who did nothing to get in their way, but kept a close watch with intimidating frowns. The blade of a short sword worn by one of the men flashed in the sunlight that filtered down directly from above between buildings. He was at the very front of the line of cervids. Noticing that his sword was exposed, he covered it with his robe as he and his companions approached the back of the inn, looking around and behind them to make sure they were not being followed.

They dismounted from their cervids, and two of the so-called thugs came over to take their mounts. The man who led the group nodded to them, and headed towards the back entrance of the building. He was a thickly bearded and well-muscled man, his hair somewhat long and tied into a ponytail, and he held a look of constant suspicion as he scanned his surroundings one more time, while his companions did the same. He motioned all of them to follow him. He opened the door, revealing steps that descended into the basement.

The bearded man exhaled heavily as he began to descend the steps. "Dammit. I was really looking forward to spending time with my wife and kids today. What the hell are we doing here?"

Another man, younger and clean-shaven, his hair already thinning despite his age, followed the bearded man down the steps. "We don't have a choice, Adrel. Given our roles, quality time with family can be hard to come by sometimes."

Adrel waved his hand dismissively. "Ah, that's ridiculous, Laren."

Laren shrugged. "Still, I wonder why we were called to Ethereal Daydreams."

In the basement were several sets of tables and chairs, each of which varied in size and shape, as if they all came from different places at different times. The floor was made of a cold stone, cracked in some places where water had seeped in sometime in the past. There was a bar at one side of the room, and bottles of liquor were arranged neatly on a rack behind it. Eight people were already in the room, four men, three women... and one child, a young girl who sat on a chair, wearing a shimmering black cloak, her face partially hidden by her hood, and her back towards the entrance. Everyone in the room was familiar to Adrel and Laren, except for the young girl.

Dellen was in an old long-sleeved dress shirt and trousers, a short sword inside a scabbard hanging from his belt. "Good of you to join us, Sir Adrel."

Adrel snorted upon seeing him. "If it isn't Sir Dellen. I'm assuming we have some business?"

Dellen approached Adrel with a smile, and extended a hand. "Of course, Sir Adrel." They both shook hands. "I'm glad you could make it. It's been a whole month since I last saw you here at Ethereal Daydreams. We should have a drink again."

Adrel chuckled. "Yeah, we should." He regarded a young woman who stood farther into the room. She was slim and toned, clad in a blouse and trousers, also with a short sword in a scabbard hanging from her belt. Her black boots were shin-high, and a knife was strapped to the side of one of her boots. Standing with confidence, her hands were clasped together behind her back. She had mid-back-length blonde hair that was tied into a ponytail. "And how is the lovely Miss Feldia today?"

Feldia smiled. "I'm fine, thanks, Sir Adrel."

"That's good." Adrel turned back to Dellen. "So...

now that we're here, what's the reason why we were called? Did something happen?"

"You could say that," said Dellen.

Adrel eyed him with a hint of suspicion. "Care to fill me in?"

"Yes, of course. I'd like to introduce you to someone."

Adrel became very puzzled. "Who is it?"

Laren stood beside Adrel, and then whispered. "The little kid behind all of them."

Adrel saw who Laren was referring to. He was familiar with everyone in the room, but not the child. "Someone we should know?"

Dellen turned towards Feldia, and nodded towards the young girl.

Feldia walked over to the young girl, stopping in front of her.

Princess Mika looked up at Feldia, who gave her an encouraging smile. Mika tried to push back her nervousness. She turned in her chair, and stood up slowly, pushing back her hood, and pulling on a single string that loosened the front of her cloak, opening it up completely at the front, revealing the sparkling diamond around her neck that represented her identity. As she turned towards the people who had just arrived, Mika tried to appear confident, despite her trepidation.

"Betrayal!" Adrel drew out his sword from inside his robe.

Laren immediately did the same. The others who had by now come in behind them followed suit, the sounds of metal scraping against scabbards echoing throughout the room.

Feldia, along everyone else behind her, drew out her sword in response as she stepped closer towards Dellen, who was in the middle of all this.

"What the hell is going on here?!" shouted Laren.

Feldia shouted back. "Put your sword down, you fool!"

"No, wait, everyone!" Dellen put up his hands, standing in between the two opposing forces. They pointed their swords at each other, ready to attack if anyone on the other side of the room made a sudden move. Holding their swords defensively, they all hurled angry shouts across the room.

"Are you betraying all of us to this?!"

"What do you think you're doing?!"

"I always thought you people couldn't be trusted!"

"You bastards, how dare you?!"

"Put your swords down!"

Mika was terrified, her heart racing, her hands over her mouth. Any sudden move would result in a bloodbath!

Dellen tried very hard to bring down the tension in the room. "Everyone, calm down! Lower your weapons! This is not what it looks like!"

Adrel growled. "How can I believe you, Dellen?!"

"Curse you, Dellen!" said Laren. "You're betraying us to the Royal Family, to the Nobility?!"

"No! That is not what's going on!" replied Dellen.

"Then what the hell *is* going on, Dellen?!" demanded Adrel, his sword pointed at Dellen. "Have you all lost your minds?! Are you betraying our cause?! The nation of Melodice?!"

"You do know that having a Royal here means death to all of us, don't you?!" said Laren.

"No!" Dellen shouted again. "We are all on the same side here! Don't forget that! We are all fighting against tyranny and oppression, and we have not forgotten what we're trying to do, that is, to free the people of Melodice! In fact, the Princess of Melodice, Princess Mika Silveraine, is on our side!"

"Preposterous!" roared Adrel.

Mika observed the exchange with great fear. Dellen was in the middle of it, and was the only one who did not have his sword drawn. She watched as he tried to convince the two sides to stop and put away their swords. She could see that his life was in danger. If anything were to happen, he would be the first to die. After that, everyone in the room would slaughter each other. Mika would be one of the last to die. Her hands and knees trembled, her body frozen in place, and their furious clamours rang in her ears, impossible to shut out.

"You cursed bastard, Dellen. I'm going to tear your heart out of your chest," exclaimed Adrel.

Feldia accidentally bumped into a table beside her, causing a glass on top of it to fall off and shatter into pieces on the floor. For a brief moment, the angry shouts intensified, and everyone gripped their swords even more tightly, ready to strike, as the two groups took one more step closer to each other.

However, the sound of glass breaking caused Mika to unfreeze. "No!" Her high-pitched voice carried throughout the room.

Everyone stopped shouting, their attention suddenly diverted to the Princess, but they still held their swords defensively. Mika surprised herself as she rushed past tables and chairs and men and women holding their short swords, eventually past Feldia, who looked on with surprise. Mika reached Dellen, gently pushing him aside.

To Dellen's great shock, Mika put herself between him and Adrel. "Princess!"

Mika cast her eyes upwards to the tall and intimidating stature of Adrel, who pointed his sword directly at her. "Please don't kill him!" she said, her voice shaking.

Adrel took one step towards the Princess, his blade now pointing at her throat.

Mika gasped.

The others in the room on Dellen's side moved another step closer in response, including Feldia, who took two steps.

Dellen was alarmed as he put up his hand towards her. "No, don't!"

"What the hell is going on?" whispered Laren, watching the Princess, Adrel, and everyone else in the room. He had taken another step closer as well.

Mika felt cold steel against her neck, just barely touching her. But she did not look at the blade, despite feeling the sharp, pointed end. She remained still. One false move, and he would stab her neck, bleeding her to death. She could tell he was more than strong enough to swing the blade across her thin neck and separate her head from her body, and he would not need much strength to do so. She was tempted to step back... but she forced herself to stand her ground. She planted her shoes firmly on the stone floor, and looked straight at Adrel, fear in her eyes, straight into his eyes that were full of anger. However, anger was not the only thing Mika saw in them.

He's afraid. Just as afraid as I am.

Everyone in the room was quiet, looking on, breaths held with great tension. The only thing Mika could hear now was her own heartbeat, racing within her chest. She felt cold all over her body. She also felt tense, making her body ache even more, because her bruises were still far from completely healed.

Mika pleaded to Adrel, her frightened whispering voice barely audible. "Sir, please believe me... I am... I *am* on your side...."

Adrel glared at Mika, his hands clamped tightly around the hilt of his sword.

The tip of his blade touched her neck gently. It was sharp enough to cause a tiny drop of blood to appear. Mika felt what seemed to her like a tiny pin prick. The tiny wound was superficial, barely noticeable... yet terrifying.

"Please... I am on your side, sir," Mika whispered again.

"I should cut off your head, you damn Royal bitch," growled Adrel.

Feldia slowly took yet another step closer, her grip on her sword tighter than ever. "If the Princess is harmed in any way, Adrel, I promise you, everyone in this room will die, and it'll be by each other's hand, not by the blades of knights."

Dellen deliberately took a step towards Adrel and Mika, his hands held up so Adrel and the others with him could see them clearly. One false move and the Princess would die. "Come on, Adrel. You know we all hold high positions in our groups. We're the leaders who do our best to inspire the peasants, and to keep them looking towards the future, hoping for a better world. If everyone died here today... then it's all over."

"The Peasantry would continue to live under tyranny," added Feldia.

Laren kept his watchful gaze upon Dellen and Feldia as he spoke. "Adrel... you know, they're right about this. If we all die here, everything we've accomplished so far would become meaningless. And if you kill the Princess... the entire city might be razed under the King's wrath."

Adrel's hands were beginning to cramp while holding his sword. "How can I believe... how can I believe this... this scrawny little girl?"

"Sir... I..." Mika remembered the name Dellen and the others called him. "Sir Adrel... if... if you don't believe me... then... then you may strike me with your fist... as hard as you can."

Dellen was stunned. *Princess, what are you saying?!*

Several tense moments passed. Mika watched as Adrel drew in a quick breath, drew back his sword, and made a fist. She closed her eyes, anticipating a hard blow to the face from a man who was easily a hundred times stronger than she was. However, instead of a painful punch that would knock her out in one blow, she felt a gentle slap on the side of her face that felt like nothing. Mika opened her eyes, gasped again. She looked up at Adrel.

"I want to know what the hell is going on here." Adrel put his sword back into his scabbard.

Laren breathed a sigh of relief, as did Feldia. Both of them put their swords down. Dellen bowed his head, exhaling slowly, feeling the tension decreasing in the room. Everyone began to sheathe their swords.

Mika was the most relieved as she took a step back, her hand on the side of her neck. She pulled her hand away, and saw a tiny smear of blood on her palm. Still somewhat fearful, she took several long, deep breaths, almost to the point of hyperventilation, to try to calm her rapidly beating heart.

Dellen smiled at Adrel. "Well, then, Adrel, maybe now... we can have a drink. What do you say?"

Adrel regarded him with annoyance. "Don't choose that foul concoction from last time. Over drinks, I will have the explanation I'm looking for." He stepped past the Princess, giving her one last glare, and headed for the bar.

Mika was at least relieved now. She cast her eyes down on the stone floor as Laren passed her, as did the rest of Adrel's companions. She slowly turned around, and observed the change in everyone's composure. Everyone in the room was suddenly much more relaxed than even just a few moments ago. It was like the tense situation from earlier never happened.

* * *

Exhausted after explaining her story and her goals to Adrel and his group, Mika sat down at a large round table, the largest in the basement of the inn, situated in the darkest back corner. Earlier, her entire body had been tense. Now, she felt the resulting aches and pains, especially in many of the areas that had been bruised by her father's beating. She had removed her cloak, which now hung over the back of her chair. Leaning forward, she rested her chin on her hands on the table. She was still in the same white dress that she had been wearing since she left the castle. Mika thought to herself that this was the longest she had worn the same thing without changing. After more than a day, she was beginning to feel uncomfortable. Seated at the table with her were Dellen and Feldia.

Mika had met the young woman named Feldia Saramis yesterday. She was the first peasant with whom she'd become acquainted outside of the Balias family. Sometime before noon, Dellen had left the house, and returned a short time later with Feldia and two men named Peter and Galien. As soon as Feldia and her companions entered the house and saw her, Peter and Galien had tried to draw their swords, but Feldia ordered them not to, because Dellen and Zima's children might be present. Fortunately, they were at school at the time. Feldia had tried to be level-headed and open-minded, despite her distrust of the Nobility and the Royal Family. Mika had told Feldia the same thing she had told Dellen and Zima, about her desire to understand the truth about the nation and to change it for the better. Feldia had seen Mika's bruises as well, and was shocked and saddened by them. After that, Feldia had accepted Mika, thinking there were some things about the little girl that were endearing to her, such as her honour and kindness.

"How are you feeling, Princess?" asked Feldia.

"I'm fine, Miss Feldia," said Mika.

"This must have been frightening for you. Sorry about earlier," said Dellen.

Mika sat up straight, resting her feet on a wooden support underneath her chair. She clasped her hands together on top of the table. "My nerves have been frayed, my heart has been beating so fast, and my whole body aches from tension. Many frightening things have happened to me and around me lately."

Feldia leaned forward slightly in her chair. "Unfortunately, Princess, this is the reality of the lives of peasants. Many frightening things happen around them all the time. It's something they've become used to."

Mika observed Adrel, who was seated at the bar beside Laren. As they talked, they occasionally looked back at them, only to turn back to each other and talk some more after a moment. They were probably talking about her and what she was doing here. After the tense moment earlier, and after Dellen had poured a relaxing alcoholic drink for Adrel, Dellen had explained to him what had happened, starting from when Mika suddenly appeared at his doorstep. He had told him about her desire to understand the true state of the nation and of her people, which he and his wife, Zima, explained to her. The young Princess wished to free the peasants from tyranny and oppression. That was what she had set out to do, and now that she was here, there was no turning back for her. Adrel and Laren were skeptical for a while, thinking there might be knights on the way here. Adrel had gone as far as sending out some of his companions to scout the area outside, but they soon returned afterwards, and confirmed that no knights were anywhere near. They were safe.

As for how they had managed to bring the Princess from Dellen's house all the way to the inn, it was somewhat difficult. Mika's cloak was far too lovely to be shown in public. She would have drawn unwanted attention from the peasant civilians, so Feldia had her cover up in a blanket that concealed her cloak and part of her face and head.

Before traveling to Ethereal Daydreams from the Balias residence, Mika had become unusually tense and fearful when Dellen asked her if she would like to ride on his cervid. She refused, so Feldia asked her if she wanted to ride with a girl instead, and Mika immediately accepted her offer. Dellen had been very confused by her reaction, but dismissed it as some childish reaction. Once that was settled, Dellen, Feldia, and their companions had managed to sneak Mika through the crowded city streets without being noticed.

Once at the inn, gaining the favour of the rest of Dellen's group had been a little harder than convincing Feldia. However, the others trusted Dellen and Feldia, and after letting Mika tell them her story and what she wanted to do, she pleaded with them for their help. She explained to them that she could never hope to ask the nobles to help her free the peasants from a life of tyranny and oppression. That was just not going to happen, given the current state of affairs. It took a little while, but they managed to see things her way, and were sufficiently convinced she was on their side, not against them.

"Sir Dellen?" whispered Mika.

Dellen turned to her.

"Is Sir Adrel... the leader of one of the major rebel groups you told me about?"

"Yeah, he is. Adrel Savarian. He is the leader of the rebel group called the Scarletia Liberation, a very large rebel group, more organized than most other groups. Many people are secretly loyal to him and his cause. The man beside him is Laren Caldest, and he's his Second Command, meaning he reports to Adrel as his second-in-command."

"Adrel is quite hot-headed, as you probably noticed earlier," said Feldia. "But he's a good man. Laren is the opposite of his hot-headedness. Both are good men who would die for their nation and their people. They love their people just as much as you do, Princess."

"I see." Mika smiled. "So... what about the other major rebel group? That's you and Sir Dellen, isn't it? Is your leader here?"

Feldia looked sharply at Dellen. "You didn't tell her yet?"

"Ah, I forgot about that." Dellen laughed. "Feldia, you know how I prefer to keep a low profile."

Feldia shook her head while Mika looked confused. "I am the Second Command for the rebel group called the Hope of Scarletia. Sitting with you right now is the leader of our group, Dellen Balias. I'm sure you're both acquainted by now," she said sarcastically as she rolled her eyes at Dellen.

Mika gasped. "Oh my... you didn't tell me that!"

Dellen shrugged, and then smiled smugly. "Like I said, I like to keep a low profile."

Feldia just shook her head again. "In reality, all of us keep low profiles out of necessity. Anyway, there you have it. These are the leaders of the two largest rebel groups in the city of Scarletia, the Hope of Scarletia and the Scarletia Liberation."

After a moment, Adrel approached them, along with Laren. Adrel stopped, resting his hands on the back of an empty chair, and looked down at Mika, while Laren stood close by. Mika, Dellen, and Feldia met their gazes.

"How was that drink, Adrel?" asked Dellen.

"Not bad. It's got a hell of a kick. What was that called again?"

"Wild Heaven, imported straight from South Alenshire. The amount of alcohol in it sure pushes the boundaries of legality."

"It's pretty good. But... I will only have one, and no more than that. I must keep my mind clear because I might have duties to perform today."

"Good man," said Dellen.

"And one of those duties, Princess Mika, is to talk to you about your decision, your goals, and what you're trying to accomplish."

Mika gasped softly, staring up at Adrel. "Sir Adrel?"

"Thanks for your explanation earlier. I think it's very honourable of you to want to free the peasants. Considering who you are and where you come from, it would be a very difficult goal for you, made even more difficult by the fact that... well, you're still a kid. I must ask you... how old are you?"

"I'm... eleven."

Adrel shook his head, his eyes holding a hint of sadness. "My heart feels heavy for you, Princess. You may be the Princess of Melodice... but you're still a little kid. Do you truly understand what you're doing?"

Mika was quiet for a moment, casting her eyes back down on the table as Adrel spoke. Her fingers nervously traced the rough creases in the wooden tabletop.

"Right now, My Lady, you're surrounded by people who, if given the chance and if circumstances were different, would kill you. They might hesitate at first, seeing you're still a kid, but they would remember that you're a member of the Royal Family. To some of these people, taking your life would be justice. Don't you understand the kind of danger you're in, Princess Mika?"

"You do remember, Adrel," said Feldia, "that if the Princess was killed, it would bring down the wrath of the King upon us all, and none of us would survive."

"I know that, Feldia. But that possibility still exists. There are people in this city who are too stupid to think of the consequences."

The basement became noticeably silent. The conversations between Adrel and Dellen's companions in other parts of the room had ceased. When Mika turned her head to the side, she noticed that all eyes were upon her. Their expressions were calm. Any of these people could kill her, if they truly wanted to. Mika stole a quick glance towards Dellen, who smiled at her discreetly, and then nodded to her, as if to boost her confidence, to encourage her to say what she needed to.

Mika sat up straight in her chair, and looked Adrel in the eyes. "I know I'm still young. I'm terribly scared by what I'm going through right now. I've honestly never been more scared in my entire life. I know I'm surrounded by people who might kill me. Someone has already tried to kill me. Twice. This might... sound rather strange but... I'm starting to get accustomed to that terrible feeling. I feel I have to watch my surroundings more carefully, and be more aware of the people who are near me."

There was silence. Feldia felt a lump in her throat as she stared at the Princess. She cast her eyes down at the table, and closed them for a moment.

Adrel again regarded her with sadness. After a moment, he let out a heavy sigh. "Princess Mika, I'm not sure if I should be commending you for your honour and courage... or if I should pity you for the terrible things you've experienced and will continue to experience while you're on the path you've chosen."

Mika was speechless.

Dellen shifted forward in his chair, his hands clasped together on the table. "I'm sorry for this, Princess. This is the way our nation is, and it's a terrible state. It's been like this for over a century, as my wife told you the other night. The peasants have been suffering under the tyranny of nobles and the Royal Family for a long time, and have experienced a lot of distressing circumstances. I'm sorry about the merchant assassin who tried to kill you. That must have been the turning point for you, and set you on this path... a path that you don't actually have to take, Princess Mika."

"But I do!" said Mika, raising her quivering voice. "In fact, I've already started on that path. As I've stated before, I'm doing this because this is who I am. I know I'm still a child. But, now that I've seen the truth, I have to do something about it. A hundred years of suffering *has* to end at some point, and I believe *now's* the time for that. I know that... I know I might die in this conflict. It could be sometime today or tomorrow or any day after. I'm risking my life for my people, but I'm doing this out of love for them. I'm not trying to be heroic or anything. I don't even care if people don't remember me after everything's over. I just... want to save them from their pain and suffering."

Dellen, Feldia, Adrel, and Laren were silent. The Princess had made up her mind.

Mika knew what she was doing, and decided for herself that she would see it through to the end. "I wonder... the castle must be in an uproar by now."

Feldia nodded. "I'm sure it is, Princess."

"No doubt," said Laren. "They must realize you're missing by now. They'll be searching the entire castle for you."

Mika nodded as well. "Yes, and my father will be furious, and my mother will be worried. I suppose... I only have a couple of regrets."

"And they are...?" asked Dellen.

"First, I regret that I'm making my mother worry about me, and making my father angry at me. But most of all...." Mika's voice trailed off.

Feldia looked puzzled. "Most of all...?"

Mika glanced up at Feldia. "I also have my best friend and my maidservant who I'm close to. I'm certain they're terribly worried about me. Those are the things I regret the most right now."

Adrel smiled as he pulled out a chair at the table, and sat down. "Princess Mika, despite the fact you're so young, you are the most honourable noble I have ever met in my life. You're young and probably stupid for doing what you're doing."

"Adrel," said Laren, firmly, reminding him of his demeanour.

"However, that being said," Adrel continued, "I've done a lot of stupid things in my time for the sake of others, and because of the stupid things I've done, because of my actions that risked my own life, people's lives were saved, men and women and especially children. I don't doubt your honour, and I can see you have a frightening wisdom despite your age. I haven't known you that long, and it already makes me seriously uncomfortable."

Mika blinked a couple of times with confusion. "Should I... take that as a compliment?"

Dellen chuckled. "Yeah, you should. Adrel may be rough, but that's high praise coming from him."

"I see. Sir Dellen, when you said earlier that the turning point of my life might have been when I was attacked by the merchant assassins, I believe you're right. That's what set me on this path. A path toward equality and the end of oppression, but, more than that... more than anything... it's because of love."

"It's as simple as that... and I totally agree with you, Princess," said Feldia, her voice softened. "And I think that's all you need, more than anything."

"But I must admit that I don't know anything about rebellions. Maybe Miss Helen was right... and I do have the beginnings of a rebellious streak."

"Miss Helen? Who's that?" asked Adrel.

"Her guard from the other night," replied Dellen.

Adrel chuckled. "Well, I agree with her, Princess. Maybe you do have a rebellious streak in you. Maybe it's because you're coming of age. At your age, some children begin to question the world around them and the things that adults tell them. They begin to test their limits. They begin to think they're somehow invincible. You also seem to be an incredibly stubborn little girl. Once you've made a decision, you stick to it, and there doesn't seem to be anything anyone can say or do about it. A girl your age, no matter how intelligent, shouldn't know anything about rebellions. But don't worry. We'll teach you everything you need to know."

Mika gasped, not believing what he said for a moment. She began to smile. When she looked at Dellen, he smiled as well, and nodded to her, wordlessly telling her the same thing, that he would help her as well.

"Your cause is the same as ours, My Lady," said Laren.

Feldia agreed with a nod. "It looks like your path and ours have crossed, and are heading in the same direction, Princess Mika."

Mika felt even more relieved. "Thank you...."

Adrel's smile was replaced with irritation. "But, you know, there's still one thing that really pisses me off."

"Huh? Pisses you off? What does that mean?" asked Mika.

Feldia rolled her eyes. "It means he's angry about something. He's just choosing derogatory words to describe what he's feeling."

Mika was surprised, gently biting her own tongue, because she was not one to curse or say anything that was considered derogatory. "Oh. But what is it that angers you, Sir Adrel?"

"When you told us earlier what your father, the King of Melodice, does to you whenever he gets angry with you."

Dellen shook his head. "It's not that she even does anything that's necessarily wrong. Bottom line is that if the King thinks it's wrong, then it's wrong no matter what. My guess is that the Princess is more often right, given her strong sense of right and wrong."

Feldia's expression turned somber. "Yet, he still beats her. I saw her bruises. Dellen and his family saw them, too."

"The King punishes his daughter almost the same way as he rules his people with an iron fist. There are parallels between how he treats Princess Mika and the people of Melodice," said Dellen.

Adrel felt pity for Mika. "That's probably why you always look so frightened, Princess Mika. This has been happening most of your life, hasn't it?"

Mika hesitated for a moment. She did not really want to talk about it. She nodded, but she had to change the subject quickly in order to avoid it. "But I'm not at the castle anymore. I'm out here in the city. I'm certain they're looking for me because they've discovered I'm missing by now."

Mika thought about everything that could be happening right now in the castle, and what could happen later on.

"My maidservant, Miss Angelica, would have been the first to find out. She would have entered my room to serve breakfast, and noticed when she tried to wake me up that something wasn't right. I put my pillows underneath my blankets to make it look like I was under them. As soon as she tried to wake me up, she would have realized I wasn't there. She would have been frantic, and notified my mother right away. My mother would have told Sir Collin, the Supreme Captain. My father would have found out soon after that, and he would have ordered the knights and servants to search the entire castle for me. I'm sure the gates have been secured, and many more knights are patrolling the Grounds and the castle itself and the top of the walls. They won't allow anything to enter or exit the castle without being thoroughly scrutinized."

Mika then looked up at the others thoughtfully.

"Very soon, they'll find out I'm not in the castle at all, and the King will order the search to be taken beyond the gates. These are the things that they will do, all of them."

Feldia blinked with surprise at Mika. "How do you know...?"

"Because that's how they are."

She's anticipating their actions, thought Feldia.

"That's why... while I'm doing this... I still need to keep a very low profile. No one can know where I am."

"Whether they are peasant or noble, Princess, no one will know you're here," said Dellen. "This inn, Ethereal Daydreams, is owned and run by members of the Hope of Scarletia. There are people who keep constant watch, including those so-called thugs in the alleyways outside, who are actually hired guards. They just pretend to be street thugs. You will be safe, and no one will know you're here."

"Thank you, Sir Dellen," said Mika as she smiled again, dispelling her seriousness from just a moment ago.

CHAPTER 19

IMPOSING QUESTIONS

SEC 3566, Morrighan 41

ANOTHER DAY PASSED, AND DESPITE the efforts of everyone involved in the search, they could not find any trace of Princess Mika. They searched every single room and residence in the castle, every storage area, every nook and cranny, everywhere, and still, there was no sign of her. The knights were extremely thorough in their search. They even considered that she might have been injured somewhere and could not move or call for help, so they searched in places where this was a possibility, and still, they could not find her. As far as anyone could determine, it was as if she had simply vanished into thin air.

"You have nearly a thousand people helping you, and you still cannot find Princess Mika?!" said the King, yelling across the table in the King's Conference at Sir Collin.

The Supreme Captain stiffened at the reproach as he stood with Maleth at his side. "My... apologies, My Lord. We have searched every room in every corner of the castle. We've even searched in places where the possibility of finding her would be remote, but we still haven't found her."

The King raised his hands in the air with great frustration. "Ridiculous!" he shouted, startling Queen Maiya, who was seated next to him.

"We will continue our search, My Lord. But the possibility of finding her within the castle and around the Grounds somewhere is now becoming quite remote."

"How can so many people be so incompetent that they can't even find one little girl?" asked the King.

Feeling his pride as a senior member of the Scarletia Royal Guard attacked, Maleth tightened his fist at his side.

Collin sighed for a moment, unable to think of what else to say to the King.

"Ralphen," said Maiya, placing her hand on his arm.

King Ralphen turned to her.

"What about that possibility we discussed last time? What if she was taken by someone?"

The King turned once again to Collin and Maleth. "If you can't find her in the castle... then what is the possibility that she could have been truly abducted?"

Collin shook his head. "As I said when we discussed that possibility before, for the Princess to be abducted, it would have been a daunting task for the abductors." He turned to Maleth. "What do you think, Sir Maleth?"

"I would have to agree," said the Supreme Commander. "The castle gates are always closed and locked up, and are never opened unless absolutely necessary. One person alone would not be able to accomplish such a monumental undertaking, and would need the cooperation of many. They would have to find a way to sneak through the castle gates. Ever since the incident with the merchant assassins, security has been tightened at the gates. Everything that passes through them from the outside is thoroughly checked. If any group of people was planning to enter the castle intent on taking the Princess, they would have been found right away."

The Queen leaned forward. "But suppose that somehow they did manage to slip through, Sir Maleth. What do you think?"

Maleth clasped his hands together behind his back. "Well, if our potential abductors somehow did slip through the gates despite the security, they would have to make their way across the Grounds, completely unprotected and without cover. They would have to enter the building, navigate dozens of hallways, and ascend stairways, while at the same time preventing themselves from being noticed by the people in the castle. About ten thousand people live in the castle, and slipping anyone suspicious past such a large concentration of people would prove to be extremely difficult. Let's remember that knights patrol not just the gates and the Grounds, but the inside of the building as well."

"Agreed," said Collin. "Also, they would have to know the location of the Princess's bedchamber. They would have to know when her maidservant Miss Angelica is not with her. Given that the Princess disappeared during the night, it would be likely that she was sleeping in her bedchamber. Anyone with the intent of taking her would have to know when and where she slept and when she would be alone."

"And, then," continued Maleth, "there's the even more daunting task of removing the Princess from the premises. Could a group of abductors take the Princess from her bedchamber, and move through the castle unnoticed? That would be extremely unlikely. Would she not have tried to fight them off? To scream? Someone would have seen or heard them, and alerted the knights right away. That she could have been taken past the heavily secured gates, without being caught by the knights, is just utterly impossible."

"So, as you can see, it wouldn't be possible for potential abductors to even accomplish such a crime. There are far too many obstacles," said Collin.

Frustrated, Maiya put a hand on her forehead. "My little Mika. Where could she have disappeared to?"

Collin thought of something as he stepped forward. "My Lord, My Lady, I do have a suggestion."

"What is it, Sir Collin?" asked Ralphen.

"There are people who regularly spend time with Princess Mika. Perhaps we can ask them questions to see if they might know anything about what's happened to her."

Ralphen found the idea preposterous as he frowned. "Are we going to ask our own people if they had anything to do with the disappearance of the Princess? Surely, you jest, Sir Collin. How can you think that our own nobles could be involved in such a crime?"

Collin shook his head quickly, hoping he didn't offend his King. "That's not what I meant, My Lord. I'm certain that none of our honourable nobles have anything to do with the disappearance of the Princess. Nobles could never perform such an act as horrendous as abducting a member of the Royal Family. But there is the possibility they might have noticed something, something small, something that looked unimportant to them. They might believe what they noticed was insignificant, but a seemingly insignificant clue might point us in the right direction."

Ralphen and Maiya exchanged intrigued glances. They leaned towards each other, and whispered for a brief moment about Collin's proprosition. After a moment, Maiya stood up from her seat. "That's certainly a very interesting possibility, and it's worth considering, Sir Collin. I'm glad you thought of it."

"Very good, Sir Collin," said Ralphen. "Let's think about those who spend time with the Princess. Obviously, there's myself and the Queen, but, unfortunately, we ourselves have noticed nothing."

"Yes, My Lord," said Collin. "There's Miss Angelica, her maidservant. She spends much of her time with the Princess, since that is her role. I've also found that our young Magic Knight, Miss Helen Renier, spends some of her time with the Princess as well. Then, there's young Sir Mirin, who is Princess Mika's best friend. We also have Sir Galner, her professor of magical studies. There are also a few other professors who teach her on various subjects and the children who attend her same classes."

"A few adults, but most of the others are children," said Maleth.

Ralphen rose from his seat. "This is an excellent idea, Sir Collin. Please proceed with questioning these individuals. Find out as much information as you can, no matter how insignificant it might be. We must find the Princess!"

Collin bowed his head slightly, as did Maleth. "Yes, My Lord."

* * *

Feldia walked down the busy Valderia Pathway as she headed towards a store called Arayia Textiles. In order to conceal the scabbard which hung from her belt at her side, she wore a cloak that was tied closed at the front and was long enough that only her knee-high boots could be seen. She also wore the hood over her head to conceal part of her face. She entered the textile store, and proceeded past patrons towards the back, where she pushed back her hood. Various fabrics such as wool and cotton hung from racks on every wall, and carpets of different sizes and textures were piled high on many wooden tables. Her hand brushed past some smooth silk that felt cool to her skin. When she looked around at the patrons, she could tell they were all most likely to be peasants, but she knew that the store's most affluent customer was the Scarletia Royal Castle itself.

The elderly woman who was the store owner greeted Feldia. "Welcome, Miss Feldia. I'm assuming you're here for the item."

Feldia looked around to make sure there was no one nearby who might hear their conversation. She spoke softly as she answered the store owner. "Yes, I am, Miss Sednia. Please tell me it wasn't damaged in any way... considering what happened that day with the peasant mob."

The elderly woman spoke in a hushed voice as well. "I inspected it myself when I found it on the street. I had my grandsons carry it inside. All the fine and beautiful things in it are still in good condition. There was some dirt on some of the clothes from the street, but I washed them."

"Thank you. The original owner will appreciate it."

A sparkle in the woman's eyes as she smiled. "I'm sure she will. Come."

Sednia led the way into the storage area at the back. As soon as Feldia went inside, Sednia closed the door, and made sure it was locked. Feldia walked farther into the room that was piled full of textiles. In one corner of the room, she saw what she was looking for.

A travel chest made of fine algerwood.

Feldia knelt down beside it, and opened it, revealing beautiful dresses, shoes, and many other items that belonged to a young girl. She closed it right away as she rose. Feldia went to the back door, and opened it. Outside the store, in the alleyway, two cloaked and hooded young men looked around to make sure that they themselves were not seen.

Feldia motioned them to come in. "Galien, Demias."

The two complied, pushing back their hoods as soon as they went inside.

Feldia gestured towards the travel chest. "There it is. Make sure no one sees you taking this back," she ordered, referring to the inn Ethereal Daydreams.

Demias groaned at seeing how elaborate the travel chest appeared. "That's going to be feat, Feldia, walking down the street with something made of algerwood."

"Cover it up with something then," said Galien.

Sednia quickly approached them, carrying an old carpet that had been rolled up. "Here. Use this to cover it."

Demias took the carpet. "Thanks, Miss Sednia. That should help." He and Galien wrapped the travel chest with the old carpet that was long enough to go around the chest three times. They lifted it up by the handles at each end, and proceeded through the exit and into the alleyway beyond.

Feldia turned to the store owner. "Thanks again, Miss Sednia."

"You're welcome, Miss Feldia." Sednia put a hand on Feldia's arm. "And good luck."

Feldia smiled. "We need as much luck as we can get."

* * *

In the Supreme Captain's Office, Collin sat behind a large desk examining the list of individuals regularly seen with Princess Mika... and he had to admit, it was a rather short list. The names were divided into two groups. The first group listed the individuals who Mika spent more time with than others. This group included Miss Angelica, Sir Galner, Miss Helen, and Mirin. The second group listed the individuals with whom Mika came into contact regularly, but did not necessarily spend time with. They included the professors who educated her and her classmates, and this group numbered no more than twelve people, three of them professors and the rest children close to Mika's age.

The only list truly worth looking at here is the first list, thought Collin. *But, of course, I must interview everyone, even the children. However... the first list... it's so short. The Princess truly does spend her time with only a select few. She doesn't socialize very much.*

His thoughts became a whisper. "I wonder why that is. Children her age tend to be more social... but the Princess tends to keep to herself."

There was a knock on one of the double doors that led into his office.

"Come!" ordered Collin.

A knight opened the door, and standing in the doorway was Angelica.

"Ah, the lovely Miss Angelica. Please do come in," said Collin, as he put on the smile of a gentleman. "You're as beautiful as always."

Angelica walked into the room, finding slight annoyance over his unsuccessful attempt at flattery.

The office of the Supreme Captain was sparsely decorated, unlike how it looked when Sir Terren Rinaldia was the Supreme Captain of the Scarletia Royal Guard. Since Collin had taken over after Terren's retirement, he had been taking his time truly moving into this office. Half the shelves were devoid of anything. There were wooden bins that carried some of Collin's belongings against one of the side walls. Many of them had not been unpacked. The windows behind Collin were covered in white curtains as the morning sun was angled in such a way that if the curtains were opened, it would be too bright in the room.

"You wanted to see me, Sir Collin." Angelica walked farther into the room, dressed in her maidservant's uniform. The door was closed behind her.

"Yes, Miss Angelica. Please have a seat." Collin motioned her towards one of the two chairs in front of his desk.

Angelica stiffened as she sat down. She then gave Collin a serious stare, and stayed silent, waiting for Collin to speak, as she pushed back a lock of her long brown hair.

Collin noted her expression. "I'm assuming I caught you at a bad time. I do apologize."

"Not at all, Sir Collin," said Angelica.

"Well, then, let's get right to business so you can get back to work. The reason why I summoned you here is simple. As you know, Princess Mika has disappeared. We've searched the entire castle, every single room in every corner of this entire complex, and we haven't found any sign of her. We've even searched the Grounds. We have found no clues that tell us what could have happened to her. It is very concerning for me."

Angelica was speechless. She wanted to tell him that they were not looking hard enough. She also wanted to tell him that she was greatly concerned for the Princess, even more so than he was.

"One of my tasks now is to interview those who are regularly found with Princess Mika, and that includes you, of course, among many others. The clues we're looking for that could help us in our search for the Princess may not always be tangible. They could be intangible, in the form of observations, for example. I wanted to ask you if you have noticed anything strange lately."

"Strange? Like what, exactly?" asked Angelica.

Collin shrugged. "It could be anything. Have you seen anything that might be out of the ordinary? It could be something insignificant. You might think it's not important, but it might help us in our search."

Angelica thought about that for a moment, and tried to recall if there was anything she might have seen, but she shook her head. "I don't recall seeing anything out of the ordinary, Sir Collin."

"All right. It may also not necessarily something you might have seen, but something you might have heard.

What about hearing anything out of the ordinary? This could be spoken words, either from other people or perhaps even from the Princess herself."

Angelica shook her head again. "I don't remember anything of the sort."

"Not even a few words?" asked Collin. "Has the Princess said anything that you yourself might have thought was out of the ordinary?"

Angelica remembered the Princess talking about the peasants and how she was obsessed over why they tried to kill her and why they said certain things. Angelica had told her that she should not think about it too much, because, according to her, peasants often say incomprehensible things.

I don't like where these questions are going. Should I tell Sir Collin about that? No. She was just wondering about something. It's natural for her curious mind. She has always been like that. No, I can't let Sir Collin know about that. I'm Princess Mika's maidservant, and my duty is to her. Whatever the Princess discusses with me is confidential. No one should ever know unless the Princess wills it.

"Miss Angelica?"

Angelica blinked, realizing she had been thinking in front of him, completely silent.

"You look like there's something on your mind. Does this mean the Princess has told you something?"

Angelica shook her head. "No. I was just thinking as hard as I could. What you're asking me to do, Sir Collin, is actually quite difficult. How do I distinguish what isn't strange and what is, especially if both are insignificant?"

"You do have a point. It's very difficult to recall something if it's insignificant, regardless of its strangeness. Why did you look so irritated when you came into my office, Miss Angelica? Did I truly catch you at a bad time?"

"No."

"What were you doing, exactly?"

Angelica frowned at him. "Performing my day-to-day duties, Sir Collin," she answered confidently. "By the way, can I ask you something?"

Collin was taken aback. "Go ahead."

"Am I here so you can find out if I had anything to do with the disappearance of the Princess, and pass it off as an interview?"

"Excuse me?" Collin was surprised by that question, and a hint of irritation appeared in his voice.

"Should I repeat my question?"

Collin paused for a moment, and leaned back in his chair. He chuckled. "Not at all, Miss Angelica. I simply want to find the Princess and bring her back safely. I do apologize if you believe being here suggests I'm accusing you of something. I assure you, I'm not accusing you of anything. I'm *fairly* certain you wouldn't have anything to do with the disappearance of the Princess."

"You should be *completely* certain." Angelica leaned forward in her seat. "I've been waiting on Princess Mika since she was eight years old, for the last three years, Sir Collin. Ever since I reached the age of majority, I have performed my duties for the Princess beyond the best of my abilities. I take great pride in my work as her maidservant. I wouldn't care to look after anyone else but her. She may be the Princess, and I may be her personal maidservant, but we are also friends. I have grown to love her very much, like a younger sister. It's very difficult for the King and Queen to spend time with her, because they are very busy with their own day-to-day duties, so I do my very best to take care of her. You ask me these questions, but by doing so, you insult me and my relationship with Princess Mika."

Collin stared hard at Angelica, trying to see if what she was saying contained any clues. However, he could see that she was becoming somewhat agitated. He leaned forward in his seat, his arms on his desk. "If you have truly heard and seen nothing, Miss Angelica, if you truly have noticed nothing, no matter how unimportant it might seem, then I can only take your word for it. I'm not accusing you of anything here. You and I want to find the Princess. But I need all the help I can get with such a daunting task."

"Then, perhaps, you should take your knights beyond

the castle gates. We've all searched the entire castle. Shouldn't it be obvious by now that she's not here?"

"I don't see any reason why she would be beyond the gates. Why would she be in the city? A noble child of the Royal Family would never want to venture beyond the gates. There would be no reason to, unless she truly was abducted, which is, of course, extremely unlikely."

"I suppose you're right," said Angelica.

Collin stood up. "I have no more questions for you. You may proceed with performing your regular day-to-day duties, Miss Angelica."

Angelica stood up. "Thank you." She immediately turned around, headed for the doors, and left.

Sir Collin sat down in his chair, and then leaned back. "Her loyalty to the Princess is admirable." He began to think about his interview with Angelica just now.

What is the possibility that she knows something, but just can't remember if it's important? Rather high, I must admit. But she doesn't think it's important. That means... she would have to think about it some more. I should interview her again in a few days. Perhaps it'll come back to her. She knows something. She just doesn't realize she does.

Taking a fountain pen, he wrote notes beside Angelica's name on his list.

* * *

Later in the morning, it was Helen sitting in front of Collin's desk. Clad in her knight's uniform with a cape, she sat with her usual air of confidence, well back into her chair. Collin had asked her the same question he had asked Angelica.

"I haven't seen or heard anything that might seem important or provide clues as to what might have happened to the Princess, Sir Collin," answered Helen.

"You're certain about this?" asked Collin.

Helen nodded. "Absolutely certain."

Collin leaned forward, rubbing his head for a moment as if he was feeling a headache coming on. "I have noticed something interesting between you and Princess Mika lately, Miss Helen."

Helen frowned. "Pardon me?"

"The two of you actually spend quite a bit of time together."

"What do you mean by that?"

"I mean just that. The two of you spend time together, perhaps not to the same degree as the Princess and her maidservant Miss Angelica, but you are sometimes found near the Princess."

"I'm not certain I understand, Sir Collin. Is there something wrong with a knight who spends some of her time near the Princess?"

Collin shook his head. "Not at all. I was simply wondering about it. I suppose the question I want to ask is... why?"

"Why? Well, both the Princess and I are under the mentorship of Sir Galner. We're both his students of magical studies. We're both learning under him, and the Princess and I are often together when these lessons with Sir Galner take place. You're aware of this, Sir Collin."

"Of course. But, sometimes, I've noticed and heard from others that it's not just during the lessons when you and Princess Mika are found together. Sometimes, you've been seen speaking with her on other occasions, perhaps in the hallways or out on the Grounds."

Helen sighed. "Sometimes the Princess and I do talk outside of our lessons, Sir Collin. Is that wrong somehow?"

"Not at all. I am just curious as to what two lovely young girls could be talking about."

"All right." Helen sighed at his strange attempt to flatter. She remembered him complimenting her during Sir Terren Rinaldia's Retirement Ceremony. His reputation for attempting to flatter young women was well-known among maidservants and female knights... and his lack of success was even more so.

Helen tried to think of what she should say to answer Collin's question.

I used to bully her, even though I knew it wasn't right.

Sometimes, her personality is irritating, but I shouldn't bully her because of that. I always think of myself as a proper lady, far more mature than the Princess, but I contradicted myself by treating her that way. And I've tried to curb that of late. By the way, this line of questioning is annoying and pointless. What does the Supreme Captain hope to achieve? I better think of something... and fast.

"Well?" said Collin, expecting an answer.

Helen thought of an idea, one that she felt would put a stop to the interview. "Are you certain you want to know what we sometimes talk about?"

Collin seemed annoyed. "Should I give you an order as your superior officer, Miss Helen?"

Helen shrugged. "There's no need, sir. I'll tell you if that's what you wish."

"Tell me."

Helen leaned forward. "Menstruation."

Collin was taken aback. "What...?"

"Among other things young girls talk about in private, Sir Collin." She leaned back in her chair. "That's all. I'm only a few years older than the Princess, as I'm sure you're aware. Sometimes there are certain topics a young girl will want to discuss with a slightly older girl as she matures. As I've already experienced some of the things that she herself will eventually experience as a growing young girl, it's only natural for us to discuss the changes that occur in our minds and bodies."

Fighting back his discomfort, Collin waved his hand to dismiss her. "Never mind. I don't need to hear about it. You may go."

"Thank you, Sir Collin." Helen rose, made her way towards the double doors to exit, and soon left Collin's office.

Looks like I was successful in ending this pointless questioning by playing with his insecurity. I've heard that most men are squeamish when it comes to hearing girls and women talk about such issues. What kind of man would want to hear about menstruation unless he was a physician? Yes, I do talk to the Princess quite a bit, don't I? It's usually just so I can have a little fun with her, that's all. But I can't tell the Supreme Captain that. If I did, I would be disciplined. Though... I must admit... the more time I spend with Princess Mika, the more I am actually starting to like her. Scary thought... but I suppose... I don't mind....

Helen smiled to herself as she headed down the hallway. She continued to think to herself.

I've witnessed the suffering of the peasants personally, and I've seen the terrible conditions they live under. Perhaps... now that I've become part of the Scarletia Royal Guard, I can do something. It may take time... but I must do something! I am a knight, after all. Isn't that the duty of a knight? To protect those who can't protect themselves? There must be something I can do.

Collin leaned back, thinking about his latest interview.

She is a young girl herself, just like the Princess. If they talk to each other the way young girls do, then... there could be many things they could talk about. It is possible that she might know something, but doesn't realize it.

After thinking through the exchange, he wrote notes beside Helen's name on the list.

* * *

Sir Galner sat in Collin's office, but he was in a much better mood than Angelica or Helen when they had been here.

"So if you're offended in any way by what I'm doing, Sir Galner, I hope that you'll understand and forgive me," said Collin.

Galner simply laughed. "You don't need to be so concerned, boy."

Collin made a fist underneath his desk upon hearing how Galner sometimes referred to him. He could not remember how many times the mage called him "boy" instead of by his first name or title. Each time, he found it very irritating.

"I understand your duties perfectly well. If you weren't questioning the people who spend much of their time with the Princess, then I would be concerned. You should definitely question them to find out if they know something. Of course, I'm not surprised that you wanted to speak with me, as I am in charge of Princess Mika's magical training. I would be glad to cooperate."

Collin smiled, relieved. "Thank you."

"To answer your question, Sir Collin, unfortunately, I was nowhere near the Princess before or during the night of her disappearance. On Morrighan 35, four days before the night of her disappearance, I journeyed to the city of Cerulean on business, to the Cerulean Magic Academy. My superiors and colleagues will tell you where I was and what I was doing, if you wish to speak with them as well, to verify my whereabouts. In fact, I only returned the day before yesterday... and I was very surprised to find the guards at the castle gates searching me and my carriage. At first, I wasn't too happy with such treatment, but I found that security was definitely much tighter than it normally was. Before I even arrived at my office, I was told by the King that the Princess was missing. Needless to say, I was quite shocked."

"We all were, Sir Galner. I very much would like to find her as soon as possible. We have searched everywhere in the castle and on the Grounds, and we still can't find her. She has been missing for two days now, and it's extremely concerning. The more time passes, the higher the possibility that we may not find her safe."

Galner stiffened at that. "That's true, Sir Collin. I'm certain you've read about crimes where a child is abducted. It doesn't happen in our castle or in other places where the Nobility reside, but it often occurs in cities, where these peasant dogs would abduct a child of a noble family that's simply passing through. When a child is abducted, time is of the essence. As you mentioned, the more time that passes, the more dangerous it becomes. When these incidents occur in the cities, very often, the child is found dead."

Collin waved his hand away. "Please... don't remind me, Sir Galner. But what about before the Princess disappeared? Have you noticed anything out of the ordinary? Have you seen or heard anything that might lead us to a clue, no matter how small that might be?"

"The only thing I found, you are already aware of, and that would be the behaviour of the Princess during our failed excursion to the city of Cerulean."

"Ah, that's right," said Collin.

"As you may recall in my report, read by you, the Princess was behaving erratically. She questioned the normality of the world around her, the status quo, and the way in which these peasant dogs lived in comparison to the way we live. She believed it was unnatural, and there was something not quite right about it. Of course, we all know that what was not quite right was her behaviour."

Collin chuckled. "I believe the young Princess, despite her age, has a reputation for being extremely opinionated and naturally curious, or perhaps, unnaturally, depending on what she wants to know. She has a sharp and inquisitive mind, far more than other children her age."

"Yes, Sir Collin." Annoyed, Galner groaned as he was reminded of Mika's character. "Though it has helped her become a very proficient user of magic, perhaps she is far too sharp and inquisitive for her own good."

Collin nodded to that. "Agreed. Is there anything else you can think of that might help us with our search for our missing Princess?"

"Unfortunately, that's all I know. As for anything seemingly small and insignificant that I might not remember but is nevertheless important, I would have to dig deeper into my mind. But know that I can't promise anything, Collin. There may be nothing."

"Please let me know of anything you might think of, if you do."

"I will. Well, if there is nothing further…?"

"That's all for now."

Galner rose, and then headed for the exit.

As soon as he left, Collin leaned forward towards his desk. He thought about Galner's words and the interviews he'd conducted so far.

Perhaps the clue we're looking for is one Galner already

found, and it's staring at us in the face, making itself very obvious, and yet we're not looking at it. Should we be looking at it? The Princess... is a child, eleven years old, and yet... is extremely intelligent, highly educated, has an opinion about everything all her own, keeps to herself, always thinks deeply, extremely stubborn, seems to have been terribly surprised that peasants and nobles live completely different lives, and questions the way they live, perhaps thinking there's something wrong with it. Once again, I'm thinking of this list of people who are regularly found with the Princess... a very short list. The Princess keeps to herself. A young girl who keeps to herself... would also think to herself very often... and would have plenty of time to do it. Who knows what truly goes on in her mind?

Collin suddenly looked up at the double doors, as if coming to a possible realization.

Does that sound like the characteristics of someone who has the potential to betray the Nobility and the Royal Family?

Surprised at himself, Collin shook his head, brushing that last thought away.

"Impossible. She's just a child."

He picked up his pen, and wrote some notes from his meeting with Galner.

* * *

Collin had already interviewed the professors who taught Mika, but they really didn't know anything. He interviewed them one at a time, having one of his knights summon them out of their classes temporarily. They proved to be very short interviews.

The Supreme Captain walked down a hallway towards a room whose doors were wide open. He heard the lecturing of a professor inside and the voices of young children. He stood at the doorway, and watched Miss Aryn Mayfeld, a highly educated woman in her late twenties, as she asked her students some questions while holding a book. The students each sat at their desks, arranged in a circular pattern around the professor. Collin had already interviewed Miss Aryn in his office earlier today.

Mirin was among the students. He saw Collin at the door.

When the professor saw Mirin's distracted eyes, Aryn turned to the door, and saw Collin there as well. She stopped, and walked over to him. "Sir Collin, is this an appropriate time? I've already told you everything I know, which is nothing."

"My apologies, Miss Aryn, but it's not you to whom I want to speak with this time," answered Collin, keeping his voice down so none of the students would hear.

Aryn frowned at Sir Collin. "What do you mean?"

"Actually, before that, I want to thank you for coming to my office earlier. I didn't have the chance, as you left so quickly after you perceived some unintended offense on my part, to apologize to you. I take no pleasure in offending beautiful young women."

Aryn sighed at Collin's obvious attempt to flatter her. "I already told you. I haven't noticed anything strange lately, not with my surroundings or with the Princess. She keeps to herself, and she is very quiet in class. She only speaks when she is spoken to."

Collin was surprised. "Hold on a moment. That, you did not tell me. I'm aware that she keeps to herself but... even among her professors and peers?"

"Does it matter to a Supreme Captain? I don't know why it would, but, yes, the Princess keeps quiet unless spoken to. She does extremely well in class, but she's painfully shy and reserved. She'll talk to me if I talk to her, such as if I'm asking her a question. If the other students talk to her, she becomes timid. She talks to them, but with very little confidence and with a very soft voice. The only one in class she's comfortable speaking with is...." Aryn looked back at her students, seeing Mirin. "It's only Mirin she speaks to comfortably."

Mirin stiffened, hearing his name whispered. Seeing that the professor turned to him just now made him wonder what was happening.

Collin hesitated for a moment. "Perhaps it's not that important. It's good to know, however, as further insight into Princess Mika's personality and her highly secretive mind."

Aryn eyed him with confusion. "All right...."

"Now, for the reason why I came. Actually, I was wondering if I could speak to young Mirin out here in the hallway for a few minutes, and perhaps a couple of his classmates as well. Any would do, as long as they have interacted with the Princess."

Aryn tried to hide her annoyance. "Other than Mirin, there are a couple of students who interact with her more than the others." She turned to her students. "Mirin, Taria, Sheena, will you please speak to our Supreme Captain for a moment?"

Mirin stiffened some more as he stood up. He looked behind him, and saw the two girls who were also called out. They slowly stood up from their seats.

Out in the hallway, as Collin spoke to them, Mirin took the lead, standing in front of the two girls. He reminded them that the Princess was missing, and that he and his knights were tasked with finding her.

"So, Sir Mirin, I hope you understand the importance of finding the Princess, and I hope you can help me. Is there anything at all that you might have seen or heard that could help us? Anything at all?"

Oh no. Does he think I know about the Princess going out into the city and staying with the peasants? Does he know she's out there? What's she doing anyway? I better stop thinking too much, or Sir Collin will think I'm hiding something.

Mirin just shook his head. "I don't know, Sir Collin. I haven't seen or heard anything strange."

"What about from the Princess herself?"

Mirin shook his head again. "She hasn't said anything strange either. I'm worried about her, Sir Collin. When are you going to find her?"

"As soon as possible, I assure you." Collin regarded the young girls next. "What about you lovely ladies?"

The two girls appeared confused as they exchanged glances. Sheena smiled sweetly as she spoke with a calm voice. "I'm sorry, Sir Collin, but we haven't seen anything either."

Taria groaned softly, annoyed as she remembered Mika's usual demeanour. "The Princess doesn't usually talk to us, so even if there were anything strange, we certainly wouldn't have noticed anything."

"The Princess doesn't talk to you? Why do you think that is, Miss Taria?" asked Collin.

Taria held out her hands at either side of her. "I don't know."

Sheena spoke with a soft voice beside Taria. "I thought I told you. She doesn't talk to us because she's better than us. She's the Princess."

Taria was alarmed. "You fool! Be quiet! Don't say that!"

Sheena gasped, her hands covering her mouth. "I'm sorry!"

Mirin, hearing what they said, turned to them. "How can you think that about the Princess? Is that what you truly think? That's the reason why you don't talk to her?"

Sheena sighed wistfully. "Sorry, Mirin, but... she doesn't talk to us either."

Taria shook her head. "Well, then... now that Sheena's mentioned it, I have to say the same thing. She's the one who doesn't talk to us."

Annoyed, Mirin snapped back. "She doesn't talk to you because you don't talk to her!"

Sheena stepped back, intimidated by Mirin's outburst.

"Calm down, why don't you?" demanded Taria, staring back at Mirin with irritation.

"All right, now, that's enough." Collin straightened up. "All of you may go back into your classroom. Thank you."

The two girls gave a quick curtsy, and headed back into the classroom.

Mirin stayed behind for a moment. "Sir Collin?"

"Yes, Sir Mirin?"

What am I doing? I don't know anything, remember? Come on, Mirin! Think quickly, because now he thinks you have something to say!

Seeing that Mirin paused for a very brief moment, Collin wondered what he had to say. "What's on your mind?"

Mirin kept his voice calm despite his apprehension. "I hope the Princess is safe. I'm worried about her."

Collin smiled. "I hope so as well."

"Thank you." Mirin headed back into the classroom.

Collin headed down the hallway on his way back to his office. "Well, then. That was a waste of time."

Except for Mirin, these children couldn't have noticed anything strange. If they don't talk to her, if the Princess keeps to herself around them and doesn't interact with them in any meaningful way, then the children probably don't know anything that would be of use to me. But, Mirin... he's always with Princess Mika. He says he hasn't heard or seen anything strange. Well... I suppose that's possible. But the two of them are very close. He's the only child that the Princess feels comfortable enough to interact with. From what I've seen, the other children are probably intimidated by her position, even though it's actually she who feels intimidated by them. There appears to be a misunderstanding between her and the other children.

Sir Mirin, like Helen, probably knows more than he realizes, but doesn't understand the importance of these simple observations.

CHAPTER 20

THE BEGINNING

"PRINCESS MIKA."

Mika glanced up as she heard her name being called. She was seated at a table in the basement of the inn called Ethereal Daydreams, snacking on biscuits and sipping a cup of hot green tea. She saw Feldia at the bottom of the stairs that led down into the basement from the outside.

"Miss Feldia?"

"We found something for you." Feldia walked farther into the room, followed by Demias and Galien, who carried something long and covered by some kind of carpet. They held on to the object using the handles at each end.

Mika stood up, and approached it. "What is it?"

"I think you'll be pleasantly surprised."

Mika watched as Demias and Galien put the object down on the floor, and removed the carpet that was wrapped around it. As soon as it was removed, she gasped. "It's my travel chest! The one I lost!" She knelt down beside it, feeling the smooth algerwood exterior.

Feldia turned to her companions. "Demias, Galien, thanks for your help."

"Not a problem," said Galien.

Demias nodded. "You're welcome, Feldia."

Mika watched as Demias and Galien left the room, and as soon as they left, she opened up the lid. She saw all her beautiful belongings from that day when she was on an excursion to the Cerulean Magic Academy. "How did you manage to find it?"

Feldia smiled, shrugging her shoulders. "I heard about a textile shop owner who somehow took ownership of a certain travel chest that had been dropped by the Princess while she was escaping. I had to see this woman. She took care of all your stuff for you."

Mika smiled. "I would like to meet with her someday. I am very thankful to her. I've been desperate to get out of these clothes for the past couple of days." She pointed to the old purple and white dress she was wearing. "I've been wearing Miss Zima's old hand-me-down dress and undergarments from when she was a young girl. She apparently keeps old clothes just in case she births a daughter someday. They don't fit me properly. I've been embarrassed to appear in someone else's old clothes."

Feldia stifled a laugh. "Clothes are expensive to peasants, My Lady. She has to save what she can, even used undergarments, unfortunately. Personally, I don't feel right about wearing someone else's knickers."

"I don't feel right about it either."

"When I saw you in Miss Zima's things, I remembered this shop owner's having mentioned the travel chest, and had to pay her a visit."

"Thank you so much, Miss Feldia," said Mika. "I've been bathing in the Balias family's bathroom. I feel like I'm imposing. Can I use the one here?"

Feldia blinked with surprised. "You mean you haven't used the one in the back? Seriously, Princess?"

Mika shook her head.

"It might not be as nicely decorated as the one in Dellen's house, but the water is a lot warmer, because you have the entire building's hot water supply at your disposal. It would be more convenient for you."

* * *

SEC 3566, Morrighan 42

"Tell me, Princess. Why do you think revolutions occur, now that you know they do?" asked Adrel, as he ascended the steps of a tall stone tower.

Mika stopped for a moment as she ascended with him. She was a few steps behind him, holding on to the cold metal rails on the wall as she ascended slowly, like the others in front of her and behind her. Because she'd finally had the opportunity to bathe properly and change into her own clothes, she felt much more comfortable. Her plain light blue dress with rosettes at the hem was sleeveless and had a somewhat low neckline. She wore a white cloak obtained from a nearby clothing store by Feldia over it to make it look like she was a peasant, but her fine white shoes certainly gave that disguise away. Her Princess Gem peeked out from underneath her cloak.

Leading the way up the stairs in front of Mika were Adrel and Dellen, wearing cloaks over their usual street clothes. Behind her were Laren and Feldia, followed by ten others. They made sure no one was following them. Mika continued to ascend the steps as she thought about Adrel's question, running her hands gently against the ancient wall and feeling its smoothness, which was occasionally interrupted by the tiny cracks that snaked across its surface.

"Revolutions occur because of various reasons," answered Mika. "It could be because people who start revolutions seek to change the political structure of a nation. Those people can be within the government itself, within the military, or the general population."

Adrel chuckled. "Very good. Looks like I've taught you well."

"Hey, come on, Adrel. You weren't the only one teaching her these kinds of things," said Dellen. "Don't forget about my contribution to her newfound knowledge."

Shaking her head at their boasting about their ability to pass on their knowledge to Mika, Feldia chimed in. "I think you gentlemen are forgetting that the Princess has been educated in the matters of politics. Get over yourselves."

Laren, upon hearing that, started laughing.

Adrel snorted, feeling his pride wounded. "So based on what you've learned, not just from us but your professors back at the castle, when it comes to politics, what can you tell me about what's going on? Are we in a state of revolution?"

Mika nodded. "Yes. We're in a constant state of revolution because there are always rebel groups fighting against the Nobility and the Royal Family. The government calls this a time of peace. There's no war at the moment. But there is a revolution. War, peace, and revolution are like a never-ending waltz, I suppose."

"That's right."

"But, Sir Adrel...."

"What?"

"Revolutions, just like wars, must have a terrible impact on the people. Their lives are disrupted. Sometimes they're forced to move somewhere else. Their homes might be destroyed. Sometimes they end up killed because they are caught up in a battle between the two sides of a revolution."

"Damn right. It's regrettable, Princess, that so many have to die because they're caught between two opposing forces. But is it avoidable?"

Mika sadly shook her head. "No, it isn't. It's... completely unavoidable. That's what's happening right now. The Nobility are oppressing the Peasantry, ruling over them with an iron fist. The Peasantry form rebel groups that try to fight back against the Nobility. They're trying to fight for their freedom from tyranny... but at the same time, people's lives are put in danger."

"I prefer to avoid bloodshed. But, unfortunately, we have to fight against all this. If we don't, our nation will be lost, our people will keep on suffering... and our children won't have a future to look forward to. That's why we fight, Princess Mika."

Mika took it all in, as she has taken in many things since the very beginning, when the merchant assassins attacked. They continued to ascend the steps of the tower until they reached the fifteenth floor, the highest floor of the tower. As soon as they reached it, Mika leaned against the wall to catch her breath. She pushed back the hood of her cloak.

"Are you all right, My Lady?" asked Feldia.

Mika nodded slowly. "I'm fine. It's just... that's a lot

of steps to climb. I'm sorry, but my body is not accustomed to that. I should be fine very soon."

After a couple of minutes' rest, she regarded her surroundings. The top floor of the tower was partially damaged. Pieces of broken white stone littered the floor, heavy and impossible to carry and move out of the way. The makeshift windows were actually rectangular openings that allowed viewing of the outside. An entire wall was missing as well, but because of that missing wall, Mika and the others had a perfect view of the Scarletia Royal Castle that stood about three kilometres away.

"What is this place?" asked Mika.

Laren stood beside Mika. "It's called the Eldoria Watchtower. It was built over a thousand years ago to watch over the city of Scarletia. It was said to have been built by the race of Spires."

"How did it get so damaged?" Mika walked around, examining the ruined stone. "Was it something that happened a long time ago?"

"No one knows exactly, but it was suggested that our neighbouring nation to the west, the nation of Tashar, launched some kind of attack on the city of Scarletia about seven hundred years ago. Dragons flew overhead, and destroyed much of the city with a terrible flame. It's a wonder that the tower still stands after such an attack and after all this time."

Feldia sat on a stone boulder. "This is the tallest structure in the entire city. I'm surprised you never saw this from your castle, Princess Mika."

"It looks like we're almost directly in front of the castle gates, since the tower is on a side street that connects to the Valderia Pathway," said Mika. "My bedchamber faces a different direction so I wouldn't have seen it."

"Ah. And if you were outside the castle, but within the walls, you probably wouldn't have noticed it because the walls were too high."

Mika suddenly remembered seeing the tower previously. "Wait, I do remember now. I passed by it that day, before we were surrounded by the peasant mob. I wondered what it was because it was so tall."

Adrel and Dellen stood a few steps from the edge of the floor, where the missing wall used to be. They could see people walking up and down the city streets, including the Valderia Pathway.

Dellen turned around to face Mika, who was still busy exploring her surroundings. "Princess Mika."

Mika joined Dellen and Adrel. From where she was, she saw that the castle walls were rectangular in shape. They were also much higher at the back of the castle than at the front and the sides. The entire building of the castle was five floors in height, but was extremely wide at the base. It was no wonder ten thousand nobles could live comfortably within its walls. But there was something about the castle that Mika saw for the first time that she could not have seen from within. From where she stood, Mika saw that the castle was not quite one enormous building, but actually several interconnected buildings of varying shapes, sizes, and ages. She remembered reading about the history of the castle. At one point, it had been much smaller, and had grown overtime as more buildings were added to it. It was a strange sensation Mika felt, seeing the castle from this perspective. Normally, she would see the castle from within the walls, but now she was seeing it in its entirety from a distance.

As Mika watched the castle, Dellen spoke to her. "You've decided to help the Peasantry. The future starts here, at the top of this tower. You're the Princess of Melodice. Because of that, we would appreciate any suggestions you may have that would help us help you achieve your goal, which is also our goal, a goal that you've made your own."

Mika appeared calm as she looked at each of them: Dellen, Feldia, Adrel, and Laren. She also regarded their companions. She was still having trouble remembering the names of all ten of them. They all waited for her to speak to them as the Princess of Melodice. Had this happened another time, before the merchant assassins had tried to take her life, she would have been completely surprised and intimidated by this situation. But it was different now. She was changing. Her experiences, both past and present, had made her into a different kind of person, making her stronger and more courageous inside. From near the missing wall, Mika stared at the castle in front of her, her home, the home of her family and friends Angelica and Mirin, and of the Nobility and the Royal Family.

"There's no turning back," whispered Mika. "I chose this path for myself and for the people of Melodice."

Mika was on the side of her people. The leaders of the two largest rebel groups in the entire city were here with her, along with their companions. They had listened to her and acknowledged her when she told them what she wanted to do. She wanted to help them in any way she could. If that was to counsel them as the Princess of Melodice, then she would do that. Mika turned to face them. "What about a revolt of the workers?"

"A revolt?" asked Feldia.

The Princess nodded. "Yes, and I'm not just thinking of a small one. I'm thinking of a revolt that spans the entire city of Scarletia."

Laren stared wide-eyed. "The entire city?"

"Yes. Is that doable?"

Dellen thought about that for a moment. "I believe so, Princess. It's pretty big, what you're thinking about. We need the coordination of many people, thousands of people. We have to be able to send word in secret to all the members of both rebel groups. If you want to do something like that, we have to plan soon. We have to spread word as quickly as possible while remaining covert."

"Do you think it could work, Sir Dellen?" asked Mika.

"It's a good start."

Adrel snorted in irritation. "What? Are you serious? You're suggesting a revolt among the workers that spans an entire city of one million people? What do you propose they do? Hold up signs?"

Mika shook her head, trying to push away her timid feelings. "Not exactly. All the peasants who work in industries that support the castle will be instructed to stop working. That'll stop supplies from reaching the castle, including food supplies. Services will stop running as well.

They will not provide the castle with anything since all work will stop. The workers will march throughout the city, and they'll vocally protest against tyranny. They'll demand freedom from it so they can live a better life."

"Hmmm... that sounds interesting," said Feldia.

Mika continued. "But they are not to cause any damage to the city or harm anyone. They mustn't fight against the knights, who will likely only attack large groups of peasants if they're attacked themselves. The Supreme Captain would never order them to attack large groups of peasants unless the peasants are causing a problem, which they won't, because the workers will be instructed to remain peaceful."

"A peaceful revolt," said Laren. "One that spans an entire city. That's quite a feat, Princess, but I think it's doable."

Dellen nodded slowly. "That's a good idea, Princess Mika."

"Not aggressive enough!" shouted Adrel.

Everyone turned to him, including Mika.

"Nobles regularly travel through the city. I think we should capture every single noble that we run across, and take them prisoner. It can be a mass hostage-taking, and we'll demand our freedom in exchange for theirs."

Dellen shook his head. "No. If we do that, you risk the knights attacking peasants blindly. They'll be ordered to deploy, and find every peasant who's involved in the mass abduction and their families, too. A lot of people would die, Adrel, including entire families."

Feldia agreed with Dellen. "That's happened before. In fact, many times."

Adrel groaned with impatience, but he understood why Dellen and Feldia didn't agree with his idea. "I did say I wanted to avoid bloodshed, but sometimes, violence has been necessary. It's unfortunate, but that's the reality of our situation. What do you think, Princess Mika?"

Mika held a somber expression. "I'm sorry, Sir Adrel, but... I don't like the idea of having people taken prisoner like that. And like Sir Dellen said, the knights would retaliate and kill everyone who's involved, including women and children. I'm sorry, but I'm not comfortable with that."

Adrel raised his hands in frustration. "Like I said before, everyone, a revolution, unfortunately, has casualties. But... I do see your point. Never mind then." He turned back to Mika. "Do forgive me, My Lady. I am a man who wants results. Please tell me that this revolt of the peasant workers will have results."

"It will have results. I even mentioned them," said Mika. "While the peasant workers are marching and demanding their freedom, they will only stop if the Nobility and the Royal Family acknowledge their demands and grant them what they want. That's the only time they'll stop the revolt, not before."

"Okay," said Dellen. "I will send word to all the members of the Hope of Scarletia."

"Thank you, Sir Dellen. I want to avoid bloodshed. I don't want anyone to have to die needlessly. I've... already seen more than enough people die, most of them innocent people." Mika remembered the mother and the baby, burning inside a wall of flame that was the result of Sir Galner's magic attack. "I don't want people to die if we can avoid it, and I don't care whether they're nobles or peasants. Everyone has the right to live, and that includes both nobles and peasants."

"I understand."

"Fine!" Adrel capitulated, raising his hands above his head. "I'll send word to all the members of the Scarletia Liberation. This had better work."

"Sir Adrel, thank you." Even though she could tell that Adrel didn't fully agree with her idea but was going through with it anyway, Mika smiled. "If we could get the entire labour force to do this, then it might be too much for the Nobility to handle. How many workers are there in the entire city?"

"I would say around three hundred thousand peasants are part of the labour force," answered Feldia.

"That's a lot of workers. The Nobility will not be able

to handle that many protesting workers. That would just be far too much for them. I think this'll work."

Adrel shook his head. "That's also a lot of people to be sending word out to. It will take far too much time to coordinate with that many peasant workers."

"It certainly is a lot of people, but I don't think we have to reach all three hundred thousand of them. We just have to reach a small but significant number. Then we can ask the ones we're able to reach to spread the word and encourage others to join them in the revolt. The message will spread by word of mouth, and the number of protesting workers will increase. Hopefully, they can reach the majority of workers and get them involved. I think what we should do is to give ourselves a timeline, and schedule the revolt to begin on a certain day at a certain time. Those who've received word will be ready to join us"

Dellen snapped his fingers. "That's an excellent idea, Princess. Yes, we should reach out to as many people as possible, say, maybe in the next three days. By the time we start the revolt, we will have a good number of workers on board. The longer the revolt lasts, the more people will get involved."

"Of course, it may take some time to organize the revolt. We have to coordinate this properly and quickly," said Laren.

Dellen turned to Adrel. "What do you think of that?"

Adrel paused for a moment. Although he hesitated, after a while, he nodded. "Okay, that sounds like a plan to me then. There is no way we can reach three hundred thousand peasants in three days. But we can definitely reach out to as many people as we possibly can before the revolt."

Mika smiled as a sense of excitement filled her, but she tried hard to keep her calm composure. "That's fine. Thank you, everyone."

They're going to do it. They're taking me seriously. They're going to take my counsel, and organize the workers' revolt. I can't believe it! I sincerely hope this works!

CHAPTER 21

THE WORKERS REVOLT

SEC 3566, Morrighan 45

THREE DAYS HAD PASSED SINCE Princess Mika suggested that the workers revolt. It was time. Workers throughout the entire city watched the horizon. They were instructed by members of the Hope of Scarletia and the Scarletia Liberation rebel groups to begin their revolt at the exact moment when the sun crested the horizon. Everyone, farmers working on the fields, miners of Starstone, those who melted down different types of metals to forge them into various objects, waited in anticipation. Soon, a crimson sliver of the sun appeared.

"The sun is rising!" shouted a farmer. "The sun is rising!"

Elsewhere, throughout the city, these words were repeated. Those who supervised workers saw this as well, and announced the same to those who worked under them.

"Today, it begins! We protest against tyranny!" announced an elderly blacksmith master. Everyone around him, people who worked with him, clamoured, raising their fists into the air, as the azure sky above them began to brighten.

"Careful with those carts!" said a caretaker at one of the Starstone mines. "Set them down gently! Today, we protest against the oppression of the Nobility!"

The miners around him had been loading carts of Starstone. They complied with the caretaker.

"Let's go, everyone!" shouted one miner, and

others around him raised their fists, and shouted with determination. They walked out of a wooden building that was constructed above a mine.

A well-dressed noble man saw this as he came out of his office overlooking a gaping chasm in the ground. He demanded to know what was going on. "Hey! What are you doing? I didn't order you maggots to stop working!"

"We protest against tyranny!" shouted the miners, as they headed towards the entrance, and filed out onto the streets.

The streets of Scarletia were usually mostly empty around this time. However, workers from every industry began to fill them, gathering into groups. The peasant workers shouted into the air, demanding an end to tyranny. People living in homes along the streets were awakened by this, and rushed to the windows, through which they saw large numbers of people.

A knight patrol station noticed this as well. The knights were awakened from their slumber by their Sergeant.

"Gentlemen, look at what's happening!" said the Sergeant, putting on his helmet and scabbard.

The knights saw what was going on, and began putting on their armour.

"What's going on, Sir Alvian?" said one of the young knights.

"I don't know, Renar, but be on your guard," said the Sergeant.

Mounted knights galloped along the city streets from one patrol station to another. It was a little more challenging to navigate the streets as some of them were blocked by large groups of peasants. Some knights gathered together on cervids at each patrol station.

"Miss Emera, what are we supposed to do," asked one knight.

"You're asking me? How the hell should I know, Perrin?" said another.

"I've never seen anything like this before! Should we attack?" Perrin began to unsheathe his sword, but only halfway.

Emera gasped, grabbing Perrin's arm to try to stop him. "No, wait! We haven't received orders to attack!"

"Stop right there!" shouted their own Sergeant, as he galloped towards them. He and his knights watched the protesting peasants. "Take a look around you. Have the peasants done anything that could endanger lives and property?"

Both Emera and Perrin replied in unison. "No, Sir Ravean!"

"Then calm yourselves," ordered Ravean. "I have sent someone to the castle. We'll wait for instructions. Put away your sword, Perrin!"

Startled, Perrin sheathed his sword. "Yes, sir! Sorry, sir!"

Several knights galloped right past them, down the Valderia Pathway, on their way towards the Scarletia Royal Castle.

About one hour after sunrise, dozens of groups walked up and down the major streets of the city. The groups were large, some of them with thousands of peasants. They marched the city streets, chanting and shouting their demands, and encouraging others to join them and do the same.

"We demand freedom!"

"Freedom from tyranny!"

"Freedom from oppression!"

"We want our freedom!"

"Everyone, join us as we demand freedom from tyranny and oppression!"

* * *

"What the hell is going on out there, Sir Collin?" demanded King Ralphen, clad in his dress shirt, waist coat, full coat, trousers, and boots, all of which had been put on with haste. He tied his cape around his neck as he and Collin quickly walked down the hallway on their way to one of the highest balconies in the entire castle. "What is this I'm hearing about a revolt? It's too early in the morning for this."

"My apologies, My Lord," said Collin, fully dressed in his knight's uniform. "But it appears this began at sunrise."

"So what are they doing?" Ralphen opened a large set of double doors that led out onto a balcony, and stepped right out, followed by Collin. The balcony extended from the front side of the fifth floor of the castle, surrounded and supported by a white stone railing and a balustrade made of the same material. They were at the very front of the castle, overlooking the Grounds, from which they could see the castle gates directly ahead of them. Ralphen and Collin watched as large numbers of knights gathered at the castle gates and on the top of the walls and watchtowers. Collin had deployed them earlier to ensure maximum security at the gates.

Collin turned to the King. "The peasants stopped working."

Surprised, Ralphen glared at the Supreme Captain. "Why?!"

"Knights from patrol stations throughout the entire city have reported that the labour force had ceased work. These workers are of every single industry in the entire city, My Lord. They walked out of businesses, and marched onto the streets, many of them forming large groups everywhere."

"Isn't anyone telling them to return to work?!"

"Yes, My Lord. I've received word that business and industry owners have ordered the peasants to return to work, but they refused."

"They refused!? They *cannot* refuse orders from members of the Nobility! They don't have a choice! How dare they?!" shouted the King. "Why are they doing this? What exactly are they doing?"

Collin paused for a moment, trying to find the right words so that the King would not explode with fury. "It would appear that the peasants are protesting, My Lord."

"Protesting against what?"

"Apparently, what they perceive to be tyranny and oppression."

Ralphen turned towards Collin. "I don't understand, Sir Collin."

"They say they are demanding freedom from tyranny and oppression. I don't know what they're talking about exactly, My Lord, but that's what they're doing. They're accusing us of oppressing them and making them suffer. They say the Nobility and the Royal Family are tyrants."

The King turned his glaring eyes towards the castle gates. "Tyrants?!"

"Yes, My Lord. They're also encouraging others to join them and to protest with them, to demand their so-called freedom from this perceived tyranny and oppression."

Ralphen leaned his hands against the side of the stone balcony as he watched the castle gates and the knights gathered there. He looked down for a moment, and started making an odd sound.

Puzzled and somewhat concerned, Collin stared at the King, wondering what he was doing. "My Lord, are you all right?"

Ralphen straightened up, and the odd sound turned out to be a laugh, which grew louder by the second. Soon, his laugh became hysterical. "These peasants are calling us tyrants?" The King laughed again. "Ludicrous! Preposterous! These peasants... they're nothing but animals!"

Collin made no reaction as he watched the King express loudly his amusement. Soon, Ralphen turned towards him, smacking his palm down on the white stone railing. The laughter of the King was so loud that Collin noticed the curious gazes of noble civilians on the Grounds below them.

"That is hilarious, Sir Collin! Animals are calling us tyrants!"

* * *

Later in the day, one of the large groups of protesting workers, about five thousand strong, walked up the Valderia Pathway. They did what all the other groups were doing, and that was to demand their freedom in a peaceful way. However, unlike the other groups who marched around the city in predetermined routes that had them circle around the entire city, this group began to march up the wide street towards the Scarletia Royal Castle.

"Join us as we demand our freedom, everyone!"

"We demand freedom from tyranny and oppression!"

Many civilians—men, women, and children—looked on from the sides of the streets, and watched the group pass by them. They themselves were inspired by the actions of this particular group heading for the castle, and encouraged them.

However, one of the members of the Hope of Scarletia, a young man by the name of Peter Aldias, saw what they were doing. He rode alongside the group on a cervid, and called out to some of the peasant workers in the group.

"Why are you all marching to the castle gates?" he asked.

"We're protesting like everyone else!" answered one of the workers.

"We're keeping it peaceful like we were told!" replied another worker.

Peter slowed down his cervid, and urged it to turn around and gallop the opposite way, down the Valderia Pathway as quickly as possible. He needed to return to Ethereal Daydreams and let Dellen and Feldia know.

Soon, the group of workers reached the castle gates. They stopped some distance away from it because there was a small group of mounted knights there who watched them but did not do anything. They kept watch only to make sure that the peasant workers did not do anything that would cause damage to property or harm to anyone.

"We demand our freedom and respect!"

"We want to be treated with fairness and dignity!"

"We're sick and tired of being tools to be used by the Nobility and the Royal Family!"

The peasant workers shouted their demands continuously, their fists rising into the air, their loud voices carrying quite a long distance around them, including the castle. As they continued their protest, the knights observed them from cervids on the ground at the sides of the castle gates and from the top of the walls, as well as the watchtowers nearby.

* * *

Dellen and Feldia came down the steps that led into the basement of Ethereal Daydreams, where Mika took her seat at one of the tables.

"Princess," said Dellen.

"What is it, Sir Dellen?" asked Mika.

Dellen strode over to the table, and sat down, as did Feldia beside him. "One of our people just found out that a large group of peasant workers is on its way to the castle gates. In fact, they should already be there by now."

Mika was surprised. "Huh? Why?"

Feldia put her hands together on the table. "I was wondering the same thing."

"There are about five thousand workers in that group. Peter told us just now. He saw the group, went alongside them, and asked them why they were headed to the castle gates. They said they were protesting like all the other groups."

"They also said they're going to keep things peaceful, also like the other groups."

"I see," said Mika. "But they are following the same instructions, aren't they?"

Feldia nodded her head. "It looks like it. The only difference is that it looks like they're planning to take their protest to the castle gates."

"I was planning on having Feldia go out there with some of our people to remind them of their instructions," said Dellen.

Though Mika was concerned with what the group of peasant workers was doing, she remembered they weren't doing anything that could be considered contrary to what they had agreed to do. "But from what we've just been told, it looks like they are aware of their instructions, and are following them."

"Yes." Dellen leaned forward, and clasped his hands together on top of the table. "My Lady, you're not just our counsel. You're also our Princess. I may be the leader of the Hope of Scarletia, but many of these people are just regular peasant civilians, workers who decided to participate in the revolt. They aren't really rebels. Because of that, I can't always be telling the people what to do. They have to decide to listen to me first."

Feldia was puzzled as she turned to Dellen. "What are you talking about?"

Mika was just as puzzled, regarding Dellen with curious eyes.

"You said before that we're your people," said Dellen. "So I'm going to start asking you this from now on, because I think you're ready for it."

Mika tilted her head slightly. "Ready for...?"

"What do you think we should do, Princess Mika?"

Mika was startled. She gasped softly as she stared up at Dellen. "You're... you're asking me what I think you should do? But...."

Feldia smiled. "I think I understand."

"I'm not certain I understand," said Mika. "You're asking me as if I'm the leader of...."

Dellen turned his chair slightly towards Mika. "But you are the Princess of Melodice, My Lady. You are the leader of your people. That's actually a fact, Princess Mika. You know it. So as the Princess of Melodice, I'm asking you... what do you think we should do?"

Mika was taken back. She has never been asked such a question before as the Princess of a nation. She was being asked as a leader, and was not sure what to say or think. She did not feel enough confidence to be able to answer a question like that. Mika put her hands together at her heart. This was not something that she expected.

"I'm not sure if...." Mika's voice trailed off, not certain how to answer Dellen.

Dellen shook his head, disagreeing with Mika's lack of confidence. "My Lady, you decided as the Princess that you would be on the side of your people. You've told us that you think of every single person in the entire nation, whether peasants or nobles, to be your people, and that's honourable of you. However, if you really want to help your people, regardless of whether they're nobles or peasants, you have to take responsibility for your role... as the Princess of Melodice, the Princess of our great nation."

Feldia agreed with a nod. "Yes, that's right. You're a leader of our nation and our people. This revolt was your idea. Because you're the Princess, it also means that you're the leader of this revolt."

Mika was speechless as she thought about their words. She let them sink in for a moment.

"What do you think of that, Princess Mika?" asked Dellen.

Mika's voice was just barely above a whisper as she stared down at the top of the table. "Me? I'm the leader? I know I wanted to help you as the Princess of Melodice so that the peasants could live a better life. I've told you what I wanted to see in the end, the goal that I want to accomplish."

"But to accomplish that goal, you must become our leader. You must be willing to take your title and use it, My Lady. It doesn't matter how old you are. I know you're still young. In the eyes of the world, you're still a child." Dellen reached out a hand towards her.

Mika's eyes shifted to his hand, a hand that reached out to her heart. It seemed to her that Dellen truly believed in her and the goal that she wanted to see done, the goal of seeing the Peasantry to freedom from tyranny, even though he knew full well that she was still just a child. After some hesitation, she put her hand in his.

Dellen held her small hand gently. "But you're still our Princess."

Feldia rose from her seat, and went around the table. She knelt down beside Mika's chair. "My Lady, as the Princess, you'll need to make some decisions. You decided for yourself to do these things, all these things you've done so far. Your people will follow you, Princess Mika, as long as you make sound decisions that will help them in the end."

"Of course, if you make decisions the way a child would, out of compulsion or immaturity, that's a totally different matter. You'd lose support very quickly if you did that," Dellen let out a slow breath, as he thought of the best words he could say to the young Princess. He reminded himself that she was not just a child. She was also a Princess, and not just any other. "But I've come to know you over the last several days, and I can see you're not like that at all. For someone your age, you're highly educated and extremely intelligent. You've been educated in the matters of politics because of your upbringing. You're knowledgeable and have plenty of common sense. You have a strong sense of right and wrong. You've seen how people in leadership use their authority. They do it with confidence, and with a goal in mind. You have your own goals, as you've said several times. If you want to achieve your goals, you'll need to assert yourself as a leader."

That's right. After understanding the state of the nation through the peasants, I decided to help my people. I decided to free my people from this living hell. I've met with those who can help me achieve that goal. Now that I have Dellen, Feldia, Adrel, Laren, and all the people who follow them on my side, it looks like it'll be possible for me to help the peasants. But in order to do that, I must be their leader. Yes... that's right. I am their Princess.

Now I know who I truly am.

Mika looked up, closing her hand gently around Dellen's fingers. He had reached out to her heart, the heart of someone who was more than just a child, the heart of a Princess who loved her people.

"I suppose you're right, Sir Dellen... but I'm just... I've never truly been a leader, even though it was expected of me from the day I was born. I may be the Princess, and I naturally have authority bestowed upon me, but... I don't think I've ever used that authority."

Feldia simply smiled. "Yes, you have. Remember? You ordered your knights to stop attacking the peasants during the incident with the peasant mob."

Mika suddenly remembered that moment. That time, she had given the order for the knights to stop the fighting... and they did. The knights had obeyed her.

Dellen held on to Mika's hand a little more firmly

but gently, as if to transfer some of his leadership ability to her. "You have the ability to lead, Princess. You have the qualities of a leader. All you have to do is believe in yourself. You have that courage and bravery. You just need to reach into yourself to find it. I'm sure you've done it before and more than just once. Otherwise, you wouldn't be here."

Mika paused for a moment, thinking about the last thing Dellen told her. "I wouldn't be here if I didn't have any courage or bravery...."

Dellen smiled as he nodded. "That's right. So I'm going to ask you again as our Princess, our leader. What do you think we should do? Right now, this group of peasant workers is at the castle gates protesting. They're still following our instructions. They said they're going to keep things peaceful."

"What if I end up making a wrong decision?"

Feldia answered the Princess. "That's what we're here for, My Lady. We are by your side. If you suggest or decide on something, we'll tell you what we think. We will give you as much information and support as we can to make a sound decision, and hopefully, the chances of making a wrong decision would be diminished."

Mika remembered Sir Terren's words. He had told her that she was a far stronger individual and had more courage than she gave herself credit for, and that she should not put herself down the way she sometimes did. He had told her that her courage came from her love of others. Mika smiled. Then, she remembered what he had whispered to her that day. He had told her that he knew of her love for her people, peasants and nobles alike, and her love for her nation, and that she would use her love to free the people from tyranny and oppression when the time comes.

Feldia rose from her kneeling position, and stood beside the Princess. "So what do you think we should do, My Lady?"

Mika pulled her hand away from Dellen as she slowly stood up. She took a few steps around the table as Dellen and Feldia watched her, waiting, while she imprinted the words of Sir Terren into her heart. She thought about everything Dellen and Feldia talked to her about just now. She stood up straight, closed her eyes, and calmed herself.

"I wonder... if Sir Terren knew I was going to do all this, that I was going to take this path."

"Huh? Pardon?" asked Dellen.

Feldia tilted her head with curiosity. "What do you mean?"

Mika opened her eyes. Smiling serenely at Dellen and Feldia and standing up straight with as much confidence as she could muster, she appeared quite regal while at the same time maintaining her kind and gentle demeanour. As she turned to them, she reached up to her Princess Gem, sparkling in front of her white dress of silk and lace.

This is who I am.

Mika clasped her hands together in front of her. "Sorry. It was nothing. The group of peasant workers that is protesting at the castle gates...."

"Yes, Princess?" asked Dellen.

"Please let them continue," ordered the Princess.

Dellen smiled. "As you wish, Princess Mika."

"That will send the message of the Peasantry of our city to the castle directly. They must still follow instructions and remain peaceful, as previously agreed. However, at the first sign of trouble, they are to move on somewhere else immediately. I don't want anyone getting injured or killed if anything happens."

Feldia smiled while Dellen stood up from his chair. They acknowledged the order of the Princess in unison.

"Yes, My Lady."

CHAPTER 22

AN UNPLEASANT DISCOVERY

SEC 3566, Morrighan 46

BY THE FOLLOWING DAY, THE number of peasant workers who participated in the workers' revolt had increased significantly. More groups of workers appeared, and marched up and down major streets throughout the city, while existing groups became much larger. Also, the group that was protesting at the castle gates had doubled in size to more than ten thousand peasants. They continued their protest without respite throughout the night and into the next day. People started organizing their protests as if they were work shifts, with some protesting during the morning, some during the afternoon, and the rest during the evening and overnight. At the castle gates, on the top of the walls, and up in the watchtowers, the knights continued to keep watch. A few of the knights were itching to draw their swords to attack the peasants, but were ordered not to do anything because the peasants remained peaceful.

Maleth, fully armoured but without his helmet, headed down one of the hallways on the fifth floor of the castle, on his way towards the highest forward-facing balcony in the castle. As soon as he exited through the doors, he found Collin, also armoured but with no helmet.

"Ah, good of you to join me, Sir Maleth." Collin held up a telescope, and peered through its lens, through which he observed the castle gates. Because of the height of the balcony above the ground, he could actually see some of the large crowd of peasants beyond the gates.

"How is this revolt going on? I trust that nothing has happened?"

"No, nothing has happened, and we are fortunate," said Collin. "These peasants have caused no harm to other civilians, to nobles that are out in the city, or to our knights. They have also caused no damage of any sort to property. Although it's a large protest, it has remained peaceful."

Maleth leaned against the balcony railing. "Well, I'm glad they're not doing anything to escalate the situation. If they did, it would become very dangerous for them, as well as our knights. Whoever's leading this must have their safety in mind."

Collin nodded in agreement as he lowered his telescope, and turned towards Maleth. "I have been wondering who might be leading them. Due to their peaceful strategy, it's likely someone I would respect, unlike that last rebel group leader I had to deal with, the one who was talking about raping the Princess."

Maleth narrowed his eyes, remembering Reid Alviana. "The man had no sense of honour. I wanted to kill him myself."

"Indeed." Collin tightened his hand around the telescope as the image of Reid bleeding to death profusely from his neck in front of him flashed in his mind. "Sir Reid had been expecting a standard execution, and he was going to hold up his head high as if he had done a great service to Melodice somehow. But after his disgraceful words... I decided he didn't deserve what he wanted. Instead, I gave him what he truly deserved: an equally disgraceful execution."

Maleth looked up at the castle gates and the part of the crowd that was visible beyond. "Then the leader of this revolt is the exact opposite. Someone who isn't filled to overflowing with hatred and bitterness."

"A respectable individual, from what I can tell." Collin raised his telescope again to observe the crowd and the knights at the gates. "However, though these peasant workers are protesting peacefully... one thing is for sure. They are blocking the Valderia Pathway, the only path into and out of the castle."

"Yes." Maleth sighed. "And that's the reason why the King has given his next order."

Collin put down the telescope, and turned to Maleth.

"Unfortunately, the peaceful nature of this protest will soon be reversed. The King has issued the following order. We are to remove the peasant workers from blocking the gates. The peasants there are to be forced to disband, and to return to work immediately."

Collin paused for a long time, mulling over the order that has just been passed on to him. He raised the telescope again. "So the King has ordered us to physically and forcibly remove the peasant workers who are protesting in a peaceful fashion...."

Maleth nodded slowly, regret in his eyes. He turned towards Collin, wondering what he thought of about the King's order.

That's a very dangerous order, thought Collin. *One that will be considered highly controversial. What is King Ralphen thinking? Is he planning something? Wait, hold on a moment... I can't think like this.* Collin put down the telescope, and turned back to Maleth.

"What do you think, Sir Collin?" asked Maleth.

"I think orders are orders, especially when they are issued by a member of the Royal Family." Collin handed his telescope to Maleth, who took it from him. "These are orders from the King."

Maleth held the telescope in his hand, hesitation in his mind as he thought about the order. He recalled the images of death on the Valderia Pathway, when he and his knights fought to protect Princess Mika from attacking peasant rebels while on her failed excursion to the city of Cerulean, as well as the images of many peasant civilians dying in a magical wall of flame invoked by Sir Galner. He stared at Collin, silent.

Collin paused one more time, deep in thought. Doubt

regarding this order was in his mind and heart, but he did his very best to push it away. Eventually, he cleared his throat and straightened. "Such is our duty, Sir Maleth. As the King has ordered, it shall be done."

* * *

At the top of the Eldoria Watchtower, clad in all white, the Princess of Melodice stood in the middle of the floor, watching the Scarletia Royal Castle.

A gentle breeze blew through the rectangular openings in the wall behind her, tugging at the hem of her mid-thigh-length summer dress whose fabric was of thin cotton. Her long sleeves reached just past her wrists. The Princess Gem sparkled as it rested high on her chest between prominent collarbones. Very subtle but intricate designs covered her sheer stockings, and her flat shoes were shiny and brand new. A long, thin ribbon was tied into her hair. In her hands, she held the old white cloak, whose inferior quality in fabric was a stark contrast to her dress. When she had reached the top of the tower with her companions earlier, she had removed it and held it in her arms as she clasped her hands together.

From her vantage point, she could see the large group of peasants in front of the castle gates. She could not see individuals very well because she was too far away, but the group of peasants appeared like a sea of people from where she was, extending quite a distance back from the castle gates.

Dellen and Adrel stood together close to the edge of the floor at the missing wall. Dellen held a telescope, and peered through its single lens, watching the peasants and what they were doing. Feldia and Laren stood close to the Princess.

Mika was starting to become familiar enough with Feldia and Laren's companions that she could remember their names and match them with the right faces. Those who reported directly to Feldia were Peter Aldias, Sorianne Edariast, Demias Kataria, Galien Saldiest, and Dayna

Tarias, while those who reported directly to Laren were Lauria Alkarias, Elsia Callen, Tavien Delcrest, Marik Eldwars, and Eduard Samarel. All of them wore robes or cloaks over their regular clothing to ensure no one could see the short swords they wore at their belts.

Dellen put down the telescope, and turned towards Princess Mika. "Princess, here, take a look."

Mika noted the cloak she was still holding, and looked confused, wondering where she should put it.

Lauria noticed her distraction. "I'll take your cloak, My Lady."

"Thank you, Miss Lauria," whispered Mika, handing her cloak to her. She joined Dellen, who gave her the telescope. Mika peered through its lens, and observed what was happening. She watched the peasants protesting without causing any problems. She saw the knights at the gates and at the top of the walls. They simply observed the peasants, not doing anything that could be considered hostile.

"I think it's as you expected, Princess," said Adrel, who held up his own telescope. "The knights aren't attacking the peasants. As long as the peasants remain peaceful while they protest, the knights can't do a damn thing."

Mika smiled. "I'm glad things have remained peaceful."

"All the groups of protesters are still marching throughout the city. They've been joined by more workers," said Dellen. "So each group has gotten larger. And there have been more groups. The people are urging others to join us. The revolt is escalating. More and more people are participating. This is going surprisingly well."

Feldia stepped forward. "But I heard that other peasant groups might be on their way to the gates. They want to join the group that's already there."

"That's fine." Mika put down the telescope. "That means more people will have their voices heard at the castle gates."

"There will be a lot more people there very soon," said Laren. "I think there are already over ten thousand people there right now. That number could double."

Mika peered through the telescope again. "Let them continue, as long as they remain peaceful. They've already been told that they are to leave the area and move elsewhere at the first sign of trouble."

Mika desperately wanted this to work. She hoped those in the castle would listen to the protests of the people. The Nobility had to be forced to listen to the demands of the Peasantry, and this was what was happening now. Perhaps, they were listening now, because work throughout the entire city had stopped. Food and supplies were not being sent to the castle. As long as the peasants continued their revolt, there would be no services provided for the castle, and the Nobility would feel the effects of that. Once they feel those effects, perhaps they will be more willing to listen to the Peasantry.

Listen to them, Father! All of you of the Nobility! Listen to our people!

* * *

A few hours later, a side door opened beside the castle gates. Collin, fully armoured from head to toe with helmet and scabbard, exited through the doorway, riding on his cervid, whose sides were also covered in some light armour. Collin was followed by Maleth, equally armoured and mounted. They were followed by a line of mounted knights. More and more of them came out, and began to position themselves between the peasant workers and the castle gates. Above the gates, knights carrying bows and arrows started filling the bridge.

The peasants watched the knights, some of them feeling a sense of possible dread, but all of them stood their ground, and continued their protest.

Adrel saw all this through his telescope. "Princess, something's happening."

Mika looked up from where she was, sitting on a boulder while chatting with Feldia, Sorianne, and Dayna. She stood up, and peered through her telescope at the castle gates. As soon as she did, she gasped, her eyes widened. She adjusted the telescope so it would zoom in closer to the knights. "Sir Collin... and Sir Maleth... what are they doing?"

"I don't like the looks of this." Adrel gave his telescope to Dellen.

Dellen peered through the telescope as well. "Damn! But wait! Nothing is happening yet. Those knights are just standing there."

Down at the castle gates, one hundred knights on cervids formed a line, standing side by side, facing the peasant workers. Collin and Maleth were at the centre of the line. Collin sighed as he watched the protesting peasants in front of him.

"Freedom from tyranny, freedom from oppression!" they shouted.

"We will not work until our voices are heard!"

"Give us our freedom and dignity!"

Collin and Maleth stole a glance at each other, speechless for a moment.

"What do we do, sir?" asked the knight beside Collin. "Do we start attacking now?"

Collin paused, recognizing the knight as Serian Avenar. He could see the bloodlust in the young man's eyes. He turned back to Maleth. "We have our orders from the King, don't we, Sir Maleth?" he asked, trying to speak over the loud voices of the peasants in front of him so Maleth could actually hear him.

"Yes, we do, Sir Collin."

"However... there's something I'd like to try before we carry out the King's orders. I want to see if I can ask the peasants to disband from this area and to return to work. There's been enough bloodshed of late, and I'd like to see if we can avoid that here. I will give them the chance to leave here peacefully." Collin put a hand on Maleth's shoulder. "What do you think of that?"

Maleth smiled, and then nodded. "An excellent idea."

Serian had been listening to their exchange, and was puzzled. "But, Sir Collin, Sir Maleth, shouldn't we pacify this threat here and now through strength of arms? It's the only way they can understand that they can't be blocking the gates and the Valderia Pathway like this."

Maleth calmly stared at Serian, but his voice easily hinted displeasure upon hearing his words. "I suggest you follow the Supreme Captain's direction, Serian. You will draw your sword *only if* instructed to do so. Is that understood?"

Serian stiffened. "Yes, sir. Understood, sir."

Mika and Dellen observed through their telescopes. A sense of dread welled up in Mika's heart. It was the same with everyone else around her at the moment. She felt frightened for the peasants down at the castle gates.

"I'm worried about them," said Mika. "Why aren't they leaving? I thought we instructed them to leave at the first sign of trouble!"

Adrel groaned. "We did. What the hell are they doing?"

Dellen let out a shallow breath. "The knights aren't doing anything yet, and neither are the peasants. They're just staring each other down while the peasants are continuing their protest. Dammit. We told them to move along if they see danger, but they're still standing there." He shook his head with frustration.

Mika could see that Collin was starting to speak. "He's saying something to the peasants. What is he saying?"

At the castle gates, Collin urged his cervid to step forward, and spoke as loudly as he could over the clamours of the peasant workers.

"Hear me, Peasantry! Listen to my words! I am the Supreme Captain of the Scarletia Royal Guard and the Royal Army of Melodice, Collin Gagnier!"

"What do you want, you damn soldier!"

"Give us what we want! Give us our freedom!"

"We will not tolerate being stepped on by the Nobility any longer!"

Collin continued. "By the order of the King of Melodice, you are all to disband immediately! Do not block the castle gates! You are to leave immediately, and return to work! Otherwise, you will face the consequences!"

The shouting of the peasants only became louder and,

this time, angrier. They heard Collin's words. Instead of complying, however, the peasants continued screaming their protests, as well as their anger.

"You are nothing but a damn noble!"

"Take our message to the King! Tell him we're not going anywhere!"

"Give us our freedom! Only then will we disband and return to work!"

"The Nobility and the Royal Family have made us suffer long enough!"

"It is time you give us back our freedom!"

"We want our freedom from tyranny and oppression!"

"You and the Royal Family and the Nobility can all go to hell!"

At the Eldoria Watchtower, Feldia joined Mika's side. "Princess, can I see through the telescope for a moment?"

Mika gave her the telescope.

Feldia peered through it, and watched Collin. As he was speaking, he was making certain hand motions. From his body language, Feldia could see what he was saying. "I think the Supreme Captain is asking the peasants to disband. He's telling them to leave that area and return to work. The fact that there are a hundred knights to either side of him tells me he's warning them of possible consequences."

Mika gasped upon hearing that. "How can you tell?" *Wait... how can she tell...? That's strange....*

"I think you're right, Feldia," said Dellen, looking through Adrel's telescope.

Adrel clenched his fist. "Dammit! This is getting uglier by the minute! That means they're in danger!"

Dellen gave Adrel's telescope to Laren. "We've got to get down there. Adrel, we need to tell the workers there at the gates to get out of there! They need to obey the orders of the Supreme Captain immediately!"

"Right," said Adrel. "Laren, Lauria, Elsia, all of you stay with the Princess. The rest of you are with me."

"Okay," acknowledged Laren.

"That goes for you as well, Feldia," said Dellen. "Dayna, Sorianne, both of you stay with the Princess. The rest of you are coming with me!"

Feldia nodded. "All right."

Dellen, Adrel, and their companions joined together.

Mika called out to them as they were about to leave. "Everyone, please be careful!"

"We will, My Lady." Dellen disappeared down the stairway.

"It'll be damn hard to get through so many people on cervids, but we have to try anyway!" said Adrel, his voice echoing up the stairwell loud enough that Mika could still hear it. Eventually, his voice faded.

Mika stood several steps away from the edge of the floor. Feldia gave Mika back the telescope, through which she observed the peasant workers and Sir Collin. Laren did the same with the telescope given to him just now.

Mika watched as Collin was still trying to convince the peasants to leave, but they shouted back at him, and did not cease their protests. Watching them, Mika felt her fear escalating, her heart starting to race.

"It's happening all over again," she said, her voice quivering with terrible apprehension. "They're not following Sir Collin's orders. They're not following our direction anymore, probably because they're too caught up in the moment. It's getting more and more dangerous every second." She gripped the telescope tightly, her hands trembling as she lowered it, and held it at her chest. She closed her eyes tight. "More people are going to die once again...."

Feldia and Laren watched Mika's reaction while others in the room looked on. She was so frightened that it made them worry about her just as much as they were worried about the peasants whose lives were now in danger.

"Princess." Laren took a step towards Mika. "Dellen and Adrel should be able to take care of this. They'll have the workers obey the orders of the Supreme Captain."

Mika opened her eyes, and stared up at him with agitation. "There's no time! They won't be able to get there in time and warn them! Things are about to go dreadfully wrong down there! The lives of the peasants are in danger!"

Feldia sighed with anxiety, her hand on her heart. "I

have to say she's right. The chances that the peasants will follow the orders of the Supreme Captain aren't good, from what I'm seeing."

Laren raised his telescope again, as did Mika.

Mika moved the view of her telescope to the back of the crowd, seeing more peasant workers joining. "How many people are there right now?"

"I'd say nearly twenty thousand by now," answered Feldia.

Laren noticed something as he quickly adjusted the telescope to zoom in as close as possible on the castle gates. "Sir Collin... wait, he's doing something."

Mika moved her view back towards Collin. She saw him raise his hands in front of him, palms forward. "What's he doing?"

Laren gritted his teeth. "He's planning to count down... before he attacks!"

Mika gasped as she shot a look of alarm at Laren. "A countdown?" *How does he know that?*

Collin spoke loudly to the peasants. "I'm going to start counting down! If you do not obey my orders, I will have no choice but to implement the King's order! As I have already instructed, you are all to disband immediately, and return to work! You cannot block the Valderia Pathway! I am going to count down, starting from ten!"

The peasants continued shouting. They also added insults against the Supreme Captain to go along with their demands for freedom.

"We're not going anywhere, noble maggots!"

"We want our freedom! Give us our freedom now!"

"Fucking nobles! We're not going anywhere!"

"Give us our freedom from tyranny!"

"Go to hell, Supreme Captain! Damn you to hell!"

Collin closed his hands, and then opened them, with one hand showing five fingers and the other with four. "Nine!"

The peasants did not cease.

The Supreme Captain gave them about half a minute. Soon, he closed his hands again, and reopened them. "Eight!"

Mika stared intently through the telescope, seeing the hand signals. "He's counting down!"

"When he reaches zero, he's going to attack the peasants!" said Laren.

"Damn!" exclaimed Feldia.

The others behind them—Lauria, Elsia, Dayna, and Sorianne—were horrified by this as well.

"What are we going to do?" asked Elsia.

"Where are Dellen and Adrel?" demanded Dayna.

Feldia turned to Laren. "See if you can find them."

Laren moved his telescope's view throughout the back of the crowd. "I can't find them! There are too many people out there!" He paused. "Wait! There they are. But they're too far away! They're trying to get through the crowd on cervids! Princess, you're right. They're not going to make it on time!"

"And they don't know Sir Collin has started counting down before he orders his knights to attack. They can't see him from where they are!" said Mika.

Collin's hands closed, and then reopened. "Seven!"

Mika saw the number where Collin was. *What am I going to do? The peasant workers are going to die! There must be something... anything! Oh, please, someone, tell me what I should do! What should I do?!* "How far away are we from the castle gates?"

"About... three kilometres, Princess," replied Feldia.

The peasants stood their ground. Mika remembered that night when she and Helen traveled through the city, shortly after they escaped from the cervid carriages that had taken them out of the castle. They had navigated the streets, and found themselves in an alleyway where they were confronted by several thugs. Mika had asked Helen if it was possible for them to fly over the thugs and to safety, but Helen had reminded her that magical flight was a skill that both of them were still working on. Both of them had been having a difficult time learning this particular skill.

Could I...?

Then Mika remembered their conversation in Galner's office. Before Galner had told them he wanted to invite them to the Cerulean Magic Academy, he had talked to them about the lesson on magical flight, and asked them how they were faring. Both Mika and Helen had to admit that they were having difficulty with it. Galner had told them it was a difficult spell to learn. Mika remembered him saying that students who attempt to learn the spell have to do so as carefully as possible, because there was a real threat of serious injury. She also remembered him telling them that some students had learned the skill by subjecting themselves to a life-threatening situation, such as by jumping out of a building. It was true that some students had learned it that way, but others were not so lucky.

Can I do this? Can I...?

Mika put down the telescope, closed her eyes, and inhaled deeply. "I have to do this," she whispered. "This is who I am."

Feldia looked confused. "I'm sorry, Princess, what did you say?" she asked, not hearing her clearly.

Laren was just as confused. "Huh?"

Mika handed the telescope to Feldia, who, along with Laren and the others, watched as she backed away from them by a few steps. She stared hard at the edge of the floor.

"Princess?" said Feldia.

I can do this. I must do this. I have the power to save them. "I'm going to save them... because they're my people... and I'm their Princess!" Mika ran towards the edge of the floor as fast as her legs could take her.

Feldia, Laren, and everyone else around them watched in utter shock.

"No, Princess!" shouted Laren.

Feldia tried to grab onto the Princess, but she had been taken completely by surprise, and was not fast enough in catching her.

Mika pushed off at the very last step at the edge of the floor, closed her eyes, and jumped. For a very brief moment, she felt like a bird, but that feeling of complete freedom from the confines of gravity disappeared almost right away as she plummeted towards the street below, fifteen floors down. She fell with her body parallel to the ground below with her arms held out at either side of her... and she screamed with absolute terror.

"No!" shouted Feldia, as she, Laren, and the others ran to the edge of the floor, and watched in shock as the Princess fell towards the ground with great speed.

Mika felt the wind blowing past her hair and her dress, which did little to slow down her fall even though it was pushed against her body as she fell straight down. She opened her eyes, and saw the street coming up fast.

The peasants on the ground who heard her scream looked up, and watched in disbelief. From their perspective, a little girl was falling from the sky to her death.

"I'm not going to die!" Mika shouted as she closed her eyes again. Her desire to live clashed with the fear of death, and tapped into her ability of powerful magic. She imagined wings at her feet and flying like a bird. Just before Mika was about to strike the sidewalk below, a magic circle appeared directly beneath her.

The people on the street below her hurried to get out of the way. They all looked on with widened eyes as the girl stopped falling just a metre above the ground.

Mika opened her eyes as she gasped, seeing the magic circle. She remembered the lesson on magical flight, and willed her body to an upright position. The magic circle disappeared, but she felt something strange. As she hovered, she looked down at her feet, and noticed pink, semi-transparent wings, but they were not truly wings. They were actually tiny magical symbols, characters, and shapes that moved along lines and curves that combined to form the shape of wings. There were four of them, two on both sides of each foot. Mika was so surprised by this that she did not notice the dozens of peasants watching her with awe. She breathed hard from the stress of falling, but she began to calm down.

"I've done it. I've completed the lesson!" Mika exclaimed in victory. She looked up towards the top of the tower above her, and saw Feldia and Laren watching her with amazement. "I've done it!"

"By the Matriarch..." Feldia whispered with shock.

"She... used her magic." Laren shook his head to regain his senses as he remembered that Collin was still counting down. He raised his telescope to see, and when he saw the Supreme Captain's hands, he called out to Mika. "Princess, Sir Collin is at five!"

"She can make it." Feldia cupped her hands around her mouth, and called out to Mika. "Princess Mika, you can make it! You can get there before Dellen and Adrel, and tell the peasants to get out of there!"

Mika nodded with determination as she looked forward. "Yes, most definitely!" she exclaimed. "Magical wings... please guide me. Take me to my people. For Melodice!"

A flash of light from her magical wings appeared. They pointed backwards, causing Mika to fly forward. The wings guided her a little higher, just above the sea of people. Very soon, she found that she could move herself to the left and right, up and down, slower and faster as easily as she could move her arms and legs. The wings had become part of her. Her magic was always a part of her, but she felt like she had grown an extra pair of unseen limbs. Mika flew over the peasants at a pretty good speed.

As she flew by them, the peasants looked up at the young girl clad in pure white and watched in awe. The Princess Gem sparkled around her neck.

Mika saw Dellen and Adrel struggling through the crowd along with their companions, all of them on cervids. She smiled as she sped past them through the narrow space in between them. "Sir Dellen, Sir Adrel, please don't worry! I'll take care of this!"

Adrel looked on with shock. "What the—?"

Dellen watched as well with amazement. "Princess?!"

"Three kilometres to fly." Mika felt the wind at her face, tugging at her hair and ribbons, at the sleeves and the hem of her dress. She flew forward with her arms at her sides and slightly back, her body angled forward about forty-five degrees from the ground, head first and face down, as instructed in the lesson on magical flight. Three kilometres was a long distance to travel, and she had only a few minutes to get to the castle gates. She saw right away that she did not have enough time to get there judging by the speed in which she flew.

Mika willed her wings to take her forward as quickly as possible. She watched down below, seeing the blurred faces of the thousands of peasants that filled the Valderia Pathway as she passed them. She glanced up ahead of her at her destination, the knights and the main group of peasant workers who refused to leave. She could see Collin from a distance, her vision sharp. Mika could not see his hands, so she could not distinguish how many fingers were up, but she knew there were very few remaining.

Up above in the watchtower, Feldia and Laren watched with extreme anticipation through their telescopes, almost holding their breaths.

"Come on, Princess... you're almost there!" exclaimed Laren.

Feldia shook her head, her voice dropping to a fearful whisper. "No... no, she's still too far away... and he's down to three...."

Mika watched, her feeling of dread escalating.

Collin closed his hands, and reopened them once again. He called out to the peasants. "Two! Peasants, you are running out of time! I urge you to leave right away! Disband your protest, and leave the castle gates! Disband immediately, or suffer the consequences!"

"Dammit!" Maleth held onto the reins of his cervid tightly. "They're not listening, Sir Collin!"

The peasants continued to shout their angry protests. They were not relenting, not one bit. If anything, their protests escalated.

"Go back to the sewer you crawled out of, you bastard noble!"

"We want our freedom from tyranny! We want it now!"

"Give us our freedom!"

"No more bending over backwards for the sake of the Nobility and the Royal Family!"

Feldia gasped. "No! He's down to one!"

"Princess!" shouted Laren, as if calling out to her,

but it would not be possible for Mika to hear him from this distance.

"What the hell is going on up there?" shouted Dellen.

"I can't see a damn thing with all these people!" exclaimed Adrel.

Mika drew in a quick breath. Despite the distance, she could see Collin a little more clearly. She could see his hands, though they were still difficult to distinguish. However, she could tell they were about to close. "No. Oh no, please don't... please...."

Their time was up.

* * *

Collin held up his hands, both of them now fists. He lowered his hands, and sighed with regret as he watched the protests of the peasants grow louder than they were before, hurling angry words, demanding their freedom without any hint of ceasing.

"It would seem... I no longer have a choice," said the Supreme Captain.

Maleth shook his head. "Do they think you're bluffing somehow?"

"No, that's not it. They're just determined, perhaps to the point of foolishness. I believe there is a term for this. Mob mentality." Collin began to address the crowd again. "Time has run out, everyone! I have given you the chance to leave peacefully, but you have chosen to ignore my orders! It is with regret that I must now follow the orders of our King, and apply the consequences of your decision!"

The peasants continued to shout over him.

Collin drew out his sword, and raised it above his head straight up. "Arrows!"

The knights on the bridge above the castle gates stepped towards the crenulated wall, bows ready. Holding their long-range weapons over the wall, they pulled on their bowstrings, and let go, unleashing a storm of arrows. The peasants on the ground were alarmed. As soon as they saw the bows and arrows aiming for them, some of them froze while others looked on. Arrows fell like a deadly rain, and struck peasants dead, some in the head and some on their chests. Shouts of angry protest were replaced immediately by screams of fear and terror.

"No!" Mika's magical wings glowed brighter as another flash of light appeared behind them. Stricken with shock, she watched as peasants were felled by flying arrows.

"Swords!" Collin pointed his sword forward, signalling the other knights to begin their charge.

The blades of the knights screeched against the metal interiors of their scabbards, painful to the ears of peasants nearby. Sunlight reflected off their swords as the knights held them up high or in front of them. Peasants at the front watched with panic as Collin, Maleth, and their knights charged forward on their cervids.

Chaos broke out and moved through the crowd like a wave. At the very front, peasants were cut down, felled by the cutting blades of the knights. Heads and limbs flew as the knights slashed at them. Bodies fell down on the street with terrible wounds. Those who were not caught by the swords and arrows of the knights screamed, and struggled to turn around and flee, but they were met by a wall of people that could not move as quickly. Peasants forced themselves through the crowd, some of them jumping over others. Some fell down, crushed by the crowds that trampled over them. It did not take long for the people at the back of the main group to realize that death was occurring at the front near the castle gates.

Adrel and Dellen watched helplessly as a wave of peasants started running towards them. They stopped along with their companions behind them.

Instinctively, Dellen's hand reached for the hilt of his sword, but there was nothing he could do from here. "We're too late...."

Agape, Adrel felt his heart sink. "No...."

Feldia's knees weakened as she fell to the floor, holding the telescope in her hands. "No... they're... they're dying."

Laren could not bear to watch any longer as he looked away from the lens of the telescope. "Damn... we didn't have enough time."

Their companions looked on, feeling powerless, as they watched the crowd of thousands of peasants forcing themselves to back away from the castle gates.

Mika watched agape. She struggled to fly faster, but she had not become accustomed to this magical ability. It would take her time yet, but time was not on her side. She stared at the absolute chaos. She tightened her hands into fists as she stared ahead at the knights who were killing her people and at Sir Collin who commanded them to do this. Feeling utter helplessness, she clenched her teeth.

Can I do anything about this? What am I supposed to do next?! It's happening all over again... people dying... dying everywhere. Can't I do anything?! Why not?! Because I'm a child?! Just because I'm a child, am I being foolish?!

Images of people dead or dying, trying to escape... these all flashed in her mind in rapid succession. The crowd at the front was beginning to thin out as the crowd in the back was finally loosened just enough that the rest could start to get through. But it was far too late for many. An enormous wall of thousands of peasants ran down the Valderia Pathway away from the castle gates, leaving behind dead and injured in their wake. Some of the dead and injured lay in pools of blood, and some areas of the street were smeared with red. Mika watched them on the ground as tears streamed down her cheeks.

Collin stopped, seeing something approaching in the sky... or rather, someone. "What is that?" He held his bloodied sword at his side, still mounted on his cervid.

Maleth wondered what he meant as he looked up.

Mika flew closer to the ground, right past peasants who were running away. *Remember the lesson on magical flight, Mika. As I prepare to land, I have to slow down to as fast as my normal run... and then put my body in an upright position... and then touch down gently with my feet in a running position. I must be careful. Otherwise, I could fall down and get injured. And the peasants will trample all over me.*

She eased herself closer to the ground to a position where she could run as soon as the magical wings disappeared, as instructed in the lesson given to her by Sir Galner. The peasants who saw her were alarmed and moved out of the way. As soon as the wings disappeared, she ran down the street, but there were so many peasants in front of her that she could barely squeeze through. They ran past her, some of them brushing against her and others bumping into her, causing her to fall down on the ground. Some of them stepped on her dress, causing stains to appear from the dirt on their shoes and on the street.

Mika forced herself to get up. *I'm just a child. That's all I am... but... but I'm also the Princess of this nation! If I can do something... anything... to stop this massacre, I will do it!*

"It disappeared into the crowd. Who did we just see?" asked Maleth, as the knights continued their killing.

Baffled, Collin could only shake his head. "I'm... not sure."

Mika ran towards the knights through the crowd that was beginning to thin out, and cried out as loudly as she could with a high-pitched voice. "Stop killing! Stop killing!"

Someone beside her was felled by an arrow, and she yelped. She stared at the man who fell forward as he was running, an arrow in his back, his body now motionless. That could have been her just now had the arrow veered to the side just a little. She forced herself to turn away, and instead looked ahead towards the knights. She continued running through the crowd. More peasants were felled by arrows farther to her left and right.

The peasants around her paid little attention to her, whether or not they knew she was the Princess of Melodice, because their highest priority was to save themselves. This was no time for them to stop and be surprised by her sudden appearance.

"Please stop your attack! By order of Princess Mika Silveraine, stop your attack!"

"That voice!" Maleth shouted, hearing the order.

The knights were confused. The voice was also familiar to them. Some of them stopped slashing at the peasants, and looked around, searching for the source of that voice.

Some of the knights who were above stopped firing their arrows, wondering what was going on.

Soon, all the peasants who were still able to escape ran past the Princess. Mika emerged from the throng, her hair disheveled, her dress dirtied from the crowd of people that rushed past her.

The Supreme Captain exclaimed as soon as he saw her. "Princess Mika!"

Maleth turned his cervid around, and saw the Princess. "What...?"

"Please stop your attack!" Mika clamoured, and finally, all of the knights ceased their attack on the peasants, including all of the knights who had been firing arrows from above.

"What's going on?" whispered Maleth.

"By my order, the Princess of Melodice, stop your attack immediately!"

CHAPTER 23

FOR MY PEOPLE

"COME ON, FELDIA, LOOK THROUGH the telescope! Look at what's happening!" urged Laren as he helped Feldia get back up on her feet.

Feldia wiped her tears away with her sleeve as she straightened up, and looked through her telescope.

Laren looked through his as well. They watched as the crowd thinned out at the front near the castle gates. The knights had stopped attacking the peasants. The Princess had just emerged from the crowd. Judging by what they had seen so far, it looked like Princess Mika had just ordered the knights to stop their attack on the peasant workers.

"She stopped them. She really did. She ordered them to stop." Feldia pointed her telescope to the area surrounding the Princess, and saw all the dead bodies scattered all over the street. "So much death... so many... it's horrible...."

Laren saw Mika walk towards the knights a certain distance, and then she stopped, but she was still quite far away from them. "What's going to happen now?"

* * *

Over a hundred people gathered around Dellen, Adrel, and their companions in the middle of the Valderia Pathway. People continued running past them on the sides of the street, screaming, trying to get away as quickly as possible from the carnage near the castle gates. Dellen, Adrel, and their companions were still mounted on their cervids.

"What's going on up there?" exclaimed Adrel.

"The Princess!" shouted one of the retreating peasant workers. "That was the Princess, wasn't it?"

"I thought I saw the girl with the Princess Gem!"

"The girl was flying through the sky. I couldn't believe it!"

"Was that the Princess?"

"It had to be! There's no mistake! That was the Princess of Melodice!"

One of the young women called out to Adrel and Dellen to get their attention. "She came and flew right over us! She used her magic! When she came, she ordered the knights to stop killing! She told them to stop killing!"

"That really was Princess Mika Silveraine!" said a young man. "She saved our lives!"

Some peasants were still somewhat skeptical despite what they saw. "But why would she do that? Isn't she a member of the Royal Family?"

"Isn't she part of the Nobility? Why would a Royal save us?"

"Does it matter right now? A lot of people died out there today, and it's a fact that she told the knights to stop killing!"

"Yeah, that's right! She ordered them to stop killing!"

"If she hadn't ordered the knights to stop, more people would have died!"

"I don't care if she's a Royal right now! I am thankful to the Princess!"

"Is it really true?! Tell me it's true that a Royal saved us!"

"I can't believe it! Is that really true?!"

"The Princess saved us!"

Adrel groaned in frustration as he tried to look over the sea of people between where he was and the castle gates. "I can't see the Princess from here! Dammit! I don't know what's going on up there! I can't see anything!"

Dellen turned to the crowd. "What's happening up there right now? What's happening at the gates?"

"The Princess is there right now, and I think she's talking to the knights!" said a middle-aged man.

Adrel was taken aback. "Talking to the knights? What do you mean?"

Dellen turned to Adrel, and moved his cervid closer to his. He kept his voice low as he spoke, so none of the peasants would hear him. "I hope that doesn't mean she's going back to them."

Adrel shook his head in disagreement. "How can she go back? After what's happened, there's no way she can go back now."

Dellen thought about that for a moment. "That's true, Adrel. If she goes back now, after the way she appeared to those knights just now like the peasants said she did, she could be taken prisoner."

"Yeah, that's what I'm afraid of. If not, then this will be a test of character for Princess Mika, Dellen."

* * *

Collin tried very hard to regain his composure as he got off his cervid, and removed his helmet. He watched Princess Mika as she stood among the dead peasants.

Mika looked around, her eyes shifting from one dead peasant to the next. Blood smeared some of the bodies. Others had no visible injuries but must have been crushed to death or were suffocated by the panicking crowd. A few of the dead had missing heads or limbs, which were scattered elsewhere. This was worse than the time when she was attacked by the peasant mob. She remembered the piles of bodies then as well. The stench of death hung stagnant in the air.

Except this time, she did not feel sick to her stomach.

"Princess Mika!" Collin called out to her as Maleth and the other knights looked on.

Mika looked up, hearing Collin's voice.

"My Lady, I had mistakenly believed you were missing. We've been searching the entire castle for you!"

Mika did not answer. *What can I say? I suppose you should be searching for me, since I'm supposed to be missing.*

Collin continued. "It would seem that… we should've been searching outside the castle! We searched thoroughly, and found no sign of you, My Lady! The idea that you would have left the castle did not seem possible. It would seem... I was mistaken."

Mika glanced behind her, seeing the peasants continuing to run away. The area around her was quite open now. She took a few steps and stared at the faces of the dead peasant workers, trying to memorize their faces. *These are the faces of my people. The faces of the peasant workers who died today. I will try to remember as many of you as I can.*

"What's going on? What is she doing?" asked Maleth, as he removed his helmet, and dismounted from his cervid.

Collin took a few steps forward. "Princess!"

Mika looked up again at Collin.

"It's time to come home, My Lady. The King and Queen are deeply concerned for your safety. I'm glad to see you safe. Please come back into the castle."

There was no outward reaction from the Princess. *You ask me to come back to the castle... but how could I? How can I go back to my mother and father? After all this... after all this death and chaos... how can I go back? How can I go back when I now know the truth?*

"Something's not right," muttered Collin. "She should have approached us by now. Is she afraid? Why would she be?"

Maleth observed Mika's facial expression despite her distance from them, and came up with a possible answer. "Sir Collin, it's not just fear. I believe she doesn't trust us."

"She doesn't trust us? I don't understand."

Mika closed her eyes for a moment. She felt terrible fear, but she did not tremble from it. She was surprised at herself, realizing that she was much calmer than she had expected, despite the situation. She opened her eyes, wiped away the remaining tears with her long sleeves, and looked up at Collin.

"Princess?"

"Sir Collin!" Mika tried to speak loudly so her voice could carry over the distance between her and the knights. "Thank you! Thank you very much for stopping your attack on my people!"

Collin was taken aback. "Your people, Princess?"

Mika nodded slightly. "I don't want any more of them to die so needlessly."

Collin looked around at the dead. "I do apologize, My Lady. I was left with no other choice. These workers have been protesting in front of the castle gates, blocking the road into and out of the castle. The King ordered that they be removed forcibly."

Mika gasped softly.

"However, I gave them a chance. I gave them the opportunity to leave peacefully. That wasn't part of the King's order. That was my order. I ordered the peasants to disband. Unfortunately, they didn't listen to me, and they chose to stand their ground. I had no choice but to follow the orders of the King."

Mika stared at him, horrified. *He ordered this?! The King, my father, ordered this?! So much death!*

"Princess Mika!"

"Sir Collin!" Mika quickly looked behind her again to see how far away the peasant workers had gotten, and was relieved to see they were now a safe distance from the knights. She turned back to Collin. "The peasant workers have left! You need not kill anymore!"

"Yes, My Lady, and I'm glad. I'm glad they finally obeyed, and removed themselves from this area."

Mika clenched her fists at her sides. *Not before killing so many of them!*

She once again regarded the dead around her. As she stepped around bloody corpses, she noticed a young man who still moved. She took several steps around more corpses to get to him, and knelt down beside him. The young man had lost an arm, and there was a gash on his chest. Mika watched, one hand covering her mouth, his blood bubbling up from inside his chest through the large tear in his waistcoat, which was completely soaked in red. Blood pooled on the street around him as his own weakening heart pumped it out of his own body. When he saw her, he knew right away who she was.

"Princess... Mika..." whispered the young man

between laboured breaths. He slowly tried to reach up with his one remaining hand.

Mika took his hand right away, the blood on his hand still warm on hers. Some of it dripped down onto her white dress. "Sir... sir, please don't move too much."

"Princess... Mika... I saw you... you saved us...."

Mika could feel her eyes tearing again but she forced herself to smile a little. "Yes, sir... I tried to...."

"Thank you... My Lady... for saving us...." The young man had tears in his eyes, but they were beginning to close, and the image of the Princess sitting beside him blurred, and then darkened. He began to smile.

Mika felt his hold on her hand quickly softening. "Sir...." She held on to his hand more tightly, this time with both of hers.

"My... loyalty... is... yours...."

Mika paused for a moment as his eyes closed. "Thank you...."

The young man drew in one last breath. His hand lost all of what little strength it had left. Mika lowered his hand, and laid it on his chest, placing her hand on top of his and her other hand on his forehead, stroking his hair, comforting him in death. "I'm your Princess..." she whispered, as tears fell down her cheeks.

Collin, Maleth, and all the other knights watched. Collin stepped forward again. "Princess Mika!"

He's dead...

"Please, My Lady! Return to the castle! Leave the peasants be!"

Leave the peasants be?! Return to the castle?!

"Princess Mika!"

Mika stood up, her knees feeling weak for a moment. She turned to face Collin and the knights. Blood from the young man stained the front of her dress. Her palms were almost completely red with the blood from the man's hand, and there were blood stains at the ends of her sleeves. Because she had been kneeling down on a pool of blood, her white stockings from the knee down to her ankle were now red. Her white shoes were stained as well. Without realizing it, she wiped her bloodied hands on her skirt, transferring some of the blood to her white dress. Mika stared at Collin with a somber expression.

"Sir Collin, please forgive me!" Mika began to take a few steps back, away from the knights.

Collin was confused. "Princess?"

"My people need me!"

Collin gripped his sword tightly, and slammed the pointed tip into the ground with frustration, cracking the weakened pavement.

The sound it made startled Mika.

"Princess Mika! Please tell me what the hell is going on! Your people are in the castle, and they are waiting for you to come home!" exclaimed Collin.

"My people include everyone in the nation! Nobles and peasants alike! Every man, every woman, every child... in the entire nation of Melodice, all of them, every single one!"

Collin glared at the Princess. "What...?"

"I'm sorry, Sir Collin. I can't return home!" More tears came down her cheeks. "Please... please tell my father and my mother... I'm sorry for being a failure of a daughter."

Collin was speechless. He watched agape as Mika turned around, and started to walk away from them, away from the knights, away from the castle gates... and towards the peasants in the distance, down the Valderia Pathway. Mika quickened her pace, and after a short distance, she started running. Maleth and all the knights around him were very surprised by the actions taken by the Princess just now.

One of the knights turned to Collin, who recognized him as Palind Emarias. "Sir, what should we do?"

"Should we ride out and capture her?" asked another knight, Belian Soraisa.

"The Princess... she's betraying the nation," commented Serian.

Maleth shot a glare at him. "Govern your tongue, Serian! Do not start making accusations like that against a member of the Royal Family!"

"My apologies, Supreme Commander!" replied the surprised Serian.

"We don't know what's truly going on or why the Princess is doing this!" Maleth quickly walked over to Collin, and spoke to him with his voice lowered. "What do you think we should do, Sir Collin?"

For the first time in his military career, Collin felt indecisive. He removed his long sword from the pavement. He took a step forward, holding his weapon at his side, staring at the Princess, then turned back to Maleth, trying to find his words. He knew what he wanted to do, but that was different from what he was supposed to do as the Supreme Captain of the Scarletia Royal Guard and the Royal Army of Melodice. Collin shot a glare towards Belian, startling him. He turned back to Maleth.

"To answer Sir Belian's question. Do I want to ride out and capture her? Of course, I do!" Collin pointed his sword towards the Princess with frustration. "We can ride on our cervids, catch up to her, capture her, and bring her back into the castle against her will! That's what I want to do!"

"However, Sir Collin." Maleth raised his voice to its normal level since Collin was voicing his frustration quite loudly. "If you ride out and capture the Princess and bring her back, as soon as you return to the castle, you will be executed before you can explain yourself. The reason why you captured the Princess would only be understood after you're dead."

Collin sheathed his sword. "I'm perfectly aware of that, Sir Maleth! That's why I haven't done it!"

The eyes of every knight were on him, including the ones on the bridge above the castle gates. Collin looked at the questioning faces. Some of them probably did want to ride out to capture the Princess, but a majority of them probably thought that would not be a beneficial idea. Nevertheless, they waited for him for instructions as their commanding officer.

"Everyone, stand down!"

All his knights obeyed, putting away their swords.

The knights above the castle gates put down their bows and arrows.

"Sir Maleth, we need to go back inside. I must speak with the King and Queen regarding this unexpected event. In their minds, the Princess has been missing, but now, we have just witnessed an unpleasant discovery. Princess Mika is with the peasants and has been with them all this time. It suggests that the Princess has betrayed the nation. This cannot be taken lightly. They must be made aware of this right away... and I imagine they will not be pleased. Not one bit."

"Agreed, Sir Collin." Maleth put his sword away.

Collin turned to the knights again. "Knights, return to the castle!"

The knights obeyed Collin's order. They began to head towards the side door through which they had exited earlier. The door was opened by knights who were on the other side.

Collin turned back to Maleth, keeping his voice down. "If Princess Mika was any other peasant or noble civilian, I would have easily given the order to capture her right away, but she's of the Royal Family, and as such, I cannot give such an order until I have sought counsel from the King and Queen. We need to speak with them first before doing anything. This is a very delicate situation, Sir Maleth. We have to think about our actions very carefully."

Maleth nodded. "I imagine the King will be quite furious."

Collin sighed heavily. "Furious? Considering what has just happened, that would be a grave understatement."

CHAPTER 24

THE WHITE PRINCESS

MALETH LED THE MOUNTED KNIGHTS single file through one of the side entrances beside the castle gates. The knights on the bridge above the gates climbed down the steps that led back down to the Grounds below.

Collin paused outside the gates, and turned to look down the Valderia Pathway for quite a long distance. He could no longer see Princess Mika. There was a sea of people out there, around a kilometre away. Mika must be within the crowd of peasants by now.

"Dammit…." Collin turned his cervid towards the entrance. "I must see the King right away."

* * *

Mika alternated between walking and running until she was quite a distance from the castle gates. She slowed one last time to a walk, breathing heavily from her physical exertion. The section of the wide street behind her was now empty except for the dead, but she knew there were people still hiding within the buildings, most of which were businesses. She stopped to look back for a moment, and saw that the knights were no longer there. On the street close to the castle gates, hundreds of dead peasants lay, the rays of the summer sun beating down on them. She could already see a handful of crows circling in the sky above them. An otherwise beautiful summer day was made ugly by the events that took place.

Mika turned away, and continued down the street

towards the crowd of thousands of peasants ahead of her, many of them looking in her direction. The Princess Gem around her neck sparkled under the sun. As she approached the peasants, some of them stood along the sides of the streets, their eyes upon her, now knowing who she was. However, by this time, they knew her by face and appearance, and not just because of a diamond around her neck. Mika walked with eyes downcast, avoiding some of their gazes. When she realized she was doing this out of habit, she forced herself to look ahead. There were still tears in her eyes.

When she saw their facial expressions, they were far different from the ones she had seen that day when she was surrounded and attacked by the peasant mob during her failed excursion to the Cerulean Magic Academy. They were not expressions of hate and anger. These peasants regarded her with expressions of confusion and shock over what had happened and what she had done. They were also unnerved by her appearance... her once-beautiful white dress of silk and lace now dirty and stained with blood. She was not only the Princess. She was also a little girl, one whose innocence had been taken away from her, replaced by a new awareness of the harsh realities of the world around her.

"Princess..." a young woman called out with a soft voice as she passed.

Mika watched her for a moment. *She's confused. She's not sure how to react to me... seeing what just happened.*

She continued through the thin crowd, but as she walked down the Valderia Pathway, the crowd began to thicken.

"Princess Mika..." another peasant worker called out, this time a young man.

I'm a member of the Royal Family, the highest of the Nobility, the group that is the object of their anger and hatred. They consider the Royal Family and the Nobility to be their mortal enemy because of what they've done to them. Who can blame them for being so angry, for having so much hatred for the Nobility? Their current situation is because of the Nobility.

Mika stopped for a moment, and turned back once more towards the castle gates. She had to be absolutely certain that no knights were headed this way. All of them were gone. Sir Collin, Sir Maleth, and the knights were not going to pursue them, or her.

Just as I expected. They aren't going to pursue me. They can't. But Sir Collin must have wanted to pursue me. He must have wanted very badly to ride out and capture me and force me to return to the castle. But he knows he can't do that without seeking the advice of the Royal Family first. He will talk to the King.

Mika sighed, knowing what was going to happen next as she thought about this. She had anticipated Sir Collin's moves with precision just now. She knew that the Supreme Captain would follow protocol, even against what he truly wanted to do.

However... when the King is told that I'm out here with the peasants, that I'm not simply missing, he will be furious. He will surely order Sir Collin to secure my capture.

Mika wrapped her arms around her body, feeling somewhat cold as she continued to walk through the crowd of peasants. She was terrified. She knew that her father would brand her as a traitor now, a traitor to the Royal Family, the Nobility, the city of Scarletia, and the entire nation of Melodice. She would be chased down, captured, tortured, and then finally executed. A soft breeze blew by her, sending shivers throughout her body. Her entire being had been held in the grips of fear since the day when she had nearly been killed by a merchant assassin, and it had only escalated since then. She has never been more frightened in her entire life. Normally, she would cower in fear, which would paralyze her. However, today was different. After going through so much, having experienced chaos and death all around her, the terrible fear she felt no longer affected her so severely.

I can't be more frightened than I already am. I feel so numb.

Mika used her sleeve to wipe her tears away. She also came to another realization.

My life at the castle... all of that is over now. I can't possibly live the same life as I lived before. The world has revealed itself to me. My life has changed. I have changed. However, for some reason, I think I can live with this. I've chosen this path. I've decided to change our nation so the peasants can live a better life. That's what I intend to do because I'm their Princess. I have no regrets.

Mika looked up at the peasants as more of them surrounded her. She passed by two young men who calmly stared at her. Their reaction to her was one she did not expect.

"Princess," they said, bowing their heads with respect.

Mika saw a middle-aged woman that she was about to pass. The woman smiled at her serenely. She did not expect that reaction either.

"The Princess! She saved us!" shouted another man.

Very soon, Mika started hearing these words repeated by other peasants around her.

"Yes, it's true. I saw her!"

"She saved our lives!"

"The Princess saved us all!"

An elderly woman stepped forward. "If the Princess hadn't been there and ordered the knights to stop, they'd have slaughtered us all! Some of us wouldn't even be here right now!"

More and more peasants repeated these words out loud as Mika stopped within the crowd. They were far from being angry with her. They appreciated what she had done for them earlier! They proclaimed that she saved them! Mika stood motionless and speechless, unsure how to react.

"Princess!"

Mika glanced ahead of her. Dellen and Adrel moved through the group of peasants that had crowded around the Princess. Laren and Feldia were behind them. The peasants made way for them as they approached her. When they reached her, they all stood together, and Mika looked up at them, speechless.

"Princess Mika!" Feldia called out.

Laren stood beside her, trying to catch his breath. "Princess...."

Feldia, Laren, and their companions had seen everything that happened. After Sir Collin and his knights left, they had rushed down the steps of the Eldoria Watchtower, and rode their cervids all the way to where Dellen and Adrel were among the crowd on the Valderia Pathway. Together, they rushed over to where the Princess was, and dismounted from their cervids.

They had all witnessed what Princess Mika, a shy and timid little girl of eleven years, was capable of. She proved that she had far more courage and bravery than she gave herself credit for. She had the ability to stand up against tyranny and oppression. She even had the power of magic on her side, which very few people have.

"Clad in white... she's the White Princess!"

"Yes, that's right! She saved us all! The White Princess!"

"The White Princess saved us!"

The White Princess? Mika was confused. Some of the peasants around her started calling her that. To Mika, it appeared that she had gained a new identity.

"The White Princess, huh?" Dellen stepped towards Mika with a smile. "Princess Mika, you don't know how proud I am of you right now."

"Sir Dellen?" said Mika, still confused.

"You're definitely our Princess, dear Mika Silveraine. You are worthy of my loyalty... until the end of time."

Mika gasped softly. A tear streamed down her cheek as warmth enveloped her heart.

Feldia stepped forward as well. Her eyes were also teary as she smiled. "Princess Mika, you have my loyalty as well. I am your servant."

"Whatever you decide to do, we will follow you to the ends of this world."

Laren nodded as he stepped forward next. "That's right, Princess Mika. My loyalty is yours. I'm also your servant."

Adrel forced himself to swallow a lump that was building up in his throat as he turned to the crowd of peasants, and spoke to them with a loud voice that carried over them. "Everyone, the Peasantry of Melodice, citizens of the city of Scarletia! She is the Princess of Melodice,

Mika Silveraine, and she saved all your lives here today! Unlike the rest of the Nobility and the Royal Family, she genuinely cares for your well-being!"

"That's right! The White Princess... she cares for us!"

"We're alive because of the White Princess!"

"You have our loyalty!"

Similar words were uttered all around Mika. More peasants in the crowd proclaimed their loyalty to the Princess of Melodice.

"You are our Princess!"

"We pledge our loyalty!"

Mika was surprised, overwhelmed with great humility. The many hundreds of peasants around her all voiced their loyalty to her in unison, loudly and proudly. Her heart was touched as she closed her eyes, trying to stop the tears that continued to stream down her cheeks. She opened her eyes again, looking up at each peasant near her, listening to their loud clamours of pride proclaiming that she was their Princess. Eventually, their proclamations reached the thousands of peasants that were gathered farther away.

"Thank you... so very much..." Mika whispered as her lips formed a smile of heartfelt gratitude. *They have accepted me as their Princess. They have called me the White Princess. I could get accustomed to that name. I reached out my hand to them... and they have taken it. I promise you... all of you... I will never... never ever let go.*

* * *

On the Grounds, directly in front of the steps that led up to the front doors of the castle, Collin dismounted from his cervid. He was surrounded by several other knights on their cervids, doing the same. Collin removed his gauntlets, and then his gloves. He turned to his knights.

"Knights, I will go into the castle to seek counsel from the King. I must do this immediately. Please wait here for my return. It's possible the King will order us to go out into the city again," ordered the Supreme Captain.

Collin was about to turn and head for the steps when he felt a hand on his shoulder.

Maleth stopped him. "Hold on, Sir Collin."

"What is it, Sir Maleth?"

Maleth spoke to him with a somewhat hushed voice. "You do realize that nothing like this has happened for a very long time. It's been over a century since a Royal betrayed their family and the Nobility. I'm certain you remember reading that it did not end well for anyone, Nobility and Peasantry alike."

"I remember my history lesson quite well, Sir Maleth," said Collin. "That certainly was a tragedy, one that led to civil war. But I also remember that the Royal who betrayed the Nobility was no child."

Maleth was speechless for a moment.

"A child will be much easier to deal with. We need not... worry," Collin assured him.

"Worry?" said Maleth, hearing a slight expression of doubt in Collin's voice.

Collin realized he had doubted his own words just now, and took a deep breath to regain his composure. He remembered that Princess Mika, as expected of a member of the Royal Family, was well versed in politics and was highly educated. Some of that education even came from Sir Terren Rinaldia, the former Supreme Captain of the Scarletia Royal Guard and the Royal Army of Melodice. It was also known that she was extremely intelligent. He gave a pat on Maleth's shoulder and smiled.

"Definitely, we need not worry," repeated Collin. "I will see the King. In fact, we should see him together as Supreme Captain and Supreme Commander. Come."

Maleth acknowledged with a nod. "As you wish."

Collin and Maleth left the knights, and ascended the steps to the castle front doors that were already opened by their guards.

* * *

Mika walked down the middle of the Valderia Pathway. Crowds of peasants still lined the sides of the streets while others stood around, watching her and her companions.

Dellen and Feldia walked with her on her right, and Adrel and Laren were on her left. Some of the peasants who were behind them followed, loudly proclaiming their loyalty to the White Princess, and telling others who did not know yet that she had saved all their lives today from the blades of the Scarletia Royal Guard.

"We need to get back to our place quickly," said Dellen, referring to the inn Ethereal Daydreams. It was a code word shared among them that meant nothing to anyone else.

Adrel agreed. "We've much to discuss after what's happened."

Mika watched her surroundings, noting the thousands of peasants that regarded her. They have seen her, and for those who have not, they have heard what happened. They watched her in awe as she and her companions passed by. Mika also saw a group of knights on cervids, standing in front of a patrol station. They stared at her, but they stood their ground.

Feldia quickly pulled her hood over her head. "What are those knights doing?"

Laren did the same in order to conceal his face. "Don't worry. They can't do anything."

"That's right," said Mika. "They will do nothing while I'm out here with you, so you need not worry."

Feldia sighed. "It's strange walking out here in the open being stared at by people who would capture you if they had the chance. You're the Princess. If the circumstances were different, they would arrest us for simply walking with you like this."

After a few minutes, their other companions of the Hope of Scarletia and the Scarletia Liberation joined them. Their cervids were brought along as well. Dellen got on his, as did Adrel.

As Laren climbed onto his cervid, he turned to Mika. "Princess Mika, care for a lift?"

Mika gasped softly, staring up at him with hesitation and apprehension. "Um… Sir Laren, I…" she said softly, her voice somewhat quivering. She felt an odd discomfort throughout her body, a cold feeling of sickness.

Laren appeared confused. "Are you all right, My Lady?"

Feldia quickly intervened as she pulled her cervid closer to Mika. "Princess, you can ride on my cervid."

Mika smiled at Feldia, calm returning to her. "Thank you, Miss Feldia."

Feldia helped Mika climb onto her cervid. When Mika was comfortable, Feldia herself got on as well. Mika was positioned behind Feldia, who took hold of the reins. Feldia gave Laren one look with no expression, and then turned away.

Laren looked even more confused, wondering what had just happened, and spoke with a voice just above a whisper. "What was that about?"

Dellen moved his cervid closer to Laren's, and spoke in a somewhat hushed voice. "Don't worry about it, Laren. The Princess wouldn't ride on my cervid either. She did ride on Feldia's though."

"What's the difference between riding on your cervid or Feldia's? It's the same animal, isn't it? Strange reaction, Dellen."

Dellen shrugged. "I don't know. But, like I said, don't worry about it."

Adrel turned his cervid towards Feldia's. "Princess Mika."

Mika met his gaze. "Yes, Sir Adrel?"

"Do you think the King is about to order the Scarletia Royal Guard to go out into the city, now knowing you're out here?"

Mika sighed with a bit of apprehension. "I believe so."

"If he does that—and I believe he will—there will be hell to pay. It's possible that many more people are going to die."

Mika shook her head. "It's not exactly going to happen like that, Sir Adrel."

Dellen heard Mika's response. "You just said you believe the King will order his knights to go out into the city."

"Yes, and he will," said Mika. "But not right away."

"What do you mean?" asked Feldia.

"The King of Melodice has a tendency to act on his emotions. He will most certainly become enraged and furious. He will definitely give the order to the Scarletia Royal Guard to head out and capture me. He will order them to search for me, and to kill anyone in their way in order to bring me back. However, the Queen of Melodice will not have it that way."

"Really?" said Laren. "Why do you think that?"

Princess Mika is once again anticipating their actions, Feldia thought. *How does such a young girl know how to think this way?*

"Because the Queen will be more concerned over my safety above all else."

* * *

"Ralphen!" shouted the angry Queen.

In the Scarlet Chamber, in front of the many members of his noble court, the King of Melodice picked up an algerwood chair, and screamed in a fit of rage as he threw the chair through the air and into one of the decorative stained-glass windows. Glass broke into thousands of tiny pieces. The chair smashed into the adjacent hallway outside, startling and frightening the passing maidservants who screamed. Fortunately, they stopped short just in time and were not injured.

Collin and Maleth stared with shock at what the King had just done, as did everyone else.

The large double doors of the Scarlet Chamber were wide open. Out in the hall, Helen and Galner stood with surprised expressions as well. They had a perfect view of the manifestation of the King's violent rage just now. They had been talking when they saw what happened.

"The Princess has betrayed the Royal Family and the Nobility!" shouted the King.

A few maidservants gathered in the hall where Helen and Galner were. They looked into the room, frightened but curious.

"Our daughter, Princess Mika Silveraine, the Princess

of Melodice, was not abducted at all! She somehow willingly exited the castle, and sided with the Peasantry!" Ralphen turned to Collin and Maleth. "After all the things she has said and done so far, it all makes sense now! I speculate that this revolt of the peasant workers is her doing! She ordered your knights to stand down! She used her authority inappropriately! She abused her power!"

Ralphen kicked another chair, and it fell on its side in front of a noble woman, who yelped and got out of the way. Ralphen ignored her.

Maiya stared at him, her hands trembling.

"Sir Collin, Sir Maleth, I want you to take your knights, and head out into the city in full force! Search for the Princess! Leave no stone unturned! You are to find her, restrain her, and bring her back here!"

Maiya walked quickly towards Ralphen, who had his back to her.

Collin and Maleth saw her approach.

"If anyone interferes, kill them! Kill anyone and everyone in your path! I don't care if you have to kill entire families and destroy whole buildings and businesses! Bring the Princess back here immediately!"

"Ralphen, stop!" Maiya grabbed Ralphen.

Ralphen suddenly turned to Maiya.

"Stop this immediately!" shouted the Queen. "You need to calm down, and think about what you are ordering our knights to do!"

"Maiya, we have to find our daughter and bring her back!"

"I am aware of that!"

Maiya's chest heaved up and down as she stared into Ralphen's eyes with anger. Tension filled the air within the Scarlet Chamber and outside as others looked on. She took a few deep breaths to try to calm down, and put her hands on Ralphen's shoulders.

"Ralphen, we must think of the safety of our daughter first before doing anything else! She is out there in the city surrounded by peasants. If she has been out there all this time and, according to what Sir Collin and Sir Maleth saw, is obviously unharmed, then they likely haven't done anything to her. If you order our knights to head out in full force to search for her and to kill anyone in their path, things might change, and the peasants might kill Mika!"

Ralphen and Maiya stared at each other for a moment. Silence filled the room.

"All right," whispered Ralphen as he, too, took several deep breaths to try to regain his composure. He nodded slowly, and then straightened as he looked around at the stunned faces of the members of his court, political leaders among the Nobility.

"Ralphen."

The King turned back to Maiya.

"From what has happened, from what it looks like, it appears that Mika is on the side of the Peasantry. However, she's still the Princess of Melodice. If she's still the Princess, they might recognize her as such, and they might even obey her commands. She's not in immediate danger... at least, not yet. We have to think carefully about what we need to do."

Ralphen thought carefully about Maiya's words, and knew she was right. He turned back to Collin and Maleth. "Sir Collin, Sir Maleth, wait for my decision."

Collin and Maleth stole a quick glance at each other showing expressions of relief. "Yes, My Lord," they said in unison.

* * *

Helen tightened one fist at her side as she watched what happened within the Scarlet Chamber. Seeing the King's outburst regarding the Princess, she felt a flood of emotions within her, but she tried her very best to keep them in check. From what she heard, it sounded like Princess Mika had become part of the rebellion of the Peasantry, just as she predicted would happen. The revolt of the peasant workers, the largest protest in the history of the capital city of Scarletia, must have been instigated by her. She thought back to that night when she had helped Mika sneak out of the castle so she can meet with the Balias family. She remembered hearing the truth about the state of their nation from the mouths of the peasants. Both she and the Princess had agreed on one thing for the first time. They had agreed that the Peasantry were suffering under the Nobility. Mika had wanted to change the nation so the peasants can live a better life.

Damn you, Princess Mika! You have started a revolution!

The members of the court, the highest ranking politicians of the nation and representatives of various departments of government, streamed out of the Scarlet Chamber. Helen saw Collin and Maleth inside the room talking, while the King and Queen exited through the back doors.

Galner, who stood beside her, let out a heavy sigh. He closed his eyes, and then rubbed his forehead, feeling a headache coming on. "I should have known this was going to happen. Why did I not see this? One of my own students!"

"Sir Galner?"

"I've always known that the Princess had a... certain level of inquisitiveness. She was always asking questions about anything and everything. She always had a strong desire to learn as much as she possibly could about every single topic that she could get her hands on. If there was something she didn't understand, she would fight and struggle with it until she did. In some circumstances, that's admirable. As a student of magic, it has helped her become extremely proficient. It has also helped her to become an excellent student of every possible subject that has been taught to her by all her professors. She has an unnatural curiosity and wisdom and some unusual ideas, even for a child. The Princess saw the world for the first time, and sought to understand it. Because of this unnatural curiosity, she has sided with the Peasantry! She has chosen to betray the Nobility and the Royal Family!"

Helen was speechless. She could only agree with Galner.

The Princess genuinely cares for her people, and that's admirable. But how far will she go for her own people?

How far will she go to free the Peasantry from tyranny and oppression? However, Sir Galner, you're right about one thing. The Princess has betrayed the Nobility and the Royal Family.

Galner turned to Helen. "The Princess has an unusual character, Miss Helen. When you take all these things we know about her, and combine them with the fact that she is the Princess of Melodice with power and authority, and has been educated as such, then this means... we are seeing the makings of an extremely dangerous individual."

"Dangerous?" Helen was taken aback by the professor's words, but listened as he continued on, his anger and frustration clearly growing.

"Her age matters not. She's a child. But she's a Princess at the same time with power, authority, intelligence, education, wisdom, the ability of magic, and an inquisitive mind with deviant ideas all her own. Despite being a child... the Princess... is dangerous."

Galner struggled to keep his emotions in check, tightening his fist in front of him. He exhaled slowly as he brought it down, meeting Helen's gaze.

"Do forgive me, Miss Helen. If you'll excuse me, I'll be in my office."

Helen nodded. "Of course, Sir Galner."

She watched Galner leave. As she watched him, she thought about his words. With all these characteristics that Princess Mika was exhibiting, she agreed that she could potentially be a dangerous person, even for a child.

I was a fool. She and I may have believed in the same things... but I question her methods, and I question the methods the Peasantry are using to fight for their freedom. I shouldn't have helped her.

Collin exited the Scarlet Chamber, and saw Helen standing in the outside hall so he approached her.

When he came near, Helen noticed him. She stood straight at attention. "Supreme Captain."

"As you were, Miss Helen," said Collin.

Helen relaxed.

Collin stood beside Helen as he faced the entrance into the Scarlet Chamber, shaking his head. "So, Miss Helen...

I'm assuming you heard and saw everything, including our King's childish outburst?"

Helen raised an eyebrow. "Yes, Sir Collin. Although, with all due respect... I would be careful with the comment you made just now."

Collin was taken aback, and looked around to make sure there was no one nearby. He turned back to Helen. "I do apologize. As the Supreme Captain, I should be a better example by choosing my words correctly. For something like that, I suppose it would be the end of me if the King were to hear about it."

"Yes, sir. I do agree with your assessment of that outburst. But that's something we need to keep to ourselves, I suppose."

"I agree. As you must now be aware, the peasant workers organized a revolt. A group of them blocked the Valderia Pathway beyond the castle gates. The King issued an order to remove them... and we have. Unfortunately, many lives were lost. More lives would have been lost if the Princess hadn't appeared just in time, and given the order for us to cease. Now you know that the Princess has betrayed the Royal Family and the Nobility."

Helen frowned as she glared into the Scarlet Chamber, clenching her fists again. "Yes, Sir Collin. I am aware of this."

"Good. You should also be made aware that the King may issue an order for the Scarletia Royal Guard to deploy into the city."

Helen turned to Collin. Her expression turned to that of concern.

"You are a member of the Scarletia Royal Guard, and you have the unique position of reporting directly to me because of the influence of your professor of magical studies, Sir Galner. That didn't change when I ascended to the position of Supreme Captain after Sir Terren's retirement."

Helen was confused. "Sir Collin?"

Collin hesitated for a moment, and stepped closer to her, keeping his voice down. "You and Princess Mika are colleagues. You're both students of magic under the mentorship of Sir Galner. But you're also a member of the Scarletia Royal Guard. If the King orders us to head out in full force to find and capture the Princess, I need to know if you'll be willing to make some difficult decisions."

"Are you asking me if I would be willing to do anything to capture Princess Mika?"

"That's correct," said Collin.

Helen hesitated for a moment, turning towards the Scarlet Chamber as she thought about Collin's words.

She's my classmate, my colleague. She's my Princess, and I'm her knight. Even though I bullied her somewhat, she still treated me with kindness. She... is a good person. Will I be willing to capture her? I'm not certain if....

Wait, I need to think about this more clearly. Her actions lately have been irrational. She has decided to stay with the Peasantry, and because of her actions, has shown that she's involved in their rebellion. So will I be willing to capture someone who is my classmate, my colleague, my Princess... someone who I have recently begun to understand, someone who shares my beliefs... and someone who has shared intimate thoughts with me?

"Yes, Sir Collin. You can depend on me." Helen turned back to Collin, holding an expression of determination. "She may be my colleague and my Princess, but, as you said, she has betrayed the Royal Family and the Nobility of Melodice. I will not hesitate to capture her and bring her back here. That is by sworn duty as a knight of the Scarletia Royal Guard. Such is my duty, Supreme Captain."

Collin smiled. "I thank you, Miss Helen."

Helen stared at her commanding officer as he began to walk away. He headed for the hallway that would take him to the front lobby of the castle. Helen glanced around once more, and noticed that all of the members of the King's court were no longer there. She decided to head back to her room. But as she proceeded down the long hallways of the castle and up a few flights of stairs, her thoughts raced.

That's right. Princess Mika, you have good intentions. But I made a terrible decision that night when I helped you. You have made enemies of the Nobility. You wanted to change the nation of Melodice for the benefit of the peasants. But your methods are wrong. I knew it all along. You would start a rebellion for the sake of changing our nation. This is wrong. There are far better ways to change it. If you want to bring about change, it should not be through revolution, but instead through political reformation. However, Princess Mika, you have chosen revolution. So... that means... I will capture you.

I have to think of a plan. After everything that has happened, after what Princess Mika has done, there must be something I can do. The Peasantry will continue to suffer even after the rebellion led by their Princess is over. It will have changed nothing. I must think of something... in order to end all of this.

* * *

"Mirin!" some young girls called out from down the hallway.

Mirin, along with Angelica, turned around. He saw three of his female classmates running towards them, Taria, Sheena, and another girl named Collete Valeris.

Angelica recognized them as students who attended the same classes as Mirin and sometimes with Princess Mika as well.

"What's going on?" asked Mirin. "You three look so flustered."

Taria glared at Mirin. "You mean to tell me you haven't heard yet?"

Mirin stared at Taria blankly. "Heard about what?"

Sheena grabbed Taria's arm. "Calm down, Taria! That's not how a young lady should speak," she said softly.

Taria turned her glare towards Sheena. "Right now, I don't care!"

Mirin frowned. "What are you talking about?"

"I'll tell you what happened," said the oldest girl in the group, Collete, who was more than a year older than Princess Mika and much taller. She was just as annoyed as Taria. "Princess Mika has betrayed us all!"

"Betrayed us?" Angelica was taken aback. "What do you mean by that?"

"Will someone tell me what's going on here?!" Mirin shouted with frustration.

Taria stepped closer to him. "Mirin, you know our parents are political leaders and part of the Royal Family's court. They just had a meeting in the Scarlet Chamber."

"You should know this already, but the Peasantry are protesting outside the castle," said Collete. "We were told that Sir Collin and his knights were sent to remove the peasants from the castle gates. Everyone knows that the Princess has been missing... but she was found! She came and stopped the knights from attacking the peasants! She ordered them to! She was on the side of the Peasantry!"

"That means she has betrayed the Nobility, Mirin!" shouted Taria.

"We all know she disappeared one night without a trace, but she was found with the peasants! She must have somehow snuck out of the castle to be with them!"

"Will you two please calm down?" asked Sheena, trying to plead with them with a soft voice, but to no avail. Her two companions were quite furious. However, she herself was quite annoyed with her friends for behaving the way they were.

Mirin stiffened. He remembered what Helen had told him. *No... surely, you jest. I know Helen said Mika stayed with the peasants. But, if what they're telling me is true... that means she's involved in the revolt of the peasants in the city?!* Mirin looked up at Angelica, who was just as shocked as he was, but her reason for being shocked was different. Mirin knew what was going on in Mika's mind. Angelica, however, did not.

"Ladies, is this true?! You heard this from your parents?" asked Angelica.

Sheena shook her head. "I'm afraid so, Miss Angelica."

Angelica felt her heart sink as she put one hand on the middle of her chest and her other hand on Mirin's shoulder. "No, that can't be... that can't be true!"

Collete shrugged. "But that was what our parents learned in the Scarlet Chamber. The King was so furious that he threw a chair through a window."

Taria crossed her arms against her chest. "We didn't see it happen, but when we heard about it, we decided to go down and see. We saw the broken chair and broken glass everywhere. The King's anger must have been terrifying. Princess Mika betrayed us."

Angelica and Mirin looked on, speechless.

Sheena pulled on Taria's sleeve, her voice somewhat hushed as she spoke. "I've always thought she was a little strange."

Taria blew out an irritated sigh. "The Princess thinks she's far too good to talk to us, and she always sits pretty in the back of the classroom. She never talks to any of us, and she just studies and studies to her heart's content."

Collete rolled her eyes. "She's the most intelligent girl I've ever met. She thinks like an adult, and speaks like one as well. That is, of course, when she actually does speak. It's… rather unnerving, I must say. Whenever I hear anything out of her, I always feel like I'm so much smaller than she is, even though she is younger than I am and far shorter as well."

Sheena corrected Collete. "I believe you mean to say that you feel intimidated by her."

"Yes, that's it. Even if she's timid and shy, like everyone says."

Mirin clenched his teeth, and then narrowed his eyes as the girls continued to talk amongst themselves.

Angelica did not like how they were speaking either.

Taria turned to Collete. "Sometimes she says strange things. But, like you said, Collete, that's only if she actually does say something. Sometimes she says things that are well above our understanding. Even though she's close to our age, she thinks differently, like she's much older than the rest of us."

"Enough already!" shouted Mirin.

The girls gasped, startled, as they turned towards him.

"I've heard enough of this ridiculous talk about Princess Mika! And I don't believe any of what you're saying about her! She's my best friend, and I know her better than any of you! She would never betray anyone!" Mirin started running away.

Angelica called out to him. "Mirin, wait!"

Taria, Sheena, and Collete watched him run, speechless.

Angelica took one look at them, showing them that she was disappointed with the way they spoke. She started running after Mirin. After rounding a corner, Angelica saw Mirin standing in the middle of another hallway. "Mirin!"

Mirin turned towards Angelica, who caught up to him. He was furious, his tense fists at his sides. "Miss Angelica," he said softly. "I'm sorry. What those girls said about Mika made me so angry."

Angelica shook her head. "I know. It's all right, Mirin. I didn't like what they were saying about Princess Mika either."

Mirin stayed silent, trying to calm down and listening to Angelica as she continued.

"They were told she was found outside the castle. I am so relieved that she's unharmed. However, I'm even more worried now because she's out there among the peasants. I'm her maidservant. Her well-being, her safety, those are the things I'm most concerned about. Why is she out there anyway? Why is she with the peasants? How did she end up with them?"

Angelica closed her eyes, and knelt down beside Mirin. She covered her eyes with her hands for a moment, and then pushed her hair back. She was visibly shaken by what was going on. All Angelica knew was that the Princess disappeared one night. Now, she has learned that Mika has been with the peasants all this time. Shortly after that, the revolt of the peasant workers began. The flow of goods and services to the castle stopped because of that revolt. The knights were ordered to remove the peasants from the castle gates, and the Princess appeared to stop them. Was it all a strange coincidence?

"I can't believe this. That's... not something Princess Mika would do, right, Mirin?" she asked.

Mirin was speechless. He knew all along that Mika was out in the city, but that was all he knew. However, this was not something he could tell Angelica. No matter what, he could not tell her. Mika had made him promise to keep everything he knew a secret, and Helen had threatened him so he would not say anything about her sneaking out of the castle and not coming back. "I… I don't know, Miss Angelica… I… I'm just worried about her."

"I know, Mirin. You're her best friend. Of course, you'd be worried about her. As long as she's out there with the peasants, she's in great danger. But I don't understand any of this. Why is this happening? What is going on?"

CHAPTER 25

RISKING OUR LIVES AND FAMILIES

SEC 3566, Morrighan 47

A NEW DAY BEGAN OVER THE city of Scarletia as the sun rose. Its morning rays dispelled the darkness of night. However, all over the entire city, the peasant workers continued their revolt. There were over a hundred groups of peasant workers that marched up and down the major streets. They varied in size from about a few hundred people to several thousand. On the Valderia Pathway, just in front of the castle gates, the bodies of peasants had already been removed, and the area was now devoid of people. No one wanted to be anywhere near the castle gates right now, not even the bravest of the peasant worker groups.

At Ethereal Daydreams, Mika was already awake. Though she'd not had much sleep, she felt quite alert.

The leaders of the Hope of Scarletia and the Scarletia Liberation were very much awake this morning, as they had been for the last few hours. They had been busy coordinating with the various minor rebel groups to continue with the rebellion. In fact, there had been reports that some of the minor rebel groups were actually merging with either the Hope of Scarletia or the Scarletia Liberation, further increasing their forces and resources.

Mika sat on a tall chair in front of the bar. To her left and right where Feldia and Laren.

Adrel served her a glass of orange juice as she requested. "Here you go, Princess. Try this out, and see if you like it."

Mika who took the glass. "Thank you." She observed the sparkling orange juice for a moment, wondering what Adrel meant about trying this drink out to see if she liked it. From what it looked like, it appeared to be like any other plain orange juice.

Feldia regarded Adrel with a frown. "Hey, Adrel, you didn't by any chance put anything strange in her juice that would make her pass out, did you?"

"Now what the hell do you think I am, Feldia?"

"Where's Dellen?" asked Laren.

Mika answered. "He's with his family, but he said he'll return shortly. They must be worried about him right now."

"I wouldn't doubt it. Go ahead, Princess. Drink it, and see if you like it," said Adrel.

"All right." Mika took the glass with both hands, and then took a sip. At first, it seemed like any other orange juice. Its sweet taste went down smoothly. But as she sipped some more, she found that there was another flavour, one that was very subtle and added to the sweetness. As she drank, she started to feel a vague tingling sensation in her throat. She stopped, put down the glass that was now half-empty, and coughed.

Feldia was alarmed, turning to Adrel. "What did you put in there?"

Laren saw Mika's reaction, and frowned. "Adrel, what did you do?"

Adrel looked at both of them, and shrugged. "What? Nothing dangerous. Just a tiny bit of Star Spirits." He produced a bottle of the drink that he had mixed into Mika's orange juice. They had not seen him do that.

Mika saw the bottle as she coughed. "Alcohol?"

Feldia grabbed the bottle from Adrel, and stared at it for a moment. "What the hell are you doing, Adrel? She's eleven years old!"

"I didn't think she was going to start coughing! It was only a tiny bit! Even if you drank a full glass of this stuff, there's so little alcohol, even a small boy can drink it without getting drunk!"

Laren shook his head. "You wouldn't ordinarily serve alcohol of any amount to an eleven-year-old girl, Adrel."

Adrel rolled his eyes, and then turned to Mika. He started pouring her a glass of water. "Here, Princess. Have a glass of water to wash that down with."

Mika coughed one more time, and tried to force a smile. "Thank you," she said, clearing her throat. She drank the water, which cleared away some of that unusual tingling sensation.

Feldia gave the bottle of Star Spirits back to Adrel. "Are you... okay, Princess Mika?"

"I'll be fine." Mika turned to Adrel. "But... please don't feel bad. I suppose I have to have my first taste of alcohol sooner or later. However, I might delay my second taste for a few more years."

Adrel laughed. "How was the drink?"

"It was sweet but tingly. It was good, in fact, but I think I'll pass next time."

"Good idea," said Laren.

Feldia shook her head. "Alcohol at sunrise. Ordinarily, alcohol is served in the evening after dinner. Even so, it wouldn't be served to a young girl. You should be ashamed of yourself, Adrel."

Adrel waved a dismissive hand away. "Ah, don't worry about it. But, anyway, Princess Mika."

Mika looked up as she completely emptied her glass of water. "What is it?" She set the glass down gently.

"Let's talk about a certain political situation that I came up for you. I need you to listen carefully to my words. It'll be good exercise for your mind," said Adrel.

The tone of Laren's voice gave a subtle warning. "Uh oh. Here we go."

Adrel continued. "Let's say we have several nations involved in this situation, including Melodice itself. The situation spans the entire continent. We have Melodice, a nation that takes pride in producing extremely talented and powerful magic users. We have Tashar, a nation that uses armies of dragons for warfare. We have South Alenshire, a nation of vast Starstone resources and high technology. We also have North Alenshire, which has a powerful standing army that is the envy of all other nations."

Mika took in his words, committing them all into memory.

"Let's say none of these nations are friends, but they're not enemies either. Each nation wants to take advantage of the resources of all the others for their own ambitions. To simplify things, let's start with one nation. For example, Melodice wants a dragon army of their own, they want to increase the size of their standing army, and they want the latest in weapons technology. What should Melodice do?"

Mika nearly gasped, thinking as quickly as she possibly could. "Oh my, that's a rather tough question. I suppose Melodice can start with friendly political relations with the other three nations one at a time."

"But by doing that, Melodice risks alienating itself at the same time. Remember. None of the nations are friends, nor are they enemies. And this has worked because none of them has declared an alliance with another. For example, if Melodice allies itself with Tashar because they want a dragon army of their own, then what do you think would happen between Melodice and the other two nations, South Alenshire and North Alenshire?"

Mika looked down at the bar table, her fingers tracing the creases in the wood as she thought about how her solution wouldn't work. "Oh, I see. South Alenshire and North Alenshire would think something strange is going on. They would ask why Melodice and Tashar are suddenly allies. However, if Melodice tried to ally itself with all three nations at the same time, then each nation would be suspicious of each other and of Melodice. Each nation will wonder about the true intentions of the others."

Adrel nodded. "That's right. So what should Melodice do?"

Mika stole a glance at both Feldia and Laren, but they merely looked back at her with a shrug. They were not going to be much help on this one.

"Um... well, what about the leaders of Melodice? Perhaps the Royal Family can privately form relationships with the leaders of the other nations. Their nations may not be friends, but their leaders surely could be friends if they wanted to. The Royal Family could invite them to a grand social event in the nation of Melodice. The leaders of all four nations would become friends, and eventually, the Royal Family of Melodice would gain the favour of the leaders of all the other nations."

Adrel thought about that for a moment, judging whether Mika's next solution was doable. "Hmmm, yes, I guess it's possible to do that. However, leaders of nations are often cunning. Any attempt to form a personal friendship is an opportunity to backstab someone. It looks suspicious, too. It looks like you want to make deals under the table, and that's what the other leaders would think."

Mika was taken back. "I didn't think about that. What reason do the other nations have for befriending the Royal Family of Melodice? Melodice might have a reason, but the other nations don't."

"Exactly. Melodice would open itself up to a good screwing between the legs by the other nations."

Mika looked up Adrel, confused. "Huh?"

Feldia shook her head. "Adrel, watch the language."

"So what should Melodice do, Princess Mika?" repeated Adrel.

Mika thought hard as Adrel asked her the same question for a third time. *All my solutions have been ineffective. The nation of Melodice is on its own, as are all the other nations, but if Melodice were to act in any way that favours one nation over the other, it would alienate itself from the other nations. And the leaders can't just form relationships with the leaders of the other nations since that would render Melodice vulnerable. What should Melodice do? I suppose other people would try to resolve this situation by having Melodice attack one of the nations to take their resources by force, but the others would frown upon such a hostile act, and either come to the aid of the nation that was attacked by Melodice or remain neutral but outwardly and vocally question the actions of Melodice, further alienating us, and eventually, all the other nations would side against Melodice. Melodice would set itself up for defeat.*

No, that's not a solution. Such a solution would cause needless death and destruction, and I don't want that. War also has a very high resource cost. A more peaceful solution is required. Perhaps Melodice could send messages of peace and friendship to the other nations to start with. No, that wouldn't work. They'd probably see it as an act. They would see right through it, and start wondering if Melodice was planning something. They would also probably think that Melodice wanted something from them, which is actually the case. Melodice does want something from each of the nations, but they can't allow their true intentions to be revealed just like that. Sir Adrel's question is difficult, even though he said he simplified it. Maybe I can find a solution within the way he asked me the question, or maybe there are clues within the words he used. He did tell me to listen to his words very carefully.

Mika gasped suddenly.

Wait a minute! I got it!

"Trena!" exclaimed Mika.

"What?"

"The continent of Alenshire has five nations, not four! You left out the nation of Trena on purpose, Sir Adrel."

Feldia was surprised by this sudden revelation. "Wait, that's right. You didn't mention Trena."

"Really, now? What about Trena, Princess Mika?" asked Adrel.

Mika leaned forward in her seat. "Trena is a neutral nation, unlike all the others. But they're very proud of their arts and culture. The Nobility and the Royal Family are often invited to the nation of Trena, not by their political leaders, but by leading artists. I've never been there myself, but my father and my mother have. It's not just our leaders who are often invited. They also regularly invite the leaders of other nations to witness theatrical performances, art galleries, and the like. If Trena were to extend invitations to the leaders of Melodice, Tashar, South Alenshire, and North Alenshire, then all the leaders would be in one place, all at the same time, and they would be in a social situation where they could all relax and enjoy themselves."

"That's similar to your second solution, but I showed you how that wouldn't work. How will this one work, Princess?"

"My second solution wouldn't work because they would all have gathered in Melodice. In this solution, they'd all be in a neutral location, which would be better for everyone involved." Mika paused for a moment. "Also, there's something else I thought of just now."

Adrel raised an eyebrow out of curiosity. "What is it?"

"If you want something from others, people—and I suppose governments and nations as well—are usually more receptive to you if you're offering them something in return, something that they either need right away or in the future. Melodice can offer them the gift of magic. They can offer to accept students who are found to be capable of magic from every nation on the continent. The Cerulean Magic Academy would teach them, and possibly open up new academies in the other nations. The other nations would express their gratitude. It's something they wouldn't expect. By doing this, Melodice would have extended a hand to the other nations, a hand of friendship, and the other nations would reciprocate by offering Melodice what they want and need. In fact, they wouldn't have a choice. Because Melodice would have done this for them, they *have* to return the favour. If they don't, they risk alienating themselves from their neighbours."

As Mika completed presenting her proposed solution, Adrel began to laugh, one so hard and so loud that people could probably hear it just outside the entrance. It might even have been heard by the inn's patrons on the floor above them.

Feldia and Laren looked at each other with surprise and amusement.

"Well done, Princess Mika," said Laren.

Feldia smiled, shaking her head with amazement. "When Adrel starts laughing like this, that means you've answered his question, and probably beyond his expectations."

Adrel took a while to stop laughing as he poured

himself a glass of Star Spirits, and downed it in just a few gulps. He set the bottle down hard on the bar table.

Laren chuckled. "Adrel, your question was fraudulent. You made your question deliberately confusing, and you left important details out, like the fifth nation of Trena."

"Politics is full of fraud in our society, Laren. You should know that," said Adrel.

Feldia nodded. "That's true."

"Princess Mika, well done." Adrel smiled proudly. "To be honest, I didn't expect you to solve this political situation, but you did. Yes, I did leave out the nation of Trena on purpose. I was hoping you would count on the knowledge that they are a neutral nation, and you did. But I didn't expect you to have the nation of Melodice offer to fulfill a present or future need to the other nations. Very well done."

Mika smiled sweetly. "Thank you, Sir Adrel."

Feldia thought back to those times when Mika accurately anticipated the actions of the Nobility within the Scarletia Royal Castle. "I think we have the makings of a tactical and political genius here."

"A child genius," said Laren. "I can't believe you were able to think of that, My Lady. That's... actually pretty amazing."

Adrel poured himself some more Star Spirits, but just half a glass this time. "That's right. Princess Mika, yesterday, you accurately predicted that the knights wouldn't head out here to capture you just yet. You told us the King would probably order the Supreme Captain to head out with his knights and capture you, but that the Queen wouldn't have it that way."

Laren leaned one arm against the bar table. "And that's the reason why nothing's happened since. The knights are still in the castle, and the King and Queen are probably still trying to decide what they should do. Why would a mother agree to knights charging into the city to search for her daughter anyway? Your safety, Princess, is her greatest concern, more than anything."

"As expected of a mother." Feldia put a hand on Mika's shoulder.

Mika glanced up at Feldia with a smile. "I'm glad that, right now, nothing has happened. However, very soon, the Royal Family will make a decision. This calm will not last long."

Adrel nodded to that. "That's right."

The door that led down into the basement of the inn opened, and Dellen came down the stairs. As soon as he entered the basement, he saw Mika seated between Feldia and Laren at the bar and Adrel behind it. "Ah, I see everyone's here."

"Took you long enough." Adrel raised the bottle of Star Spirits. "Come, Dellen. Have a drink."

Dellen looked at Adrel with disapproval. "Alcohol in the morning? I think I'll pass on that."

"As you wish. I've already had one and a half glasses, and I think that's enough, even though Star Spirits has very little alcohol in it. You'd have to drink several bottles of this to get drunk. I wonder why they even sell this." Adrel put the bottle away.

Feldia turned to Dellen as he strode over to the seat beside her. "Everything okay, Dellen?"

Dellen paused for a moment, slight discomfort within him. "We've tallied up the casualties from yesterday."

Mika, Feldia, and Laren immediately looked somber as they met Dellen's gaze.

Adrel sighed with regret. "Let's have it."

"There were over seven hundred dead. More than one hundred fifty of those were killed by the knights. The other five hundred fifty or so deaths resulted from the stampede of the civilians as they struggled to escape. They were basically crushed to death."

Laren looked down at the bar table, closing his eyes for a moment. "That's... just horrible."

Feldia pressed her hand to her forehead as if to push away the images of the dead from her mind. She looked over towards Mika, who stared at her glass of water as she listened to the casualty report. Mika was visibly saddened to hear it, but she remained speechless and motionless.

"Damn. Let's be sure to honour them," said Adrel.

Dellen agreed. "Of course, despite all that, the workers are continuing their revolt. They're still marching all over the city. As expected, the knights are doing nothing about it. They haven't been ordered to do anything. I passed by near the castle on the way here. Nothing's stirring."

"But, as the Princess said just now, that calm won't last long."

"Exactly."

Mika chimed in, concerned for the safety of the civilians. "I trust that the many groups of peasant workers are still following their instructions?"

Dellen nodded. "Yeah, they are. After what happened yesterday, no one's marching up to the gates."

A moment of silence. Adrel leaned forward against the bar table, positioning himself directly in front of Mika as he looked down at her. "Princess Mika, there's something we need to tell you."

Mika glanced up to meet his gaze. "What is it?"

"It's extremely important that you remember this, so listen carefully." Adrel held a look of utter seriousness. "You *cannot*, under any circumstances, tell anyone about this hideout and where it is. We chose the basement of Ethereal Daydreams because it's an old, well-established, and unassuming inn that no one would think was special in any way. You *cannot* tell anyone about this, not even the Peasantry. You can't even tell anyone who's involved with our rebel groups. The only ones who know about this place are the five of us, our immediate reports, like Demias, Eduard, and the others, and the owners and workers of this inn. Between the Hope of Scarletia and the Scarletia Liberation, rebel groups with thousands of members in each, only forty people know about this place. Not even their families and closest friends know about it."

"Not even families and closest friends? Why not?" asked Mika.

It was Laren's turn to speak. "Unfortunately, Princess, there's another fact you must realize. People might reveal information that's supposed to be kept secret if they know the lives of their own families were being threatened. To protect themselves and their families, they might reveal the location of this hideout. They might exchange that information for their safety. If that happens, we're all dead."

Mika's voice dropped to a whisper. "I see...."

"It's not that we don't trust them. We need to protect ourselves and our goals, and it's also for their own safety," said Feldia.

Dellen leaned forward in his seat. "That means you must limit your trust, Princess Mika, even among the Peasantry. It wouldn't be a problem if we were an army, but we're far from that. We're only rebels."

Mika acknowledged with a nod. Although she was very surprised to hear this, she understood why it was important that she kept their location a secret. She thought about Dellen and Adrel. They were risking their lives as leaders of the two major rebel groups. Mika stared at both of them.

"You both amaze me, Sir Dellen and Sir Adrel," said Mika.

"Hmm? How so?" asked Dellen.

"As leaders, many people follow you and look up to you. But you both realize that you're risking your lives, given your positions. You're risking your lives for a greater purpose."

Adrel nodded to that. "It's not just us who are risking our lives, Princess Mika. Our families are also at risk."

Mika gasped softly. "Why? I thought you mentioned they don't know the location of this hideout."

"They don't. But that's not what risks their lives. Our position as leaders... that's what puts our families at risk."

"Oh... that's why...."

Dellen nodded as well. "You know I have a wife and two sons. Adrel has a family, too."

"You do, Sir Adrel?"

"Yes. I have a wife and three daughters who are ages three, six, and nine. Only my wife knows about my involvement with the rebellion as the leader of the Scarletia Liberation. My daughters are completely unaware... and it must stay that way. At this point in their lives, they must know *nothing*. In fact, my wife shouldn't even know, but it's only fair to her that I let her know who I am, and who I'm involved with. None of them know about this place." Adrel looked up at Dellen. "The same goes for Dellen's wife and his sons."

Dellen rested his arms on the bar table, turning back towards Mika. "We need to keep them as safe as possible. Zima knows who I am, and what my involvement is. My sons don't. But I do wonder sometimes if Jaren suspects that I might have some involvement with a rebel group, because Feldia and her reports sometimes pass by to talk to me. He is of that age, and he's very intelligent. However, none of them know about this place, this inn. The less they know, the safer they will be."

Mika nodded. "I understand. What about those young men outside who pretend to be street thugs? They're your sentries. Do they know what truly goes on in the basement of Ethereal Daydreams?"

Dellen shook his head. "They think there are illicit business transactions occurring in the basement of the inn. They've been contracted to act as sentries, but they don't know—and don't need to know—what really goes on here."

"All right. Sir Adrel?"

Adrel looked at Mika. "What?"

Mika smiled at him as she leaned forward, and rested her cheek against one hand. "I've met Sir Dellen's wife and sons, and they're lovely. I'd love to meet your family someday."

Adrel smiled. "I'm sure they'd love that, especially my daughters."

"What are their names? What are they like?"

Adrel chuckled. "My wife's name is Vera. She's the most beautiful woman I've ever laid my eyes upon."

Laren smirked. "For a rough-looking man, Adrel, you can be quite the romantic."

"Quiet," said Adrel, without looking back at Laren, and continued. "As I was saying, before I was rudely interrupted, Vera is very beautiful. Her hair is like yours, Princess Mika, light blonde, although longer. It reaches past her waist, and is very smooth and straight. When you see her, you'll find that she's quite lovely."

"I can't wait to meet her then," said Mika.

"And then, there are our three sweet daughters. Harsia is the youngest. She's three years old. I love the hilarious questions she asks, and the comments she makes about various things. Very honest, and to the point. She'll constantly question why things are the way they are. I guess her level of curiosity is almost comparable to yours, Princess."

Feldia smiled, remembering meeting Adrel's youngest daughter once. "She's a very cute girl, Adrel. Very smart, too."

"That she is. Our middle daughter, Emelia, is six years old. She and her younger sister are partners in mischief. She likes to play the part of the explorer, and likes to go outside and pretend she's exploring the world. We have to make sure she doesn't go too far, or she'll get lost, but she usually knows how far she should go, and doesn't go any farther."

Mika gasped with delight. "Oh, a little explorer." She giggled. "That's so cute."

Adrel chuckled. "And then, we have our eldest daughter, Anira. She is nine years old. I suppose I could compare her to you, too, Princess Mika. She's bright, mature for her age, and very sophisticated. She won't admit it, but she enjoys playing with her younger sisters. She sometimes takes part in their pretend activities. But, of course, if you say anything about it, she'll deny it. Anira is also very protective of her younger sisters. She likes to be thought of as a mature young lady."

Mika smiled. "They all sound lovely, Sir Adrel. I very much hope I can meet them someday."

"Of course. When this revolt is over, I will introduce you to them. I'm sure they'll grow to love you very quickly, Princess Mika."

* * *

The revolt of the peasant workers continued throughout the day. Above them, the clouds thickened, blocking out the sun, its orb appearing ominous as clouds that looked like smoke moved across its face. The number of people who protested and demanded their freedom now exceeded a hundred thousand, about one-third of the total labour force. Businesses and industries throughout the city remained closed. The Scarletia Royal Castle was isolated from the goods and services that were usually provided to it on a normal day.

As peasant workers continued their revolt, knights stayed at their patrol stations. They took turns guarding their posts, mounted on cervids. They were fully armoured, their swords in scabbards at their sides. The knights still had not received any orders from the castle, so they continued to stand their ground, and did nothing but watch the peasants protest. As long as they themselves were not attacked by the peasants and as long as the peasants did not damage property, they had no reason to take action.

Two of Laren's direct reports, Marik and Tavien, were on cervids as they galloped alongside a group that marched down one of the major streets.

"Where is this group headed?" asked Marik.

One of the peasants who led the group answered. "Nowhere specific, sir. We're continuing our march around the city. We're taking this road that leads all the way around in a never-ending circle."

"Good. I'm sure you already know not to protest near the castle gates for now, unless specifically instructed to do so. And you are clear on all your other instructions," said Tavien.

"Don't provoke the knights," said Marik. "Don't do anything that would allow them to take action against you."

"We know that already. Don't worry about us," said another member of the group.

After their brief discussion, Marik and Tavien rode on to the next group of peasant workers to ensure they were also following instructions, and that they were not going to do anything that would provoke the knights who stood guard.

* * *

The civilians living within the Scarletia Royal Castle had started complaining. Because goods and services were no longer being provisioned for the castle, food supplies were being rationed. The complaints of the Nobility made their way to the King and Queen.

"Our people are asking when this revolt will be over." Queen Maiya turned away from one of the windows overlooking the Grounds from the King's Conference, and faced King Ralphen.

The King remained silent as he sat in his designated chair, his elbows on the table, his hands clasped together.

Maiya continued. "They're complaining that the food rations are affecting their ability to have a decent meal. They're eating smaller portions, and they're not able to eat whatever they want. Choices in meals have been limited."

Ralphen shook his head. "Humph. They're complaining like a group of toddlers who haven't been given their toys." He leaned back in his seat. "Still, I suppose I can't blame them."

"They are the Nobility, Ralphen. They're not accustomed to food rationing. I doubt they've heard of the term until recently."

"Yes, I suppose you're right," said Ralphen. "Dammit. We have to do something about this, and soon. Over ten thousand nobles live within the castle. Food and supplies will not last long with that many people."

Silence filled the room. Ralphen leaned back in his chair, rubbing his face in frustration.

Maiya sat on one of the chairs closest to him.

Ralphen was deep in thought. "Why does Mika have to do this? Why did she sneak out of the castle? Did she do this without help, or was there someone with her? I haven't heard about anyone helping her. But, either way, how did she do it? Was there someone she needed to meet in the city? If so, it could only be some peasant."

Maiya looked on, unable to offer any answers or ideas.

"Who might she meet in the city? Rebel leaders? How

could that be? She doesn't know a soul in the city. Or does she? In that case, how did she come to know them? There are so many questions, but the answers are few." Ralphen set his hands down on the smooth algerwood table, and looked up at Maiya. "How could our daughter do this, Maiya? How could she be on the side of the Peasantry, as Sir Collin, Sir Maleth, and our knights have witnessed?"

Maiya shook her head, the calm expression on her face giving way to sadness. "We can only find the answers to these questions when we find our Mika, and hear them from her own lips."

"Yes. We must find her, and bring her back to the castle. We have to stop this revolt, and force them to return to work. However, as you said, if I send out the knights, there's a possibility that Mika will be killed. If the knights were to attack the peasant workers and kill those who are participating in this revolt...."

Maiya waited for a moment, and then completed his thoughts for him. "The workforce will dwindle, Ralphen. A battle between the knights and the peasant workers will have an enormous death toll, as well as extensive property damage. Replacing the workers and cleaning up the damage would cause resources to dwindle even more so. It'll be a cycle that will be extremely difficult to get out of. That's why... that's why you need to think about this very carefully, Ralphen."

"If only we had more information. If we could just find something—anything—that could help us make the right decision. This would be so much easier if the Princess were not in the city. But she is making this very difficult for me."

Ralphen stood, and began to pace about the room.

"Think about this very carefully," he whispered. He paused as he looked down at the Queen. "I need to take a walk for a moment. Forgive me, Maiya, but I would like to take this walk alone for now. Hopefully, I'll come back with a decision."

"Of course," said Maiya. "Take your time."

"Time is not on our side, Maiya. Eventually, food will

run out within the castle, and it'll be the nobles who will be next in line to protest. That's something I don't want to have to deal with."

Ralphen headed for the doors to exit the King's Conference. Maiya stood up from her chair, and walked over to the windows once more.

* * *

Helen left her bedchamber, and proceeded down the hallways of the castle, clad in her knight's uniform with a knee-length black cape, which was tied together with a ribbon in front of her chest. Her hand subconsciously went to her breast pocket, where there were two folded sheets of paper. When she realized what she was doing, she drew her hand back. She stopped in the middle of the hallway, her hands tightly fisted at her sides. She held a look of frightening determination.

"I hope I'm doing the right thing. Never again will I make such a stupid mistake," whispered Helen. She continued down the hallways of the castle.

Eventually, she passed by the Scarlet Chamber. Its doors were wide open. When she looked inside, she saw a few noble workers fixing the stained-glass window that the King had broken in his fit of rage. There was nothing here for her. She continued on her way.

After everything that has happened, there are two things I have decided on.

First, the Princess has indeed done a terrible thing. She has sided with the Peasantry, and led them into rebellion. All of this has to stop. I will capture Princess Mika, and by doing that, I will bring an end to this revolt of the peasant workers.

But there's another. The Peasantry continue to live under tyranny and have been suffering for a very long time... and this has to stop. The first step, of course, is to stop this damn revolt. The next step after that... actually, it's a whole series of steps that must be taken. No one in the Nobility is willing to put an end to the status quo, as far as I know. No one among the Peasantry has the power and resources sufficient enough to escape the tyranny that has become the norm. They may form rebel groups and start rebellions… but that's not enough, and it's certainly not the right way to bring about change. It would only bring more suffering, because they would surely lose. Someone in the Nobility must take action on their behalf. Someone must climb up the ladders of authority, and attain power and influence. Someone must change the government from within once he—or she—has attained enough authority, and then she can change our nation. That is what needs to be done.

"And I… will be the one… who will end the suffering of the Peasantry," she said aloud, assured that there was no one nearby to hear her words.

However… in order for me to begin, sacrifices have to be made. There's no way around it. What I'm about to do… must be done in order to achieve a greater good.

After a few more minutes, Helen found herself in the main lobby. The great steel and algerwood front doors of the castle loomed in front of her. Knights in uniform stood guard at the sides of the doors. Up above her, hung high along the walls of the lobby, were portraits of the various individuals who have ruled the nation of Melodice over the years. She followed the line of portraits from one side of the room all the way up to the walls above a balcony that overlooked the main lobby, where she spotted the person that she was hoping to run into, leaning over the balcony with his hands on the rails.

"My Lord!" Helen called out.

King Ralphen smiled as he looked down at her from above. "Good afternoon, Miss Helen."

Helen cleared her throat, and stood at attention. "Good afternoon, My Lord. I trust you are well?"

"I am, and I hope you are as well. I was just taking a walk. I've been thinking about what we need to do about this current unfortunate situation in which we have found ourselves. I'm certain you've been made fully aware of what we're facing."

"Yes, My Lord. The peasant workers continue to revolt as we speak."

"Correct."

Helen hesitated for a moment. She did her very best to project an air of confidence. It was not usually a problem for her, but considering what she was planning, it seemed more difficult than usual. Once again she touched her breast pocket that held the folded papers. She drew her hand away.

"Pardon me, My Lord, but you mentioned you were taking a walk. Would it be acceptable for a knight of the rank of Private Enlist to join you?" asked Helen.

Ralphen nodded. "I see no harm in that."

"Thank you, My Lord." Helen ascended the stairs that led her up to the second-floor balcony. After a moment, she joined the King.

"Well, then, shall we?" The King held out his hand towards one of the hallways.

"Yes, My Lord."

Helen and Ralphen proceeded quietly down a hallway. The King walked casually, so Helen matched his steps, holding her hands together behind her back as she kept her body straight. One side of the hallway was lined with glass windows, some of them opened, allowing a breeze to enter. The sunlight outside dwindled somewhat as the clouds continued to thicken. Helen looked for an opportunity to start speaking, but the silence continued as they walked. She was unsure how to begin a conversation with the King.

Eventually, Ralphen broke the silence between them. "I must thank you again, Miss Helen."

"My Lord?" Helen was confused.

"It was you who saved our daughter from those wretched merchant assassins. If it hadn't been for you, she would be dead right now. I can never thank you enough for your heroic deed that day."

Helen looked on ahead. "Such is my duty, My Lord, as a knight of the Scarletia Royal Guard."

"You have exceptional skill despite your extreme youth. You joined the Scarletia Royal Guard as soon as you turned sixteen years old, Miss Helen. In such a short time, you've proven yourself to be highly committed to your duties.

I'm impressed. Word has reached me of your commitment, your positive and enthusiastic attitude towards duty and honour, and your great skill in magic and swordsmanship. I see greatness in your future."

"Thank you, My Lord. And I would like to thank you as well for the commendation you bestowed upon me for saving the life of the Princess that day. I am truly honoured."

Ralphen smiled. "You deserved it, Miss Helen."

"I must admit that, after receiving it, other knights have regarded me slightly differently. I'm accustomed to being seen as a child. However, ever since that day, it appears as if some of them now regard me more as a young woman rather than a little girl in a knight's uniform."

"But you are no child, Miss Helen. You are of the age of majority. You report directly to Supreme Captain Collin Gagnier. You deserved the commendation. You have earned the respect and admiration that you are now receiving from your fellow knights."

"Thank you, My Lord. I greatly appreciate your kind words."

"You are most welcome."

More silence between them. Helen took this opportunity to try to push away whatever doubt that remained from within her.

That was my first step, wasn't it? Saving the life of Princess Mika... it earned me some honour and prestige, even if it's just a little, among my peers. Perhaps that was the beginning for me, the turning point of my life. And now, this is the next step... the next step that will help me change our beloved nation of Melodice for the better.

It was Helen's turn to break the silence. "My Lord, I am fortunate for crossing paths with you just now."

Ralphen was puzzled. "Why is that, Miss Helen?"

"I'm assuming you're still trying to decide what we should do? The Princess is out in the city of Scarletia, and the peasants continue to revolt. I've heard the Nobility within the castle have begun to speak out against the rationing of food and supplies."

Ralphen shook his head. "You're right. It's very

frustrating, Miss Helen. As King, I have to think about our next course of action, and I must think of the best possible solution. I wanted to order Sir Collin to take his knights into the city to find Princess Mika, but that would have caused her life to be endangered, because she's surrounded by peasants. Also, attacking the peasant workers would be detrimental because it would cause extensive damage to the city. Our workforce would be reduced, and the ability of the city proper to provision goods and services to the castle would be severely hampered."

"Yes, My Lord. I can see this would be a very difficult decision to make, especially because we know so little about what's happening out there. We know the peasant workers are continuing the revolt. From what we've heard, it seems the Princess is involved in their revolt. If that's true, then there must be someone who is helping the Princess, someone who has plenty of resources and influence, someone who can relay messages to thousands of people in a very short period of time to organize this revolt. The Princess couldn't have done all that on her own, especially since the Peasantry don't trust the Nobility. It appears to me that this could only have been organized by the leaders of one or more rebel groups. These leaders must be the ones who are helping the Princess. They must have organized this workers' revolt."

The King watched Helen through the periphery of his vision as she spoke, hanging on to each word she uttered. To him, there was something interesting about what she was saying and how she was saying it.

Helen continued. "Unfortunately, we don't know of any peasants who might be involved with the revolt, specifically those who are their leaders. There's still much we don't know. Because of that, we don't have a starting point."

Ralphen slowed his pace, and looked over at Helen, wondering what she was going on about. "You sound like you know something, Miss Helen."

Helen turned towards the King. "I have some information that I'm certain may be of use to you, My

Lord. It might prove to be the starting point you're looking for. It may help you in making your decision."

Ralphen suddenly stopped in the hallway.

Helen stood beside one of the windows. The breeze from outside tugged at her locks of red hair and her ponytail, as well as the edges of her cape.

The King's cape moved as well as he took a few steps towards the window, and turned to face Helen. "I suppose this is the reason why you wanted to join me."

"It's one of the two reasons."

"Truly, now? What was the second reason?"

"The second reason would be to simply walk with the King, an honour that I have not yet experienced."

Ralphen chuckled, forming his lips into a cunning smile. "You are well versed in what words to use when speaking with political leaders, Miss Helen."

"Thank you, My Lord."

"What is this information, or rather, this starting point you speak of?"

"Before I speak of this starting point, My Lord, I would like to request something of you," said Helen.

"A request?"

"Yes, My Lord. Because of your commendation, Sir Collin and Sir Maleth regard me as a soldier worthy of their respect and praise. For saving the life of the Princess, I've gained your admiration and your favour."

"That you have, Miss Helen. What is your request?"

"I would like to request a promotion in rank, My Lord."

Ralphen chuckled again as he turned towards the window.

Helen stayed quiet. It was now up to the King to either honour her request in exchange for her information, or to force it from her by having her arrested. For a moment, she didn't realize she was holding her breath in anticipation.

Eventually, the King turned back towards her. "I see no harm in granting your request, but I must first know what kind of information you're about to provide me. Promotions in rank aren't just handed out to anyone, Miss Helen. They are usually earned with hard work. Knights desiring promotion must be exceptional at what they do, and go beyond the call of duty, exceeding the expectations of their superiors. That normally takes at least a few years of experience. You're asking me to promote you without having to work nearly as long as most of your fellow knights of the same rank. So my decision depends on how helpful your information will be, if at all."

"My Lord, I believe you will find it useful. Would you like to discuss the information here, or in a different location?"

"You're willing to give me this information regardless of whether or not I honour your request?"

"As you said, My Lord, whether I'm promoted or not depends on how useful this information will be to you. Since I do believe that it will prove very useful, then my request for a rank promotion will surely be granted."

Ralphen laughed, more loudly this time. "You have a way with words, Miss Helen. We can discuss it out here."

"Yes, My Lord." Helen moved one step closer to the King as she drew out the papers she was carrying, and unfolded them. "Miss Angelica, the maidservant of the Princess, handed these to me in private. She found them while cleaning in Princess Mika's bedchamber the other day."

The King was curious. "What's on them?"

Helen handed the two sheets of paper to him. "One of them is information on the identities of a certain peasant family, the Balias family, along with their whereabouts. The exact address of their household is shown."

Ralphen looked down at the paper, holding them in the sunlight. "Hmmm. Dellen Balias, his wife Zima, and sons Tyrel and Jaren. Avencial 560." He looked up at the young knight. "Who are these people, Miss Helen?"

"I'm not certain, but seeing their names on a piece of paper that was found in Princess Mika's bedchamber shortly after her disappearance leads me to believe that the Princess may have left the castle to find these people. This is only an assumption, but it's too much of a coincidence not to consider the possibility. The possibility... is made more plausible by the map on the second page."

Ralphen turned to the other sheet of paper. "A map..." he whispered.

"Yes, My Lord. Perhaps the Princess needed a map to locate this family. The address of the Balias family is indicated on the map as well."

Ralphen folded the sheets of paper, and looked up at Helen with a serious expression. "Miss Helen, I thank you for this information. You originally requested a promotion in rank? Would you care for two ranks instead of one?"

Helen was taken aback. *Two ranks?! This is more than I hoped for!*

"This is more than a starting point, Miss Helen! This will greatly help us. You will receive a promotion of two ranks for this and another commendation from me."

Helen wanted to shout in celebration, but she kept her composure. She smiled at the King. "Thank you very much, My Lord. I am deeply grateful."

"It might be possible that, whoever these people are, they may be involved with the revolt of the peasant workers."

"That possibility has crossed my mind as well, Your Highness," said Helen.

Ralphen extended a hand. After a brief moment, Helen took it, and the King shook her hand firmly. "You have brought honour to us again with this information, Miss Helen. I will make your request a reality."

Helen thought of something else. "My Lord, there is one more thing...."

"What is it?" asked Ralphen.

"I do have one more request."

Ralphen stared into Helen's eyes with a hint of disapproval. "Be careful, Miss Helen. Don't ask for the entire world just yet."

"No, My Lord, it's not another request of you. Rather, it's one that I would hope you could pass on to Sir Collin, as you are his direct superior."

Ralphen chuckled. "Ah, my apologies, Miss Helen. A request for Sir Collin? What is it?"

"If and when you do decide to issue the order for Sir Collin to deploy the Scarletia Royal Guard into the city, if possible, I would like to be the one to..." Helen paused for a moment.

Ralphen was puzzled. "Go on, Miss Helen."

"I would like to be the one to bring back the Princess, My Lord."

Ralphen stared at Helen, thinking about her request. No doubt, Sir Collin can facilitate the request, but only he can grant it, because the request would be to capture a Royal. If Helen approached Collin, he would have to go to the King to clear such a request anyway. Since Helen was approaching him directly, this was probably personal. Helen and Mika were, after all, colleagues in the study of magic. They have spent a great amount of time together. Seeing that Helen was also volunteering information that could potentially help him find Princess Mika, it would seem that her loyalty was in the right place. "Miss Helen, I will speak to Sir Collin, and tell him to facilitate your request."

"Thank you, My Lord."

Ralphen put the papers in a pocket inside his coat, and then turned once more to face Helen. "However, if I may ask, Miss Helen, why do you wish to be the one to capture the Princess?"

Helen was taken aback, but she did her best to keep her composure in check. She thought about her reply very carefully, reminding herself of what she has decided to do... to save the Peasantry from the tyranny of the Nobility. She met the King's gaze with confidence and determination.

"Because of the time I have spent with Princess Mika as my colleague in the study of magic, I have come to a better understanding of how she views the world. I can't condone her disregard for our accepted status quo. She has clearly chosen a rebellious path, siding with the Peasantry. I was willing to give my life to protect her, as was my duty as her knight, but I can no longer turn a blind eye to her recent actions."

"Do you feel a sense of betrayal?" asked Ralphen.

"Yes, My Lord. She has betrayed the Royal Family, the Nobility, the city of Scarletia, and the entire nation of Melodice."

The King was again impressed by Helen's loyalty. "You're not the only one who feels betrayed, Miss Helen. Surely, many among the Nobility feel betrayed as well. I feel the same way, not only as her King, but as her father. It's very disheartening for any parent when a child has taken actions like this."

Helen nodded. "Agreed, sir."

"As I said before, Miss Helen. I see greatness in your future. I must see your Queen about this, and then I will speak with Sir Collin. I believe I've come to a decision on what we'll do next. Thank you again."

Helen bowed her head as she smiled. "You are most welcome, My Lord."

After their conversation, King Ralphen left, and Helen headed back towards her bedchamber. As she walked down the hallways, she tightened her fists at her sides, her heart racing.

This is it! I've done it! Power and authority and influence... they are already within my reach. All because I have given the King the information he needs. The fact that it was information drawn by my own hand is of no consequence. I provided it at the request of my Princess. Princess Mika... I will defeat you, and I will be the one to save the Peasantry from tyranny and oppression, even if I have to make sacrifices... like the one I have just made.

Sir Dellen, Miss Zima, Sir Jaren, Sir Tyrel, I hope you will all eventually forgive me.

CHAPTER 26

RETRIBUTION

SEC 3566, Morrighan 48

HOURS AFTER MIDNIGHT, RAIN FELL on the city of Scarletia. Lightning flashed occasionally, followed by roars of thunder. The heavy rain hammered on the rooftops and glass windows of the houses in the residential area. The kerosene street lamps that lined the sides of the streets continued to burn brightly in defiance of the rain.

Inside the Balias family home, in the master bedroom, a lone candle flickered in a bowl on an old table beside the window, whose black curtains were closed. A half-filled wooden bucket, sitting on the floor near the bed, collected rain that dripped from the ceiling. In addition to the sounds of raindrops on the windows and the water dripping into the bucket, the sound of Zima's soft, breathless ecstasy filled the air.

"Does that feel good, Zima?"

"Ah, oh, Dellen... yes, very much so."

Zima, the front of her sleeping robe open, revealing the smooth curves of her small breasts, ran her hands through Dellen's hair as she closed her eyes. She let out moans of deep pleasure, taking in the loving sensation of Dellen inside of her.

Fully clothed but with his trousers pulled down to his knees, Dellen pushed himself into her soft flesh. His hand touched hers, their fingers intertwined. He leaned down, and pressed his lips against hers.

Zima opened her eyes wide as she felt tension building up, yearning desperately for release. She stifled her moans by putting her free hand over her mouth, hoping she would not awaken their sons. She felt Dellen lean down even closer, until his flushed face was right next to hers. She felt his hot breath against the side of her neck. She listened to his heavy breathing, which soon became groans, and at the same time, she shut her eyes tight.

"Come inside me, Dellen." Zima gasped loudly as she felt a warm wetness between her smooth thighs. Her hands grabbed hold of the blanket tightly, and her back arched as her muscles tensed, pushing her breasts against Dellen's chest. As Dellen thrust himself into Zima with even more vigor, she jerked several times as her loins sent waves of euphoria throughout her body.

They stayed that way for a long moment to catch their breaths. Zima looked deep into his eyes, and felt as if she was being pulled into them. She watched him intently as his hand gently pushed back locks of her beautiful hair, and then she held his other hand, her thin fingers around his, feeling the calluses on his palms just below his fingers that resulted from practicing his swordsmanship.

"I love you so much." Dellen kissed her deeply.

Zima caressed the warmth of his cheeks. "Oh, I love you, too. But you made a mess in our bed again. You're cleaning it up in the morning."

Dellen let out a breath of feigned exasperation as he held a smug grin. "Well, that's just great. My apologies, my lady."

After their intense love-making, Dellen pulled up his trousers, and then lay beside her, while Zima closed her sleeping robe.

In the room next door, Jaren and Tyrel slept on two beds on opposite sides of the room. They slept peacefully despite the rain tapping relentlessly on their windows. Water flowed down one of the walls as the roof leaked, eventually crossing the floor and finding its way into a makeshift drain in the wooden floorboards that had been cut open.

Outside, Collin glared at the house of Dellen Balias. Standing on the side of the street, he raised his head, rain dripping down his helmet. Light from the street lamps reflected off his polished full armour. He wore a layer of leather armour underneath to keep out the rain.

"So... it begins here." Collin raised his hand, and pointed his gauntlet towards the house. That was his signal for the other knights to make their move.

Several fully armoured knights ran along the sidewalk. Some of them circled around to the back of the house to make sure that, if there was a back exit, they would be able to cover it. Six of the knights ran for the front door, one of them brandishing a mace, and they all stood there waiting for their next orders.

Two peasants were walking the streets in the rain, clad in poorly designed cloaks that did nothing to keep their clothes underneath from getting wet. They saw the movement of the knights.

"Wait! Go back! Go back! Knights of the Scarletia Royal Guard!" one of them whispered desperately. "Let's get out of here!"

Collin watched the two men leave as quickly as possible, but they were no one to be concerned about. He turned his attention back to the house of the Balias family, and crossed the street. When he reached the other side, he stood on the pavement in front of the house.

One of the knights near the door, Serian Avenar, was holding a kerosene lamp. He turned towards Collin. "Everyone is in position, sir."

Collin watched the knights at the door. Palind Emarias held the mace as he stood nearest the front door. Alryn and Sorial stood closest to him. Dereas and Belian stood a little further back. Reland, one of the younger knights in the Scarletia Royal Guard, watched them all from a short distance away. Serian walked over to him, holding on to the kerosene lamp.

"Proceed," ordered Collin.

"Yes, sir." Gripping the handle of his mace and taking a deep breath, Palind applied the first swing against the door handle, making a terrible sound that reverberated throughout the entire house.

Dellen sat up in bed with a start.

Zima opened her eyes immediately, and turned towards Dellen. "What was that?"

"The Royal Guard," whispered Dellen.

Zima gasped. "No!"

Dellen pushed the blankets off him, and jumped out of bed. "Protect the children, Zima. You know what you need to do. Protect them right now!"

They heard another loud crunch of wood being broken down. Zima got up as well. As he was about to leave through the bedroom door, she managed to grab onto his arm. "No, Dellen, you can't go! I'll take the children, but you must come with us!"

Dellen held Zima firmly by her upper arms. "Zima, you have to go! You have to protect our children! Go!"

The desperation in Dellen's voice frightened Zima as he forced her out of the bedroom and toward the children's room. When Zima opened their door, Jaren and Tyrel were already awake, fear etched into their faces. They heard another loud sound.

"Mother, what's going on?!" Tyrel asked, his voice quivering.

Zima clenched her teeth, trying hard to push away her own fear while in front of her sons. "We have to go now! They're here!"

"The knights." Jaren understood right away. He jumped out of his bed, grabbing the startled Tyrel out of his.

"What are you doing?!" cried out Tyrel.

"Shut up! We have to go!" exclaimed Jaren. "Mother, let's go! Father!"

Zima turned towards the doorway, where Dellen was standing. Another loud sound reverberated throughout the house. She quickly ran to him, and they kissed.

"You know I love you, Zima," he whispered.

Zima's eyes began to tear slightly. "I love you, too, Dellen...."

"Now, go. Right now! Our first priority... is to make

sure Jaren and Tyrel are safe."

Zima nodded. "Okay...."

Dellen closed the bedroom door.

"Father!" cried out Tyrel.

Zima pushed both Jaren and Tyrel towards a closet. "Come on, we have to go right now. Don't worry about your father. He'll join us...." A lump was caught in her throat, but she forced herself to swallow. "He'll join us later. Now, go!"

Inside the closet, in the darkness, Jaren fumbled around, and found what he was looking for: a narrow gap between the floorboards. Placing his fingers in the gap, he pulled on the floorboards, and a trapdoor swung upwards, revealing a space underneath the floor that Dellen had built, which would take them under the house and to an ancient network of tunnels that would lead them to safety.

Outside, Collin was growing impatient as he took several steps towards the knights at the door. "Come on, Palind. Hurry with that mace!"

"Yes, sir. I'm going as fast as I can," said Palind.

Alryn shook his head. "Something's wrong, Sir Collin. The mace should have smashed the door by now."

Dereas examined the door for a moment, pushing on it. "I believe the door is barricaded from the inside, sir."

"Agreed. We need more power to force it open," said Sorial.

"Very well, then. Sorial, Alryn, when Palind strikes with the mace, you two try to kick the door down," ordered Collin.

Sorial and Alryn acknowledged the order in unison. "Yes, sir."

Now, with each sound of the mace striking the barricaded door, there were other sounds, not as loud as the first, that followed it as the knights tried to kick the door down. Dellen could hear these sounds as he hid around a corner. He looked back at the bedroom door that led to the room of his children, hoping that his family was making their escape without any difficulty. He watched the front door from around the corner. The entire door shook each time it was struck. As was standard at night, the thick wooden barricade was in place across the door, but it shook violently, and the steel braces that held it in place were starting to give way.

Dellen reached to the side, his hand finding the shape of his scabbard in the darkness. He thought about going back into the room where Zima was helping Tyrel and Jaren escape through the trapdoor. However, by staying out here, he would be able to buy them some time.

"For Melodice... for my family."

Dellen held his scabbard in front of him, holding on to the hilt of his short sword. He felt his heart pounding in his chest, and his breathing became shallow in anticipation. Beads of sweat ran down his back.

Zima gave a small kerosene lamp and a set of matches to Jaren, her hands trembling slightly. "Take this with you. Be very, very careful with it."

Jaren was already under the floor as he reached up to take the lamp and the matches, and then set them down. He looked down at Tyrel, who was already beside him in the dark tunnel underneath the house. Tyrel was terrified.

He reached up for his mother. "Come on, Mother. I'll help you get down here."

"You take your brother and go. Right now!" ordered Zima.

Jaren's eyes widened. "Mother?"

Zima closed the trapdoor, and prevented it from opening by turning a piece of wood that was screwed into the floorboard beside it.

Jaren was alarmed. He tried to push the trapdoor open. "Mother!"

"Get out of here now!" Zima exclaimed.

"What...? Oh no...."

"Mother!" exclaimed Tyrel.

Jaren could feel his tears about to come down. Fear gripped his entire body as he came to a sudden realization. It was not just the knights who were pounding the door of his family's home that frightened him. His mother and father have both decided to stay behind. He wanted to pound on the trapdoor. But he remembered the words of his parents from a long time ago. They told him that if this time ever came, he would run away with his brother as fast as he could, and then disappear. Jaren shook his head, and tears came down.

"Jaren..." whispered Tyrel. Tears came down his cheeks as well.

No, I have to protect you. I've made a promise to Mother and Father, thought Jaren. *I have to fulfill that promise, don't I?*

Holding the lamp with one hand, Jaren wiped his tears away with the other. He reached up, and locked the trapdoor from the underside using the same locking mechanism that was on the other side, where Zima was. This way, it could not be opened from above either. He put the box of matches in the breast pocket of his nightshirt.

"Come on, Tyrel. Let's go. We've got to get out of here."

"But what about Mother and Father?" he exclaimed.

"We have to go, Tyrel! Shut up! Go that way, down the tunnel ahead of you! Go! I'm right behind you!"

Tyrel, more frightened than he'd ever felt in his life, shut his eyes, and gritted his teeth. As soon as he opened them again, he began to crawl down the long tunnel underneath his house, the long tunnel that led into the darkness, but would eventually take them outside.

Jaren was right behind him. "That's it, Tyrel. I'm proud of you. Keep going," he said, holding the kerosene lamp with one hand and easing his body forward with the other. He had to be careful with the lamp so that its full tank of kerosene would not spill. If it did, there was a possibility that he and his younger brother would be burned alive. In this tunnel, escape would be impossible.

Zima closed the closet door, then stood behind the door to the hallway, waiting. She heard another loud sound, followed by softer ones, as the knights continued to try to break down the barricaded entrance.

Out in the hallway, Dellen's eyes went wide as he saw one of the steel braces almost completely give way. He slowly drew out his sword from its scabbard, his grip tightened around its hilt.

"Ah, shit. Almost there." Almost breathless from physical exertion, sweat dripping down from his forehead, Palind readied himself for another strike with his heavy mace.

"Keep at it, Palind," said Sorial.

Collin stepped over to Belian, and put a hand on his shoulder. He also motioned towards Dereas. "Dereas, Belian, I need both of you to draw your swords. As soon as the door comes down, both of you will storm in. It'll be dark in there, so be careful."

"Yes, sir," they replied.

Collin pointed at Serian and Alryn. "Alryn, Serian, both of you will storm in right after Dereas and Belian. Alryn, get your crossbow ready just in case. Serian, you hold that lamp to brighten the interior, but stay behind Alryn. Draw your sword, just in case you're attacked."

"Yes, sir," they replied in unison.

Collin turned next to Reland. "I need you to watch their backs. Stay behind them as they enter the house."

"Yes, sir," acknowledged Reland, drawing out his long sword as well.

Palind smashed the door one more time as hard as he could with his mace, letting out a loud grunt. The barricade behind the door finally gave way.

"Go!" ordered Collin.

Dereas and Belian burst in through the broken door, but they could not see anything.

However, Dellen's eyes were already adjusted to the darkness. He saw their dark figures. He assumed where the neck of one of the knights was, and jumped out of the corner.

Belian suddenly felt cold steel pushing itself down into the interior of his chest through the side of his neck. His eyes went wide, and his grip on his long sword loosened. His sword clattered against the floorboards as he struggled to reach for the blade that had been plunged through him, but he felt his life leaving him. His entire body trembled from his death throes, and then fell.

Dereas saw Belian's dark figure collapse, and was

alarmed. "Belian!"

Alryn quickly entered the room with his crossbow, and right behind him was Serian with his long sword and the kerosene lamp. The room brightened. As soon as Alryn saw Dellen standing in the room with a bloodstained short sword and Belian lying motionless on the floor, he fired his crossbow.

The steel tip of the quarrel embedded itself into Dellen's thigh. Pain twisted his face as he screamed.

"Get down!" Dereas punched him in the face with his gauntlet.

Dellen fell backwards against the wall dazed, dropping his short sword on the floor.

Zima gasped with fear when she heard Dellen scream. "No, Dellen...."

Jaren and Tyrel heard their father's scream. It sounded far away from where they were. Jaren could see Tyrel's fear, and hoped desperately that he was not about to scream.

"Tyrel... please... don't..." whispered Jaren.

"I'm not... I'm not going to scream." Tyrel closed his eyes, and let out a soft sob as tears came down.

Jaren wanted to cry as well, but he had to remain strong at this moment. There would be time to cry later. "Come on, let's keep going."

Tyrel continued crawling through the dark tunnel with Jaren behind him.

* * *

Reland lit up a couple more kerosene lamps in the living room, providing plenty of light.

Dellen grimaced in pain as Sorial and Dereas forced him to kneel down in the middle of the living room. The crossbow quarrel was still embedded in his leg, and the tip scraped against this thighbone, causing excruciating pain. His hands were bound tightly behind his back, and his resistance only caused further discomfort as the rope scraped his wrists.

Collin stood in front of him, removing his wet helmet,

and giving it to Serian. "Sir Dellen Balias, I presume?"

Dellen looked up at Collin's face, intent on remembering every detail, if he survived this. He immediately recognized him. It was the Supreme Captain of the Scarletia Royal Guard, the one who led the knights in the attack against the group of peasant workers who protested outside the castle gates. "Yes. Sir Collin Gagnier, I presume?"

Collin nodded slightly. "That's correct. Good of you to recognize me."

Zima was still in the bedroom, quivering in fear. She could not hear Dellen's voice anymore, but she did hear the voices of the knights. In addition to their voices, she could also hear the rapid beating of her heart and her shallow breathing. She felt around for the scabbard that was hidden underneath Jaren's bed. When she found it, she gripped it hard with both trembling hands.

"For our children... for Melodice."

She carefully drew out the short sword from the scabbard, then slowly and quietly, she made her way to the door, which was slightly ajar. She opened it just enough so that she could slip through it. Fortunately, the door was not within the view of the knights, as it was farther down the hallway from the living room. Her footsteps were soft as she moved to the side of the hallway and behind a corner. The rain tapping on the rooftop and on the windows masked the sound of her approach. She looked around the corner, and saw Dellen kneeling down on the floor, surrounded by knights.

"As you might have already noticed, we know who you are," said the Supreme Captain. "We know the identities of the members of your family. Dellen Balias, age forty. Married to Zima Balias, age thirty-eight. Her maiden name was Falcrest. You were married in 3551. You have two children, Tyrel, age ten, and Jaren, age fourteen."

Dellen glared at Collin as he spoke the names of his family.

"I need a favour from you, Sir Dellen."

Dellen responded with a hostile tone. "What would that be?"

"As you know, peasants have ceased work throughout the city. They started a revolt, and have been marching around the city protesting. You will tell me the names and the whereabouts of the people who are responsible for this revolt."

Dellen gritted his teeth. "Go to hell, bastard!"

Palind, standing between Reland and Dereas, removed his helmet, feeling very uncomfortable due to the rainwater that seeped into it. He was also tired from pounding on the front door with the mace, and was trying to cool off. Sweat and rainwater made his hair stick to his scalp.

Zima held her short sword with both hands. She glared at the soldier who had removed his helmet and was closest to her. She came out of the shadows of the hallway, and screamed out a battle cry.

Collin raised his head, alarmed. The other knights turned, but it was too late for Palind.

Zima, swinging her short sword downwards as hard as she could, embedded the blade into the back of his head.

Reland and Dereas heard the crunch of broken skull, and felt splatters of blood on the sides of their faces. Palind's hold on his helmet loosened. It made a loud sound as it struck the floorboards. His body collapsed onto the floor.

Dellen looked in the direction of the sudden commotion. "No, Zima! Run away!"

Although Zima managed to kill Palind using the element of surprise, she was no fighter. Reland grabbed the sword out of her hands, and Dereas punched her in the abdomen. She doubled over, and fell to the floor on all fours.

Collin glared at his knights. "Must I give orders for everything? Alryn, Sorial, search the rest of the house! They have two children! This should have been done already! Find them!"

"Yes, sir!" said Alryn.

"No!" exclaimed Dellen.

Alryn and Sorial drew out their long swords, and went further into the house to check every single room.

Collin grabbed Dellen by the neck with his gauntlet,

and reached down for the quarrel that was embedded in his thigh. Collin twisted the quarrel, and Dellen screamed in agony.

Hearing her husband's painful scream, Zima tried to look up. "Dellen!"

"Shut up!" ordered Dereas.

Serian angrily slammed his fist against a wall. "This is no ordinary civilian family, Sir Collin! They took out Belian and Palind!"

"I'm aware of that," said Collin, his voice low but his tone angry. "And that's why...."

Collin gave a hard twist to the quarrel in Dellen's thigh, moving it forcibly in a circular motion several times, tearing flesh.

Dellen screamed so loud that the neighbours could definitely hear him. But there was no way any of them could help, as the house was surrounded by knights on all sides.

"Once again, I'm asking you for a favour, and it'll be in your best interest to honour it, Sir Dellen. You will tell me who is responsible for this revolt, and then you will tell me their whereabouts. This peasant revolt is far too large and far too organized to be a random event. This revolt was put together by leaders with plenty of resources at their disposal. Who are the leaders?!"

Dellen glared at Collin with rage despite the pain. "I am, you son of a bitch! I'm the leader of this revolt!"

"What..." whispered Reland, surprised. The other knights who heard were in shock as well.

However, Collin held a completely calm exterior as he let go of the quarrel and Dellen's neck. He straightened up, standing in front of Dellen. "Who else is responsible? Who else is leading this revolt?"

"No one. I'm the only one who's leading this revolt," said Dellen, forcing his words through despite the pain he felt. His breathing was laboured. He looked up at Collin, and formed his lips into a mocking smile. "Congratulations, Sir Collin. You've found the leader, the instigator, the organizer of the revolt of the peasant workers."

Collin stared at him, expressionless.

"What? You don't believe I can do it? I've stopped food and supplies from reaching your precious Nobility within the castle, haven't I? My plan is working perfectly."

"I do believe you, Sir Dellen." Collin grabbed him by the neck again, and leaned forward. "I believe you're telling me the truth when you say you're the leader of this revolt. However...." He reached down to grab the quarrel again, and twisted it even harder than before.

Dellen screamed.

"Stop it!" shouted Zima.

Collin clenched his teeth, putting his face right in front of Dellen's. "You're not the only leader of this revolt, Sir Dellen! There's someone else! Tell me who else leads this revolt!"

"No one! Just me!" yelled Dellen.

"I don't believe you!"

"Believe me! I'm not lying! Why do you think there's more than one?!"

What I want you to tell me is that Princess Mika Silveraine is involved in this revolt of the peasant workers! I want you to confirm it! From what I have seen so far, I know she's involved in this!

The horrified Zima pleaded to the Supreme Captain. "Please, stop it!"

"How do I know you're not lying to me?!" shouted Collin, ignoring Zima. "You had better tell me names and places very soon because I am running out of patience!"

Collin stopped twisting the quarrel, and let go of Dellen. He straightened up, and turned to the knights. After a moment, Alryn and Sorial returned.

"Did you find the children?" asked the Supreme Captain.

Sorial shook his head. "No, sir. We looked in every room and every closet. There is no sign of them."

"How can that be? This house is surrounded on all sides. They couldn't have escaped!" Collin looked down at Dellen. "Unless, of course, they were not here to begin with tonight. Is that the case, Sir Dellen?"

Dellen said nothing.

Zima stared at the floorboards, desperately hoping the knights would not discover the trapdoor in the children's bedroom. For now, however, it looked like the knights had already stopped looking for their children.

Collin turned to Dereas and Reland, who were restraining Zima. "Dereas, Reland, bring her here. Let husband and wife kneel together."

Dereas and Reland dragged Zima on her knees along the floor, scraping her skin. She tried to stand, but they pulled on her too fast. They forced her to kneel beside Dellen, and bound her hands behind her back with the same rope. She grimaced as the rope cut into her skin.

Collin grabbed a chair from the kitchen, and set it down in front of Dellen and Zima. Sitting down on the chair, he paused for a moment to regain his composure. "Let me tell you a little about my life, Sir Dellen, Miss Zima."

Dellen and Zima looked on, wondering what he was up to.

"I'm a single man. I don't have a female partner, although sometimes I wish I did. Do you know why?"

The tension in the air kept them silent.

"The reason why I don't have a female partner is because of my profession. I am a knight of high rank within the Scarletia Royal Guard and the Royal Army of Melodice. I have just recently gained the rank of Supreme Captain. As a knight, my hands are stained with blood. I have killed many for various reasons. I have terminated the lives of people out of self-defence. I have terminated lives while administering justice. I've also been directly ordered by the Royal Family to take people's lives. I don't want to have to explain to a female partner why I killed someone. After a while, if you were in my position, you'd grow weary of telling the same story, the same reason. You'd grow tired of having to explain why you've had to terminate the life of someone's father, someone's mother, someone's son or daughter. Eventually, it eats away at your heart."

Other knights remained quiet as they listened to their commanding officer.

Serian, however, glared at Dellen and Zima from behind the other knights. He clenched his fists so hard that they shook.

"There is another reason why I don't have a female partner. My profession is filled with danger. If I had a wife and child, Sir Dellen, I would love them with all my heart. After a hard day, protecting the nation from its enemies, I would come home to them. I would enjoy their love, and they would enjoy mine, as families do. However, there's the possibility that they would face danger at some point in their lives because of my profession. I'm not prepared to risk their lives, and I don't wish to face the possibility of losing them. That is not something I've prepared myself for. My enemies might learn of them, and they would be taken away from me. So it would be best to avoid the possibility of losing them by not having them in my life in the first place."

His story felt condescending to Dellen and Zima as they both glared at him.

"It would appear that you, Sir Dellen, are in the situation that I described in the latter part of my story." Collin leaned towards him, his voice more gentle as he appeared somewhat more sympathetic. "As you said, you are the leader of this revolt. That must mean you're the leader of a major rebel group. No small rebel group could have organized such a large-scale revolt. Only a large one could have, one with many resources at its disposal. Despite your position, you still have a wife and two children. It's unfortunate. But I suppose, in your case, you may not have anticipated becoming the leader of rebels and unruly peasants. You were already married and with children, weren't you?"

Dellen was tempted to answer, but he kept his mouth closed. He felt the sickly warmth of the Supreme Captain's breath as he leaned even closer towards them, his face and voice dangerously calm as he spoke.

"I do know the names of your children, Sir Dellen, Miss Zima. I don't want to have to search for them, and deal them a harsh punishment. Punishing children is not one of the duties I take pride in. Dealing punishment to those who are innocent, to those who have done nothing wrong, to those who have nothing to do with revolts and rebellions... I take no pleasure in such horrendous acts. It's the most difficult part of my profession. In fact, I hate it more than anything in this entire world."

Dellen glared into Collin's eyes so hard he wished he could set him on fire just by looking. He let out an angry breath.

Behind the other knights, Serian faced the wall, his forehead resting on his arm that was pressed up against the wall. He was breathing hard.

Reland heard him. "Serian, are you all right?"

"After everything they've done... killing our own Belian and Palind, I want to kill these peasant bastards so badly... in the cruelest way possible." Serian spoke softly but angrily. No one else heard him except Reland.

Reland stared at Serian for a while, wondering what was going through his mind. He turned back to Collin, who continued speaking to Dellen and Zima.

"But if I have to do such unbearable things, Sir Dellen," continued Collin, "if doing such hateful things means following the orders of the King and gaining his favour... then I will continue to do them. If ordered by the King, I will go hunt down entire families, and I will kill parents and children and elderly. If it means gaining the favour of the King, then I will do these things. At the end of the day, I will return home, and mourn the lives of the people I had to kill, as ordered by the King. Such is my duty, but I will still mourn."

"You talk much, but say nothing, Sir Collin," said Dellen, his tone full of fury, and his eyes full of hatred for this man who was the Supreme Captain.

Zima turned to him with tears in her eyes.

Collin stared back at Dellen, speechless, but with no facial expression as he kept his emotions in check.

"You insult me and my wife and my children with these hateful words. You, who rampage through the city streets of Scarletia, terminating the lives of innocent men, women, and children, are telling me that you're being forced to do evil things, but at the end of the day, you mourn their deaths? You're a fool."

Collin narrowed his eyes slightly, the only outward hint of his pride as the highest-ranking noble knight in the entire nation being tarnished.

Dellen chuckled with mockery and sarcasm, and then continued. "A man who follows the orders given to him by an evil man is just as evil as the one who gave him those orders. In the end, Sir Collin, you're just a small man without honour, one who denies his own free will, and follows the orders of a tyrant, believing that it somehow makes him greater."

Collin exchanged hostile glares with Dellen for a long moment. He remembered the words of the former Supreme Captain, Sir Terren Rinaldia, who told him that, while he had demonstrated most of the qualities of a great leader as a Supreme Commander, the one and only thing he still needed to work on was to stop holding back on what he truly thought and felt. Sir Terren had told him as well that he had his own opinions, just like everyone else.

Tense silence filled the room. Every knight heard Dellen's words. Serian looked up, glaring angrily at Dellen. Alryn, Dereas, Sorial, and Reland stole glances at each other, thinking about Dellen's words.

Collin stood up from his chair, giving Dellen a dismissive look. He slowly walked around them. From behind, he stared into the back of Dellen's head, trying hard to contain his fury. His eyes shifted to Zima. His gloved hands suddenly went around her neck.

Zima, startled, felt panic as her throat was sealed. She struggled to breathe as her eyes widened.

Dellen was alarmed as he watched Collin strangling his wife. "No! Sir Collin! Stop!"

"Tell me who else leads the revolt, Sir Dellen," said Collin, his voice unusually calm.

Alryn, Dereas, Sorial, and Reland were surprised as they watched Collin strangling Zima.

Serian stepped forward, and stood between Alryn and Dereas, deadly fury and bloodlust in his eyes. "That's right. Kill that bitch."

The other knights heard his whisper, and stared at him for a moment.

Dellen panicked inside. *It's over isn't it? He's not buying it! I'm telling him that I'm the only leader, but he's not buying it!*

"I think she's about to pass out, Sir Dellen," said Collin.

"Stop!" Dellen stared with great horror at his beloved wife, as her life was slowly being snuffed out by the Supreme Captain of the Scarletia Royal Guard. Her eyes began to close. "Adrel Savarian!"

Collin stopped, immediately letting go of Zima, who slumped forward, and started coughing as she drew in quick breaths.

Dellen was trembling as his head went down, staring with eyes wide open at the floorboards. Tears started to build up and fell.

After a moment, Zima looked to the side, and saw his tears. She began to cry as well as she cast her eyes down.

Dellen was broken inside, his emotions torn to shreds, his pride as a leader trampled to nothing. "I'm the leader of the rebel group... called the Hope of Scarletia. Adrel Savarian... is the leader of the rebel group called... the Scarletia Liberation. He lives on... Terestia 1289. Together, he and I conspired... to join forces and organize the revolt of the peasant workers." He spoke softly, his words occasionally interrupted by sobs.

Zima stared with frightened disbelief at what her husband had just done.

Dellen looked up at Collin, tears streaming down his face. "We're the leaders of this revolt! There's no one else! I swear it!"

Collin stared down at Dellen with pity. *He didn't mention anything about the Princess. He has strength of character, but I nearly killed his wife just now. I have broken this man down. Does this mean he truly knows nothing about the Princess? Is it true that the only leaders of this revolt are Sir Dellen and the man he mentioned, Adrel Savarian? Something doesn't quite add up here. I absolutely know the Princess is involved in this... but how is she involved?*

Dellen turned towards his wife. "Zima... are you all right?"

Zima nodded. "I'm fine...." But soon, she shook her head at him, disapproving of his revealing of information that should not have been shared. Though she understood why he had done it, she still felt extreme disappointment.

Collin slowly went back to the chair he had put in front of them. "Thank you for your cooperation, Sir Dellen."

When Dellen and Zima glanced up at him, they saw something in his expression that surprised them. If Dellen did not know any better, he could have sworn he saw regret in the eyes of the Supreme Captain. Dellen stared at him, wondering what was going to happen next.

"I truly am thankful. I believe what you have told me. However...." Collin reached for his belt, and slowly drew out a long knife.

Dellen and Zima stared at the blade, and then at Collin, their eyes wide with shock.

Collin held the knife in front of them, turning it over a couple of times, the bright glare of the kerosene lamp nearby reflecting off its silver blade. "Orders are orders. I hope you will forgive me... in the afterlife."

Dellen glared at Collin, willing death to come to him someday for everything he had done so far and what he was about to do. Lightning flashed outside, causing the room to brighten for a moment. Thunder roared through the air like a wild beast, as if the storm outside felt his anger.

"Curse you, you fucking noble!"

* * *

The White Princess was kneeling down on a layer of several blankets that had been laid out in one of the corners of the basement of Ethereal Daydreams. Clad in yet another beautiful white dress, her bare legs were folded back on either side of her as she watched a pot of soup that had been brought to her and her companions who sat nearby. Steam slowly drifted upwards from the inside of the pot. Her feet bare, her white shoes were beside her.

"What kind of soup is it?" asked Mika.

Dayna, Elsia, Galien, and Peter all knelt down on the blankets with her, clad in ordinary long-sleeved dress shirts, trousers, and high boots, along with capes over their shirts. Their scabbards were on the floor beside them, within easy reach if needed.

Dayna used a large ladle to pour a bowl of soup, and then offered the soup to Mika. "It's some kind of chicken and beef soup. The owner is always good enough to provide us with some. He's really kind. Here you go, My Lady."

"Be careful. It's hot," said Elsia.

Mika picked up a thick cloth to protect her hand from the heat of the bowl as she accepted it. "Thank you, Miss Dayna."

"You're welcome." Dayna proceeded with pouring the others their own bowls of soup as well.

Mika took a soup spoon, and inhaled the smooth fragrance. "It smells so good. Far better than the strange concoction that Sir Adrel provided me with yesterday morning."

"What concoction?" Galien asked, as he accepted the next bowl.

Peter shook his head. "I heard the story from Feldia. Trust me, Galien. You don't want to know."

Galien was taken aback, even more curious. "Really, now?"

Mika blew at the soup gently to cool it down before taking a sip. When she tried it, her eyes lit up with contentment. "Oh my, it's good!"

Dayna smiled. "I'm glad you like it, Princess."

Eventually, everyone was given their soup, and ate heartily. As the Princess ate, the others watched her.

Mika consumed her soup with much enjoyment. After a moment, she noticed them all staring at her with confusion and amazement. However, she was not sure how to interpret their expressions, and began to blush. "Um... I'm sorry... I suppose I'm not eating like a proper lady?"

Elsia quickly waved her hand. "No, no, it's not that, Princess."

Peter smiled with amusement. "Princess, I think

everyone's just amazed because this is the first time we've seen you eat our food."

Galien chuckled. "Yeah, that's it. Since you've been out here in the city for days now, I'm sure you've eaten the food of peasants, but this is the first time we've seen you do it."

Mika smiled while her cheeks were still red from her blush.

Dayna gently patted Mika's shoulder. "I hope you're not offended or anything. We're just not used to seeing a Royal eating the food of peasants. From our experience, Royals and nobles would rather eat their own food, and wouldn't have anything to do with ours."

"This tastes just like some of the soups I've been served at the castle. It tastes exactly the same. If there is a difference... I haven't noticed it," said Mika.

Elsia responded with a laugh. "Well, that figures! I've always suspected there wasn't anything special about noble food."

"Yeah, it's the same thing," said Peter.

"But one thing that's even more surprising is..." said Galien, but he stopped before continuing, hoping his next words wouldn't be considered rude by the young Princess.

"What is it, Sir Galien?" asked Mika.

"Well... it's that you're eating with us, My Lady."

They all fell silent as they gazed over at Mika, who paused for a moment. This truly was the first time she was eating with them. Mika smiled sweetly, and regarded them with a gentle and kind expression. "This may be the first time I'm eating breakfast with you, but hopefully not the last. I am truly enjoying the food, as well as your company. Thank you for eating breakfast with me. I'm glad that, even though I'm the Princess, you'll still share breakfast with me, and speak to me like this. It warms my heart."

All of them smiled as well.

"We're glad you're here with us, Princess Mika," said Dayna.

Mika nodded, and continued with her soup. "Whoever made this soup has great skill in the art of cooking."

"Oh, absolutely." Galien downed his bowl of soup.

The sounds of commotion emanated from the door that led up to the outside. As everyone turned their attention to the door, Dayna and Peter put their hands down on their scabbards just in case.

The door opened, revealing one of their companions. Eduard closed the door behind him, and came rushing down the steps. "Princess Mika!"

Mika put her bowl down, and stood up. Everyone did the same.

"What's the matter, Eduard?" asked Galien.

Eduard ran to Mika and the others, his face ashen. "Thank goodness I found you all here! Thank the Matriarch I found you, Princess! It's a tragedy! Something terrible has happened! The most awful thing I've ever…."

Mika stared into Eduard's face. He was in complete shock. His facial expression immediately sent chills down her back.

"What's going on, Eduard?" said Dayna.

Eduard leaned against the wall, and closed his eyes. "Please… Princess… all of you… something tragic."

Mika stepped forward, putting her hands on his arms. "Sir Eduard…."

Eduard glanced down at her as tears came down his cheeks. He covered his face to hide them as they fell, and then he shook his head, as if to shake away some kind of terrible image that was now imprinted within his mind. But no matter how hard he tried to push that image away, no matter how hard he tried to shake it from his mind, it was still there.

Mika could feel his body trembling. He had seen something. Whatever it was, it devastated this large man, and reduced him to tears. "Sir Eduard, please take us there," she said, her voice gentle and soft.

Eduard hesitated, putting his hands down. "But… Princess, maybe it's better if you stayed here. The others can come…."

Mika thought his suggestion was odd. "Why?"

"Please… Princess Mika…."

The expression on his face frightened Mika, but she tried to push away that fear. There was something not quite right about it. The part of her that was still a child was telling her that perhaps she should heed his suggestion and stay while the others go, but another part of her, the part of her that was the Princess of Melodice, told her that she should go with them. She decided to listen to the more mature part of her. "I'll go with the others," she said, ensuring her voice carried.

Eduard was shocked by this. "But...."

"You heard the Princess." Peter turned to the others. "Come on, everyone. Let's get ready."

The others prepared themselves. Unfortunately, their soup would have to wait for them as Dayna placed it on the bar. Mika's companions put on cloaks with large hoods over their capes. They attached their scabbards to their belts. Mika put on her shoes, and then draped her white cloak over her shoulders, ensuring that the Princess Gem was hidden underneath it. Before leaving the basement, she pulled her large hood over her head. They followed Eduard out of the basement to cervids that were waiting in the alleyway. They passed by their confused sentries, who must have sensed that something was not quite right, but said nothing.

Mika got on the cervid that belonged to Elsia, seated behind. Her companions all glanced at her. She felt a sense of dread. Something was not right.

"Let's go," ordered the Princess, her voice subdued.

The cervids galloped down the alleyway. Water in puddles splashed as the cervid hooves rode over them. The rain had stopped earlier this morning just before sunrise, but the clouds still covered the sky. Because the sun was blocked out, it was darker than it should be. She put her arms around Elsia tighter as they rode into the city streets. Eduard led the way.

What's going on? Why do I have this feeling of impending doom?

A few more minutes passed as they galloped down the city streets. Eventually, they came upon a large intersection where there was a city square. Mika saw the Eldoria Watchtower, which was close by. She looked ahead of her, peering around Elsia, and saw a large crowd of people gathered at the square. As Mika passed by some of the people in the crowd, she saw that some of them were crying while others were wailing with grief. Others stood motionless, their faces covered with deep shock. Mika's companions urged their cervids to a complete stop, and began to dismount.

Mika heard a retching sound, and quickly turned. She witnessed a young man vomiting, fear etched into his face. Mika remembered doing the same after the attack of the peasant mob, an event that felt like such a long time ago. At the time, she had been surrounded by dead bodies, and involuntarily discarded her breakfast because of it.

He saw something... something terrible... something... ghastly.

"What the hell is going on?" whispered Peter.

Elsia voiced her discomfort. "I don't like the looks of this."

Some people ran away from the square, one of them brushing past Mika, nearly knocking her over. They paid no attention to her as they ran. Mika could see that they wanted to get away as quickly as they could.

"Stop looking! Stop looking!" a peasant shouted.

"You don't have to see this! Get out of here!" shouted another peasant. They were ordering younger people to move along.

But people continued to look on. Mika drew back her hood, and opened her cloak, revealing the Princess Gem. She exchanged worried glances with her companions. She went over to Eduard, and put her hand on his arm gently to comfort him. He seemed to be frozen in place. "Sir Eduard?"

"Please, Princess... you don't need to see this," he whispered.

"What's going on, Eduard?" demanded Peter, grabbing him by his other arm.

People around them started to notice that the Princess

was among them. However, they did not react with shock. Mika saw the horror on their faces... but she also noticed that some of them held expressions of concern.

Are they concerned... for me? Mika found that to be odd, and at the same time, strangely worrisome. "I'm going on ahead." She began to walk through the crowd towards the city square. As the peasants noticed her, they began to make way for her.

"Princess, wait for us." Dayna and the others followed her.

Eduard was alarmed. "No... please don't... Princess...."

Peter stayed behind with Eduard, his arm around his shoulder.

An elderly man saw Princess Mika and her companions making their way through the crowd. "Oh... Princess Mika...."

Mika noticed him right away. "Yes, sir?"

The elderly man was deeply worried. "I don't think... you should continue... for your own good, My Lady. Please, I beg of you not to continue."

Another man, middle-aged, stood nearby. "He's right, Princess. It might be best if you didn't look."

Fear was creeping up on Mika, but she tried to push it away. She steeled herself for something unknown as she continued to make her way through the crowd.

One of the men in the crowd grabbed her by the upper arm. "Princess!"

Mika gasped, startled, her eyes widened.

Galien pressed a clip that loosened his short sword from his scabbard, exposing part of the blade, and glared at the man. He spoke with a hint of warning in his voice. "Please keep your hands to yourself, sir."

The man quickly let go of the Princess, realizing what he had done. "Please forgive me! But... but I'm afraid what'll happen if you see... if you see what's up ahead."

Mika paused for a moment. Although Galien kept his glaring eyes on him, she saw that the man was genuinely concerned for her. It seemed that, for a moment, he had forgotten that she was a Princess, and instead looked at her as a child. She figured that was probably the reason why he grabbed her just now.

The Princess gently touched his arm. "I must see. Whatever this is, I have to see it."

The man cast his eyes down with great sadness. "Yes, My Lady...."

Mika continued on ahead. Elsia, Dayna, and Galien were not far behind her. After another moment, Mika managed to make it through the crowd. She took a few steps out of the crowd, her eyes downcast. As soon as she looked up ahead of her, she froze.

In the middle of the square, seven headless bodies were arranged around seven stakes, which had been hammered into the soil. More frightening than that, Mika saw that three of the seven bodies were small. They were definitely children. She stared at the stakes and at the heads that were mounted on top of them. She recognized three of them immediately.

Sir Dellen? Miss Zima? Sir Adrel?

The other four bodies were that of a woman she had not met before and three children. Mika suddenly remembered Adrel's words yesterday morning. He mentioned he was married and that he had three daughters, ages three, six, and nine. Mika stared at the woman's face. She had light-blonde hair that was smooth and straight, just like hers. Her hair, which Mika remembered was supposed to reach past her waist, according to Adrel, had been cut by the same blade that detached her head from her body. Her face had very soft and gentle features, even in death. Mika remembered her name.

Miss Vera?

Mika turned her gaze to the bodies of the three children and their heads whose eyes stared back at her from the stakes, their frozen expressions completely blank. They were Adrel's three little girls. Judging by their sizes, they were of the right ages. Each girl also had smooth and straight light-blonde hair, just like their mother and just like Mika. Their faces also held soft and gentle features. Mika remembered telling Adrel that she wanted to meet them someday... and Adrel told her that they would love to. She remembered their names.

Miss Harsia? Miss Emelia? Miss Anira?

Behind her, Elsia, Dayna, and Galien stared with cold shock, just like Mika. Galien felt sickness in his stomach as he looked away, and fell to the ground on his knees. His hand covered his mouth, but it did nothing to stop the regurgitation of this morning's breakfast.

Dayna looked sideways, and saw Feldia on her knees, staring at the severed heads of their leaders and their families, as tears streamed down her cheeks. "Feldia!" she cried out.

Feldia looked in Dayna's direction, and then saw Mika.

Laren was nearby as well. He was alarmed when he realized that their young Princess had just witnessed the most awful thing that they themselves have ever seen. Laren turned to his other companions nearby, Marik and Tavien, as he clenched his teeth. "Marik! Tavien! Everyone! Cover their bodies! Cover their heads! Don't let anyone see them anymore!" he ordered, hastily removing his cloak.

"Princess!" Feldia got up, and rushed over to Mika as fast as she could. She dropped down to her knees in front of Mika, obstructing her view.

At the same time, behind her, Laren, as well as Marik and Tavien, covered the bodies and their heads with their cloaks. Elsia followed suit, throwing her cloak over to Laren. Dayna did the same. Eventually, the sickening sight was completely covered.

Mika could no longer see them, but she stared through Feldia.

"Princess..." Feldia whispered, as tears filled her eyes. She wanted to take hold of the little Princess. She wanted to take the young girl into her arms, and embrace her to comfort her. She began to reach out to her.

But Mika's knees felt weak, and she fell on them. She cast her eyes down at the soil in front of her, and then closed them as tears streamed down like torrents. Emotions filled her heart to overflowing. She raised her fists, and pounded them hard into the damp soil, still somewhat wet from last night's rain. She lashed at the earth, taking hard, crumbling soil into her hands, and again raising her fists in the air in emotional turmoil. Again and again, Mika pounded her fists into the ground as hard as her feeble strength could muster.

Everyone around her, Feldia, Laren, Eduard, Peter, Elsia, Dayna, Galien, Marik, Tavien, and the peasants who had gathered watched Mika... as she raised her head towards the overcast skies, her face full of despair and soaked with her tears. Completely stricken with panic, grief, horror, despair, and anger, she screamed into the sky, the high pitch of her terrified voice echoing throughout the city square and beyond.

"WHY?!"

CHAPTER 27

THE REVOLT
CONTINUES

T HE GHASTLY SIGHT WAS NO longer present in the city square. The headless bodies of the leaders of the Hope of Scarletia and the Scarletia Liberation, along with the corpses of their families, had been covered up in thick shrouds and removed. Many of the peasants who had gathered in that area still remained. Some of them still wailed in grief, while others looked on with expressions of shock, speechless and motionless.

News of the deaths of Dellen Balias and Adrel Savarian was passed on from peasant to peasant in the area. It spread like wildfire as people galloped away on cervids to tell others. Some of the nearby groups of peasant workers who continued to march around the city protesting and demanding their freedom very soon heard of the terrible news.

The knights at the patrol stations who stood their ground watched with surprise as some of the peasant groups actually started disbanding. They wondered what had happened as men and women cried out in grief. While some of the worker groups disbanded, others stopped and stood around, trying to determine what they should do next. Still others were so distraught and confused, but they decided to wait for instructions.

About one hour after the tragic discovery, Princess Mika stood in the middle of the Valderia Pathway. She stared directly in front of her at the Scarletia Royal Castle, its castle gates distant but observable. She felt numb inside, and her skin felt cold. Her eyes were red from crying. Peasants stood around to her left and right and behind her, all of them in a state of shock. The breeze tugged at the hem of her cloak and her white dress, causing her to shiver as she wrapped her arms around herself.

After all this... after everything... after what I've seen and experienced... after all the horror and suffering, if ever I set foot in that cursed castle again... it will not be as the Princess... but as a prisoner... and the manner of my return will not be peaceful.

Mika slowly walked towards a side street. Some of the peasants watched her as she passed by with her eyes downcast. Her entire body felt weak from the grief and despair she had earlier displayed. She still felt those emotions, along with many others. She could hear elderly women crying and their husbands attempting to comfort them. In the periphery of her vision, she saw men standing around, their expressions bleak. Mika continued down the side street until she came upon another group of peasants. She stopped in the middle of the street, and then looked upwards. Above her, the Eldoria Watchtower loomed as if it were a lone observer that searched in vain for the sun beyond the overcast skies.

Mika noticed her companions, scattered among the peasants—Dayna, Demias, Galien, Peter, Sorianne, Eduard, Elsia, Lauria, Marik, and Tavien—all of them with somber faces.

Laren and Feldia were seated on the steps that led up to the entrance of the watchtower. Feldia was still crying, and Laren sat beside her with one arm around her, doing his best to try to comfort her, but to no avail. As Mika watched them, she let out a sigh filled with sorrow, pain, and defeat. Emotions no young girl of eleven years should face.

The knights had found Sir Dellen and Sir Adrel, and killed them, along with their families. They must have done this during the night. No doubt, Sir Collin was with them. The knights wouldn't have been deployed to find the leaders of the rebel groups without Sir Collin, and they certainly wouldn't have been sent out into the city without the order of the King. My father... he found out, didn't he? He found out who the leaders of the Hope of Scarletia and the Scarletia Liberation were and where they lived... and sent Sir Collin and the Royal Guard to find them and... and execute them.

As Mika thought about this, something did not make sense to her.

But... how did my father about Sir Dellen and Sir Adrel? Their status as leaders of the rebel groups is a well-kept secret. And how did he find out where they lived?

She looked up at Feldia and Laren.

Miss Feldia and Sir Laren are still here. They're also leaders of the same rebel groups, and they reported directly to Sir Dellen and Sir Adrel. They're still alive. That means... the King doesn't know about them. And then... there's the Ethereal Daydreams inn. No knights barged in overnight. None of us were captured. Sir Dellen and Sir Adrel knew of this place. But no one came. That means... the King doesn't know about our meeting place either.

Feldia's words of sorrow became louder as Mika approached her and Laren. Her voice was racked by sobs. "How... how are we... supposed to continue like this? How are we supposed to?!"

Laren could not find his words as he held his eyes downcast. He himself was far too stricken with grief to offer any answers.

"Our leaders are gone. Dellen and Adrel... even their wives... and Adrel's children." Feldia saw Mika in front of her, and their somber gazes met. "How can they kill their wives and children? What the hell did they do? They haven't done anything! And Dellen and Adrel... they were our leaders. How are we supposed to do anything without them?"

Mika felt the compulsion to continue to cry, but she felt so numb now that she could not shed any more tears even if she willed herself to.

"Princess... we've seen so much death and violence. You yourself have seen so much of it lately. Our leaders are gone, the leaders of the two largest rebel groups in the city... gone! So many of the smaller groups try their very best to support us... but now there's no point! It's hopeless, My Lady. The Nobility and the Royal Family are far too strong. We're just a bunch of rebel groups. We don't have any real power, and our resources are nothing compared to theirs. In our circumstances, there's no way we can win against such overwhelming power."

Laren put a hand over his forehead, feeling defeated himself.

Mika fixed her eyes upon the cracked sidewalk, thinking about Feldia's words just now.

Feldia wrapped her arms around her knees, and put her face down, her tears falling and soaking into her trousers. "How can we win the freedom of the Peasantry like this?! It's hopeless!"

"No... that's wrong," whispered Mika.

Feldia and Laren looked up at the Princess, surprised by what she said.

Mika took a step closer to them, and met their gazes. "Miss Feldia, Sir Laren... that's wrong. Sir Dellen and Sir Adrel were heroes!" She voiced her last words loudly enough that a few people nearby heard, along with Elsia and Peter.

Laren stared at Mika blankly. "Heroes, Princess?"

"That's right! They were heroes! They wouldn't want their cause to just disappear into history as yet another failed rebellion. If we don't continue, then that's what will happen. Everything that they've done so far... will become meaningless. They loved the people of Melodice just as much as I do!"

Mika's voice quivered, but she continued to speak. Even though she felt somewhat numb from tears shed earlier, she could feel a lump in her throat. However, her voice carried a little more as she spoke.

What's coming over me? I'm nothing but a child... but I'm still a Princess. I suppose... if I have something to say... if I have something that I feel deeply in my heart... I should express it with all I have!

"I didn't know Sir Adrel and Sir Dellen for very long. I had just recently met them. But in such a short time, I grew to like them. I saw how much they loved the people of their nation. They continued to be proud of the nation of Melodice despite the circumstances. No matter how difficult it was, they did anything and everything they could to help the Peasantry. Even though they had very little power and very few resources compared to the Nobility, they still tried. I imagine that, sometimes… they probably felt overwhelmed, but it didn't matter to them because their love for all their people was far too great. They used that to fill themselves with powerful determination. They were charismatic and highly intelligent. People around them listened to them, and followed them wherever they went. They were true leaders. They did everything that was necessary to help their people."

Tears finally did come down Mika's cheeks, even when she thought she had no tears left to cry.

"As I got to know them a little better, as I watched them do the things they did as leaders of the Hope of Scarletia and the Scarletia Liberation… I was so impressed by them. They could do things that I could only dream of doing. They fought and died for the nation of Melodice, the nation they loved, for the people they loved! Everything they did, everything they fought for… it was all for their people, who are still being oppressed by the tyranny of the Nobility!"

Feldia and Laren did not take their eyes off her as they sat on the steps. They took a quick glance at the peasants and their rebel group companions who gathered around them as Mika spoke. They regarded her with surprise and admiration.

Mika turned around slightly to face the people around her. They listened to the determined words of the White Princess as she continued. "I know we're fighting against oppression. I know we're fighting for the sake of freedom. Unfortunately, while we continue to do this, sacrifices will be made, and friends will be split apart. Some of us might not even see the results of what we're trying to do. Sir

Dellen and Sir Adrel had a dream! Their dream was to at least see the people of the city of Scarletia lead a better life, free from the oppression of people who horde riches and power. We have to continue! We can't just stop now! Sir Dellen and Sir Adrel wouldn't want that! We have to continue their legacy! If we don't continue their legacy, if we don't finish what they started... then everything we've done so far will be meaningless, and the lives of the people will never change for the better!"

Laren slowly rose. "Princess... you're right."

Feldia wiped her tears away with her sleeves, stood up from the steps, and smiled. She stepped towards Mika. "Yes, My Lady, you're absolutely right. We can't just stop here and let tyranny rule our lives forever! Dellen and Adrel are dead! They fought hard for us and for our freedom! They gave their lives for our cause. We can't just stop because they're gone!"

Laren stepped towards the Princess as well. "Princess Mika, the legacy of our leaders will not die with them! Dellen and Adrel had a vision, and we are *not* going to let that fade away! We love this nation as much as they did!"

"Yes, that's right!" shouted a peasant from behind.

"We love this nation, too!" shouted another.

"Dellen and Adrel's deaths will not be in vain!"

Variations of these cries were repeated by the peasants behind Mika, who turned around to face them.

Feldia and Laren watched as the peasants were starting to become determined once more despite their grief and despair.

Eduard stepped forward. "Princess Mika, you've been an inspiration to us all!"

"You've been beside Dellen and Adrel... and you helped them in our cause," said Elsia.

Marik walked over to them, and raised his fist in front of him with determination. "Our leaders may be gone, but they left behind a legacy that we must continue!"

"No more tyranny! No more oppression! We will continue to fight for our nation and our people, because that's what Dellen and Adrel would want!" shouted Peter.

"Princess Mika." Laren stood beside the Princess. "You must realize by now that you've been a leader to us as well. It wasn't just Dellen and Adrel who were our leaders. You've stood by their side, and supported them ever since you left the castle, and this revolt was planned and implemented with your assistance. Remember, My Lady, that we pledged our loyalties to you, that we considered ourselves your servants, when you saved the peasant workers at the castle gates when Sir Collin and his knights attacked! You saved our lives! Because of that, we recognized you as our Princess! As such, you are our inspiration, and the right person to lead us all to freedom!"

Feldia put a hand on Mika's shoulder to draw her attention. "Yes, Princess Mika, we are your servants. You may think yourself a child, but you are far more than that. You're the Princess of this nation, with power and authority as her birthright. You've been brought up as such, with great intelligence and wisdom for someone your age. You also hold the power of magic, and that's something that very few people in our nation have. We will serve you, and we will follow you to the end of this!"

Mika let out a deep breath as she heard these words. Her eyes still damp with tears, she smiled, and turned to face the people who gathered around her.

"Please lead us, Princess!"

"Only you can lead us to freedom!"

Lauria stepped forward with resolve. "If you lead us, Princess Mika, I'll make sure to follow you until the day I die."

"I commit my loyalty to you as well," said Demias. "Our rebellion will continue with its goal to win freedom for the Peasantry. I'll follow your orders."

Tavien smiled as he approached the Princess. "As will I," said Tavien.

Galien nodded. "And you can count on me, too."

Mika smiled at each and every one of them. She could feel warmth enveloping her heart once more as she was surrounded by the peasants she'd come to know, her people. The peasants all around her clamoured with determination as they pledged their loyalty to their Princess. A part of Mika was surprised that they would follow a child, but it looked to her that they saw her as more than that, just as Feldia mentioned. She was more than just a child. She was the Princess of Melodice, a Royal who was meant to lead. She gave them new determination, and for that, they would follow her. Mika watched as the chants of support from the peasants attracted the attention of more peasants down the street, and they started to join in. When they realized what was going on, they voiced their new determination as well.

Yes, that's right, I had held out my hand to reach out to them... and they had taken hold of it. I had promised that I would never let go. I will continue to hold on. I will, as the Princess of Melodice, lead you to freedom! Such is my duty!

Mika began to nod just a little. "I'll do my best... for all of you. I hope I will be good enough... because I still have a lot to learn." She turned to Feldia and Laren. "I hope you will be by my side through this. I hope to ask you for advice every time I need it."

Laren smiled, and then nodded to her. "You can count on us, Princess Mika."

"We are yours, Princess." Feldia put a hand on Mika's shoulder. "We'll advise you to the best of our ability."

The determined shouting of the peasants drew much attention from all around. More and more people continued to gather around Princess Mika and her companions. Their loud cheering and applauding was like a wave that was completely unstoppable. While the deaths of Dellen and Adrel may have brought them down to great despair, the Princess was successful in picking them up and giving them hope once again.

"We will now be your Second Commands, Princess Mika," said Feldia. "We will now report directly to you."

"Your first order, please, My Lady," said Laren.

Mika smiled. "Let the peasant workers continue with the revolt. Let them continue to march through the city streets all over Scarletia, and demand their freedom. Have them encourage others to join them, and make this revolt even larger than ever before. Send my words of inspiration to everyone!"

"Yes, Your Highness!" acknowledged both Feldia and Laren, with much enthusiasm.

Mika wiped away her remaining tears with her sleeve. "I wonder if Sir Dellen and Sir Adrel are proud of this moment."

Feldia felt her eyes tearing up again, but she willed herself not to cry. "Princess Mika, I'm sure they are... very, very proud of this... and of you."

* * *

Princess Mika's words spread like a wildfire that could not be contained. Those who were around her to hear her words of inspiration went out to spread the word, and those people, in turn, spread the message even further. Nearby peasant worker groups were made aware of her words of determination, and found new hope, despite the deaths of Dellen and Adrel. Those groups grew in size once more, and their members spread the word. Other groups began to follow them. In the next few hours, the revolt of the peasant workers continued as if nothing had affected them.

They also spread the word that the new leader of the Hope of Scarletia and the Scarletia Liberation was Princess Mika Silveraine. Those who were part of the rebel groups were amazed by this. They had heard about the recent actions of the Princess and, despite her youth, had been very impressed by them. While some may have questioned her tender age, many of those who held higher positions in the groups recognized her courage and bravery, and began to acknowledge her as their new leader. Though they all knew her Royal name was Princess Mika Silveraine, they began referring to Mika as the White Princess.

In addition to referring to Mika as such, people throughout the city were starting to call their group the White Princess Liberation Army, whether they were actually of the Hope of Scarletia or the Scarletia Liberation. The members of both groups put aside any differences that they may have had remaining up until then, and decided to combine their forces.

Laren galloped on his cervid, and stopped in front of a large group of workers of over a thousand members.

"People of Scarletia, my brothers and sisters! Peasants who have been trampled on by the Nobility! You have pledged your allegiance to the White Princess and to this nation! Now, fulfill your promises, and demand freedom for the sake of your families and for the future of your children! Fulfill them all for the glory of your land!"

The peasants around him cheered as loud as thunder with newfound hope.

"Everyone!" Feldia rode by a group of peasants a short distance away, another group of over a thousand workers. "The White Princess has spoken! Our rebel groups who fight for your freedom have become one at last! The White Princess Liberation Army will continue where the Hope of Scarletia and the Scarletia Liberation left off! Your love for this nation knows no bounds! Show your pride for Melodice, and demand your freedom from the oppression of the Nobility!"

The same loud cheer came over Feldia like a torrent.

"This will be the greatest rebellion in the history of Melodice!" shouted the peasants.

"We will demand our freedom! We will demand respect and dignity!"

"Dellen and Adrel are our heroes! Their deaths will not be in vain!"

"The White Princess will lead us to freedom!"

Knights at every patrol station continued to watch worker groups pass peacefully by. Many of them stood their ground outside the patrol stations while mounted on cervids, their weapons at their sides, while wearing full armour.

"What are our orders, sir? The revolt of the peasants is continuing! They're never going to stop!" shouted a knight named Perrin.

Ravean, the Sergeant who was behind him, glared at him. "We do nothing! We have received no orders from the castle! Until then, you stand your ground!"

"But what if they attack, sir?" asked the female knight named Emera.

"That's the only time when you can counterattack. At that point, you may pay back whatever harm they cause a hundredfold!"

But the peasants continued to leave them alone. As much as some may have wanted to cause harm to the knights and the nobles that were still living in the city, no peasant caused any disturbances. They also left property untouched. There was no reason for the knights to counterattack.

However, Mika was deep in thought as she rode on a cervid seated behind Elsia. She may have given her people around her inspiration... but something was nagging at her. A possibility crept up from within her, a possibility that she dreaded and was very frightened of. But it was a possibility she felt she had to deal with, just in case it became reality. As she rode behind Elsia, surrounded by some of Feldia and Laren's direct reports, her hood covered part of her face. This way, the knights would be less likely to see her should she pass by them.

Mika tugged at Elsia's sleeve. "Miss Elsia?"

Elsia turned her head slightly towards Mika. "What is it, My Lady?"

"Where are Feldia and Laren?"

"They're up ahead."

"I need to speak with them."

"Yes, My Lady." Elsia urged the cervid to gallop towards them.

As soon as they reached Feldia and Laren near the base of the Eldoria Watchtower, both still on their cervids, Mika called out to them. "Miss Feldia! Sir Laren!"

Feldia turned around to face her. "What is it, Princess?"

When Elsia stopped in front of them, Mika carefully climbed down from the cervid, and because she was awkward in doing so, Elsia helped her by holding her hands. As soon as she was on the ground, Mika took a few steps towards Feldia and Laren.

"There's something I need to talk to you about, and it's very urgent," said Mika. "I've been thinking about it for the past hour or so."

There was a look of fear in Mika's eyes, which Feldia and Laren could see. However, Mika was getting better at being able to control her fear so it did not take command of her entire being.

Feldia dismounted from her cervid. "What's going on?"

"We need to make certain plans."

Laren was confused. "What kind of plans? What do you mean?" Seeing Mika's facial expression, he, along with Feldia, immediately felt uncomfortable.

Mika hesitated for a moment, trying to think of the right words to express the growing anxiety she felt. "Miss Feldia, Sir Laren... after everything that's happened, I'm worried."

"Worried about what?" asked Feldia.

"I'm worried that certain terrible things might happen, and I believe we need to get together, and think of plans that could help us counteract them... just in case. Just in case anything bad happens."

Feldia and Laren looked at each other, still somewhat confused, but Mika's anxious expression certainly was not something they could just ignore. Based on their experience with Mika so far, whenever she was worried about something, it was likely to be something very much worth worrying about.

"Let's head back to our place," said Feldia.

* * *

Several hours later, Collin walked past several knights, and ascended the steps that led up to the top of the castle walls. He made his way to the bridge above the gates. Once there, he leaned against the crenulated wall, and looked out towards the city. He raised a telescope, and peered through its single lens. Far down the Valderia Pathway, he saw large groups of peasant workers continuing their revolt. He looked towards various main streets that branched off from the Valderia Pathway, and saw more of the same. What they were doing was no different from yesterday or the day before.

Collin put down the telescope. "I see the deaths of their leaders had no effect," he muttered under his breath.

A few minutes later, he heard the knight Dereas announce the approach of the King of Melodice. "The King arrives!"

Collin watched several of his knights stand at attention as King Ralphen reached the top of the wall. When Ralphen saw him, he made his way towards the bridge.

"As you were," ordered Collin, and the knights went back to what they had been doing before.

Ralphen stood beside Collin at the middle of the bridge. "So how are things going here, Sir Collin?"

"Not well, My Lord," answered Collin.

Ralphen narrowed his eyes. "What? What do you mean?"

"It would appear that the deaths of the leaders of the Scarletia Liberation and the Hope of Scarletia had no effect on the revolt. I did observe a temporary drop in enthusiasm among the groups of peasant workers, but it has dramatically escalated back to its previous level. The people are protesting as fervently as they were before I executed their leaders."

The King glared out toward the city. "Truly?!"

"And, of course, because of this, businesses and industries all over the city that support our castle are still not operating. Nothing is being manufactured or produced for us. The workers continue to march throughout the city. The only industries that are still working are the ones that support the peasants directly. Of course, even they are not working at their full capacity."

Ralphen slammed his fist against the wall in frustration, but he stopped himself from doing it again when he realized he needed to stay calm if he wanted to resolve this situation and to keep himself from breaking his own hand. "Damn peasant animals! The deaths of their leaders did nothing to discourage them?!"

"That's correct, My Lord," said Collin.

Ralphen shook his head as he let out a long breath.

"In fact... I believe the deaths of their leaders only

served to inspire them. They continue to protest, and more people are protesting as well. More people have joined their cause."

"How could this have happened?!"

Collin had no answer.

Ralphen lowered his head in frustration. Despite the information that was provided to him by Miss Helen, his plan had failed. He raised his head, and glared at the groups of peasants protesting in the distance. His voice was an ominous calm as he spoke. "This... must be my daughter's doing. These are not the results of the actions of rebel groups that are scattered throughout the city with no sense of unity."

Collin knew the King was deeply angry inside, but the calm of his voice was certainly uncomfortable.

However, after what has happened, since finding out about how the Princess had ordered the Scarletia Royal Guard to stop their attack on the peasants the other day, Ralphen could only think of one conclusion. "After everything that has happened, and judging by her personality and her unusual tendency to question everything around her, even accepted facts, and the way she behaved after seeing the city and lives of the Peasantry for the first time, it's obvious to me that Princess Mika... is now the new leader of this revolt."

Collin stiffened slightly as he held his breath for a moment. When he thought about it, it certainly seemed like a possibility, however remote. But even though it was just a possibility, it was still something that needed to be looked at, because of who they were dealing with. They were dealing with a member of the Royal Family.

"We have all watched Mika over the years. She's just a meek little girl. But that doesn't matter at all, does it? Though she may be easily frightened and speak in that annoying timid manner, it doesn't matter. In the end, she's also a stubborn, spoiled child who thinks she's always right. She has certain opinions, feelings, ideas... all potentially dangerous to the status quo." Ralphen straightened up, and turned towards Collin. "What happens, Sir Collin, when you question the accepted status quo, and then perform actions that are against it based upon your own opinions, feelings, and ideas?"

Collin paused thoughtfully for a moment. "I believe such behaviour leads to anarchy, My Lord."

"Precisely. Princess Mika's authority is her birthright. She is of the Royal Family. Unfortunately, she is abusing that right based on her own opinions about how the world should be. Our society thrives because of normality, because of a status quo. People are content to live in a society that is stable. However... Mika doesn't agree with the accepted status quo. We have seen that in her words and actions. As the Princess of Melodice, she has the authority to disrupt the status quo, but as King, I have the right and responsibility to maintain it. But how? Look at what has happened lately. The peasant workers are rampaging throughout the city unchecked. We have taken measures to stop this revolt... but we have been unsuccessful, and it's all because of our very own Princess Mika. With the way her mind works, Sir Collin, no one else in our entire nation is capable of disrupting the lives of the Nobility to this degree, and this cannot be allowed to continue."

Listening to the words of King Ralphen, there could only be one thing left now that he was going to order Collin to do. A certain feeling crept up to him and gnawed at him from deep inside. It was the same feeling he'd had just before he was ordered by the King to take a hundred knights to the castle gates and remove the peasants that were blocking it. It was a feeling of dread. That was only a mere two days ago. Many peasant workers died that day because of the King's order.

Collin kept his outward composure calm as he spoke. "Your orders, My Lord?"

Ralphen smiled. "You know what my next orders will be. We are left with no other choice, Sir Collin. Starting tomorrow, take the Scarletia Royal Guard, as many knights as you can spare, and head out into the city. You have two tasks that you must perform. The first task is to subdue the peasant revolt."

Collin paused for a moment, and then he nodded. "Yes, My Lord." He knew the first task would certainly involve the deaths of many peasants.

"Your second task, Sir Collin, is to find Princess Mika. Find her, capture her, and bring her back to the castle."

Collin thought about the second task the King ordered. That would actually prove to be far more difficult than subduing the peasant revolt. The Princess could be anywhere, and would most likely be in hiding.

"Also, as we briefly discussed earlier today... one of your young knights, Miss Helen Renier, has a request. She has requested to be the one who captures Princess Mika. She's a very honourable young woman. I've also promoted her myself on paper. I've promoted her from the rank of Private Enlist, past the rank of Corporal... to the rank of Sergeant. She now has authority over groups of knights, Sir Collin."

"I'm pleased to hear that, and I support her promotion in rank. She certainly deserves it after she provided you with the information that allowed us to seek out the leaders of the rebel groups. They've been a major inconvenience for us for the longest time. And Miss Helen's request to capture the Princess is further evidence of her loyalty to her King. But, sir...."

"What is it?"

"We should have a formal ceremony for Miss Helen."

Ralphen chuckled and nodded. "Of course, Sir Collin. We absolutely must. After all this is over, we will certainly perform a ceremony for all to see. She is already officially a Sergeant. But we must also inform everyone else through a formal ceremony."

Collin smiled as well. "Excellent, My Lord. Also, with these orders you've given to me, I will ensure that Miss Helen is given the special task of capturing the Princess."

"Very good. In the meantime, you now know your orders, Sir Collin. You've done well so far as the new Supreme Captain of the Scarletia Royal Guard and the Royal Army of Melodice. I trust that you will fulfill my expectations well."

Collin nodded with determination as he stood at attention. "Yes, My Lord. I will carry out these tasks. As you have ordered, it shall be done."

Ralphen put a hand on Collin's shoulder. "Very good. By doing this, you will bring honour to the Royal Family and to the Nobility, the city of Scarletia, and the greater nation of Melodice."

The Supreme Captain bowed his head slightly. "I will do my utmost to serve you, My Lord. Now and forever."

"Thank you. It's late in the afternoon. You should rest for now so you are better prepared for tomorrow. It will no doubt be a long and difficult day for you and the knights of the Scarletia Royal Guard."

"Thank you, My Lord."

CHAPTER 28

HELEN'S
DETERMINATION

AFTER HIS CONVERSATION WITH KING Ralphen, Collin headed down some walkways that took him through the Grounds. He was headed for the back of the castle, where he was expecting to find Helen. Based on her daily schedule, she was probably attending a lesson with Sir Galner. As he walked, he thought about what had recently occurred with his subordinate, the young Helen Renier.

Two ranks in promotion... and just for providing the King with the information he needed to make an informed decision. A very important decision. Her information helped us find the leaders of this revolt of the peasant workers, and bring down justice upon them. It may not have ended the revolt, but it was an honourable attempt, and because of that, she certainly deserved her reward.

The sun was descending closer to the walls to the west. As he watched it, he estimated that it would disappear behind the castle walls in a quarter hour. As night drew closer, the light breeze that stirred his cape felt cooler. The pastel colours of sunset slowly changed to varying shades of crimson.

And she wants to be the one who captures the Princess as well. I find that interesting. I have seen them spending time together, and they are colleagues in their study of magic. Have they become friends? Might she know more about what the Princess is thinking? From what the King shared of her request, she seems to believe the Princess has betrayed her country, and has shown blatant disregard for the laws of our land.

However, it still seemed odd to him that Helen would make such a request, when other knights could also be sent to secure the capture of the Princess. It was odd as well that she would approach the King directly to request it. She could have approached him instead, and he would have been open to honouring such a request with approval from the King.

Why would you make your request directly to the King, Miss Helen? Let's think about this for a moment. Is your relationship with Princess Mika deeper than what others think? Have you and she shared your thoughts on matters of government? Maybe because of the incident in the city with the peasant mob? Perhaps you're angry with her because it appears she's siding with the Peasantry, and you disagree with her actions? Your reasons… are personal, aren't they, Miss Helen?

"Hmmm… interesting." whispered Collin.

Also, your choice to bypass your commanding officer and go directly to the King seems to have a professional motive, perhaps one that is political in nature. Miss Helen, are you trying to maneuver your way into the King's favour? Your latest rank hike would seem to be evidence of that. I will have to keep my eye on you.

Collin chuckled at that thought. "This whole story is getting more amusing every day. Nevertheless, this task shall be yours, Miss Helen… as you've requested."

Eventually, Collin reached the area behind the castle that Galner had unofficially designated as his own training ground for teaching his students of magic. The area looked like any other part of the Grounds, although this area had more opens spaces. There were fewer trees and no flower gardens, no obstacles that can get in the way. As he stood on one of the walkways that encircled the area, he watched Sir Galner and Miss Helen.

Galner was hovering over the ground just above Helen. Blue semi-transparent wings, a total of four of them, two at either side of each of his boots, kept him afloat. He faced Helen, who stood on the grass, looking up at him attentively. When he saw Collin standing on the walkway a short distance away, he nodded to him in greeting. Collin returned the same.

"Now, Miss Helen, let's again have you try." Galner slowly floated down. When he was very close to the ground, he dispelled the magical wings that kept him afloat, and landed on the grass gracefully.

Helen sighed. "Yes, Sir Galner."

Galner looked up at Collin. "Why don't you come closer, Sir Collin?"

Helen stiffened slightly, and turned around, and as soon as she saw her superior officer, she stood at attention. "Supreme Captain!" she said, standing with the heels of her knee-high boots clicking together. She was in civilian clothing. A black knee-length cape hung over a white blouse with rounded collars. Her blouse was tucked into snug-fitting trousers, which accentuated the shape of her long slim legs.

Collin smiled as he approached them. "As you were, *Sergeant* Helen Renier," he said.

Helen relaxed. "Yes, sir."

Galner chuckled. "How do like this new title of yours, Miss Helen? Two ranks in promotion. Not bad at all."

"I'm grateful to the King of Melodice and the Supreme Captain, Sir Galner. It'll take some time to get accustomed to, knowing I now have authority over most knights."

"You will become accustomed to it soon enough, Miss Helen." Collin stood in front of both of them, one hand on his belt, as he gestured with his other hand to Galner to continue what he was doing. "Sir Galner, I see you're in the middle of a magical flight lesson. Please don't let my presence interrupt you."

Galner grinned, shaking his head. "No, Collin, you're not interrupting us at all."

"Thank you, Sir Galner." Collin turned back to Helen. "So, Miss Helen, how are you faring with this lesson? Magical flight is one of the more complex magic spells to learn. It's like controlling a pair of arms or legs that you don't see."

Helen was amused by that analogy. "That's exactly what it's like, sir. I must admit I'm still having difficulty understanding the lesson. However, today, I'm determined to learn this once and for all."

"We've been at this on and off since morning." Galner chuckled again. "I don't mind at all. We have taken breaks, but Miss Helen is very determined to learn this as soon as possible no matter what."

"Although I've been at it for quite some time, I'm still having difficulty."

It was Collin's turn to be amused. "Try not to worry too much, Miss Helen, because the more you worry about the lesson, the harder it will be to understand."

"Yes, sir," said Helen.

"Magical flight is not too terribly difficult once you become accustomed to it. If you treat it as something your body can naturally do, such as breathing, it becomes easier. It'll become natural for you, and thus, it'll become involuntary."

Slightly frustrated, Helen was taken aback. "You make it sound so easy. However, Sir Collin, breathing is an involuntary action of the body while magical flight is a voluntary action. You have to make it happen. Breathing happens automatically. Besides, if you compare it to breathing, as you have, and if breathing were voluntary, how does one breathe if one doesn't know how to move the diaphragm in order to inflate and deflate their lungs?"

Collin laughed. "That's a good point."

"As for you, Collin," said Galner, "I think you should use your magic more often. You're quite the powerful Magic Knight yourself. There's no need for you to be so humble about it."

Helen was surprised by this, and regarded Collin with awe. "Sir Collin, I didn't know you could also use magic."

"It's not about humility, but rather, caution. I think it's better to hide one's true abilities. I normally only use my magic for... special occasions. Sir Galner knows what

I'm capable of." Collin turned to Galner with a smug grin. "Isn't that correct, Sir Galner?"

"Ah, yes, of course. You're one of the most powerful Magic Knights in the entire army. That's one of the reasons why you were promoted to the rank of Supreme Captain shortly after the departure of Sir Terren," said Galner. "You are doing well to fill such a large role. Sir Terren was quite possibly the most powerful knight in the entire nation, but you yourself are not too far behind. I see great things in your future, boy."

Collin narrowed his eyes for a brief moment. *Still calling me "boy," aren't you?*

"That's amazing, Sir Collin. I would very much like to see you use magic at some point," said Helen.

Collin nodded as he clasped his hands behind his back. "In time, you will, Miss Helen, and I will make sure to put on a good show for you when I do."

"Are you capable of great offensive and defensive magic as well? Are you able to cast magic spells that can temporarily enhance speed, strength, and other attributes?"

"Well… let me tell you something about my specialty, Miss Helen, which a few know about, including Sir Galner, the King and Queen, and Sir Terren. I trust that you will keep this to yourself as well."

"Of course, I will, sir."

"I have focused all of my efforts in offensive magic. I have no defensive magic or any other magic that can be used for support."

Galner snorted at that. "Yes, well, it is a good idea to be able to defend yourself as well. You do know that, don't you?"

"In fact, I do. I believe the best defense is a strong and overwhelming offense. I prefer to strike hard and fast against my enemies. I prefer not to give them the chance to strike back."

Helen nodded with agreement. "I suppose it's similar with me. I do have knowledge when it comes to defensive magic and support magic, but most of my efforts have been focused on offensive magic as well."

Galner shook his head. "Yes, but unlike you, Collin, Helen is not completely defenseless. Armour and shields may be able to defend you against swords and spears, but they will not defend you against magic unless they have been magically enchanted."

Collin only smiled at that. "However, if I were to strike the enemy hard and fast enough, then, as I said, they wouldn't be able to strike back. Instead, they would be dead."

"Let's hope, for your sake, Collin, that you're right. We would hate to lose such a fine soldier."

"I have no regrets, Sir Galner."

"I'm sure you don't." Galner turned to Helen. "Shall we continue with our lesson, Helen?"

"Yes, Sir Galner." Helen turned to Collin, wondering what he was going to do now.

"I'll stand back here and watch." Collin found a wooden bench nearby where he could take a seat.

"As you wish." Galner and Helen continued with the lesson on magical flight.

Helen concentrated while standing still on the grass. She closed her eyes, and imagined herself as a bird flying freely in the sky. She felt her wings at her sides, the wind flowing over and under her wings, guiding her through the air. She imagined flying among clouds, soaring over the city of Scarletia and the countryside that surrounded it.

Galner's voice was calm and soothing, which helped Helen calm down. "Free your mind of all that stresses you, Miss Helen. Magic, as you know, requires a clear mind, one that is at peace. You don't have to reach the level of mental calmness and inner peace that a wise old sage might have. You just have to relax your mind. You have already memorized the design of this magic spell, the circles, the lines that pass through those circles and cross each other, the shapes, and the symbols that run along the circles and lines. You simply call it up from your memories, as you would with any other memory. Free your mind, Helen."

Helen continued to concentrate. The great wings of the bird in her imagination flapped in the wind, picking up altitude. Eventually, she let out a quick breath, and a magic circle appeared on the ground. Helen opened her eyes, and was surprised when she looked down. Semi-transparent wings, similar to those of Sir Galner's but with the colour pink instead of blue, appeared on either side of her boots. "I... I've done it?"

"No, you haven't, Miss Helen. You still have to fly," said Galner. "I need you to close your eyes again."

Helen was fascinated by the symbols and characters that appeared on the magic circle. Eventually, the circle faded, but the magical wings stayed. The strange symbols and characters now made up the semi-transparent lines that formed the shape of wings at her feet. She forced herself to close her eyes once more.

"You're not moving yet, Miss Helen. The wings have appeared... but you haven't started flying. You need to concentrate harder."

Helen continued to concentrate on the mental image that she had earlier. The bird flew higher in the sky. Soon the bird flew so high in the sky that she saw the tops of mountains and the land beyond them. The wind blew by as the bird ascended effortlessly.

I don't have to think about it. They are wings... they should be a part of me... a bird doesn't have to think about flying. It just... flies....

Galner thought about something else that could motivate the young girl. She was not moving at all. The magical wings glowed, waiting for her mental commands, but nothing was happening. He stood a few metres in front of her, and began to speak to her loudly.

"Miss Helen! Do you remember the report given by Sir Collin and Sir Maleth on what happened outside the castle gates when the peasant workers were blocking the Valderia Pathway? You do remember the report, don't you?"

Collin watched. Listening to Galner's words, he could tell he was trying to motivate Helen. He knew what was coming next, and hoped it would work.

"Do you remember who it was who came down from the sky, and then ordered Sir Collin's knights to stop their attack on the peasants?!"

The image of Princess Mika Silveraine appeared in Helen's mind. She suddenly opened her eyes, her expression quickly changing from one of calm to one of anger. She remembered the anger she felt towards Mika when she decided she would stay with the peasants. She remembered the report that Collin and Maleth gave. They reported seeing Mika flying over the peasants with her semi-transparent magical wings at her feet.

"Evidently, she has completed the lesson on magical flight... ahead of you!"

Helen closed her eyes again, more tightly this time. *Yes, she certainly has, hasn't she? I wish I had been there to see it. I would have liked to see Princess Mika flying. She's better than me at everything! She's more beautiful than I am! She's more talented at magic than I am! She's generally a nicer person! She's likely to be more intelligent than I am! Damn you! And here you are, as the Princess of Melodice, leading a rebellion! Like I said before... this is not the way to save the people of Melodice! You've branded yourself a criminal!*

"She must have learned it on her own! How she learned it, we don't know. But I can't say I'm surprised. She has always been highly talented when it comes to magic!"

The one who will save the Peasantry will not be you, Princess Mika! It will not be done through revolution! It will be done the right way! The one who will save the people of Melodice will be me!

"Princess Mika has learned to fly before you have, Miss Helen! What are you going to do about it?!"

I've been outdone by a scrawny little girl! Unacceptable!

"You need to learn this magical ability as soon as possible if you hope to catch up to her, and then surpass her!"

Helen opened her eyes, and clenched her teeth. She tightened her hands into fists at her sides underneath her cape. "And that, Sir Galner, is what I vow to do!" A flash of light appeared at her wings, and Helen's body suddenly moved upwards. She gasped with surprise.

"Calm down, Helen!" exclaimed Galner.

Collin stood up from the bench, walked over to Galner's side, and watched Helen.

Helen flew straight up into the sky just a short distance, but it was extremely awkward. She lost her balance, and tried to stifle a scream. Fear gripped her, something that did not usually happen to her. She was surprised at herself for feeling this way. She flailed her arms a couple of times as her widened eyes looked down below. She tried to turn her body towards one direction, but ended up upside down. She gasped loudly, and let out a brief scream this time.

Collin called out to her. "Miss Helen!"

Galner raised his hand to silence Collin. "Helen, you must calm yourself! You are in control of your wings! They're a part of you! Remember that!"

About twelve metres above the ground, Helen closed her eyes again, and drew in a few quick breaths. She listened to Galner's words. She knew he was right. The magical wings were a part of her, an extension of her body, although not physical. She could not touch them nor feel them, but they were definitely a part of her.

Concerned, Collin spoke to the mage in a whisper. "If she loses all of her concentration and control of the magic spell due to her fear, she might fall and seriously injure herself, Sir Galner."

Galner raised his hand again, whispering back to the Supreme Captain. "No, she won't. Be quiet. Have some confidence in your own subordinate."

Helen stopped moving as she continued to concentrate. If the magical wings were a part of her, it meant that she was in control of them. She willed herself to remember, to believe, that she should be able to control them as easily as she can control her arms and legs.

"Concentrate, Miss Helen. Remember to relax your mind," said Galner.

Helen slowly opened her eyes as she willed her body to move to an upright position. She watched as the horizon righted itself in her vision. She saw the castle walls in the distance to her right and the building of the castle to her left. She saw the setting sun and the beautiful pastels that surrounded it as it inched closer to the horizon. Helen closed her eyes again, and exhaled slowly, and when she opened her eyes, she felt much more relaxed. Her arms held out at her sides, she glanced down at Galner and Collin.

Relieved, Collin smiled. "Miss Helen, you've done it!"

Galner laughed. "Yes, she certainly has! Very good, Helen! Very good! Well done!"

I'm floating. I... I can't believe it! I've done it!

Galner stepped forward. "Now, Helen, try to use your wings to turn your body to the left and right. Do it slowly and carefully."

Helen did as he asked. She willed her body to turn instead of doing it physically. She moved according to her mind's wishes.

"Next, instead of just turning, try to move towards the left and then towards the right. Try to move forward and backwards, up and down. It's just like any other magic spell. Practice makes perfect. The more you do this, the better you will be at it."

Helen willed her body to move forward, and a flash of light appeared at her feet. She started moving forward. After a few slightly awkward attempts, she was able to will her body to move towards the left and right. She felt a slight wind brushing gently past her cheeks, tugging at her hair and the edges of her cape. As she moved forward while moving from side to side, her body positioned itself in such a way that she faced forward while slanted in a forty-five degree angle from the ground. She looked ahead of her, and held out her arms at her sides. Helen smiled brightly. She felt so good.

"You're doing well, Miss Helen. Remember to try to move backwards."

Helen complied. She willed herself to stop in mid-air, and that is exactly what happened. Her wings guided her as she moved backwards, leaning back against the wind. As she moved backward, her magical wings pointed forward. They pointed in the opposite direction of her movements. She moved left and right, and then up and down. She turned her body gracefully as she started moving forward in a different direction. She headed straight for the sky above her. The feeling of what seemed like absolute freedom filled her heart.

"This... this is fun!" she exclaimed, her smile brilliant and beautiful.

Hearing what Helen said and the way she said it, Galner exchanged amused glances with Collin. "Just a like a child."

Collin chuckled. "While a legal adult, at sixteen, you could say she still is a child."

After a few more maneuvers in the air, Helen began to fly downwards, her feet first. She landed on the ground gracefully, and her magical wings disappeared.

Galner approached her, with Collin following closely behind. "That was excellent, Helen! I must congratulate you! You've completed the lesson!"

Collin extended his hand to Helen in a handshake, which she reciprocated. "Well done, Miss Helen."

Helen smiled at both of them. "Thank you."

"You were having quite a bit of fun up there, weren't you?" asked Galner.

Helen blushed somewhat, but she made no effort to hide it, like she normally would. "Yes! And it felt so natural, Sir Galner. After I realized how I could move in the air, I'm starting to wonder to myself why it's taken me so long to learn this lesson. It was far easier than I imagined!"

Collin was amused by her reaction. "It is."

Galner patted Helen on the shoulder. "You can only truly find out how easy it actually is when you've done it. Now that you have, Miss Helen, you realize that it's just like moving any part of your body and moving your body in any direction that you want to go. Words can't truly describe how to begin to fly. It's something you have to feel in your heart."

"I understand now, Sir Galner. Thank you."

"Princess Mika must have felt the same way. I still wonder how she managed to complete the lesson without my assistance, even if I'm not surprised," said Galner.

Helen frowned, and then turned to Collin. Hearing the name of the Princess again, she was reminded of the request she made to King Ralphen. "Sir, I was wondering...."

"What is it, Miss Helen?" asked Collin.

"I made a request to the King which I had hoped he would pass on to you."

Collin paused for a moment, reminding himself that he needed to keep an eye on this young woman because of her newfound power. He smiled. "Ah, yes, of course. The King has passed on your request to me."

Galner looked confused. "What are the two of you going on about?"

Collin ignored him, and continued speaking to Helen. "Before I talk about that, I would like to make you aware of the orders the King has given."

"Orders, sir?" asked Helen.

"Now we're getting somewhere," said Galner.

"The Scarletia Royal Guard has been ordered to perform two tasks in regards to this revolt. The first task is to subdue the protesting peasant workers. We are to force them to stop their revolt."

Force them to stop?! Helen thought.

"I'm certain you know what that entails, don't you, Miss Helen?"

"Yes, sir. It means we must attack them. No doubt, there will be many deaths."

Galner let out a quick breath of disdain. "So much for their revolt. They have been inconveniencing the entire castle, the Nobility, with their pathetic claims that they're somehow being ruled by oppression and tyranny. It's time for these peasant dogs to be forced back to work. I'm glad that the King has finally taken action."

Damn! I was hoping it wouldn't come to this... but I can't say I'm truly surprised. Princess Mika... you have brought this burden upon us all. If you hadn't become involved with the peasants, this wouldn't have to happen.

Collin continued. "It's unfortunate that we will have to stain our hands with their blood, but it must be done. We are the Scarletia Royal Guard, and we must do this for the sake of the Nobility and the Royal Family."

"Understood, sir." Helen forced herself to keep her composure, despite the sick feeling within her. They were being ordered to head out into the city and kill innocent people. Such an order made her stomach turn, but she did her very best to keep her discomfort from being noticed by Collin and Galner. "You mentioned there are two tasks we've been ordered to perform. What's the second?"

"The second task, which goes back to your request to the King, is to find and capture Princess Mika Silveraine. She is to be brought back to the castle."

"I see," said Helen.

Galner snorted. "Good! That little girl has caused enough trouble!"

Collin clasped his hands together behind his back. "The Royal Guard will proceed with the first task. You, Miss Helen, will proceed with the second."

Helen was relieved. "Thank you, Sir Collin. You had asked me before if I was willing to make some difficult decisions should we be ordered to find and capture the Princess. Now that we have, I'll certainly do my best to perform this task. And I'm grateful that this task has been given to me."

"It's what you wanted, Miss Helen. It must be important to you, since you went straight to the King with your request. I have no problem with assigning you to that task," said Collin. "And I understand why you would want to. You feel that she has betrayed you, that she has betrayed us all."

"Yes, sir. I'm glad you understand," said Helen. "She certainly has betrayed everyone. Me, you, Sir Galner, and her own mother and father."

Galner chuckled. "Well, then, Helen, it looks like you have the most important task of all. You're one of my best students. I think it's most appropriate that you capture another one of my best students, one who has disrupted our lives to such a degree with her treachery. You will capture Princess Mika."

"I intend to. I will bring her back."

Collin smiled and nodded, impressed by the young warrior.

"However, Sir Collin, there's something I feel I must ask," said Helen.

"What is it?"

Helen cleared her throat, and ensured that she kept her air of confidence. "Is it truly necessary to kill so many peasants to stop this revolt?"

Galner looked up, confused. "What?"

Collin paused for a moment. He asked himself that question as well. *That's an excellent question, Miss Helen. Is there a better way? Perhaps there is a better way... but I don't know what it is.*

At that moment, he remembered the exchange he had with Dellen Balias, the now-dead leader of the Hope of Scarletia. He remembered the words that struck him deeply, so deeply that he felt like he was attacked. The thought of being attacked at a personal level by a mere peasant made him uneasy. Dellen had told him that a man who followed the orders of an evil man was himself evil, and that he was just a small man without honour for denying his own free will while following the orders of a tyrant, believing that doing so makes him greater.

Collin tightened his fist at his side but he kept it hidden. *Is that so, Sir Dellen? Am I a small man without honour, who denies his own free will? By following the orders of the King, I have made myself a great man, haven't I? I'm fighting for our nation!*

The image of Sir Terren Rinaldia appeared in his mind for a moment, reminding him once again of the one and only thing he still needed to work on, that he needed to stop holding back on what he truly thought and felt, that he had his own opinions, just like everyone else. Collin cleared his throat, pushing those thoughts and images away. "It is the order of the King, Miss Helen. As ordered by the King, it shall be done."

Helen paused as well, and eventually nodded. "Very well."

"Any more questions regarding our orders?" asked Collin.

"Yes, sir."

Collin looked at her expectantly.

"I will most certainly do my best to bring back the

Princess. But, as you're aware, Princess Mika is highly proficient with magic as well. Once I find her, it will be likely that she'll resist, and use her magic to do so. It's possible that... I may have to use magic as well."

Collin thought about that for a moment. "That's true, Miss Helen. Because you are both very proficient with magic, I will tell you this right now. You are authorized to use force, *if necessary*."

"Yes, Supreme Captain."

"However, please remember what I have emphasized. This is extremely important. If you feel you need to use magic to capture and restrain the Princess, then you may do so. If you feel you need to use offensive magic to accomplish your task, then proceed. However, this also means that the power you use must be reasonable. You don't want to kill the Princess. Bring her back alive. If you must attack her, keep injury to a minimum."

Helen nodded with acknowledgment. "Of course, Sir Collin. Understood."

* * *

That night, about an hour before midnight, Helen lay in bed, staring at the ceiling. She pulled her blankets up to her chest. A kerosene lamp continued to burn, along with a few candles. Eventually, they would all burn out, and darkness would envelope her bedchamber.

Helen's bedchamber was much smaller than Princess Mika's. The walls were covered with textured wallpaper that was plain white. Like Mika's bedchamber, one wall was covered with windows along its entire length, and half of them were covered by curtains while the others had their curtains pushed back. One window was open, allowing the fresh midsummer night's air to cool the room. There were couches that faced each other, separated by an algerwood table on one side of the room. A dressing table with a large mirror was on the opposite side of the room from her bed.

Helen turned to her side, her back to the windows, closing her eyes in a futile attempt to fall asleep. However, her thoughts about tomorrow were racing through her mind. She thought about the task that was assigned to her.

She remembered the day when she spoke to the King and showed him the information that led him to the location of Dellen Balias and his family. She had read Collin's report about what had happened that night, when he had led several knights into the house. The report had indicated that both Dellen and Zima were executed by Collin, their throats slashed. Before they were killed, Dellen had revealed the location of another rebel group leader, Adrel Savarian. He and his entire family had been executed as well in the same manner.

"According to the report, all seven of them were executed. Sir Collin slashed their throats. Even the children. But their wives and children… what did they have to do with any of it? Why did they have to be killed as well?" Helen wondered if she had done the right thing. "What was I thinking? They died because of me… didn't they?"

However, she reminded herself that what she had done was necessary. It meant that the leaders of the two largest rebel groups in the entire city were eliminated. They were leaderless, and no longer had any direction. Because of that, she had assumed it would bring an end to the revolt of the peasant workers. However, she was wrong. The revolt continued. Now that Princess Mika was among the Peasantry, it was very likely that she was the new leader of this revolt. Helen opened her eyes.

"Well, then… I suppose there's no more avoiding our eventual confrontation. Sacrificing the lives of their leaders and their families…." She swallowed hard. "I led them to their deaths. I thought it would stop their revolt, but it didn't. A wasted sacrifice. The next step is to find Princess Mika and capture her. That's the only way this revolt will stop now."

As she closed her eyes, Helen suddenly remembered something about the report. She was surprised. But it was not what was on the report that surprised her. Rather, it was what was not on the report.

Hold on a moment. There was no mention of Sir Dellen's

sons. What happened to them? If they were captured and executed along with their mother and father, it would have been mentioned. Does that mean... they somehow escaped? "What happened to them?"

Laughter, eerie and cold, resonated softly throughout the room.

Helen's eyes widened. She turned in her bed towards the windows. It took her a very brief moment to recognize the dark figure who was seated on her windowsill. "Mother?!"

The woman laughed again, completely clad in black. She sat with one leg crossed over the other, leaning against the side of the windowsill, her back straight and her arms crossed against her chest. Her long red hair, straight, smooth, and mid-back in length, fluttered in the wind like the curtain beside her. Her obsidian eyes were darker than the room itself, piercing and cold. In her long-sleeved, tight-fitting blouse with rounded collars, a knee-length cape that was tied around her neck with small ribbons and buttons, knee-high leather boots, and a snug-fitting but extremely short skirt that revealed much of her slim thighs, she was beautiful but, at the same time, strangely seductive in appearance.

Daria Renier grinned. "Can't sleep, Helen?"

Helen narrowed her eyes.

Daria leapt off the windowsill, and landed on the carpeted floor, but made no sound, as if she were as light as a feather. Even though the floor was covered by carpeting, her boots should have made at least a soft, muffled sound. However, there was none. Daria was as tall as Helen, and just as thin. There was a strong family resemblance. The only difference was that Daria was more than double Helen's age.

Helen crawled out of bed, and took a few steps towards Daria. Clenching her fists at her sides, she glared at Daria. The hem of her sleeveless white nightgown reached down to mid-thigh, and was stirred by the gentle breeze that came in through the window. "Mother, what the hell are you doing here?"

Daria frowned as well. "That's the second time you've

called me Mother, and I find it highly distasteful. Hearing it makes my stomach turn. I feel like I'm going to vomit."

Helen felt some of the wind knocked out of her as Daria shoved her backwards. She fell against her bed, but she regained her balance as she sat up, her arms supporting her. She looked up at Daria, her heart racing, her eyes widened. A strange feeling came over her, a feeling that she normally did not experience.

She felt fear. Fear of this woman before her.

Daria put one hand on her waist, shifting her weight to one leg while slightly bending the other. "As usual, my daughter is impertinent."

Helen frowned again, clenching her teeth. Her eyes shifted down briefly to Daria's unusually short skirt, revealing a shockingly large proportion of her smooth, unblemished thighs. She wondered how she could wear such a skirt, also noting that it could not possibly get any shorter. "And, as usual, you're dressed like a whore."

"That's one of the things I hate about this pompous aristocratic society. Ignorance. Short skirts do not necessarily mean that a person is a whore. Keep up the ignorance, and I will show you the true meaning of pain, my dear daughter Helen."

Helen leaned forward on the edge of her bed. "You refer to me as your daughter, but you won't let me call you Mother?"

"Yes. And I won't have you question that." Daria took a few steps around the room for a moment, noting the lack of decoration. "This is the room they gave you after you joined the Scarletia Royal Guard? They certainly lack a sense of style."

"What do you expect? They're the military," said Helen.

Daria shrugged. "So... I see you've gained two ranks, and you've personally requested to be the one who captures Princess Mika Silveraine and bring her back to the castle. Well... good luck with that."

"Good luck? Why? Is there something I'm doing wrong?"

"You tell me. What's the real reason why you want to capture the Princess?"

Helen's jaw stiffened with anger as she rose up from her bed, and stood in front of her mother. "That is my duty as a knight!"

Daria just smiled. "Really? Are you sure it's not to fulfill some political ambition?"

Helen was taken aback, her eyes wide.

"Having the King of Melodice grant you two ranks in promotion in exchange for information that led to the deaths of the leaders of the Hope of Scarletia and the Scarletia Liberation rebel groups... smells of political ambition to me."

Perhaps you're right, bitch, at least to a certain extent. By rising through the ranks of the Royal Guard, I will gain power through politics... but this is not for personal gain. When I have attained enough power, I'll be able save the Peasantry of our nation. I'll be able to change the government from within, and free the peasants from tyranny and oppression! Of course, I can't let you know my true intentions... not yet.

"Tell me, Helen...."

"What?"

"Does political ambition require the sacrifice of whole families? Fathers and mothers and children?"

"Of course not! And I don't have any political ambitions!" Helen crossed her arms against her chest. "What are you doing here anyway? Surely, you didn't come here to mock me. The Blood Roses wouldn't come to the city of Scarletia for no reason."

Daria's formed her lips into a mocking grin. "I'm the only one of my group here. The only reason why I'm here... is to see the King, and let him know that...." She paused for a moment, unsure of what to say next, but her mocking grin did nothing to show any of that hesitation.

Helen unleashed her infamous frown yet again. "Let him know what?"

Daria dismissed her frown with a calm shrug. Her grin never left her lips. "I'm here to let him know that our services are at his disposal, if ever he requires them. Which I've already done. That's all."

"That can't be the only reason why you're here! How

did you know I was promoted two ranks? How did you know about the information I handed to the King? How did you know these things? Were you here in the city all this time?"

"Few things escape my knowledge. My powers are diverse, my dear daughter Helen." Daria chuckled softly. She turned around, and headed for the open window.

Helen realized that she was about to leave, and took a step forward. "Wait!"

Daria turned around. "We'll meet again soon, Helen. I promise you that. It's been nearly a year since I last saw you. There's much we need to catch up on. Besides...." She looked around again at Helen's bedchamber, shaking her head with disapproval. "We need to fix this place up, give it a woman's touch. No daughter of mine should be sleeping in a room that looks like it belongs to a man."

Helen was taken aback by that as she looked around her own bedchamber as well.

Daria smiled. "See you soon, Helen."

Helen reached out for her mother hesitantly, but she was too late. She watched as her mother took two large steps towards the window, and jumped right through.

"Mother, wait!"

Helen ran to the window, and looked out. She saw a flash of light down below. The dark figure of her mother ascended into the night sky on blue semi-transparent wings at either side of her boots. Another flash of light appeared. Helen blinked only once, and Daria was gone. She flew so fast that she disappeared into the darkness of the night.

"She's fast..." Helen whispered.

Daria certainly flew much, much faster than Helen did when she first learned the ability of magical flight.

"Why is she here? Is it only because of what she said? What's going on here?"

CHAPTER 29

THE REVOLT
ESCALATES

SEC 3566, Morrighan 49

I N THE SCARLET CHAMBER, KING Ralphen and Queen Maiya, while seated on their thrones, listened as the leaders of the Nobility voiced their anger and frustrations over the revolt of the peasant workers. Because of the revolt which has continued into its fifth day, the patience of the Nobility was wearing very thin indeed.

"My Lord, the supply levels of this castle are dangerously low!" shouted one of the noble civilians, Arian Denara, Premier of the Department of Education for the entire nation of Melodice.

"Food has been rationed ever since the first day of this ridiculous ploy perpetrated by the filth of the Peasantry!" said the Premier of the Department of Agriculture, Shelia Talsien.

The Administrator of Castle Planning, Miria Darielle, raised a fist in the air. "We cannot allow this to continue, King Ralphen!"

"How long is this revolt going to last, My Lord? How long is it going to be allowed to continue?" asked Tamar Eldias, the Administrator of Social Events and Activities for the Scarletia Royal Castle.

"Because of this preposterous game these peasants are playing, we haven't received any supplies from the city in days!" shouted the Administrator of City Planning for Scarletia, Erias Paledor.

Ralphen glared at the nobles, and quickly stood up. "Silence, you insolent brats!"

The nobles stopped their protests, at least, for the moment. However, some still spoke in soft whispers in the back.

"Do you people realize you sound very much like those peasant animals that are protesting outside?!"

Maiya watched from her throne as Ralphen headed towards the top of the steps that led down to the lower level of the Scarlet Chamber. He stood tall with authority in front of the leaders of the Nobility.

"We mean no disrespect, Your Highness," said one soft-spoken noble named Jeran Alevars, the Administrator of Hospitality Services in the Scarletia Royal Castle, to whom all the maidservants of the castle reported.

"We are merely concerned with what appears to be inaction, My Lord!" shouted Tamar.

"This revolt must stop immediately! We cannot go on like this!" said Erias.

"Quiet!" ordered the King.

After a moment, the nobles finally complied.

Ralphen shook his head at the impertinence of the nobles in front of him. "I understand we are in a crisis situation. I am aware that food and supplies are at dangerously low levels. However, I've come up with a plan that will stop this revolt once and for all, and force the peasants to return to work. Today will be the day when all this will be over."

"What is your plan, My Lord?" asked another noble, the Premier of the Department of Military Technology and Research, Kelvin Isarias.

Ralphen took a quick glance at his timepiece. "Preparations began early this morning, in fact, long before sunrise. In about two hours, feel free to look outside, ladies and gentlemen, and when you do, direct your gazes upon the castle gates. This ridiculous workers' revolt is going to end one way or another."

* * *

Laren rode down one of the major streets of the city of Scarletia. He urged his cervid to go as fast as it could. Its hooves thundered upon the pavement, kicking up dust. Peasants crowded the sides of the streets. Ahead of him, he saw a knight on another cervid heading in the opposite direction. Laren and the knight exchanged glances as they were about to pass each other. Laren saw the expression on the knight's face. The knight gave him a dirty look, but they passed each other without incident.

After a moment, Laren brought his cervid to a halt to look back. The knight stopped at a patrol station. He noticed movement among the knights already there. It looked like their newcomer was passing on a message to them, or perhaps, an order. Laren could see that something was not quite right. He turned back around, and continued on his way.

Laren rode past a couple of large groups of peasant workers. He was glad to know that the revolt continued, and was even escalating. The groups of peasant workers had increased again in number throughout the city, and each group had become progressively larger. However, as he headed down an alleyway, something on his mind made him uneasy. Laren travelled down a few more alleyways, and then past the street thugs who were really sentries. He urged his cervid to a halt, and dismounted at the back door of Ethereal Dreams. He descended the steps that led him into the basement.

"Princess Mika, Feldia," he called out.

Mika was seated beside Feldia at a large round table. They were the only ones in the basement at the moment. Everyone else was coordinating with the groups of peasant workers, other members of the White Princess Liberation Army, and any other minor rebel groups involved, or observing the movements of the knights in the city and at the castle gates. When Laren reached their table, Mika and Feldia saw his facial expression, and were immediately concerned.

"You look troubled, Laren," said Feldia.

"Sir Laren, what's wrong?" asked Princess Mika.

"I've come here to let you know, Princess, that it's just as you suspected."

Mika stared up at him, and let out a small gasp, but she was not as surprised as she thought she would be.

Laren continued with his report. "Several knights left the castle. They rode quickly to the various patrol stations throughout the city. I was told by some of our people, and I saw it myself, too. It looked like they were relaying orders to the knights at the patrol stations."

"Oh... I see...."

Feldia was not surprised either. "What about at the castle gates? What about within the castle itself? Has anyone seen anything?"

Laren nodded. "As expected... large numbers of knights are gathering. They're gathering on the Grounds. It's begun."

Mika placed her hands together, and rested her forehead on them, her elbows on the table. She let out a deep breath. Her heart raced, but she did not feel as frightened as she used to. She had been through too many frightening events by this point, and was becoming accustomed to it. She wondered if it was fortunate for her or unfortunate. She supposed it could be either, depending on one's perspective. After a moment, Mika stood up.

"Princess Mika," said Feldia. "It really is as you expected. Brilliant, yet frightening."

"You anticipated this, My Lady." Laren let out a somber sigh.

"Things are beginning to escalate. I truly wished it wouldn't come to this." Mika leaned her hands on the edge of the table, her eyes downcast for a moment. She shook her head as she closed her eyes. "I truly wished it wouldn't happen this way."

Feldia agreed. "Same here."

Mika held her hands together against her chest for a moment. She tried to stifle the slight trembling of her hands, but to no avail. "I don't want to cry anymore. I don't want to cower in fear anymore like I always used to." She brought her hands down. "We no longer have a choice... so we have to do it."

Laren nodded. "This is it, isn't it?"

"Everything's in position, My Lady. Those who agreed to this plan have made the necessary preparations... to the best of their ability, and with the limited amount of time they had. Those who didn't agree with it... they'll disband as soon as they see trouble, and look for a safer place. As for everyone else, the majority... they don't know about this, but...."

Mika nodded. "The majority will win their freedom... if we are successful, Miss Feldia, Sir Laren."

Laren stiffened with discomfort. "This is a daring plan, My Lady, but I have agreed to follow you to the ends of this world, and that's what I'll do. I have no regrets."

"As promised, Princess Mika, you have my full support," said Feldia, as she stood up.

Mika smiled at both of them. "Thank you so much. But there's one thing I need to do... before we do anything else."

"What is it?" asked Laren.

Mika reached up to touch the Princess Gem. She detached the diamond from her golden necklace. She held it in her hand, and stared at it for a moment as she thought to herself that this item has been either a curse or a blessing. If she had not been identified as the Princess, maybe a lot of dangerous things would not have happened. But without it, a lot of people would not have recognized her as the Princess when she proclaimed she would lead the peasants to freedom. Mika she set down the diamond on the middle of the table.

"What are you doing, Princess Mika?" asked Feldia.

"In the event that the worst possible outcome of our plan occurs, no one must be allowed to find this."

Mika placed her hand on the table next to the Princess Gem. A pink magic circle appeared on the table, and surrounded the diamond. The symbols and circles glowed with power, and after a moment, tiny strands of light surrounded the diamond. The strands combined into a sphere of light, covering the diamond completely. When the light and the magic circle disappeared... so did the Princess Gem.

Feldia's eyes widened with great surprise. "What the...? Princess, where did it go?"

"Did you destroy it with your magic?" asked the alarmed Laren.

Mika shook her head. "No. It's not destroyed. It's simply hidden."

"Where?" asked Feldia.

"In a place where no one can ever hope to find it." Mika reached up to put her necklace underneath her dress collar.

* * *

One of the side doors at the castle gates opened just enough to allow a small figure to sneak through. As soon as the figure was clear of the door, it was closed from the inside, and locked tight. The figure quickly darted into the shadows cast by the high walls that surrounded the castle. The sun beat down on this rather hot summer day. The skies were clear and appeared pleasant, but it was the complete opposite in the city of Scarletia.

Helen, covered in a black and gold-trimmed cloak, whose hood covered most of her face, looked around to make sure no one had seen her. Clad in black protective gear, her leather armour with intricate golden designs peeked out of the front of her cloak, and her long sword, protected by its scabbard, hung from a large belt. A long dagger was sheathed in a smaller scabbard on the other side of her belt. Her leather greaves covered her legs from above her boots and all the way up to just above her knees. Two throwing knives were strapped to the sides of each boot. Soon, she disappeared into the shadows of an alleyway.

A moment later, the castle gates began to part. They slid sideways along tracks that had been laid into the pavement. As the gates parted, civilians on the Valderia Pathway took notice, and faced the gates to see what was happening.

The parting gates revealed an army of knights, all on cervids, all wearing full battle armour of black and gold from head to toe. They carried various weapons, such as long swords, spears, poleaxes, axes, halberds, maces, bows, and crossbows. Most of them were equipped with multiple weapons, but all of them were equipped with swords. Flags and banners fluttered in the wind, tied to some of their pole weapons. Even their cervids were armoured, the front and sides of their heads covered with metal plate, as well as the sides of their necks and bodies. Their legs were covered with loose leather armour, because metal armour would have restricted their ability to move swiftly.

At the very front of the Scarletia Royal Guard, Collin and Maleth waited, both of them mounted on their cervids like all their other knights, and just as fully armoured.

Collin met the Supreme Commander's gaze. "This is it, Sir Maleth."

Maleth nodded with agreement. "Yes, indeed."

As soon as the peasant civilians saw this, they were terrified. They screamed and ran away, some jostling past each other, and others running into their fellow civilians. Many of them crammed into nearby buildings. Businesses barricaded their doors.

Galner ascended the stairs leading to the top of the walls, where many other knights were stationed, knights who were not part of the large group on the Grounds. He approached the bridge above the castle gates, and stood beside King Ralphen and Queen Maiya, both of them surrounded by knights and servants.

"Thank you for joining us, Sir Galner," said Ralphen.

Maiya looked up at Galner with a somber expression. When Galner met her gaze, she looked away immediately.

Galner looked over the crenulated wall, and watched the Royal Guard all gathered together. "It looks like everyone's ready. It's been a while since you've had to deploy nearly the entire Scarletia Royal Guard, My Lord."

"That's correct. Do they not look distinguished, fully armed and armoured, their flags and banners fluttering in the breeze, signifying who they are, who they represent, and the nation they proudly protect?"

Galner grinned as he took one more look at the army of knights. "They certainly do appear distinguished."

Ralphen smiled. "I'm glad you approve."

Galner looked down the Valderia Pathway. He saw peasants rushing into buildings for safety and many more running away down the street, away from the castle gates. The mage snorted with disdain as he watched the groups of peasant workers in the distance who continued their revolt. "Humph. It's unfortunate, My Lord, that it has come to this. It's a shame that these peasant dogs have chosen death. I can't say I'm surprised. They truly are the scum of this world, their intelligence and comprehension barely above that of animals."

Ralphen stepped closer to the crenulated wall, and stood beside Galner, indicating his agreement with a nod. "They truly are fools for choosing to disrupt the lives of the Nobility and the Royal Family. These animals don't recognize danger when they see it. It's like a moth that intentionally flies towards a flame, not realizing that injury or death can result."

"I'll be glad when this is finally over."

"I vow that this will be dealt with as quickly as possible."

"Ralphen," said Maiya.

The King turned towards the Queen.

"Don't forget that Mika is still out there. She's in danger as long as she's surrounded by the peasants. We must get her back as quickly and as safely as possible. You do know this, don't you?"

"Yes, of course, Maiya." Ralphen smiled. "That's already being taken care of. It's all part of the plan."

A moment later, several knights from the Grounds below sounded horns. Galner, Ralphen, Maiya, and everyone on the bridge above the castle gates turned towards the knights of the Scarletia Royal Guard.

Collin, on his cervid, turned to face his knights. "Knights of the Scarletia Royal Guard! Today, we fight for the honour of our people! We fight for the honour of the Royal Family and the Nobility! The Peasantry of Melodice has stained the honour of our glorious nation by partaking in anarchy and revolution!" The Supreme Captain drew out his sword, and raised it high above him. "Raise your swords, and protect the honour of our nation! The King and Queen have given you their blessings!"

All the knights, around two thousand strong, drew out their long swords. The sound of metal on metal echoed, and was carried away by the breeze. Their voices shouted in unison as they cheered.

"Ride out, knights! Ride out into the city!" Collin turned his cervid around towards the city of Scarletia proper. He swung his sword through the air, and then brought it down, its blade pointing towards the direction of the peasant workers in the distance. "For our honour! For Melodice!"

And the knights chanted as they cheered again, their swords raised above them.

"FOR OUR HONOUR!"

"FOR MELODICE!"

Collin gave the command. "Scarletia Royal Guard, ride forth!"

The horns once again sounded. The knights urged their cervids to walk through the castle gates.

The King and Queen, along with Sir Galner, their knights who patrolled the walls, and the servants with them, watched as the army moved into the city proper. Ralphen smiled with pride as Collin led the Royal Guard down the Valderia Pathway.

The remaining peasants nearby continued to run into buildings, their frightened screams carrying far, as they saw the approaching army, while others scurried away into side streets and alleyways, desperately looking for protection.

* * *

Feldia and Laren exited the basement of Ethereal Daydreams into the alleyway, followed by Mika. All of them wore their cloaks with their hoods covering their heads. At the same time, cervids galloped towards them, ridden by Demias, Galien, Elsia, and Marik. Feldia and Laren headed for their own cervids, which were already prepared for them.

"Princess, it's begun!" shouted Marik.

Demias stepped forward with his cervid. "The Scarletia Royal Guard has begun its march through the gates!"

Mika gazed up at them with a frightened expression, but she knew this was going to happen, and because of that, she knew exactly what she needed to do.

As Laren and Feldia made their way to their cervids, Feldia looked back at Mika, wondering how she was feeling, and hoping she was going to be fine despite all this. She was still a child, after all.

Mika nodded with acknowledgment. "Well, then... we ourselves must begin."

"Okay. Elsia, take the Princess with you to the Eldoria Watchtower," said Feldia.

Elsia nodded. "Yes, Feldia."

"All of you, it's time for us to split up, and give the others the signal!" ordered Laren. "You know what your jobs are!"

"Send word as quickly as possible!" shouted Feldia.

"Come, Princess!" Elsia held out her hand for Mika.

However, Mika hesitated. She cast her eyes down on the ground, and put her hands on the sides of her head. She knelt down on the ground as she closed her eyes, and clenched her teeth. "I can't believe this is happening!"

Feldia knelt down beside her. "Princess!"

"More people are going to die because of all this!" Mika looked up at Feldia as her hands trembled and her lips quivered. "I may be considered the leader of the White Princess Liberation Army, but despite all that... I'm still a child! Am I doing the right thing?! Everyone who agreed to this plan is already in the right position, all over the city, and all the groups we've coordinated with are at the right places at the right time! Everything's been planned out, and much of the Starstone has been moved! I can't believe this, Miss Feldia! I may be the Princess, but... in the end, I'm still a child! Am I good enough for this?!"

"You are our Princess, the White Princess, and the leader of the White Princess Liberation Army... *Princess Mika Silveraine!*" exclaimed Feldia, her voice with a somewhat frightened tone herself. "I am frightened as well!

I'm scared to death! I don't know how we can do what needs to be done! But we have all come together, and we're now fighting for our freedom and our future!"

"And if it doesn't work... then we're all dead!" shouted Mika.

"If it doesn't work, Princess Mika," said Laren, stepping closer to her, "then our legacy will continue through others, and they will fight for the freedom of our people. We will light the Flame!"

Feldia continued. "You have given us your orders, My Lady! We have helped you put this plan together. We will follow your orders because we know they are our best opportunity to achieve our greater goal!"

That's right... I'm their Princess. I must once again remind myself of that.

Mika forced herself to stand up. "Yes, of course, Miss Feldia, Sir Laren...."

She met the gazes of everyone around her, and then closed her eyes, took a deep breath, and let it out slowly. In front of her, she held her cold hands together tightly, and then loosened them as she tried her very best to calm down and put on the composure of a leader, one who was worthy to lead the White Princess Liberation Army. "We fight for the freedom of our people, the honour of our nation. The King has sent forth the Scarletia Royal Guard. We've made the necessary preparations. We push on forward, everyone!"

Laren and the others let out a battle cry as their raised their fists into the air.

Feldia wasn't sure how to react when Mika put her hands on her, and then embraced her. "My Lady...."

"Miss Feldia, I haven't known you for very long, but I've come to think of you as a friend. After such a short time, we've already been through much together. I hope we'll see each other again very soon."

Feldia returned Mika's embrace. "We will, Princess Mika. We'll see each other again. I promise you that. I don't really agree with letting you go by yourself. But this is all part of our plan... or, rather, your plan, since you thought up most of it. It's a bold and daring plan."

"I know. I don't want to go either. I wish we could all stay together."

After a moment, Mika pulled away from Feldia, and looked up at Laren, who had stepped closer to her. Mika extended both her hands up towards him.

It was obvious to Laren that she wanted to embrace him as well. He shrugged, and knelt down so that the Princess could hug him.

"Sir Laren, please don't forget me," said Mika.

"Princess, please don't talk like you'll never see me again." Laren returned Mika's embrace. He held out his hand towards Feldia, who took his. "All of us will see each other again, and that's a promise, I swear it. When that day comes, we'll continue where we left off."

Feldia nodded, holding his hand tight. "Yes, you're right, Laren."

"And you'll both have stories to tell me. We'll have much catching up to do. We'll be together again." Laren looked up at their other companions. "In fact, all of us will have stories to tell, and I'm going to want to hear all of them."

Demias, Galien, Elsia, and Marik all smiled, and then nodded with agreement and determination.

"It's a promise, Laren," said Demias.

Galien chuckled. "I'll want to hear your stories, too, Laren, when we're all together again. So you better have some good ones to share."

Mika pulled away from Laren, and glanced at everyone around her, inspired by the inner strength they have all shown so far. "If this plan works, and I know it will, we will grant freedom to the Peasantry, perhaps not in this city, but beyond the city gates. Beyond the city, they will rebuild their lives in peace."

As Feldia and Laren climbed onto their cervids, Elsia took hold of Mika's hand, and helped the Princess hop onto hers.

Feldia. "Let this be the day we bring freedom to our people."

Laren. "This is the day where everything truly begins."

"To freedom," said Princess Mika, a new look of determination and confidence expressed. "Liberation Army, let's ride!"

Feldia and Laren headed one direction down the alleyway. Behind them, Mika's group, consisting of Elsia and the others, headed in the opposite direction.

Feldia clenched her teeth as she urged her cervid to go faster. "We're about to fight against knights. It's been a while since I've had to do anything like this."

Laren rode alongside her. "What? Don't tell me you've forgotten everything."

Feldia shook her head. "I haven't. Deserters like us do not forget their training."

Laren smiled. "That's right."

Eventually, Feldia and Laren arrived at a branching alleyway. They both headed in different directions. Mika, Feldia, and Laren headed for their separate but related objectives as part of a plan they hoped desperately would bring freedom to the Peasantry of the city of the Scarletia.

* * *

One large group of peasant workers, about five thousand strong, marched up the Valderia Pathway, completely blocking it. Among them were members of various rebel groups who had combined themselves with the White Princess Liberation Army. Those who were at the front saw the castle gates ahead of them as well as the Scarletia Royal Guard now marching towards them. They were still quite a distance away from each other.

"Stop! Stop! Stand your ground!" shouted a peasant who led the workers.

The entire group slowly came to a halt. The group consisted of mostly men, but there were women and children there as well. Some of the women were workers, but others were wives of men in the group. The men began to ask their wives and children to leave the group and head for a safer location. After tearful goodbyes and heartfelt embraces, the wives and children began to leave the group through the back. Some of them hesitated to leave while others ran away as quickly as possible.

"We'll get through this!" said one father.

"I'll come back home when this is over. I promise!" said another.

When the wives and children had left, the men looked ahead of them, fear in their eyes, but they stood their ground. The knights were coming closer.

"Draw your swords, the ones we smuggled at the cost of so many lives!" ordered one of the workers. "Draw whatever weapon you found!"

Few people in the group were actually armed, but there were some who had managed to obtain short swords, and others who had obtained crossbows and quarrels or bows and arrows. But the majority were without such weapons. Instead, they had obtained items that would not normally be considered weapons or items they had put together to turn into makeshift weapons. These consisted of wooden clubs, iron bars, kitchen knives, axes used for wood-cutting, pitchforks, shovels, pokers used for prodding firewood, and many others. In terms of body protection, very few peasants had anything that could be of use, as most of them wore ordinary clothes. Some managed to obtain pieces of leather armour and a few pieces of metal armour here and there.

Someone in the group signaled to some youths and young adults at the sides of the street. One of them was a boy who was no more than twelve. He, along with the others, held bottles filled with kerosene. The bottles had pieces of cloth hanging out of their narrow openings. One of their companions held out a burning wooden torch, which the others used to light their makeshift incendiaries. When they were ready, they ran down the street to their predetermined destinations, including the young boy.

As Collin's army marched down the Valderia Pathway, each time he passed a major street either to his left or to his right, he gave a signal for some of the knights to proceed down those streets. Companies separated from the main group, and proceeded in whichever direction Collin indicated.

Maleth looked ahead, and saw the group of workers blocking the street. "It appears, Sir Collin, that the group in front of us will be the first."

"Remind me again the reason why we're out here, Sir Maleth," said Collin, with a hint of hesitation in his voice, as he held his sword beside him while his cervid trotted forward.

"The order of the King." Maleth raised his sword in his right hand a little higher.

Collin pointed his sword towards the group. "Charge forth!"

"Charge forth!" shouted Maleth, relaying the order of the Supreme Captain, raising his sword in the air.

The knights behind them let out battle cries in acknowledgment. Collin and Maleth urged their cervids to a gallop, and the knights behind them almost immediately followed suit. The thundering hooves of the cervids sent vibrations down the streets, which the peasants felt under their feet.

The leaders of the group of peasant workers ahead of them stared at the approaching knights, their eyes widened, some of them even frozen in place as fear gripped their hearts.

"Go! Go!" shouted one of them, pointing at the approaching knights.

With some hesitating and others letting out battle cries, peasants began running forward. Those who wielded weapons at the front of the group began running as fast as they could towards the knights of the Scarletia Royal Guard. They ran hard as their battle cries echoed, and with their various crude weapons raised high and ready to strike.

Collin raised his sword. "Arrows!"

Knights who held crossbows and bows aimed high and fired. Quarrels and arrows flew, and rained down upon the peasants who charged towards them. Death came to many peasants as arrows and quarrels tore into their flesh, their everyday clothes doing nothing to deflect them. Some of the charging peasants were felled, along with some of those who were still standing back.

Collin roared out a battle cry as he beheaded an axe-wielding man coming towards him with one swift swing of his sword.

The mounted knights clashed with the peasants. The blades of the knights reflected sunlight as they slashed away at the charging peasants. Clamours of fury and screams of pain competed with the sounds of blades striking other blades as well as the sounds of flesh tearing and bones cracking. More quarrels and arrows flew, and felled peasants who were pushing forward from the middle of the group.

The peasants flailed wildly with their weapons, many of them untrained in combat. Those who had some form of training fared somewhat better. The peasant workers were cut down to shreds as if they were nothing, although some managed to swarm a few knights by overwhelming them with their numbers and forcing them off their cervids. Peasants who forced knights to the ground opened their helmets or removed them and stabbed them in the face or neck. But many of those peasants were eventually slaughtered by the mounted knights who speared them from above.

Cervids were part of the battle as well as they trampled on peasants who found themselves on the ground, crushing them to death. Cervids that saw the peasants charging towards them were trained to recognize their behaviour as a threat, so they glared at them and pointed their sharp antlers forward, spearing and slashing some of the peasants who came dangerously close.

"Reland!" Collin galloped towards one of his knights.

Reland had been swarmed by several peasants, and cried out for help as he flailed, dropping his sword on the ground in panic. His sword was taken away by a peasant, who disappeared into the crowd. His cervid was trying to fight off some the peasants with its pointed antlers.

Collin's cervid speared a peasant with its antlers as it approached Reland. As soon as Collin arrived, he slashed at the legs of someone trying to climb on to Reland's cervid, and stabbed another who was already upon him. They fell dead, while others with them scrambled away, only to be cut down by nearby knights with halberds and maces.

"Don't let your guard down, Reland! Where's your sword?!" shouted Collin.

"I don't know, sir! They swarmed me, and I panicked! I must have dropped it!" said Reland.

"You can't fight without a sword! Find someone with a spare weapon! Otherwise, you need to be escorted back to the castle!"

Maleth saw a flying rock about to strike him so he dodged it. However, another rock struck one of the other knights beside him in the chest. Although the knight was dazed by it, he was uninjured because of his thick armour. Maleth swung his long sword at either side of his cervid, cutting down more attacking peasants. One managed to get past his cervid's pointed antlers, and struck the side of his mount with a wooden club. The cervid reeled from the blow, but it was protected by metal plate. Maleth embedded his sword into the junction between the man's shoulder and neck.

Collin ran down another peasant, trampling him to death with his cervid, and cut down another with his long sword. Several peasants made a run for him, brandishing axes, short swords, and metal pokers. When one of them was close enough, Collin slashed the peasant's chest, felling him instantly. But during that attack, another worker managed to climb onto the back of Collin's cervid. Collin immediately felt the balance of his cervid shift, and just as he was turning to look behind him, Alryn, one of the nearby knights, fired his bow and arrow. The arrow embedded into the worker's forehead, and he fell off Collin's cervid.

"You have my thanks, Sir Alryn!" said Collin, as he continued to slash away at the peasant workers.

"You're welcome, sir!" shouted Alryn as he quickly reloaded and fired another arrow, felling a peasant who was coming towards him.

Near the area where Collin's group of knights and the peasant workers clashed, Feldia rode on her cervid, brandishing a long sword at her side, which she managed to steal from a knight, who lay dead on the street bleeding from his neck. She urged her cervid to gallop as fast as it could down a major street which led away from the Valderia Pathway. Down the street, thousands of peasants flocked in loosely formed groups.

As she raised her sword high in the air, she clamoured the order that was understood by members of various rebel groups, including the White Princess Liberation Army, who were among the groups of peasant workers.

"Light the Flame! Light the Flame of the White Princess!"

Feldia's voice echoed, carrying beyond the buildings and down the city streets.

Collin looked up, hearing the voice. He heard the command, and then looked around, trying to find out where it was coming from.

As knights and peasants fought each other all around Collin, he saw movement in the periphery of his vision. He saw a boy, no more than twelve years old, running down the side of the street towards a building. The boy held a bottle of kerosene with a flame burning at the top, a crude incendiary. He faced a building beside Collin's group of knights. Although it was dark inside the building, Collin saw something sparkle inside through its windows. As soon as he saw the sparkle, his eyes widened.

Starstone!

"We will light the Flame of the White Princess!" The young boy threw the incendiary into the building's opened windows with as much strength as his arms could muster. By the time he'd finished shouting his battle cry, the entire front of the first floor of the brick-and-mortar building exploded into a bright ball of deep blue flame, consuming the boy instantly... and his entire surroundings, along with a handful of peasants and dozens of knights on their cervids.

CHAPTER 30

THE FLAME OF THE WHITE PRINCESS

FROM FAR AWAY, THE LOUD explosion was heard. The black smoke that rose up from it could be seen for kilometres. King Ralphen watched from a distance, his eyes wide with shock. Maiya and Galner were the same as they looked on. The knights and the servants around them saw, and wondered what had just happened.

Feldia saw the black smoke beyond the buildings as she galloped away on her cervid.

Laren saw it as well as he turned around on his cervid when he heard the explosion.

On the ground, Helen turned towards the source of the sound of what seemed to her like thunder. She saw the towering black cloud. "What just happened?"

The Starstone within the building had ignited, causing the fiery blast. Thousands of pieces of wood, brick, and glass flew out on everyone in the area. Some of the debris burned, and as soon as the dark blue flames touched anyone, mostly knights and their mounts but some peasants as well, their bodies burned as they screamed with terrible agony. The knights were literally cooked within their armour. Other knights nearby tried to raise their shields in defense, but the flames were so hot that their shields became impossible to hold, and burned their hands through their gauntlets.

However, the carnage did not end there. Because the first floor exploded, the entire building, which consisted of three more floors above the first, became unstable. Support columns broke, metal screeched, and wood cracked near the front of the building. Knights nearby who had survived the initial explosion heard the sounds, looked up, and knew right away that there was no escape as the entire building began to fall towards the street. Those who were not injured tried to run away, but many of them were crushed by the falling building. Large pieces of the building came crashing down into a cloud of debris, providing the dark blue flames with even more fuel to burn.

Collin pushed himself off the ground. The force of the explosion had knocked him and many of his knights off their cervids. Some of the cervids had fallen as well. Some of them could not get back up, and others were dead or severely injured. For a moment, Collin could only hear faint muffled sounds around him that seemed like desperate cries for help. As he slowly got up, his hearing began to sort itself out. The explosion temporarily deafened him. Soon, the muffled cries became loud and desperate clamours of chaos all around him. He turned towards the source of the explosion and at the building that had collapsed and crushed his knights. He saw the approaching flames that could not be quenched, reaching out to anything they could consume.

"Get away from the flames! Everyone, get back!" shouted Collin.

Maleth was very much alive as he ran and helped knights get back up on their feet. He and a few knights passed by one of their own who stood burning in his armour, screaming for help.

"No! No, don't touch him! He's already dead!" Maleth and the other knights backed off. The burning knight fell, and soon, his screams became silent. His body, red and black underneath the blue flames, became motionless.

"Get away from this area now! Move back!" ordered Collin. He found his sword, and picked it up from the ground. When he straightened up, he looked down the street, and saw what was left of the peasant group they had been in battle with. They were running away from them, but it was not to escape.

Another explosion occurred further down the street. The blue flames appeared, and destroyed small buildings.

* * *

"What the hell is going on?!" King Ralphen, alarmed, peered through the single lens of his telescope. He saw the explosion that nearly took out Collin. He could see the carnage the explosion caused.

A moment later, Galner heard another explosion. "My Lord, look!"

The explosions followed some sort of predetermined pattern. As each explosion occurred, another one appeared a moment later farther away. It was as if whoever was setting them off was using the previous explosion as a signal to proceed with the next. Flashes of dark blue flame appeared, followed by black smoke that rose ominously into the otherwise clear blue skies from various parts of the city.

Ralphen put down the telescope, anger twisting his face. "What is the meaning of this?!"

"Those distinct blue flames are the result of Starstone exploding, My Lord!" replied Galner.

"Starstone?! How can that be?! It is mined by the peasants under orders of noble masters in mines that are owned by the Nobility! How can they—?!"

Galner stared ahead as he placed his tense hands on the crenulated wall. "Many of the Nobility within the city have retreated into the castle. That means much of the property we own has been left unguarded. The peasants must have moved the Starstone during the night, and stored it away in various locations!"

Ralphen roared with fury into the sky. "How can peasant animals plan such a devious act?! How can lower forms of life have the mental capacity to plan something like this?! Curse them all! Kill them all!"

Maiya held up her telescope, and watched through its lens the carnage the Starstone flames caused. Burning rubble filled a few of the side streets from buildings that collapsed from the explosions. Knights and cervids lay dead on the streets, either crushed by falling debris or burned to death by the flames of the ignited Starstone. "Sir Galner, please tell me there's a way to extinguish those flames."

Galner shook his head with regret. "I'm afraid not, My Lady. Starstone is made of materials we don't yet have the technology to identify. When brought near any conventional flame, such as a flame started with kerosene or even a candle, the results are disastrous. The Starstone explodes into a ball of dark blue fire. The flame burns so hot that not even water can be used to extinguish it. There's no known method to extinguish Starstone flames. It must consume everything around it until there is nothing left to consume, and it must spread until it is stopped by an obstacle that has a sufficiently high ignition or melting point... and only then will the flames fizzle out."

Ralphen pounded his fist on top of the crenulated wall at the side of the bridge. "Bastards! The peasants stockpiled the Starstone where the explosions are occurring right now?!"

"It would appear so, My Lord," said Galner.

"I don't understand this! How can this be happening?!"

Maiya gave her telescope to Galner, who used it to observe the explosions and the typical blue flames he recognized. He observed the burning buildings, trying to ascertain which ones were being targeted. After a moment, he felt a sinking feeling within him as his eyes became wide with alarm. "My Lord, My Lady...."

Ralphen turned to Galner. "What is it now?!"

Galner met Ralphen's gaze. "The buildings where the Starstone explosions are occurring...."

"What about them?" Maiya asked.

"They are buildings that manufacture goods for the castle, places that process food, buildings that store our food and supplies. The peasants are deliberately torching the buildings that directly support our castle. These places are essential to the survival of the Nobility living within the Scarletia Royal Castle! These peasant dogs are burning them to the ground!"

Ralphen and Maiya turned towards the city, watching the distant explosions and the black smoke that rose from them.

"No. How can this be? Sir Collin, you must stop these peasant animals from causing any further damage!" shouted the King.

* * *

A pink magic circle appeared on the ground beneath Helen's feet, and magical wings appeared at the sides of her boots. She floated upwards as the magic circle disappeared. She rose up higher, and was soon above most of the buildings. She looked over them, and saw the black smoke.

"What is this?" she whispered.

Helen saw a distant explosion while hovering above a building, and was shocked as she watched. Parts of another building blew out, and fiery debris fell upon the street, crushing knights, cervids, and peasants under them. Those who were too close were burned alive by the sinister blue flames.

"A blue flame? What... kind of flame is that?"

As the minutes passed by, a few more explosions occurred. Although they were far away, she heard their sounds like distant thunder. Helen flew from one building roof to another. She hovered over the side of a building, and watched with horror.

Knights and peasants clashed on the streets below. As trained warriors, with their armour and weapons, and the advantage of being mounted on cervids, the knights were far superior fighters. They easily overtook the peasants, who used crude weapons and had little to no combat training. Up and down the street, she saw death. Peasants lay on the streets, their bodies crushed by cervid hooves, slashed by swords, stabbed by spears, dismembered, or decapitated. Most of the dead were peasants, but occasionally, she saw a dead knight. Helen calculated that for around every hundred dead peasants, there were probably just one or two knights that lay motionless.

"This is the level we've fallen to. The killing of peasant civilians...." Helen shut her eyes, and shook her head to push away the terrible images for now. She looked at her surroundings. "Dammit! I must find the Princess! Only then can this useless bloodshed be stopped!"

The magical wings flashed, and Helen flew over the buildings as she looked for any sign that could lead her to Princess Mika's location. It was like looking for a needle in a haystack. But she was desperate. She had to find the Princess in order to end this massacre. Otherwise, this would never end, and the peasant population of the city would be decimated.

* * *

A knight ran down the street as he held his sword with both hands. He roared out a battle cry, and raised his long sword above him as he charged towards Feldia.

Feldia saw him approaching, and switched her long sword from her left hand to her right. A blue fireball appeared behind her. Despite her safe distance from it, the wind from the explosion pushed her hair forward. As soon as the knight arrived, he swung his sword at her, but Feldia ducked to dodge it. His momentum carried him forward as Feldia maneuvered around him. With great accuracy, she embedded the blade of her sword into the man's armpit, where his armour was weak. The blade passed between armour pieces, tearing through his flesh. She withdrew the blade, and the knight fell dead at her feet.

Feldia ran a short distance down the street, her bloodied sword at her side. She watched as peasants ran farther ahead. They carried the flaming bottles, throwing them into buildings. There were two buildings on opposite sides of the street ahead of her a short distance away, both of them food storage facilities. Blue flames tore through the buildings, and the explosions were so powerful that the shock wave threw her down, along with everyone else on the street.

She struggled to get up, then looked down the road

where she saw peasants and knights burned alive by the flames. She could feel the terrible heat of the nearest flames, even though they were a good distance away from her.

"Feldia, here!" Lauria rode towards Feldia, pulling along the cervid that Feldia had been using by its reins.

When Lauria arrived, Feldia climbed onto her cervid, and they rode down the street past the peasants still fighting the fight.

"Keep lighting the Flame of the White Princess!" ordered Feldia.

The peasants cheered with determination.

"Don't stop until you have your freedom!"

* * *

Two peasants, a man and a woman, ran away as fast as they could down one of the major streets. Two knights chased them, brandishing bloodied long swords. The woman tripped, and the man tried to go back to her, but it was too late. One of the knights plunged his sword into her back. She tried to scream, but blood spilled out of her mouth. The man screamed for his wife, but the other knight slashed at him as he ran by, and the man's head went flying.

Laren roared with a battle cry as he thundered towards the two knights on his cervid, his bloody short sword at his side.

The knight who had just killed the woman looked up, and saw him for only a split second as his eyes widened. He did not have time to defend himself as Laren slashed. Blood sprayed out of his neck, and the knight fell dead.

The other knight ran for his own cervid, but Laren urged his cervid to chase him down. When the knight realized he could not outrun Laren on his cervid, he turned around, and raised his sword. The knight charged on foot towards Laren, who thought the man was a fool. The knight slashed at him, but Laren deflected it with his short sword. The knight had a better weapon, but Laren was mounted. The shock of the impact between their blades reverberated into Laren's arm, distracting him for only a moment, but as the knight tried to strike him a couple of more times, Laren slashed back to deflect them.

Next, the knight stabbed Laren's cervid on the side. The cervid reeled, screaming with excruciating pain as the blade tore through its innards. However, the blade was embedded too deeply into the cervid's body so the knight could not pull it out, forcing him to become off-balanced as the cervid began to fall, pulling him with it. Laren quickly removed his feet from the stirrups, and jumped towards the knight, who let go of the hilt of his now-useless sword. Laren landed on the knight, and the two of them fell into a crumpled heap on the pavement.

Another large explosion went off nearby. Blue flames appeared, incinerating buildings, and causing severe damage to nearby structures as well death to anyone who happened to be too close. Both Laren and the knight felt the searing heat. The knight tried to punch Laren in the face, but Laren dodged as he struggled to gain a hold on the knight's neck. The knight tried to reach for the knife on his belt with one hand while he slammed his other fist into Laren's side. Laren jerked in pain, but managed to raise his short sword, and land it in the knight's neck. The knight lay motionless as Laren struggled to stand up.

Laren went to his fallen cervid, and sheathed his short sword. He pulled the knight's long sword from the side of the cervid, which screamed in pain as he did. Now, he had a new weapon that was far superior. He spotted the armoured cervid that one of the knights used, now abandoned, and as he walked toward it, he picked up the long sword of the dead knight who had killed the peasant woman. Then he saw Tavien riding towards him.

"Tavien, take this! It's yours now!" Laren tossed the long sword to Tavien.

"Thanks!" Tavien caught the long sword perfectly by the hilt.

As Laren mounted the abandoned armoured cervid, he met the gazes of the peasants nearby.

"Keep lighting the Flame! You know what you have to do! Go!"

He urged the cervid to a gallop down the street as Tavien followed him.

* * *

Each time a flash of light appeared at her feet, Mika's pink magical wings took her forward and then up the stairways. She held on to the ancient stone walls of the Eldoria Watchtower and the metal railings that had been recently installed along the sides of the stairways. When she reached the fourteenth floor, she looked behind her, and watched her companions, Demias, Galien, Elsia, and Marik, struggling up the steps. Even from the watchtower's interior, all five of them could hear the sounds of distant fiery explosions, the screams of peasants, and the battle cries of knights.

Demias and the others panted as they continued up the stairs. He looked up at the Princess, who had not broken a sweat because she was using her flight magic. "My Lady, any chance you could teach us how to fly someday?"

Mika was taken aback, and was not sure how to answer. She could see they were labouring as they climbed the steps while she simply used her flight magic. "I'm sorry... I'm not certain how to teach magic if you don't already have it."

Galien patted him on the shoulder. "Come on, Demias. Keep going. It's good exercise."

"We're almost at the top," said Marik, who was bringing up the rear.

Elsia wiped away sweat from the side of her head with her sleeve. "We'll be right there, Princess! Please go on."

Mika went ahead. As soon as she reached the fifteenth floor, she released her magic spell, and the wings at her white knee-high boots disappeared. She landed on the floor gracefully, and then took a few steps forward, thinking to herself that she was definitely becoming more accustomed to her magical flight ability from the way she touched the floor. Very soon, the others joined her on the top floor of the Eldoria Watchtower.

Demias struggled to catch his breath. "Why does this tower have to be so damn high? Why fifteen floors?"

Elsia shrugged. "Ask the Spires. They're the ones who built it."

Immediately, another explosion occurred at a nearby building, and the black smoke appeared, startling Mika. She took several steps forward, stopping a short distance from the edge of the floor. The missing wall gave her a perfect view of the castle towards the north and the surrounding areas.

On the streets below, she saw the knights and the peasants clashing against each other, but the knights easily overpowered the peasants, causing serious injury and death. Many peasants escaped into buildings, trying to find shelter and protection. The streets were littered with dead, mostly peasants and a handful of knights. She saw the flames reaching into the air from the explosions. She had never seen such strange flames before, especially with the colour of deep blue. She and her companions watched peasant workers as they ran down the streets with flaming bottles and threw them into buildings where they had stockpiled Starstone. Those buildings exploded into balls of blue flame, incinerating those who threw the incendiaries and everyone else near them.

Mika watched agape. Because she no longer wore her hood, a breeze tugged at her hair, as well as the hem of her white dress and cloak. "How many of them are dead? Hundreds upon hundreds of them... maybe a few thousands by now."

"Princess, look over there at the major side streets." Galien handed her a telescope. He pointed to some of the major streets that branched off from the Valderia Pathway.

Mika took the telescope, and peered through. Down these streets, more groups of knights rode on their cervids, tearing through groups of peasants. "Sir Collin's army separated into several groups, and they're rampaging all over the city, slaughtering the peasants."

Elsia observed through her telescope as well, and spoke with a somber tone. "So many people dying. This is awful. I can't believe it's come to this."

"But the peasants are lighting the Flame of the White Princess," said Marik, as he also observed through his telescope. "Some of the knights are being killed, too."

"I wasn't looking for bloodshed in the first place," Mika said firmly. "But it had to come to this nevertheless. We're fighting for the freedom of the people, and we're going to have it no matter what, even if we have to make terrible sacrifices. It's something terrible I have learned about revolutions. But no matter what, I'll win you the freedom you deserve, freedom from this tyranny."

Demias nodded. "That's right. We'll have our freedom."

"You left me with no choice, Father," said the Princess.

Mika's companions glanced at her.

She shook her head. "No, not just my father. The Nobility and the Royal Family. They left me with no choice. What could a child do against an overwhelming force like this? The only reasons why I've been able to do these things are because I'm the Princess of Melodice, and because I've gained the support of the people around me, the people whom I love. Without my identity, I'm just a child. Without the support of my people, I'm nothing.

"I knew you would send out Sir Collin and the Scarletia Royal Guard into the city eventually, Father. You would send him out to find me and to capture me, and at the same time, you would order the knights to subdue the peasant workers and force them into submission. You would order their deaths. You would order this massacre. You would kill those who are protesting and demanding their freedom from those who hold power and authority. Sir Collin had seen me arrive at the castle gates, and I had ordered him and his knights to stop killing my people. I knew he would have reported this to you. And you would have realized I'm out here with the peasants."

Another explosion went off nearby. A hot wind came from it, and black smoke floated by the watchtower. Its smell was like that of burnt flesh. Mika saw soot forming on the floor and on her white cloak. The others noticed it as well as they shook it off their cloaks.

"Father, I know you had ordered the deaths of Sir

Dellen and Sir Adrel. You had ordered the deaths of their wives as well. You had ordered the deaths of Sir Adrel's children, all of them even younger than I am. But what about Sir Dellen's children? What happened to them? They weren't among the dead."

Elsia stole a glance towards Mika, putting down her telescope. "We haven't been able to find them, My Lady. Tyrel and Jaren are still missing."

Mika nodded. "I hope we can find them soon. They must have escaped somehow."

"I hope so, too," said Elsia.

Mika watched the castle again, envisioning her father standing on the wall above the gates. "Father, if you had ordered the deaths of the leaders of the Scarletia Liberation and the Hope of Scarletia, and seeing that Sir Collin and the Royal Guard have been deployed into the city, seeing that you obviously want me captured, then you must know... that I'm now the leader of this rebellion, the White Princess Liberation Army."

Elsia turned to Marik. "We need to watch the other side of the tower. Come, Marik." She headed towards the other side of the floor.

"Okay," said Marik.

Marik and Elsia went to the wall opposite of the missing one. They stood at two different windows that were really rectangular openings within the walls. Elsia observed towards the southeast, and Marik observed towards the southwest. Demias and Galien stayed with the Princess at the missing wall.

Mika continued. "I've already anticipated all this. I know what you're thinking, all of you at the castle. I've lived among you. I know you all so well. Now, having lived among the peasants, I also know what the rebels are capable of. They're willing to make terrible sacrifices to serve a higher purpose. They're risking themselves and sometimes even their entire families, even when they don't want to, by their actions. They are very resourceful. They can send messages to each other in secret, and pass them along from one person to another, and they wouldn't be intercepted by anyone. They can secretly stash away items they need, such as weapons and armour. They can smuggle them from someplace else or steal them. They can even transport Starstone secretly from the mines, and stockpile it in buildings, all under the cover of nighttime darkness. They can hide from the knights, and disappear without a trace if they needed to. They are completely familiar with the network of hidden alleyways throughout the city. They're willing to do whatever is necessary in order to win the freedom of the people of their nation, the nation they love and are proud of. One million peasant civilians live in the city of Scarletia, and only about one thousand knights patrol the city streets. When it comes to covert operations, the knights are outnumbered and disadvantaged. I suppose there's one thing I should be thankful for while I was living at the castle."

"What is it, Princess?" asked Galien.

Mika realized she'd been speaking aloud as she blinked a couple of times, bringing herself back into the present moment. She answered Galien's question. "I'm thankful that I've been educated well by the finest professors in the entire nation despite my age. They've taught me everything I know, and they've taught me to think for myself. I can anticipate things that might happen, and I can plan my way around them. I've already thought about this deployment of the Scarletia Royal Guard. I've already thought about the King ordering Sir Collin to head out to massacre the peasant workers who continue to revolt. I've already thought this far ahead and more. The peasants are willing to destroy the buildings of the city that directly support the Scarletia Royal Castle. They'll destroy places that store food and manufacture goods and provide various services for the castle. This is what we've done. We've started destroying these places. This is in response to the deployment of the Royal Guard. But there's more to it than just that. I've already thought about the worst possible outcome... and in the event that occurs, something else will happen.

"I suppose... I've become a woman just a little. I've

grown up ever so slightly. I don't know if it's enough. But I'll try my very hardest to win the freedom of my people."

Marik saw something in the periphery of his vision as he looked through the large opening on the side of the wall. He turned his head in that direction, and could have sworn he saw someone leaping from the roof of one building to another, and then disappeared behind yet another building. "Princess!"

Mika, Demias, Galien, and Elsia looked in his direction. Mika headed to where he was, and stood beside him. She stood on the tips of her boots to look, but the bottom of the opening was as high as her chest and she had difficulty seeing. "What is it?"

"I thought I saw something."

Elsia was listening. "What did you see?"

"I'm... I'm not sure. I thought...."

Mika put a gentle hand on Marik's shoulder. "Tell me...."

Marik looked again through the opening. "I thought I saw someone jumping from one building to another. If I didn't know any better, I'd swear they were flying, whoever it was... but I'm not sure what I saw. It disappeared so quickly."

"You probably just saw a large bird," said Elsia.

"Maybe. I... I don't know what I saw. It's gone. I can't find it anywhere." Marik tried to look again.

"Did you see how large it might have been?" asked Mika.

"I'm... not sure. Maybe almost the size of a person?"

Mika thought that was very strange. As far as she knew from her studies, no birds existed in the nation of Melodice that were as large as people. She glanced over at Elsia. "You didn't see anything, did you, Miss Elsia?"

Elsia shook her head. "No. Nothing."

The Princess looked around on the floor, and found a nearby rock. She bent down to try to move it, but it was heavy.

Marik knew right away what she wanted to do. He bent down to pick up the rock, and placed it on the floor against the wall below the opening.

"Thank you, Sir Marik."

"You're welcome, My Lady."

Mika stepped onto the rock, which allowed her to have a better view of the city below. She could not see anything different from where she had been observing from. She looked over the tops of the buildings. Nothing stirred. She stepped off the rock. "Sir Marik, please let me know if you see anything else." She turned to Elsia. "You as well, Miss Elsia."

Elsia nodded. "Sure."

"I better keep my eyes focused," said Marik.

Mika wondered what Marik had seen, if he had seen anything at all. If he had seen something, she wondered what it meant.

* * *

Collin's cervid trotted down a major street that connected to the Valderia Pathway. Maleth was beside him on a cervid as well. They both held their swords at their sides, their blades stained with blood. Their armour had been damaged in the many fights they have been through with the peasants, as well as from nearby explosions of Starstone. Their faces were dirty with soot. They were forced to open their helmets in order to wipe their faces. The flames of the explosions blew in hot wind from all directions, causing everyone around them to feel uncomfortable within their full suits of black armour. It was hot enough inside their armour with the summer sun beating down on them. It was made worse by Starstone flames. Behind them, knights followed, either on foot or on cervids. They were as disheveled as Collin and Maleth. The knights on foot had lost their cervids, either because they had run away in panic or had been injured or killed.

Collin looked up for a moment. He saw Helen flying overhead, heading from one building roof to another, crossing above the pathway where he was. He voiced his thoughts out loud. "Come on, Miss Helen. Find the Princess. Find her with haste so we can end this."

Maleth saw peasants running away from them up ahead. They were not part of any worker groups. They were merely civilians who hoped to get away from the rampaging knights and the groups of peasant workers. "Let's hope she finds her soon, Sir Collin. Otherwise, there will be more civilian deaths on our hands. More civilian blood spilled for the sake of His Highness."

"How many civilians do you think we've killed for... the sake of His Highness, Sir Maleth?" asked Collin. His voice held a hint of frustration and irritation. It was frustration and irritation that was not directed at any of his knights in particular, and certainly not Sir Maleth. In fact, it was directed at King Ralphen.

"I don't know. I would estimate several hundred. But that's not counting the peasants killed by the other groups of knights who have separated from us."

"Some of our knights have been killed as well. Most of our people who were killed were burned alive or crushed to death. Dammit! These peasants are resilient... and desperate. Something's strange here... when you think about it."

Maleth raised an eyebrow as he turned his gaze towards the Supreme Captain. "What do you mean?"

Collin shook his head. "I'm not certain yet. The peasants were prepared for our knights. They were prepared to fight us. Normally, they would just run away. Don't you think these peasants are fighting much harder than they normally would? It's like they're being driven by something. They're being driven by some greater purpose. What is it that they're planning? I don't like this strange feeling of dread that's been gnawing at me since the first explosion, Sir Maleth. There's something going on here. Have you noticed something special about those buildings they've torched?"

Maleth thought about that for a moment. "They're burning down places that provide food, supplies, and services for the castle, for the Nobility and the Royal Family."

"Exactly," said Collin. "Seeing this happening all

around us is doing nothing to quell my suspicions... that something very strange is going on. And what about the timing? All this time, they were peaceful."

"They only started attacking us and burning down the buildings that serve the castle when our knights were deployed into the city."

"Doesn't that seem rather reactive to you?" Collin sighed deeply. "What the hell is going on? This must be her doing. The Princess must have planned this. That's the way she is. That's how her mind works. That's what I've learned about her after all this."

In the distance, a group of peasant workers were rampaging down the streets with crude weapons. They clamoured a battle cry as they charged on foot towards the knights.

"Ride forth, knights!" commanded Maleth, pointing the blade of his sword towards the incoming group.

The knights behind them rode forward, brandishing their various weapons. One knight threw a spear towards a peasant who was brandishing a stolen long sword. The spear tore through the heavyset man's body, and he was thrown backwards, falling onto a broken wooden crate and crushing it underneath him. Arrows and quarrels flew, and struck down more peasant workers.

Collin climbed off his cervid, and walked past his knights as they fought with the peasants. One tried to strike him with a short sword, but Collin deflected it. The sound of their blades clashing rang loud in his ears, but he was unfazed as he turned around, and then used his momentum to cause a gash in the man's side with his long sword. The man fell dead while Collin continued his pace. Another one charged towards him with a wooden club with nails sticking out of it, but Collin simply slashed in front of him to cut the man's arm off, spraying blood on Collin's armour as the club fell to the ground. The man collapsed in pain as he fell to his knees. Collin promptly stabbed him through the heart. The Supreme Captain was well ahead of his knights at this point, walking towards the group of hostile peasant workers as he glared at them.

"Sir Collin!" Maleth watched as a group of ten armed peasants charged towards his commanding officer.

Collin embedded the tip of his sword into the pavement, and a blue magic circle appeared on the ground. His sword glowed brightly, drawing the attention of Maleth and the other knights, as well as some of the attacking peasants.

The peasants charging towards Collin were alarmed, but they had no time to stop and turn back.

Collin raised his glowing sword, and then slashed forward. A bright crescent-shaped wave of white magical energy left his sword, and streaked through the air. As soon as it struck the ten peasants who were almost upon him, their bodies exploded. There were no traces of blood, clothes that might have been burned, or flesh that might have been torn. The only traces left of the peasants were scattered bones, completely clean of anything that used to be attached to them.

The knights behind Collin cheered loudly as if victory was upon them. It gave the knights more determination while the peasants who watched were shocked. Their alarm distracted them, and they were struck down by the knights. The bodies of peasants littered the streets. Knights walked over them, sometimes stepping into pools of blood.

Maleth stood beside Collin, who stared at the bones, littered across the dusty street among random detritus from fallen buildings and discarded wood, paper, glass, and other garbage. He raised his head, meeting Collin's gaze. "Please tell me the Supreme Captain didn't lose control just now."

"I haven't had to use Forbidden Magic in a long time." Collin looked up, and searched the sky for any trace of Helen. "Dammit, Miss Helen, find the Princess so we can end this bloodshed!"

* * *

Mika felt a strange tingling that came from the depths of her subconscious. She looked up and around her, as if searching for something. Her companions continued to observe the city from where they were. She stood at the very centre of the floor. She reached up, and touched the sides of her neck and then her cheeks, feeling apprehensive. She stayed motionless and quiet for a long moment, until....

She gasped. "Magic!"

Everyone turned to face her.

"What's wrong, My Lady?" asked Demias.

Mika looked up at the others. "I feel magic. Someone used magic nearby. All of you, did you see anything?"

Everyone turned back towards the directions they were observing, and looked through their telescopes, searching the city streets for anything out of the ordinary, anything that hinted at the use of magic.

Galien had seen something. "Sir Collin, the Supreme Captain of the Scarletia Royal Guard, did use magic just now. I'd prefer not to say too much about what he just did, My Lady. He's very powerful."

"That's fine," said Mika. "Where did he use it?"

"About three kilometres from here, down that street over there." Galien pointed, but only Demias, who was beside him, could see what he was referring to.

Mika thought about the location, and asked herself if that was what she had felt. She then shook her head. "I don't think that's what I felt. That's too far away. In fact, I still feel it. I feel like someone is using magic, and it's nearby. Are all of you sure you don't see anything?"

"There's nothing, Princess. I don't see anything, not from here," said Elsia, as she observed from where she was.

"I don't see anything out of the ordinary either, Princess Mika." Marik continued looking through his telescope.

Mika sighed. "Then what is it I'm feeling? Am I... just feeling paranoid after everything that's happened?" She looked behind her at the large rectangular opening at the centre of the south wall. She looked out at the clear sky, but saw nothing.

What is this... feeling?

CHAPTER 31

MIKA AND HELEN

"THIS IS THE TALLEST STRUCTURE in the entire city," whispered Helen. "It's a good place for a leader of a rebellion to keep watch over what's going on. The perfect place, in fact. Perhaps, too perfect. You're not the only one blessed with incredible intelligence. You may be intelligent, Princess Mika... but, as expected of a child, one of your greatest weaknesses... is your lack of experience."

Helen hovered in the air as her pink semi-transparent wings of magic glowed at the sides of her boots. Her cloak fluttered in the wind, which pushed her hood off her head. The wind blew at her hair, which was restrained in a ponytail so it would not get in her eyes and interfere with her search. Her eyes moved from the base of the Eldoria Watchtower and slowly up its imposing structure, and eventually, she fixed her eyes upon the missing wall at the top of the tower. She quietly drew out her long sword, its blade shining in the sunlight. As she slowly floated up, she kept herself as close to the exterior wall as possible.

Near the edge of the floor, Demias continued observing through his telescope alongside Galien. "Damn. People are dying everywhere out there, Galien." His hands gripped the metal body of the telescope hard.

Galien watched the carnage below. He raised his telescope to his eye. "The people are desperately fighting for their freedom now, Demias. This is the nature of revolution... I guess. It doesn't make me feel any better though."

Mika had her back to them as she stared at the opening in the south wall, still thinking to herself, wondering about this strange tingling sensation that indicated the presence of magic nearby.

Elsia and Marik continued to observe from where they were, facing away from Mika. Marik turned to Elsia. "You don't see anything strange from there like I did earlier, do you?"

Elsia shook her head. "I don't see anything, Marik."

As Demias looked through his telescope, darkness blocked his view. "Huh?" He put down his telescope… and gasped as his eyes widened.

Helen tore her blade through his chest. He fell over the edge of the floor and fifteen floors down. His body slammed against the cracked pavement.

Galien was alarmed as he turned around, his hand hastily reaching for the hilt of his sword. "Princess!"

Mika suddenly turned around, and gasped.

Helen plunged her sword through Galien's back, and out through the middle of his chest.

Elsia and Marik saw, and were horrified.

Helen pulled her sword out of Galien, which caused his body to be pulled backwards. He fell all the way down to the street below, joining Demias, who lay sprawled on a pool of blood. Peasants nearby screamed when they saw their two bodies.

"Princess, get away!" Elsia shouted. She and Marik drew out their short swords.

Mika did not have time to react. All she could do was scream her name. "Miss Helen!"

A flash of light appeared, Mika saw Helen burst forward with great speed. She blinked once only, and already, Helen was upon her. Elsia and Marik, although they were close by, did not have enough time to get to her and protect her. Helen grabbed her by the front of her dress and cloak with only one hand. Mika felt the wind knocked out of her as Helen slammed her hand into her chest. Helen flew through the opening in the south wall, pulling Mika through with her, and let go. Mika screamed as she fell while Helen continued to fly upwards.

Elsia and Marik rushed back to the observation windows, and watched with shock as the White Princess plunged towards the street below.

"Princess Mika!" shouted Elsia.

Helen's lips formed a mocking smile. "She won't die."

In a flash of light, a pink magic circle appeared, followed by Mika's magical wings at her feet. Mika looked upwards, breathing hard to try to catch her breath. In the periphery of her vision, she saw Elsia and Marik up in the tower, looking on with great surprise. Her eyes moved upwards, higher and higher, until she saw Helen hovering above. "Miss Helen...." She saw the semi-transparent wings at Helen's feet. "I see she completed the lesson on magical flight as well. But... but what's going on?"

Helen stared down at Mika from above, her cloak fluttering in the wind. Mika's cloak fluttered as well, along with her hair and the hem of her dress and cloak. Helen held her bloody sword at her side, which she slowly brought forward. She pointed the blade directly at the Princess.

Mika gasped as she stared at Helen. Behind each of them, more black smoke reached into the sky.

"Princess Mika Silveraine!" called out Helen.

Mika was speechless. *What's going on? What is this?! Why is Miss Helen...?!*

"I, Helen Renier, Sergeant of the Scarletia Royal Guard, hereby take you into custody as ordered by the King of Melodice!"

Sergeant? She was a Private Enlist! A rank promotion? Two ranks?! And she's here to capture me?! Instead of Sir Collin, she's the one who's been ordered to capture me?!

"Dammit!" Marik pounded his fist against the wall while his other hand gripped his sword tightly. "We can't help her from here!"

Elsia looked behind her at the edge of the floor, her sword at her side. It took a moment for the deaths of Demias and Galien and the appearance of this woman with the intent to capture the White Princess to sink in. "Who is that young woman? She killed Demias and Galien, and now she's here to capture the Princess?"

Mika clenched her fists. "I was wrong. It wasn't Sir Collin who was sent to capture me. It was you who was sent to capture me and take me back to the castle?!"

"Correct, Princess," said Helen.

Wait. Hold on a moment. She was with me. At the home of the Balias family. I asked her to come with me. She helped me. She's the only other person who knew where they lived. That means.... Mika stared with antipathy, her mouth open. Her eyes narrowed somewhat. Her fists tightened even harder as anger welled up from within her. She was surprised at herself for a very brief moment for feeling this way, because she was usually slow to anger. However, this time, as she came to a sudden realization, she had every reason to feel angry. "I see. So that's how it is, is it, Miss Helen?"

Helen's eyes narrowed as well as she held her sword beside her. "What?"

"You knew where the Balias family lived. You knew where Sir Dellen, Miss Zima, and their children lived, and that's how the King and the Scarletia Royal Guard found them! You told them where they lived, didn't you?!"

Helen gripped her sword harder.

Hot tears of anger streamed down Mika's cheeks as she glared at Helen. "It was all you! They were executed along with another leader of the rebels, along with his family! The knights beheaded them!"

Helen was taken aback. *Beheaded? What is she talking about? Their throats were slashed... according to Sir Collin's report.*

"Even the children!" shouted Mika.

Helen glared at Mika so hard that if she glared any harder, she imagined that an explosion might appear in between them and consume them both.

Mika continued. "If it weren't for that information, it would have taken them much longer to find the leaders of the rebel groups!"

"What of it?!" shouted Helen, anger welling up from inside of her as well. "I was fulfilling my duty as a knight of the Royal Guard!"

Mika was aghast by her reaction, her dismissive words. To her, it seemed as if Helen had become a different person. She had just started to get to know her. Mika had even started to like her. However.... "You... all this is happening... because of you...."

"You're an intelligent young girl, Princess Mika. I suppose I shouldn't be surprised that you figured this out. Yes, the information I showed you so that we could locate the Balias family... I gave that information to the King. Because of that, the leaders of your precious rebel groups were found and executed. And I've been promoted by two ranks."

"I see. A promotion! Is that why you gave that information to my father?! So you could become a Sergeant?! No, there has to be more than that! Why?! You must have another reason, Miss Helen!"

Helen's lips formed a smile of mockery. "You suspect another reason. Very good. You amaze me, little girl. I suppose you truly are getting to know me better. You know I'm not so shallow that I'd do something like that just to boost myself in rank."

"Then why?!"

"You want to know why? I'll tell you! Don't misunderstand me, Princess. I agree with you that the peasants are being treated unfairly by the Nobility and the Royal Family. They've suffered so much in the past century, and it's time for that suffering to stop. They must find their freedom from this terrible oppression. However... your methods are wrong!"

Mika stared at Helen, eyes widened.

"This freedom you seek for the Peasantry will not be obtained through revolution! You will only make them suffer! Don't you see the death and chaos occurring on the streets below you?! People are dying! They're being cut down by the knights of the Royal Guard, as ordered by their King! This is what revolution is about! This is not the correct method for obtaining freedom! Once they do find their freedom, most of them will have died! If you truly want to change this nation, you need to do it through political reformation! You need to change the government from within! If you do that, eventually, that change will spread throughout Melodice, and the Peasantry will know true freedom! That's the only way to change our nation, Princess Mika! Not through bloodshed and revolution!"

Mika looked down below for a brief moment, knowing full well the results of a revolution. She watched as death and chaos filled the city streets. She glanced back up at Helen. "If you want to change Melodice for the better from within the government, judging by the way they think right now, do you seriously believe the Nobility will listen to you?! They'll think you're a fool!"

Helen slashed the air in front of her with her sword. "Enough talk! I will take you into custody as ordered! Right now!"

A flash of light appeared at Helen's magical wings… and she charged forward through the air with great speed. Mika gasped, surprised by how fast Helen could fly. She turned, and a flash of light appeared at her wings of magic as well, and she surged through the air in a different direction.

Helen followed her. "Damn… she's faster than I thought." She willed herself to go faster. She felt the wind against her face. She remembered how fast her mother flew away, and wished she had that kind of speed already, but her mother, having much more experience with magic, was far ahead of her ability in magical flight.

Mika flew overhead. Below, she saw carnage. Blood smeared the streets where bodies of peasants lay, men and women alike. Knights and peasants clashed weapons. Another Starstone explosion appeared in the distance. The black smoke that rose up from it blocked out the sun from Mika's view as she flew underneath its shadow. The summer wind felt cool against her cheeks, but also carried with it the smell of the smoke that was like that of burnt flesh as she passed over areas where Starstone flames were burning.

"You're not getting away from me, Princess Mika!" Another flash of light appeared at Helen's feet, and she surged forward faster.

Mika willed herself to go faster, and then she started to arc upwards, higher into the sky. She looked behind her. "She's... flying faster!" She closed her eyes tight, and willed herself to go faster still, but nothing was happening. Her fear was probably interfering with her mind. In order to properly focus her magic, she needed to calm her mind, but she was far from calm right now. Behind her, she saw Helen closer than she was just a moment ago.

"Come here!" shouted Helen, reaching out towards Mika's feet.

Mika suddenly jerked to the right, and Helen stopped in midair. The Princess flew in a different direction. Helen groaned in frustration, and flew towards her again, but Mika was flying in different directions to try to confuse her. Helen continued after her, and tried to follow along with her sharp maneuvers.

"You are perfectly capable of fighting back against me, Princess! Your magic is strong, but you're too weak inside! That's what you are! A coward and a weakling!"

Mika maneuvered sharply through the air, but it made her somewhat queasy inside. As she flew upwards, she shook her head vigorously to try to rid herself of the uncomfortable sensation she felt deep within her ears, but doing so only made it worse.

Down below, Collin looked up, and saw Helen and Mika. Helen was flying faster than Mika, who tried to dodge her.

"Miss Helen, you almost have her!" shouted Collin.

Feldia looked up from where she was. On another street, Laren saw as well. They saw Mika flying, desperately trying to get away from her pursuer.

"No! Princess!" shouted Feldia.

Laren watched with shock. "No! Get away, Princess!"

As knights and peasants continued to battle each other in the city, and more explosions occurred, Mika struggled against the forces that racked her body as she made unusual sharp turns and maneuvers to try to outrun Helen.

"You can't get away!" shouted Helen.

Mika flew in another direction, backwards. She

watched Helen from a distance, and pointed her hand towards her. She thought of the same magic spell she had used to stop the peasant thugs from attacking her and Helen while they were trapped in the alleyways of the city. A magic circle appeared in the air. It was supposed to appear in the same location as Helen as she flew by, but it missed and disappeared.

Helen shouted again. "You think you can stop me with that?!"

Mika turned away, and flew in yet another direction. *It missed her! She's going too fast for me! Too fast for my magic!* After a moment, she stopped in midair, and concentrated harder. Perhaps it would work if she stopped for a split second. She tried again. The magic circle appeared in the air... but it missed Helen again. That was a mistake. It gave Helen time to catch up. Mika gasped as Helen reached out, and took her by the arm.

"I have you!"

"Get away from me!" Mika closed her eyes. A quick magic circle appeared underneath her feet, and a spherical barrier appeared around her. In just a split second, the barrier pushed outwards, pushing Helen away from Mika by quite a long distance. The barrier disappeared when it became too large.

Helen was somewhat dazed for a moment. She shook her head, her eyes closed, feeling somewhat dizzy. After a moment, she recovered, stopping in midair. "Impressive. She used a repulsion barrier."

Mika willed her wings to take her away with due haste. Her heart and her thoughts raced. She tried to think of what she was going to do. She looked around for a place to hide, but she knew Helen would follow her and find her. There was no escaping her.

Helen watched Mika, who started arcing upwards again, flying higher into the air. She remembered that she was authorized to use force, if necessary, in order to accomplish her task of capturing the Princess.

"Ah, that's right. You're not getting away from me, little girl!" Helen hovered in the air, and held her sword at her side as she stared up at Mika. A massive magic circle suddenly appeared, larger than any of the others she had ever produced. Its lines of power glowed brightly, along with the characters and symbols that were arranged in various intricate patterns throughout.

Collin, Maleth, the knights, the peasants, Laren, and Feldia could see the enormous glowing magic circle above them, nearly twenty metres wide.

Mika felt it, the same strange feeling she experienced while still in the Eldoria Watchtower, just before Helen appeared. She looked down below, and saw the magic circle. Helen appeared tiny from this far away, but the magic circle was large. When Mika saw this, she gasped.

Helen brought her sword up, and held it sideways in front of her, the flat side of the blade against the palm of her other hand. The steel blade felt warm against her palm as it glowed brightly due to the effects of the magic spell she was casting. In front of the middle of the blade, a sphere of magical energy appeared. It grew in size and power, and its brightness increased. Soon, the brightness was so intense that it stung Helen's eyes slightly, causing her to stop looking directly at it. She focused her eyes on Mika instead, far above her.

Mika stopped in midair. She watched the magical power that gathered where Helen was, and she was alarmed. "Oh my... she's going to...."

The sphere brightened further, and a beam of light erupted out of it, streaking through the air upwards into the sky towards Mika.

Mika gasped. Multiple flashes of light appeared at her feet, and her wings pointed downward as she charged upward. She flew facing downwards, so in a sense, she was flying backwards. She watched the beam of magic approaching her with great speed. Since it was a beam, she figured she could move sideways and avoid it. Mika willed herself to make a sharp maneuver sideways, and continued to fly as fast as she could.

Helen grinned mockingly. The beam curved.

Mika gasped again. She flew in another direction, and

yet another. No matter what she did, the beam curved to follow her, until it formed a strange shape of light in the sky that everyone in the entire city of one million could see. Mika looked back, and turned around again as she flew away.

"I can't avoid it. That means... I have to somehow stop it!" She raised her hands in front of her, palms out towards the approaching beam. Several large magic circles appeared, one after another. They formed defensive barriers. They were enormous, similar in size to the gigantic magic circle that Helen produced to create the beam of light that followed her. Eventually, Mika formed a total of seven magic barriers, each of them as powerful as she could make them.

The beam struck the first barrier, and was stopped there, but did not cease. Where the beam struck the barrier, a sustained explosion occurred that sent out waves and beams of bright magical energy. The sound it made was like a frightening thunder, just as loud as the Starstone explosions. It also disrupted the atmosphere around Mika, causing a great tempest that whirled around her immediate vicinity, tugging at her hair and her clothes.

Helen struggled for more power as she narrowed her eyes, and cried out. The beam brightened as she poured as much of her magical power as she could muster.

The first barrier broke into pieces like glass, and then disappeared. Mika's eyes widened. The beam struck the second barrier. She cried out as well to try to keep them all held up at the same time as she continued to fly upwards and backwards. After just a moment, the second barrier broke to pieces as well. The beam brightened some more, causing the sustained explosion to also brighten. Mika was forced to look away from it, as the light stung her eyes. The third barrier broke... and then the fourth... and then the fifth.

"No!" shouted Mika as she closed her eyes.

The sixth barrier was struck. It broke to pieces, and then disappeared. The beam exploded against the seventh and final magic barrier. Mika poured out as much of her magical power as she could. She opened her eyes again, trying to endure the brilliant light of the sustained explosion. A much brighter flash of light appeared in front of her as the seventh magical barrier was completely destroyed. She closed her eyes again, and threw up her hands in front of her as if to defend herself one last time. The beam of light consumed her. Mika screamed in terrible pain, as if her entire body was being torn apart, but the pain was not physical. The feeling was as if a part of her that she couldn't see with her own physical eyes was torn asunder.

Helen stopped, and the curving beam of light faded away. She breathed hard as she watched.

Mika was still in the air, hovering. Her cloak and her dress were perfectly intact. However, she felt incredible pain in her entire body as her eyes began to close. The semi-transparent wings at her feet started to fade. Very soon, the magical wings disappeared... and Mika started falling.

"I've got you," said Helen, as she quickly sheathed her sword. A flash of light appeared at her feet, and her wings took her forward. She surged through the air as Mika fell.

Over one and a half kilometres above the ground... that gives her perhaps about twenty seconds to fall to her death!

Helen clenched her teeth, willing herself to fly as fast as possible. She estimated where she needed to be to catch the Princess as she fell from the sky. Eventually, she was directly below Mika's path, so she changed the direction of her flight to a downwards direction, and matched the speed of Mika's fall. Helen reached out to put her arms under Mika's frail body, and began to slow herself down so Mika's weight would press against her arms. They fell together towards the street below.

Feldia ran down the street, seeing where Mika was about to land. She ran as fast as her legs could take her, her sword at her side. "Princess Mika!"

A few metres above the pavement, a flash of light appeared at Helen's wings of magic, and she soared upwards again, with Mika in her arms, and carried her away. Helen looked down for a moment, and saw a young woman carrying a sword at her side, who stopped where Mika could have landed had she been allowed to fall.

Feldia looked up, stunned. She met the gaze of the young lady knight who caught Mika in the air. "Princess!"

All around Feldia, the peasants watched with horror as the Princess was taken away.

Helen held Mika as she flew upwards to avoid the range of anyone who might fire a crossbow or bow and arrow.

Laren looked up. "No...!" He saw Mika, her body motionless. Another explosion of Starstone went off a safe distance behind him. The hot wind from the blast blew by him, but he was far too shocked by what he was seeing to pay any attention to it.

"Sir Collin!" said Maleth, pointing at the sky.

Collin saw the successful capture of Princess Mika. He raised his sword high in the air. "Victory!" shouted the Supreme Captain.

Most of the knights around Collin, with the exception of Sir Maleth, shouted in unison as they raised their weapons high above their heads. Maleth looked on without any expression, and said nothing. They watched as the Princess of Melodice was being brought back to the Scarletia Royal Castle by Helen. Their clamours echoed down the streets. Peasants watched, utterly helpless.

* * *

Helen carried Mika's frail body as she slowly flew back towards the castle. The spectacular display of magical power in the skies over Scarletia had been seen by the entire city, by every knight and peasant. Some of the fighting between the knights and the peasants had paused as they were interrupted by the magical battle above them. Now, they watched, as the Princess was being taken back to the Scarletia Royal Castle.

Mika was motionless, feeling extremely weak. When she attempted to move, she found that only her fingertips obeyed her command, and just barely. She opened her eyes just a little. Through her blurry vision, she saw Helen's face, as beautiful and as radiant as hers. As she lay in Helen's arms, Mika watched her.

Helen noticed Mika trying to move her lips, and hesitated. The Princess was trying to say something. Helen watched her for a moment, and sighed as she looked at Mika's lovely face, bewildered, but completely unharmed. "What is it?" she asked, leaning her face a little closer.

The young Princess tried to whisper again.

"What are you trying to say, Princess Mika?"

Mika forced herself to swallow to clear her throat, and let out a slow breath. "I suppose... this means... I need to... practice more... with... my magic."

"Oh?" whispered Helen, confused.

"Your magic... is so powerful... Miss Helen. I... couldn't... defend myself. You... were too... too strong."

Helen paused for a moment, and then shook her head. She could not help but smile just a little. "No, Princess. It was only because your defensive magic was so powerful. I had to use all my offensive power to break through it. You're very strong."

Mika opened her eyes just a little more, and saw the small smile on Helen's lips. But just opening her eyes a little more took quite a bit out of her. She thought about what had just happened earlier and what was happening now. "Miss Helen...."

"Yes, Princess?"

Mika paused before she said anything. There was something she wanted to say to her, but a part of her wanted to hold back. However, she thought about what had happened just now. Helen had just attacked her and captured her, and was now taking her back to the castle. She thought back to Dellen and his wife Zima, to Adrel, his wife, and three young daughters. All of them died because Helen revealed the identities of Dellen, Zima, and their family to the King. Also, Dellen's sons Tyrel and Jaren were missing. No, she was not going to hold back. She was angry enough with Helen that holding back was no longer an option. "I... honestly... very honestly... thought... we were... starting to... understand... each other, Miss Helen."

Helen was taken aback. "What?"

"I was... truly... starting to like... you... very much."

Helen was speechless, staring into Mika's eyes.

"I had... hoped that... we could become... friends someday. I truly... would have... loved that... Miss Helen... very much."

More silence. Helen gently bit her lip.

"But... it appears... I was... mistaken."

Helen looked ahead towards the Scarletia Royal Castle, avoiding Mika's gaze. She frowned as a heavy feeling enveloped her heart. She held onto the Princess as she hovered closer to the castle. Helen closed her eyes for a moment, and when she reopened them, she looked quite furious. *How dare you say that to me? You betrayed the Royal Family, the Nobility, and your own nation. Are you angry with me because of what I did? Because I revealed to the King the information that led to the deaths of Sir Dellen and Miss Zima? No, that sacrifice was necessary. It was... it was necessary.... It might appear wrong to you, and maybe it is, but I'm trying to achieve a greater good!*

Mika watched her reaction, but she was feeling weaker by the minute as her eyes began to close a little more.

* * *

The knights and the servants atop the bridge above the castle gates did not know how to react to the capture of Princess Mika. Some of them wanted to cheer with victory like the knights did farther away, but in the presence of the King and Queen, it might have been inappropriate, considering who had just been captured.

Helen slowly hovered downwards towards the bridge, carrying Mika in her arms. She watched everyone's reactions. King Ralphen had a hard facial expression while Queen Maiya appeared to be shocked. Galner held an expression of relief and anger at the same time. She eased herself onto the bridge, and knelt down, carefully laying Mika down on the bridge. Without letting anyone notice, she put a gentle hand on Mika's arm, as if to try to comfort her.

Mika felt her hand. *Don't touch me.*

"Mika!" shouted Maiya, rushing over to her daughter.

As Queen Maiya arrived, Helen stood back, and bowed her head. "I apologize, My Lady, for using force to capture the Princess."

Maiya glared at Helen. However, there was nothing that she could say.

Helen could not say anything either as she backed away a few steps to give Maiya and Mika some room. She was taken aback by the Queen's reaction to her just now, but understood why. She had just attacked and captured her daughter, the Princess of Melodice. What mother wouldn't be angered by such action?

King Ralphen arrived, putting a comforting hand on Helen's shoulder, and nodded to her.

"My Lord, please forgive me for having to use force." Helen bowed slightly.

"Do not be troubled, Miss Helen. You did well. You will be commended for this, I promise you." Ralphen stepped closer to Mika, and knelt down. "I don't believe she's hurt. You can tell, can't you, Maiya?"

Mika could feel the gentle touch of her mother, who examined her from head to toe, caressing her arms, forehead, hair, and face, but her eyes were almost closed. She could barely even see her mother's face.

"Mika... please be all right." Maiya looked up at Ralphen. "She's not injured... but being struck by magical energy can be very painful. I'm certain you know that. It feels like a part of you was torn to pieces. The pain is unimaginable."

"But as users of magic, we know she'll recover quickly, since the injury is magical rather than physical."

"I know that!" snapped Maiya.

Ralphen looked down at Mika, shaking his head. "I am disappointed."

Mika's lips parted slightly as she tried to whisper.

"What is she saying?" asked Ralphen.

"What is it, Mika?" Maiya leaned closer to the Princess. She put one ear close to Mika's lips, and strained to hear what she was trying to say.

There was only one thing Mika could say at this point. "Mother, please... forgive me."

Maiya pulled away after a moment, and stared down at her. She thought about what had happened so far. She thought about that night when Mika had disappeared from her bedchamber. She thought about that morning when Angelica had found that she was missing. However, it turned out Mika had snuck out into the city, and had joined the rebellious peasants. Tears appeared in Maiya's eyes as she glared at Mika. "How dare you ask me for forgiveness after all this?!"

Ralphen put a hand on Maiya's shoulder in an attempt to comfort her. He waved Galner to come closer. Galner complied, and stood near the severely weakened Princess. "Seal her magic away, Sir Galner."

"Gladly, My Lord." Galner raised his hand directly above Mika. A blue magic circle appeared underneath her, and her entire body glowed for a brief moment. The glow disappeared almost as quickly as it came.

No... I can't... no... my magic.... Mika suddenly felt empty, as if she had been separated from the rest of the world. She felt complete isolation. She realized this was what it felt like to have one's magic power sealed away. She could not sense any magic at all.

"The seal I've placed upon her is a strong one," said Galner. "It's strong enough that she won't be able to use her magic for a month. She'll have no hope of being able to break the seal, and only I will be able to remove it. If needed, I can cast an even more powerful one, My Lord, one that can potentially last a year."

"That should suffice for now. We'll decide later what we need to do. But, right now... I'm just glad this is finally over," said the King.

No! The Peasantry! No... no, it's not over... it's not... I promise you, it's not!

As Ralphen rose, Mika stared at him through eyes that were almost completely closed by now, feeling what was left of her strength ebbing away. She saw her mother's face, full of worry, but also disappointment. Galner appeared to be angry. Ralphen stared down at her with no outward expression, but she knew he was seething with rage inside. Around them, the knights and the servants gathered. They watched as they bore witness to the capture of the young Princess who had rebelled against the Nobility.

"Princess Mika Silveraine," said King Ralphen. "You are hereby taken into custody for the charge of high treason."

High treason? Is this... how it ends for me? I suppose we've done everything we needed to do, or rather... what I needed to do. It's up to Sir Laren and Miss Feldia and the others now, starting from here.

Ralphen turned to the knights around them. "Take her into the dungeon. She's a criminal, a prisoner. Treat her as such,"

Maiya shot a glance at him. "Ralphen, she's our child, our eleven-year-old daughter!"

"Yes, our child, our eleven-year-old daughter, who has committed high treason!" Ralphen looked up at the knights again. He could see the hesitation and confusion in their faces. They were unsure on what they were supposed to do, and though he was somewhat irritated by their reaction, he understood why they felt the way they did. They were being ordered to take Princess Mika prisoner. "Take her now!"

"Y-yes, My Lord!" said the knights, their voices expressing uneasy tension.

Mika felt her tiny body being turned over to its side, and her hands being brought together behind her back. She closed her eyes. The sounds of the voices around her became muffled as her consciousness began to fade. She felt sharp pain as her hands were tied together at the wrists by the same rope the knights used to tie the hands of peasants behind their backs. The rope scraped the soft skin of her thin wrists. She felt the strong hands of the knights lifting her up by her armpits as her head slumped forward. Her feet were dragged against the floor of the bridge. As the child Princess of the nation of Melodice was dragged away by the knights, she continued to speak defiantly in her thoughts.

It's not over... it's not over yet... there's still... one more....

CHAPTER 32:

GAMBIT OF THE PRINCESS

SEC 3566, Morrighan 50

E VEN WITH THE CAPTURE OF the White Princess, the revolt did not cease. Over a hundred thousand peasant workers continued to fight against the knights of the Scarletia Royal Guard. Groups of peasants continued to march throughout the city of Scarletia. Some of those groups continued burning down buildings that supplied goods and services directly to the Scarletia Royal Castle. As the night passed, the dark blue flames of Starstone that consumed whole buildings and their surroundings glowed ominously. As the next day dawned, they continued to burn.

The peasant workers did not just destroy buildings that supplied goods and services to the castle. Many knight patrols stations were also attacked. While the knights put up a good fight to defend them, the peasants eventually overwhelmed them with their sheer numbers. Many peasants died, but eventually, the knights were slaughtered mercilessly. This allowed the peasants to steal weapons, armour, and other equipment from the patrol stations.

Bloodied, bruised, and battle-scarred, Feldia and Laren walked down one of the major streets as confident and battle-hardened warriors, followed by peasants behind them. They now wore full armour from head to toe, and they carried shields as well as long swords. After attacking a few knight patrol stations overnight, they managed to find armour that fit them perfectly. They also wore knives at their boots and daggers at their belts. Some of the peasants were fully armoured as well. Others wore metal armour on their torso or just gauntlets or greaves or helmets. Others wore leather armour. They were also able to obtain the superior weapons of the knights, such as long swords, maces, spears, crossbows with large supplies of quarrels, and bows and arrows. Around them, the streets were littered with debris and the dead, both peasants and knights alike. The knights who had been killed had their armour and weapons removed, taken by the peasants.

"We're not done yet!" Feldia struck the flat side of her sword against her shield. "We haven't given up!"

Laren swung his sword in front of him, shaking off drops of blood. "This fight is not over! It's far from over!"

Feldia glared ahead as knights approached on foot. "The White Princess was aware of the possibility that she was going to be captured, and made it clear what we must do! We have our final orders!"

Laren observed their approach as well, the sounds of their battle cries competing with those of the peasant fighters behind him. "And those orders are... to fight hard for our freedom! We're going to force our way out of this city, and destroy it in the process!"

"As the White Princess has ordered!"

"It shall be done!"

Feldia and Laren swung their swords, and clashed against the blades of the knights. The peasant workers, now armed and armoured, fought against the attacking knights. Blades struck shields. The sounds of metal scraping metal and tearing flesh competed with cries of battle and screams of death that echoed down the streets of Scarletia.

* * *

The double doors to the King's Conference were opened wide, and Collin entered. He removed his dirt-smeared helmet, and held it underneath his arm. His full armour was damaged, and it was stained by blood, dirt, and soot. He had a bloody bruise on the side of his head, and sweat made his hair stick to his scalp. He glanced up at King Ralphen and Queen Maiya, who were seated at the table, and stood straight at attention.

"Sir Collin, where is Sir Maleth?" asked Ralphen.

"My Lord, in command of the Royal Guard while I'm here about to provide you with the report you requested."

"All right. Now, about those peasant animals! Why the hell are they still fighting?!"

Collin paused for a moment, trying to gather his thoughts despite the tension he felt.

However, Ralphen continued. "We have captured Princess Mika! She's locked up in the dungeon where she belongs! I had thought this would stop the revolt of the peasant workers! Why are they still fighting, Sir Collin?!"

Collin stiffened. "I'm... not certain, My Lord."

Ralphen slammed his palm against the table, startling Maiya beside him. "Dammit, Sir Collin, how can you not be certain? Perhaps that new rank of Supreme Captain doesn't fit you well after all!"

Filled with frustration that he tried to contain as much as possible, Collin clenched his free hand into a fist beside him.

Maiya put a hand on Ralphen's arm to try to calm him down.

Ralphen took a deep breath, and then cleared his throat. "Your report on the current situation, Sir Collin."

"Yes, My Lord. Despite the capture of Princess Mika, they're continuing their revolt. In fact, that's an understatement. Before, they were destroying the facilities that provided goods and services for the castle. However, we've observed that they've started destroying more than just our facilities."

Ralphen glared at him. "What do you mean?"

"They've started targeting... infrastructure, My Lord, such as the provision of water. They're burning down farmland. They've targeted our patrol stations, killed our knights, and stolen our equipment for their own use.

They've also targeted all property owned by the Nobility, including the mines. Some of those mines still have ample amounts of Starstone. If those mines explode, My Lord, the consequences could be dire. We don't know how far and how deep those mines go."

Maiya stared with shock. "How?! Why?!"

"I'm sorry, My Lady, but I'm not certain why they're doing this. The peasants have escalated their revolt even further."

"I see," said Ralphen.

"It's estimated, My Lord, My Lady, that the number of peasant workers who are now participating in this ongoing revolt has reached over one hundred thousand. More are joining them every hour, and it continues to escalate. We have lost many knights despite having the training to fight in wars, despite having superior weapons and armour."

"What are the casualties, Sir Collin?"

"My Lord, we have lost over four hundred knights."

Maiya gasped. "Over four hundred of our knights?!"

The King shouted with great fury. "Unacceptable, Sir Collin! How can we lose so many knights against peasant animals?! They don't have the mental capacity to be able to do something of that magnitude! Your numbers must be wrong!"

Collin swallowed hard. "Nevertheless, that's the body count we have gathered. That's how many of our men and women are unaccounted for. There may be more."

"These are *peasant animals*!"

"However, My Lord!" interrupted Collin. "That's how many of our people these peasants have killed. Regardless of their mental capacity, they've been able to overwhelm our patrol stations, and burn them down. They've been able to put up a fight, using anything and everything they can get their hands on as weapons. They have, in secret, moved large quantities of Starstone from the mines to various buildings, which they detonated using makeshift incendiary devices. They have targeted facilities that provide the castle with day-to-day goods and services."

Ralphen glared at him, not appreciating being interrupted just a moment ago.

"In addition, they have targeted other infrastructure vital to the survival of the Nobility, My Lord! Food, apothecaries, hospitals, everything! We are severely outnumbered, and we are losing ground! We are down to about twenty-six hundred knights in the city, and there are still over a hundred thousand peasants we have to contend with! We cannot fight against that many rampaging peasant workers!"

"I still can't understand how they can be doing all these things!"

Maiya looked up. "I can."

Collin glanced towards the Queen. "My Lady?"

"Do you not agree that the Peasantry are often disorganized, that they often employ primitive tactics, Sir Collin?" asked Maiya.

"Yes, My Lady, that's correct."

The Queen sighed softly with a somber expression. "It's because of our daughter. Mika Silveraine. As the Princess of Melodice, she gathered them together, and turned them all into one unified force. The peasants are united because of her. They followed her direction because she promised them this so-called freedom. Because of that, look at what's happened."

Ralphen rose from his chair with such fury that the chair flew back and crashed to the floor. He put his hand on his forehead. "Dammit... what the hell are we going to do?" After a moment, he looked up at Maiya, and then at Collin. "Mika... she must know something."

* * *

Mika wore the same dress, cloak, and boots from yesterday. Normally, as a prisoner, her clothes would have been replaced with a plain gray uniform made from rags. She remembered hearing about what was done to prisoners in the dungeon. Sometimes, men were beaten and women were raped to the point that they ended up becoming nothing more than the physically battered and emotionally broken outer shells of their former selves. Their clothes were removed, and then examined for anything that could be used as evidence against them. Their naked bodies were laid flat on the cold, hard dungeon floor, their hands and feet bound together, and every possible place that could be used to hide anything was poked and prodded with various instruments of torture. If she had been any other prisoner, they would have forced her to spread her legs, and then probing fingers would have searched inside of her. Mika shuddered at the thought.

Right now, I'm completely defenseless. Perhaps they believe I couldn't possibly have anything on me that I could use to escape from the dungeon. Perhaps they believe I'm no longer a threat because my magic is sealed. Perhaps the knights still look at me as a child, and refused to defile me. For any and all of those reasons, I'm still relieved.

Mika opened her eyes, taking a moment to adjust to the darkness of the dungeon. She took a deep breath, and found the air to be stale, as if it had not been circulated for months, perhaps years. She observed her surroundings. Her cell was completely enclosed on all four sides with stone walls. One of the walls had a wide door made of thick iron bars welded together in a diagonal formation. The door had an enormous padlock on the outside. There was some light that filtered into her cell from kerosene lamps mounted on the walls outside. Through the bars of the door, she could see brighter lights from the hallways beyond. It meant that her cell was close to the entrance of the dungeon.

She felt the rope that bound her wrists together. If she moved them by just a little, she felt them scrape the delicate and soft skin on her wrists, causing her pain. She felt the intangible seal that prevented her from using her magic. The magic seal Sir Galner used against her was powerful. She truly felt as if something precious had been taken away from her, as if she had been separated from a dear loved one. However, she noticed she had recovered from the magic attack Helen had unleashed upon her. Last night, as soon as she was placed in this dungeon, she had fallen into a very deep sleep. She had awakened a couple of times throughout the night, only to fall back asleep. Now, she was wide awake.

Mika looked up at one of the shafts of light that filtered between the iron bars, and saw two dark silhouettes farther away. She focused her eyes on them. With a wistful voice, she spoke the names of the people standing outside. "Miss Angelica... and Mirin."

Angelica, along with Mirin, stood near the entrance of the dungeon as they tried to look in. "Where is she? Do you see her, Mirin?"

After a moment, Mirin saw Mika, and their eyes met through the iron bars of the nearest cell. Mirin gasped, and pulled on Angelica's sleeve. His soft voice quivered as he spoke. "Angelica, look."

Angelica looked in the direction he was pointing, and one of her hands flew to her mouth. She saw Mika, her precious little Princess, lying down in the dungeon cell on her side. In the darkness of her cell, she could barely see Mika, but she did manage to make out parts of her face and her dress, illuminated by the narrow shafts of light that filtered through the bars. "Oh, Princess Mika... I...."

She could not find the words. She wanted to call out to her to comfort her. She wanted to go to her to embrace her as tightly as she could. However, the impenetrable iron bars separated them, as well as the watchful eyes of Sir Collin, who appeared in front of them. She and Mirin gasped together.

"What are you two doing here?" asked the Supreme Captain. "This area is off limits to civilians."

Mika stared, seeing the dark silhouette of Collin. He had cleaned up, and wore a new suit of black armour without a helmet. He had his back to her, and blocked her view of the outside.

Mirin was absolutely speechless as he held Angelica's arm.

Angelica put her arm around him to comfort him, and then she looked up at Collin, trying to appear as confident as she normally would. "Sir Collin, would it be too much to ask if we could... see Princess Mika?"

"Why?"

"Why, you ask?" Angelica searched for an answer. "Well... I'm her maidservant, Sir Collin, that's why. And Mirin here, he's her friend. I'm also her friend. We both are. We love her dearly! Would you be so kind as to let us see her?"

Collin thought for a moment as Angelica and Mirin waited for his answer. He stepped closer towards them as he expressed regret, lowering his voice with due respect to their relationship with the Princess. "I'm sorry, Miss Angelica, Sir Mirin. The King had ordered that no one is to see her. Only the King, the Queen, Sir Maleth, Sir Galner, and I are allowed to see her. Other knights may see her, but only under our supervision. Unfortunately, he didn't make any exceptions. That means... even her friends can't see her."

Angelica and Mirin were speechless. Angelica wanted to say something. She tried to think quickly.

"Now, if you will please leave the dungeon area, I would most appreciate it."

"Sir Collin...."

Collin's voice grew louder and more authoritative. "Now, please."

Mirin was startled by Collin's order. He felt Angelica take his hand. He watched her gaze up at Collin with a hint of defiance in her face, but she relented, and bowed her head slightly.

"Come, Mirin," Angelica said with a wistful voice.

A terrible sadness came over Mirin. As he and Angelica turned around, they both tried to look at Mika one more time. They did see a glimpse of her face through the iron bars.

Mika watched them, her heart full of despair. She watched as Angelica and Mirin took one more glance at her. She could see they were painful glances. She watched them slowly walk away, and eventually, they moved out of sight. Her feeling of isolation stabbed at her heart as her tears welled up.

* * *

Mirin held his head low, tears streaming down his cheeks, but he did not wail, nor did he sob. He held tightly onto Angelica's hand. As Angelica led him down one of the hallways of the castle, he reached up to wipe his tears away with the sleeve of his coat. "Miss Angelica... why did this have to happen?"

Angelica sighed as they walked together in silence. A few nobles passed by them, and gave Mirin a curious look. Some of them who knew of his relationship with the Princess understood why he was crying, and gave him a look of sympathy. After a moment, Angelica saw someone in the hallway she did not really want to see. "Miss Helen...."

Mirin raised his head. He and Angelica stopped just a few steps away from Helen.

Helen stood in the hallway, looking out an opened window. She had changed out of her leather armour, and wore her knight's uniform. Her uniform was more decorated now, with a few more gold pins at the collar. She wore her light red hair down, and it fell down her back, smooth and straight. Her face held a somber expression. When she heard their footsteps as they approached, she looked up.

Angelica met Helen's gaze. *The young girl knight who captured Princess Mika, and brought her back to the castle. I've seen her so many times, and yet... I didn't think she would do something like that, let alone volunteer for such a task. Despicable.*

"Are you happy now, Helen?" asked Mirin, his voice at the edge of breaking.

Helen looked down at him, confused.

"You attacked the Princess, and brought her back, didn't you? You must be happy now, aren't you? You made fun of her again, and hurt her, and now she's in the dungeon, right?"

Angelica stared at Helen as Mirin tried to talk to her. She wanted an answer out of her as much as Mirin did.

Helen said nothing as she stared right back.

Angelica noted her speechlessness. *Is she feeling bad about what she did? If I didn't know any better, she looks like she is. She looks just like a child herself, especially with her hair down. Not much younger than I am, and not that much older than Princess Mika. Only sixteen years old.*

"You bitch, say something!" Mirin attempted to launch himself towards Helen, ready to strike her face with his palm. In his rage, he forgot himself, but Angelica caught him, and then held on to him.

Helen was so surprised by his sudden outburst that she took a step back. However, her expression remained unchanged from a moment ago.

Angelica knelt down behind Mirin, her arms around him. "Mirin, I know it's infuriating... but please try to calm down."

Mirin felt weak as more tears came down his cheeks. He cast his eyes down on the floor, avoiding the surprised gazes of the few nobles in the hallway who watched the scene. "Mika... in the dungeon... my poor Mika... she's...." He finally let out his sobs, no longer able to keep them within.

Tears came down Angelica's cheeks as well, but she made no sound as she held on to Mirin, and looked up at Helen.

Helen cast her eyes down on the floor, awkward discomfort taking over her entire being. There was absolutely nothing that she could say to them.

Angelica stood up, and then took hold of Mirin's hand. She wiped away her own tears with her sleeve. "Come, Mirin, let's go." They walked away, leaving Helen by herself at the window.

When they were gone, Helen turned towards the window again. Her somber expression never left her face. "I've done the right thing, haven't I? I know I did. But... why am I feeling so sad? Why?"

* * *

After some struggling, Mika managed to sit up. She looked around and above her as she sat in the middle of the floor. She felt the coldness of the stone through the thin fabric of her dress and cloak. She still felt a slight headache, but it was tolerable. Fear gripped her mind and heart, but she knew this was one of the possible consequences of her actions. She knew she would probably be captured, and this was the result. However, knowing what the future might hold did nothing to make her feel any less frightened. She wondered what was going to happen next. As for the peasants in the city, she hoped they would be successful in implementing the plans she had laid out for them. She cast her eyes down.

"I suppose this is the end of me."

A silhouette appeared beyond the door. Mika saw Sir Collin some distance away, staring at her through the spaces between the iron bars without any expression. She wondered what he was thinking as he regarded her with a blank look. It made her uneasy.

Why am I here? A natural consequence of my actions. However... there's more to it than any of this. There's a consequence to my capture... and everyone is going to know about it. Every member of the Peasantry, the Nobility, the Royal Family, the Royal Guard, everyone in the Scarletia Royal Castle, and everyone in the city of Scarletia... they will all know... very, very shortly. That's right. I can't fall into despair just yet. I did, after all, plan for this outcome. There's still more work that needs to be done.

Everything... is going according to plan.

Mika watched as Collin gave a signal to several knights who joined him, and wondered what was about to happen. All of them, including Collin, wore their uniforms instead of their armour.

"Bring her to the Scarlet Chamber," ordered Collin.

"Yes, sir," said the knights.

The knights approached, and Mika stiffened as she watched them. One of them unlocked the heavy padlock, and then removed it, and then another knight swung the door open. When Mika looked up at the knights, two of them were familiar to her. She recognized them as Tanari and Caylen, two of the knights who were with her on her failed excursion to the city of Cerulean. Tanari and Caylen, along with two other knights, entered the dungeon cell. Another four knights watched from beyond the door. Mika felt small as the eight knights looked down at her, their imposing shadows falling upon her.

Caylen stood above her, and regarded her with a regretful expression.

Mika looked up at him, and noticed what he was feeling right away. "Sir Caylen...."

He spoke with a somber tone of voice. "My Lady, we have orders to escort you—I mean... to bring you—to the Scarlet Chamber."

Mika stared into his eyes. She could see in his face and hear in his voice the sadness he felt. He tried to look away from the gaze of the fallen Princess.

The female knight, Tanari, knelt down on the stone floor, and spoke to her in a soft voice. "Princess, please come with us. I beg of you."

The young Princess looked up at her. "Miss Tanari...."

Tanari nodded, silently encouraging her to comply.

Mika watched the other knights. When they met her gaze, they looked away, either ashamed or saddened. She realized that the knights did not like doing this to her one bit. They felt no satisfaction in throwing her into this dank dungeon and in tying her hands together behind her back with rope that dug into her skin. They now had to bring her to the Scarlet Chamber. They did not enjoy treating her like a prisoner. They still tried to respect her and speak to her calmly to preserve her dignity as the Princess of Melodice.

She moved her legs into a position that would help her stand up, but her bound hands were of no use to her. Tanari and Caylen stood at either side of her, and held her gently by the arms to help her get up. As soon as they did that, they stepped away from her.

"Thank you."

"Please, Princess, we must go," said one of the other knights from outside the cell. "It is... in your best interest."

Mika hesitated for a short moment longer. *To the Scarlet Chamber. No doubt, I am to be publicly humiliated.* However, remembering that her people referred to her as the White Princess, she gathered her strength, stood up straight, and slowly stepped towards the door. The knights watched her as she passed through it. Beyond the iron door, she looked up at Collin.

"This way, Princess Mika." Collin turned away, and then walked ahead.

Four of the knights walked in front of her, and the other four, including Tanari and Caylen, gently urged her to follow them. After another moment of hesitation, Mika followed Collin and the four knights ahead of her while the other four brought up the rear. She was led out of the dungeon area, up some stairs that led to the ground floor, and into the public hallways.

The hallways felt much longer than they normally did. Mika cast her eyes down on the floor as she walked. Noble civilians lined the sides of the wide hallways, all staring at her, some with shock, others with terrible disapproval, and still others with sadness. She saw others who even appeared to be extremely angry because of what had happened. Mika could not really blame them too much. The revolt of the peasant workers disrupted the lives of the people in the castle, so she felt their anger towards her was justified to a certain extent.

Eventually, Mika was led to the large lobby surrounding the Scarlet Chamber. The doors to the room were wide open, and there were many nobles who crowded the lobby. Among them were Angelica and Mirin. When Mika saw them, she was surprised. Her calm expression suddenly turned into a look of sadness.

Mirin nearly stepped away from Angelica to try to run to Mika, but Angelica stopped him. Angelica knelt on the floor beside him, and put her comforting arms around him. Mirin had tears in his eyes as he regarded Mika with terrible sadness.

"Princess Mika...." whispered Angelica. She looked up at Mika with eyes full of grief, as if Mika herself had died.

"Mika…" whispered Mirin. His voice was so soft that Mika could not hear it at all from where she was.

As Mika was about to pass them, she slowed, and then looked over to them. Her lips formed their names. "Miss Angelica… Mirin…."

Although they could not hear her, Angelica and Mirin could tell what she was saying through the movement of her lips.

"Keep going, please, Princess," said Caylen, keeping his voice humble.

Angelica and Mirin watched her as she approached the entrance to the Scarlet Chamber. Many more nobles looked on with various expressions. There were also many knights who watched.

As she approached the Scarlet Chamber's entrance, Mika's eyes fixed upon Helen, who stood beside one of the doors, staring back at her without expression. Their gazes met, and then locked, as if to pierce through each other. Both girls clenched their fists.

Because her hands were tied behind her back, Mika wasn't able to hide her tightened fists, but she was certain that no one even noticed. If they had, they would have just assumed she tightened her hands into fists because they felt uncomfortable being restrained the way they were. *Normally, you intimidate me, but… today… I feel like I want to stare you down until you look away, Miss Helen.*

Helen hid her hands behind her back. *What? Staring at me with those kinds of eyes? I'm impressed. Do you think you can look at me like that and get away with it, Princess Mika?*

The two of them stared each other down, until Mika could no longer do so as she passed by, straining her neck. Mika was forced to look ahead. Not a single person, except Helen, noticed the anger within her that was now personal in nature. *I didn't lose that staring match. I was forced to look away. That doesn't count.*

Bitch, thought Helen, her eyes narrowed.

Mika tried to calm down as she entered the Scarlet Chamber. She took another deep breath to cool down her anger. All that was left now was her fear of what was going to happen next. She saw political leaders everywhere in the room, crowding the sides, along with people who worked with them. At the back, she saw King Ralphen and Queen Maiya seated on their thrones, waiting for her. Sir Galner was also in the room, near the front, close to the steps.

Collin stopped, letting the first four knights pass him. He took the Princess by the shoulder, forcing her to stop. He signaled the other knights to stand at the sides of the room.

"Mika," whispered Maiya.

Hearing her voice, Ralphen hushed her. "Don't..." he said softly. He clenched his fists at his sides as he stared at Mika.

Maiya wanted so much to reach out to her daughter to embrace her and tell her that everything was going to be all right. But nothing was all right. The Princess of Melodice had committed high treason, one of the worst crimes that anyone could commit.

Collin gently pushed the fallen Princess along. Mika walked slowly with small footsteps as Collin led her to the bottom of the steps. He bowed his head towards the King and Queen, and then stood back.

As Mika stood motionless with her heels together, she kept her eyes downcast on the steps in front of her. Silence filled the room.

Ralphen got up from his throne, and then walked towards the top of the steps. He went down the steps, and stood directly in front of her. His eyes were full of anger, but he was doing his best to keep himself calm for now. He stared down at her.

Mika stiffened, seeing her father's boots.

"Look at me," ordered the King.

She hesitated. She tried to comply with her father's order, her eyes moving up, but they went back down to his boots.

"I said look at me!"

Mika nearly jumped from the sound of his angry voice. She eventually forced herself to set her eyes upon his. His eyes raged with fury, piercing deep into her soul.

Mika's hands and knees trembled. She only looked at him for a very brief moment when he slapped her. She felt pain so great that it might as well have been a punch. She fell sideways with a yelp, and she fell on her side, unable to balance herself because her hands were bound. The side of her head struck the floor as well, but fortunately not as hard.

Helen cast her eyes down, hearing the gasps of people in the Scarlet Chamber.

Still seated on her throne, Maiya was startled as she looked away.

Outside, Angelica had Mirin turn away so he would not see what had just been done to Mika by her own father's hand.

Mika lay trembling on the floor.

Collin grabbed hold of her as he motioned one of the knights to help him get her back up. "Reland, come."

Reland rushed over to Collin, and both of them grabbed her by the armpits, and forced her to stand up in front of the King once again. They could feel her body trembling as they held on to her.

As Mika stood, hunched over because of the pain on the left side of her face, on her right hip, right shoulder, and the right side of her head.

"Do you realize what you've done, Princess Mika?!" shouted the King.

Mika said nothing. Saying anything would just earn her yet another slap. Tears immediately came down her cheeks. She felt her left cheek starting to swell up ever so slightly. She kept her eyes down on the floor.

"You've betrayed the proud nation of Melodice! You've betrayed the great city of Scarletia! You've also betrayed the Nobility and the Royal Family! You've betrayed your mother, the Queen of Melodice, and me, you father and your King!"

Mika grimaced as Ralphen shouted his last few words with his mouth close to her face. His words struck her just as hard as his slap from just a moment ago.

"Why would you do this?! Why would you betray us all?!"

Mika tasted blood as she licked her lips, and realized she had bitten her lip without noticing. She wondered if it happened when her father slapped her, or just now when she grimaced.

"I expect an answer!"

The little Princess hesitated.

Ralphen reached out, grabbed her shoulder, and twisted.

Mika screamed out loud with terrible pain.

"When I tell you to answer, I expect you to obey me! Answer me now!"

Mika sobbed, and then screamed once more as Ralphen handled her roughly. He pulled away. Mika's knees grew weak from the pain. However, Collin and Reland kept her from falling to her knees as they continued to hold her with their arms underneath her armpits.

"What is your answer, Princess Mika?!" shouted the King.

Mika looked up just a little. After another moment, her eyes finally met the King's. "I... the people of... the people of Melodice. They've been forced to live under tyranny and oppression for over a century. They want freedom. They want to live with dignity and with respect!"

Ralphen glared at her, and immediately slapped her again, this time on the right cheek. He slapped her so hard that even Collin and Reland felt the force.

Mika cried out, falling against Collin, but he kept her from falling any further. Her knees felt weak again, but Collin and Reland held her up. Pain stung the right side of her face. When the slap landed, she had bitten the inside of her right cheek hard. She also felt at least one of her teeth jarred loose. As Ralphen stood back, Mika put her face down, and felt something in her mouth. She coughed, and one of her last primary premolars that had been somewhat loose to begin with fell out, along with several drops of blood. She whimpered like a frightened kitten.

Helen covered her eyes, and then turned away. She could not bear to look at Princess Mika any longer while her father was physically abusing her in front of everyone.

When she looked up, she watched the horrified faces of the nobles outside the Scarlet Chamber.

Angelica pulled Mirin along as she moved a little farther away, but they did not leave just yet. As much as it pained them, they stayed to listen to Mika's words, but they did not want to see her abused by the King.

Mika breathed heavily. Blood stained her lips, and dripped down the corner of her chin.

"These peasant animals have poisoned your mind with these ridiculous ideas, Mika!" shouted Ralphen.

Mika inhaled deeply as she gathered up the courage she had learned from Feldia, Laren, and all the others, including Dellen and Adrel. She began to look up again slowly, higher and higher, and soon met her father's gaze. "Father...."

Ralphen narrowed his eyes. "What?"

"I... I am... I am...."

"What are you trying to say?!"

"I am... their Princess! They are my people... and I love them with all my heart!"

There were gasps in the audience from behind her. Mika could hear the whispers. As she gazed up at her father through her tears, his eyes went wide with almost uncontrolled rage as his fists began to tremble at his sides.

"Because... I'm their Princess... because... I love them... it's my responsibility to take care of them and make sure they live comfortably!"

Ralphen stepped forward. He slammed his fist into Mika's abdomen.

Mika felt terrible pain as she reeled backwards, her eyes wide, but Collin and Reland continued to hold on to her. They themselves nearly fell backwards, but they stood their ground so the Princess herself did not fall. However, pain racked her entire body as she lost her balance, and most of the strength she had left to stay standing. The force threw blood out of her mouth as the wound inside her cheek bled. Eventually, she was able to scream as she sobbed with horrendous pain.

Helen walked away a short distance, stepping past

nobles who watched with horror. Although she did not want to see Mika being abused like she was, she still wanted to hear what she had to say.

On her throne, Maiya closed her eyes, and then put her head down, covering her face as tears streamed down her cheeks.

Even Sir Galner had to look away.

Ralphen stood back, and stared down at her again. "Are you, Princess Mika, the leader of this rebellion?"

Mika looked up slightly again, but did not meet his eyes. "Yes, Father..." she whispered, but her voice was still loud enough to be heard by the nobles nearby. "This rebellion... this group I lead... is called the White Princess Liberation Army."

Galner looked on with shock, as did everyone else in the room.

Collin listened, absolutely stunned. *This is ridiculous! The King is wasting his time brutalizing his own daughter in public! While he's doing this, the peasants are still rampaging throughout the city!*

Ralphen just chuckled, and then spoke with a mocking tone. "Humph. The White Princess Liberation Army? I've never heard of that group, but I'm certain it's nothing more than a ragtag group of peasant animals who feast on the litter of rats and mice, believing they can fight against something bigger than they are!"

Collin looked up at the King. "My Lord, if I could speak for a moment...."

"What is it, Sir Collin?"

"The peasants continue to rampage throughout the city of Scarletia. Forgive me, My Lord, but I believe you wanted to find out why they were still doing this even after the Princess was captured."

"Ah, yes, of course. Thank you, Sir Collin." Ralphen returned his angry gaze to Mika. "As Sir Collin said, I had believed the revolt of the peasant workers would stop with your capture, but that clearly hasn't happened. Why are the peasants still rampaging throughout the city? Why are they still protesting? Why are they causing so much destruction? Why the change in tactics? Why?!"

Mika hesitated for a moment. *Is this where I tell him the real reason? The consequences of my capture?*

"Answer me!"

"Because...."

Ralphen stared with anticipation, waiting for her response, as did everyone else in the room and out in the lobby.

Soon, once again, Mika's eyes met his. "Because... it's all part of my plan, Father."

Everyone responded with consternation, their faces ashen.

Mika continued. "The peasants are fighting for freedom from tyranny. I left orders that, if I was captured, the peasant workers would change their tactics, and escalate the destruction. They will not stop until either they have that freedom... or everything that gives life to the Nobility living in the city of Scarletia and the Scarletia Royal Castle is razed to the ground!"

The entire room exploded with clamours of anger from the nobles.

And then they can escape. The infrastructure that allows the city to provide for the castle will be destroyed. The Nobility within the castle will have no hope of survival. The peasants will use the Starstone to destroy the city gates, and then they will escape into the countryside. Away from this cursed city, they can start a new life. That was my plan.

"Traitor to Melodice! Traitor to Scarletia! Traitor!"

"What the hell kind of a child are you?!"

"You are not a Princess! You are a witch!"

"You damn demon child, you have betrayed us all!"

"Traitor! Execute her! Traitor!"

Ralphen, enraged, lunged forward. He grabbed Mika by the neck with one hand.

Mika was terrified as she felt her tiny neck squeezed shut.

Collin, along with Reland beside him, watched with shock as Ralphen strangled Mika out of fury. "My Lord!" shouted the Supreme Captain.

Distressed, Maiya stood from her throne, and rushed

towards the steps. "Ralphen, stop!" she shouted, but over the angry clamours of the nobles, he could not hear her. She walked down the steps quickly, and grabbed Ralphen's hands.

Ralphen, surprised, pulled his hands away.

Mika drew in a quick breath as she slumped forward. She started coughing, and then inhaled and exhaled deeply in order to catch her breath.

"I can't believe it," whispered Galner. "This is a tragedy. The Princess of Melodice is only eleven years old. Timid, shy, meek, and gentle, the little Princess Mika... planned the destruction of the city's infrastructure if the peasants were not granted their freedom?!"

Mika listened to the angry voices echoing throughout the room and beyond.

Collin pulled Reland closer to tell him something. "Reland, you and Tanari hold on to her."

"Yes, sir." Reland waved Tanari over.

Tanari quickly approached, and helped him hold onto the Princess. As soon as she took hold of Mika, she felt the young girl's body trembling... and immediately felt a great deal of heartache. Watching the proud young Princess being demoralized like this was painful.

Collin pulled away, and approached King Ralphen. "My Lord!"

Ralphen was so shocked that he could not hear Collin. "My Lord, King Ralphen!"

Ralphen blinked, and then glanced at him. "What, Sir Collin?"

Collin leaned closer to Ralphen, and spoke to him in a whisper so no one else around them could hear, but loud enough so that they could still hear each other despite the shouting of the nobles. "My Lord, it might be wise to ask the Princess if she has terms."

Horrified, Ralphen stared at him. "Ridiculous! Why?!"

"Our first priority is to stop the ongoing destruction in the city. We can't allow the city's infrastructure to be destroyed. Otherwise, the Nobility living within the city and the castle will not survive. If you give them what they want, they'll stop!"

"Give them what they want?! You must be mad, Sir Collin!"

"My Lord, please hear me out! I'm not saying to give in! I'm saying…." Collin cupped his hand over his mouth as he spoke into Ralphen's ear. After a moment, they pulled away.

Maiya took a few steps back, but she saw the King and the Supreme Captain whispering to each other, and wondered what they were talking about.

"Very good, Sir Collin." Ralphen turned to everyone in the room who continued their shouting. "Silence! Be silent!"

As the King's command echoed throughout the room, the nobles stopped.

Ralphen climbed the steps, and then turned back to Mika, who was still hunched over with her head down while Reland and Tanari supported her.

Mika breathed heavily from the pain she felt throughout her body and the fear that gripped her heart. There was silence in the room, until Ralphen once again addressed her.

"Princess Mika, look at me."

Slowly, Mika complied.

"I am concerned with the well-being of the city of Scarletia. I wouldn't want the city's lifeblood, its infrastructure, to be burned to the ground by the peasants. In exchange for halting the destruction, what do the peasants want?"

Mika tried to keep her surprised reaction in check. *Am I dreaming? My father is asking for terms? Does this mean… does this mean the peasants of Scarletia will have their freedom?*

Ralphen looked at her expectantly. "Well?"

"Father, you know what the Peasantry of Scarletia want, as I've explained it. They… want their freedom from tyranny and oppression. They want to leave the city of Scarletia. They don't wish to live under the rule of the Nobility any longer. They're tired of living like slaves, constantly being abused by the Nobility. They want to live under their own terms, with dignity and respect."

"Truly? How many peasants want to leave the city?"

Mika remembered how many people were participating in the revolt, as well as the size of the entire city's labour force. She opted for the higher number. "About... three hundred thousand, Father."

Ralphen glared at Mika. "Three hundred thousand?!"

"That's how many people want to live in peace, away from the Nobility. They want to start a better life somewhere else. They want to build their own community, where everyone can live in harmony with each other, under their own terms... a place that everyone, either peasant or noble, can live without being discriminated against. They want to live in a place where they can all be treated equally."

Silence filled the room. The leaders of the Nobility looked on as King Ralphen and Princess Mika watched each other's reaction, as if trying to read each other's thoughts.

"Are these your terms for the cessation of the activities of the White Princess Liberation Army?" asked the King, looking for confirmation.

Mika nodded. "Yes, Father."

"Then I accept. Under these terms, I will grant safe passage to any peasants who wish to leave and start a life somewhere else."

Mika stared up at the King agape. However, the nobles behind her erupted with angry clamours once again.

"No, My Lord! How can you do this to us?!"

"These peasants who have participated in this revolt have committed a terrible crime!"

"They are criminals! They should all be put to death!"

Ralphen glared at the nobles in the room, and pointed at them as if they were nothing more than unruly dogs. "Silence! Still your impertinent tongues!"

Mika was shocked by the King's decision. *I can't believe it! I... I won?!*

"My immediate concern is to preserve ourselves, the Nobility of Scarletia! We cannot have the city's infrastructure burned to the ground! I have made my decision as the King of Melodice!"

Eventually, the nobles stopped shouting.

"Any peasants who wish to leave the city may leave and do as they please. However, once they have exited, they will *not* be allowed to return. That's what they wanted after all. They wanted to live a better life somewhere else. Is that not fair, Princess Mika?"

Mika thought about that for a moment. If the peasants were allowed to leave, they would not want to return anyway. "Yes, Father."

"There we have it. However, there is one thing, Princess Mika."

The Princess tried to calm herself from the surprise she had just been given. She looked up at the King once again.

"Regretfully... I cannot allow you to go freely with the Peasantry."

Mika stared into her father's eyes.

"You were captured as a traitor. You have committed high treason, and the standard punishment for high treason... is death."

The angry clamours of the nobles became shouts of victory, as if they themselves had won something. Mika cast her eyes down onto the floor, and closed them. She imagined Queen Maiya was terribly saddened by what was happening and what was going to happen. She imagined Angelica and Mirin's reactions as well, as they stood outside the Scarlet Chamber. They must be filled with shock and despair, just like her mother. She could even hear the deep sighs of the two knights who held onto her, Tanari and Reland. It was obvious to her that they regretted hearing the words of King Ralphen just now.

I see... but I suppose a part of me expected this. I've won the freedom of the Peasantry. That's what I set out to do, and I've done it. It's unfortunate that I will not see them enjoy that freedom. But I've won... and I have... no regrets.

CHAPTER 33:

JUDGEMENT

SEC 3566, Morrighan 54

A FEW DAYS AFTER THE CAPTURE of Princess Mika, all the flames caused by the Starstone explosions throughout the city burned themselves out as they ran out of things to consume. The flames had consumed entire city blocks, but they could not cross streets to consume adjacent blocks because the streets provided a natural barrier. Within affected city blocks, nothing remained except a fine black ash. Black smoke continued to rise from these areas as they cooled, but it would take several more days for them to sufficiently cool to allow the cleanup process to begin.

On the city streets, no peasant workers protested, and no worker groups fought against the knights of the Scarletia Royal Guard. The knights had been ordered to stand down. No one, not a single peasant, was told to surrender. They were also never told to surrender any of the equipment they had stolen from the knights and their patrol stations, such as various weapons and armour. The revolt of the peasant workers was over. Some of the businesses and industries that provided goods and services to the castle, what was left of them, had opened up while others still had some cleanup work to do.

However, at the castle gates, tens of thousands of peasants gathered to fill the entire width of the Valderia Pathway. The sea of people continued down the street for quite a distance. A small group of people tried to get through the crowd as they headed for the gates.

Feldia looked back at her companions. "Come on! Hurry up!"

"Don't go so far ahead, Feldia." Laren pushed through the crowd.

Eventually, both of them made it through, and ended up at the very front. The castle gates towered in front of them. Clad in gray cloaks that hid their weapons underneath, they used their hoods to conceal a good portion of their faces. Feldia and Laren looked around, and found their remaining direct reports from the White Princess Liberation Army among the crowd, Dayna, Eduard, Elsia, Lauria, Marik, Peter, Sorianne, and Tavien. As Feldia and Laren met their gazes, they saw their somber expressions because they knew the reason why they were here.

Sir Collin faced the people of Scarletia from the bridge above the castle gates, accompanied by several knights who stood guard and kept watch over the peasants below. Behind him, on the Grounds, many nobles gathered as well. Some of the nation's political leaders were also present on the top of the walls and the bridge. "His Highness, King Ralphen, and Her Highness, Queen Maiya, arrives!"

As every knight stood at attention, King Ralphen ascended the steps that led up to the top of the walls. He was followed by Queen Maiya as he headed for the bridge. As soon as they reached the bridge, they stood near Collin. Maiya stood near the crenulated wall next to Maleth. Ralphen nodded to Collin, who issued the next command.

"Bring the traitor!"

On the Grounds, a cell made of wood and iron sitting on top of a flatbed cart with a set of four large wheels was pulled by a group of eight strong cervids, driven by two knights, while several other knights walked alongside, in front, and behind it. The cervids pulled the cell closer towards the castle gates, and the nobles there looked on as it approached. When it stopped, one of the knights unlocked the iron door, and opened it.

A moment passed, and the lone occupant of the cell slowly stepped out. As soon as she appeared, angry shouts from the nobles filled the air as they hurled words of hateful condemnation. She carefully placed her bare feet on the metal steps leading down to the grass below. She stepped on the grass, and felt a small rock dig into the bottom of her foot, causing her to adjust her footing.

Mika stood with her feet together, her hands bound tightly together behind her back with brand new ropes that scraped her wrists even further, causing her skin to become raw. Her hair, which had not been brushed for days, was now disheveled. Fresh bruises darkened areas of her arms and legs, and her knees were scraped. Her right eye had turned black and blue, while marks on her neck, forehead, and on the sides of her cheeks were a dull red, all of which were results of yet another beating from her father. The fabric of the thin rag dress she was forced to wear made her skin itch, but there was nothing she could do about it. Plain gray in colour, it reached down to just above her knees, its loose threads unwinding at the ends of the short sleeves and at the hem. The dress was much like the ones worn by children who begged for money on the streets of Scarletia.

Angelica, holding on to Mirin beside her, saw from far away that Mika was in terrible shape. They were stricken by her appearance. "Princess Mika... what have they done to you?"

"Her father did all that to her, didn't he?" said Mirin, his voice soft. He cupped his hands around his mouth, and tried to call out to her. "Mika!"

Angelica took his hands away from his mouth. "She can't hear you, Mirin. Not with all these people shouting at her."

The knights urged Mika to head towards the steps leading up to the top of the walls. She complied, but walked slowly and carefully as she grimaced with every step. Pain racked her entire body, pain caused by the beatings her father had again given to her. Mika walked up the cold stone steps. She kept her eyes downcast as she walked in order to avoid the gazes of people as much as possible. She nearly tripped as she failed to negotiate a step, but a knight was behind her to grab her by the back of her rag dress. The knight righted her up easily, and she regained her balance.

Mika tried not to listen to the furious shouts of the nobles as she was made to walk along the walls. As she passed by political leaders, she recognized each of them, and remembered a time when they respected her. She remembered the times she had conversations with them, all of the pleasant and friendly. This time, they hurled comments full of hatred.

"You are a traitor, little girl!"

"A demon child! A witch! That is what you are!"

"You have betrayed your own family and all of us, the entire city and the entire nation!"

"No one will ever forgive you! It'll be better if you just die!"

"May death come to you, you evil witch!"

Mika continued, trying to keep those words from reaching her heart, but nevertheless, they were hurtful. She had heard many angry words of condemnation the last few days. Every single one struck at her heart like a thousand daggers. They continued to do so.

Soon, Mika saw a familiar pair of boots, which made her look up. She saw Sir Galner, who glared at her with eyes full of disdain. Mika cast her eyes down again as she walked past him, but his scornful expression followed her.

The voices of condemnation continued from one side. However, as she stepped onto the bridge, they were joined next by vocalized expressions of shock as the peasants on the other side of the castle gates began to call out to her with sorrow. Feldia and Laren were horrified by the appearance of their Princess.

"No... Princess..." whispered Feldia.

Laren forced himself to swallow. "How can they do this to you?"

Their other companions, like Lauria, Elsia, Marik, and Peter, all stared, speechless as Mika was forced to walk around as a humiliated and fallen Princess, her body visibly broken.

Peter clenched his teeth, his hand reaching for the hilt

of his sword underneath his cloak. "Those bastards. How dare they do this to our Princess?!"

Marik firmly grabbed his arm. "Hey, stop it. Not here, not now."

Fury twisted Peter's face. "Look at what those fucking nobles have done to our Princess, Marik. Just look at her!"

"I understand, but right now, you need to be mindful of our surroundings. Look." Marik nodded toward the mounted knights who trotted up the sides of the street. "And let's not forget that we're surrounded by thousands of innocent bystanders."

Peter turned to see the approaching knights. They joined other knights who were on foot, and were standing guard at either side of the castle gates.

Mika was made to stand near the crenulated wall, overlooking the peasants crowding the Valderia Pathway. The cries of the peasants and their words of sympathy reached out to her, but behind her, the words of hatred from the nobles counteracted them.

Ralphen approached her, and looked down at her. He noticed the golden necklace around her neck, and his eyes narrowed.

Mika felt her father's hands forcibly turn her towards him. He roughly groped for the necklace, and pulled it out of the collar of her rag dress. He glared at her, and pulled it roughly, causing it to snap and her to gasp loudly with pain. It also caused red marks to appear at the back of her neck as the chain scraped against her skin.

Ralphen held the golden chain in his hands, and then he glanced up at Collin while holding up the chain for the Supreme Captain to see. "Sir Collin."

Collin came over, and saw the golden chain. "Yes, My Lord."

"What happened to the Princess Gem?"

The Supreme Captain was confused. "Sir?"

Ralphen glared at Mika, and then back at Collin. "She wears a diamond around her neck attached to this golden chain! The Princess Gem! You know of it, Sir Collin! What happened to it? Where is it? Didn't your knights search her?"

"My Lord, we didn't find anything on her except that golden chain. We... did not think to remove the chain from her."

"Why the hell not?" Ralphen shook his head, and then he looked down at the Princess, who kept her head down. "Now that she's a traitor, she doesn't need finery such as this." He threw down the necklace, and stepped on it.

Mika stared at the necklace. She grimaced as Ralphen grabbed her under her chin, and forced her to look up at him. Fear was written all over her face.

"Where is the Princess Gem, Mika?"

Mika hesitated. "I... I'm sorry... Father, I must have lost it... during my confrontation with Miss Helen."

Ralphen exhaled furiously as he let go of Mika while Collin returned to where he was. He turned her around to make her face the peasants of Scarletia. He imagined there was nothing he could do about the Princess Gem for now. It could be anywhere if she had dropped it during her confrontation with Helen in the skies over the city.

A perfect lie... a perfect situation... a perfect excuse... to explain the disappearance of the Princess Gem, thought Mika. She stole a glance sideways just a little towards Galner, who looked ahead. *Sir Galner, thank you for casting the magic seal upon me. By doing that, you've made my diamond impossible to find. Now, the only way it can be found is if you knew about it and where I hid it, and if you removed the magic seal from me. I've placed the Princess Gem in a lockbox, and I've hidden away the key, and by sealing my magic, you have unwittingly thrown that key away.*

Ralphen raised his hands to call for silence. After a moment, the nobles and the peasants fell silent. "Ladies and gentlemen of the Nobility, peasants, citizens of the city of Scarletia. Hear me as I reiterate what we've done to stop the chaos that had befallen us. In exchange for the preservation of our great city, I have granted safe passage to any and all peasants who wish to leave the city to find a better life on their own. You may leave and do as you please. However, once you exit the city, you will not be allowed to return. You have been demanding your freedom from us? Then you can have it!"

The peasants began to cheer as they heard this. Feldia, Laren, and the others, however, did not react. They were definitely happy that the peasants were now granted their freedom, but they were deeply worried about Princess Mika.

"However!" shouted Ralphen, raising both of his hands again. The peasants stopped. "Although I'm letting you peasants leave on your own, I cannot and will not ignore one glaring fact. The young girl you see before you, Mika Silveraine, the Princess of Melodice, the leader of the so-called White Princess Liberation Army, has committed the most heinous crime in the entire nation of Melodice. She has committed the crime of high treason!"

Mika heard the expressions of despair among the peasants. She shifted her eyes, and for a moment, she thought she saw Feldia and Laren. She looked again, and soon realized she was not seeing things. However, they were far away from her.

"I am deeply troubled—no, deeply disturbed—that our daughter, a little girl who is only eleven years old, could do these things. Part of me tells me I shouldn't be surprised. She was, after all, educated by the finest professors in the entire nation. She has been educated in the matters of politics. She studied subjects normally enjoyed by students several years her senior. She also has the power of magic!"

Mika cast her eyes down as tears streamed down her cheeks.

"However, these are not excuses! Being intelligent and educated does not mean a person has to choose to cause chaos and destruction. She has an inquisitive mind. She questioned the world around her, a world she saw for the first time. She sought answers to her questions in order to understand a world that was different from what she expected. There's nothing wrong with doing this. However, one has two choices once one finds the answers to these questions. The first choice, the right choice, would be to accept the world as it is... and the second choice, the wrong choice, is to reject it!" Ralphen turned to Mika. "Princess Mika Silveraine, you have chosen to reject the world as it is! And because of this, you have chosen the

path of rebellion! You are a traitor! Your crime of high
treason... is punishable by death!"

Mika shut her eyes, and her knees and hands trembled
as her heart raced. However, what upset her was not that
she was being branded a traitor. She knew that would
be the result of her actions. She knew her return to the
castle would be as a prisoner... and as a traitor. As she
had anticipated, her return to the castle had not been
peaceful. She knew that the Nobility and her father would
use such hurtful words to stab at her. She knew she was
going to endure isolation. However, she realized she was
not going to see the peasants enjoy the freedom they had
all fought so hard to achieve. Now, after it all, she realized
she was truly afraid of death. Even though she knew it was
inevitable, and had tried to prepare herself mentally, the
days in the dungeon had not given her sufficient time to
preparing emotionally.

The nobles called out for her execution while the
peasants called for mercy. Their conflicting clamours rang
in her ears.

Ralphen raised his hands again, and everyone fell silent.
"As you all know, execution is the standard punishment for
high treason. However, that will not be her punishment."

Maiya looked up with surprise.

Sir Galner, Sir Collin, Sir Maleth, all the knights and
servants and political leaders, the nobles behind the castle
gates, and the peasants who stood in front of it, Feldia,
Laren, and their direct reports, as well as Angelica and
Mirin among the crowd of nobles, all regarded the King
with great surprise.

Mika was surprised herself, as she opened her eyes
wide. She straightened, and looked up towards her father.
*Huh? I'm... going to live? I'm not going to be executed? I had
already prepared myself to a certain extent. Over the past few
days, I've been thinking about the manner of my execution.
How was I going to meet my death? Would I be beheaded?
Poisoned? Drowned? Doused with kerosene and burned?*

"Instead of execution, Princess Mika, your punishment
will be exile," announced the King. "You will be stripped

of your title and status. You will no longer be known as the Princess of Melodice. You will no longer be part of the Royal Family, and therefore, you will have no right to use the name of Silveraine. Your status as a member of the Nobility will be no more. Instead of Princess Mika Silveraine, you will simply be called Mika. You will be bound and blindfolded, and you will be taken by cervid carriage to the farthest reaches of the nation of Melodice. You will be dropped off in the wild with nothing but the rag dress that you wear today. You will wander the wild plains, forests, and grasslands, and there will be nothing for you as far as the eye can see. You will be far away from any hint of civilization. You can go anywhere as you please, but you will be alone, and you will have to fend for yourself. You will wander aimlessly in the vast wilderness... until the day you die."

Feldia, Laren, and the others looked on, aghast. The peasants shouted with anger.

"That's an unfair punishment!"

"How can you do this to your own child?!"

"A child, on her own, can't fend for herself out in the wild!"

"This is worse than execution!"

Ralphen raised his hand towards the peasants. "Silence!" he ordered. After a moment, the shouting stopped. "I believe I'm being quite generous, not to mention reasonable! I'm even going as far as giving her a pair of shoes to walk in as she wanders the wilderness! Had I not been generous and reasonable, I would have had her killed instantly as soon as she was captured and brought back to the castle, even if she is my own daughter! She has betrayed this nation! No one, not even a child of the Royal Family, is exempt from the laws of our land! I would have had every single one of you burned to the ground before you had a chance to do the same to the city's infrastructure, even if you threatened to destroy everything yourselves!"

The peasants were silent, shocked by the words of the King.

"You are all replaceable! Don't forget that! The

only reason why I agreed to these terms was to stop the destruction of the city's infrastructure, which would have caused the destruction of the Nobility! I am willing to go so far as to let you animals leave in peace and rebuild your lives somewhere else and do as you wish! I think I am being very generous and reasonable! Don't make me change my mind!"

Mika stole a glance towards the peasants, and saw their various expressions of despair, sadness, anger, and shock. She saw Feldia, and Laren, and their companions with the same expression written all over their faces. She turned slightly towards her mother, but as soon as their gazes met, Maiya gave her a sharp look, and then turned away, refusing to look at her. Maleth did not look at her either, probably because he might be in trouble if he did meet her gaze. Mika turned towards Collin, who also refused to meet her gaze, and then, there was Sir Galner, who eyed her with great disdain and fury, but he kept quiet.

Ralphen pointed at the peasants. "Now, we're done here. I want you all to get out of my sight!" He turned to Collin. "Take her away!"

Collin waved the knights over, and ordered them to take Mika. The knights urged Mika gently to walk along the bridge, back to the top of the walls, and then back down the steps.

Ralphen stepped away from the crenulated wall, and was soon joined by Maiya, and then by Collin, who stood at attention in front of the King.

"My Lord, My Lady," said the Supreme Captain.

"What is it?" asked Ralphen.

"Please accept my sincerest apologies regarding the Princess Gem. However, there is something I would like to point out."

"Oh? What is that, Sir Collin," said Maiya.

"Although you have publicly and officially removed the status of Princess from... our prisoner, according to our laws, the Princess Gem must also be retrieved. If she lost the diamond while flying over the city, I can send out knights to attempt to narrow down its possible location."

Maiya agreed. "That's true. The Princess Gem is the

physical and legal representation of her identity as the Princess of Melodice. We need to locate it. If we don't, the legal document that declares her status as Princess as nulled is incomplete." She turned to the King. "What do you think, Ralphen?"

The King shook his head. "Don't bother."

Maiya was surprised by this, as well as Collin. "But... why?"

"Do you actually believe we're going to find the Princess Gem in a crowded city of one million people? It'll be a waste of time. Surely, we can make an exception. We are the lawmakers, after all." Ralphen looked up at Collin. "What we have done is sufficient."

Collin nodded, and then bowed his head slightly. "Yes, My Lord."

As Mika walked with her head down, she listened to the various clamours of the peasants. Some of them were furious as they condemned the punishment given to her, and some of them cried out for mercy.

Feldia closed her eyes as she put her head down. "How is she going to survive out there in the wilderness all by herself?"

Laren went over to her and put a hand on her shoulder. "Feldia..."

"She won't survive out there on her own!" Tears came down as Feldia sobbed. "She doesn't have any skills that can help her survive in the wild! Even if she somehow survives the hazards of nature, eventually, winter will come, and she'll die from the cold!"

"I know." Laren looked up at the bridge above the castle gates, giving the knights stationed up there a death stare. However, there was nothing they could do for now. He put a comforting hand on Feldia's shoulder as he turned away. "Come on, let's get out of here."

As the peasants continued to shout, the nobles did the same. They again hurled their words of condemnation at Mika as she was escorted by the knights.

Angelica and Mirin watched as she was led back into the cell. As soon as she was made to climb the steps to enter it, the impenetrable iron doors were shut.

CHAPTER 34:

MY ONE AND
ONLY REGRET

SEC 3566, Morrighan 61

URING THE NEXT SEVERAL DAYS after Mika's sentence was handed to her, many people were leaving the city of Scarletia, venturing forth into the countryside. Long lines of people, whole families and their relatives and friends, filed through the many city gates, taking with them their cervids, carriages, and wagons filled with their belongings. The knights of the Scarletia Royal Guard did nothing to get in the way of the mass exodus.

Among those already in the grassy plains outside the city were Feldia and Laren. Clad in gray cloaks that concealed their long swords and with hoods down, they rode slowly on their cervids. In front of them, thousands of people formed lines that snaked away from the city gates, and behind then, there were thousands more, all of them traveling on the many long dirt roads that led from each city gate.

Laren looked ahead, noting how many people had chosen their freedom. He thought to himself he should be happy, but something was nagging at him.

Feldia rode alongside him, and noticed his expression, so she patted him on the back, startling him. "What's on your mind?"

Laren met her gaze. "I'm still having trouble believing

it, but it looks like we were victorious... somehow. I don't know how we won this freedom, but luck was clearly on our side."

Feldia paused for a moment as she thought about his words. "I don't think it's about luck, Laren. We did our best. Princess Mika did her best, too. We all fought hard for this."

"We certainly did. We're finally free from the tyranny of the Nobility, at least, here in the city of Scarletia."

Feldia nodded, but her expression became serious. "But... we have to remember that this freedom, this victory, was won with a high cost. A lot of people died for this freedom. Over ten thousand peasant civilians and fifteen hundred members of the White Princess Liberation Army dead. We lost two of our friends, Demias and Galien. We lost Dellen and Zima. Adrel, his wife, and his children were all killed. Many of the smaller rebel groups were decimated. And, of course, Princess Mika is to be exiled."

Laren nodded as he sighed with regret. "Yeah, I know."

"Dellen and Zima's children are still missing, and we have no idea where to look for them. I can only hope they're part of this crowd of people leaving the city, if they haven't left already, and if not, I hope we'll be able to find them. That's one of the things I want to do, in fact. I want to find Jaren and Tyrel. It probably means I will have to return to Scarletia someday, but covertly. Some of our friends are staying behind to look for them, and I want to help them."

"I'll help you with that."

Feldia smiled. "Thanks."

"But you're right. This has been a very costly victory. Thousands died, but a million people were saved. A lot of people sacrificed themselves for this victory."

"That's right, Laren."

"I'm worried about her though. The Princess...."

A somber expression appeared on Feldia. "So am I. She's an amazing little girl... no, an amazing young woman. That's what she is after all the things she's done. She may have been just a young girl, but she was able to lead the

White Princess Liberation Army. She had anticipated the actions of the Royal Family and the Nobility with disturbing precision, and had used her insight into their minds to our advantage. But... I don't know how she's going to survive out there in the wilderness with nothing but the clothes on her back. She's going to face her toughest challenge yet... and I have no idea how she's going to do it."

Laren looked up at Feldia, wanting to express what he has been thinking about for quite some time. "Hey, Feldia...."

"What is it?"

"I'm planning to go to the city of Platinar. We have a few friends out there who should know what happened here. Raisa will definitely want to know, if she doesn't know already. Do you want to come with me?"

Feldia chuckled. "Raisa? Good luck finding her. She's always up and about."

"I know. She's very busy with a lot of things. We haven't heard from her in a while though. She's been working hard on something... something big."

Feldia became curious. "Really? Well, then, I wonder what that is. And, yes, I'll come with you. It'll be a long journey though. It's the farthest city from here, deep in the Northeast Frontier."

"Great. And after we've reached Platinar, when enough time has passed, we should set out to try to find Princess Mika."

Feldia nodded with determination. "Absolutely. She's one of our own. She helped us in so many ways. It's our turn to help her. It's going to be difficult to find out where they're taking her, but we will... and we'll find her. I promise you that."

Determination came to Laren as he began to smile. "Yes, of course. Together, we will find her, Feldia."

* * *

Mika lay flat on her side on the cold floor of the dungeon cell. For days, she had been locked up with absolutely nothing to do except to think and sleep. Eating and going to the lavatory proved to be cumbersome and extremely humiliating. The knights would temporarily remove the rope that bound her wrists together behind her back, watch her as she ate or used the lavatory, and then tied her wrists again. No one talked to her, not even Angelica or Mirin. She was certain they wanted to see her, but the dungeon was off-limits to them. Mika also noticed that neither her father nor her mother had come down to see her since the day of her public sentencing in front of the Nobility and the Peasantry. Absolutely no one had seen her, except for various knights who worked shifts in the dungeon, some of whom she recognized, others she did not.

She sometimes kept watch through the iron bars on the door, trying to see what was going on. Usually, nothing happened. Occasionally, a knight passed by. Other than that, there was no noise or any other form of stirring. The dungeon was empty. Apparently, she was the only prisoner.

Mika heard loud footsteps and some voices in the background. She recognized Collin's voice. There was someone else with him. The voice was unmistakably that of Galner. Other footsteps accompanied them, which belonged to several knights.

Collin, Galner, and a total of six knights appeared, including Tanari, Caylen, and someone whom she recently identified as Reland. They gathered just outside the door of her dungeon cell. All six of the knights wore full armour without their helmets, and each of them wore travel capes, ready for a long excursion.

"It's about time we get rid of her," said Galner, standing at the entrance into the dungeon area.

Collin eyed him with irritation. "Is that what you truly think, Sir Galner? Is that how you truly feel about your own student?"

"My student?!" Galner chuckled with disgust. "Don't make me laugh, boy."

Collin glared at the mage. "That's Supreme Captain to you, you decrepit old man."

Galner frowned with offense. "Excuse me?!"

Mika was surprised. Collin was in a bad mood, and she wondered why. Normally, Galner calling him "boy" would not provoke a reaction of that magnitude.

"Are you offended, Sir Galner?" Collin pointed his finger at Galner as he spoke. "Next time, if you want respect, you had better learn to give it. Otherwise, it will be a blade that will teach you a lesson."

Galner's frown deepened. "You've got some nerve, Sir Collin, just like Sir Maleth."

"That's much better." Collin turned to the other knights. "Open these doors. It's now time to take our Princess...." He stopped, and then cleared his throat to correct himself. "I mean, our prisoner, to her place of exile."

Galner looked at him with a raised eyebrow.

"Yes, sir." Reland unlocked the dungeon cell.

Mika watched the iron door open. More light came from the kerosene lamps outside. When Tanari and Caylen entered the cell, she looked up at them, but said nothing.

Caylen knelt down beside her, and spoke to her gently. "It's time to go."

Galner frowned. "Why do you all still talk to her with reverence? She is no one now! She's even less than these peasant dogs."

"Silence, Sir Galner," said Collin. "Let them speak to her however they please. It's... only natural for them to speak to her that way."

Galner shook his head. "Despicable."

Mika struggled to a sitting position, but Caylen was there to take her by the shoulders to help her. As she brought her legs underneath her, Caylen and Tanari helped her get up. The raw skin on her wrists itched, but there was nothing she could do about it. Scraping them against the rope that bound them together certainly would not help her, because that only caused a stinging sensation. She was forced to wear the same rag dress from the day of her sentencing, and she was given plain old shoes to walk in, but they were so badly worn that she could feel the shape of the creases in the stone floor underneath her feet even with them on. She had been allowed to bathe. However, bathing was nothing more than wiping her skin with a wet cloth while sitting in front of an old bucket of cold, soapy water, but it also meant a knight had to untie her wrists, watch what she was doing while completely nude to make sure she did not do anything suspicious, and then tie her wrists again. She also had to be careful with the bruises on her legs and arms, still in the final stages of healing.

I wonder if these clothes originally belonged to someone else. Did this rag dress belong to a little peasant girl? What about the knickers? And the shoes? Probably. And why would I be forced to wear them? Is this... little peasant girl already dead? If she is, I hope that she... at least forgives me for wearing her clothes.

The strange feeling of wearing the clothes of a little girl who was probably dead had haunted her for the first few days she wore them, but somehow, she had become accustomed to it. She only hoped that the girl was resting in peace. Assuming, of course, that they truly had belonged to a nameless dead girl she did not know.

"Come," said Collin, ordering Mika to move.

Mika did not hesitate. She headed for the doorway, followed by the knights behind her. She stopped in front of Collin, who stood in front of her, and she became puzzled, but she dared not look up at him. She kept her eyes downcast.

Collin turned to the mage at the dungeon entrance. "Sir Galner, as ordered, please recast the magic seal upon her."

"Gladly." Galner approached her.

Mika's eyes went wide as her entire body stiffened. The magic seal that had been placed upon her on the day of her capture was strong, but it was not the kind that would last a very long time. She had actually started feeling signs of her magic ability starting to return, but it was still very weak. She wondered what kind of magic seal Galner was going to cast upon her this time.

Galner stood beside Mika. "This is the most powerful magic seal that I can cast. It is so powerful that it will normally last for one year. In her case, this one will last through the fall, the winter, and into the spring. About three months."

"There are four months in the year. Why would it last only three-quarters of a year?"

"The duration will depend on the strength of the target. As you should be aware, Collin, her magic is quite powerful. Will this suffice?"

"It'll have to do. You may proceed."

Galner put his hand over Mika's head. A blue magic circle appeared on the ground.

Mika gasped. She stared at the magic circle as fear gripped her entire body, deep down into her soul. She felt that same terrible isolation as before, when Galner cast a magic seal on her the first time. She was hoping never to feel such a depressing sensation again. However, Galner was casting an even more powerful seal. Her body glowed brightly, and then the magical energy disappeared, along with the magic circle. Mika stared at the ground with cold shock, her mouth hung open, and her eyes wide. She was almost completely frozen.

Galner grinned as if enjoying what he had just done to Mika. "Done. She has been completely cut off from her magic. I imagine that to be a very depressing feeling for her, but she brought it upon herself."

Collin looked down at Mika for a moment. He had to admit that a part of him felt pity for her, after everything that had happened to her since the night of her disappearance. Actually, even before that. From the day the merchant assassins attacked and nearly killed her, he felt pity for her. She had been through hell and back several times since then, and managed to survive each time. However, he was not certain if she was going to be able to survive her exile. *One thing is for certain. Princess Mika is going to die out there in the wilderness, either from malnutrition, or from exposure during the winter season. There's no question about it.*

The Supreme Captain turned to the knights. "You may proceed."

"Yes, sir," said Caylen.

Collin and Galner stepped aside.

Mika felt Tanari's gentle hand on her back as she was urged to walk. She began to walk with them, three knights in front and three more behind her. They led her out of the dungeon. She walked with her eyes cast down on the floor, her tears drying up. She paid no attention to what was in front of her. All she had to do was to follow the knights leading her down a dark hallway. This was one of the passages that led from the dungeon to the back of the castle. It was separate from other hallways within the castle, and was used for transporting prisoners only.

After a long walk, the hallway began to brighten as Mika saw daylight at the end. She was led by the knights in front of her up some stone steps, eventually taking her to the outside. Mika breathed in the fresh air, which was certainly much better than breathing in the stagnant air of the dungeon. She squinted, waiting a moment for her eyes to adjust to the brightness of the outside. She was led down a walkway, and eventually to a cervid carriage.

Mika looked up at the cervid carriage made of wood and some iron. It was plain, and had absolutely no identifiable marks. Two cervids stood in front of the carriage. Stable boys who had prepared the cervids for their journey left when two of the knights took over.

An unmarked carriage. They're planning to take me away in secret. No one will know that the carriage is transporting a traitor to her exile.

One of the knights opened the door at the back. Reland urged Mika to get in. She stepped up carefully on the iron beams below the door. As soon as she was inside, Reland, Tanari, Caylen, and a fourth knight Mika had not yet acquainted herself with followed her into the carriage.

Through one of the open windows on the second floor of the castle, Queen Maiya watched, tears rolling down her cheeks.

"Mika, wait." Maiya was about to run down to stop the carriage. However a hand around her arm stopped her. She looked up at King Ralphen.

"Don't, Maiya. You have to let her go. You must," said Ralphen.

Maiya glared at him. "Ralphen, she's... our daughter."

"Not anymore."

The Queen gasped as her eyes widened. "How can you be so cruel to her? You always have been! You monster! Ever since that day on her sixth birthday, when you took her out riding on your cervid around the Grounds and you got angry with her—!"

Ralphen slapped her.

Maiya's hand reached up to her cheek, and she looked away from Ralphen as she supported herself with one hand on the windowsill.

The King regarded her with a look of terrible rage. "She was misbehaving, and she deserved it!"

Still higher above, on a balcony that overlooked the back of the castle, Helen sighed deeply as she watched Mika disappear into the cervid carriage. She leaned against the balcony railing as the breeze stirred her long cape, which she wore over her distinguished knight's uniform.

Helen recalled the day when she had captured the Princess. As Helen was taking her back to the castle, Mika had whispered to her. Mika had told Helen that she thought she was beginning to understand her, and that she had mistakenly believed the two of them could have been friends someday. As Helen replayed that brief conversation, she straightened up with a deep frown, and then clenched her fists.

"You're not the only one who thought that, Mika." Helen turned away, sat on the railing, and closed her eyes for a moment. She refused to watch the carriage any longer. She shook her head as she opened her eyes, this time with a saddened expression. "I suppose... nothing has truly changed. I may have started to understand you... and I think I would have loved to be your friend as well. But it's too late for that now. We were never meant to be friends."

With that, Helen left the balcony, and went back into the castle.

In the carriage, Tanari helped Mika sit on the floor at the very front of the cabin, her back against the corner, her hands still tied behind her back. In the corner of the cabin,

Tanari observed her with a heavy heart. Mika appeared even smaller than she already was.

Reland knocked on the front wall of the cabin to give his signal to the two knights who were to drive the carriage. "Let's go!"

Mika felt the carriage begin to move. She listened to the sound of cervid hooves against the pavement as they pulled it around the back of the castle, along the side, and towards the castle gates.

The knight who Mika did not yet know held out a piece of thick black cloth to Tanari. "Tanari, here. Remember what we were supposed to do."

Filled with regret, Tanari took hold of the cloth. "Thanks, Serian."

Mika stared at the black cloth as Tanari knelt down beside her, and wondered what it was to be used for.

"Um... Princess... I'm sorry, but I need to blindfold you... using this cloth," said Tanari. "I'm not certain how else to say this but... we're under orders to prevent you from seeing anything as we travel to your place of exile."

Caylen, Reland, and the knight named Serian, who were all seated on comfortable seats at both sides of the cabin, looked down at her calmly. However, Mika could almost see the pity in their eyes. She glanced up at Tanari, and then nodded. "Orders are orders, Miss Tanari."

"Thank you... and once again, please forgive me." Tanari began to wrap the cloth around Mika's head, completely covering her eyes.

Mika turned her head a couple of times, and saw only darkness. However, she could still hear what was going on around her to a certain extent. Eventually, the carriage reached the castle gates, and it stopped. She heard the gates grinding against the rails in the pavement as they slid open. She could tell they opened only as much as needed to let the carriage through. As soon as the carriage passed through, they began to close.

Mika listened to the sound of the cervid hooves against the pavement and the wheels of the carriage. She felt the vibrations of the carriage as it moved over the surface of the Valderia Pathway, and made a note in her mind of how it felt. As moments passed, the knights stayed quiet. However, Mika continued to listen. She heard the usual sounds of the city of Scarletia. She heard the people minding their own business, going back and forth down the street, and running their errands. She also heard the sounds of people leaving the city, or still preparing to leave. She identified them by the words she sometimes heard them utter, depending on what they were doing.

Outside, peasants passed by without giving the carriage a second look or thought. To them, it was just another cervid carriage driving down the crowded city streets.

Sometime later, the carriage stopped at one of the main city gates as it waited for large groups of peasants to thin out in front of them. Knights on cervids guarded the gates that were wide open. The city gates were larger than the castle gates, but were made of the same heavy algerwood as well as metal beams and panels that provided strength and support. The gates had been slid sideways along the thick stone walls that surrounded the city and tracks that were installed in the pavement to their fully opened position. Peasants moved through the gates as they continued their journey out of the city and into the plains beyond.

When the groups of people thinned out just enough, the cervid carriage proceeded through the gates.

At that point, the sound of the wheels and the cervid hooves changed, as did the vibrations Mika felt throughout the carriage. They were now riding on a dirt road, and she could hear the peasants as they passed.

Mika lips formed a small smile. "I must remind myself... that I truly have won something."

Tanari, as well as the other knights, looked up, hearing her unusual words. "Princess... what do you mean?"

"I won the freedom of the Peasantry. Even though the price of this victory was so high... I still won them their freedom. I have no regrets."

After a brief moment of awkward silence, Caylen spoke. "I suppose... you're probably right, Princess Mika."

Mika smiled again, this time more broadly. *It's not over*

yet. I may have won the freedom of the Peasantry of the city of Scarletia, but there's plenty of work that still needs to be done. Miss Feldia and Sir Laren have probably left the city by now. They're probably already far from here. They're the leaders of the White Princess Liberation Army now. They will be the ones who will continue to fight for the freedom of all the Peasantry for the entire nation. Many more people are being oppressed by the Nobility in all the other cities. They need to be freed as well. Perhaps, word will reach them, and they'll learn of the actions of the King, to allow the peasants of the oppressive city of Scarletia to leave and rebuild their lives elsewhere, free from the tyrannical rule of the Nobility.

Yes, there truly is more work that needs to be done. This is only the beginning. Right here... in the city of Scarletia... is the beginning of everything.

"Perhaps... I'm mistaken about one thing and one thing only," said Mika.

"What is it, Princess Mika?" asked Tanari.

Mika thought for a moment, hesitating at first. "My only regret... is that I won't see the results of my own victory, that I won't be part of any of it. I will not see the Peasantry enjoy their newfound freedom. For I am now just the exiled former Princess of Melodice...."

EPILOGUE

INTO THE ISOLATED HINTERLANDS OF Melodice, where life and death was decided in the blink of an eye, the fallen young princess was ostracized by those who brutally held sway over a dying nation.

Of the lowborn citizens of the capital city of Scarletia, over a hundred thousand chose to leave to start a new life elsewhere, away from the shackles of tyranny. The companions of the princess followed their own paths to fulfill their separate but related objectives. However, there was still much work to be done. Though the commoners of Scarletia were allowed to go freely, millions were still ruled by the heavy hand of the corrupted highborn.

The fallen princess was completely unaware that her adventures had only just begun.

The History of Elladrel: Volume 176, Book 22 (p. 548)
Neirute, "The Matriarch" (b. unknown)

DRAMATIS PERSONAE

THE ROYAL FAMILY OF MELODICE

Maiya Silveraine (MY-uh SIL-ver-reyn):
> The Queen of the nation of Melodice, she is the mother of Mika Silveraine and the wife of Ralphen Silveraine. Her maiden name is Satielle. She is also a skilled user of magic.

Mika Silveraine (MEE-kah SIL-ver-reyn):
> The Princess of the nation of Melodice. At eleven years old, she is exceptionally talented at magic, extremely intelligent, and highly educated, but is terribly shy, timid, and lacks confidence in herself. She is also a novice practitioner of Forbidden Magic. She is also known as the "White Princess."

Ralphen Silveraine (RAHL-fen SIL-ver-reyn):
> The King of the nation of Melodice, he is the father of Mika Silveraine. His wife is Maiya Silveraine.

THE SCARLETIA ROYAL GUARD

Collin Gagnier (CALL-in GAG-nee-ur):
> One of the two Supreme Commanders of the Scarletia Royal Guard, he is later promoted to the

rank of Supreme Captain, after the retirement of Terren Rinaldia.

Helen Renier (HEL-uhn REN-yur):
A young knight of the Scarletia Royal Guard, she is also considered to be a Magic Knight. She holds the rank of Private Enlist. She is a colleague of Mika Silveraine in her studies of magic, and is sixteen years old.

Maleth Arlistia (MAL-ith ar-LIST-ya):
The Supreme Commander of the Scarletia Royal Guard and the Royal Army of Melodice.

Terren Rinaldia (TER-ren rin-ALL-dee-AH):
The former Supreme Captain of the Royal Army of Melodice. He retired at the age of sixty years after forty-two years of service with the Scarletia Royal Guard. He was succeeded by Collin Gagnier. He was in charge of Princess Mika Silveraine's education in the areas of politics, military studies, and battle strategies. He is one of the most powerful knights, as well as one of the strongest Magic Knights, in the entire nation of Melodice, and is known as the "Knight of the Dark."

CIVILIANS OF THE SCARLETIA

ROYAL CASTLE

Angelica Ruviel (an-JUH-li-kuh ROO-vee-el):
The maidservant of Mika Silveraine, and the legal guardian for Mirin Gothwald. She is nineteen years old. She became both the maidservant to Mika and guardian to Mirin when she was sixteen years old, when she reached the age of majority.

Mirin Gothwald (MEE-rin GOTH-wuld):
> The best friend of Mika Silveraine. He is the only one who regularly calls the Princess by her first name. His legal guardian is Angelica Ruviel.

CIVILIANS OF THE CERULEAN

MAGIC ACADEMY

Galner Ciannar (GAL-nuhr SEE-uhn-ar):
> A professor of magical studies, he is also the Royal Representative of the Cerulean Magic Academy. While he is employed by the Academy, he is stationed at the Scarletia Royal Castle. As an elite professor, his current students include Princess Mika Silveraine and Helen Renier. He is a highly skilled practitioner of Forbidden Magic.

MEMBERS OF THE HOPE

OF SCARLETIA

Feldia Saramis (FEL-dee-ah SA-RA-miss):
> One of the leaders of the rebel group called the Hope of Scarletia. She is the group's Second Command, and reports to Dellen Balias.

Dellen Balias (del-len BAL-ee-as):
> The leader of the rebel group called the Hope of Scarletia, one of the two largest rebel groups in the city of Scarletia.

MEMBERS OF THE

SCARLETIA LIBERATION

Laren Caldest (LA-rin CAL-dist):
> One of the leaders of the rebel group called the Scarletia Liberation. He is the group's Second Command, and reports to Adrel Savarian.

Adrel Savarian (ey-drel sa-VAR-ee-an):
> The leader of the rebel group called the Scarletia Liberation, one of the largest rebel groups in the city of Scarletia.

GLOSSARY

NAMES OF LOCATIONS

Alenshire (AL-in-shire):
>One of the major continents of the world of Elladrel, where the nation of Melodice is located.

Cerulean (sir-ROO-lee-uhn):
>The second largest city in the nation of Melodice. It lies to the northwest of the city of Scarletia. It has a population of seven hundred thousand. It is also home to the Cerulean Magic Academy.

Cerulean Magic Academy:
>A revered academy of magic located in the city of Cerulean, one of very few academies of magic located throughout the world of Elladrel. It was established over one thousand years ago by a Spire woman named Muriel of Tarslyn.

Eldoria (el-DOOR-ee-ah) Watchtower:
>An ancient stone tower built within the city of Scarletia by the race of Spires about one thousand years ago. Fifteen floors high, it was damaged when the city was attacked by a dragon army from the nation of Tashar approximately seven hundred years ago.

Elladrel:
>   The world in which Humans and Spires flourish.

Ethereal Daydreams:
>   An inn located in the city of Scarletia, it is also the hideout of the leaders of the two largest rebel groups in the city, the Hope of Scarletia and the Scarletia Liberation.

Grounds:
>   See Scarletia Royal Castle Grounds.

King's Conference:
>   A conference room within the Scarletia Royal Castle used mainly by the King to hold meetings. It overlooks the southern Grounds and the castle gates. The room also contains a bar.

Melodice (MEL-oh-DEES):
>   One of the five nations located on the continent of Alenshire, bordered by Tashar in the west, South Alenshire in the north, and Trena in the northeast. While its government considers itself an absolute monarchy, neighbouring nations also consider it to be an autocracy.

Scarlet Chamber:
>   The main audience hall in the Scarletia Royal Castle. It is the place in which the Royal Family of Melodice conducts most of their official events, including conferences with political leaders.

Scarletia:
>   The capital city of the nation of Melodice, with a population of approximately one million. It is located in the southeast corner of the nation of Melodice.

Scarletia Royal Castle:

The centre of government for the nation of Melodice. It is a large complex that appears to be one very wide building, but is actually several smaller buildings connected to each other by constant reconstruction and maintenance. Parts of the castle were built up to a maximum height of five floors, but a majority of the castle is composed of just two to three floors. The entire complex can comfortably accommodate about ten thousand people.

Scarletia Royal Castle Grounds:

More commonly known as the Grounds, it is a vast open area of concrete walkways, gardens, and grass lawns surrounding the Scarletia Royal Castle. The Grounds are surrounded by a defensive wall, separating the property of the castle from the rest of the city of Scarletia.

Valderia Pathway:

The longest and widest street in the city of Scarletia. It extends from the front of the Scarletia Royal Castle, through the city, and all the way to the main southern exit of the city of Scarletia.

TITLES

Corporal:

The second rank in the Royal Army of Melodice. Men and women who gain this rank have seniority over Private Enlists, but do not take leadership roles.

King:

The male monarch of a nation. The people of Melodice write this title with an uppercase first letter out of reverence. This is not standard practice in most other nations on the world of Elladrel, where the title is written in lowercase unless used in direct address.

Princess:

> The female child of a King and Queen. The people of Melodice write this title with an uppercase first letter out of reverence. This is not standard practice in most other nations on the world of Elladrel, where the title is written in lowercase unless used in direct address.

Private Enlist:

> The first and the lowest rank in the Royal Army of Melodice. Men and women who enlist in the army gain this rank after training for one year under a professor of military studies.

Queen:

> The female monarch of a nation. The people of Melodice write this title with an uppercase first letter out of reverence. This is not standard practice in most other nations on the world of Elladrel, where the title is written in lowercase unless used in direct address.

Second Command:

> A formal term used by large, highly structured, and organized rebel groups such as the Hope of Scarletia and the Scarletia Liberation. It is used to refer to the individual who is next in line in the chain of command, starting from the top. This individual may act on behalf of the leader of the group. The Second Command reports directly to the group's leader.

Sergeant:

> The third rank in the Royal Army of Melodice. Men and women who attain this rank gain the ability to lead others of lower rank. This is the lowest rank one requires to be in a leadership position, and to command small companies of soldiers.

Supreme Captain:
> The highest rank in the Royal Army of Melodice. The holder of the rank is a member of the Scarletia Royal Guard. The Supreme Captain reports directly to the Royal Family of Melodice.

Supreme Commander:
> The second-highest rank in the Royal Army of Melodice. The holder of the rank is a member of the Scarletia Royal Guard. The Supreme Commander reports directly to the Supreme Captain.

GROUPS

Hope of Scarletia:
> One of the two largest rebel groups based in the city of Scarletia, led by Dellen Balias, and his Second Command, Feldia Saramis. The group consisted of thousands of members.

Nobility of Melodice:
> A small minority of the population of the nation of Melodice is considered the Nobility, also known as the highborn or the upper class. This small minority of the population owns and controls a vast majority of the nation's financial assets, goods, and services.

Nobility of Scarletia:
> See Nobility of Melodice.

Peasantry:
> An outdated term used by the population of the nation of Melodice to refer to anyone who is not of the Nobility or who is of the working class. The term dates back to a time when the nation was an agrarian society well over a thousand years ago. However, the term has persisted over the centuries.

Peasantry of Melodice:
> A large majority of the population of the nation of Melodice is considered the Peasantry, also known as the lowborn or the working class. This large majority of the population is able to use only a tiny percentage of the nation's financial assets, goods and services.

Peasantry of Scarletia:
> See Peasantry of Melodice.

Royal Army of Melodice:
> The military force of the nation of Melodice. Every city in the entire nation holds an army, including the capital city of Scarletia, where the army stationed there is called the Scarletia Royal Guard. The Supreme Captain is the highest-ranking officer of the entire military force.

Royal Family of Melodice:
> The family originally appointed by the Nobility as the ruler of the nation of Melodice. Eventually, the relatives of the family became the only ones who were allowed to decide which immediate family was the ruler of the nation. Currently, Ralphen Silveraine and his immediate family are the rulers of the nation of Melodice, with Ralphen as King.

Royal Guard:
> See Scarletia Royal Guard.

Scarletia Liberation:
> One of the two largest rebel groups based in the city of Scarletia, led by Adrel Savarian, and his Second Command, Laren Caldest. The group consisted of thousands of members.

Scarletia Royal Guard:
> A branch of the Royal Army of Melodice, it is a large

group of soldiers primarily stationed in the city of Scarletia as well as the Scarletia Royal Castle. It is sometimes simply referred to as the Royal Guard.

MAGICAL STUDIES

Forbidden Magic:

A term used by the race of Spires and adopted by the race of Humans to refer to a higher class of magic that is capable of manipulating and disrupting normal non-living matter. Typically, an offensive magic spell that is directed at an individual will cause damage to his body, but will leave his clothing unscathed. It also has no effect on inanimate objects such as buildings. A typical defensive magic spell can only protect against other magic, but not against physical objects such as swords or arrows. Magic spells of the Forbidden Magic category are free of these limitations, but also induce increased mental and physical stress, increased energy reduction, and increased risk of injury or death to the magic user.

Magic Circle:

A component of magic. When a magic spell is invoked by its caster, a magic circle appears that indicates the design of the magic spell. This normally appears just below the person who is casting the magic spell, but will also appear in front of them if it is rather small. The larger and more complex the magic circle, the more advanced and more powerful the magic spell is.

Magic Knight:

An unofficial term used by the Royal Family, the Nobility, and the Peasantry of the nation of Melodice to refer to anyone who is able to use the power of magic and that is of the race of Humans. It is not legally adopted by the government, and as such, there is no rule that defines a person to be a Magic Knight, except for the obvious fact that he or she uses magic. It is not used to refer to anyone of the race of Spires, since all Spires are able to use the power of magic.

DATES AND TIMES

Demetre (de-MEH-tree):
> Also known as the spring season. The second month of the year, it consists of ninety calendar days.

Half-Month:
> Any period of time that is forty-five days in length, either within a month, or from one month to the next.

Morrighan (MORE-ig-ghun):
> Also known as the summer season. The third month of the year, it consists of ninety calendar days.

SEC:
> See Spire Elladrel Calendar.

Spire Elladrel Calendar:
> The calendar originally used by the race of Spires. It was adopted by the race of Humans on the world of Elladrel. Each calendar year has four months, and a total of three hundred sixty days. Each month in the calendar consists of ninety days, and corresponds to a season.

CULTURE

Age of Majority:

In the nation of Melodice, the age when one is considered to be a legal adult is sixteen years.

Honourifics ("Sir" / "Miss"):

In the nation of Melodice, adult men and women generally refer to each other with the "Sir" and "Miss" honourifics. (i.e., "Sir Terren", "Miss Angelica") unless they are in close relationships, such as family members or romantic partners. Friends may sometimes omit using them. Children use them as well when addressing each other, and also when addressing adults. Adults are not required to use these honourifics to address children, but sometimes use it anyway to teach them proper etiquette.

Retirement Ceremony:

When an individual who has served under the Royal Army of Melodice or the government of the nation of Melodice reaches the age of sixty years and has had a long and distinguished career, they have the option of having a ceremony performed by the Royal Family of Melodice. This public ceremony recognizes the achievements of the individual during their years of service. Part of the ceremony also involves the reciting of a Royal Message for the individual by a member of the Royal Family.

Royal Message:

Any formal written message recited by a member of the Royal Family of Melodice in front of an audience for any special occasion, such as for a Retirement Ceremony. It is often written down on and read from a ceremonial scroll.

ITEMS

Algerwood (AL-jer-wood):
> A very strong, but extremely rare wood used for fine furniture. It is derived from the Algera Tree. Prized for its beauty and texture, as well as its durability, only the Nobility are able to obtain algerwood furniture, due to its extremely high cost.

Crystium (KRIS-tee-uhm):
> The standard currency used by the race of Humans as well as the race of Spires. The currency exists as either thin, semi-transparent, square-shaped coins for lower denominations, or official promissory paper notes for higher denominations.

Princess Gem:
> A deep blue diamond that is flat and circular, measuring four centimetres in width. It is handed down through the generations of females from mother to daughter within the Royal Family of Melodice. There can be more than one Princess Gem, such as in cases where the Royal Family may have more than one daughter and therefore more than one Princess. It is used as the legal and physical representation of the daughter's identity and birthright as the Princess of Melodice.

Starstone:
> A black, rocky material that crumbles easily, and is composed of unidentified organic and inorganic materials that have been compressed together over millions of years. When brought into contact with fire, it ignites and explodes violently with a deep blue flame. Starstone flames are so hot that not even water can extinguish them. It burns everything in its proximity until there is nothing left to burn, and all that is left is a fine black ash. However, it cannot burn anything that has a sufficiently high ignition or melting point, such as concrete or granite.

PLANTS AND ANIMALS

Algera (AL-jer-uh):

A tree or shrub similar to oak, but much stronger. Algera are difficult to find, and exist only deep inside forests on mountain slopes, and only at certain altitudes, where temperature, pressure, and humidity allow for them to flourish. Cutting down Algera trees is an extremely difficult task because of the toughness of their barks.

Cervid (SIR-vid):

A four-legged, even-toed, hoofed mammal common throughout the world of Elladrel. They have sharp, forward-pointing antlers that can be used as defensive weapons. They are also large and muscular. There are two types of cervids: wild and domesticated. Wild cervids can be captured and trained easily to become domesticated. Domesticated cervids live and work alongside Humans and Spires by performing a variety of tasks, such as pulling carriages and wagons for transporting cargo. They are also used in the military by mounted soldiers. Cervids in the military are trained to recognize hostile threats and react accordingly, as well as to remain calm during adverse situations.

RACES

Humans:

One of the major races that inhabit the world of Elladrel. They inhabit much of the world. They have a natural affinity to technology, and are extremely ingenious when it comes to its use. A Human has a natural lifespan of eighty to one hundred years.

Spires:

> One of the major races that inhabit the world of Elladrel. Most of them live in a different part of the world far from the race of Humans. They have a natural affinity to magic, and are extremely powerful. A Spire has a natural lifespan of nine hundred to one thousand years.

ACKNOWLEDGMENTS

I would like to thank the following people who helped me get this project off the ground. I couldn't have done it without their help and support.

- My loving wife Nadia who provided so much encouragement.

- My adorable daughter Olivia Rose who inspires me in everything I do.

- The staff at Jasvere Nights Studios (Terry, Cherly, Edwin, Nancy T, Nancy H, Joyce, Ivy) for banding together to get this book published.

BIOGRAPHY

Michael Santos was born in Manila, Philippines in 1978, and moved to Toronto, Canada with his family when he was ten years old. As a child, he was an avid book reader, and loved to write stories for others to read. At the age of fourteen, he started creating a "constructed universe" for various fantasy and science fiction story ideas with the help of one of his friends. He has worked various jobs including Information Technology. He is currently working as a Project Manager at Jasvere Nights Studios where he is working on several projects including the Ethereal Daydreams epic fantasy series.